THE YEARS

BETWEEN THE ACTS

The Years

Between the Acts

VIRGINIA WOOLF

with Introductions and Notes by
LINDEN PEACH

WORDSWORTH CLASSICS

For my husband
ANTHONY JOHN RANSON
with love from your wife, the publisher.
Eternally grateful for your unconditional love,
not just for me but for our children,
Simon, Andrew and Nichola Trayler.

Readers who are interested in other titles from
Wordsworth Editions are invited to visit our website at
www.wordsworth-editions.com

For our latest list and a full mail-order service, contact
Bibliophile Books, 5 Datapoint, South Crescent, London E16 4TL
TEL: +44 (0)20 7474 2474 FAX: +44 (0)20 7474 8589
ORDERS: orders@bibliophilebooks.com
WEBSITE: www.bibliophilebooks.com

First published in 2012 by Wordsworth Editions Limited
8B East Street, Ware, Hertfordshire SG12 9HJ

ISBN 978 1 84022 681 2

Typeset in Great Britain by Antony Gray
Printed and bound by Clays Ltd, St Ives plc

CONTENTS

GENERAL INTRODUCTION
page VII

INTRODUCTION TO
The Years and *Between the Acts*
page VII

BIBLIOGRAPHY
page XXV

THE YEARS
page 3

NOTES TO *The Years*
page 299

BETWEEN THE ACTS
page 305

NOTES TO *Between the Acts*
page 411

GENERAL INTRODUCTION

Wordsworth Classics are inexpensive editions designed to appeal to the general reader and students. We commission teachers and specialists to write wide-ranging, jargon-free introductions and in some cases to provide notes that will assist the understanding of our readers rather than interpret the stories for them. In the same spirit, because the pleasures of reading are inseparable from the surprises, secrets and revelations that all narratives contain, we strongly advise you to enjoy this book before turning to the Introduction.

General Adviser: KEITH CARABINE
Rutherford College, University of Kent at Canterbury

INTRODUCTION

Virginia Woolf (1882–1941) has long been recognised as one of England's most prestigious authors whose work has significantly influenced the course of twentieth-century fiction and continues to inspire many women writers across the world, including the first African American woman novelist to win the Nobel Prize for Literature, Toni Morrison, in 1993. Until recently, she has been best known for her experimental novels written in the 1920s: *Jacob's Room* (1922); *Mrs Dalloway* (1925); *Orlando* (1928); and *The Waves* (1931). They belong to an exciting and richly innovative period for the arts, known as 'modernism', to which many of her novels still remain one of the best introductions. For nearly a century, her modernist work has been valued for its prose style and structure, especially the way in which it captures the multilayered, and often random, nature of individual consciousness. Until recently, her less modernist and more socio-historical work of the 1930s, *The Years* (1937) and *Between the Acts* (1941), written in the last six years of her life, have not received the same degree of critical attention. In some respects, they are the least understood of her novels even though they constitute her most intriguing explorations of English identity and personal relationships.

The Years was originally conceived as a new genre, a 'Novel Essay', on which Woolf began work between October and December 1932. Entitled *The Pargiters*, it consisted of fictional accounts of the Pargiter family interleaved with essays which placed them in their historical contexts and pursued themes from *A Room of One's Own* (1929), a work of non-fiction based on a series of lectures that she delivered at Newham and Girton Colleges. However, the project was jettisoned at the end of the year and some of the fictional chapters were then incorporated in an entirely fictional work which eventually became the novel *The Years*. Some of the material in the essays constituted a new work of non-fiction, *Three Guineas* (1938). In the twelve months following the publication of *The Years*, Woolf began *Between the Acts*, originally entitled 'Pointz Hall', the draft of which was completed in 1940 and published posthumously the following year.

Although Woolf left behind diaries, letters and memoirs, and has been the subject of a handful of biographies, a definitive picture of her still eludes us and her politics, feminism, sexuality and even her recurring mental illness continue to be subjects of controversy and debate.[1] She was born Adeline Virginia Stephen in 1882 and mostly brought up in prestigious areas of London. While she is associated with the periods of change and innovation in literature, culture and the arts that followed the First World War, it is important to remember that her childhood was lived in what seems by contrast to have been the relatively less exciting end of the Victorian period. Parents invariably inculcate their children in the experiences and values of their own era but, because of the celebration of her modernism, the tension in Woolf's work between the traditional and the new has been generally overlooked.

Woolf's life has intrigued readers and critics almost as much as the novels themselves, not least because of the way in which her early years were overshadowed by family deaths. Her mother, Julia Jackson

---

1   Quentin Bell, *Virginia Woolf: A Biography*, 2 volumes, Hogarth Press, London, 1972; Julia Briggs, *Virginia Woolf: An Inner Life*, Penguin, London, 2005; Gordon Lyndall, *Virginia Woolf: A Writer's Life*, Oxford University Press, Oxford, 1984; Hermione Lee, *Virginia Woolf*, Chatto and Windus, London, 1996; Panthea Reid, *Art and Affection: A Life of Virginia Woolf*, Oxford University Press, New York, 1996; Phyllis Rose, *Woman of Letters: A Life of Virginia Woolf*, Routledge, London, 1978

Duckworth (1846–1895), was a widow when she married Woolf's father, Sir Leslie Stephen (1832–1904), himself a widower, in 1878. She was to die from influenza in 1895 when Virginia was only thirteen years old. Woolf's half-sister Stella Duckworth died only two years later and her favourite brother, Thoby, in 1906. As an adolescent, following her mother's death, Woolf was brought up by her father and the impact of this upon her life has been the cause of some speculation, even with suggestions that she suffered abuse. A number of aspects of her work, such as its interest in relationships between women (Woolf's most emotionally intimate relationships were with women), and its representation of masculinity and of the mother figure, can be attributed to these formative years. These early experiences no doubt contributed also to the bouts of mental illness which dogged her entire life, and proved particularly relevant to her last novel. Although the traumatic and tragic events of her early years occurred, of course, long before she began thinking about the *The Years* and *Between the Acts*, they never left her and, at the start of the 1930s, she returned to thinking about father-and-daughter relationships after seeing a stage play in London based on the life of the Victorian poet Elizabeth Barrett Browning (1806–61) which inspired her spoof biography of Barrett Browning's dog, *Flush* (1932).

Woolf recognised much in Elizabeth Barrett Browning's life that was also true of her own, not only the complex relationship between Barrett Browning and her father but how remarkable it was that any woman writer should achieve the status and influence that as a poet she acquired. Of course, Elizabeth Barrett Browning never achieved the recognition enjoyed by her husband Robert Browning and this exemplified for Woolf the dilemma that all artistic and professional women faced. Like her sister, and unlike her brothers, Woolf did not attend school and was largely educated at home by her parents. The different education opportunities afforded men compared with women in the late nineteenth and early twentieth centuries is one of the main themes of *A Room of One's Own* (1929). However, Woolf's father, who was the editor of the *Dictionary of National Biography* and of two prestigious journals, had an extensive library and the use which Woolf made of it is evident in the references and allusions in all her fiction, not least in her last two novels, to subjects that extend beyond literature and the arts to newspaper stories, popular songs and nursery rhymes as well as to buildings, street names and monuments. Two female tutors had a particular impact upon her: Clara Pater (1841–1910), who was the sister of the influential Victorian essayist and critic Walter Pater (1838–94), and Janet Case, one of the first graduates of Girton College, Cambridge, established in 1869 to provide residential higher education for women. As a feminist, Case encouraged Woolf's interest and involvement in the suffragette movement.

Following Leslie Stephen's death in 1904, the family moved from Kensington to Bloomsbury. There they hosted meetings that brought leading figures in the arts, politics and economics to their house, some of whom eventually constituted what became known as the Bloomsbury Group. In 1910, the Group achieved notoriety when Roger Fry (1866–1934) organised an exhibition of 'Post-Impressionist' painting, including canvases by the French artist Henri Matisse (1869–1954). Reviews of the exhibition were almost wholly hostile, with some critics dismissing it as crude and even degenerate. However, the period which Woolf spent with the Bloomsbury Group provided her with a liberal, as well as liberating, education.

At the age of thirty, Virginia married Leonard Woolf, a Cambridge University graduate who, after seven years in the Colonial Civil Service, became a passionate anti-imperialist and socialist who published novels, pamphlets and essays on national and international politics. He undoubtedly influenced his wife's view, evident in the pageant in *Between the Acts*, that imperialism was an essential part of 'Englishness'. Although their marriage has been the subject of critical commentary, Virginia and Leonard remained together until Woolf's death. In one of her final letters to him, written while *Between the Acts* lay unfinished, she speaks perhaps more coherently to him about their relationship and her lifelong anxieties than she did when they were together.[2] It is a reminder that what also recommends these last two novels to the twenty-first-century reader is their preoccupation with characters who seem to be struggling to communicate with each other and to grasp something that is evading them.

---

2   'What I want to say is I owe all the happiness of my life to you. You have been entirely patient with me and incredibly good. I want to say that – everybody knows it. If anybody could have saved me it would have been you. Everything has gone from me but the certainty of your goodness. I can't go on spoiling your life any longer. I don't think two people could have been happier than we have been.' *The Letters of Virginia Woolf*, Nigel Nicolson and Joanne Trautman (eds), Hogarth Press, 6 volumes, London, 1975–80, VI, p. 481. See also, Lee, *Virginia Woolf*, pp. 756–65.

2

As suggested above, when they are read together, *The Years* (1937), a long but engaging novel based on the lives of members of a dispersed middle-class family between 1880 and 1937, and *Between the Acts* (1941) reflect the shifting mood and ambience of the late 1930s and the early 1940s and provide important insights into the changing nature of Englishness and British identity in the first half of the twentieth century. Given what was happening in Europe in the 1930s – mass unemployment, the rise of Fascism, and the prospect of war – and the events of the year in which *Between the Acts* was written, it is not surprising that each of these works pursues Woolf's long-standing concern not only with history but with the very concept of history itself. The chronological sweep of *The Years* places the time in which it was written (the closing chapter, 'The Present Day', is the longest) in a wider perspective, as does *Between the Acts* through its historical pageant and the memories of its characters.

The period which *The Years* covers, virtually corresponding with Woolf's own life, 1882–1941, is represented through only eleven chapters, each of which does not have a title but bears a date. At first, these dates seem to have been chosen at random: 1880, 1891, 1907, 1908, 1910, 1911, 1913, 1914, 1917, 1918, 'Present Day'. However, *The Years* presents the reader with a history of 1880–1937 from a woman's perspective in that the selected dates are significant to women's lives generally and to the private lives of the women in the dispersed Pargiter family, and ultimately the two are interrelated throughout the book. Woolf demonstrates in *The Years* that when women's lives have become as fragmented and dispersed as the lives of the Pargiter family, they have to be mapped differently from official histories which frequently overlook the contributions and achievements of women in such circumstances. Thus, one way of reading the novel is to examine how the content of each chapter relates to and encourages us to see the year in question from the perspective of women and particularly of the Pargiter women. For example, 1918 is of particular importance to the dispersion of the women members of this family because in that year the bill was passed that granted the vote to women over the age of thirty who were householders, the wives of householders, the occupiers of property with an annual rent of £5 or graduates of British universities. Also significant to the theme of social fragmentation is Woolf's decision to begin the novel in the 1880s when the West End of Mayfair and St James's became secure as the centre of finance, commerce and entertainment but when women were perceived very differently from men in relation to these social and political foundations.

Central to the theme of the social fragmentation of women's lives in *The Years* is the way in which their new and often contradictory roles were becoming more visible in public places. Up to a point, this explains why the novel is more of a social realist text than her experimental, modernist work of the 1920s. However, Woolf was always fascinated by public thoroughfares as places where groups of people who might not ordinarily interact with each other might share the same social space. The main thoroughfares of London gave the diversity of women's lives visibility, as, for example, business people, secretaries, typists, nurses, shoppers, wives and mothers, and even prostitutes, and in their own way suggested that throughout history women's lives have been a fragmented fusion of emergent opportunity, inequality and oppression. Thoroughfares are places where lives interact with each other only briefly and where people rarely become more than strangers to each other. In this regard, they reflect many aspects of the book including its representation of broader political themes and social contexts.

The Years is not a political novel as such for its political themes are often vague and only introduced through incidental details and conversations. Indeed, the book marginalises the Boer War, the death of Queen Victoria, the rise of the Labour Party, the demise of the Liberals, the General Strike, the Wall Street Crash, the First World War and even the suffragettes. This is not simply because these subjects are associated with traditional histories of the times, after all the suffragettes are especially relevant to Woolf's historical emphasis upon the lives of women in the book, but because its focus, as the title suggests, is upon time, memory and identity which places its concern with social fragmentation and dispersion in a wider context. At its heart, there are even deeper psychological themes which give the book a sense of profound melancholy that critics have generally overlooked. This in turn is evident in subjects also suggested by the title such as time passing, dispersion, human isolation, how people are always strangers to each other and the difficulties many people have in articulating what they really want to say.

At one level, *The Years* might be seen as a family or generational saga, a genre which in the hands of writers like John Galsworthy (1867–1933), who is best remembered today for *The Forsyte Saga* (1906–21), proved extremely popular with the Edwardian reading public. However, *The Years* is a different kind of family-centred historical novel from that.

It questions the nature of the traditional family and examines the changing family structure over the period in which the book is set. From the outset, the book scrutinises what holds the traditional family together. The father figure is portrayed as a strong unifying force within the family and, hence, society as a whole. Colonel Pargiter drinks from a special cup, symbolic of the law of the father within the household and of the public endorsement of the male as head of the family in Victorian society. Inherited from his father, the cup implies that the father's authority is passed down through the various generations but the ritual of afternoon tea also links the family, society and, ultimately, Englishness itself to empire, and especially to India and Ceylon. The importance of the ritual in preserving the family hierarchy is underscored by the fact that Colonel Pargiter actually hates tea and only takes a few sips from his symbolic cup.

The father, however, is a disturbing as well as a powerful force, signified by his mutilated, claw-like hand and by the way in which his children are bonded together through fear of him. Indeed, the family structure, together with the social hierarchy which it mirrors, seems to be crumbling from within. When he sits in his father's chair, Martin mimics but also mocks the patriarchy of which he is a part but against which he rebels. Further suggestions that the Victorian family is disintegrating are Eleanor being late for tea, Rose breaking the family and social code in going alone to Lamley's and, most seriously of all, Colonel Pargiter having a mistress in a less salubrious part of the city.

The Years traces the dissolution of the traditional family which we see in the first chapter through the dispersion of the Pargiter family following the death of their father who failed to provide adequately for them in his will. It becomes concerned with forms of living which undermine any single identifiable notion of the family. Thus, Eleanor achieves physical and emotional independence; Edward lives in his college; Rose lives with a female lover and then alone; and Delia lives in a flat above offices. The book does not simply explore the nature of these new forms of living but their relationship to the historical *a priori* of the family.

3

The dispersion of the Pargiter family, the emphasis on achievement and frustration in women's lives, and the focus on diverse forms of living outside of the traditional family not only informs but determines the seemingly randomised structure and fragmentation of the narrative.

As mentioned earlier, the novel does not simply map the period from 1880–1937 from a woman's perspective but from the perspective of lives that have become as fragmented and isolated as they have become dispersed from their familial centre. This creates a narrative which, in addition to alternating between different characters and between the private lives of women and public themes, frequently interrupts itself. Not only are the public sphere and private lives interrupted by un-foreseen circumstances and events, but characters frequently fail to finish their sentences either because they seem to have lost their words or because they are interrupted by others. The family find that 'they scarcely spoke, or only in little formal sentences' (p. 61), and when, for, example, the elderly maid, Crosby, is taking leave of what then remains of the family, it is said that 'tears checked her speech' (p. 151). Such interruptions determine the overall mood of the novel which is not so much about social change as the interruption of social change and the further uncertainty which this creates. The frequent interruption of the narrative disrupts the reading process so that the reader is forced to experience, as it were, the fragmentation and disruption of the lives of the book's characters.

Thus, Woolf does not only return to the interrelationship between private and public histories, the subject of The Pargiters, but examines the way in which the inability to access fully and articulate convincingly the innermost self reflects, if it does not actually constitute, a fundamental sense of isolation within the self and between individuals. Once again what is happening in the lives of the novel's characters is embodied in the reading process. The dispersal, interruption and fragmentation which characterises the narrative makes it difficult for the reader to become fully involved with them and fully to understand them as they experience difficulty in getting to know each other fully. In suggesting that this is a part of the modern human condition, the novel echoes existentialism, associated with early twentieth-century philosophers such as Gabriel Marcel (1889–1973), Martin Heidegger (1889–1976) and Jean-Paul Sartre (1905–80), who stressed individual existence, freedom and choice. Thus, there are frequently implied connections between the overall national mood in the novel and the choices, dilemmas and actions of its characters. For example, at one point, a woman whistles the wrong dog, and at another Sara and Martin seem to embrace the modern condition when they find 'they had been walking in the wrong direction' (p. 166).

Criticism of The Years has focused upon its traditional social-realist features which has led to the book being seen as a rather bewildering return to the 'realism' of Woolf's first two novels, *The Voyage Out* (1915) and *Night and Day* (1919), which some twenty years previously she had rejected. While this is not a fair assessment of the book overall, it is impossible to deny that *The Years* harks back to the traditional nineteenth-century novel. For example, as in the traditional English novel, meals, parties and banquets are important to the structure of the narrative and to the interaction, or lack of interaction, of the characters.

A noticeable feature of the book is the tension throughout between the fragmented sentences through which members of the dispersed family attempt to talk about themselves and their pasts and the more confident and fluent descriptions of landscapes and the weather. Each chapter is not only located at a point of time within the year in which it is set but in a particular moment of weather. The references to the weather create particular moods at different points in the text; for example, the snowflakes that fall as Crosby, the elderly maid, leaves the house in which she has been employed most of her life, covering her past and occluding what has given her life meaning, and the setting summer sun which sets the mood of the last chapter and of the closing years of the decade. Frequently, in the description of the weather, the emphasis, as in the account of the fine rain which opens the book, is upon people's reactions to it in different situations and places. The rain seems to create a universal mood of indecision in which people, unable to decide whether or not they should open their umbrellas, are caught. This notion becomes more and more explicit and pervasive the more the chapter returns to the weather: 'It was an uncertain day, with passing shadows and darting rays of bright sunshine' (p. 61). Indeed, the weather becomes a technique in the book as a whole by which Woolf creates the pervasiveness of different and changing moods within the country. Thus, the chapter '1908' is set in March and, recalling the opening of the poem 'The Wasteland' by T. S. Eliot (1888–1965), 'the wind was blowing . . . It was so cruel' (p. 103). While the cold is vividly described, the focus is upon how it drove people off the streets and 'worked its way under the doors, through the window frames' (p. 103). A particular dimension of this chapter, and indeed of the novel as a whole, is encapsulated in the wind's 'power to peel off the bark, the bloom, and show the bare bone' (p. 103).

The way in which the weather is used to encapsulate and create mood is true also of objects in the novel. In this regard, Woolf was probably influenced by the relationship between people and objects in the socio-realist paintings of Walter Sickert (1860–1942), on which she wrote an essay, 'Walter Sickert: A Conversation' (1934), shortly before she began

The Years.[3] Some of his paintings, as Woolf suggests in her essay, portray people in whose fragmented lives communication appears strained, and in many of the works, as in *The Years*, objects carry a social inflection. In Woolf's novel, for example, the books that once constituted the Pargiters' library, the kind upon which Woolf herself relied for her education, now 'exist silently with dignity, by themselves, for themselves' (p. 191). At one level, as part of a middle-class family's library, they carry a similar social inference to the account of 'soaring spires of slumbering university cities, over the leaded libraries, and the museums' (p. 36), which suggests that an educational elite had a singular hold on knowledge and learning. However, at another level, the dispersion of the library reinforces one of the book's key themes, encapsulated in Martin's comment upon 'the identity of different objects and their differences' (p. 173). This observation often proves true of people in the novel, too, such as the fashionable lady in Kensington Gardens who has, in the sunlight, 'a curious look of transparency, as if she were caught in a net of light' (p. 168). Here there is an interesting dynamic between the binding ritual of the season, of taking tea in the Gardens, and the sense of insubstantiality and movement created by the interplay of object and light which furthers the sense of fragmentation, as if the latter itself 'were broken into separate points' (p. 168). Although the narrative relies upon the materiality of objects to create a sense of environment and mood, they contribute, often subtly, to a heightened sense of time and movement, as in the attention to creases in shoes, dresses trailing over steps and the movement of clock hands.

4

Between the Acts is a much shorter and more streamlined work than *The Years*, focused on a family home, Pointz Hall, in an English village in mid-June 1939 in the last few months before the outbreak of the Second World War, where everyone seems surprisingly preoccupied with the summer pageant. In an earlier novel, *Mrs Dalloway* (1925), Woolf borrowed a technique from the Irish writer James Joyce of setting a story within a twenty-four-hour time span. In *Between the Acts*, Woolf returns to this technique, setting her novel on a summer evening and the following day when the village's annual pageant takes place.

---

3   For a fuller discussion of this subject, see Linden Peach, 'Woolf's Camden: Virginia Woolf and Walter Sickert', in Anna Snaith (ed.), *Locating Woolf: The Politics of Space and Place*, Palgrave Macmillan, Basingstoke, 2007.

However, through the pageant, concerned with English history over the centuries, and all kinds of techniques borrowed from Joyce, including stories and memories related by the different characters, it has an unexpectedly broad frame of reference, reaching well beyond the twenty-four hours in which it is set.

The prospect of war and the ensuing uncertainty is the principal focus of *Between the* Acts. The year in which it was written, 1940, saw the capitulation of France, the Dunkirk evacuation, the Battle of Britain and the beginning of the Blitz, which Woolf witnessed first hand; and the year in which it is set, 1939, saw the fall of Barcelona, the conquest of Austria and Czechoslovakia and the imminent invasion of Poland. Although the war has not begun in the novel, it is clearly influenced by the events and the national mood of 1940. For example, at one level, a Victorian constable's reference in the pageant to the fireplaces of an English house – 'Don't I see the fire […] blazing ever higher?' (p. 387) – evokes the domestic hearth, as symbolic of the English home and the family around which the myths of England and Englishness were constructed. But, viewed through the lens of 1940, this image suggests what everyone in Britain feared in 1940, the bombing which eventually came with the Blitz on London and other major British cities.

Even the descriptions of the English countryside in the novel cryptically allude to the politics of the 1930s. At one point, brambles are said to have 'mobbed themselves together' (p. 333), a surprising image by which the organised violence of fascist mobs in Europe in the 1930s infiltrates the pastoral context. In some respects, the mood of the novel brings to mind Kitty's feelings on the train in *The Years*, in the chapter '1914', when she is said to 'hardly believe that so great a monster could start so gently on so long a journey' (p. 186). This reference to the train could also be an allusion to the way in which the events that eventually led to the Second World War developed out of the way in which the armistice which brought the First World War to an end left Germany humiliated. The rise of the Nazi party, the way in which Hitler gradually secured the position of Chancellor and the re-arming of Germany were among a series of incremental steps by which Germany repositioned itself so as to regain its national esteem and take revenge on the nations which punished it so excessively at the Treaty of Versailles (1919).

The village encapsulates a sense of a mythical Englishness which seems to have endured over generations. Indeed, so little appears to have changed that an 1833 guidebook is said to reflect the area in 1939. But outside this rural enclave there is change which interrupts tradition, ritual and custom. Church attendances are said to have fallen because of motorbikes, motor cars and the movies. The pageant begins as what is described as 'our pageant' but is interrupted by a faulty gramophone. The gramophone is the first of a number of intrusions which, as in *The Years*, occur throughout the book. The pageant is subsequently interrupted by an aircraft overhead anticipating how the Luftwaffe will disrupt the peace of Britain, and, throughout, it is threatened by the possibility of rain. The private fantasies on which the lives of the villagers are focused are also disrupted. Isa Oliver desires Rupert Haines, a married gentleman-farmer; her husband, Giles, is attracted by Mrs Manresa, a guest who has come for lunch, while her companion, William Dodge, a homosexual, has feelings for him although he is emotionally close to Isa. The mood of the novel as a whole infiltrates sexual relations and desires in the text where there is, as Lady Harpy says in the pageant, a tension between a sense that 'the dog days are over' and the conviction that 'where there's a will there's a way' (p. 366). Her point is not lost on Bartholomew and especially Giles who determines, 'Off to Gretna Green with his girl; the deed done. Damn the consequences' (p. 374).

The fragility of England's institutions and its independence in whatever structure is to follow the war is suggested by the stage props left over from the pageant, the crown made of cardboard, the swords made from silver paper and turbans made from dishcloths (p. 336). The representation in the pageant of the Elizabethan period, England's Golden Age, closes optimistically with Elizabeth I's words, 'the flower has fallen./ But soon will rise another dawning' (p. 351). However, hardly any of the audience is listening because they have noticed the word 'Interval' in the programme. One of the few to do so, Isabella, demonstrating how the responses of the audience are as least as important as the pageant itself, pointedly contradicts the Queen, 'All is over. The wave has broken' (p. 352). Mrs Manresa, on the other hand, places the institutions of Englishness in a wider perspective when she declares, 'I'm dying for my tea' (p. 355). Beyond its literal meaning, this seemingly innocuous exclamation suggests that she and others are about to die in defence of England, Englishness and its rituals of which the taking of tea is one of the best known that has its less than innocent origins in the days of empire.

The villagers find themselves at a time which not only has its roots in the past but is a time when, with the prospect of war, 'the future shadowed their present' (p. 361). The novel's tone, captured by William when he talks of 'the doom of sudden death hanging over us' p. (361), is established at the outset by the reference to a nightingale heard 'chuckling' over the 'substance and succulence of the day' (p. 307). However, there is nothing for the audience to do as they take their seats but wait for the unfolding of events over which they have no control. In this regard, they epitomise the English nation waiting for the outbreak of the war. The different ways in which characters respond to, and conceptualise, this waiting is evident in the conversations between them in which some talk of 'marking' time, how time does not exist, how now there is only the present and how the present is interrupted by the future, while for some, there is no future.

Throughout the book, there is a sense of things increasingly failing to cohere, signified in the image of the 'many-veined transparent vine leaf' where there is 'a criss-cross of lines making no pattern' (p. 361). Miss La Trobe typifies the condition of the artist/producer in the 1930s struggling to make sense of everything, believing that 'a vision imparted was relief from agony . . . for one moment' (p. 353) when reality is constituted of only 'scraps and fragments' (p. 364). Her frustration, bordering on violence, she 'gnashed her teeth. She crushed her manuscript' (p. 364), reflects her exasperation with her audience with whom she is no longer confident of connecting, for they have 'slipped the noose' (p. 364). The novel is haunted by the image of the impotent artist whose 'vision [had] escaped her' (p. 353) and whose 'power had left her' (p. 372). At the end, Miss La Trobe discovers, perhaps like Woolf herself in the months leading up to her suicide, that 'illusion had failed' (p. 372), and finds herself, as Woolf thought of a number of her own works, with 'another damned failure' (p. 353).

5

The title, *Between the* Acts, suggests that it can be seen as a drama, a sequence of scenes which are interwoven through recurring imagery and themes, but more important that it is concerned with events that are occurring off-stage, between the Acts, which in turn is a reference to what is happens during the intervals in the pageant, the two world wars and even sexual acts. Certainly, it is not a novel in the conventional sense of the term, as there is no plot or character development and it is not divided into chapters. However, the novel is divided into sections through the division of the pageant itself into periods of time, the ellipses in the text, the comments of the audience and the intervals. The selection of periods in the pageant is as pertinent to the interrogation of history as the chapters into which *The Years* is divided, with a particular focus this time on the Elizabethan and the Victorian periods and mock Shakespearian rustic comedy and Restoration pastiche.

At one level, the periods of the pageant may represent an unusual choice, as Colonel Mayhew finds, bewildered by the exclusion of the British army, the epitome of a particular type of masculinised pageant and ritual and ultimately 'Englishness'. But there are profound and thought-provoking similarities between them, not least in the evidence each provides of the tension between the rhetoric of a unified 'England' and a more dispersed and socially fragmented nation in reality. The often lofty, serious parts of the pageant espouse a unified sense of Englishness, mocked and undermined in the rustic, Shakespearian comedy, the pastiche of Restoration comedy and the behaviour of the audience, members of which betray their own preconceptions and prejudices.

One member of the audience is overheard suggesting, in an interval, 'Hear rather the shepherd, coughing by the farmyard wall, the withered tree that sighs . . . the brawl in the barrack room when they stripped her naked' (p. 380). This story is based on an actual reported incident from the previous year in which some guards at Whitehall tricked a young woman into their stables to see a horse with a green tail where they then sexually assaulted her. The judge in the case reprimanded the soldiers for letting down their regiment as the woman, as indeed the nation itself a few years later, would have expected to be able to look to them for protection. It is impossible to forget that soldiers like these would soon be sent into occupied Europe where many of them would suffer injury and death. But their act of rape also reminds us that in war soldiers like these sometimes take advantage of the situations of power in which they find themselves and perform acts of rape and brutality on enemy women. Typical of these last novels, the allusion to this event is further complicated through repetition. The newspaper in which the rape is allegedly reported is the one which Isa's father-in-law uses playfully to terrify her three-year-old son, George, whom he then reproaches as a coward and a cry baby. The incident is disturbing because the rolled-up newspaper becomes a phallic, club-like object which, together with the father-in-law's labelling of George as unmanly, even though he is only a child, suggests that the traditional definition of masculinity, as ever, was bound up with violence.

Although *Between the Acts* is a poetic, at times lyrical, text, it is also, as here, deeply disturbing. Often the most shocking images are mediated by the consciousness of the characters which in turn makes them harder to grasp than those in *The Years*. The image of the snake with a toad caught in its throat, 'unable to swallow, the toad was unable to die' (p. 353), is disturbing in itself, but when Giles stamps on it, Woolf intensifies the horror by describing what he sees: 'The mess crushed and slithered. The white canvas on his tennis shoes was bloodstained and sticky.' The crushed, sticky mess takes the reader not only beyond life but beyond death as does the line which Isa mutters to herself later in the novel, 'Four and twenty blackbirds, strung upon a string' (p. 390). The effect of this is to render the individual consciousnesses as 'strange', as does the way in which Giles imagines himself at the pageant, 'manacled to a rock he was, and forced passively to behold indescribable horror' (p. 334), and the behaviour of Giles and Isa at the end of the book when they are compared to a dog fox with a vixen where 'enmity was bared and also love' (p. 409).The reference in the book to the increasing darkness (p. 409) suggests that its world is becoming increasingly unfathomable and disingenuous to a range of uneasy consciousnesses. In the microscopic description of violence within nature, as in the blue-bottle on a piece of cake 'which stabbed its yellow rock with its short drill' (p. 354) or the wasps burrowing holes (p. 331), it is difficult to distinguish the 'reality' from the mediating consciousness.

6

Pageants were originally brought to England from France at the Norman Conquest. They often took the form of religious plays of the sort which T. S. Eliot adapted in his first drama, *The Rock: A Pageant Play* (1934). However, the pageant in *Between the Acts* is of the kind of which Woolf would have been made aware in the pageant plays of her friend E. M. Forster (1879–1970). How he defined the characteristics of an English pageant play, covering about a thousand years of history, and occurring close to a village or a manor house, is reflected in the type of tableau which Woolf creates in *Between the Acts*. His writing about the English pageant, for example in *England's Pleasant Land* (1940),[4] which was published by the Hogarth Press while Woolf was working on *Between the Acts*, anticipates Woolf's pageant also in the way in which he perceives them as not so much representing tradition but a national identity which has evolved historically. Viewed in this way, the pageant provides Woolf with a vehicle to interrogate the concept of history as narrative, not least because there was always, as Forster highlights, a satirical edge to them.

4   E. M. Forster, *England's Pleasant Land*, Hogarth Press, London 1940

In its opening lines, the pageant celebrates England as an 'isle', reminding its audience that at one level English identity has evolved from its geographical separation from Europe. It rejoices in how the seas around Britain have afforded a degree of protection from its aggressive neighbours since the Norman Conquest but anticipates how these seas are once again to become a scene of battle. When a girl representing the country in the pageant comes to the point when she says 'England am I' (p. 342), she suddenly forgets her lines, as does Mrs Clark when she is playing Queen Elizabeth later. As in the case of some of the characters in *The Years* who forget their lines, it is as if the words no longer exist to articulate the uncertainty of what is to come. And there is also the sense here that the old languages and concepts are redundant. The word 'lines' is revealingly ambiguous. At one level, it refers to the spoken lines of the pageant but, at another level, it suggests the various ancestral and cultural lines which the war threatens to bring to an end.

Woolf's critical rendering of hundreds of years or so of English history in her fictional pageant betrays a further anxiety which she shares with Forster, namely the way in which Englishness, as celebrated in the pageant, was prone to develop into xenophobic patriotism.[5] However, Woolf does not see this, like Forster, as the product of the pageant as such but of an inherent dimension of Englishness which the pageant reveals. Although the novel's run up to the pageant depicts the mood and fears of a country as ominous events unfurl overseas, it also sows the seeds of subjects explored in the pageant such as the part which colonialism, conquest, oppression, violence, intolerance and prejudice have played in creating that country's sense of identity. For example, consider the seemingly innocuous description of red admiral butterflies as having 'gluttonously absorbed richness from dishcloths' (p. 336). The name 'admiral' might suggest the role which the English navy had in the development of the colonies and the exploitation of their riches. Red is also the colour of the ensign of the Merchant Navy, and both Royal and Merchant navies, or 'the seafaring men' as they are romantically described in the Pageant (p. 346), like the butterfly are involved in their own ways in the extraction of richness/riches. The dishcloth is made no doubt from imported cotton which can be traced back to the cotton plantations in the colonies and the various parts of

5   Joshua Esty, *A Shrinking Island: Modernism and National Cultures in England*, University of Princeton Press, Princeton, 2003, pp. 80-1

the empire. In the pageant itself, the Elizabethan Age is marked by ships 'tumbling their oranges, ingots of silver,/Cargoes of diamonds, ducats of gold,/ Down on the jetty . . . ' (p. 346).

Woolf's pageant highlights what has been written out of the history of Englishness and makes clear that Englishness is a way of life in which not everyone had an equal part on account of the circumstances of their birth, gender, sexuality, race or age. Woolf's novel develops the sardonic nature of the English pageant to the point where it makes English identity itself a problem. In the course of the tableau, the nursery is referred to as the 'cradle of our race' (p. 340) but the pageant encourages the audience to ask themselves where exactly is this. The extent to which the once fixed and knowable concept of Englishness has become complex, if not confused, is reflected in the way in which the audience is disorientated at the outset of the tableau, unable to distinguish between the prologue and the play. Thus, not all the violence to which the pageant alludes comes from outside England. Working-class districts of London, such as Cripplegate, St Giles and Whitechapel, are invoked as sites of anxiety and linked in the constable's monologue with those who 'sweat at the mines' and 'cough at the looms' in the colonies (p. 383). Other references suggest that sexual violence has long been a feature of rural England, the mythical centre of Englishness. The seemingly innocuous description of wasps burrowing in fruit (p. 333) when considered more closely has a menacing sexual connotation which comes to the fore in the pageant in the image of the rustics 'tumbling' with girls (p. 346). The word 'tumbling' disguises what in reality would have involved non-consensual as well as consensual sex and the social exclusion and hardship that would follow for the girls if they became pregnant. Mrs Manresa – ironically her name is a generic one for Jesuit novice-houses but also suggests the teasing and arousing of men – sees this scene as 'Merry England' (p. 346). She apparently fails to recognise, even though she is herself a woman, the dark side of this holiday merriment. Indeed, the novel encourages us to ask where is the distinction between the behaviour of the rustics and their attitude towards women and those of the guardsman who raped a young woman.

One of the themes developed through the pageant, and shared with *The Years*, is the way in which the full potential and creativity of women are occluded by the achievements of men and the domestic roles which they invariably have had to assume. This a theme which Woolf pursues in her non-fiction, *A Room of One's Own* (1929) and *Three Guineas* (1938), as well as in her earlier novels. The former interrogates the production of literary criticism and literary works by women while

Three Guineas examines the male-centred institutions and social practices which oppress women, drawing parallels between the public and domestic spheres.

Three Guineas is in many ways the link between *The Years* and *Between the Acts* for it, too, is concerned with the repressive nature of the house and the family and the way in which they traditionally blocked alternative opportunities for women in terms of how they might live and also in regard to female sexuality. Woolf's further thoughts about the oppressive nature of the family and patriarchy in this essay were inspired by the death and funeral of George V when she was in the final stages of completing *The Years*. His funeral reignited her concern with militarism, spectacle, symbolism and sentimentality in English ritual. An important difference between *The Years* and *Between the Acts*, however, is the greater emphasis in the latter upon the complicity of women in maintaining the family and domestic structures that oppress them, as when Lucy Swithin shows a guest, William Dodge, around the house in which she was born. The theme is wittily satirised in the parody of Restoration drama when Lady Harpy brings to the fore the complicity of her class in oppressing lower-class women, bemoaning the fact that her maid has deserted her, 'she that I fed on apple parings and crusts from my own table, she that I taught to play cribbage and sew chemises' (p. 376).

A member of the audience observes, somewhat ironically considering what happened to the rape victim in the barracks, 'it's a good day, some say, the day we are stripped naked. Others, it's the end of the day.' Pertinently, they go on to comment how 'none speaks with a single voice' (p. 380). One of the most disturbing aspects of England being 'stripped naked' in the novel is the way in which it blurs the boundary between events in England and Europe in the 1930s, such as the rise of Fascism, the annexation by Germany of neighbouring territories, anti-Semitism and the outbreaks of violence in European capitals. Rather worryingly, it invites us to consider how the factors which gave rise to and characterised Fascism in 1930s' Europe, including violence, power, hierarchy and oppression, were also part of English history. At the end of the pageant the audience is not presented with a comfortable historical narrative but a tableau which reflects back to them uncomfortable truths and interrogates much that they have taken for granted.

Much of the imagery at the end of the novel, such as the garden covered by shadow and the house seemingly brittle and dry, conveys a sense of traditional England coming to an end. Giles crumples up the newspaper and, again in an act appropriate to the ending of something, turns out the light. The increasing darkness could be the blackout that is to come, the blackness between plays in a theatre or the blackness of death. At this point, the novel looks back to prehistory, when England was not separated from the continent by a channel, of which Mrs Swithin is again reading as she was at the outset of the book. Implicitly the coming war, when German bombers and submarines would effectively join England with the continent once again, could spell the end of human civilisation, as the Ice Age destroyed the age of the giant reptiles.

The novel ends with the curtain rising and people speaking, suggesting that another pageant is beginning. But it is not clear what will be revealed, what is being said or indeed who is speaking, a problem we have in the intervals throughout the pageant. *Between the Acts* ends on a note of uncertainty, like *The Years* where Eleanor asks, 'And now?' The uncertainty in *Between the Acts* is undermined by the final image of the curtain rising and in *The Years* by the sun rising in a sky that has 'an air of extraordinary beauty, simplicity and peace' (p. 298). The rising curtain recalls both Elizabeth's conviction in the Pageant that 'soon will rise another dawning' (p. 351) and a snippet from a member of the audience, 'the Jews . . . People like ourselves, beginning life again' (p. 364), which suggests not only hope but diaspora, reminding us of the refrain created by the faulty gramophone, 'Dispersed are we' (p. 352).

Bibliography

Jane Goldman, *The Cambridge Introduction to Virginia Woolf*, Cambridge University Press, Cambridge, 2006

Clare Hanson, *Virginia Woolf*, Macmillan, Basingstoke, 1994

Anna Snaith (ed.), *Palgrave Advances in Virginia Woolf Studies*, Palgrave Macmillan, Basingstoke, 2006

Anna Snaith (ed.), *Locating Woolf: The Politics of Space and Place*, Palgrave Macmillan, Basingstoke, 2007

Michael Whitworth, *Authors in Context: Virginia Woolf*, Oxford University Press, Oxford, 2005

THE YEARS

BETWEEN THE ACTS

The Years

♦

VIRGINIA WOOLF

A novel by
VIRGINIA WOOLF
first published in 1937

CONTENTS

1880
page 5

1891
page 62

1907
page 89

1908
page 101

1910
page 111

1911
page 132

1913
page 147

1914
page 154

1917
page 191

1918
page 206

PRESENT DAY
page 209

1880

I T WAS AN UNCERTAIN SPRING. The weather, perpetually changing, sent clouds of blue and of purple flying over the land. In the country farmers, looking at the fields, were apprehensive; in London umbrellas were opened and then shut by people looking up at the sky. But in April such weather was to be expected. Thousands of shop assistants made that remark, as they handed neat parcels to ladies in flounced dresses standing on the other side of the counter at Whiteley's and the Army and Navy Stores.[1] Interminable processions of shoppers in the West End, of businessmen in the East, paraded the pavements, like caravans perpetually marching – so it seemed to those who had any reason to pause, say, to post a letter, or at a club window in Piccadilly. The stream of landaus,[2] victorias and hansom cabs was incessant; for the season was beginning. In the quieter streets musicians doled out their frail and for the most part melancholy pipe of sound, which was echoed, or parodied, here in the trees of Hyde Park,[3] here in St James's by the twitter of sparrows and the sudden outbursts of the amorous but intermittent thrush. The pigeons in the squares shuffled in the tree-tops, letting fall a twig or two, and crooned over and over again the lullaby that was always interrupted. The gates at the Marble Arch and Apsley House were blocked in the afternoon by ladies in many-coloured dresses wearing bustles, and by gentlemen in frock-coats carrying canes, wearing carnations. Here came the Princess,[4] and as she passed hats were lifted. In the basements of the long avenues of the residential quarters servant girls in cap and apron prepared tea. Deviously ascending from the basement, the silver teapot was placed on the table, and virgins and spinsters with hands that had staunched the sores of Bermondsey and Hoxton carefully measured out one, two, three, four spoonfuls of tea. When the sun went down a million little gaslights, shaped like the eyes in peacocks' feathers, opened in their glass cages, but nevertheless broad stretches of darkness were left on the pavement. The mixed light of the lamps and the setting sun was reflected equally in the placid waters of the Round Pond and the Serpentine. Diners-out, trotting over the Bridge in hansom cabs, looked for a moment at the charming vista. At length the moon rose and its polished coin, though obscured now and then by wisps of cloud, shone out with serenity, with severity, or perhaps with complete indifference. Slowly wheeling, like the rays of a searchlight, the days, the weeks, the years passed one after another across the sky.

Colonel Abel Pargiter was sitting after luncheon in his club talking. Since his companions in the leather armchairs were men of his own type, men who had been soldiers, civil servants, men who had now retired, they were reviving with old jokes and stories now their past in India, Africa, Egypt, and then, by a natural transition, they turned to the present. It was a question of some appointment, of some possible appointment.

Suddenly the youngest and the sprucest of the three leant forward. Yesterday he had lunched with . . . Here the voice of the speaker fell. The others bent towards him; with a brief wave of his hand Colonel Abel dismissed the servant who was removing the coffee cups. The three baldish and greyish heads remained close together for a few minutes. Then Colonel Abel threw himself back in his chair. The curious gleam which had come into all their eyes when Major Elkin began his story had faded completely from Colonel Pargiter's face. He sat staring ahead of him with bright blue eyes that seemed a little screwed up, as if the glare of the East were still in them; and puckered at the corners as if the dust were still in them. Some thought had struck him that made what the others were saying of no interest to him; indeed, it was disagreeable to him. He rose and looked out of the window down into Piccadilly. Holding his cigar suspended he looked down on the tops of omnibuses, hansom cabs, victorias, vans and landaus. He was out of it all, his attitude seemed to say; he had no longer any finger in that pie. Gloom settled on his red handsome face as he stood gazing. Suddenly a thought struck him. He had a question to ask; he turned to ask it; but his friends were gone. The little group had broken up. Elkins was already hurrying through the door; Brand had moved off to talk to another man. Colonel Pargiter shut his mouth on the thing he might have said, and turned back again to the window overlooking Piccadilly. Everybody in the crowded street, it seemed, had some end in view. Everybody was hurrying along to keep some appointment. Even the ladies in their victorias and broughams[5] were trotting down Piccadilly on some errand or other. People were coming back to London; they were settling in for the season. But for him there would be no season; for him there was nothing to do. His wife was dying; but she did not die. She was better today; would be worse tomorrow; a new nurse was coming; and so it went on. He picked up a paper and turned over the pages. He looked at a picture of the west front of Cologne Cathedral. He tossed the paper back into its place among the other papers. One of these days – that was his euphemism for the time when his wife was dead – he would give up London, he thought, and live in the country. But then there was the house; then there were the children; and there was also . . . his face changed; it became less discontented; but also a little furtive and uneasy.

He had somewhere to go, after all. While they were gossiping he had kept that thought at the back of his mind. When he turned round and found them gone, that was the balm he clapped on his wound. He would go and see Mira; Mira at least would be glad to see him. Thus when he left the club he turned not East, where the busy men were going; nor West where his own house in Abercorn Terrace was; but took his way along the hard paths through Green Park towards Westminster. The grass was very green; the leaves were beginning to shoot: little green claws, like birds' claws, were pushing out from the branches; there was a sparkle, an animation everywhere; the air smelt clean and brisk. But Colonel Pargiter saw neither the grass nor the trees. He marched through the park, in his closely buttoned coat, looking straight ahead of him. But when he came to Westminster he stopped. He did not like this part of the business at all. Every time he approached the little street that lay under the huge bulk of the Abbey, the street of dingy little houses, with yellow curtains and cards in the window, the street where the muffin man seemed always to be ringing his bell, where children screamed and hopped in and out of white chalk-marks on the pavement, he paused, looked to the right, looked to the left; and then walked very sharply to number thirty and rang the bell. He gazed straight at the door as he waited with his head rather sunk. He did not wish to be seen standing on that doorstep. He did not like waiting to be let in. He did not like it when Mrs Sims let him in. There was always a smell in the house; there were always dirty clothes hanging on a line in the back garden. He went up the stairs, sulkily and heavily, and entered the sitting-room.

Nobody was there; he was too early. He looked round the room with distaste. There were too many little objects about. He felt out of place, and altogether too large as he stood upright before the draped fireplace in front of a screen upon which was painted a kingfisher in the act of alighting on some bulrushes. Footsteps scurried about hither and thither on the floor above. Was there somebody with her? he asked himself listening. Children screamed in the street outside. It was sordid; it was mean; it was furtive. One of these days, he said to himself . . . but the door opened and his mistress, Mira, came in.

'Oh, Bogy, dear!' she exclaimed. Her hair was very untidy; she was a little fluffy-looking; but she was very much younger than he was and really glad to see him, he thought. The little dog bounced up at her.

'Lulu, Lulu,' she cried, catching the little dog in one hand while she put the other to her hair, 'come and let Uncle Bogy look at you.'

The colonel settled himself in the creaking basket-chair. She put the dog on his knee. There was a red patch – possibly eczema – behind one of its ears. The colonel put on his glasses and bent down to look at the dog's ear. Mira kissed him where his collar met his neck. Then his glasses fell off. She snatched them and put them on the dog. The old boy was out of spirits today, she felt. In that mysterious world of clubs and family life of which he never spoke to her something was wrong. He had come before she had done her hair, which was a nuisance. But her duty was to distract him. So she flitted – her figure, enlarging as it was, still allowed her to glide between table and chair – hither and thither; removed the fire-screen and set a light, before he could stop her, to the grudging lodging-house fire. Then she perched on the arm of his chair.

'Oh, Mira!' she said, glancing at herself in the looking-glass and shifting her hairpins, 'what a dreadfully untidy girl you are!' She loosed a long coil and let it fall over her shoulders. It was beautiful gold-glancing hair still, though she was nearing forty and had, if the truth were known, a daughter of eight boarded out with friends at Bedford. The hair began to fall of its own accord, of its own weight, and Bogy seeing it fall stooped and kissed her hair. A barrel-organ had begun to play down the street and the children all rushed in that direction, leaving a sudden silence. The colonel began to stroke her neck. He began fumbling, with the hand that had lost two fingers, rather lower down, where the neck joins the shoulders. Mira slipped on to the floor and leant her back against his knee.

Then there was a creaking on the stairs; someone tapped as if to warn them of her presence. Mira at once pinned her hair together, got up and shut the door.

The colonel began in his methodical way to examine the dog's ears again. Was it eczema? or was it not eczema? He looked at the red patch, then set the dog on its legs in the basket and waited. He did not like the prolonged whispering on the landing outside. At length Mira came back; she looked worried; and when she looked worried she looked old.

She began hunting about under cushions and covers. She wanted her bag, she said; where had she put her bag? In that litter of things, the colonel thought, it might be anywhere. It was a lean, poverty-stricken-looking bag when she found it under the cushions in the corner of the sofa. She turned it upside down. Pocket handkerchiefs, screwed up bits of paper, silver and coppers fell out as she shook it. But there should have been a sovereign, she said. 'I'm sure I had one yesterday,' she murmured.

'How much?' said the colonel.

It came to one pound – no, it came to one pound eight and sixpence,[6] she said, muttering something about the washing. The colonel slipped two sovereigns out of his little gold case and gave them to her. She took them and there was more whispering on the landing.

'Washing . . . ?' thought the colonel, looking round the room. It was a dingy little hole; but being so much older than she was it did not do to ask questions about the washing. Here she was again. She flitted across the room and sat on the floor and put her head against his knee. The grudging fire which had been flickering feebly had died down now. 'Let it be,' he said impatiently, as she took up the poker. 'Let it go out.' She resigned the poker. The dog snored; the barrel-organ played. His hand began its voyage up and down her neck, in and out of the long thick hair. In this small room, so close to the other houses, dusk came quickly; and the curtains were half drawn. He drew her to him; he kissed her on the nape of the neck; and then the hand that had lost two fingers began to fumble rather lower down where the neck joins the shoulders.

A sudden squall of rain struck the pavement, and the children, who had been skipping in and out of their chalk cages, scudded away home. The elderly street singer, who had been swaying along the kerb, with a fisherman's cap stuck jauntily on the back of his head, lustily chanting, 'Count your blessings, Count your blessings – ', turned up his coat collar and took refuge under the portico of a public house where he finished his injunction: 'Count your blessings. Every one.' Then the sun shone again; and dried the pavement.

'It's not boiling,' said Milly Pargiter, looking at the tea-kettle. She was sitting at the round table in the front drawing-room of the house in Abercorn Terrace. 'Not nearly boiling,' she repeated. The kettle was an old-fashioned brass kettle, chased with a design of roses that was almost obliterated. A feeble little flame flickered up and down beneath the brass bowl. Her sister Delia, lying back in a chair beside her, watched it too. 'Must a kettle boil?' she asked idly after a moment, as if she expected no answer, and Milly did not answer. They sat in silence watching the little flame on a tuft of yellow wick. There were many plates and cups as if other people were coming; but at the moment they were alone. The room was full of furniture. Opposite them stood a Dutch cabinet with blue china on the shelves; the sun of the April evening made a bright stain here and there on the glass. Over the fireplace the portrait of a red-haired young woman in white muslin holding a basket of flowers on her lap smiled down on them.

Milly took a hairpin from her head and began to fray the wick into separate strands so as to increase the size of the flame.

'But that doesn't do any good,' Delia said irritably as she watched her. She fidgeted. Everything seemed to take such an intolerable time. Then Crosby came in and said should she boil the kettle in the kitchen? and Milly said no. How can I put a stop to this fiddling and trifling, she said to herself, tapping a knife on the table and looking at the feeble flame that her sister was teasing with a hairpin. A gnat's voice began to wail under the kettle; but here the door burst open again and a little girl in a stiff pink frock came in.

'I think nurse might have put you on a clean pinafore,' said Milly severely, imitating the manner of a grown-up person. There was a green smudge on her pinafore as if she had been climbing trees.

'It hadn't come back from the wash,' said Rose, the little girl, grumpily. She looked at the table, but there was no question of tea yet.

Milly applied her hairpin to the wick again. Delia leant back and glanced over her shoulder out of the window. From where she sat she could see the front doorsteps.

'Now, there's Martin,' she said gloomily. The door slammed; books were slapped down on the hall table, and Martin, a boy of twelve, came in. He had the red hair of the woman in the picture, but it was rumpled.

'Go and make yourself tidy,' said Delia severely. 'You've plenty of time,' she added. 'The kettle isn't boiling yet.'

They all looked at the kettle. It still kept up its faint melancholy singing as the little flame flickered under the swinging bowl of brass.

'Blast that kettle,' said Martin, turning sharply away.

'Mama wouldn't like you to use language like that,' Milly reproved him as if in imitation of an older person; for their mother had been ill so long that both sisters had taken to imitating her manner with the children. The door opened again.

'The tray, miss . . . ' said Crosby, keeping the door open with her foot. She had an invalid's tray in her hands.

'The tray,' said Milly. 'Now who's going to take up the tray?' Again she imitated the manner of an older person who wishes to be tactful with children.

'Not you, Rose. It's too heavy. Let Martin carry it; and you can go with him. But don't stay. Just tell mama what you've been doing; and then the kettle . . . the kettle . . . '

Here she applied her hairpin to the wick again. A thin puff of steam issued from the serpent-shaped spout. At first intermittent, it gradually became more and more powerful, until, just as they heard steps on the stairs, one jet of powerful steam issued from the spout.

'It's boiling!' Milly exclaimed. 'It's boiling!'

They ate in silence. The sun, judging from the changing lights on the glass of the Dutch cabinet, seemed to be going in and out. Sometimes a bowl shone deep blue; then became livid. Lights rested furtively upon the furniture in the other room. Here was a pattern; here was a bald patch. Somewhere there's beauty, Delia thought, somewhere there's freedom, and somewhere, she thought, *he* is – wearing his white flower . . . But a stick grated in the hall.

'It's papa!' Milly exclaimed warningly.

Instantly Martin wriggled out of his father's armchair; Delia sat upright. Milly at once moved forward a very large rose-sprinkled cup that did not match the rest. The colonel stood at the door and surveyed the group rather fiercely. His small blue eyes looked round them as if to find fault; at the moment there was no particular fault to find; but he was out of temper; they knew at once before he spoke that he was out of temper.

'Grubby little ruffian,' he said, pinching Rose by the ear as he passed her. She put her hand at once over the stain on her pinafore.

'Mama all right?' he said, letting himself down in one solid mass into the big armchair. He detested tea; but he always sipped a little from the huge old cup that had been his father's. He raised it and sipped perfunctorily.

'And what have you all been up to?' he asked.

He looked round him with the smoky but shrewd gaze that could be genial, but was surly now.

'Delia had her music lesson, and I went to Whiteley's – ' Milly began, rather as if she were a child reciting a lesson.

'Spending money, eh?' said her father sharply, but not unkindly.

'No, papa; I told you. They sent the wrong sheets – '

'And you, Martin?' Colonel Pargiter asked, cutting short his daughter's statement. 'Bottom of the class as usual?'

'Top!' shouted Martin, bolting the word out as if he had restrained it with difficulty until this moment.

'Hm – you don't say so,' said his father. His gloom relaxed a little. He put his hand into his trouser pocket and brought out a handful of silver. His children watched him as he tried to single out one sixpence from all the florins.[7] He had lost two fingers of his right hand in the Mutiny,[8] and the muscles had shrunk so that the right hand resembled the claw of some aged bird. He shuffled and fumbled; but as he always ignored the injury, his children dared not help him. The shiny knobs of the mutilated fingers fascinated Rose.

'Here you are, Martin,' he said at length, handing the sixpence to his son. Then he sipped his tea again and wiped his moustaches.

'Where's Eleanor?' he said at last, as if to break the silence.

'It's her Grove day,' Milly reminded him.

'Oh, her Grove day,' muttered the colonel. He stirred the sugar round and round in the cup as if to demolish it.

'The dear old Levys,' said Delia tentatively. She was his favourite daughter; but she felt uncertain in his present mood how much she could venture.

He said nothing.

'Bertie Levy's got six toes on one foot,' Rose piped up suddenly. The others laughed. But the colonel cut them short.

'You hurry up and get off to your prep, my boy,' he said, glancing at Martin, who was still eating.

'Let him finish his tea, papa,' said Milly, again imitating the manner of an older person.

'And the new nurse?' the colonel asked, drumming on the edge of the table. 'Has she come?'

'Yes . . . ' Milly began. But there was a rustling in the hall and in came Eleanor. It was much to their relief; especially to Milly's. Thank goodness, there's Eleanor she thought, looking up – the soother, the maker-up of quarrels, the buffer between her and the intensities and strifes of family life. She adored her sister. She would have called her goddess and endowed her with a beauty that was not hers, with clothes that were not hers, had she not been carrying a pile of little mottled books and two black gloves. Protect me, she thought, handing her a teacup, who am such a mousy, downtrodden inefficient little chit, compared with Delia, who always gets her way, while I'm always snubbed by papa, who was grumpy for some reason. The colonel smiled at Eleanor. And the red dog on the hearthrug looked up too and wagged his tail, as if he recognised her for one of those satisfactory women who give you a bone, but wash their hands afterwards. She was the eldest of the daughters, about twenty-two, no beauty, but healthy, and though tired at the moment, naturally cheerful.

'I'm sorry I'm late,' she said. 'I got kept. And I didn't expect – ' She looked at her father.

'I got off earlier than I thought,' he said hastily. 'The meeting – ' he stopped short. There had been another row with Mira.

'And how's your Grove, eh?' he added.

'Oh, my Grove – ' she repeated; but Milly handed her the covered dish.

'I got kept,' Eleanor said again, helping herself. She began to eat; the atmosphere lightened.

'Now tell us, papa,' said Delia boldly – she was his favourite daughter – 'what you've been doing with yourself. Had any adventures?'

The remark was unfortunate.

'There aren't any adventures for an old fogy like me,' said the colonel surlily. He ground the grains of sugar against the walls of his cup. Then he seemed to repent of his gruffness; he pondered for a moment.

'I met old Burke at the club; asked me to bring one of you to dinner; Robin's back, on leave,' he said.

He drank up his tea. Some drops fell on his little pointed beard. He took out his large silk handkerchief and wiped his chin impatiently. Eleanor, sitting on her low chair, saw a curious look first on Milly's face, then on Delia's. She had an impression of hostility between them. But they said nothing. They went on eating and drinking until the colonel took up his cup, saw there was nothing in it, and put it down firmly with a little chink. The ceremony of tea-drinking was over.

'Now, my boy, take yourself off and get on with your prep,' he said to Martin.

Martin withdrew the hand that was stretched towards a plate.

'Cut along,' said the colonel imperiously. Martin got up and went, drawing his hand reluctantly along the chairs and tables as if to delay his passage. He slammed the door rather sharply behind him. The colonel rose and stood upright among them in his tightly buttoned frock-coat.

'And I must be off too,' he said. But he paused a moment, as if there was nothing particular for him to be off to. He stood there very erect among them, as if he wished to give some order, but could not at the moment think of any order to give. Then he recollected.

'I wish one of you would remember,' he said, addressing his daughters impartially, 'to write to Edward . . . Tell him to write to mama.'

'Yes,' said Eleanor.

He moved towards the door. But he stopped.

'And let me know when mama wants to see me,' he remarked. Then he paused and pinched his youngest daughter by the ear.

'Grubby little ruffian,' he said, pointing to the green stain on her pinafore. She covered it with her hand. At the door he paused again.

'Don't forget,' he said, fumbling with the handle, 'don't forget to write to Edward.' At last he had turned the handle and was gone.

They were silent. There was something strained in the atmosphere, Eleanor felt. She took one of the little books that she had dropped on the table and laid it open on her knee. But she did not look at it. Her glance fixed itself rather absent-mindedly upon the farther room. The trees were coming out in the back garden; there were little leaves – little ear-shaped leaves on the bushes. The sun was shining, fitfully; it was going in and it was going out, lighting up now this, now –

'Eleanor,' Rose interrupted. She held herself in a way that was oddly like her father's. 'Eleanor,' she repeated in a low voice, for her sister was not attending.

'Well?' said Eleanor, looking at her.

'I want to go to Lamley's,' said Rose.

She looked the image of her father, standing there with her hands behind her back.

'It's too late for Lamley's,' said Eleanor.

'They don't shut till seven,' said Rose.

'Then ask Martin to go with you,' said Eleanor.

The little girl moved off slowly towards the door.

Eleanor took up her account-books again. 'But you're not to go alone, Rose; you're not to go alone,' she said, looking up over them as Rose reached the door. Nodding her head in silence, Rose disappeared.

She went upstairs. She paused outside her mother's bedroom and snuffed the sour-sweet smell that seemed to hang about the jugs, the tumblers, the covered bowls on the table outside the door. Up she went again, and stopped outside the schoolroom door. She did not want to go in, for she had quarrelled with Martin. They had quarrelled first about Erridge and the microscope and then about shooting Miss Pym's cats next door. But Eleanor had told her to ask him. She opened the door.

'Hello, Martin – ' she began.

He was sitting at a table with a book propped in front of him, muttering to himself – perhaps it was Greek, perhaps it was Latin.

'Eleanor told me – ' she began, noting how flushed he looked, and how his hand closed on a bit of paper as if he were going to screw it into a ball. 'To ask you . . . ' she began, and braced herself and stood with her back against the door.

Eleanor leant back in her chair. The sun now was on the trees in the back garden. The buds were beginning to swell. The spring light of course showed up the shabbiness of the chair-covers. The large arm-chair had a dark stain on it where her father had rested his head, she noticed. But what a number of chairs there were – how roomy, how airy it was after that bedroom where old Mrs Levy – But Milly and Delia were both silent. It was the question of the dinner-party, she remembered. Which of them was to go? They both wanted to go. She wished people would not say, 'Bring one of your daughters.' She wished they would say, 'Bring Eleanor,' or 'Bring Milly,' or 'Bring Delia,' instead of lumping them all together. Then there could be no question.

'Well,' said Delia abruptly, 'I shall . . . '

She got up as if she were going somewhere. But she stopped. Then she strolled over to the window that looked out on to the street. The houses opposite all had the same little front gardens; the same steps; the same pillars; the same bow windows. But now dusk was falling and they looked spectral and insubstantial in the dim light. Lamps were being lit; a light glowed in the drawing-room opposite; then the curtains were drawn, and the room was blotted out. Delia stood looking down at the street. A woman of the lower classes was wheeling a perambulator; an old man tottered along with his hands behind his back. Then the street was empty; there was a pause. Here came a hansom jingling down the road. Delia was momentarily interested. Was it going to stop at their door or not? She gazed more intently. But then, to her regret, the cabman jerked his reins, the horse stumbled on; the cab stopped two doors lower down.

'Someone's calling on the Stapletons,' she called back, holding apart the muslin blind. Milly came and stood beside her sister, and together, through the slit, they watched a young man in a top-hat get out of the cab. He stretched his hand up to pay the driver.

'Don't be caught looking,' said Eleanor warningly. The young man ran up the steps into the house, the door shut upon him and the cab drove away.

But for the moment the two girls stood at the window looking into the street. The crocuses were yellow and purple in the front gardens. The almond trees and privets were tipped with green. A sudden gust of wind tore down the street, blowing a piece of paper along the pavement; and a little swirl of dry dust followed after. Above the roofs was one of those red and fitful London sunsets that make window after window burn gold. There was a wildness in the spring evening; even here, in Abercorn Terrace the light was changing from gold to black, from black to gold. Dropping the blind, Delia turned, and coming back into the drawing-room, said suddenly: 'Oh my God!'

Eleanor, who had taken to her books again, looked up disturbed. 'Eight times eight . . . ' she said aloud. 'What's eight times eight?'

Putting her finger on the page to mark the place, she looked at her sister. As she stood there with her head thrown back and her hair red in the sunset glow, she looked for a moment defiant, even beautiful. Beside her Milly was mouse-coloured and nondescript.

'Look here, Delia,' said Eleanor, shutting her book, 'you've only got to wait . . . ' She meant but she could not say it, 'until mama dies.'

'No, no, no,' said Delia, stretching her arms out. 'It's hopeless . . . ' she began. But she broke off, for Crosby had come in. She was carrying a tray. One by one with an exasperating little chink she put the cups, the plates, the knives, the jam-pots, the dishes of cake and the dishes of bread and butter on the tray. Then, balancing it carefully in front of her, she went out. There was a pause. In she came again and folded the tablecloth and moved the tables. Again there was a pause. A moment or two later back she came carrying two silk-shaded lamps. She set one in the front room, one in the back room. Then she went, creaking in her cheap shoes, to the window and drew the curtains. They slid with a familiar click along the brass rod, and soon the windows were obscured by thick sculptured folds of claret-coloured plush. When she had drawn the curtains in both rooms, a profound silence seemed to fall upon the drawing-room. The world outside seemed thickly and entirely cut off. Far away down the next street they heard the voice of a street hawker droning; the heavy hooves of van horses clopped slowly down the road. For a moment wheels ground on the road; then they died out and the silence was complete.

Two yellow circles of light fell under the lamps. Eleanor drew her chair up under one of them, bent her head and went on with the part of her work that she always left to the last because she disliked it so much – adding up figures. Her lips moved and her pencil made little dots on the paper as she added eights to sixes, fives to fours.

'There!' she said at last. 'That's done. Now I'll go and sit with mama.' She stooped to pick up her gloves.

'No,' said Milly, throwing aside a magazine she had opened, 'I'll go . . . '

Delia suddenly emerged from the back room in which she had been prowling. 'I've nothing whatever to do,' she said briefly. 'I'll go.'

She went upstairs, step by step, very slowly. When she came to the bedroom door with the jugs and glasses on the table outside, she paused. The sour-sweet smell of illness slightly sickened her. She could not force herself to go in. Through the little window at the end of the passage she could see flamingo-coloured curls of cloud lying on a pale-blue sky. After the dusk of the drawing-room, her eyes dazzled. She seemed fixed there for a moment by the light. Then on the floor above she heard children's voices – Martin and Rose quarrelling.

'Don't then!' she heard Rose say. A door slammed. She paused. Then she drew in a deep breath of air, looked once more at the fiery sky, and tapped on the bedroom door.

The nurse rose quietly; put her finger to her lips, and left the room. Mrs Pargiter was asleep. Lying in a cleft of the pillows with one hand under her cheek, Mrs Pargiter moaned slightly as if she wandered in a world where even in sleep little obstacles lay across her path. Her face was pouched and heavy; the skin was stained with brown patches; the hair which had been red was now white, save that there were queer yellow patches in it, as if some locks had been dipped in the yolk of an egg. Bare of all rings save her wedding ring, her fingers alone seemed to indicate that she had entered the private world of illness. But she did not look as if she were dying; she looked as if she might go on existing in this borderland between life and death for ever. Delia could see no change in her. As she sat down, everything seemed to be at full tide in her. A long narrow glass by the bedside reflected a section of the sky; it was dazzled at the moment with red light. The dressing-table was illuminated. The light struck on silver bottles and on glass bottles, all set out in the perfect order of things that are not used. At this hour of the evening the sick-room had an unreal cleanliness, quiet and order. There by the bedside was a little table set with spectacles, prayer-book and a vase of lilies of the valley. The flowers, too, looked unreal. There was nothing to do but to look.

She stared at the yellow drawing of her grandfather with the high light on his nose; at the photograph of her Uncle Horace in his uniform; at the lean and twisted figure on the crucifix to the right.

'But you don't believe in it!' she said savagely, looking at her mother sunk in sleep. 'You don't want to die.'

She longed for her to die. There she was – soft, decayed but ever-lasting, lying in the cleft of the pillows, an obstacle, a prevention, an impediment to all life. She tried to whip up some feeling of affection, of pity. For instance, that summer, she told herself, at Sidmouth, when she called me up the garden steps . . . But the scene melted as she tried to look at it. There was the other scene of course – the man in the frock-coat with the flower in his button-hole. But she had sworn not to think of that till bedtime. What then should she think of? Grandpapa with the white light on his nose? The prayer-book? The lilies of the valley? Or the looking-glass? The sun had gone in; the glass was dim and reflected now only a dun-coloured patch of sky. She could resist no longer.

'Wearing a white flower in his button-hole,' she began. It required a few minutes' preparation. There must be a hall; banks of palms; a floor beneath them crowded with people's heads. The charm was beginning to work. She became permeated with delicious starts of flattering and exciting emotion. She was on the platform; there was a huge audience; everybody was shouting, waving handkerchiefs, hissing and whistling. Then she stood up. She rose all in white in the middle of the platform; Mr Parnell[9] was by her side.

'I am speaking in the cause of Liberty,' she began, throwing out her hands, 'in the cause of Justice . . . ' They were standing side by side. He was very pale but his dark eyes glowed. He turned to her and whispered . . .

There was a sudden interruption. Mrs Pargiter had raised herself on her pillows. 'Where am I?' she cried. She was frightened and bewildered, as she often was on waking. She raised her hand; she seemed to appeal for help. 'Where am I?' she repeated.

For a moment Delia was bewildered too. Where was she?

'Here, mama! Here!' she said wildly. 'Here, in your own room.'

She laid her hand on the counterpane. Mrs Pargiter clutched it nervously. She looked round the room as if she were seeking someone. She did not seem to recognise her daughter.

'What's happening?' she said. 'Where am I?'

Then she looked at Delia and remembered.

'Oh, Delia – I was dreaming,' she murmured half apologetically. She lay for a moment looking out of the window. The lamps were being lit, and a sudden soft spurt of light came in the street outside.

'It's been a fine day . . . ' she hesitated, 'for . . . ' It seemed as if she could not remember what for.

'A lovely day, yes, mama,' Delia repeated with mechanical cheerfulness.

' . . . for . . . ' her mother tried again.

What day was it? Delia could not remember.

' . . . for your Uncle Digby's birthday,' Mrs Pargiter at last brought out. 'Tell him from me – tell him how very glad I am.'

'I'll tell him,' said Delia. She had forgotten her uncle's birthday; but her mother was punctilious about such things.

'Aunt Eugénie – ' she began.

But her mother was staring at the dressing-table. Some gleam from the lamp outside made the white cloth look extremely white.

'Another clean tablecloth!' Mrs Pargiter murmured peevishly. 'The expense, Delia, the expense – that's what worries me – '

'That's all right, mama,' said Delia dully. Her eyes were fixed upon her grandfather's portrait; why, she wondered, had the artist put a dab of white chalk on the tip of his nose? 'Aunt Eugénie brought you some flowers,' she said.

For some reason Mrs Pargiter seemed pleased. Her eyes rested contemplatively on the clean tablecloth that had suggested the washing bill a moment before.

'Aunt Eugénie . . . ' she said. 'How well I remember' – her voice seemed to get fuller and rounder – 'the day the engagement was announced. We were all of us in the garden; there came a letter.' She paused. 'There came a letter,' she repeated. Then she said no more for a time. She seemed to be going over some memory. 'The dear little boy died, but save for that . . . '

She stopped again. She seemed weaker tonight, Delia thought; and a start of joy ran through her. Her sentences were more broken than usual. What little boy had died? She began counting the twists on the counterpane as she waited for her mother to speak.

'You know all the cousins used to come together in the summer,' her mother suddenly resumed. 'There was your Uncle Horace . . . '

'The one with the glass eye,' said Delia.

'Yes. He hurt his eye on the rocking-horse. The aunts thought so much of Horace. They would say . . . ' Here there was a long pause. She seemed to be fumbling to find the exact words. 'When Horace comes . . . remember to ask him about the dining-room door.'

A curious amusement seemed to fill Mrs Pargiter. She actually laughed. She must be thinking of some long-past family joke, Delia supposed, as she watched the smile flicker and fade away. There was complete silence. Her mother lay with her eyes shut; the hand with the single ring, the white and wasted hand, lay on the counterpane. In the silence they could hear a coal click in the grate and a street hawker droning down the road. Mrs Pargiter said no more. She lay perfectly still. Then she sighed profoundly.

The door opened, and the nurse came in. Delia rose and went out. Where am I? she asked herself, staring at a white jug stained pink by the setting sun. For a moment she seemed to be in some borderland between life and death. Where am I? she repeated, looking at the pink jug, for it all looked strange. Then she heard water rushing and feet thudding on the floor above.

'Here you are, Rosie,' said nurse, looking up from the wheel of the sewing-machine as Rose came in.

The nursery was brightly lit; there was an unshaded lamp on the table. Mrs C., who came every week with the washing, was sitting in the armchair with a cup in her hand. 'Go and get your sewing, there's a good girl,' said nurse as Rose shook hands with Mrs C., 'or you'll never be done in time for papa's birthday,' she added, clearing a space on the nursery table.

Rose opened the table drawer and took out the boot-bag that she was embroidering with a design of blue and red flowers for her father's birthday. There were still several clusters of little pencilled roses to be worked. She spread it on the table and examined it as nurse resumed what she was saying to Mrs C. about Mrs Kirby's daughter. But Rose did not listen.

Then I shall go by myself, she decided, straightening out the boot-bag. If Martin won't come with me, then I shall go by myself.

'I left my work-box in the drawing-room,' she said aloud.

'Well, then, go and fetch it,' said nurse, but she was not attending; she wanted to go on with what she was saying to Mrs C. about the grocer's daughter.

Now the adventure has begun, Rose said to herself as she stole on tiptoe to the night nursery. Now she must provide herself with ammunition and provisions; she must steal nurse's latchkey; but where was it? Every night it was hidden in a new place for fear of burglars. It would be either under the handkerchief-case or in the little box where she kept her mother's gold watch-chain. There it was. Now she had her pistol and her shot, she thought, taking her own purse from her own drawer, and enough provisions, she thought, as she hung her hat and coat over her arm, to last a fortnight.

She stole past the nursery, down the stairs. She listened intently as she passed the schoolroom door. She must be careful not to tread on a dry branch, or to let any twig crack under her, she told herself, as she went on tiptoe. Again she stopped and listened as she passed her mother's bedroom door. All was silent. Then she stood for a moment on the landing, looking down into the hall. The dog was asleep on the mat; the coast was clear; the hall was empty. She heard voices murmuring in the drawing-room.

She turned the latch of the front door with extreme gentleness, and closed it with scarcely a click behind her. Until she was round the corner she crouched close to the wall so that nobody could see her. When she reached the corner under the laburnum tree she stood erect.

'I am Pargiter of Pargiter's Horse,' she said, flourishing her hand, 'riding to the rescue!'

She was riding by night on a desperate mission to a besieged garrison, she told herself. She had a secret message – she clenched her fist on her purse – to deliver to the general in person. All their lives depended upon it. The British flag was still flying on the central tower – Lamley's shop was the central tower; the general was standing on the roof of Lamley's shop with his telescope to his eye. All their lives depended upon her riding to them through the enemy's country. Here she was galloping across the desert. She began to trot. It was growing dark. The street lamps were being lit. The lamplighter was poking his stick up into the little trap-door; the trees in the front gardens made a wavering network of shadow on the pavement; the pavement stretched before her broad and dark. Then there was the crossing; and then there was Lamley's shop on the little island of shops opposite. She had only to cross the desert, to ford the river, and she was safe. Flourishing the arm that held the pistol, she clapped spurs to her horse and galloped down Melrose Avenue. As she ran past the pillar-box the figure of a man suddenly emerged under the gas lamp.

'The enemy!' Rose cried to herself. 'The enemy! Bang!' she cried, pulling the trigger of her pistol and looking him full in the face as she passed him. It was a horrid face: white, peeled, pock-marked; he leered at her. He put out his arm as if to stop her. He almost caught her. She dashed past him. The game was over.

She was herself again, a little girl who had disobeyed her sister, in her house shoes, flying for safety to Lamley's shop.

Fresh-faced Mrs Lamley was standing behind the counter folding up the newspapers. She was pondering among her twopenny watches, cards of tools, toy boats and boxes of cheap stationery something pleasant, it seemed; for she was smiling.

Then Rose burst in. She looked up enquiringly. 'Hello, Rosie!' she exclaimed. 'What d'you want, my dear?'

She kept her hand on the pile of newspapers. Rose stood there panting. She had forgotten what she had come for.

'I want the box of ducks in the window,' Rose at last remembered.

Mrs Lamley waddled round to fetch it.

'Isn't it rather late for a little girl like you to be out alone?' she asked, looking at her as if she knew she had come out in her house shoes, disobeying her sister.

'Good-night, my dear, and run along home,' she said, giving her the parcel. The child seemed to hesitate on the doorstep: she stood there staring at the toys under the hanging oil lamp; then out she went reluctantly.

I gave my message to the general in person, she said to herself as she stood outside on the pavement again. And this is the trophy, she said, grasping the box under her arm. I am returning in triumph with the head of the chief rebel, she told herself, as she surveyed the stretch of Melrose Avenue before her. I must set spurs to my horse and gallop. But the story no longer worked. Melrose Avenue remained Melrose Avenue. She looked down it. There was the long stretch of bare street in front of her. The trees were trembling their shadows over the pavement. The lamps stood at great distances apart, and there were pools of darkness between. She began to trot. Suddenly, as she passed the first lamp-post, she saw the man again. He was leaning with his back against the lamp-post, and the light from the gas lamp flickered over his face. As she passed he sucked his lips in and out. He made a mewing noise. But he did not stretch his hands out at her; they were unbuttoning his clothes.

She fled past him. She thought that she heard him coming after her. She heard his feet padding on the pavement. Everything shook as she ran; pink and black spots danced before her eyes as she ran up the doorsteps, fitted her key in the latch and opened the hall door. She did not care whether she made a noise or not. She hoped somebody would come out and speak to her. But nobody heard her. The hall was empty. The dog was asleep on the mat. Voices still murmured in the drawing-room.

'And when it does catch,' Eleanor was saying, 'it'll be much too hot.'

Crosby had piled the coals into a great black promontory. A plume of yellow smoke was sullenly twining round it; it was beginning to burn, and when it did burn it would be much too hot.

'She can see nurse stealing the sugar, she says. She can see her shadow on the wall,' Milly was saying. They were talking about their mother.

'And then Edward,' she added, 'forgetting to write.'

'That reminds me,' said Eleanor. She must remember to write to Edward. But there would be time after dinner. She did not want to write; she did not want to talk; always when she came back from the Grove she felt as if several things were going on at the same time. Words went on repeating themselves in her mind – words and sights. She was thinking of old Mrs Levy, sitting propped up in bed with her white hair in a thick flop like a wig and her face cracked like an old glazed pot.

'Them that's been good to me, them I remember . . . them that's ridden in their coaches when I was a poor widder woman scrubbing and mangling – ' Here she stretched out her arm, which was wrung and white like the root of a tree. 'Them that's been good to me, them I remember . . . ' Eleanor repeated as she looked at the fire. Then the daughter came in who was working for a tailor. She wore pearls as big as hen's eggs; she had taken to painting her face; she was wonderfully handsome. But Milly made a little movement.

'I was thinking,' said Eleanor on the spur of the moment, 'the poor enjoy themselves more than we do.'

'The Levys?' said Milly absent-mindedly. Then she brightened. 'Do tell me about the Levys,' she added.

Eleanor's relations with 'the poor' – the Levys, the Grubbs, the Paravicinis, the Zwinglers and the Cobbs[10] – always amused her. But Eleanor did not like talking about 'the poor' as if they were people in a book. She had a great admiration for Mrs Levy, who was dying of cancer. 'Oh, they're much as usual,' she said sharply.

Milly looked at her. Eleanor's 'broody' she thought. The family joke was, 'Look out. Eleanor's broody. It's her Grove day.'

Eleanor was ashamed, but she always was irritable for some reason when she came back from the Grove – so many different things were going on in her head at the same time: Canning Place; Abercorn Terrace; this room; that room. There was the old Jewess sitting up in bed in her hot little room; then one came back here, and there was mama ill; papa grumpy; and Delia and Milly quarrelling about a party . . . But she checked herself. She ought to try to say something to amuse her sister.

'Mrs Levy had her rent ready, for a wonder,' she said. 'Lily helps her. Lily's got a job at a tailor's in Shoreditch.[11] She came in all covered with pearls and things. They do love finery – Jews,' she added.

'Jews?' said Milly. She seemed to consider the taste of the Jews; and then to dimiss it. 'Yes,' she said. 'Shiny.'

'She's extraordinarily handsome,' said Eleanor, thinking of the red cheeks and the white pearls.

Milly smiled; Eleanor always would stick up for the poor. She thought Eleanor the best, the wisest, the most remarkable person she knew.

'I believe you like going there more than anything,' she said. 'I believe you'd like to go and live there if you had your way,' she added, with a little sigh.

Eleanor shifted in her chair. She had her dreams, her plans, of course; but she did not want to discuss them.

'Perhaps you will, when you're married?' said Milly. There was something peevish yet plaintive in her voice. The dinner-party; the Burkes' dinner-party, Eleanor thought. She wished Milly did not always bring the conversation back to marriage. And what do they know about marriage? she asked herself. They stay at home too much, she thought; they never see anyone outside their own set. Here they are cooped up, day after day . . . That was why she had said, 'The poor enjoy themselves more than we do.' It had struck her coming back into that drawing-room, with all the furniture and the flowers and the hospital nurses . . . Again she stopped herself. She must wait till she was alone – till she was brushing her teeth at night. When she was with the others she must stop herself from thinking of two things at the same time. She took the poker and struck the coal.

'Look! What a beauty!' she exclaimed. A flame danced on top of the coal, a nimble and irrelevant flame. It was the sort of flame they used to make when they were children, by throwing salt on the fire. She struck again, and a shower of gold-eyed sparks went volleying up the chimney. 'D'you remember,' she said, 'how we used to play at firemen, and Morris and I set the chimney on fire?'

'And Pippy went and fetched papa,' said Milly. She paused. There was a sound in the hall. A stick grated; someone was hanging up a coat. Eleanor's eyes brightened. That was Morris – yes; she knew the sound he made. Now he was coming in. She looked round with a smile as the door opened. Milly jumped up.

Morris tried to stop her.

'Don't go – ' he began.

'Yes!' she exclaimed. 'I shall go. I shall go and have a bath,' she added on the spur of the moment. She left them.

Morris sat down in the chair she had left empty. He was glad to find Eleanor alone. Neither of them spoke for a moment. They watched the yellow plume of smoke, and the little flame dancing nimbly, irrelevantly, here and there on the black promontory of coals. Then he asked the usual question: 'How's mama?'

She told him; there was no change: 'except that she sleeps more,' she said. He wrinkled his forehead. He was losing his boyish look, Eleanor thought. That was the worst of the Bar,[12] everyone said; one had to wait. He was devilling for Sanders Curry; and it was dreary work, hanging about the courts all day, waiting.

'How's old Curry?' she asked – old Curry had a temper.

'A bit liverish,' said Morris grimly.

'And what have you been doing all day?' she asked.

'Nothing in particular,' he replied.

'Still *Evans* v. *Carter*?'

'Yes,' he said briefly.

'And who's going to win?' she asked.

'Carter, of course,' he replied.

Why 'of course' she wanted to ask? But she had said something silly the other day – something that showed that she had not been attending. She muddled things up; for example, what was the difference between Common Law and the other kind of law? She said nothing. They sat in silence, and watched the flame playing on the coals. It was a green flame, nimble, irrelevant.

'D'you think I've been an awful fool,' he asked suddenly. 'With all this illness, and Edward and Martin to be paid for – papa must find it a bit of a strain.' He wrinkled his brow up in the way that made her say to herself that he was losing his boyish look.

'Of course not,' she said emphatically. Of course it would have been absurd for him to go into business; his passion was for the Law.

'You'll be Lord Chancellor one of these days,' she said. 'I'm sure of it.' He shook his head, smiling.

'Quite sure,' she said, looking at him as she used to look at him when he came back from school and Edward had all the prizes and Morris sat silent – she could see him now – bolting his food with nobody making a fuss of him. But even while she looked, a doubt came over her. Lord Chancellor, she had said. Ought she not to have said Lord Chief Justice? She never could remember which was which: and that was why he would not discuss *Evans* v. *Carter* with her.

She never told him about the Levys either, except by way of a joke. That was the worst of growing up, she thought: they couldn't share things as they used to share them. When they met they never had time to talk as they used to talk – about things in general – they always talked about facts – little facts. She poked the fire. Suddenly a blare of sound rang through the room. It was Crosby applying herself to the gong in the hall. She was like a savage wreaking vengeance upon some brazen victim. Ripples of rough sound rang through the room. 'Lord, that's the dressing-bell!' said Morris. He got up and stretched himself. He raised his arms and held them for a moment suspended above his head. That's what he'll look like when he's the father of a family, Eleanor thought. He let his arms fall and left the room. She sat brooding for a moment; then she roused herself. What must I remember? she asked herself. To write to Edward, she mused, crossing over to her mother's writing-table. It'll be my table now, she thought, looking at the silver candlestick, the miniature of her grandfather, the tradesmen's books – one had a gilt cow stamped on it – and the spotted walrus with a brush in its back that Martin had given his mother on her last birthday.

Crosby held open the door of the dining-room as she waited for them to come down. The silver paid for polishing, she thought. Knives and forks rayed out round the table. The whole room, with its carved chairs, oil paintings, the two daggers on the mantelpiece, and the handsome sideboard – all the solid objects that Crosby dusted and polished every day – looked at its best in the evening. Meat-smelling and serge-curtained by day, it looked lit up, semi-transparent in the evening. And they were a handsome family, she thought as they filed in – the young ladies in their pretty dresses of blue-and-white-sprigged muslin; the gentlemen so spruce in their dinner jackets. She pulled the colonel's chair out for him. He was always at his best in the evening; he enjoyed his dinner; and for some reason his gloom had vanished. He was in his jovial mood. His children's spirits rose as they noted it.

'That's a pretty frock you're wearing,' he said to Delia as he sat down.

'This old one?' she said, patting the blue muslin.

There was an opulence, an ease and a charm about him when he was in a good temper that she liked particularly. People always said she was like him; sometimes she was glad of it – tonight for instance. He looked so pink and clean and genial in his dinner-jacket. They became children again when he was in this mood, and were spurred on to make family jokes at which they all laughed for no particular reason.

'Eleanor's broody,' said her father, winking at them. 'It's her Grove day.'

Everybody laughed; Eleanor had thought he was talking about Rover, the dog, when in fact he was talking about Mrs Egerton, the lady. Crosby, who was handing the soup, crinkled up her face because she wanted to laugh too. Sometimes the colonel made Crosby laugh so much that she had to turn away and pretend to be doing something at the sideboard.

'Oh, Mrs Egerton – ' said Eleanor, beginning her soup.

'Yes, Mrs Egerton,' said her father, and went on telling his story about Mrs Egerton, 'whose golden hair was said by the voice of slander not to be entirely her own'.

Delia liked listening to her father's stories about India. They were crisp, and at the same time romantic. They conveyed an atmosphere of officers dining together in mess jackets on a very hot night with a huge silver trophy in the middle of the table.

He used always to be like this when we were small, she thought. He used to jump over the bonfire on her birthday, she remembered. She watched him flicking cutlets dexterously on to plates with his left hand. She admired his decision, his common sense. Flicking the cutlets on to plates, he went on –

'Talking of the lovely Mrs Egerton reminds me – did I ever tell you the story of old Badger Parkes and – '

'Miss – ' said Crosby in a whisper, opening the door behind Eleanor's back. She whispered a few words to Eleanor privately.

'I'll come,' said Eleanor, getting up.

'What's that – what's that?' said the colonel, stopping in the middle of his sentence. Eleanor left the room.

'Some message from nurse,' said Milly.

The colonel, who had just helped himself to cutlets, held his knife and fork in his hand. They all held their knives suspended. Nobody liked to go on eating.

'Well, let's get on with our dinner,' said the colonel, abruptly attacking his cutlet. He had lost his geniality. Morris helped himself tentatively to potatoes. Then Crosby reappeared. She stood at the door, with her pale-blue eyes looking very prominent.

'What is it, Crosby? What is it?' said the colonel.

'The mistress, sir, taken worse, I think, sir,' she said with a curious whimper in her voice. Everybody got up.

'You wait. I'll go and see,' said Morris. They all followed him out into the hall. The colonel was still holding his dinner napkin. Morris ran upstairs; in a moment he came down again.

'Mama's had a fainting-fit,' he said to the colonel. 'I'm going to fetch Prentice.' He snatched his hat and coat and ran down the front steps. They heard him whistling for a cab as they stood uncertainly in the hall.

'Finish your dinner, girls,' said the colonel peremptorily. But he paced up and down the drawing-room, holding his dinner napkin in his hand.

*

'It has come,' Delia said to herself; 'it has come!' An extraordinary feeling of relief and excitement possessed her. Her father was pacing from one drawing-room to the other; she followed him in; but she avoided him. They were too much alike; each knew what the other was feeling. She stood at the window looking up the street. There had been a shower of rain. The street was wet; the roofs were shining. Dark clouds were moving across the sky; the branches were tossing up and down in the light of the street lamps. Something in her was tossing up and down too. Something unknown seemed to be approaching. Then a gulping sound behind her made her turn. It was Milly. She was standing by the mantelpiece under the picture of the white-robed girl with the flower-basket, and the tears slid slowly down her cheeks. Delia moved towards her; she ought to go up to her and put her arms round her shoulders; but she could not do it. Real tears were sliding down Milly's cheeks. But her own eyes were dry. She turned to the window again. The street was empty – only the branches were tossing up and down in the lamplight. The colonel paced up and down; once he knocked against a table and said, 'Damn!' They heard steps moving about in the room upstairs. They heard voices murmuring. Delia turned to the window.

A hansom came trotting down the street. Morris jumped out directly the cab stopped. Dr Prentice followed him. He went straight upstairs and Morris joined them in the drawing-room.

'Why not finish your dinner?' the colonel said gruffly, coming to a halt and standing upright before them.

'Oh, after he's gone,' said Morris irritably.

The colonel resumed his pacing.

Then he stopped his pacing, and stood with his hands behind him in front of the fire. He had a braced look as if he were holding himself ready for an emergency.

We're both acting, Delia thought to herself, stealing a glance at him, but he's doing it better than I am.

She looked out of the window again. The rain was falling. When it crossed the lamplight it glanced in long strips of silver light.

'It's raining,' she said in a low voice, but nobody answered her.

At last they heard footsteps on the stairs and Dr Prentice came in. He shut the door quietly but said nothing.

'Well?' said the colonel, facing up to him.

There was a prolonged pause.

'How d'you find her?' said the colonel.

Dr Prentice moved his shoulders slightly. 'She's rallied,' he said. 'For the moment,' he added.

Delia felt as if his words struck her violently a blow on the head. She sank down on the arm of a chair.

So you're not going to die, she said, looking at the girl balanced on the trunk of a tree; she seemed to simper down at her daughter with smiling malice. You're not going to die – never, never! she cried clenching her hands together beneath her mother's picture.

'Now, shall we get on with our dinner?' said the colonel, taking up the napkin which he had dropped on the drawing-room table.

It was a pity – the dinner was spoilt, Crosby thought, bringing up the cutlets from the kitchen again. The meat was dried up, and the potatoes had a brown crust on top of them. One of the candles was scorching its shade too, she observed, as she put the dish down in front of the colonel. Then she shut the door on them, and they began to eat their dinner.

All was quiet in the house. The dog slept on its mat at the foot of the stairs. All was quiet outside the sick-room door. A faint sound of snoring came from the bedroom where Martin lay asleep. In the day nursery Mrs C. and the nurse had resumed their supper, which they had interrupted when they heard sounds in the hall below. Rose lay asleep in the night nursery. For some time she slept profoundly, curled round with the blankets tight twisted over her head. Then she stirred and stretched her arms out. Something had swum up on top of the blackness. An oval white shape hung in front of her dangling, as if it hung from a string. She half opened her eyes and looked at it. It bubbled with grey spots that went in and out. She woke completely. A face was hanging close to her as if it dangled on a bit of string. She shut her eyes; but the face was still there, bubbling in and out, grey, white, purplish and pock-marked. She put out her hand to touch the big bed next hers. But it was empty. She listened. She heard the clatter of knives and the chatter of voices in the day nursery across the passage. But she could not sleep.

She made herself think of a flock of sheep penned up in a hurdle in a field. She made one of the sheep jump the hurdle; then another. She counted them as they jumped. One, two, three, four – they jumped over the hurdle. But the fifth sheep would not jump. It turned round and looked at her. Its long narrow face was grey; its lips moved; it was the face of the man at the pillar-box, and she was alone with it. If she shut her eyes there it was; if she opened them, there it was still.

She sat up in bed and cried out, 'Nurse! Nurse!'

There was dead silence everywhere. The clatter of knives and forks in the next room had ceased. She was alone with something horrible.

Then she heard a shuffling in the passage. It came closer and closer. It was the man himself. His hand was on the door. The door opened. An angle of light fell across the washstand. The jug and basin were lit up. The man was actually in the room with her . . . but it was Eleanor.

'Why aren't you asleep?' said Eleanor. She put down her candle and began to straighten the bedclothes. They were all crumpled up. She looked at Rose. Her eyes were very bright and her cheeks were flushed. What was the matter? Had they woken her, moving about downstairs in mama's room?

'What's been keeping you awake?' she asked. Rose yawned again; but it was a sigh rather than a yawn. She could not tell Eleanor what she had seen. She had a profound feeling of guilt; for some reason she must lie about the face she had seen.

'I had a bad dream,' she said. 'I was frightened.' A queer nervous jerk ran through her body as she sat up in bed. What was the matter? Eleanor wondered, again. Had she been fighting with Martin? Had she been chasing cats in Miss Pym's garden again?

'Have you been chasing cats again?' she asked. 'Poor cats,' she added; 'they mind it just as much as you would,' she said. But she knew that Rose's fright had nothing to do with the cats. She was grasping her finger tightly; she was staring ahead of her with a queer look in her eyes.

'What was your dream about?' she asked, sitting down on the edge of the bed. Rose stared at her; she could not tell her; but at all costs Eleanor must be made to stay with her.

'I thought I heard a man in the room,' she brought out at last. 'A robber,' she added.

'A robber? Here?' said Eleanor. 'But Rose, how could a robber get into your nursery? There's papa, there's Morris – they would never let a robber come into your room.'

'No,' said Rose. 'Papa would kill him,' she added. There was something queer about the way she twitched.

'But what are you all doing?' she said restlessly. 'Haven't you gone to bed yet? Isn't it very late?'

'What are we all doing?' said Eleanor. 'We're sitting in the drawing-room. It's not very late.' As she spoke a faint sound boomed through the room. When the wind was in the right direction they could hear St Paul's. The soft circles spread out in the air: one, two, three, four – Eleanor counted eight, nine, ten. She was surprised that the strokes stopped so soon.

'There, it's only ten o'clock, you see,' she said. It had seemed to her much later. But the last stroke dissolved in the air. 'So now you'll go to sleep,' she said.

Rose clutched her hand. 'Don't go, Eleanor; not yet,' she implored her.

'But tell me, what's frightened you?' Eleanor began. Something was being hidden from her, she was sure.

'I saw . . . ' Rose began. She made a great effort to tell her the truth; to tell her about the man at the pillar-box. 'I saw . . . ' she repeated. But here the door opened and nurse came in.

'I don't know what's come over Rosie tonight,' she said, bustling in. She felt a little guilty; she had stayed downstairs with the other servants gossiping about the mistress. 'She sleeps so sound generally,' she said, coming over to the bed.

'Now, here's nurse,' said Eleanor. 'She's coming to bed. So you won't be frightened any more, will you?' She smoothed down the bedclothes and kissed her. She got up and took her candle.

'Good-night, nurse,' she said, turning to leave the room.

'Good-night, Miss Eleanor,' said nurse, putting some sympathy into her voice; for they were saying downstairs that the mistress couldn't last much longer.

'Turn over and go to sleep, dearie,' she said, kissing Rose on the forehead. For she was sorry for the little girl who would so soon be motherless. Then she slipped the silver links out of her cuffs and began to take the hairpins out of her hair, standing in her petticoats in front of the yellow chest of drawers.

' "I saw",' Eleanor repeated, as she shut the nursery door. ' "I saw . . . " ' What had she seen? Something horrible, something hidden. But what? There it was, hidden behind her strained eyes. She held the candle slightly slanting in her hand. Three drops of grease fell on the polished skirting before she noticed them. She straightened the candle and walked down the stairs. She listened as she went. There was silence. Martin was asleep. Her mother was asleep. As she passed the doors and went downstairs a weight seemed to descend on her. She paused, looking down into the hall. A blankness came over her. Where am I? she asked herself, staring at a heavy frame. What is that? She seemed to be alone in the midst of nothingness; yet must descend, must carry her burden – she raised her arms slightly, as if she were carrying a pitcher, an earthenware pitcher on her head. Again she stopped. The rim of a bowl outlined itself upon her eyeballs; there was water in it; and something yellow. It was the dog's bowl, she realised; that was the sulphur in the dog's bowl; the dog was lying curled up at the bottom of the stairs. She stepped carefully over the body of the sleeping dog and went into the drawing-room.

They all looked up as she came in; Morris had a book in his hand but he was not reading; Milly had some stuff in her hand but she was not sewing; Delia was lying back in her chair, doing nothing whatever. She stood there hesitating for a moment. Then she turned to the writing-table. 'I'll write to Edward,' she murmured. She took up the pen, but she hesitated. She found it difficult to write to Edward, seeing him before her, when she took up the pen, when she smoothed the note-paper on the writing-table. His eyes were too close together; he brushed up his crest before the looking-glass in the lobby in a way that irritated her. 'Nigs' was her nickname for him. 'My dear Edward,' she began to write, choosing 'Edward' not 'Nigs' on this occasion.

Morris looked up from the book he was trying to read. The scratching of Eleanor's pen irritated him. She stopped; then she wrote; then she put her hand to her head. All the worries were put on her of course. Still she irritated him. She always asked questions; she never listened to the answers. He glanced at his book again. But what was the use of trying to read? The atmosphere of suppressed emotion was distasteful to him. There was nothing that anybody could do, but there they all sat in attitudes of suppressed emotion. Milly's stitching irritated him, and Delia lying back in her chair doing nothing as usual. There he was cooped up with all these women in an atmosphere of unreal emotion. And Eleanor went on writing, writing, writing. There was nothing to write about – but here she licked the envelope and dabbed down the stamp.

'Shall I take it?' he said, dropping his book.

He got up as if he were glad to have something to do. Eleanor went to the front door with him and stood holding it open while he went to the pillar-box. It was raining gently, and as she stood at the door, breathing in the mild damp air, she watched the curious shadows that trembled on the pavement under the trees. Morris disappeared under the shadows round the corner. She remembered how she used to stand at the door when he was a small boy and went to a day school with a satchel in his hand. She used to wave to him; and when he got to the corner he always turned and waved back. It was a curious little ceremony, dropped now that they were both grown up. The shadows shook as she stood waiting; in a moment he emerged from the shadows. He came along the street and up the steps.

'He'll get that tomorrow,' he said – 'anyhow by the second post.'

He shut the door and stooped to fasten the chain. It seemed to her, as the chain rattled, that they both accepted the fact that nothing more was going to happen tonight. They avoided each other's eyes; neither of them wanted any more emotion tonight. They went back into the drawing-room.

'Well,' said Eleanor, looking round her, 'I think I shall go to bed. Nurse will ring,' she said, 'if she wants anything.'

'We may as well all go,' said Morris. Milly began to roll up her embroidery. Morris began to rake out the fire.

'What an absurd fire –.' he exclaimed irritably. The coals were all stuck together. They were blazing fiercely.

Suddenly a bell rang.

'Nurse!' Eleanor exclaimed. She looked at Morris. She left the room hurriedly. Morris followed her.

But what's the good? Delia thought to herself. It's only another false alarm. She got up. 'It's only nurse,' she said to Milly, who was standing up with a look of alarm on her face. She can't be going to cry again, she thought, and strolled off into the front room. Candles were burning on the mantelpiece; they lit up the picture of her mother. She glanced at the portrait of her mother. The girl in white seemed to be presiding over the protracted affair of her own deathbed with a smiling indifference that outraged her daughter.

'You're not going to die – you're not going to die!' said Delia bitterly, looking up at her. Her father, alarmed by the bell, had come into the room. He was wearing a red smoking-cap with an absurd tassel.

But it's all for nothing, Delia said silently, looking at her father. She felt that they must both check their rising excitement. 'Nothing's going to happen – nothing whatever,' she said, looking at him. But at that moment Eleanor came into the room. She was very white.

'Where's papa?' she said, looking round. She saw him. 'Come, papa, come,' she said, stretching out her hand. 'Mama's dying . . . And the children,' she said to Milly over her shoulder.

Two little white patches appeared above her father's ears, Delia noticed. His eyes fixed themselves. He braced himself. He strode past them up the stairs. They all followed in a little procession behind. The dog, Delia noticed, tried to come upstairs with them; but Morris cuffed him back. The colonel went first into the bedroom; then Eleanor; then Morris; then Martin came down, pulling on a dressing-gown; then Milly brought Rose wrapped in a shawl. But Delia hung back behind the others. There were so many of them in the room that she could get no farther than the doorway. She could see two nurses standing with their backs to the wall opposite. One of them was crying – the one, she observed, who had only come that afternoon. She could not see the bed from where she stood. But she could see that Morris had fallen on his knees. Ought I to kneel too? she wondered. Not in the passage, she decided. She looked away; she saw the little window at the end of the passage. Rain was falling; there was a light somewhere that made the raindrops shine. One drop after another slid down the pane; they slid and they paused; one drop joined another drop and then they slid again. There was complete silence in the bedroom.

Is this death? Delia asked herself. For a moment there seemed to be something there. A wall of water seemed to gape apart; the two walls held themselves apart. She listened. There was complete silence. Then there was a stir, a shuffle of feet in the bedroom and out came her father, stumbling.

'Rose!' he cried. 'Rose! Rose!' He held his arms with the fists clenched out in front of him.

You did that very well, Delia told him as he passed her. It was like a scene in a play. She observed quite dispassionately that the raindrops were still falling. One sliding met another and together in one drop they rolled to the bottom of the window-pane.

It was raining. A fine rain, a gentle shower, was peppering the pavements and making them greasy. Was it worth while opening an umbrella, was it necessary to hail a hansom, people coming out from the theatres asked themselves, looking up at the mild, milky sky in which the stars were blunted. Where it fell on earth, on fields and gardens, it drew up the smell of earth. Here a drop poised on a grass-blade; there filled the cup of a wild flower, till the breeze stirred and the rain was spilt. Was it worth while to shelter under the hawthorn, under the hedge, the sheep seemed to question; and the cows, already turned out in the grey fields, under the dim hedges, munched on, sleepily chewing with raindrops on their hides. Down on the roofs it fell – here in Westminster, there in Ladbroke Grove; on the wide sea a million points pricked the blue monster like an innumerable shower bath. Over the vast domes, the soaring spires of slumbering university cities, over the leaded libraries, and the museums, now shrouded in brown holland, the gentle rain slid down, till, reaching the mouths of those fantastic laughers, the many-clawed gargoyles, it splayed out in a thousand odd indentations. A drunken man slipping in a narrow passage outside the public house, cursed it. Women in childbirth heard the doctor say to the midwife,

'It's raining.' And the walloping Oxford bells, turning over and over like slow porpoises in a sea of oil, contemplatively intoned their musical incantation. The fine rain, the gentle rain, poured equally over the mitred and the bareheaded with an impartiality which suggested that the god of rain, if there were a god, was thinking: Let it not be restricted to the very wise, the very great, but let all breathing kind, the munchers and chewers, the ignorant, the unhappy, those who toil in the furnace making innumerable copies of the same pot, those who bore red-hot minds through contorted letters, and also Mrs Jones in the alley, share my bounty.

It was raining in Oxford. The rain fell gently, persistently, making a little chuckling and burbling noise in the gutters. Edward, leaning out of the window, could still see the trees in the college garden, whitened by the falling rain. Save for the rustle of the trees and the rain falling, it was perfectly quiet. A damp, earthy smell came up from the wet ground. Lamps were being lit here and there in the dark mass of the college; and there was a pale-yellowish mound in one corner where lamplight fell upon a flowering tree. The grass was becoming invisible, fluid, grey, like water.

He drew in a long breath of satisfaction. Of all the moments in the day he liked this best, when he stood and looked out into the garden. He breathed in again the cool damp air, and then straightened himself and turned back into the room. He was working very hard. His day was parcelled out on the advice of his tutor into hours and half-hours; but he still had five minutes before he need begin. He turned up the reading-lamp. It was partly the green light that made him look a little pale and thin, but he was very handsome. With his clear-cut features and the fair hair that he brushed up with a flick of his fingers into a crest, he looked like a Greek boy on a frieze. He smiled. He was thinking as he watched the rain how, after the interview between his father and his tutor – when old Harbottle had said, 'Your son has a chance' – the old boy had insisted upon looking up the rooms that his own father had had when his father was at college. They had burst in and found a chap called Thompson on his knees blowing up the fire with a bellows.

'My father had these rooms, sir,' the colonel had said, by way of apology. The young man had got very red and said, 'Don't mention it.' Edward smiled. ' "Don't mention it," ' he repeated. It was time to begin. He turned the lamp a little higher. When the lamp was turned higher he saw his work cut out in a sharp circle of bright light from the surrounding dimness. He looked at the textbooks, at the dictionaries lying before him. He always had some doubts before he began. His father would be frightfully cut-up if he failed. His heart was set on it. He had sent him a dozen of fine old port 'by way of a stirrup-cup', so he said. But after all Marsham was in for it; then there was the clever little Jew-boy from Birmingham – but it was time to begin. One after another the bells of Oxford began pushing their slow chimes through the air. They tolled ponderously, unequally, as if they had to roll the air out of their way and the air was heavy. He loved the sound of the bells. He listened till the last stroke had struck, then pulled his chair to the table; time was up; he must work now.

A little dint sharpened between his brows. He frowned as he read. He read; and made a note; then he read again. All sounds were blotted out. He saw nothing but the Greek in front of him. But as he read, his brain gradually warmed; he was conscious of something quickening and tightening in his forehead. He caught phrase after phrase exactly, firmly, more exactly, he noted, making a brief note in the margin, than the night before. Little negligible words now revealed a shade of meaning which altered the meaning. He made another note; *that* was the meaning. His own dexterity in catching the phrase plumb in the middle gave him a thrill of excitement. There it was, clean and entire. But he must be precise; exact; even his little scribbled notes must be clear as print. He turned to this book; then that book. Then he leant back to see, with his eyes shut. He must let nothing dwindle off into vagueness. The clocks began striking. He listened. The clocks went on striking. The lines that had graved themselves on his face slackened; he leant back; his muscles relaxed; he looked up from his books into the dimness. He felt as if he had thrown himself down on the turf after running a race. But for a moment it seemed to him that he was still running; his mind went on without the book. It travelled by itself without impediments through a world of pure meaning; but gradually it lost its meaning. The books stood out on the wall; he saw the cream-coloured panels; a bunch of poppies in a blue vase. The last of the strokes had sounded. He gave a sigh and rose from the table.

He stood by the window again. It was raining, but the whiteness had gone. Save for a wet leaf shining here and there, the garden was all dark now – the yellow mound of the flowering tree had vanished. The college buildings lay round the garden in a low couched mass, here red-stained, here yellow-stained, where lights burnt behind curtains; and there lay the chapel, huddling its bulk against the sky which, because of the rain, seemed to tremble slightly. But it was no longer silent. He listened; there was no sound in particular; but, as he stood looking out, the building hummed with life. There was a sudden roar of laughter; then the tinkle of a piano; then a nondescript clatter and chatter – of china partly; then again the sound of rain falling, and the gutters chuckling and burbling as they sucked up the water. He turned back into the room.

It had grown chilly; the fire was almost out; only a little red glowed under the grey ash. Opportunely he remembered his father's gift – the wine that had come that morning. He went to the side table and poured himself out a glass of port. As he raised it against the light he smiled. He saw again his father's hand with two smooth knobs instead of fingers holding the glass, as he always held the glass, to the light before he drank.

'You can't drive a bayonet through a chap's body in cold blood,' he remembered him saying.

'And you can't go in for an exam without drinking,' said Edward. He hesitated; he held the glass to the light in imitation of his father. Then he sipped. He set the glass on the table in front of him. He turned again to the *Antigone*.[13] He read; then he sipped; then he read; then he sipped again. A soft glow spread over his spine at the nape of his neck. The wine seemed to press open little dividing doors in his brain. And whether it was the wine or the words or both, a luminous shell formed, a purple fume, from which out stepped a Greek girl; yet she was English. There she stood among the marble and the asphodel, yet there she was among the Morris wallpapers and the cabinets – his cousin Kitty, as he had seen her last time he dined at The Lodge. She was both of them – Antigone and Kitty; here in the book; there in the room; lit up, risen, like a purple flower. No, he exclaimed, not in the least like a flower! For if ever a girl held herself upright, lived, laughed and breathed, it was Kitty, in the white and blue dress that she had worn last time he dined at The Lodge. He crossed to the window. Red squares showed through the trees. There was a party at The Lodge. Who was she talking to? What was she saying? He went back to the table.

'Oh, damn!' he exclaimed, prodding the paper with his pencil. The point broke. Then there was a tap at the door, a sliding tap, not a commanding tap, the tap of one who passes, not of one who comes in. He went and opened the door. There on the stair above loomed the figure of a huge young man who was leaning over the banisters. 'Come in,' said Edward.

The huge young man came slowly down the stairs. He was very large. His eyes, which were prominent, became apprehensive at the sight of the books on the table. He looked at the books on the table. They were Greek. But there was wine after all.

Edward poured out wine. Beside Gibbs he looked what Eleanor called 'finicky'. He felt the contrast himself. The hand with which he lifted his glass was like a girl's beside Gibbs's great red paw. Gibbs's hand was burnt bright scarlet; it was like a piece of raw meat.

Hunting was the subject they had in common. They talked about hunting. Edward leant back and let Gibbs do the talking. It was all very pleasant, listening to Gibbs, riding through these English lanes. He was talking about cubbing in September; and a raw but handy hack. He was saying, 'You remember that farm on the right as you go up to Stapleys? and the pretty girl?' – he winked – 'worse luck, she's married to a keeper.' He was saying – Edward watched him gulping down his port – how he wished this damned summer were over. Then, again, he was telling the old story about the spaniel bitch. 'You'll come and stop with us in September,' he was saying when the door opened so silently that Gibbs did not hear it, and in glided another man – quite another man.

It was Ashley who came in. He was the very opposite of Gibbs. He was neither tall nor short, neither dark nor fair. But he was not negligible – far from it. It was partly the way he moved, as if chair and table rayed out some influence which he could feel by means of some invisible antennae, or whiskers, like a cat. Now he sank down, cautiously, gingerly, and looked at the table and half read a line in a book. Gibbs stopped in the middle of his sentence.

'Hello, Ashley,' he said rather curtly. He stretched out and poured himself another glass of the colonel's port. Now the decanter was empty.

'Sorry,' he said, glancing at Ashley.

'Don't open another bottle for me,' said Ashley quickly. His voice sounded a little squeaky, as if he were ill at ease.

'Oh, but we shall want some more too,' said Edward casually. He went into the dining-room to fetch it.

'Damned awkward,' he reflected as he stooped among the bottles. It meant, he reflected grimly as he chose his bottle, another row with Ashley, and he had had two rows with Ashley about Gibbs already this term.

He went back with the bottle and sat down on a low stool between them. He uncorked the wine and poured it out. They both looked at him, as he sat between them, admiringly. The vanity, which Eleanor always laughed at in her brother, was flattered. He liked to feel their eyes on him. And yet he was at his ease with both of them, he thought; the thought pleased him; he could talk hunting with Gibbs and books with Ashley. But Ashley could only talk about books, and Gibbs – he smiled – could only talk about girls. Girls and horses. He poured out three glasses of wine.

Ashley sipped gingerly, and Gibbs, with his great red hands on the glass, gulped rather. They talked about races; then they talked about examinations. Then Ashley, glancing at the books on the table, said: 'And what about you?'

'I've not the ghost of a chance,' said Edward. His indifference was affected. He pretended to despise examinations; but it was pretence. Gibbs was taken in by him; but Ashley saw through him. He often caught Edward out in small vanities like this; but they only served to endear him the more. How beautiful he looks, he was thinking: there he sat between them with the light falling on the top of his fair hair; like a Greek boy; strong; yet in some way, weak, needing his protection.

He ought to be rescued from brutes like Gibbs, he thought savagely. For how Edward could tolerate that clumsy brute, he thought looking at him, who always seemed to smell of beer and horses (he was listening to him), Ashley could not conceive. As he came in he had caught the tail of an infuriating sentence – of a sentence that seemed to show that they had made some plan together.

'Well, then, I'll see Storey about that hack,' Gibbs was saying now, as if he were finishing some private talk that they had been having before he came in. A spasm of jealousy ran through Ashley. To hide it, he stretched out his hand and took up a book that lay open on the table. He pretended to read it.

He did it to insult him, Gibbs felt. Ashley, he knew, thought him a great hulking brute; the dirty little swine came in, spoilt the talk, and then began to give himself airs at Gibbs's expense. Very well; he had been going to go; now he would stay; he would twist his tail for him – he knew how. He turned to Edward and went on talking.

'You won't mind pigging it,' he said. 'My people will be up in Scotland.'

Ashley turned a page viciously. They would be alone then. Edward began to relish the situation; he played up to it maliciously.

'All right,' he said. 'But you'll have to see I don't make a fool of myself,' he added.

'Oh, it'll only be cubbing,' said Gibbs. Ashley turned another page. Edward glanced at the book. It was being held upside down. But as he glanced at Ashley he caught his head against the panels and the poppies. How civilised he looked, he thought, compared with Gibbs; and how ironical. He respected him immensely. Gibbs had lost his glamour. There he was, telling the same old story of the spaniel bitch all over again. There would be a devil's own row tomorrow, he thought, and glanced surreptitiously at his watch. It was past eleven; and he must do an hour's work before breakfast. He swallowed down the last drops of his wine, stretched himself, yawned ostentatiously and rose.

'I'm off to bed,' he said. Ashley looked at him appealingly. Edward could torture him horribly. Edward began unbuttoning his waistcoat; he had a perfect figure, Ashley thought, looking at him, standing between them.

'But don't you hurry' said Edward, yawning again. 'Finish your drinks.' He smiled at the thought of Ashley and Gibbs finishing their drinks together.

'There's plenty more in there if you want it.' He indicated the next room and left them.

'Let 'em fight it out together,' he thought as he shut the bedroom door. His own fight would come soon enough; he knew that from the look on Ashley's face. He was infernally jealous. He began to undress. He put his money methodically in two heaps on either side of the looking-glass, for he was a little near about money; folded his waistcoat carefully on a chair; then glanced at himself in the looking-glass, and brushed his crest up with the half-conscious gesture that irritated his sister. Then he listened.

A door slammed outside. One of them had gone – either Gibbs or Ashley. But one, he rather thought, was still there. He listened intently. He heard someone moving about in the sitting-room. Very quickly, very firmly, he turned the key in the door. A moment later the handle moved.

'Edward!' said Ashley. His voice was low and controlled.

Edward made no answer.

'Edward!' said Ashley, rattling the handle.

The voice was sharp and appealing.

'Good-night,' said Edward sharply. He listened. There was a pause. Then he heard the door shut. Ashley was gone.

'Lord! What a row there'll be tomorrow,' said Edward, going to the window and looking out at the rain that was still falling.

The party at the Lodge was over. The ladies stood in the doorway in their flowing gowns, and looked up at the sky from which a gentle rain was falling.

'Is that a nightingale?' said Mrs Larpent, hearing a bird twitter in the bushes. Then old Chuffy – the great Dr Andrews – standing slightly behind her with his domed head exposed to the drizzle and his hirsute, powerful but not prepossessing countenance turned upward, gave a roar of laughter. It was a thrush, he said. The laughter was echoed back

like a hyena laughing from the stone walls. Then, with a wave of the
hand dictated by centuries of tradition, Mrs Larpent drew back her
foot, as if she had encroached upon one of the chalk marks which
decorate academic lintels and, signifying that Mrs Lathom, wife of the
Divinity professor, should precede her, they passed out into the rain.

In the long drawing-room at the Lodge they were all standing up.

'I'm so glad Chuffy – Dr Andrews – came up to your expectations,'
Mrs Malone was saying in her courteous manner. As residents they
called the great doctor 'Chuffy'; he was Dr Andrews to American
visitors.

The other guests had gone. But the Howard Fripps, the Americans,
were staying in the house. Mrs Howard Fripp was saying that Dr
Andrews had been perfectly charming to her. And her husband, the
professor, was saying something equally polite to the master. Kitty, the
daughter, standing a little in the background, wished that they would
get it over and come to bed. But she had to stand there until her mother
gave the signal for them to move.

'Yes, I never knew Chuffy in better form,' her father continued,
implying a compliment to the little American lady who had made such
a conquest. She was small and vivacious, and Chuffy liked ladies to be
small and vivacious.

'I adore his books,' she said in her queer nasal voice. 'But I never
expected to have the pleasure of sitting next him at dinner.'

Did you really like the way he spits when he talks? Kitty wondered,
looking at her. She was extraordinarily pretty and gay. All the other
women had looked dowdy and dumpy beside her, except her mother.
For Mrs Malone, standing by the fireplace with her foot on the fender,
with her crisp white hair curled stiffly, never looked in the fashion or
out of it. Mrs Fripp, on the contrary, looked in the fashion.

And yet they laughed at her, Kitty thought. She had caught the
Oxford ladies lifting their eyebrows at some of Mrs Fripp's American
phrases. But Kitty liked her American phrases; they were so different
from what she was used to. She was American, a real American; but
nobody would have taken her husband for an American, Kitty thought,
looking at him. He might have been any professor, from any university,
she thought, with his distinguished wrinkled face, his goatee beard and
the black ribbon of his eyeglass crossing his shirt-front as if it were
some foreign order. He spoke without any accent – at least without any
American accent. Yet he too was different somehow. She had dropped
her handkerchief. He stooped at once and gave it her with a bow that

was almost too courteous – it made her shy. She bent her head and smiled at the professor, rather shyly, as she took the handkerchief.

'Thank you so much,' she said. He made her feel awkward. Beside Mrs Fripp she felt even larger than usual. Her hair, of the true Rigby red, never lay smooth as it should have done; Mrs Fripp's hair looked beautiful, glossy and tidy.

But now Mrs Malone, glancing at Mrs Fripp, said, 'Well, ladies – ?' and waved her hand.

There was something authoritative about her action – as if she had done it again and again; and been obeyed again and again. They moved towards the door. Tonight there was a little ceremony at the door; Professor Fripp bent very low over Mrs Malone's hand, not quite so low over Kitty's hand, and held the door wide open for them.

'He rather overdoes it,' Kitty thought to herself as they passed out.

The ladies took their candles and went in single file up the wide low stairs. Portraits of former masters of Katharine's[14] looked down on them as they mounted. The light of the candles flickered over the dark gold-framed faces as they went up stair after stair.

Now she'll stop, thought Kitty, following behind, and ask who *that* is.

But Mrs Fripp did not stop. Kitty gave her good marks for that. She compared favourably with most of their visitors, Kitty thought. She had never done the Bodleian[15] quite so quick as she had done it that morning. Indeed, she had felt rather guilty. There were a great many more sights to be seen, had they wished it. But in less than an hour of it Mrs Fripp had turned to Kitty and had said in her fascinating, if nasal, voice: 'Well, my dear, I guess you're a bit fed-up with sights – what d'you say to an ice in that dear old bun-shop with the bow windows?'

And they had eaten ices when they ought to have been going round the Bodleian.

The procession had now reached the first landing, and Mrs Malone stopped at the door of the famous room where distinguished guests always slept when they stayed at the Lodge. She gave one look round as she held the door open.

'The bed where Queen Elizabeth did *not* sleep,' she said, making the usual little joke as they looked at the great four-poster. The fire was burning; the water-jug was swaddled up like an old woman with the toothache; and the candles were lit on the dressing-table. But there was something strange about the room tonight, Kitty thought, glancing over her mother's shoulder; a dressing-gown flashed green and silver upon the bed. And on the dressing-table there were a number of little pots and jars and a large powder-puff stained pink.

Could it be, was it possible, that the reason why Mrs Fripp looked so very bright and the Oxford ladies looked so very dingy was that Mrs Fripp – But Mrs Malone was saying, 'You have everything you want?' with such extreme politeness that Kitty guessed that Mrs Malone too had seen the dressing-table. Kitty held out her hand. To her surprise, instead of taking it, Mrs Fripp pulled her down and kissed her.

'Thanks a thousand times for showing me all those sights,' she said. 'And remember, you're coming to stay with us in America,' she added. For she had liked the big shy girl who had so obviously preferred eating ices to showing her the Bodleian; and she had felt sorry for her too for some reason.

'Good-night, Kitty,' said her mother as she shut the door; and they touched each other perfunctorily on the cheek.

Kitty went on upstairs to her own room. She still felt the spot where Mrs Fripp had kissed her; the kiss had left a little glow on her cheek.

She shut the door. The room was very stuffy. It was a warm night, but they always shut the windows and drew the curtains. She opened the windows and drew the curtains. It was raining as usual. Arrows of silver rain crossed the dark trees in the garden. Then she kicked off her shoes. That was the worst of being so large – shoes were always too tight; white satin shoes in particular. Then she began to unhook her dress. It was difficult: there were so many hooks and all at the back; but at last the white satin dress was off and laid neatly across the chair; and then she began to brush her hair. It had been Thursday at its very worst, she reflected; sights in the morning; people for lunch; under-graduates for tea; and a dinner-party in the evening.

However, she concluded, tugging the comb through her hair, it's over . . . it's over.

The candles flickered and then the muslin blind, blowing out in a white balloon, almost touched the flame. She opened her eyes with a start. She was standing at the open window with a light beside her in her petticoat.

'Anybody might see in,' her mother had said, scolding her only the other day.

Now, she said, moving the candle to a table at the right, nobody can see in.

She began to brush her hair again. But with the light at the side instead of in front she saw her face from a different angle.

Am I pretty? she asked herself, putting down her comb and looking in the glass. Her cheekbones were too prominent; her eyes were set too far apart. She was not pretty; no, her size was against her. What did Mrs Fripp think of me, she wondered?

She kissed me, she suddenly remembered with a start of pleasure, feeling again the glow on her cheek. She asked me to stay with them in America. What fun that would be! she thought. What fun to leave Oxford and go to America! She tugged the comb through her hair, which was like a fuzz bush.

But the bells were making their usual commotion. She hated the sound of the bells; it always seemed to her a dismal sound; and then, just as one stopped, here was another beginning. They went walloping one over another, one after another, as if they would never be finished. She counted eleven, twelve, and then they went on thirteen, fourteen . . . clock repeating clock through the damp, drizzling air. It was late. She began to brush her teeth. She glanced at the calendar above the washstand and tore off Thursday and screwed it into a ball, as if she were saying, 'That's over! That's over!' Friday in large red letters confronted her. Friday was a good day; on Friday she had her lesson with Lucy; she was going to tea with the Robsons. 'Blessed is he who has found his work', she read on the calendar. Calendars always seemed to be talking at you. She had not done her work. She glanced at a row of blue volumes, *The Constitutional History of England*, by Dr Andrews. There was a paper slip in volume three. She should have finished her chapter for Lucy; but not tonight. She was too tired tonight. She turned to the window. A roar of laughter floated out from the undergraduates' quarters. What are they laughing at, she wondered as she stood by the window. It sounded as if they were enjoying themselves. They never laugh like that when they come to tea at the Lodge, she thought, as the laughter died away. The little man from Balliol[16] sat twisting his fingers, twisting his fingers. He would not talk; but he would not go. Then she blew out the candle and got into bed. I rather like him, she thought, stretching out in the cool sheets, though he twists his fingers. As for Tony Ashton, she thought, turning on her pillow, I don't like him. He always seemed to be cross-examining her about Edward, whom Eleanor, she thought, calls 'Nigs'. His eyes were too close together. A bit of a barber's block, she thought. He had followed her at the picnic the other day – the picnic when the ant got into Mrs Lathom's skirts. There he was always beside her. But she didn't want to marry him. She didn't want to be a don's wife and live in Oxford for ever. No, no, no! She yawned, turned on her pillow, and listening to a belated bell that went walloping like a slow porpoise through the thick drizzling air, yawned once more and fell asleep.

*

The rain fell steadily all night long, making a faint mist over the fields, chuckling and burbling in the gutters. In gardens it fell over flowering bushes of lilac and laburnum. It slipped gently over the leaden domes of libraries, and splayed out of the laughing mouths of gargoyles. It smeared the window where the Jew boy from Birmingham sat mugging up Greek with a wet towel round his head; where Dr Malone sat up late writing another chapter in his monumental history of the college. And in the garden of the Lodge outside Kitty's window it sluiced the ancient tree under which kings and poets had sat drinking three centuries ago, but now it was half fallen and had to be propped up by a stake in the middle.

'Umbrella, miss?' said Hiscock, offering Kitty an umbrella as she left the house rather later than she should have left it the following afternoon. There was a chilliness in the air which made her glad, as she caught sight of a party with white and yellow frocks and cushions bound for the river, that she was not going to sit in a boat today. No parties today, she thought, no parties today. But she was late, the clock warned her.

She strode along until she came to the cheap red villas that her father disliked so much that he would always make a round to avoid them. But as it was in one of these cheap red villas that Miss Craddock lived, Kitty saw them haloed with romance. Her heart beat faster as she turned the corner by the new chapel and saw the steep steps of the house where Miss Craddock actually lived. Lucy went up those steps and down them every day; that was her window; this was her bell. The bell came out with a jerk when she pulled it; but it did not go back again, for everything was ramshackle in Lucy's house; but everything was romantic. There was Lucy's umbrella in the stand; and it too was not like other umbrellas; it had a parrot's head for a handle. But as she went up the steep shiny stairs excitement became mixed with fear: once more she had scamped her work; she had not 'given her mind to it' again this week.

'She's coming!' thought Miss Craddock, holding her pen suspended. Her nose was red-tipped; there was something owl-like about the eyes, round which there was a sallow, hollow depression. There was the bell. The pen had been dipped in red ink; she had been correcting Kitty's essay. Now she heard her step on the stairs. 'She's coming!' she thought with a little catch of her breath, laying down the pen.

'I'm awfully sorry, Miss Craddock,' Kitty said, taking off her things and sitting down at the table. 'But we had people staying in the house.'

Miss Craddock brushed her hand over her mouth in a way she had when she was disappointed.

'I see,' she said. 'So you haven't done any work this week either.'

Miss Craddock took up her pen and dipped it in the red ink. Then she turned to the essay.

'It wasn't worth correcting,' she remarked, pausing with her pen in the air. 'A child of ten would have been ashamed of it.'

Kitty blushed bright red.

'And the odd thing is,' said Miss Craddock putting down her pen when the lesson was over, 'that you've got quite an original mind.'

Kitty flushed bright red with pleasure.

'But you don't use it,' said Miss Craddock. 'Why don't you use it?' she added, looking at her out of her fine grey eyes.

'You see, Miss Craddock,' Kitty began eagerly, 'my mother –'

'Hm . . . hm . . . hm . . . ' Miss Craddock stopped her. Confidences were not what Dr Malone paid her for. She got up.

'Look at my flowers,' she said, feeling that she had snubbed her too severely. There was a bowl of flowers on the table: wild flowers, blue and white, stuck into a cushion of wet green moss. 'My sister sent them from the moors,' she said.

'The moors?' said Kitty. 'Which moors?' She stooped and touched the little flowers tenderly. How lovely she is, Miss Craddock thought; for she was sentimental about Kitty. But I will not be sentimental, she told herself.

'The Scarborough moors,' she said aloud. 'If you keep the moss damp but not too damp, they'll last for weeks,' she added, looking at the flowers.

'Damp, but not too damp,' Kitty smiled. 'That's easy in Oxford, I should think. It's always raining here.' She looked at the window. Mild rain was falling.

'If I lived up there, Miss Craddock –' she began, taking her umbrella. But she stopped. The lesson was over.

'You'd find it very dull,' said Miss Craddock, looking at her. She was putting on her cloak. Certainly she looked very lovely, putting on her cloak.

'When I was your age,' Miss Craddock continued, remembering her role as teacher, 'I would have given my eyes to have the opportunities you have, to meet the people you meet; to know the people you know.'

'Old Chuffy?' said Kitty, remembering Miss Craddock's profound admiration for that light of learning.

'You irreverent girl!' Miss Craddock expostulated. 'The greatest historian of his age!'

'Well, he doesn't talk history to me,' said Kitty, remembering the damp feel of a heavy hand on her knee.

She hesitated; but the lesson was over; another pupil was coming. She glanced round the room. There was a plate of oranges on the top of a pile of shiny exercise-books; a box that looked as if it contained biscuits. Was this her only room, she wondered? Did she sleep on the lumpy-looking sofa with the shawl thrown over it? There was no looking-glass, and she stuck her hat on rather to one side, thinking as she did so that Miss Craddock despised clothes.

But Miss Craddock was thinking how wonderful it was to be young and lovely and to meet brilliant men.

'I'm going to tea with the Robsons,' said Kitty, holding out her hand.

The girl, Nelly Robson, was Miss Craddock's favourite pupil; the only girl, she used to say, who knew what work meant.

'Are you walking?' said Miss Craddock, looking at her clothes. 'It's some way, you know. Down Ringmer Road, past the gasworks.'

'Yes, I'm walking,' said Kitty, shaking hands. 'And I will try to work hard this week,' she said, looking down on her with eyes full of love and admiration. Then she descended the steep stairs whose oilcloth shone bright with romance; and glanced at the umbrella that had a parrot for a handle.

The son of the professor, who had done it all off his own bat, 'a most creditable performance', to quote Dr Malone, was mending the hen-coops in the back garden at Prestwich Terrace – a scratched-up little place. Hammer, hammer, hammer, he went, fixing a board to the rotten roof. His hands were white, unlike his father's, and long fingered too. He had no love of doing these jobs himself. But his father mended the boots on Sunday. Down came the hammer. He went at it, hammering the long shiny nails that sometimes split the wood, or drove outside. For it was rotten. He hated hens too, imbecile fowls, a huddle of feathers, watching him out of their red beady eyes. They scratched up the path; left little curls of feather here and there on the beds, which were more to his fancy. But nothing grew there. How grow flowers like other people if one kept hens? A bell rang.

'Curse it! There's some old woman come to tea,' he said, holding his hammer suspended; and then brought it down on the nail.

As she stood on the step, noting the cheap lace curtains and the blue and orange glass, Kitty tried to remember what it was that her father had said about Nelly's father. But a little maid let her in. I'm much too large, Kitty thought, as she stood for a moment in the room to which the maid had admitted her. It was a small room, crowded with objects. And I'm too well dressed she thought, looking at herself in the glass over the fireplace. But here her friend Nelly came in. She was dumpy; over her large grey eyes she wore steel spectacles, and her brown holland overall seemed to increase her air of uncompromising veracity.

'We're having tea in the back room,' she said, looking her up and down.

What has she been doing? Why is she dressed in an overall? Kitty thought, following her into the room where tea had already begun.

'Pleased to see you,' said Mrs Robson formally, looking over her shoulder. But nobody seemed in the least pleased to see her. Two children were already eating. Slices of bread and butter were in their hands, but they stayed the bread and butter and stared at Kitty as she sat down.

She seemed to see the whole room at once. It was bare yet crowded. The table was too large; there were hard green-plush chairs; yet the tablecloth was coarse; darned in the middle; and the china was cheap with its florid red roses. The light was extraordinarily bright in her eyes. A sound of hammering came in from the garden outside. She looked at the garden: it was a scratched-up, earthy garden without flower-beds; and there was a shed at the end of the garden from which the sound of hammering came.

They're all so short too, Kitty thought, glancing at Mrs Robson. Only her shoulders came above the tea things; but her shoulders were substantial. She was a little like Bigge, the cook at the Lodge, but more formidable. She gave one brief look at Mrs Robson and then began to pull off her gloves secretly, swiftly, under the cover of the tablecloth. But why does nobody talk? she thought nervously. The children kept their eyes fixed upon her with a look of solemn amazement. Their owl-like stare went up and down over her uncompromisingly. Happily before they could express their disapproval, Mrs Robson told them sharply to go on with their tea; and the bread and butter slowly rose to their mouths again.

Why don't they say something? Kitty thought again, glancing at Nelly. She was about to speak when an umbrella grated in the hall; and Mrs Robson looked up and said to her daughter: 'There's dad!'

Next moment in trotted a little man, who was so short that he looked as if his jacket should have been an Eton jacket, and his collar a round collar. He wore, too, a very thick watch-chain, made of silver, like a schoolboy's. But his eyes were keen and fierce, his moustache bristly, and he spoke with a curious accent.

'Pleased to see you,' he said, and gripped her hand hard in his. He sat down, tucked a napkin under his chin so that it obscured his heavy silver watch-chain under its stiff white shield. Hammer, hammer, hammer came from the shed in the garden.

'Tell Jo tea's on the table,' said Mrs Robson to Nelly, who had brought in a dish with a cover on it. The cover was removed. Actually they were going to eat fried fish and potatoes at teatime, Kitty remarked.

But Mr Robson had turned his rather alarming blue eyes upon her. She expected him to say, 'How is your father, Miss Malone?'

But he said: 'You're reading history with Lucy Craddock?'

'Yes,' she said. She liked the way he said Lucy Craddock, as if he respected her. So many of the dons sneered at her. She liked feeling too, as he made her feel, that she was nobody's daughter in particular.

'You're interested in history?' he said, applying himself to his fish and potatoes.

'I love it,' she said. His bright blue eyes, gazing straight at her rather fiercely, seemed to make her say quite shortly what she meant.

'But I'm frightfully lazy,' she added. Here Mrs Robson looked at her rather sternly, and handed her a thick slice of bread on the point of a knife.

Anyhow their taste is awful, she said by way of revenge for the snub that she felt was intended. She focused her eyes on a picture opposite – an oily landscape in a heavy gilt frame. There was a blue and red Japanese plate on either side of it. Everything was ugly, especially the pictures.

'The moor at the back of our house,' said Mr Robson, seeing her look at a picture.

It struck Kitty that the accent with which he spoke was a Yorkshire accent. In looking at the picture he had increased his accent.

'In Yorkshire?' she said. 'We come from there too. My mother's family I mean,' she added.

'Your mother's family?' said Mr Robson.

'Rigby,' she said, and blushed slightly.

'Rigby?' said Mrs Robson, looking up. 'I wur-r-rked for a Miss Rigby before I married.'

What sort of wur-r-rk had Mrs Robson done? Kitty wondered. Sam explained.

'My wife was a cook, Miss Malone, before we married,' he said.

Again he increased his accent as if he were proud of it. I had a great-uncle who rode in a circus, she felt inclined to say; and an aunt who married . . . but here Mrs Robson interrupted her.

'The Hollies,' she said. 'Two very old ladies: Miss Ann and Miss Matilda.' She spoke more gently. 'But they must be dead long ago,' she concluded. For the first time she leant back in her chair and stirred her tea, just as old Snap at the farm, Kitty thought, stirred her tea round and round and round.

'Tell Jo we're not sparing the cake,' said Mr Robson, cutting himself a slice of that craggy-looking object; and Nell went out of the room once more. The hammering stopped in the garden. The door opened. Kitty, who had altered the focus of her eyes to suit the smallness of the Robson family, was taken by surprise. The young man seemed immense in that little room. He was a handsome young man. He brushed his hand through his hair as he came in, for a wood shaving had stuck in it.

'Our Jo,' said Mrs Robson, introducing them. 'Go and get the kittle, Jo,' she added; and he went at once as if he were used to it. When he came back with the kettle, Sam began chaffing him about a hencoop.

'It takes you a long time, my son, to mend a hencoop,' he said. There was some family joke which Kitty could not follow about mending boots and hencoops. She watched him eating steadily under his father's banter. He was not Eton or Harrow; or Rugby or Winchester; or reading or rowing. He reminded her of Alf, the farmhand up at Carter's, who had kissed her under the shadow of the haystack when she was fifteen, and old Carter loomed up leading a bull with a ring through its nose and said, 'Stop that!' She looked down again. She would rather like Jo to kiss her; better than Edward, she thought to herself suddenly. She remembered her own appearance, which she had forgotten. She liked him. Yes, she liked them all very much, she told herself; very much indeed. She felt as if she had given her nurse the slip and run off on her own.

Then the children began scrambling down off their chairs; the meal was over. She began to fish under the table for her gloves.

'These them?' said Jo, picking them up off the floor. She took them and crumpled them up in her hand.

He cast one quick sulky look at her as she stood in the doorway. She's a stunner,[17] he said to himself, but my word, she gives herself airs!

Mrs Robson ushered her into the little room where, before tea, she had looked in the glass. It was crowded with objects. There were bamboo tables; velvet books with brass hinges; marble gladiators askew on the mantelpiece and innumerable pictures . . . But Mrs Robson, with a gesture that was exactly like Mrs Malone's when she pointed to the Gainsborough[18] that was not quite certainly a Gainsborough, was displaying a huge silver salver with an inscription.

'The salver my husband's pupils gave him,' Mrs Robson began, pointing to the inscription. Kitty began to spell out the inscription.

'And this . . . ' said Mrs Robson, when she had done, pointing to a document framed like a text on the wall.

But here Sam, who stood in the background fiddling with his watch-chain, stepped forward and indicated with his stubby forefinger the picture of an old woman looking rather over life-size in the photographer's chair.

'My mother,' he said and stopped. He gave a queer little chuckle.

'Your mother?' Kitty repeated, stooping to look. The unwieldy old lady, posed in all the stiffness of her best clothes, was plain in the extreme. And yet Kitty felt that admiration was expected.

'You're very like her, Mr Robson,' was all she could find to say. Indeed they had something of the same sturdy look; the same piercing eyes; and they were both very plain. He gave an odd little chuckle.

'Glad you think so,' he said. 'Brought us all up. Not one of them a patch on her though.' He gave his odd little chuckle again.

Then he turned to his daughter, who had come in and was standing there in her overall.

'Not a patch on her,' he repeated, pinching Nell on the shoulder. As she stood there with her father's hand on her shoulder under the portrait of her grandmother, a sudden rush of self-pity came over Kitty. If she had been the daughter of people like the Robsons, she thought; if she had lived in the north – but it was clear they wanted her to go. Nobody ever sat down in this room. They were all standing up. Nobody pressed her to stay. When she said that she must go, they all came out into the little hall with her. They were all about to go on with what they were doing, she felt. Nell was about to go into the kitchen and wash up the tea things; Jo was about to return to his hencoops; the children were about to be put to bed by their mother; and Sam – what was he about to do? She looked at him standing there with his heavy watch-chain, like a schoolboy's. You are the nicest man I have ever met, she thought, holding out her hand.

'Pleased to have made your acquaintance,' said Mrs Robson in her stately way.

'Hope you'll come again soon,' said Mr Robson, grasping her hand very hard.

'Oh, I should love to!' she exclaimed, pressing their hands as hard as she could. Did they know how much she admired them? she wanted to say. Would they accept her in spite of her hat and her gloves? she wanted to ask. But they were all going off to their work. And I am going home to dress for dinner, she thought as she walked down the little front steps, pressing her pale kid gloves in her hands.

The sun was shining again; the damp pavements gleamed; a gust of wind tossed up the wet branches of the almond trees in the villa gardens; little twigs and tufts of blossom whirled on to the pavement and stuck there. As she stood still for a second at a crossing she too seemed to be tossed aloft out of her usual surroundings. She forgot where she was. The sky, blown into a blue open space, seemed to be looking down not here upon streets and houses, but upon open country, where the wind brushed the moors, and sheep, with grey fleeces ruffled, sheltered under stone walls. She could almost see the moors brighten and darken as the clouds passed over them.

But then in two strides the unfamiliar street became the street she had always known. Here she was again in the paved alley; there were the old curiosity shops with their blue china and their brass warming-pans; and next moment she was out in the famous crooked street with all the domes and steeples. The sun lay in broad stripes across it. There were the cabs and the awnings and the bookshops; the old men in black gowns billowing; the young women in pink and blue dresses flowing; and the young men in straw hats carrying cushions under their arms. But for a moment all seemed to her obsolete, frivolous, inane. The usual undergraduate in cap and gown with books under his arm looked silly. And the portentous old men with their exaggerated features looked like gargoyles, carved, medieval, unreal. They were all like people dressed up and acting parts, she thought. Now she stood at her own door and waited for Hiscock, the butler, to take his feet off the fender and waddle upstairs. Why can't you talk like a human being? she thought, as he took her umbrella and mumbled his usual remark about the weather.

Slowly, as if a weight had got into her feet too, she went upstairs, seeing through open windows and open doors the smooth lawn, the recumbent tree and the faded chintzes. Down she sank on the edge of her bed. It was very stuffy. A bluebottle buzzed round and round; a lawn mower squeaked in the garden below. Far away pigeons were cooing – Take two coos, Taffy.[19] Take two coos. Tak . . . Her eyes half shut. It seemed to her that she was sitting on the terrace of an Italian inn. There was her father pressing gentians on to a rough sheet of blotting paper. The lake below lapped and dazzled. She plucked up courage and said to her father: 'Father . . . ' He looked up very kindly over his spectacles. He held the little blue flower between his thumb and finger. 'I want . . . ' she began slipping off the balustrade upon which she was sitting. But here a bell struck. She rose and crossed to the washing-table. What would Nell think of this, she thought, tilting up the beautifully polished brass jug and dipping her hands in the hot water. Another bell tolled. She crossed to the dressing-table. The air from the garden outside was full of murmurings and cooings. Wood shavings, she said as she took up her brush and comb – he had wood shavings in his hair. A servant passed with a pile of tin dishes on his head. The pigeons were cooing – Take two coos, Taffy. Take two coos . . . But there was the dinner bell. In a moment she had pinned her hair up, hooked her dress on and run down the slippery stairs, sliding her palm along the banisters as she used to do when she was a child in a hurry. And there they all were.

Her parents were standing in the hall. A tall man was with them. His gown was thrown back and one last ray of sunshine lit up his genial, authoritative face. Who was he? Kitty could not remember.

'My word!' he exclaimed, looking up at her with admiration.

'It *is* Kitty, isn't it?' he said. Then he took her hand and pressed it.

'How you've grown!' he exclaimed. He looked at her as if he were looking not at her but at his own past.

'You don't remember me?' he added.

'Chingachgook!'[20] she exclaimed, recalling some childish memory.

'But he is now Sir Richard Norton,' said her mother, giving him a proud little pat on the shoulder; and they turned away, for the gentlemen were dining in Hall.

It was dull fish, Kitty thought; the plates were half cold. It was stale bread, she thought, cut in meagre little squares; the colour, the gaiety of Prestwich Terrace was still in her eyes, in her ears. She granted, as she looked round, the superiority of the Lodge china and silver; and the Japanese plates and the picture had been hideous; but this dining-room with its hanging creepers and its vast cracked canvases was so dark. At Prestwich Terrace the room was full of light; the sound of hammer, hammer, hammer still rang in her ears. She looked out at the fading greens in the garden. For the thousandth time she echoed her childish wish that the tree would either lie down or stand up instead of doing neither. It was not actually raining, but gusts of whiteness seemed to blow about the garden as the wind stirred the thick leaves on the laurels.

'Didn't you notice it?' Mrs Malone suddenly appealed to her.

'What, mama?' Kitty asked. She had not been attending.

'The odd taste in the fish,' said her mother.

'I don't think I did,' she said; and Mrs Malone went on talking to the butler. The plates were changed; another dish was brought in. But Kitty was not hungry. She bit one of the green sweets that were provided for her, and then the modest dinner, retrieved for the ladies from the relics of last night's party, was over and she followed her mother into the drawing-room.

It was too big when they were alone, but they always sat there. The pictures seemed to be looking down at the empty chairs, and the empty chairs seemed to be looking up at the pictures. The old gentleman who had ruled the college over a hundred years ago seemed to vanish in the daytime, but he came back when the lamps were lit. The face was placid, solid and smiling, and singularly like Dr Malone, who, had a frame been set round him, might have hung over the fireplace too.

'It's nice to have a quiet evening once in a way,' Mrs Malone was saying, 'though the Fripps . . . ' Her voice tailed off as she put on her spectacles and took up *The Times*. This was her moment of relaxation and recuperation after the day's work. She suppressed a little yawn as she glanced up and down the columns of the newspaper.

'What a charming man he was,' she observed casually, as she looked at the births and deaths. 'One would hardly have taken him for an American.'

Kitty recalled her thoughts. She was thinking of the Robsons. Her mother was talking about the Fripps.

'And I liked her too,' she said rashly. 'Wasn't she lovely?'

'Hum–m–m. A little overdressed for my taste,' said Mrs Malone dryly. 'And that accent – ' she went on, looking through the paper, 'I sometimes hardly understood what she said.'

Kitty was silent. Here they differed; as they did about so many things.

Suddenly Mrs Malone looked up: 'Yes, just what I was saying to Bigge this morning,' she said, laying down the paper.

'What, mama?' said Kitty.

'This man – in the leading article,' said Mrs Malone. She touched it with her finger. ' "With the best flesh, fish and fowl in the world," ' she read, ' "we shall not be able to turn them to account because we have none to cook them" – what I was saying to Bigge this morning.' She gave her quick little sigh. Just when one wanted to impress people, like those Americans, something went wrong. It had been the fish this time. She foraged for her work things, and Kitty took up the paper.

'It's the leading article,' said Mrs Malone. That man almost always said the very thing that she was thinking, which comforted her, and gave her a sense of security in a world which seemed to her to be changing for the worse.

' "Before the rigid and now universal enforcement of school attendance . . . "?' Kitty read out.

'Yes. That's it,' said Mrs Malone, opening her work-box and looking for her scissors.

' " . . . the children saw a good deal of cooking which, poor as it was, yet gave them some taste and inkling of knowledge. They now see nothing and they do nothing but read, write, sum, sew or knit," ' Kitty read out.

'Yes, yes,' said Mrs Malone. She unrolled the long strip of embroidery upon which she was working a design of birds pecking at fruit copied from a tomb at Ravenna. It was for the spare bedroom.

The leading article bored Kitty with its pompous fluency. She searched the paper for some little piece of news that might interest her mother. Mrs Malone liked someone to talk to her or read aloud to her as she worked. Night after night her embroidery served to weave the after-dinner talk into a pleasant harmony. One said something and stitched; looked at the design, chose another coloured silk, and stitched again. Sometimes Dr Malone read poetry aloud – Pope, Tennyson.[21] Tonight she would have liked Kitty to talk to her. But she was becoming increasingly conscious of difficulty with Kitty. Why? She glanced at her. What was wrong? she wondered. She gave her quick little sigh.

Kitty turned over the large pages. Sheep had the fluke; Turks wanted religious liberty; there was the General Election.

'Mr Gladstone[22] – ' she began.

Mrs Malone had lost her scissors. It annoyed her.

'Who can have taken them again?' she began. Kitty went down on the floor to look for them. Mrs Malone ferreted in the work-box; then she plunged her hand into the fissure between the cushion and the chair frame and brought up not only the scissors but also a little mother-of-pearl paper-knife that had been missing for ever so long. The discovery annoyed her. It proved Ellen never shook up the cushions properly.

'Here they are, Kitty,' she said. They were silent. There was always some constraint between them now.

'Did you enjoy your party at the Robsons', Kitty?' she asked, resuming her embroidery.

Kitty did not answer. She turned the paper. 'There's been an experiment,' she said. 'An experiment with electric light. "A brilliant light," ' she read, ' "was seen to shoot forth suddenly, shooting out a profound ray across the water to the Rock. Everything was lit up as if by daylight." ' She paused. She saw the bright light from the ships on the drawing-room chair. But here the door opened and Hiscock came in with a note on a salver.

Mrs Malone took it and read it in silence.

'No answer,' she said. From the tone of her mother's voice Kitty knew that something had happened. She sat holding the note in her hand. Hiscock shut the door.

'Rose is dead!' said Mrs Malone. 'Cousin Rose.'

The note lay open on her knee.

'It's from Edward,' she said.

'Cousin Rose is dead?' said Kitty. A moment before she had been thinking of a bright light on a red rock. Now everything looked dingy. There was a pause. There was silence. Tears stood in her mother's eyes.

'Just when the children most wanted her,' she said, sticking the needle into her embroidery. She began to roll it up very slowly. Kitty folded *The Times* and laid it on a little table, slowly, so that it should not crackle. She had only seen Cousin Rose once or twice. She felt awkward.

'Fetch me my engagement book,' said her mother at last. Kitty brought it.

'We must put off our dinner on Monday,' said Mrs Malone, looking through her engagements.

'And the Lathoms' party on Wednesday,' Kitty murmured, looking over her mother's shoulder.

'We can't put off everything,' said her mother sharply, and Kitty felt rebuked.

But there were notes to be written. She wrote them at her mother's dictation.

Why is she so ready to put off all our engagements? thought Mrs Malone, watching her write. Why doesn't she enjoy going out with me any more? She glanced through the notes that her daughter brought her.

'Why don't you take more interest in things here, Kitty?' she said irritably, pushing the letters away.

'Mama, dear – ' Kitty began, deprecating the usual argument.

'But what is it you want to do?' her mother persisted. She had put away her embroidery; she was sitting upright, she was looking rather formidable. 'Your father and I only want you to do what you want to do,' she continued.

'Mama, dear – ' Kitty repeated.

'You could help your father if it bores you helping me,' said Mrs Malone. 'Papa told me the other day that you never come to him now.'

She referred, Kitty knew, to his history of the college. He had suggested that she should help him. Again she saw the ink flowing – she had made an awkward brush with her arm – over five generations of Oxford men, obliterating hours of her father's exquisite penmanship; and could hear him say with his usual courteous irony, 'Nature did not intend you to be a scholar, my dear,' as he applied the blotting-paper.

'I know,' she said guiltily. 'I haven't been to papa lately. But then there's always something – ' She hesitated.

'Naturally,' said Mrs Malone, 'with a man in your father's position . . . '

Kitty sat silent. They both sat silent. They both disliked this petty bickering; they both detested these recurring scenes; and yet they seemed inevitable. Kitty got up, took the letters she had written and put them in the hall.

What does she want? Mrs Malone asked herself, looking up at the picture without seeing it. When I was her age . . . she thought, and smiled. How well she remembered sitting at home on a spring evening like this up in Yorkshire, miles from anywhere. You could hear the beat of a horse's hoof on the road miles away. She could remember flinging up her bedroom window and looking down on the dark shrubs in the garden and crying out, 'Is this life?' And in the winter there was the snow. She could still hear the snow flopping off the trees in the garden. And here was Kitty, living in Oxford, in the midst of everything.

Kitty came back into the drawing-room and yawned very slightly. She raised her hand to her face with an unconscious gesture of fatigue that touched her mother.

'Tired, Kitty?' she said. 'It's been a long day; you look pale.'

'And you look tired too,' said Kitty.

The bells came pushing forth one after another, one on top of another, through the damp, heavy air.

'Go to bed, Kitty,' said Mrs Malone. 'There! It's striking ten.'

'But aren't you coming too, mama?' said Kitty, standing beside her chair.

'Your father won't be back just yet,' said Mrs Malone, putting on her spectacles again.

Kitty knew it was useless to try to persuade her. It was part of the mysterious ritual of her parents' lives. She bent down and gave her mother the little perfunctory peck that was the only sign they ever gave each other outwardly of their affection. Yet they were very fond of each other; yet they always quarrelled.

'Good-night, and sleep well,' said Mrs Malone. 'I don't like to see your roses fade,' she added, putting her arm round her for once in a way.

She sat still after Kitty had gone. Rose is dead, she thought – Rose who was about her own age. She read the note again. It was from Edward. And Edward, she mused, is in love with Kitty, but I don't know that I want her to marry him, she thought, taking up her needle. No, not Edward . . . There was young Lord Lasswade . . . That would be a nice marriage, she thought. Not that I want her to be rich, not that I care about rank, she thought, threading her needle. No, but he could give her what she wants . . . What was it? . . . Scope, she decided, beginning to stitch. Then again her thoughts turned to Rose. Rose was dead. Rose who was about her own age. That must have been the first time he proposed to her, she thought, the day we had the picnic on the moors. It was a spring day. They were sitting on the grass. She could see Rose wearing a black hat with a cock's feather in it over her bright red hair. She could still see her blush and look extremely pretty when Abel rode up, much to their surprise – he was stationed at Scarborough – the day they had the picnic on the moors.

The house at Abercorn Terrace was very dark. It smelt strongly of spring flowers. For some days now wreaths had been piled one on top of another on the hall table. In the dimness – all the blinds were drawn – the flowers gleamed; and the hall smelt with the amorous intensity of a hot-house. Wreath after wreath, they kept arriving. There were lilies with broad bars of gold in them; others with spotted throats sticky with honey; white tulips, white lilac – flowers of all kinds, some with petals as thick as velvet, others transparent, paper-thin; but all white, and clubbed together, head to head, in circles, in ovals, in crosses so that they scarcely looked like flowers. Black-edged cards were attached to them, 'With deep sympathy from Major and Mrs Brand'; 'With love and sympathy from General and Mrs Elkin'; 'For dearest Rose from Susan.' Each card had a few words written on it.

Even now with the hearse at the door the bell rang; a messenger boy appeared bearing more lilies. He raised his cap, as he stood in the hall, for men were lurching down the stairs carrying the coffin. Rose, in deep black, prompted by her nurse, stepped forward and dropped her little bunch of violets on the coffin. But it slipped off as it swayed down the brilliant sunlit steps on the slanting shoulders of Whiteleys' men. The family followed after.

*

It was an uncertain day, with passing shadows and darting rays of bright sunshine. The funeral started at a walking pace. Delia, getting into the second carriage with Milly and Edward, noticed that the houses opposite had their blinds drawn in sympathy, but a servant peeped. The others, she noticed, did not seem to see her; they were thinking of their mother. When they got into the main road the pace quickened, for the drive to the cemetery was a long one. Through the slit of the blind, Delia noticed dogs playing; a beggar singing; men raising their hats as the hearse passed them. But by the time their own carriage passed, the hats were on again. Men walked briskly and unconcernedly along the pavement. The shops were already gay with spring clothing; women paused and looked in at the windows. But they would have to wear nothing but black all the summer, Delia thought, looking at Edward's coal-black trousers.

They scarcely spoke, or only in little formal sentences, as if they were already taking part in the ceremony. Somehow their relations had changed. They were more considerate, and a little important too, as if their mother's death had laid new responsibilities on them. But the others knew how to behave; it was only she who had to make an effort. She remained outside, and so did her father, she thought. When Martin suddenly burst out laughing at tea, and then stopped and looked guilty, she felt – that is what papa would do, that is what I should do if we were honest.

She glanced out of the window again. Another man raised his hat – a tall man, a man in a frock-coat, but she would not allow herself to think of Mr Parnell until the funeral was over.

At last they reached the cemetery. As she took her place in the little group behind the coffin and walked up the church, she was relieved to find that she was overcome by some generalised and solemn emotion. People stood up on both sides of the church and she felt their eyes on her. Then the service began. A clergyman, a cousin, read it. The first words struck out with a rush of extraordinary beauty. Delia, standing behind her father, noticed how he braced himself and squared his shoulders.

'I am the resurrection and the life.'

Pent up as she had been all these days in the half-lit house which smelt of flowers, the outspoken words filled her with glory. This she could feel genuinely; this was something that she said herself. But then, as Cousin James went on reading, something slipped. The sense was blurred. She could not follow with her reason. Then in the midst of the argument came another burst of familiar beauty: ' . . . and fade away suddenly like the grass. In the morning it is green, and groweth up; but in the evening it is cut down, dried up, and withered.' She could feel the beauty of that. Again it was like music; but then Cousin James seemed to hurry, as if he did not altogether believe what he was saying. He seemed to pass from the known to the unknown; from what he believed to what he did not believe; even his voice altered. He looked clean, he looked starched and ironed like his robes. But what did he mean by what he was saying? She gave it up. Either one understood or one did not understand, she thought. Her mind wandered.

But I will not think of him, she thought, seeing a tall man who stood beside her on a platform and raised his hat, until it's over. She fixed her eyes upon her father. She watched him dab a great white pocket-handkerchief to his eyes and put it in his pocket; then he pulled it out and dabbed his eyes with it again. Then the voice stopped; he put his handkerchief finally in his pocket; and again they all formed up, the little group of the family, behind the coffin and again the dark people on either side rose, and watched them and let them go first and followed after.

It was a relief to feel the soft damp air blowing its leafy smell in her face again. But again now that she was out of doors, she began to notice things. She noticed how the black funeral horses were pawing the ground; they were scraping little pits with their hooves in the yellow gravel. She remembered hearing that funeral horses came from Belgium and were very vicious. They looked vicious she thought; their black necks were flecked with foam – but she recalled herself. They went straggling in ones and twos along a path until they reached a fresh mound of yellow earth heaped beside a pit; and there again she noticed how the grave-diggers stood at a little distance, rather behind, with their spades.

There was a pause; people kept on arriving and took up their positions, some a little higher, some a little lower. She observed a poor-looking shabby woman prowling on the outskirts, and tried to think whether she were some old servant, but she could not put a name to her. Her Uncle Digby, her father's brother, stood directly opposite her, with his top-hat held like some sacred vessel between his hands, the image of grave decorum. Some of the women were crying, but not the men; the men had one pose, the women had another, she observed. Then it all began again. The splendid gust of music blew through them – 'Man that is born of a woman': the ceremony had renewed itself; once more they were grouped, united. The family pressed a little closer to the graveside and looked fixedly at the coffin which lay with its polish and its brass handles there in the earth to be buried for ever. It looked too new to be buried for ever. She stared down into the grave. There lay her mother; in that coffin – the woman she had loved and hated so. Her eyes dazzled. She was afraid that she might faint; but she must look; she must feel; it was the last chance that was left her. Earth dropped on the coffin; three pebbles fell on the hard shiny surface; and as they dropped she was possessed by a sense of something everlasting; of life mixing with death, of death becoming life. For as she looked she heard the sparrows chirp quicker and quicker; she heard wheels in the distance sound louder and louder; life came closer and closer . . .

'We give thee hearty thanks,' said the voice, 'for that it has pleased thee to deliver this our sister out of the miseries of this sinful world – '[23]

What a lie! she cried to herself. What a damnable lie! He had robbed her of the one feeling that was genuine; he had spoilt her one moment of understanding.

She looked up. She saw Morris and Eleanor side by side; their faces were blurred; their noses were red; the tears were running down them. As for her father he was so stiff and so rigid that she had a convulsive desire to laugh aloud. Nobody can feel like that, she thought. He's overdoing it. None of us feel anything at all, she thought: we're all pretending.

Then there was a general movement; the attempt at concentration was over. People strolled off this way and that; there was no attempt now to form into a procession; little groups came together; people shook hands rather furtively, among the graves, and even smiled.

'How good of you to come!' said Edward, shaking hands with old Sir James Graham, who gave him a little pat on the shoulder. Ought she to go and thank him too? The graves made it difficult. It was becoming a shrouded and subdued morning party among the graves. She hesitated – she did not know what she ought to do next. Her father had walked on. She looked back. The grave-diggers had come forward; they were piling the wreaths one on top of another neatly; and the prowling woman had joined them and was stooping down to read the names on the cards. The ceremony was over; rain was falling.

1891

THE AUTUMN WIND blew over England. It twitched the leaves off the trees, and down they fluttered, spotted red and yellow, or sent them floating, flaunting in wide curves before they settled. In towns, coming in gusts round the corners, the wind blew here a hat off, there lifted a veil high above a woman's head. Money was in brisk circulation. The streets were crowded. Upon the sloping desks of the offices near St Paul's, clerks paused with their pens on the ruled page. It was difficult to work after the holidays. Margate, Eastbourne and Brighton had bronzed them and tanned them. The sparrows and starlings, making their discordant chatter round the eaves of St Martin's,[24] whitened the heads of the sleek statues holding rods or rolls of paper in Parliament Square. Blowing behind the boat train, the wind ruffled the channel, tossed the grapes in Provence, and made the lazy fisher boy, who was lying on his back in his boat in the Mediterranean, roll over and snatch a rope.

But in England, in the North, it was cold. Kitty, Lady Lasswade, sitting on the terrace beside her husband and his spaniel, drew the cloak round her shoulders. She was looking at the hilltop, where the snuffer-shaped monument raised by the old earl made a mark for ships at sea. There was mist on the woods. Near at hand the stone ladies on the terrace had scarlet flowers in their urns. Thin blue smoke drifted across the flaming dahlias in the long beds that went down to the river. 'Burning weeds,' she said aloud. Then there was a tap on the window, and her little boy in a pink frock stumbled out, holding his spotted horse.

In Devonshire where the round red hills and the steep valleys hoarded the sea air leaves were still thick on the trees – too thick, Hugh Gibbs said at breakfast. Too thick for shooting, he said, and Milly, his wife, left him to go to his meeting. With her basket on her arm she walked down the well-kept crazy pavement with the swaying movement of a woman with child. There hung the yellow pears on the orchard wall, lifting the leaves over them, they were so swollen. But the wasps had got at them – the skin was broken. With her hand on the fruit she paused. Pop, pop, pop sounded in the distant woods. Someone was shooting.

The smoke hung in veils over the spires and domes of the university cities. Here it choked the mouth of a gargoyle; there it clung to the walls that were peeled yellow. Edward, who was taking his brisk constitutional, noted smell, sound and colour; which suggested how complex impressions are; few poets compress enough; but there must be some line in Greek or Latin, he was thinking, which sums up the contrast – when Mrs Lathom passed him and he raised his cap.

In the Law Courts the leaves lay dry and angular on the flagstones. Morris, remembering his childhood, shuffled his feet through them on his way to his chambers, and they scattered edgeways along the gutters. Not yet trodden down they lay in Kensington Gardens, and children, crunching the shells as they ran, scooped up a handful and scudded on through the mist down the avenues, with their hoops.

Racing over the hills in the country the wind blew vast rings of shadow that dwindled again to green. But in London the streets narrowed the clouds; mist hung thick in the East End by the river; made the voices of men crying, 'Any old iron to sell, any old iron,' sound distant; and in the suburbs the organs were muted. The wind blew the smoke – for in every back garden, in the angle of the ivy-grown wall that still sheltered a few last geraniums, leaves were heaped up; keen fanged flames were eating them – out into the street, into windows that stood open in the drawing-room in the morning. For it was October, the birth of the year.

Eleanor was sitting at her writing-table with her pen in her hand. It's awfully queer, she thought, touching the ink-corroded patch of bristle on the back of Martin's walrus with the point of her pen, that *that* should have gone on all these years. That solid object might survive them all. If she threw it away it would still exist somewhere or other. But she never had thrown it away because it was part of other things – her mother for example . . . She drew on her blotting paper; a dot with strokes raying out round it. Then she looked up. They were burning weeds in the back garden; there was a drift of smoke; a sharp acrid smell; and leaves were falling. A barrel-organ was playing up the street. 'Sur le pont d'Avignon'[25] – she hummed in time to it. How did it go? – the song Pippy used to sing as she wiped your ears with a piece of slimy flannel?

'Ron, ron, ron, et plon, plon plon,' she hummed. Then the tune stopped. The organ had moved farther away. She dipped her pen in the ink.

'Three times eight,' she murmured, 'is twenty-four,' she said decidedly; wrote a figure at the bottom of the page, swept together the little red and blue books and took them to her father's study.

*

'Here's the housekeeper!' he said good-humouredly as she came in. He was sitting in his leather armchair reading a pinkish financial paper. 'Here's the housekeeper,' he repeated, looking up over his glasses. He was getting slower and slower, she thought; and she was in a hurry. But they got on extremely well; they were almost like brother and sister. He put down his paper and went to the writing-table.

But I wish you would hurry, papa, she thought as she watched the deliberate way in which he unlocked the drawer in which he kept his cheque-book, or I shall be late.

'Milk's very high,' he said, tapping the book with the gilt cow.

'Yes. It's eggs in October,' she said.

As he made out the cheque with extreme deliberation she glanced round the room. It looked like an office, with its files of papers and its deed-boxes, except that horses' bits hung by the fireplace, and there was the silver cup he had won at polo. Would he sit there all the morning reading the financial papers and considering his investments, she wondered? He stopped writing.

'And where are you off to now?' he asked with his shrewd little smile.

'A committee,' she said.

'A committee,' he repeated, signing his firm heavy signature. 'Well, stand up for yourself; don't be sat on, Nell.' He entered a figure in the ledger.

'Are you coming with me this afternoon, papa?' she said as he finished writing the figure. 'It's Morris's case you know; at the Law Courts.'

He shook his head.

'No; I've got to be in the City at three,' he said.

'Then I shall see you at lunch,' she said, making a movement to go. But he held up his hand. He had something to say, but he hesitated. He was getting rather heavier in the face, she noted; there were little veins in his nose; he was getting rather too red and heavy.

'I was thinking of looking in at the Digbys',' he said, at length. He got up and walked to the window. He looked out at the back garden. She fidgeted.

'How the leaves are falling!' he remarked.

'Yes,' she said. 'They're burning weeds.'

He stood looking at the smoke for a moment.

'Burning weeds,' he repeated, and stopped.

'It's Maggie's birthday,' at last he came out with it. 'I thought I'd take her some little present – ' He paused. He meant that he wished her to buy it, she knew.

'What would you like to give her?' she asked.

'Well,' he said vaguely, 'something pretty you know – something she could wear.'

Eleanor reflected – Maggie, her little cousin; was she seven or eight? 'A necklace? A brooch? Something like that?' she asked quickly.

'Yes, something like that,' said her father, settling down in his chair again. 'Something pretty, something she could wear, you know.' He opened the paper and gave her a little nod. 'Thank you, my dear,' he said as she left the room.

On the hall table, between a silver salver laden with visiting-cards – some with their corners turned down, some large, some small – and a piece of purple plush with which the colonel polished his top hat – lay a thin foreign envelope with 'England' marked in large letters in the corner. Eleanor, running down the stairs in a hurry, swept it into her bag as she passed. Then she ran at a peculiar ambling trot down the Terrace. At the corner she stopped and looked anxiously down the road. Among the other traffic she singled out one bulky form; mercifully, it was yellow; mercifully she had caught her bus. She hailed it and climbed on top. She sighed with relief as she pulled the leather apron over her knees. All responsibility now rested with the driver. She relaxed; she breathed in the soft London air; she heard the dull London roar with pleasure. She looked along the street and relished the sight of cabs, vans and carriages all trotting past with an end in view. She liked coming back in October to the full stir of life after the summer was over. She had been staying in Devonshire with the Gibbses. That's turned out very well, she thought, thinking of her sister's marriage to Hugh Gibbs, seeing Milly with her babies. And Hugh – she smiled. He rode about on a great white horse, breaking up litters. But there are too many trees and cows and too many little hills instead of one big one, she thought. She did not like Devonshire. She was glad to be back in London, on top of the yellow bus, with her bag stuffed with papers, and everything beginning again in October. They had left the residential quarter; the houses were changing; they were turning into shops. This was her world; here she was in her element. The streets were crowded; women were swarming in and out of shops with their shopping baskets. There was something customary, rhythmical about it, she thought, like rooks swooping in a field, rising and falling.

She, too, was going to her work – she turned her watch on her wrist without looking at it. After the committee, Duffus; after Duffus, Dickson. Then lunch; and the Law Courts . . . then lunch and the Law Courts at two-thirty, she repeated. The bus trundled along the Bayswater Road. The streets were becoming poorer and poorer.

Perhaps I oughtn't to have given the job to Duffus, she said to herself – she was thinking of Peter Street where she had built houses; the roof was leaking again; there was a bad smell in the sink. But here the omnibus stopped; people got in and out; the omnibus went on again – but it's better to give the work to a small man, she thought, looking at the huge plate-glass windows of one of the large shops, instead of going to one of those big firms. There were always small shops side by side with big shops. It puzzled her. How did the small shops manage to make a living? she wondered. But if Duffus, she began – here the omnibus stopped; she looked up; she rose ' – if Duffus thinks he can bully me,' she said as she went down the steps, 'he'll find he's mistaken.'

She walked quickly up the cinder path to the galvanised iron shed in which the meeting took place. She was late; there they were already. It was her first meeting since the holidays, and they all smiled at her. Judd even took his toothpick out of his mouth – a sign of recognition that flattered her. Here we all are again, she thought, taking her place and laying her papers on the table.

But she meant 'them', not herself. She did not exist; she was not anybody at all. But there they all were – Brocket, Cufnell, Miss Sims, Ramsden, Major Porter and Mrs Lazenby. The major preaching organisation; Miss Sims (ex-mill hand) scenting condescension; Mrs Lazenby, offering to write to her cousin Sir John, upon which Judd, the retired shopkeeper, snubbed her. She smiled as she took her seat. Miriam Parrish was reading letters. But why starve yourself, Eleanor asked as she listened. She was thinner than ever.

She looked round the room as the letters were read. There had been a dance. Festoons of red and yellow paper were slung across the ceiling. The coloured picture of the Princess of Wales had loops of yellow roses at the corners; a sea-green ribbon across her breast, a round yellow dog on her lap and pearls slung and knotted over her shoulders. She wore an air of serenity, of indifference; a queer comment upon their divisions, Eleanor thought: something that the Lazenbys worshipped; that Miss Sims derided; that Judd looked at cocking his eyebrows, picking his teeth. If he had had a son, he had told her, he would have sent him to the varsity. But she recalled herself. Major Porter had turned to her.

'Now, Miss Pargiter,' he said, drawing her in, because they were both of the same social standing, 'you haven't given us your opinion.'

She pulled herself together and gave him her opinion. She had an opinion – a very definite opinion. She cleared her throat and began.

*

The smoke blowing through Peter Street had condensed, between the narrowness of the houses, into a fine grey veil. But the houses on either side were clearly visible. Save for two in the middle of the street, they were all precisely the same – yellow-grey boxes with slate tents on top. Nothing whatever was happening; a few children were playing in the street, two cats turned something over in the gutter with their paws. Yet a woman leaning out of a window searched this way, that way, up and down the street as if she were raking every cranny for something to feed on. Her eyes, rapacious, greedy, like the eyes of a bird of prey, were also sulky and sleepy, as if they had nothing to feed their hunger upon. Nothing happened – nothing whatever. Still she gazed up and down with her indolent dissatisfied stare. Then a trap turned the corner. She watched it. It stopped in front of the houses opposite which, since the sills were green, and there was a plaque with a sunflower stamped on it over the door, were different from the others. A little man in a tweed cap got out and rapped at the door. It was opened by a woman who was about to have a baby. She shook her head; looked up and down the street; then shut the door. The man waited. The horse stood patiently with the reins drooping and its head bent. Another woman appeared at the window, with a white many-chinned face, and an underlip that stood out like a ledge. Leaning out of the window side by side the two women watched the man. He was bandy-legged; he was smoking. They passed some remark about him together. He walked up and down as if he were waiting for somebody. Now he threw away his cigarette. They watched him. What would he do next? Was he going to give his horse a feed? But here a tall woman wearing a coat and skirt of grey tweed came round the corner hastily; and the little man turned and touched his cap.

'Sorry I'm late,' Eleanor called out, and Duffus touched his cap with the friendly smile that always pleased her.

'That's all right, Miss Pargiter,' he said. She always hoped that he did not feel that she was the ordinary employer.

'Now we'll go over it,' she said. She hated the job, but it had to be done.

The door was opened by Mrs Toms, the downstairs lodger.

Oh dear, thought Eleanor, observing the slant of her apron, another baby coming, after all I told her.

They went from room to room of the little house, Mrs Toms and Mrs Grove following after. There was a crack here; a stain there. Duffus had a foot-rule in his hand with which he tapped the plaster. The worst of it is, she thought, as she let Mrs Toms do the talking, that I can't help liking him. It was his Welsh accent largely; he was a charming ruffian. He was as supple as an eel, she knew; but when he talked like that, in that sing-song, which reminded her of Welsh valleys . . . But he had cheated her at every point. There was a hole you could poke your finger through in the plaster.

'Look at that, Mr Duffus, there – ' she said, stooping and poking her finger. He was licking his pencil. She loved going to his yard with him and seeing him size up planks and bricks; she loved his technical words for things, his little hard words.

'Now we'll go upstairs,' she said. He seemed to her like a fly struggling to haul itself up out of a saucer. It was touch and go with small employers like Duffus; they might haul themselves up and become the Judds of their day and send their sons to the varsity; or on the other hand they might fall in and then – He had a wife and five children; she had seen them in the room behind the shop, playing with reels of cotton on the floor. And she always hoped that they would ask her in . . . But here was the top floor where old Mrs Potter lay bedridden. She knocked; she called out in a loud cheerful voice, 'May we come in?'

There was no answer. The old woman was stone deaf; so in they went. There she was, as usual, doing nothing whatever, propped up in the corner of her bed.

'I've brought Mr Duffus to look at your ceiling,' Eleanor shouted.

The old woman looked up and began plucking with her hands like a large tousled ape. She looked at them wildly, suspiciously.

'The ceiling, Mr Duffus,' said Eleanor. She pointed to a yellow stain on the ceiling. The house had only been built five years; and yet everything wanted repairing. Duffus threw open the window and leant out. Mrs Potter clutched hold of Eleanor's hand, as if she suspected that they were going to hurt her.

'We've come to look at your ceiling,' Eleanor repeated very loudly. But the words conveyed nothing. The old woman went off into a whining plaint; the words ran themselves together into a chant that was half plaint, half curse. If only the Lord would take her. Every night, she said, she implored Him to let her go. All her children were dead.

'When I wake in the morning . . . ' she began.

'Yes, yes, Mrs Potter,' Eleanor tried to soothe her; but her hands were firmly grasped.

'I pray Him to let me go,' Mrs Potter continued.

'It's the leaves in the gutter,' said Duffus, popping his head in again.

'And the pain – ' Mrs Potter stretched out her hands; they were knotted and grooved like the gnarled roots of a tree.

'Yes, yes,' said Eleanor. 'But there's a leak; it's not only the dead leaves,' she said to Duffus.

Duffus put his head out again.

'We're going to make you more comfortable,' Eleanor shouted to the old woman. Now she was cringing and fawning; now she had pressed her hand to her lips.

Duffus drew his head in again.

'Have you found out what's wrong?' Eleanor said to him sharply. He was entering something in his pocket-book. She longed to go. Mrs Potter was asking her to feel her shoulder. She felt her shoulder. Her hand was still grasped. There was medicine on the table; Miriam Parrish came every week. Why do we do it? she asked herself as Mrs Potter went on talking. Why do we force her to live? she asked, looking at the medicine on the table. She could stand it no longer. She withdrew her hand.

'Goodbye, Mrs Potter,' she shouted. She was insincere; she was hearty. 'We're going to mend your ceiling,' she shouted. She shut the door. Mrs Groves waddled in advance of her to show her the sink in the scullery. A wisp of yellow hair hung down behind her dirty ears. If I had to do this every day of my life, Eleanor thought, as she followed them down into the scullery, I should become a bag of bones like Miriam; with a string of beads . . . And what's the use of that? she thought, stooping to smell the sink in the scullery.

'Well, Duffus,' she said, facing him when the inspection was over, with the smell of drains still in her nose. 'What d'you propose to do about it?'

Her anger was rising; it was his fault largely. He had swindled her. But as she stood facing him and observed his little underfed body, and how his bow tie had worked up over his collar, she felt uncomfortable.

He shuffled and squirmed; she felt that she was going to lose her temper.

'If you can't make a good job of it,' she said curtly, 'I shall employ somebody else.' She adopted the tone of the colonel's daughter; the upper-middle-class tone that she detested. She saw him turn sullen before her eyes. But she rubbed it in.

'You ought to be ashamed of it,' she told him. He was impressed she could see. 'Good-morning,' she said briefly.

The ingratiating smile was not produced for her benefit again, she observed. But you have to bully them or else they despise you, she thought as Mrs Toms let her out, and once more she observed the slant in her apron. A crowd of children stood round staring at Duffus's pony. But none of them, she noticed, dared stroke the pony's nose.

*

She was late. She gave one look at the sunflower on the terracotta plaque. That symbol of her girlish sentiment amused her grimly. She had meant it to signify flowers, fields in the heart of London; but now it was cracked. She broke into her usual ambling trot. The movement seemed to break up the disagreeable crust; to jolt off the grasp of the old woman's hand that was still on her shoulder. She ran; she dodged. Shopping women got in her way. She dashed into the road waving her hand among the carts and horses. The conductor saw her, curved his arm round her and hauled her up. She had caught her bus.

She trod on the toe of a man in the corner, and pitched down between two elderly women. She was panting slightly; her hair was coming down; she was red with running. She cast a glance at her fellow-passengers. They all looked settled, elderly, as if their minds were made up. For some reason she always felt that she was the youngest person in an omnibus, but today, since she had won her scrap with Judd, she felt that she was grown up. The grey line of houses jolted up and down before her eyes as the omnibus trundled along the Bayswater Road. The shops were turning into houses; there were big houses and little houses; public houses and private houses. And here a church raised its filigree spire. Underneath were pipes, wires, drains . . . Her lips began moving. She was talking to herself. There's always a public house, a library and a church, she was muttering.

The man on whose toe she had trodden sized her up; a well-known type; with a bag; philanthropic; well nourished; a spinster; a virgin; like all the women of her class, cold; her passions had never been touched; yet not unattractive. She was laughing . . . Here she looked up and caught his eye. She had been talking aloud to herself in an omnibus. She must cure herself of the habit. She must wait till she brushed her teeth. But luckily the bus was stopping. She jumped out. She began to walk quickly up Melrose Place. She felt vigorous and young. She noticed everything freshly after Devonshire. She looked down the long many-pillared vista of Abercorn Terrace. The houses, with their pillars and their front gardens, all looked highly respectable; in every front room she seemed to see a parlourmaid's arm sweep over the table, laying it for luncheon. In several rooms they were already sitting down to luncheon; she could see them between the tent-shaped opening made by the curtains. She would be late for her own luncheon, she thought as she ran up the front steps and fitted her latchkey in the door. Then, as if someone were speaking, words formed in her mind. 'Something pretty, something to wear.' She stopped with her key in the lock. Maggie's birthday; her father's present; she had forgotten it. She paused. She turned, she ran down the steps again. She must go to Lamley's.

Mrs Lamley, who had grown stout these last years, was masticating a mouthful of cold mutton in the back room when she saw Miss Eleanor through the glass door.

'Good-morning, Miss Eleanor,' she began, coming out.

'Something pretty, something to wear,' Eleanor panted. She was looking very well – quite brown after her holiday, Mrs Lamley noticed.

'For my niece – I mean cousin. Sir Digby's little girl,' Eleanor brought out.

Mrs Lamley deprecated the cheapness of her goods.

There were toy boats; dolls; twopenny gold watches – but nothing nice enough for Sir Digby's little girl. But Miss Eleanor was in a hurry.

'There,' she said, pointing to a card of bead necklaces. 'That'll do.'

It looked a little cheap, Mrs Lamley thought, reaching down a blue necklace with gold spots, but Miss Eleanor was in such a hurry that she wouldn't even have it wrapped in brown paper.

'I shall be late as it is, Mrs Lamley,' she said, with a genial wave of her hand; and off she ran.

Mrs Lamley liked her. She always seemed so friendly. It was such a pity she didn't marry – such a mistake to let the younger sister marry before the elder. But then she had the colonel to look after, and he was getting on now, Mrs Lamley concluded, going back to her mutton in the back shop.

'Miss Eleanor won't be a minute,' said the colonel as Crosby brought in the dishes. 'Leave the covers on.' He stood with his back to the fireplace waiting for her. Yes, he thought, I don't see why not. 'I don't see why not,' he repeated, looking at the dish-cover. Mira was on the scene again; the other fellow had turned out, as he knew he would, a bad egg. And what provision was he to make for Mira? What was he to do about it? It had struck him that he would like to put the whole thing before Eleanor. Why not after all? She's not a child any longer, he thought; and he didn't like this business of – of – shutting things up in drawers. But he felt some shyness at the thought of telling his own daughter.

'Here she is,' he said abruptly to Crosby, who stood waiting mutely behind him.

No, no, he said to himself with sudden conviction, as Eleanor came in. I can't do it. For some reason when he saw her he realised that he could not tell her. And after all, he thought, seeing how bright-cheeked, how unconcerned she looked, she has her own life to live. A spasm of jealousy passed through him. She's got her own affairs to think about, he thought as they sat down.

She pushed a necklace across the table towards him.

'Hello, what's that?' he said, looking at it blankly.

'Maggie's present, papa,' she said. 'The best I could do . . . I'm afraid it's rather cheap.'

'Yes; that'll do very nicely,' he said, glancing at it absent-mindedly. 'Just what she'll like,' he added, shoving it to one side. He began to carve the chicken.

She was very hungry; she was still rather breathless. She felt a little 'spun round', as she put it to herself. What did you spin things round on? she wondered, helping herself to bread-sauce – a pivot? The scene had changed so often that morning; and every scene required a different adjustment; bringing this to the front; sinking that to the depths. And now she felt nothing; hungry merely; merely a chicken-eater; blank. But as she ate, the sense of her father imposed itself. She liked his solidity, as he sat opposite her munching his chicken methodically. What had he been doing, she wondered. Taking shares out of one company and putting them in another? He roused himself.

'Well, how was the committee?' he asked. She told him, exaggerating her triumph with Judd.

'That's right. Stand up to 'em, Nell. Don't let yourself be sat on,' he said. He was proud of her in his own way; and she liked him to be proud of her. At the same time she did not mention Duffus and Rigby Cottages. He had no sympathy with people who were foolish about money, and she never got a penny interest: it all went on repairs. She turned the conversation to Morris and his case at the Law Courts. She looked at her watch again. Her sister-in-law Celia had told her to meet her at the Law Courts at two-thirty sharp.

'I shall have to hurry,' she said.

'Ah, but these lawyer chaps always know how to spin things out,' said the colonel. 'Who's the judge?'

'Sanders Curry,' said Eleanor.

'Then it'll last till Domesday,' said the colonel. 'Which court's he sitting in?' he asked.

Eleanor did not know.

'Here, Crosby – ' said the colonel. He sent Crosby for *The Times*. He began opening and turning the great sheets with his clumsy fingers as Eleanor swallowed her tart. By the time she had poured out coffee he had found out in which court the case was being heard.

'And you're going to the City, papa?' she said as she put down her cup.

'Yes. To a meeting,' he said. He loved going to the City, whatever he did there.

'Odd it should be Curry who's trying the case,' she said, rising. They had dined with him not long ago in a dreary great house somewhere off Queen's Gate. 'D'you remember that party?' she said, getting up. 'The old oak?' Curry collected oak chests.

'All shams I suspect,' said her father. 'Don't hurry,' he expostulated. 'Take a cab, Nell – if you want any change – ' he began, fumbling with his curtailed fingers for silver. As she watched him Eleanor felt the old childish feeling that his pockets were bottomless silver mines from which half-crowns could be dug eternally.

'Well, then,' she said, taking the coins, 'we shall meet at tea.'

'No,' he reminded her, 'I'm going round by the Digbys'.'

He took the necklace in his large hairy hand. It looked a little cheap, Eleanor was afraid.

'And what about a box for this, eh?' he asked.

'Crosby, find a box for the necklace,' said Eleanor. And Crosby, suddenly radiating importance, hurried off to the basement.

'It'll be dinner then,' she said to her father. That'll mean, she thought with relief, that I needn't be back for tea.

'Yes, dinner,' he said. He held a spill of paper in his hand which he was applying to the end of his cigar. He sucked. A little puff of smoke rose from the cigar. She liked the smell of cigars. She stood for a moment and drew it in.

'And give my love to Aunt Eugénie,' she said. He nodded as he puffed at his cigar.

It was a treat to take a hansom – it saved fifteen minutes. She leant back in the corner, with a little sigh of content, as the flaps clicked above her knees. For a minute her mind was completely vacant. She enjoyed the peace, the silence, the rest from exertion as she sat there in the corner of the cab. She felt detached, a spectator, as it trotted along. The morning had been a rush; one thing on top of another. Now, until she reached the Law Courts, she could sit and do nothing. It was a long way; and the horse was a plodding horse, a red-coated hairy horse. It kept up its steady jog-trot all down the Bayswater Road. There was very little traffic; people were still at luncheon. A soft grey mist filled up the distance; the bells jingled; the houses passed. She ceased to notice what houses they were passing. She half shut her eyes, and then, involuntarily, she saw her own hand take a letter from the hall table. When? That very morning. What had she done with it? Put it in her bag? Yes. There it was, unopened; a letter from Martin in India. She would read it as they drove along. It was written on very thin paper in Martin's little hand. It was longer than usual; it was about an adventure with somebody called Renton. Who was Renton? She could not remember. 'We started at dawn,' she read.

She looked out of the window. They were being held up by traffic at Marble Arch. Carriages were coming out of the park. A horse pranced; but the coachman had him well in hand.

She read again: 'I found myself alone in the middle of the jungle . . .'

But what were you doing? she asked.

She saw her brother; his red hair; his round face; and the rather pugnacious expression which always made her afraid that he would get himself into trouble one of these days. And so he had, apparently.

'I had lost my way; and the sun was sinking,' she read.

'The sun was sinking . . . ' Eleanor repeated, glancing ahead of her down Oxford Street. The sun shone on dresses in a window. A jungle was a very thick wood, she supposed; made of stunted little trees; dark green in colour. Martin was in the jungle alone, and the sun was sinking. What happened next? 'I thought it better to stay where I was.' So he stood in the midst of little trees alone, in the jungle; and the sun was sinking. The street before her lost its detail. It must have been cold, she thought, when the sun sank. She read again. He had to make a fire. 'I looked in my pocket and found that I had only two matches . . . The first match went out.' She saw a heap of dry sticks and Martin alone watching the match go out. 'Then I lit the other, and by sheer luck it did the trick.' The paper began to burn; the twigs caught; a fan of fire blazed up. She skipped on in her anxiety to reach the end . . . – 'once I thought I heard voices shouting, but they died away.'

'They died away!' said Eleanor aloud.

They had stopped at Chancery Lane.[26] An old woman was being helped across the road by a policeman; but the road was a jungle.

'They died away,' she said. 'And then?'

' . . . I climbed a tree . . . I saw the track . . . the sun was rising . . . They had given me up for dead.'

The cab stopped. For a moment Eleanor sat still. She saw nothing but stunted little trees, and her brother looking at the sun rising over the jungle. The sun was rising. Flames for a moment danced over the vast funereal mass of the Law Courts. It was the second match that did the trick, she said to herself as she paid the driver and went in.

*

'Oh, there you are!' cried a little woman in furs, who was standing by one of the doors. 'I had given you up. I was just going in.' She was a small cat-faced woman, worried, but very proud of her husband.

They pushed through the swing doors into the court where the case was being tried. It seemed dark and crowded at first. Men in wigs and gowns were getting up and sitting down and coming in and going out like a flock of birds settling here and there on a field. They all looked unfamiliar; she could not see Morris. She looked about her, trying to find him.

'There he is,' Celia whispered.

One of the barristers in the front row turned his head. It was Morris; but how odd he looked in his yellow wig! His glance passed over them without any sign of recognition. Nor did she smile at him; the solemn sallow atmosphere forbade personalities; there was something ceremonial about it all. From where she sat she could see his face in profile; the wig squared his forehead, and gave him a framed look, like a picture. Never had she seen him to such advantage; with such a brow, with such a nose. She glanced round. They all looked like pictures; all the barristers looked emphatic, cut out, like eighteenth-century portraits hung upon a wall. They were still rising and settling, laughing, talking . . . Suddenly a door was thrown open. The usher demanded silence for his lordship. There was silence; everybody stood up; and the judge came in. He made one bow and took his seat under the lion and the unicorn.[27] Eleanor felt a little thrill of awe run through her. That was old Curry. But how transformed! Last time she had seen him he was sitting at the head of a dinner-table; a long yellow strip of embroidery went rippling down the middle; and he had taken her, with a candle, round the drawing-room to look at his old oak. But now, there he was, awful, magisterial, in his robes.

A barrister had risen. She tried to follow what the man with a big nose was saying; but it was difficult to pick it up now. She listened, however. Then another barrister rose – a chicken-breasted little man, wearing gold pince-nez. He was reading some document; then he too began to argue. She could understand parts of what he was saying; though how it bore on the case she did not know. When was Morris going to speak, she wondered? Not yet apparently. As her father had said, these lawyer chaps knew how to spin things out. There had been no need to hurry over luncheon; an omnibus would have done just as well. She fixed her eyes on Morris. He was cracking some joke with the sandy man next to him. Those were his cronies, she thought; this was his life. She remembered his passion for the Bar as a boy. It was she who had talked papa round; one morning she had taken her life in her hand and gone to his study . . . but now, to her excitement, Morris himself got up.

She felt her sister-in-law stiffen with nervousness and clasp her little bag tightly. Morris looked very tall, and very black and white as he began. One hand was on the edge of his gown. How well she knew that gesture of Morris's, she thought – grasping something, so that you saw the white scar where he had cut himself bathing. But she did not recognise the other gesture – the way he flung his arm out. That belonged to his public life, his life in the courts. And his voice was unfamiliar. But every now and then as he warmed to his speech, there was a tone in his voice that made her smile; it was his private voice. She could not help half turning to her sister-in-law as if to say, How like Morris! But Celia was looking with absolute fixity ahead of her at her husband. Eleanor, too, tried to fix her mind upon the argument. He spoke with extraordinary clearness; he spaced his words beautifully. Suddenly the judge interrupted: 'Do I understand you to hold, Mr Pargiter . . . ?' he said in urbane yet awful tones; and Eleanor was thrilled to see how instantly Morris stopped short; how respectfully he bent his head as the judge spoke.

But will he know the answer? she thought, as if he were a child, shifting in her seat with nervousness lest he might break down. But he had the answer at his finger-ends. Without hurry or flutter he opened a book; found his place; read out a passage; upon which old Curry nodded, and made a note in the great volume that lay open in front of him. She was immensely relieved.

'How well he did that!' she whispered. Her sister-in-law nodded; but she still grasped her bag tightly. Eleanor felt that she could relax. She glanced round her. It was an odd mixture of solemnity and licence. Barristers kept coming in and out. They stood leaning against the wall of the court. In the pale top light all their faces looked parchment-coloured; all their features seemed cut out. They had lit the gas. She gazed at the judge himself. He was now lying back in his great carved chair under the lion and the unicorn, listening. He looked infinitely sad and wise, as if words had been beating upon him for centuries. Now he opened his heavy eyes, wrinkled his forehead, and the little hand that emerged fraily from the enormous cuff wrote a few words in the great volume. Then again he lapsed with half-shut eyes into his eternal vigil over the strife of unhappy human beings. Her mind wandered. She leant back against the hard wooden seat and let the tide of oblivion flow over her. Scenes from her morning began to form themselves; to obtrude themselves. Judd at the committee; her father reading the paper; the old woman plucking at her hand; the parlourmaid sweeping the silver over the table; and Martin lighting his second match in the jungle . . .

She fidgeted. The air was fuggy; the light dim; and the judge now that the first glamour had worn off, looked fretful; no longer immune from human weakness; and she remembered with a smile how very gullible he was, there in that hideous house in Queen's Gate, about old oak. 'This I picked up at Whitby,' he had said. And it was a sham. She wanted to laugh; she wanted to move. She rose and whispered: 'I'm going.'

Her sister-in-law made a little murmur, perhaps of protest. But Eleanor made her way as silently as she could through the swing doors, out into the street.

The uproar, the confusion, the space of the Strand came upon her with a shock of relief. She felt herself expand. It was still daylight here; a rush, a stir, a turmoil of variegated life came racing towards her. It was as if something had broken loose – in her, in the world. She seemed, after her concentration, to be dissipated, tossed about. She wandered along the Strand, looking with pleasure at the racing street; at the shops full of bright chains and leather cases; at the white-faced churches; at the irregular jagged roofs laced across and across with wires. Above was the dazzle of a watery but gleaming sky. The wind blew in her face. She breathed in a gulp of fresh wet air. And that man, she thought, thinking of the dark little court and its cut-out faces, has to sit there all day, every day. She saw Sanders Curry again, lying back in his great chair, with his face falling in folds of iron. Every day, all day, she thought, arguing points of law. How could Morris stand it? But he had always wanted to go to the Bar.

Cabs, vans and omnibuses streamed past; they seemed to rush the air into her face; they splashed the mud on to the pavement. People jostled and hustled and she quickened her pace in time with theirs. She was stopped by a van turning down one of the little steep streets that led to the river. She looked up and saw the clouds moving between the roofs: dark clouds, rain-swollen; wandering, indifferent clouds. She walked on.

Again she was stopped at the entrance to Charing Cross Station. The sky was wide at that point. She saw a file of birds flying high, flying together; crossing the sky. She watched them. Again she walked on. People on foot, people in cabs were being sucked in like straws round the piers of a bridge; she had to wait. Cabs piled with boxes went past her.

She envied them. She wished she were going abroad: to Italy, to India
. . . Then she felt vaguely that something was happening. The paper-
boys at the gates were dealing out papers with unusual rapidity. Men
were snatching them and opening them and reading them as they
walked on. She looked at a placard that was crumpled across a boy's
legs. 'Death' was written in very large black letters.

Then the placard blew straight, and she read another word: 'Parnell'.
'Dead.' . . . she repeated. 'Parnell.' She was dazed for a moment. How
could he be dead – Parnell? She bought a paper. They said so . . .

'Parnell is dead!' she said aloud. She looked up and saw the sky again;
clouds were passing; she looked down into the street. A man pointed at
the news with his forefinger. Parnell is dead he was saying. He was
gloating. But how could he be dead? It was like something fading in the
sky.

She walked slowly along towards Trafalgar Square, holding the paper
in her hand. Suddenly the whole scene froze into immobility. A man
was joined to a pillar; a lion was joined to a man; they seemed stilled,
connected, as if they would never move again.

She crossed into Trafalgar Square. Birds chattered shrilly somewhere.
She stopped by the fountain and looked down into the large basin full
of water. The water rippled black as the wind ruffled it. There were
reflections in the water, branches and a pale strip of sky. What a dream,
she murmured; what a dream . . . But someone jostled her. She turned.
She must go to Delia. Delia had cared. Delia had cared passionately.
What was it she used to say – flinging out of the house, leaving them all
for the Cause, for this man? Justice, Liberty? She must go to her. This
would be the end of all her dreams. She turned and hailed a cab.

She leant over the flaps of the cab looking out. The streets they were
driving through were horribly poor; and not only poor, she thought,
but vicious. Here was the vice, the obscenity, the reality of London. It
was lurid in the mixed evening light. Lamps were being lit. Paper-boys
were crying, Parnell . . . Parnell. He's dead, she said to herself, still
conscious of the two worlds; one flowing in wide sweeps overhead, the
other tip-tapping circumscribed upon the pavement. But here she was .
. . She held up her hand. She stopped the cab opposite a little row of
posts in an alley. She got out and made her way into the square.

The sound of the traffic was dulled. It was very silent here. In the
October afternoon, with dead leaves falling, the old faded square looked
dingy and decrepit and full of mist. The houses were let out in offices,
to societies, to people whose names were pinned up on the door-posts.
The whole neighbourhood seemed to her foreign and sinister. She

came to the old Queen Anne doorway with its heavy carved eyebrows and pressed the bell at the top of six or seven bells. Names were written over them, sometimes only on visiting-cards. Nobody came. She pushed the door open and went in; she mounted the wooden stairs with carved banisters that seemed to have been degraded from their past dignity. Jugs of milk with bills under them stood in the deep window-seats. Some of the panes were broken. Outside Delia's door, at the top, there was a milk-jug too, but it was empty. Her card was fixed by a drawing-pin to a panel. She knocked and waited. There was no sound. She turned the handle. The door was locked. She stood for a moment listening. A little window at the side gave on to the square. Pigeons crooned on the tree-tops. The traffic hummed far off; she could just hear paper-boys crying death . . . death . . . death. The leaves were falling. She turned and went downstairs.

She strolled along the streets. Children had chalked the pavement into squares; women leant from the upper windows, raking the street with a rapacious, dissatisfied stare. Rooms were let out to single gentlemen only. There were cards in them which said 'Furnished Apartments' or 'Bed and Breakfast'. She guessed at the life that went on behind those thick yellow curtains. This was the purlieu in which her sister lived, she thought, turning; she must often come back this way at night alone. Then she went back to the square and climbed the stairs and rattled at the door again. But there was no sound within. She stood for a moment watching the leaves fall; she heard the paper-boys crying and the pigeons crooning in the tree-tops. Take two coos, Taffy; take two coos, Taffy; tak . . . Then a leaf fell.

The traffic at Charing Cross thickened as the afternoon wore on. People on foot, people in cabs were being sucked in at the gates of the station. Men swung along at a great pace as if there were some demon in the station who would be enraged if they kept him waiting. But even so they paused and snatched a paper as they passed. The clouds parting and massing let the light shine and then veiled it. The mud, now dark brown, now liquid gold, was splashed up by the wheels and hooves, and in the general churn and uproar the shrill chatter of the birds on the eaves was silenced. The hansoms jingled and passed; jingled and passed. At last among all the jingling cabs came one in which sat a stout red-faced man holding a flower wrapped in tissue-paper – the colonel.

'Hi!' he cried as the cab passed the gates, and drove one hand through the trap-door in the roof. He leant out and a paper was thrust up at him.

'Parnell!' he exclaimed, as he fumbled for his glasses. 'Dead, by Jove!'

The cab trotted on. He read the news two or three times over. He's dead, he said, taking off his glasses. A shock of something like relief, of something that had a tinge of triumph in it, went through him as he leant back in the corner. Well, he said to himself, he's dead – that unscrupulous adventurer – that agitator who had done all the mischief, that man . . . Some feeling connected with his own daughter here formed in him; he could not say exactly what, but it made him frown. Anyhow he's dead now, he thought. How had he died? Had he killed himself? It wouldn't be surprising . . . Anyhow he was dead and that was an end of it. He sat holding the paper crumpled in one hand, the flower wrapped in tissue paper in the other, as the cab drove down Whitehall [28] . . . One could respect him, he thought, as the cab passed the House of Commons, which was more than could be said for some of the other fellows . . . and there'd been a lot of nonsense talked about the divorce case.[29] He looked out. The cab was driving near a certain street where he used to stop and look about him years ago. He turned and glanced down a street to the right. But a man in public life can't afford to do those things, he thought. He gave a little nod as the cab passed on. And now she's written to ask me for money, he thought. The other chap had turned out, as he knew he would, a bad egg. She'd lost all her looks, he was thinking; she had grown very stout. Well, he could afford to be generous. He put on his glasses again and read the City news.

It would make no difference, Parnell's death, coming now, he thought. Had he lived, had the scandal died down – he looked up. The cab was going the long way round as usual. 'Left!' he shouted, 'Left!' as the driver, as they always did, took the wrong turning.

In the rather dark basement at Browne Street, the Italian manservant was reading the paper in his shirt sleeves when the housemaid waltzed in carrying a hat.

'Look what she's given me!' she cried. To atone for the mess in the drawing-room, Lady Pargiter had given her a hat. 'Ain't I stylish?' she said, pausing in front of the glass with the great Italian hat that looked as if it were made of spun glass on one side of her head. And Antonio had to drop his paper and catch her round the waist from sheer gallantry, since she was no beauty, and her action was merely a parody of what he remembered in the hill towns of Tuscany. But a cab stopped in front of the railings; two legs stood still there, and he must detach himself, put on his jacket and go upstairs to answer the bell.

*

He takes his time, the colonel thought, as he stood on the doorstep waiting. The shock of the death had been absorbed almost; it still swept round in his system, but did not prevent him from thinking, as he stood there, that they had had the bricks re-pointed; but how had they money to spare, with the three boys to educate, and the two little girls? Eugénie was a clever woman of course; but he wished she would get a parlourmaid instead of these Italian dagos[30] who always seemed to be swallowing macaroni. Here the door opened, and as he went upstairs he thought he heard, from somewhere in the background, a shout of laughter.

He liked Eugénie's drawing-room, he thought, as he stood there waiting. It was very untidy. There was a litter of shavings from something that was being unpacked on the floor. They had been to Italy, he remembered. A looking-glass stood on the table. It was probably one of the things she had picked up there: the sort of thing that people did pick up in Italy; an old glass, covered with spots. He straightened his tie in front of it.

But I prefer a glass in which one can see oneself, he thought, turning away. There was the piano open; and the tea – he smiled – with the cup half full as usual; and branches stuck about the room, branches of withering red and yellow leaves. She liked flowers. He was glad he had remembered to bring her his usual gift. He held the flower wrapped in tissue paper in front of him. But why was the room so full of smoke? A gust blew in. Both windows in the back room were open, and the smoke was blowing in from the garden. Were they burning weeds, he wondered? He walked to the window and looked out. Yes, there they were – Eugénie and the two little girls. There was a bonfire. As he looked, Magdalena, the little girl who was his favourite, tossed a whole armful of dead leaves. She jerked them as high as she could, and the fire blazed up. A great fan of red flame flung out.

'That's dangerous!' he called out.

Eugénie pulled the children back. They were dancing with excitement. The other little girl, Sara, ducked under her mother's arm, seized another armful of leaves and flung them again. A great fan of red flame flung out. Then the Italian servant came and mentioned his name. He tapped on the window. Eugénie turned and saw him. She held the children back with one hand and raised the other in welcome.

'Stay where you are!' she cried. 'We're coming!'

A cloud of smoke blew straight at him; it made his eyes water, and he turned and sat down in the chair by the sofa. In another second she came, hurrying towards him with both her hands stretched out. He rose and took them.

'We're having a bonfire,' she said. Her eyes were glowing; her hair was looping down. 'That's why I'm all so blown-about,' she added, putting her hand to her head. She was untidy, but extremely handsome all the same, Abel thought. A fine large woman, growing ample, he noted as she shook hands; but it suited her. He admired that type more than the pink-and-white pretty Englishwoman. The flesh flowed over her like warm yellow wax; she had great dark eyes like a foreigner, and a nose with a ripple in it. He held out his camellia; his customary gift. She made a little exclamation as she took the flower from the tissue paper and sat down.

'How very good of you!' she said, and held it for a moment in front of her, and then did what he had often seen her do with a flower – put the stalk between her lips. Her movements charmed him as usual.

'Having a bonfire for the birthday?' he asked . . . 'No, no, no,' he protested, 'I don't want tea.'

She had taken her cup, and sipped the cold tea that was left in it. As he watched her, some memory of the East came back to him; so women sat in hot countries in their doorways in the sun. But it was very cold at the moment with the window open and the smoke blowing in. He still had his newspaper in his hand; he laid it on the table.

'Seen the news?' he asked.

She put down her cup and slightly opened her large dark eyes. Immense reserves of emotion seemed to dwell in them. As she waited for him to speak, she raised her hand as if in expectation.

'Parnell,' said Abel briefly. 'He's dead.'

'Dead?' Eugénie echoed him. She let her hand fall dramatically.

'Yes. At Brighton. Yesterday.'

'Parnell is dead!' she repeated.

'So they say,' said the colonel. Her emotion always made him feel more matter-of-fact; but he liked it.

She took up the paper. 'Poor thing!' she exclaimed, letting it fall.

'Poor thing?' he repeated. Her eyes were full of tears. He was puzzled. Did she mean Kitty O'Shea? He hadn't thought of her.

'She ruined his career for him,' he said with a little snort.

'Ah, but how she must have loved him!' she murmured.

She drew her hand over her eyes. The colonel was silent for a moment. Her emotion seemed to him out of all proportion to its object; but it was genuine. He liked it.

'Yes,' he said, rather stiffly. 'Yes, I suppose so.' Eugénie picked up the flower again and held it, twirling it. She was oddly absent-minded now and then, but he always felt at his ease with her. His body relaxed. He felt relieved of some obstruction in her presence.

'How people suffer! . . . ' she murmured, looking at the flower. 'How they suffer, Abel!' she said. She turned and looked straight at him.

A great gust of smoke blew in from the other room.

'You don't mind the draught?' he asked, looking at the window. She did not answer at once; she was twirling her flower. Then she roused herself and smiled.

'Yes, yes. Shut it!' she said with a wave of her hand. He went and shut the window. When he turned round, she had got up and was standing at the looking-glass, arranging her hair.

'We've had a bonfire for Maggie's birthday,' she murmured, looking at herself in the Venetian glass that was covered with spots. 'That's why, that's why – ' she smoothed her hair and fixed the camellia in her dress. 'I'm so very – '

She put her head a little on one side as if to observe the effect of the flower in her dress. The colonel sat down and waited. He glanced at his paper.

'They seem to be hushing things up,' he said.

'You don't mean – ' Eugénie was beginning; but here the door opened and the children came in. Maggie, the elder, came first; the other little girl, Sara, hung back behind her.

'Hello!' the colonel exclaimed. 'Here they are!' He turned round. He was very fond of children. 'Many happy returns of the day to you, Maggie!' He felt in his pocket for the necklace that Crosby had done up in a cardboard box. Maggie came up to him to take it. Her hair had been brushed, and she was dressed in a stiff clean frock. She took the parcel and undid it; she held the blue-and-gold necklace dangling from her finger. For a moment the colonel doubted whether she liked it. It looked a little garish as she held it dangling in her hand. And she was silent. Her mother at once supplied the words she should have spoken.

'How lovely, Maggie! How perfectly lovely!'

Maggie held the beads in her hand and said nothing.

'Thank Uncle Abel for the lovely necklace,' her mother prompted her.

'Thank you for the necklace, Uncle Abel,' said Maggie. She spoke directly and accurately, but the colonel felt another twinge of doubt. A pang of disappointment out of all proportion to its object came over him. Her mother, however, fastened it round her neck. Then she turned away to her sister, who was peeping from behind a chair.

'Come, Sara,' said her mother. 'Come and say how-d'you-do.'

She held out her hand partly to coax the little girl, partly, Abel guessed, in order to conceal the very slight deformity that always made him uncomfortable. She had been dropped when she was a baby; one shoulder was slightly higher than the other; it made him feel squeamish; he could not bear the least deformity in a child. It did not affect her spirits, however. She skipped up to him, whirling round on her toe, and kissed him lightly on the cheek. Then she tugged at her sister's frock, and they both rushed away into the back room laughing.

'They are going to admire your lovely present, Abel,' said Eugénie. 'How you spoil them! – and me too,' she added, touching the camellia on her breast.

'I hope she liked it?' he asked. Eugénie did not answer him. She had taken up the cup of cold tea again and was sipping it in her indolent Southern manner.

'And now,' she said, leaning back comfortably, 'tell me all your news.'

The colonel, too, lay back in his chair. He pondered for a moment. What was his news? Nothing occurred to him on the spur of the moment. With Eugénie, too, he always wanted to make a little splash; she put a shine on things. While he hesitated, she began: 'We've been having a wonderful time in Venice! I took the children. That's why we're all so brown. We had rooms not on the Grand Canal – I hate the Grand Canal – but just off it. Two weeks of blazing sun; and the colours' – she hesitated – 'marvellous!' she exclaimed, 'marvellous!' She threw out her hand. She had gestures of extraordinary significance. That's how she rigs things up, he thought. But he liked her for it.

He had not been to Venice for years.

'Any pleasant people there?' he asked.

'Not a soul,' she said. 'Not a soul. No one except a dreadful Miss —. One of those women who make one ashamed of one's country,' she said energetically.

'I know 'em,' he chuckled.

'But coming back from the Lido [31] in the evening,' she resumed, 'with the clouds above and the water below – we had a balcony; we used to sit there.' She paused.

'Was Digby with you?' the colonel asked.

'No, poor Digby. He took his holiday earlier, in August. He was up in Scotland with the Lasswades shooting. It does him good, you know.' There she goes, rigging thing's up again, he thought.

But she resumed.

'Now tell me about the family. Martin and Eleanor, Hugh and Milly, Morris and . . . ' She hesitated; he suspected that she had forgotten the name of Morris' wife.

'Celia,' he said. He stopped. He wanted to tell her about Mira. But he told her about the family: Hugh and Milly; Morris and Celia. And Edward.

'They seem to think a lot of him at Oxford,' he said gruffly. He was very proud of Edward.

'And Delia?' said Eugénie. She glanced at the paper.

The colonel at once lost his affability. He looked glum and formidable, like an old bull with his head down, she thought.

'Perhaps it will bring her to her senses,' he said sternly. They were silent for a moment. There were shouts of laughter from the garden.

'Oh those children!' she exclaimed. She rose and went to the window. The colonel followed her. The children had stolen back into the garden. The bonfire was burning fiercely. A clear pillar of flame rose in the middle of the garden. The little girls were laughing and shouting as they danced round it. A shabby old man, something like a decayed groom to look at, stood there with a rake in his hand. Eugénie flung up the window and cried out. But they went on dancing. The colonel leant out too; they looked like wild creatures with their hair flying. He would have liked to go down and jump over the bonfire, but he was too old. The flames leapt high – clear gold, bright red.

'Bravo!' he cried, clapping his hands. 'Bravo!'

'Little demons!' said Eugénie. She was as much excited as they were, he observed. She leant out of the window and cried to the old man with the rake: 'Make it blaze! Make it blaze!'

But the old man was raking out the fire. The sticks were scattered. The flames had sunk.

The old man pushed the children away.

'Well, that's over,' said Eugénie, heaving a sigh. She turned. Someone had come into the room.

'Oh, Digby, I never heard you!' she exclaimed. Digby stood there with a case in his hands.

'Hello, Digby!' said Abel, shaking hands.

'What's all this smoke?' said Digby, looking round him.

He's aged a bit, Abel thought. There he stood in his frock-coat with the top buttons undone. His coat was a little threadbare; his hair was white on top. But he was very handsome; beside him the colonel felt large, weather-beaten and rough. He was a little ashamed that he had been caught leaning out of the window clapping his hands. He looks older, he thought, as they stood side by side; yet he's five years younger than I am. He was a distinguished man in his way; the top of his tree; a knight and all the rest of it. But he's not as rich as I am, he remembered with satisfaction; for he had always been the failure of the two.

'You look so tired, Digby!' Eugénie exclaimed, sitting down. 'He ought to take a real holiday,' she said, turning to Abel. 'I wish you'd tell him so.' Digby brushed away a white thread that had stuck to his trousers. He coughed slightly. The room was full of smoke.

'What's all this smoke for?' he asked his wife.

'We've been having a bonfire for Maggie's birthday,' she said as if excusing herself.

'Oh yes,' he said. Abel was irritated; Maggie was his favourite; her father ought to have remembered her birthday.

'Yes,' said Eugénie, turning to Abel again, 'he lets everybody else take a holiday, but he never takes one himself. And then, when he's done a full day's work at the office, he comes back with his bag full of papers – ' She pointed at the bag.

'You shouldn't work after dinner,' said Abel. 'That's a bad habit.' Digby did look a bit off-colour, he thought. Digby brushed aside this feminine effusiveness.

'Seen the news?' he said to his brother, indicating the paper.

'Yes. By Jove!' said Abel. He liked talking politics with his brother, though he slightly resented his official airs as if he could say more but must not. And then it's all in the papers the day after, he thought. Still they always talked politics. Eugénie lying back in her corner always let them talk; she never interrupted. But at length she got up and began tidying the litter that had fallen from the packing-case. Digby stopped what he was saying and watched her. He was looking at the glass.

'Like it?' said Eugénie, with her hand on the frame.

'Yes,' said Digby; but there was a hint of criticism in his voice. 'Quite a pretty one.'

'It's only for my bedroom,' she said quickly.

Digby watched her stuffing the bits of paper into the box. 'Remember,' he said, 'we're dining with the Chathams tonight.'

'I know.' She touched her hair again. 'I shall have to make myself tidy,' she said. Who were 'the Chathams'? Abel wondered. Bigwigs, mandarins, he supposed half contemptuously. They moved a great deal in that world. He took it as a hint that he should go. They had come to the end of what they had to say to each other – he and Digby. He still hoped, however, that he might talk with Eugénie alone.

'About this African business – ' he began, bethinking him of another question – when the children came in; they had come to say good-night. Maggie was wearing his necklace and it looked very pretty, he thought, or was it she who looked so pretty? But their frocks, their clean blue and pink frocks, were crumpled; they were smudged with the sooty London leaves that they had been holding in their arms.

'Grubby little ruffians!' he said, smiling at them.

'Why d'you wear your best clothes to play in the garden?' said Sir Digby, as he kissed Maggie. He said it jokingly, but there was a hint of disapproval in his tones. Maggie made no answer. Her eyes were riveted on the camellia that her mother wore in the front of her dress. She went up and stood looking at her.

'And you – what a little sweep!' said Sir Digby, pointing to Sara.

'It's Maggie's birthday,' said Eugénie, holding out her arm again as if to protect the little girl.

'That is a reason, I should have thought,' said Sir Digby, surveying his daughters, 'to – er – to – er – reform one's habits.' He stumbled, trying to make his sentence sound playful; but it turned out as it generally did when he talked to the children, lame and rather pompous.

Sara looked at her father as if she were considering him.

'To – er – to – er – reform one's habits,' she repeated. Emptied of all meaning, she had got the rhythm of his words exactly. The effect was somehow comic. The colonel laughed; but Digby, he felt, was annoyed. He only patted Sara on the head when she came to say good-night; but he kissed Maggie as she passed him.

'Had a nice birthday?' he said, pulling her to him.

Abel made it an excuse to go.

'But there is no need for you to go yet, Abel?' Eugénie protested as he held out his hand.

She kept hold of his hand as if to prevent him from going. What did she mean? Did she want him to stay, did she want him to go? Her eyes, her large dark eyes, were ambiguous.

'But you're dining out?' he said.

'Yes,' she replied, letting his hand fall, and as she said no more there was nothing for it, he supposed – he must take himself off.

'Oh, I can find my way out alone,' he said as he left the room.

He went downstairs rather slowly. He felt depressed and disappointed. He had not seen her alone; he had not told her anything. Perhaps he never would tell anybody anything. After all, he thought as he went downstairs, slowly, heavily, it was his own affair; it didn't matter to anybody else. One must burn one's own smoke, he thought as he took his hat. He glanced round.

Yes . . . the house was full of pretty things. He looked vaguely at a great crimson chair with gilt claws that stood in the hall. He envied Digby his house, his wife, his children. He was getting old, he felt. All his children were grown-up; they had left him. He paused on the doorstep and looked out into the street. It was quite dark; lamps were lit; the autumn was drawing in; and as he marched up the dark windy street, now spotted with raindrops, a puff of smoke blew full in his face; and leaves were falling.

1907

IT WAS MIDSUMMER; and the nights were hot. The moon, falling on water, made it white, inscrutable, whether deep or shallow. But where the moonlight fell on solid objects it gave them a burnish and a silver plating, so that even the leaves in country roads seemed varnished. All along the silent country roads leading to London carts plodded; the iron reins fixed in the iron hands, for vegetables, fruit, flowers travelled slowly. Heaped high with round crates of cabbage, cherries, carnations, they looked like caravans piled with the goods of tribes migrating in search of water, driven by enemies to seek new pasturage. On they plodded, down this road, that road, keeping close to the kerb. Even the horses, had they been blind, could have heard the hum of London in the distance; and the drivers, dozing, yet saw through half-shut eyes the fiery gauze of the eternally burning city. At dawn, at Covent Garden,[32] they laid down their burdens; tables and trestles, even the cobbles were frilled as by some celestial laundry with cabbages, cherries and carnations.

All the windows were open. Music sounded. From behind crimson curtains, rendered semi-transparent and sometimes blowing wide came the sound of the eternal waltz – After the ball is over, after the dance is done – like a serpent that swallowed its own tail, since the ring was complete from Hammersmith to Shoreditch. Over and over again it was repeated by trombones outside public houses; errand boys whistled it; bands inside private rooms where people were dancing played it. There they sat at little tables at Wapping in the romantic inn that overhung the river, between timber warehouses where barges were moored; and here again in Mayfair. Each table had its lamp; its canopy of tight red silk, and the flowers that had sucked damp from the earth that noon relaxed and spread their petals in vases. Each table had its pyramid of strawberries, its pale plump quail; and Martin, after India, after Africa, found it exciting to talk to a girl with bare shoulders, to a woman iridescent with green beetles' wings in her hair, in a manner that the waltz condoned and half concealed under its amorous blandishments. Did it matter what one said? For she looked over her shoulder, only half listening, as a man came in wearing decorations, and a lady, in black with diamonds, beckoned him to a private corner.

As the night wore on a tender blue light lay on the market carts still plodding close to the kerb, past Westminster, past the yellow round clocks, the coffee stalls and the statues that stood there in the dawn holding so stiffly their rods or rolls of paper. And the scavengers followed after, sluicing the pavements. Cigarette ends, little bits of silver paper, orange peel – all the litter of the day was swept off the pavement and still the carts plodded, and the cabs trotted, indefatigably, along the dowdy pavements of Kensington, under the sparkling lights of Mayfair, carrying ladies with high headdresses and gentlemen in white waistcoats along the hammered dry roads which looked in the moonlight as if they were plated with silver.

'Look!' said Eugénie as the cab trotted over the bridge in the summer twilight. 'Isn't that lovely?'

She waved her hand at the water. They were crossing the Serpentine; but her exclamation was only an aside; she was listening to what her husband was saying. Their daughter Magdalena was with them; and she looked where her mother pointed. There was the Serpentine, red in the setting sun; the trees grouped together, sculptured, losing their detail; and the ghostly architecture of the little bridge, white at the end, composed the scene. The lights – the sunlight and the artificial light – were strangely mixed.

' . . . of course it's put the Government in a fix,' Sir Digby was saying. 'But then that's what he wants.'

'Yes . . . he'll make a name for himself, that young man,'[33] said Lady Pargiter.

The cab passed over the bridge. It entered the shadow of the trees. Now it left the park and joined the long line of cabs, taking people in evening dress to plays, to dinner-parties, that was streaming towards the Marble Arch. The light grew more and more artificial; yellower and yellower. Eugénie leant across and touched something on her daughter's dress. Maggie looked up. She had thought that they were still talking politics.

'So,' said her mother, arranging the flower in front of her dress. She put her head a little on one side and looked at her daughter approvingly. Then she gave a sudden laugh and threw her hand out. 'D'you know what made me so late?' she said. 'That imp, Sally . . . '

But her husband interrupted her. He had caught sight of an illuminated clock.

'We shall be late,' he said.

'But eight-fifteen means eight-thirty,' said Eugénie as they turned down a side street.

All was silent in the house at Browne Street. A ray from the street lamp fell through the fanlight and, rather capriciously, lit up a tray of glasses on the hall table; a top hat; and a chair with gilt paws. The chair, standing empty, as if waiting for someone, had a look of ceremony; as if it stood on the cracked floor of some Italian ante-room. But all was silent. Antonio, the manservant, was asleep; Mollie, the housemaid, was asleep; downstairs in the basement a door flapped to and fro – otherwise all was silent.

Sally in her bedroom at the top of the house turned on her side and listened intently. She thought she heard the front door click. A burst of dance music came in through the open window and made it impossible to hear.

She sat up in bed and looked out through the slit of the blind. Through the gap she could see a slice of the sky; then roofs; then the tree in the garden; then the backs of houses opposite standing in a long row. One of the houses was brilliantly lit and from the long open windows came dance music. They were waltzing. She saw shadows twirling across the blind. It was impossible to read; impossible to sleep. First there was the music; then a burst of talk; then people came out into the garden; voices chattered, then the music began again.

It was a hot summer's night, and though it was late, the whole world seemed to be alive; the rush of traffic sounded distant but incessant.

A faded brown book lay on her bed, as if she had been reading. But it was impossible to read; impossible to sleep. She lay back on the pillow with her hands behind her head.

'And he says,' she murmured, 'the world is nothing but . . . ' She paused. What did he say? Nothing but thought, was it? she asked herself as if she had already forgotten. Well, since it was impossible to read and impossible to sleep, she would let herself *be* thought. It was easier to act things than to think them. Legs, body, hands, the whole of her must be laid out passively to take part in this universal process of thinking which the man said was the world living. She stretched herself out. Where did thought begin?

In the feet? she asked. There they were, jutting out under the single sheet. They seemed separated, very far away. She closed her eyes. Then against her will something in her hardened. It was impossible to act thought. She became something: a root; lying sunk in the earth; veins seemed to thread the cold mass; the tree put forth branches; the branches had leaves.

' – the sun shines through the leaves,' she said, waggling her finger.

She opened her eyes in order to verify the sun on the leaves and saw the actual tree standing out there in the garden. Far from being dappled with sunlight, it had no leaves at all. She felt for a moment as if she had been contradicted. For the tree was black, dead black.

She leant her elbow on the sill and looked out at the tree. A confused clapping sound came from the room where they were having the dance. The music had stopped; people began to come down the iron staircase into the garden which was marked out with blue and yellow lamps dotted along the wall. The voices grew louder. More people came and more people came. The dotted square of green was full of the flowing pale figures of women in evening dress; of the upright black-and-white figures of men in evening dress. She watched them moving in and out. They were talking and laughing; but they were too far off for her to hear what they were saying. Sometimes a single word or a laugh rose above the rest, and then there was a confused babble of sound. In their own garden all was empty and silent. A cat slid stealthily along the top of a wall; stopped; and then went on again as if drawn on some secret errand. Another dance struck up.

'Over again, over and over again!' she exclaimed impatiently. The air, laden with the curious dry smell of London earth, puffed in her face, blowing the blind out. Stretched flat on her bed, she saw the moon; it seemed immensely high above her. Little vapours were moving across the surface. Now they parted and she saw engravings chased over the white disc. What were they, she wondered – mountains? valleys? And if valleys, she said to herself half closing her eyes, then white trees; then icy hollows, and nightingales, two nightingales calling to each other, calling and answering each other across the valleys. The waltz music took the words 'calling and answering each other' and flung them out; but as it repeated the same rhythm again and again, it coarsened them, it destroyed them. The dance music interfered with everything. At first exciting, then it became boring and finally intolerable. Yet it was only twenty minutes to one.

Her lip raised itself, like that of a horse that is going to bite. The little brown book was dull. She reached her hand above her head and took down another book from the shelf of battered books without looking at it. She opened the book at random; but her eye was caught by one of the couples who were still sitting out in the garden though the others had gone in. What were they saying, she wondered? There was something gleaming in the grass, and, as far as she could see, the black-and-white figure stooped and picked it up.

'And as he picks it up,' she murmured, looking out, 'he says to the

lady beside him: "Behold, Miss Smith, what I have found on the grass –
a fragment of my heart; of my broken heart," he says. "I have found it in
the grass; and I wear it on my breast" ' – she hummed the words in time
to the melancholy waltz music – 'my broken heart, this broken glass, for
love – ' she paused and glanced at the book. On the fly-leaf was written:
'Sara Pargiter from her cousin Edward Pargiter'.

' . . . for love,' she concluded, 'is best.'

She turned to the title-page.

'The *Antigone* of Sophocles, done into English verse by Edward
Pargiter', she read.

Once more she looked out of the window. The couple had moved.
They were going up the iron staircase. She watched them. They went
into the ballroom. 'And suppose in the middle of the dance,' she
murmured, 'she takes it out; and looks at it and says, "What is this?"
and it's only a piece of broken glass – of broken glass . . . ' She looked
down at the book again.

'The *Antigone* of Sophocles', she read. The book was brand-new; it
cracked as she opened it; this was the first time she had opened it.

'The *Antigone* of Sophocles, done into English verse by Edward
Pargiter', she read again. He had given it her in Oxford, one hot
afternoon when they had been trailing through chapels and libraries.
'Trailing and wailing,' she hummed, turning over the pages, 'and he
said to me, getting up from the low armchair, and brushing his hand
through his hair' – she glanced out of the window – ' "my wasted
youth, my wasted youth".' The waltz was now at its most intense, its
most melancholy. 'Taking in his hand,' she hummed in time to it, 'this
broken glass, this faded heart, he said to me . . . ' Here the music
stopped; there was a sound of clapping; the dancers once more came
out into the garden.

She skipped through the pages. At first she read a line or two at
random; then, from the litter of broken words, scenes rose, quickly,
inaccurately, as she skipped. The unburied body of a murdered man lay
like a fallen tree-trunk, like a statue, with one foot stark in the air.
Vultures gathered. Down they flopped on the silver sand. With a lurch,
with a reel, the top-heavy birds came waddling; with a flap of the grey
throat swinging, they hopped – she beat her hand on the counterpane
as she read – to that lump there. Quick, quick, quick with repeated jerks
they struck the mouldy flesh. Yes. She glanced at the tree outside in the
garden. The unburied body of the murdered man lay on the sand.
Then in a yellow cloud came whirling – who? She turned the page
quickly. Antigone? She came whirling out of the dust-cloud to where

the vultures were reeling and flung white sand over the blackened foot. She stood there letting fall white dust over the blackened foot. Then behold! there were more clouds; dark clouds; the horsemen leapt down; she was seized; her wrists were bound with withies; and they bore her, thus bound – where?

There was a roar of laughter from the garden. She looked up. Where did they take her? she asked. The garden was full of people. She could not hear a word that they were saying. The figures were moving in and out.

'To the estimable court of the respected ruler?' she murmured, picking up a word or two at random, for she was still looking out into the garden. The man's name was Creon. He buried her. It was a moonlight night. The blades of the cactuses were sharp silver. The man in the loincloth gave three sharp taps with his mallet on the brick. She was buried alive.[34] The tomb was a brick mound. There was just room for her to lie straight out. Straight out in a brick tomb, she said. And that's the end, she yawned, shutting the book.

She laid herself out, under the cold smooth sheets, and pulled the pillow over her ears. The one sheet and the one blanket fitted softly round her. At the bottom of the bed was a long stretch of cool fresh mattress. The sound of the dance music became dulled. Her body dropped suddenly; then reached ground. A dark wing brushed her mind, leaving a pause; a blank space. Everything – the music, the voices – became stretched and generalised. The book fell on the floor. She was asleep.

'It's a lovely night,' said the girl who was going up the iron steps with her partner. She rested her hand on the balustrade. It felt very cold. She looked up; a slice of yellow light lay round the moon. It seemed to laugh round it. Her partner looked up too, and then mounted another step without saying anything for he was shy.

'Going to the match tomorrow?' he said stiffly, for they scarcely knew each other.

'If my brother gets off in time to take me,' she said, and went up another step too. Then, as they entered the ballroom, he gave her a little bow and left her; for his partner was waiting.

The moon which was now clear of clouds lay in a bare space as if the light had consumed the heaviness of the clouds and left a perfectly clear pavement, a dancing ground for revelry. For some time the dappled iridescence of the sky remained unbroken. Then there was a puff of wind; and a little cloud crossed the moon.

*

There was a sound in the bedroom. Sara turned over.

'Who's that?' she murmured. She sat up and rubbed her eyes.

It was her sister. She stood at the door, hesitating. 'Asleep?' she said in a low voice.

'No,' said Sara. She rubbed her eyes. 'I'm awake,' she said, opening them.

Maggie came across the room and sat down on the edge of the bed. The blind was blowing out; the sheets were slipping off the bed. She felt dazed for a moment. After the ballroom, it looked so untidy. There was a tumbler with a toothbrush in it on the washstand; the towel was crumpled on the towel-horse; and a book had fallen on the floor. She stooped and picked up the book. As she did so, the music burst out down the street. She held back the blind. The women in pale dresses, the men in black and white, were crowding up the stairs into the ballroom. Snatches of talk and laughter were blown across the garden.

'Is there a dance?' she asked.

'Yes. Down the street,' said Sara.

Maggie looked out. At this distance the music sounded romantic, mysterious, and the colours flowed over each other, neither pink nor white nor blue.

Maggie stretched herself and unpinned the flower that she was wearing. It was drooping; the white petals were stained with black marks. She looked out of the window again. The mixture of lights was very odd; one leaf was a lurid green; another was a bright white. The branches crossed each other at different levels. Then Sally laughed.

'Did anybody give you a piece of glass,' she said, 'saying to you, Miss Pargiter . . . my broken heart?'

'No,' said Maggie, 'why should they?' The flower fell off her lap on to the floor.

'I was thinking,' said Sara. 'The people in the garden . . . '

She waved her hand at the window. They were silent for a moment, listening to the dance music.

'And who did you sit next?' Sara asked after a time.

'A man in gold lace,' said Maggie.

'In gold lace?' Sara repeated.

Maggie was silent. She was getting used to the room; the discrepancy between this litter and the shiny ballroom was leaving her. She envied her sister lying in bed with the window open and the breeze blowing in.

'Because he was going to a party,' she said. She paused. Something had caught her eye. A branch swayed up and down in the little breeze.

Maggie held the blind so that the window was uncurtained. Now she could see the whole sky, and the houses and the branches in the garden.

'It's the moon,' she said. It was the moon that was making the leaves white. They both looked at the moon, which shone like a silver coin, perfectly polished, very sharp and hard.

'But if they don't say O my broken heart,' said Sara, 'what do they say, at parties?'

Maggie flicked off a white fleck that had stuck to her arm from her gloves.

'Some people say one thing,' she said, getting up, 'and some people say another.'

She picked up the little brown book which lay on the counterpane and smoothed out the bedclothes. Sara took the book out of her hand.

'This man,' she said, tapping the ugly little brown volume, 'says the world's nothing but thought, Maggie.'

'Does he?' said Maggie, putting the book on the washstand. It was a device, she knew, to keep her standing there, talking.

'D'you think it's true?' Sara asked.

'Possibly,' said Maggie, without thinking what she was saying. She put out her hand to draw the curtain. 'The world's nothing but thought, does he say?' she repeated, holding the curtain apart.

She had been thinking something of the kind when the cab crossed the Serpentine; when her mother interrupted her. She had been thinking, Am I that, or am I this? Are we one, or are we separate – something of the kind.

'Then what about trees and colours?' she said, turning round.

'Trees and colours?' Sara repeated.

'Would there be trees if we didn't see them?' said Maggie. 'What's "I"? . . . "I" . . . ' She stopped. She did not know what she meant. She was talking nonsense.

'Yes,' said Sara. 'What's "I"?' She held her sister tight by the skirt, whether she wanted to prevent her from going, or whether she wanted to argue the question. 'What's "I"?' she repeated.

But there was a rustling outside the door and her mother came in.

'Oh my dear children!' she exclaimed, 'still out of bed? Still talking?'

She came across the room, beaming, glowing, as if she were still under the influence of the party. Jewels flashed on her neck and her arms. She was extraordinarily handsome. She glanced round her.

'And the flower's on the floor, and everything's so untidy,' she said. She picked up the flower that Maggie had dropped and put it to her lips.

'Because I was reading, mama, because I was waiting,' said Sara. She took her mother's hand and stroked the bare arm. She imitated her mother's manner so exactly that Maggie smiled. They were the very opposite of each other – Lady Pargiter so sumptuous; Sally so angular. But it's worked, she thought to herself, as Lady Pargiter allowed herself to be pulled down on to the bed. The imitation had been perfect.

'But you must go to sleep, Sal,' she protested. 'What did the doctor say? Lie straight, lie still, he said.' She pushed her back on to the pillows.

'I am lying straight and still,' said Sara. 'Now' – she looked up at her – 'tell me about the party.'

Maggie stood upright in the window. She watched the couples coming down the iron staircase. Soon the garden was full of pale whites and pinks, moving in and out. She half heard them behind her talking about the party.

'It was a very nice party,' her mother was saying.

Maggie looked out of the window. The square of the garden was filled with differently tinted colours. They seemed to ripple one over the other until they entered the angle where the light from the house fell, when they suddenly turned to ladies and gentlemen in full evening dress.

'No fish-knives?' she heard Sara saying.

She turned.

'Who was the man I sat next?' she asked.

'Sir Matthew Mayhew,' said Lady Pargiter.

'Who is Sir Matthew Mayhew?' said Maggie.

'A most distinguished man, Maggie!' said her mother, flinging her hand out.

'A most distinguished man,' Sara echoed her.

'But he is,' Lady Pargiter repeated, smiling at her daughter whom she loved, perhaps because of her shoulder.

'It was a great honour to sit next him, Maggie,' she continued. 'A great honour,' she said reprovingly. She paused, as if she saw a little scene. She looked up.

'And then,' she resumed, 'when Mary Palmer says to me, Which is your daughter? I see Maggie, miles away, at the other end of the room, talking to Martin, whom she might have met every day of her life in an omnibus!'

Her words were stressed so that they seemed to rise and fall. She emphasised the rhythm still further by tapping with her fingers on Sally's bare arm.

'But I don't see Martin every day,' Maggie protested. 'I haven't seen him since he came back from Africa.'

Her mother interrupted her. 'But you don't go to parties, my dear Maggie, to talk to your own cousins. You go to parties to – '

Here the dance music crashed out. The first chords seemed possessed of frantic energy, as if they were summoning the dancers imperiously to return. Lady Pargiter stopped in the middle of her sentence. She sighed; her body seemed to become indolent and suave. The heavy lids lowered themselves slightly over her large dark eyes. She swayed her head slowly in time to the music.

'What's that they're playing?' she murmured. She hummed the tune, beating time with her hand. 'Something I used to dance to.'

'Dance it now, mama,' said Sara.

'Yes, mama. Show us how you used to dance,' Maggie urged her.

'But without a partner – ?' Lady Pargiter protested.

Maggie pushed a chair away.

'Imagine a partner,' Sara urged her.

'Well,' said Lady Pargiter. She rose. 'It was something like this,' she said. She paused; she held her skirt out with one hand; she slightly crooked the other in which she held the flower; she twirled round and round in the space which Maggie had cleared. She moved with extraordinary stateliness. All her limbs seemed to bend and flow in the lilt and the curve of the music; which became louder and clearer as she danced to it. She circled in and out among the chairs and tables and then, as the music stopped, 'There!' she exclaimed. Her body seemed to fold and close itself together as she sighed, 'There!' and sank all in one movement on the edge of the bed.

'Wonderful!' Maggie exclaimed. Her eyes rested on her mother with admiration.

'Nonsense,' Lady Pargiter laughed, panting slightly. 'I'm much too old to dance now; but when I was young; when I was your age – ' She sat there panting.

'You danced out of the house on to the terrace and found a little note folded in your bouquet – ' said Sara, stroking her mother's arm. 'Tell us that story, mama.'

'Not tonight,' said Lady Pargiter. 'Listen – there's the clock striking!'

Since the Abbey was so near, the sound of the hour filled the room; softly, tumultuously, as if it were a flurry of soft sighs hurrying one on top of another, yet concealing something hard. Lady Pargiter counted. It was very late.

'I'll tell you the true story one of these days,' she said as she bent to kiss her daughter good-night.

'Now! Now!' cried Sara, holding her fast.

'No, not now – not now!' Lady Pargiter laughed, snatching away her hand. 'There's papa calling me!'

They heard footsteps in the passage outside, and then Sir Digby's voice at the door.

'Eugénie! It's very late, Eugénie!' they heard him say.

'Coming!' she cried. 'Coming!'

Sara caught her by the train of her dress. 'You haven't told us the story of the bouquet, mama!' she cried.

'Eugénie!' Sir Digby repeated. His voice sounded peremptory. 'Have you locked – '

'Yes, yes, yes,' said Eugénie. 'I will tell you the true story another time,' she said, freeing herself from her daughter's grasp. She kissed them both quickly and went out of the room.

'She won't tell us,' said Maggie, picking up her gloves. She spoke with some bitterness.

They listened to the voices talking in the passage. They could hear their father's voice. He was expostulating. His voice sounded querulous and cross.

'Pirouetting up and down with his sword between his legs; with his opera hat under his arm and his sword between his legs,' said Sara, pummelling her pillows viciously.

The voices went farther away, downstairs.

'Who was the note from, d'you think?' said Maggie. She paused, looking at her sister burrowing into her pillows.

'The note? What note?' said Sara. 'Oh, the note in the bouquet. I don't remember,' she said. She yawned.

Maggie shut the window and pulled the curtain but she left a chink of light.

'Pull it tight, Maggie,' said Sara irritably. 'Shut out that din.'

She curled herself up with her back to the window. She had raised a hump of pillow against her head as if to shut out the dance music that was still going on. She pressed her face into a cleft of the pillows. She looked like a chrysalis wrapped round in the sharp white folds of the sheet. Only the tip of her nose was visible. Her hip and her feet jutted out at the end of the bed covered by a single sheet. She gave a profound sigh that was half a snore; she was asleep already.

*

Maggie went along the passage. Then she saw that there were lights in the hall beneath. She stopped and looked down over the banister. The hall was lit up. She could see the great Italian chair with the gilt claws that stood in the hall. Her mother had thrown her evening cloak over it, so that it fell in soft golden folds over the crimson cover. She could see a tray with whisky and a soda-water syphon on the hall table. Then she heard the voices of her father and mother as they came up the kitchen stairs. They had been down in the basement; there had been a burglary up the street; her mother had promised to have a new lock put on the kitchen door but had forgotten. She could hear her father say: ' . . . they'd melt it down; we should never get it back again.'

Maggie went on a few steps upstairs.

'I'm so sorry, Digby,' Eugénie said as they came into the hall. 'I will tie a knot in my handkerchief; I will go directly after breakfast tomorrow morning . . . Yes,' she said, gathering her cloak in her arms, 'I will go myself, and I will say, "I've had enough of your excuses, Mr Toye. No, Mr Toye, you have deceived me once too often. And after all these years!" '

Then there was a pause. Maggie could hear soda-water squirted into a tumbler; the chink of a glass; and then the lights went out.

1908

I T WAS MARCH and the wind was blowing. But it was not 'blowing'. It was scraping, scourging. It was so cruel. So unbecoming. Not merely did it bleach faces and raise red spots on noses; it tweaked up skirts; showed stout legs; made trousers reveal skeleton shins. There was no roundness, no fruit in it. Rather it was like the curve of a scythe which cuts, not corn, usefully, but destroys, revelling in sheer sterility. With one blast it blew out colour – even a Rembrandt in the National Gallery, even a solid ruby in a Bond Street window: one blast and they were gone. Had it any breeding place it was in the Isle of Dogs[35] among tin cans lying beside a workhouse drab on the banks of a polluted city. It tossed up rotten leaves, gave them another span of degraded existence; scorned, derided them, yet had nothing to put in the place of the scorned, the derided. Down they fell. Uncreative, unproductive, yelling its joy in destruction, its power to peel off the bark, the bloom, and show the bare bone, it paled every window; drove old gentlemen farther and farther into the leather-smelling recesses of clubs; and old ladies to sit eyeless, leather cheeked, joyless among the tassels and antimacassars of their bedrooms and kitchens. Triumphing in its wantonness it emptied the streets; swept flesh before it; and coming smack against a dustcart standing outside the Army and Navy Stores, scattered along the pavement a litter of old envelopes; twists of hair; papers already blood smeared, yellow smeared, smudged with print, and sent them scudding to plaster legs, lamp-posts, pillar boxes, and fold themselves frantically against area railings.

Matty Stiles, the caretaker, huddled in the basement of the house in Browne Street, looked up. There was a rattle of dust along the pavement. It worked its way under the doors, through the window frames; on to chests and dressers. But she didn't care. She was one of the unlucky ones. She had been thinking it was a safe job, sure to last the summer out anyhow. The lady was dead; the gentleman too. She had got the job through her son the policeman. The house with its basement would never let this side of Christmas – so they told her. She had only to show parties round who came with orders to view from the agent. And she always mentioned the basement – how damp it was. 'Look at that stain on the ceiling.' There it was, sure enough. All the same, the party from China took a fancy to it. It suited him, he said. He had business in the city. She was one of the unlucky ones – after three months to turn out and lodge with her son in Pimlico.

A bell rang. Let him ring, ring, ring, she growled. She wasn't going to open the door any more. There he was standing on the doorstep. She could see a pair of legs against the railing. Let him ring as much as he liked. The house was sold. Couldn't he see the notice on the board? Couldn't he read it? Hadn't he eyes? She huddled closer to the fire, which was covered with pale ash. She could see his legs there, standing on the doorstep, between the canaries' cage and the dirty linen which she had been going to wash, but this wind made her shoulder ache cruel. Let him ring the house down, for all she cared.

Martin was standing there.

'Sold' was written on a strip of bright red paper pasted across the house-agent's board.

'Already!' said Martin. He had made a little circle to look at the house in Browne Street. And it was already sold. The red strip gave him a shock. It was sold already, and Digby had only been dead three months – Eugénie not much more than a year. He stood for a moment gazing at the black windows now grimed with dust. It was a house of character; built some time in the eighteenth century. Eugénie had been proud of it. And I used to like going there, he thought. But now an old newspaper was on the doorstep; wisps of straw had caught in the railings; and he could see, for there were no blinds, into an empty room. A woman was peering up at him from behind the bars of a cage in the basement. It was no use ringing. He turned away. A feeling of something extinguished came over him as he went down the street.

It's a grimy, it's a sordid end, he thought; I used to enjoy going there. But he disliked brooding over unpleasant thoughts. What's the good of it? he asked himself.

'The King of Spain's daughter,' he hummed as he turned the corner, 'came to visit me . . .'

'And how much longer,' he asked himself, pressing the bell, as he stood on the doorstep of the house in Abercorn Terrace, 'is old Crosby going to keep me waiting?' The wind was very cold.

He stood there, looking at the buff-coloured front of the large, architecturally insignificant, but no doubt convenient, family mansion in which his father and sister still lived. 'She takes her time nowadays,' he thought, shivering in the wind. But here the door opened, and Crosby appeared.

'Hello, Crosby!' he said.

She beamed on him so that her gold tooth showed. He was always her favourite, they said, and the thought pleased him today.

'How's the world treating you?' he asked, as he gave her his hat.

She was just the same – more shrivelled, more gnat-like, and her blue eyes were more prominent than ever.

'Feeling the rheumatics?' he asked, as she helped him off with his coat. She grinned, silently. He felt friendly; he was glad to find her much as usual. 'And Miss Eleanor?' he asked, as he opened the drawing-room door. The room was empty. She was not there. But she had been there, for there was a book on the table. Nothing had been changed he was glad to see. He stood in front of the fire and looked at his mother's picture. In the course of the past few years it had ceased to be his mother; it had become a work of art. But it was dirty.

There used to be a flower in the grass, he thought, peering into a dark corner: but now there was nothing but dirty brown paint. And what's she been reading? he wondered. He took the book that was propped up against the teapot and looked at it. 'Renan,' he read. 'Why Renan?' he asked himself, beginning to read as he waited.

'Mr Martin, miss,' said Crosby, opening the study door. Eleanor looked round. She was standing by her father's chair with her hands full of long strips of newspaper cuttings, as if she had been reading them aloud. There was a chess-board in front of him; the chessmen were set out for a game; but he was lying back in his chair. He looked lethargic, and rather gloomy.

'Put 'em away . . . Keep 'em safe somewhere,' he said, jerking his thumb at the cuttings. That was a sign that he had grown very old, Eleanor thought – wanting newspaper cuttings kept. He had grown inert and ponderous after his stroke; there were red veins in his nose and in his cheeks. She too felt old, heavy and dull.

'Mr Martin's called,' Crosby repeated.

'Martin's come,' Eleanor said. Her father seemed not to hear. He sat still with his head sunk on his breast. 'Martin,' Eleanor repeated. 'Martin . . . '

Did he want to see him or did he not want to see him? She waited as if for some sluggish thought to rise. At last he gave a little grunt; but what it meant she was not certain.

'I'll send him in after tea,' she said. She paused for a moment. He roused himself and began fumbling with his chessmen. He still had courage, she observed with pride. He still insisted upon doing things for himself.

She went into the drawing-room and found Martin standing in front of the placid, smiling picture of their mother. He held a book in his hand.

'Why Renan?' he said as she came in. He shut the book and kissed her. 'Why Renan?' he repeated. She flushed slightly. It made her shy, for some reason, that he had found the book there, open. She sat down and laid the press cuttings on the tea-table.

'How's papa?' he asked. She had lost something of her bright colour, he thought, glancing at her, and her hair had a tuft of grey in it.

'Rather gloomy,' she said, glancing at the press cuttings. 'I wonder,' she added, 'who writes that sort of thing?'

'What sort of thing?' said Martin. He picked up one of the crinkled strips and began reading it: " . . . an exceptionally able public servant . . . a man of wide interests . . . " Oh, Digby,' he said. 'Obituaries. I passed the house this afternoon,' he added. 'It's sold.'

'Already?' said Eleanor.

'It looked very shut-up and desolate,' he added. 'There was a dirty old woman in the basement.'

Eleanor took out a hairpin and began fraying the wick beneath the kettle. Martin watched her for a moment in silence.

'I liked going there,' he said at length. 'I liked Eugénie,' he added. Eleanor paused.

'Yes . . . ' she said doubtfully. She had never felt at her ease with her. 'She exaggerated,' she added.

'Well of course,' Martin laughed. He smiled, recalling some memory. 'She had less sense of truth than . . . that's no sort of use, Nell,' he broke off, irritated by her fumbling with the wick.

'Yes, yes,' she protested. 'It boils in time.'

She paused. Stretching out towards the tea-caddy, she measured the tea. 'One, two, three, four,' she counted.

She still used the nice old silver tea-caddy, he noticed, with the sliding lid. He watched her measuring the tea methodically – one, two, three, four. He was silent.

'We can't tell a lie to save our souls,' he said abruptly.

What makes him say that? Eleanor wondered.

'When I was with them in Italy – ' she said aloud. But here the door opened and Crosby came in carrying some sort of dish. She left the door ajar and a dog pushed in after her.

'I mean – ' Eleanor added; but she could not say what she meant with Crosby in the room fidgeting about.

'It's time Miss Eleanor got a new kettle,' said Martin, pointing to the old brass kettle, faintly engraved with a design of roses, which he had always hated.

'Crosby,' said Eleanor, still poking with her pin, 'doesn't hold with new inventions. Crosby won't trust herself in the Tube, will you, Crosby?'

Crosby grinned. They always spoke to her in the third person, because she never answered but only grinned. The dog snuffed at the dish she had just put down. 'Crosby's letting that beast get much too fat,' said Martin, pointing at the dog.

'That's what I'm always telling her,' said Eleanor.

'If I were you, Crosby,' said Martin, 'I'd cut down his meals and take him for a brisk run round the park every morning.'

Crosby opened her mouth wide. 'Oh, Mr Martin!' she protested, shocked by his brutality into speech.

The dog followed her out of the room.

'Crosby's the same as ever,' said Martin.

Eleanor had lifted the lid of the kettle and was looking in. There were no bubbles on the water yet.

'Damn that kettle,' said Martin. He took up one of the newspaper cuttings and began to make it into a spill.

'No, no, papa wants them kept,' said Eleanor. 'But he wasn't like that,' she said, laying her hand on the newspaper cuttings. 'Not in the least.'

'What was he like?' Martin asked.

Eleanor paused. She could see her uncle clearly in her mind's eye: he held his top-hat in his hand; he laid his hand on her shoulder as they stopped in front of some picture. But how could she describe him?

'He used to take me to the National Gallery,' she said.

'Very cultivated, of course,' said Martin. 'But he was such a damned snob.'

'Only on the surface,' said Eleanor.

'And always finding fault with Eugénie about little things,' Martin added.

'But think of living with her,' said Eleanor.

'That manner – ' She threw her hand out; but not as Eugénie threw her hand out, Martin thought.

'I liked her,' he said. 'I liked going there.' He saw the untidy room: the piano open; the window open; a wind blowing the curtains, and his aunt coming forward with her arms open. 'What a pleasure, Martin! what a pleasure!' she would say. What had her private life been, he wondered – her love affairs? She must have had them – obviously, obviously.

'Wasn't there some story,' he began, 'about a letter?' He wanted to say, Didn't she have an affair with somebody? But it was more difficult to be open with his sister than with other women, because she treated him as if he were a small boy still. Had Eleanor ever been in love, he wondered, looking at her.

'Yes,' she said. 'There was a story – '

But here the electric bell rang sharply. She stopped.

'Papa,' she said. She half rose.

'No,' said Martin. 'I'll go.' He got up. 'I promised him a game of chess.'

'Thanks, Martin. He'll enjoy that,' said Eleanor with relief as he left the room, and she found herself alone.

She leant back in her chair. How terrible old age was, she thought; shearing off all one's faculties, one by one, but leaving something alive in the centre: leaving – she swept up the press cuttings – a game of chess, a drive in the park, and a visit from old General Arbuthnot in the evening.

It was better to die, like Eugénie and Digby, in the prime of life with all one's faculties about one. But he wasn't like that, she thought, glancing at the press cuttings. 'A man of singularly handsome presence . . . shot, fished, and played golf.' No, not like that in the least. He had been a curious man: weak; sensitive; liking titles; liking pictures; and often depressed, she guessed, by his wife's exuberance. She pushed the cuttings away and took up her book. It was odd how different the same person seemed to two different people, she thought. There was Martin, liking Eugénie; and she, liking Digby. She began to read.

She had always wanted to know about Christianity – how it began; what it meant, originally. God is love; The kingdom of Heaven is within us; sayings like that she thought, turning over the pages, what did they mean? The actual words were very beautiful. But who said them – when? Then the spout of the tea-kettle puffed steam at her and she moved it away. The wind was rattling the windows in the back room; it was bending the little bushes; they still had no leaves on them. It was what a man said under a fig tree, on a hill, she thought. And then another man wrote it down. But suppose that what that man says is just as false as what this man – she touched the press cuttings with her spoon – says about Digby? And here am I, she thought, looking at the china in the Dutch cabinet, in this drawing-room, getting a little spark from what someone said all those years ago – here it comes (the china was changing from blue to livid) skipping over all those mountains, all those seas. She found her place and began to read.

But a sound in the hall interrupted her. Was someone coming in? She listened. No, it was the wind. The wind was terrific. It pressed on the house; gripped it tight, then let it fall apart. Upstairs a door slammed; a window must be open in the bedroom above. A blind was tapping. It was difficult to fix her mind on Renan. She liked it, though. French she could read easily of course; and Italian; and a little German. But what vast gaps there were, what blank spaces, she thought leaning back in her chair, in her knowledge! How little she knew about anything. Take this cup for instance; she held it out in front of her. What was it made of? Atoms? And what were atoms, and how did they stick together? The smooth hard surface of the china with its red flowers seemed to her for a second a marvellous mystery. But there was another sound in the hall. It was the wind, but it was also a voice, talking. It must be Martin. But who could he be talking to, she wondered? She listened, but she could not hear what he was saying because of the wind. And why, she asked herself, did he say: We can't tell a lie to save our souls? He was thinking about himself; one always knew when people were thinking about themselves by their tone of voice. Perhaps he was justifying himself for having left the army. That had been courageous, she thought; but isn't it odd, she mused, listening to the voices, that he should be such a dandy too? He was wearing a new blue suit with white stripes on it. And he had shaved off his moustache. He ought never to have been a soldier, she thought; he was much too pugnacious . . . They were still talking. She could not hear what he was saying, but from the sound of his voice it came over her that he must have a great many love affairs. Yes – it became perfectly obvious to her, listening to his voice through the door, that he had a great many love affairs. But who with? and why do men think love affairs so important? she asked as the door opened.

'Hello, Rose!' she exclaimed, surprised to see her sister come in too. 'I thought you were in Northumberland!'

'You thought I was in Northumberland!' Rose laughed, kissing her. 'But why? I said the eighteenth.'

'But isn't today the eleventh?' said Eleanor.

'You're only a week behind the times, Nell,' said Martin.

'Then I must have dated all my letters wrong!' Eleanor exclaimed.

She glanced apprehensively at her writing-table. The walrus, with a worn patch in its bristles, no longer stood there.

'Tea, Rose?' she asked.

'No. It's a bath I want,' said Rose. She threw off her hat and ran her fingers through her hair.

'You're looking very well,' said Eleanor, thinking how handsome she looked. But she had a scratch on her chin.

'A positive beauty, isn't she?' Martin laughed at her.

Rose threw her head up rather like a horse. They always bickered, Eleanor thought – Martin and Rose. Rose was handsome, but she wished she dressed better. She was dressed in a green hairy coat and skirt with leather buttons, and she carried a shiny bag. She had been holding meetings in the North.

'I want a bath,' Rose repeated. 'I'm dirty. And what's all this?' she said, pointing to the press cuttings on the table. 'Oh, Uncle Digby,' she added casually, pushing them away. He had been dead some months now; they were already yellowish and curled.

'Martin says the house has been sold,' said Eleanor.

'Has it?' she said indifferently. She broke off a piece of cake and began munching it. 'Spoiling my dinner,' she said. 'But I had no time for lunch.'

'What a woman of action she is!' Martin chaffed her.

'And the meetings?' Eleanor asked.

'Yes. What about the North?' said Martin.

They began to discuss politics. She had been speaking at a by-election. A stone had been thrown at her; she put her hand to her chin. But she had enjoyed it.

'I think we gave 'em something to think about,' she said, breaking off another piece of cake.

She ought to have been the soldier, Eleanor thought. She was exactly like the picture of old Uncle Pargiter of Pargiter's Horse. Martin, now that he had shaved his moustache off and showed his lips, ought to have been – what? Perhaps an architect, she thought. He's so – she looked up. Now it was hailing. White rods came across the window in the back room. There was a great gust of wind; the little bushes blanched and bent under it. And a window banged upstairs in her mother's bedroom. Perhaps I ought to go and shut it, she thought. The rain must be coming in.

'Eleanor – ' said Rose. 'Eleanor' – she repeated.

Eleanor started.

'Eleanor's broody,' said Martin.

'No, not at all – not at all,' she protested. 'What are you talking about?'

'I was asking you,' said Rose. 'Do you remember that row when the microscope was broken? Well, I met that boy – that horrid, ferret-faced boy – Erridge – up in the North.'

'He wasn't horrid,' said Martin.

'He was,' Rose persisted. 'A horrid little sneak. He pretended that it was I who broke the microscope and it was he who broke it . . . D'you remember that row?' She turned to Eleanor.

'I don't remember that row,' said Eleanor. 'There were so many,' she added.

'That was one of the worst,' said Martin.

'It was,' said Rose. She pursed her lips together. Some memory seemed to have come back to her. 'And after it was over,' she said, turning to Martin, 'you came up into the nursery and asked me to go beetling with you in the Round Pond. D'you remember?'

She paused. There was something queer about the memory, Eleanor could see. She spoke with a curious intensity.

'And you said, "I'll ask you three times; and if you don't answer the third time, I'll go alone." And I swore, "I'll let him go alone." ' Her blue eyes blazed.

'I can see you,' said Martin. 'Wearing a pink frock, with a knife in your hand.'

'And you went,' Rose said; she spoke with suppressed vehemence. 'And I dashed into the bathroom and cut this gash' – she held out her wrist. Eleanor looked at it. There was a thin white scar just above the wrist joint.

When did she do that? Eleanor thought. She could not remember. Rose had locked herself into the bathroom with a knife and cut her wrist. She had known nothing about it. She looked at the white mark. It must have bled.

'Oh, Rose always was a firebrand!' said Martin. He got up. 'She always had the devil's own temper,' he added. He stood for a moment looking round the drawing-room, cluttered up with several hideous pieces of furniture that he would have got rid of had he been Eleanor, he thought, and forced to live there. But perhaps she did not mind things like that.

'Dining out?' she said. He dined out every night. She would like to have asked him where he was dining.

He nodded without saying anything. He met all sorts of people she did not know, she reflected; and he did not want to talk about them. He had turned to the fireplace.

'That picture wants cleaning,' he said, pointing to the picture of their mother. 'It's a nice picture,' he added, looking at it critically. 'But usen't there to be a flower in the grass?'

Eleanor looked at it. She had not looked at it, so as to see it, for many years.

'Was there?' she said.

'Yes. A little blue flower,' said Martin. 'I can remember it when I was a child . . . '

He turned. Some memory from his childhood came over him as he saw Rose sitting there at the tea table with her fist still clenched. He saw her standing with her back to the school-room door; very red in the face, with her lips tight shut as they were now. She had wanted him to do something. And he had crumpled a ball of paper in his hand and shied it at her.

'What awful lives children live!' he said, waving his hand at her as he crossed the room. 'Don't they, Rose?'

'Yes,' said Rose. 'And they can't tell anybody,' she added.

There was another gust and the sound of glass crashing.

'Miss Pym's conservatory?' said Martin, pausing with his hand on the door.

'Miss Pym?' said Eleanor. 'She's been dead these twenty years!'

1910

IN THE COUNTRY it was an ordinary day enough: one of the long reel of days that turned as the years passed from green to orange; from grass to harvest. It was neither hot nor cold, an English spring day, bright enough, but a purple cloud behind the hill might mean rain. The grasses rippled with shadow, and then with sunlight.

In London, however, the stricture and pressure of the season were already felt, especially in the West End, where flags flew; canes tapped; dresses flowed; and houses freshly painted had awnings spread and swinging baskets of red geraniums. The parks too – St James's, the Green Park, Hyde Park – were making ready. Already in the morning, before there was a chance of a procession, the green chairs were ranged among the plump brown flower beds with their curled hyacinths, as if waiting for something to happen; for a curtain to rise; for Queen Alexandra to come, bowing through the gates. She had a face like a flower petal, and always wore her pink carnation.

Men lay flat on the grass reading newspapers with their shirts open; on the bald scrubbed space by the Marble Arch speakers congregated; nursemaids vacantly regarded them; and mothers, squatted on the grass, watched their children play. Down Park Lane and Piccadilly vans, cars, omnibuses ran along the streets as if the streets were slots; stopped and jerked, as if a puzzle were solved, and then broken; for it was the season, and the streets were crowded. Over Park Lane and Piccadilly the clouds kept their freedom, wandering fitfully, staining windows gold, daubing them black, passed and vanished, though marble in Italy looked no more solid, gleaming in the quarries, veined with yellow, than the clouds over Park Lane.

If the bus stopped here, Rose thought, looking down over the side, she would get up. The bus stopped, and she rose. It was a pity, she thought, as she stepped on to the pavement and caught a glimpse of her own figure in a tailor's window, not to dress better, not to look nicer. Always reach-me-downs, coats and skirts from Whiteleys. But they saved time, and the years after all – she was over forty – made one care very little what people thought. They used to say, why don't you marry? Why don't you do this or that, interfering. But not any longer.

She paused in one of the little alcoves that were scooped out in the bridge, from habit. People always stopped to look at the river. It was running fast, a muddy gold this morning with smooth breadths and ripples, for the tide was high. And there was the usual tug and the usual barges with black tarpaulins and corn showing. The water swirled round the arches. As she stood there, looking down at the water, some buried feeling began to arrange the stream into a pattern. The pattern was painful. She remembered how she had stood there on the night of a certain engagement, crying; her tears had fallen, her happiness, it seemed to her, had fallen. Then she had turned – here she turned – and had seen the churches, the masts and roofs of the city. There's *that*, she had said to herself. Indeed it was a splendid view . . . She looked, and then again she turned. There were the Houses of Parliament. A queer expression, half frown, half smile, formed on her face and she threw herself slightly backwards, as if she were leading an army.

'Damned humbugs!' she said aloud, striking her fist on the balustrade. A clerk who was passing looked at her with surprise. She laughed. She often talked aloud. Why not? That too was one of the consolations, like her coat and skirt, and the hat she stuck on without giving a look in the glass. If people chose to laugh, let them. She strode on. She was lunching in Hyams Place with her cousins. She had asked herself on the spur of the moment, meeting Maggie in a shop. First she had heard a voice; then seen a hand. And it was odd, considering how little she knew them – they had lived abroad – how strongly, sitting there at the counter before Maggie saw her, simply from the sound of her voice, she had felt – she supposed it was affection? – some feeling bred of blood in common. She had got up and said, May I come and see you? busy as she was, hating to break her day in the middle. She walked on. They lived in Hyams Place, over the river – Hyams Place, that little crescent of old houses with the name carved in the middle which she used to pass so often when she lived down here. She used to ask herself in those far-off days, Who was Hyam? But she had never solved the question to her satisfaction. She walked on, across the river.

The shabby street on the south side of the river was very noisy. Now and again a voice detached itself from the general clamour. A woman shouted to her neighbour; a child cried. A man trundling a barrow opened his mouth and bawled up at the windows as he passed. There were bedsteads, grates, pokers and odd pieces of twisted iron on his barrow. But whether he was selling old iron or buying old iron it was impossible to say; the rhythm persisted; but the words were almost rubbed out.

The swarm of sound, the rush of traffic, the shouts of the hawkers, the single cries and the general cries, came into the upper room of the house in Hyams Place where Sara Pargiter sat at the piano. She was singing. Then she stopped; she watched her sister laying the table.

'Go search the valleys,' she murmured, as she watched her, 'pluck up every rose.' She paused. 'That's very nice,' she added, dreamily. Maggie had taken a bunch of flowers; had cut the tight little string which bound them, and had laid them side by side on the table; and was arranging them in an earthenware pot. They were differently coloured, blue, white and purple. Sara watched her arranging them. She laughed suddenly.

'What are you laughing at?' said Maggie absent-mindedly. She added a purple flower to the bunch and looked at it.

'Dazed in a rapture of contemplation,' said Sara, 'shading her eyes with peacocks' feathers dipped in morning dew – ' she pointed to the table. 'Maggie said,' she jumped up and pirouetted about the room, 'three's the same as two, three's the same as two.' She pointed to the table upon which three places had been laid.

'But we are three,' said Maggie. 'Rose is coming.'

Sara stopped. Her face fell. 'Rose is coming?' she repeated.

'I told you,' said Maggie. 'I said to you, Rose is coming to luncheon on Friday. It is Friday. And Rose is coming to luncheon. Any minute now,' she said. She got up and began to fold some stuff that was lying on the floor.

'It is Friday, and Rose is coming to luncheon,' Sara repeated.

'I told you,' said Maggie. 'I was in a shop. I was buying stuff. And somebody' – she paused to make her fold more accurately – 'came out from behind a counter and said, "I'm your cousin. I'm Rose," she said. "Can I come and see you? Any day, any time," she said. So I said,' she put the stuff on a chair, 'lunch.'

She looked round the room to see that everything was in readiness. Chairs were missing. Sara pulled up a chair.

'Rose is coming,' she said, 'and this is where she'll sit.' She placed the chair at the table facing the window. 'And she'll take off her gloves; and she'll lay one on this side, one on that. And she'll say, I've never been in this part of London before."

'And then?' said Maggie, looking at the table.

'You'll say, "It's so convenient for the theatres."'

'And then?' said Maggie.

'And then she'll say rather wistfully, smiling, putting her head on one side, "D'you often go to the theatre, Maggie?" '

'No,' said Maggie. 'Rose has red hair.'

'Red hair?' Sara exclaimed. 'I thought it was grey – a little wisp straggling from under a black bonnet,' she added.

'No,' said Maggie. 'She has a great deal of hair; and it's red.'

'Red hair; red Rose,' Sara exclaimed. She spun round on her toe. 'Rose of the flaming heart; Rose of the burning breast; Rose of the weary world – red, red Rose!'

A door slammed below; they heard footsteps mounting the stairs. 'There she is,' said Maggie.

The steps stopped. They heard a voice saying, 'Still further up? On the very top? Thank you.' Then the steps began mounting the stairs again.

'This is the worst torture . . . ' Sara began, screwing her hands together and clinging to her sister, 'that life . . . '

'Don't be such an ass,' said Maggie, pushing her away, as the door opened.

Rose came in.

'It's ages since we met,' she said, shaking hands.

She wondered what had made her come. Everything was different from what she expected. The room was rather poverty-stricken; the carpet did not cover the floor. There was a sewing-machine in the corner, and Maggie too looked different from what she had looked in the shop. But there was a crimson-and-gilt chair; she recognised it with relief.

'That used to stand in the hall, didn't it?' she said, putting her bag down on the chair.

'Yes,' said Maggie.

'And that glass – ' said Rose, looking at the old Italian glass blurred with spots that hung between the windows, 'wasn't that there too?'

'Yes,' said Maggie, 'in my mother's bedroom.'

There was a pause. There seemed to be nothing to say.

'What nice rooms you've found!' Rose continued, making conversation. It was a large room and the door-posts had little carvings on them. 'But don't you find it rather noisy?' she continued.

The man was crying under the window. She looked out of the window. Opposite there was a row of slate roofs, like half-opened umbrellas; and, rising high above them, a great building which, save for thin black strokes across it, seemed to be made entirely of glass. It was a factory. The man bawled in the street underneath.

'Yes, it's noisy,' said Maggie. 'But very convenient.'

'Very convenient for the theatres,' said Sara, as she put down the meat.

'So I remember finding,' said Rose, turning to look at her, 'when I lived here myself.'

'Did you live here?' said Maggie, beginning to help the cutlets.

'Not here,' she said. 'Round the corner. With a friend.'

'We thought you lived in Abercorn Terrace,' said Sara.

'Can't one live in more places than one?' Rose asked, feeling vaguely annoyed, for she had lived in many places, felt many passions, and done many things.

'I remember Abercorn Terrace,' said Maggie. She paused. 'There was a long room; and a tree at the end; and a picture over the fireplace, of a girl with red hair?'

Rose nodded. 'Mama when she was young,' she said.

'And a round table in the middle?' Maggie continued.

Rose nodded.

'And you had a parlourmaid with very prominent blue eyes?'

'Crosby. She's still with us.'

They ate in silence.

'And then?' said Sara, as if she were a child asking for a story.

'And then?' said Rose. 'Well then' – she looked at Maggie, thinking of her as a little girl who had come to tea.

She saw them sitting round a table; and a detail that she had not thought of for years came back to her – how Milly used to take her hairpin and fray the wick of the kettle. And she saw Eleanor sitting with her account books; and she saw herself go up to her and say: 'Eleanor, I want to go to Lamley's.'

Her past seemed to be rising above her present. And for some reason she wanted to talk about her past; to tell them something about herself that she had never told anybody – something hidden. She paused, gazing at the flowers in the middle of the table without seeing them. There was a blue knot in the yellow glaze she noticed.

'I remember Uncle Abel,' said Maggie. 'He gave me a necklace; a blue necklace with gold spots.'

'He's still alive,' said Rose.

They talked, she thought, as if Abercorn Terrace were a scene in a play. They talked as if they were speaking of people who were real, but not real in the way in which she felt herself to be real. It puzzled her; it made her feel that she was two different people at the same time; that she was living at two different times at the same moment. She was a little girl wearing a pink frock; and here she was in this room, now. But there was a great rattle under the windows. A dray went roaring past. The glasses jingled on the table. She started slightly, roused from her thoughts about her childhood, and separated the glasses.

'Don't you find it very noisy here?' she said.

'Yes. But very convenient for the theatres,' said Sara.

Rose looked up. She had repeated herself. She thinks me an old fool, Rose thought, making the same remark twice over. She blushed slightly.

What is the use, she thought, of trying to tell people about one's past? What is one's past? She stared at the pot with the blue knot loosely tied in the yellow glaze. Why did I come, she thought, when they only laugh at me? Sally rose and cleared away the plates.

'And Delia – ' Maggie began as they waited. She pulled the pot towards her, and began to arrange the flowers. She was not listening; she was thinking her own thoughts. She reminded Rose, as she watched her, of Digby – absorbed in the arrangement of a bunch of flowers, as if to arrange flowers, to put the white by the blue, were the most important thing in the world.

'She married an Irishman,' she said aloud.

Maggie took a blue flower and placed it beside a white flower.

'And Edward?' she asked.

'Edward . . . ' Rose was beginning, when Sally came in with the pudding.

'Edward!' she exclaimed, catching the word. 'Oh blasted eyes of my deceased wife's sister – withered prop of my defunct old age . . . ' She put down the pudding. 'That's Edward,' she said. 'A quotation from a book he gave me. "My wasted youth – my wasted youth" . . . ' The voice was Edward's; Rose could hear him say it. For he had a way of belittling himself, when in fact he had a very good opinion of himself.

But it was not the whole of Edward. And she would not have him laughed at; for she was very fond of her brother and very proud of him.

'There's not much of "my wasted youth" about Edward now,' she said.

'I thought not,' said Sara, taking her place opposite.

They were silent. Rose looked at the flower again. Why did I come? she kept asking herself. Why had she broken up her morning, and interrupted her day's work, when it was clear to her that they had not wished to see her?

'Go on, Rose,' said Maggie, helping the pudding. 'Go on telling us about the Pargiters.'

'About the Pargiters?' said Rose. She saw herself running along the broad avenue in the lamplight. 'What could be more ordinary?' she said. 'A large family, living in a large house . . . ' And yet she felt that she had been herself very interesting. She paused.

Sara looked at her. 'It's not ordinary,' she said. 'The Pargiters – ' She was holding a fork in her hand, and she drew a line on the tablecloth. 'The Pargiters,' she repeated, 'going on and on and on' – here her fork touched a salt-cellar – 'until they come to a rock,' she said; 'and then Rose' – she looked at her again: Rose drew herself up slightly ' – Rose claps spurs to her horse, rides straight up to a man in a gold coat, and says, "Damn your eyes!" Isn't that Rose, Maggie?' she said, looking at her sister as if she had been drawing her picture on the tablecloth.

That is true, Rose thought as she took her pudding. That is myself. Again she had the odd feeling of being two people at the same time.

'Well, that's done,' said Maggie, pushing away her plate. 'Come and sit in the armchair, Rose,' she said.

She went over to the fireplace and pulled out an armchair, which had springs like hoops, Rose noticed, in the seat.

They were poor, Rose thought, glancing round her. That was why they had chosen this house to live in – because it was cheap. They cooked their own food – Sally had gone into the kitchen to make the coffee. She drew her chair up beside Maggie's.

'You make your own clothes?' she said, pointing to the sewing-machine in the corner. There was silk folded on it.

'Yes,' said Maggie, looking at the sewing-machine.

'For a party?' said Rose. The stuff was silk – green, with blue rays on it.

'Tomorrow night,' said Maggie. She raised her hand with a curious gesture to her face, as if she wanted to conceal something. She wants to hide herself from me, Rose thought, as I want to hide myself from her. She watched her; she had got up, had fetched the silk and the sewing-machine, and was threading the needle. Her hands were large and thin and strong, Rose noticed.

'I never could make my own clothes,' she said, watching her arrange the silk smoothly under the needle. She was beginning to feel at her ease. She took off her hat and threw it on the floor. Maggie looked at her with approval. She was handsome, in a ravaged way; more like a man than a woman.

'But then,' said Maggie, beginning to turn the handle rather cautiously, 'you did other things.' She spoke in the absorbed tones of someone who is using their hands.

The machine made a comfortable whirring sound as the needle pricked through the silk.

'Yes, I did other things,' said Rose, stroking the cat that had stretched itself against her knee, 'when I lived down here.'

'But that was years ago,' she added, 'when I was young. I lived here with a friend,' she sighed, 'and taught little thieves.'

Maggie said nothing; she was whirring the machine round and round.

'I always liked thieves better than other people,' Rose added after a time.

'Yes,' said Maggie.

'I never liked being at home,' said Rose. 'I liked being on my own much better.'

'Yes,' said Maggie.

Rose went on talking.

It was quite easy to talk, she found; quite easy. And there was no need to say anything clever; or to talk about oneself. She was talking about the Waterloo Road as she remembered it when Sara came in with the coffee.

'What was that about clinging to a fat man in the Campagna?' she asked, setting her tray down.

'The Campagna?' said Rose. 'There was nothing about the Campagna.'

'Heard through a door,' said Sara, pouring out the coffee, 'talk sounds very odd.' She gave Rose her cup.

'I thought you were talking about Italy; about the Campagna, about the moonlight.'

Rose shook her head. 'We were talking about the Waterloo Road,' she said. But what had she been talking about? Not simply about the Waterloo Road. Perhaps she had been talking nonsense. She had been saying the first thing that came into her head.

'All talk would be nonsense, I suppose, if it were written down,' she said, stirring her coffee.

Maggie stopped the machine for a moment and smiled.

'And even if it isn't,' she said.

'But it's the only way we have of knowing each other,' Rose protested. She looked at her watch. It was later than she thought. She got up.

'I must go,' she said. 'But why don't you come with me?' she added on the spur of the moment.

Maggie looked up at her. 'Where?' she said.

Rose was silent. 'To a meeting,' she said at length. She wanted to conceal the thing that interested her most; she felt extraordinarily shy. And yet she wanted them to come. But why? she asked herself, as she stood there awkwardly waiting. There was a pause.

'You could wait upstairs,' she said suddenly. 'And you'd see Eleanor;

you'd see Martin – the Pargiters in the flesh,' she added. She remembered Sara's phrase, 'The caravan crossing the desert,' she said.

She looked at Sara. She was balancing herself on the arm of a chair, sipping her coffee and swinging her foot up and down.

'Shall I come?' she asked, vaguely, still swinging her foot up and down.

Rose shrugged her shoulders. 'If you like,' she said.

'But should I like it?' Sara continued, still swinging her foot, ' . . . this meeting? What do you think, Maggie?' she said, appealing to her sister. 'Shall I go, or shan't I? Shall I go, or shan't I?' Maggie said nothing.

Then Sara got up, went to the window and stood there for a moment humming a tune. 'Go search the valleys; pluck up every rose,' she hummed. The man was passing; he was crying 'Any old iron? Any old iron?' She turned round with a sudden jerk.

'I'll come,' she said, as if she had made up her mind. 'I'll fling on my clothes and come.'

She sprang up and went into the bedroom. She's like one of those birds at the zoo, Rose thought, that never flies but hops rapidly across the grass.

She turned to the window. It was a depressing little street, she thought. There was a public house at the corner. The houses opposite looked very dingy, and it was very noisy. 'Any old iron to sell?' the man was crying under the window, 'any old iron?' Children were screaming in the road; they were playing a game with chalk-marks on the pavement. She stood there looking down on them.

'Poor little wretches!' she said. She picked up her hat and ran two bonnet-pins sharply through it. 'Don't you find it rather unpleasant,' she said, giving her hat a little pat on one side as she looked in the looking-glass, 'coming home late at night sometimes with that public house at the corner?'

'Drunken men, you mean?' said Maggie.

'Yes,' said Rose. She buttoned the row of leather buttons on her tailor-made suit and gave herself a little pat here and there, as if she were making ready.

'And now what are you talking about?' said Sara, coming in carrying her shoes. 'Another visit to Italy?'

'No,' said Maggie. She spoke indistinctly because her mouth was full of pins. 'Drunken men following one.'

'Drunken men following one,' said Sara. She sat down and began to put on her shoes.

'But they don't follow me,' she said. Rose smiled. That was obvious.

She was sallow, angular and plain. 'I can walk over Waterloo Bridge at any hour of the day or night,' she continued, tugging at her shoelaces, 'and nobody notices.' The shoelace was in a knot; she fumbled with it. 'But I can remember,' she continued, 'being told by a woman – a very beautiful woman – she was like – '

'Hurry up,' Maggie interrupted. 'Rose is waiting.'

' . . . Rose is waiting – well, the woman told me, when she went into Regent's Park to have an ice' – she stood up, trying to fit her shoe on to her foot, ' – to have an ice, at one of those little tables under the trees, one of those little round tables laid with a cloth under the trees' – she hopped about with one shoe off and one shoe on – 'the eyes, she said, came through every leaf like the darts of the sun; and her ice was melted . . . Her ice was melted!' she repeated, tapping her sister on the shoulder as she twirled round on her toe.

Rose held out her hand. 'You're going to stay and finish your dress?' she said. 'You won't come with us?' It was Maggie she wanted to come.

'No, I won't come,' said Maggie, shaking hands. 'I should hate it,' she added, smiling at Rose with a candour that was baffling.

Did she mean me? thought Rose as she went down the stairs. Did she mean that she hated me? When I liked her so much?

In the alley that led into the old square off Holborn an elderly man, battered and red-nosed, as if he had weathered out many years at street corners, was selling violets. He had his pitch by a row of posts. The bunches, tightly laced, each with a green frill of leaves round the rather withered flowers, lay in a row on the tray; for he had not sold many.

'Nice vilets, fresh vilets,' he repeated automatically as the people passed. Most of them went by without looking. But he went on repeating his formula automatically. 'Nice vilets, fresh vilets,' as if he scarcely expected anyone to buy. Then two ladies came; and he held out his violets, and he said once more, 'Nice vilets, fresh vilets.' One of them slapped down two coppers on his tray; and he looked up. The other lady stopped, put her hand on the post, and said, 'Here I leave you.' Upon which the one who was short and stout, struck her on the shoulder and said, 'Don't be such an ass!' And the tall lady gave a sudden cackle of laughter, took a bunch of violets from the tray as if she had paid for it; and off they walked. She's an odd customer, he thought – she took the violets though she hadn't paid for them. He watched them walking round the square; then he began muttering again, 'Nice vilets, sweet vilets.'

*

'Is this the place where you meet?' said Sara as they walked along the square.

It was very quiet. The noise of the traffic had ceased. The trees were not in full leaf yet, and pigeons were shuffling and crooning on the tree-tops. Little bits of twig fell on the pavement as the birds fidgeted among the branches. A soft air puffed in their faces. They walked on round the square.

'That's the house over there,' said Rose, pointing. She stopped when she reached a house with a carved doorway, and many names on the doorpost. The windows on the ground floor were open; the curtains blew in and out, and through them they could see a row of heads, as if people were sitting round a table, talking.

Rose paused on the doorstep.

'Are you coming in,' she said, 'or aren't you?'

Sara hesitated. She peered in. Then she brandished her bunch of violets in Rose's face and cried out, 'All right!' she cried. 'Ride on!'

Miriam Parrish was reading a letter. Eleanor was blackening the strokes on her blotting-paper. I've heard all this, I've done all this so often, she was thinking. She glanced round the table. People's faces even seemed to repeat themselves. There's the Judd type, there's the Lazenby type and there's Miriam, she thought, drawing on her blotting-paper. I know what he's going to say, I know what she's going to say, she thought, digging a little hole in the blotting-paper. Here Rose came in. But who's that with her? Eleanor asked. She did not recognise her. Whoever it was was waved by Rose to a seat in the corner, and the meeting went on. Why must we do it? Eleanor thought, drawing a spoke from the hole in the middle. She looked up. Someone was rattling a stick along the railings and whistling; the branches of a tree swung up and down in the garden outside. The leaves were already unfolding . . . Miriam put down her papers; Mr Spicer rose.

There's no other way, I suppose, she thought, taking up her pencil again. She made a note as Mr Spicer spoke. She found that her pencil could take notes quite accurately while she herself thought of something else. She seemed able to divide herself into two. One person followed the argument – and he's putting it very well, she thought; while the other, for it was a fine afternoon, and she had wanted to go to Kew, walked down a green glade and stopped in front of a flowering tree. Is it a magnolia? she asked herself, or are they already over? Magnolias, she remembered, have no leaves, but masses of white blossom . . . She drew a line on the blotting-paper.

Now Pickford . . . she said, looking up again. Mr Pickford spoke. She drew more spokes; blackened them. Then she looked up, for there was a change in the tone of voice.

'I know Westminster very well,' Miss Ashford was saying.

'So do I!' said Mr Pickford. 'I've lived there for forty years.'

Eleanor was surprised. She had always thought he lived at Ealing. He lived at Westminster, did he? He was a clean-shaven, dapper little man, whom she had always seen in her mind's eye running to catch a train with a newspaper under his arm. But he lived at Westminster, did he? That was odd, she thought.

Then they went on arguing again. The cooing of the pigeons became audible. Take two coos, take two coos, tak . . . they were crooning. Martin was speaking. And he speaks very well, she thought . . . but he shouldn't be sarcastic; it puts people's backs up. She drew another stroke.

Then she heard the rush of a car outside; it stopped outside the window. Martin stopped speaking. There was a momentary pause. Then the door opened and in came a tall woman in evening dress. Everybody looked up.

'Lady Lasswade!' said Mr Pickford, getting up and scraping back his chair.

'Kitty!' Eleanor exclaimed. She half rose, but she sat down again. There was a little stir. A chair was found for her. Lady Lasswade took her place opposite Eleanor.

'I'm so sorry,' she apologised, 'to be so late. And for coming in these ridiculous clothes,' she added, touching her cloak. She did look strange, dressed in evening dress in the broad daylight. There was something shining in her hair.

'The Opera?' said Martin as she sat down beside him.

'Yes,' she said briefly. She laid her white gloves in a businesslike way on the table. Her cloak opened and showed the gleam of a silver dress beneath. She did look odd compared with the others; but it's very good of her to come, Eleanor thought, looking at her, considering she's going on to the Opera. The meeting began again.

How long has she been married? Eleanor wondered. How long is it since we broke the swing together at Oxford? She drew another stroke on the blotting-paper. The dot was now surrounded with strokes.

' . . . and we discussed the whole matter perfectly frankly,' Kitty was saying. Eleanor listened. That's the manner I like, she thought. She had been meeting Sir Edward at dinner . . . It's the great ladies' manner, Eleanor thought . . . authoritative, natural. She listened again. The great ladies' manner charmed Mr Pickford; but it irritated Martin, she knew. He was pooh-poohing Sir Edward and his frankness. Then Mr Spicer was off again; and Kitty had joined in. Now there was Rose. They were all at loggerheads. Eleanor listened. She became more and more irritated. All it comes to is: I'm right and you're wrong, she thought. This bickering merely wasted time. If we could only get at something, something deeper, deeper, she thought, prodding her pencil on the blotting-paper. Suddenly she saw the only point that was of any importance. She had the words on the tip of her tongue. She opened her mouth to speak. But just as she cleared her throat, Mr Pickford swept his papers together and rose. Would they pardon him? he said. He had to be at the Law Courts. He rose and went.

The meeting dragged on. The ashtray in the middle of the table became full of cigarette-stumps; the air became thick with smoke; then Mr Spicer went; Miss Bodham went; Miss Ashford wound a scarf tightly round her neck, snapped her attaché-case to, and strode out of the room. Miriam Parrish took off her pince-nez and fixed them to a hook that was sewn on to the front of her dress. Everybody was going; the meeting was over. Eleanor got up. She wanted to speak to Kitty. But Miriam intercepted her.

'About coming to see you on Wednesday,' she began.

'Yes,' said Eleanor.

'I've just remembered I've promised to take a niece to the dentist,' said Miriam.

'Saturday would suit me just as well,' said Eleanor.

Miriam paused. She pondered. 'Would Monday do instead?' she said.

'I'll write,' said Eleanor with an irritation that she could never conceal, saint though Miriam was, and Miriam fluttered away with a guilty air as if she were a little dog caught stealing.

Eleanor turned. The others were still arguing.

'You'll agree with me one of these days,' Martin was saying.

'Never! Never!' said Kitty, slapping her gloves on the table. She looked very handsome; at the same time rather absurd in her evening dress.

'Why didn't you speak, Nell?' she said, turning on her.

'Because – ' Eleanor began, 'I don't know,' she added, rather feebly. She felt suddenly shabby and dowdy compared with Kitty, who stood there in full evening dress with something shining in her hair.

'Well,' said Kitty, turning away. 'I must be off. But can't I give anyone a lift?' she said, pointing to the window. There was her car.

'What a magnificent car!' said Martin, looking at it, with a sneer in his voice.

'It's Charlie's,' said Kitty rather sharply.

'What about you, Eleanor?' she said, turning to her.

'Thanks,' said Eleanor: ' – one moment.'

She had muddled her things up. She had left her gloves somewhere. Had she brought an umbrella, or hadn't she? She felt flustered and dowdy, as if she were a schoolgirl suddenly. There was the magnificent car waiting, and the chauffeur held the door open with a rug in his hand.

'Get in,' said Kitty. And she got in and the chauffeur put the rug over her knees.

'We'll leave them,' said Kitty, with a wave of her hand, 'caballing.' And the car drove off.

'What a pig-headed set they are!' said Kitty, turning to Eleanor.

'Force is always wrong – don't you agree with me? – always wrong!' she repeated, drawing the rug over her knees. She was still under the influence of the meeting. Yet she wanted to talk to Eleanor. They met so seldom; she liked her so much. But she was shy, sitting there in her absurd clothes, and she could not jerk her mind out of the rut of the meeting in which it was running.

'What a pig-headed set they are!' she repeated. Then she began: 'Tell me . . .'

There were many things that she wanted to ask; but the engine was so powerful; the car swept in and out of the traffic so smoothly; before she had time to say any of the things she wanted to say Eleanor had put her hand out because they had reached the Tube station.

'Would he stop here?' she said, rising.

'But must you get out?' Kitty began. She had wanted to talk to her.

'I must, I must,' said Eleanor. 'Papa's expecting me.' She felt like a child again beside this great lady and the chauffeur, who was holding the door open.

'Do come and see me – do let us meet again soon, Nell,' said Kitty, taking her hand.

The car started on again. Lady Lasswade sat back in her corner. She wished she saw more of Eleanor, she thought; but she never could get her to come and dine. It was always, 'Papa's expecting me', or some other excuse, she thought rather bitterly. They had gone such different ways, they had lived such different lives, since Oxford . . . The car slowed down. It had to take its place in the long line of cars that moved at a foot's pace, now stopping dead, now jerking on, down the narrow street, blocked by market carts, that led to the Opera House. Men and women in full evening dress were walking along the pavement. They looked uncomfortable and self-conscious as they dodged between costers' barrows, with their high-piled hair and their evening cloaks; with their button-holes and their white waistcoats, in the glare of the afternoon sun. The ladies tripped uncomfortably on their high-heeled shoes; now and then they put their hands to their heads. The gentlemen kept close beside them as though protecting them. It's absurd, Kitty thought; it's ridiculous to come out in full evening dress at this time of day. She leant back in her corner. Covent Garden porters, dingy little clerks in their ordinary working clothes, coarse-looking women in aprons stared in at her. The air smelt strongly of oranges and bananas. But the car was coming to a standstill. It drew up under the archway; she pushed through the glass doors and went in.

She felt at once a sense of relief. Now that the daylight was extinguished and the air glowed yellow and crimson, she no longer felt absurd. On the contrary, she felt appropriate. The ladies and gentlemen who were mounting the stairs were dressed exactly as she was. The smell of oranges and bananas had been replaced by another smell – a subtle mixture of clothes and gloves and flowers that affected her pleasantly. The carpet was thick beneath her feet. She went along the corridor till she came to her own box with the card on it. She went in and the whole Opera House opened in front of her. She was not late after all. The orchestra was still tuning up; the players were laughing, talking and turning round in their seats as they fiddled busily with their instruments. She stood looking down at the stalls. The floor of the house was in a state of great agitation. People were passing to their seats; they were sitting down and getting up again; they were taking off their cloaks and signalling to friends. They were like birds settling on a field. In the boxes white figures were appearing here and there; white arms rested on the ledges of boxes; white shirt-fronts shone beside them. The whole house glowed – red, gold, cream-coloured, and smelt of clothes and flowers, and echoed with the squeaks and trills of the instruments and with the buzz and hum of voices. She glanced at the programme that was laid on the ledge of her box. It was Siegfried – her favourite opera. In a little space within the highly decorated border the names of the cast were given. She stooped to read them; then a thought struck her and she glanced at the royal box. It was empty. As she looked the door opened and two men came in; one was her cousin Edward; the other a boy, a cousin of her husband's.

'They haven't put it off?' he said as he shook hands. 'I was afraid they might.' He was something in the Foreign Office; with a handsome Roman head.

They all looked instinctively at the royal box. Programmes lay along the edge; but there was no bouquet of pink carnations. The box was empty.

'The doctors have given him up,'[36] said the young man, looking very important. They all think they know everything, Kitty thought, smiling at his air of private information.

'But if he dies?' she said, looking at the royal box, 'd'you think they'll stop it?'

The young man shrugged his shoulders. About that he could not be positive apparently. The house was filling up. Lights winked on ladies' arms as they turned; ripples of light flashed, stopped, and then flashed the opposite way as they turned their heads.

But now the conductor pushed his way through the orchestra to his raised seat. There was an outburst of applause; he turned, bowed to the audience; turned again, all the lights sank down; the overture had begun.

Kitty leant back against the wall of the box; her face was shaded by the folds of the curtain. She was glad to be shaded. As they played the overture she looked at Edward. She could only see the outline of his face in the red glow; it was heavier than it used to be; but he looked intellectual, handsome and a little remote as he listened to the overture. It wouldn't have done, she thought; I'm much too . . . she did not finish the sentence. He has never married, she thought; and she had. And I've three boys. I've been in Australia, I've been in India . . . The music made her think of herself and her own life as she seldom did. It exalted her; it cast a flattering light over herself, her past. But why did Martin laugh at me for having a car? she thought. What's the good of laughing? she asked.

Here the curtain went up. She leant forward and looked at the stage. The dwarf was hammering at the sword. Hammer, hammer, hammer, he went with little short, sharp strokes. She listened. The music had changed. *He*, she thought, looking at the handsome boy, knows exactly what the music means. He was already completely possessed by the music. She liked the look of complete absorption that had swum up on top of his immaculate respectability, making him seem almost stern . . . But here was Siegfried. She leant forward. Dressed in leopard-skins, very fat, with nut-brown thighs, leading a bear – here he was. She liked the fat bouncing young man in his flaxen wig: his voice was magnificent. Hammer, hammer, hammer he went. She leant back again. What did that make her think of? A young man who came into a room with shavings in his hair . . . when she was very young. In Oxford? She had gone to tea with them; had sat on a hard chair; in a very light room; and there was a sound of hammering in the garden. And then a boy came in with shavings in his hair. And she had wanted him to kiss her. Or was it the farmhand up at Carter's, when old Carter had loomed up suddenly leading a bull with a ring through its nose?

'That's the sort of life I like,' she thought, taking up her opera-glasses. 'That's the sort of person I am . . . ' she finished her sentence.

Then she put the opera-glasses to her eyes. The scenery suddenly became bright and close; the grass seemed to be made of thick green wool; she could see Siegfried's fat brown arms glistening with paint. His face was shiny. She put down the glasses and leant back in her corner.

And old Lucy Craddock – she saw Lucy sitting at a table; with her red nose, and her patient, kind eyes. 'So you've done no work this week again, Kitty!' she said reproachfully. How I loved her! Kitty thought. And then she had gone back to the Lodge; and there was the tree, with a prop in the middle; and her mother sitting bolt upright . . . I wish I hadn't quarrelled so much with my mother, she thought, overcome with a sudden sense of the passage of time and its tragedy. Then the music changed.

She looked at the stage again. The Wanderer had come in. He was sitting on a bank in a long grey dressing-gown; and a patch wobbled uncomfortably over one of his eyes. On and on he went; on and on. Her attention flagged. She glanced round the dim red house; she could only see white elbows pointed on the ledges of boxes; here and there a sharp pinpoint of light showed as someone followed the score with a torch. Edward's fine profile again caught her eye. He was listening, critically, intently. It wouldn't have done, she thought, it wouldn't have done at all.

At last the Wanderer had gone. And now? she asked herself, leaning forward. Siegfried burst in. Dressed in his leopard-skins, laughing and singing, here he was again. The music excited her. It was magnificent. Siegfried took the broken pieces of the sword and blew on the fire and hammered, hammered, hammered. The singing, the hammering and the fire leaping all went on at the same time. Quicker and quicker, more and more rhythmically, more and more triumphantly he hammered, until at last up he swung the sword high above his head and brought it down – crack! The anvil burst asunder. And then he brandished the sword over his head and shouted and sang; and the music rushed higher and higher; and the curtain fell.

The lights opened in the middle of the house. All the colour came back. The whole Opera House leapt into life again with its faces and its diamonds and its men and women. They were clapping and waving their programmes. The whole house seemed to be fluttering with white squares of paper. The curtains fell apart and were held back by tall footmen in knee-breeches. Kitty stood up and clapped. Again the curtains closed; again they parted. The footmen were almost pulled off their feet by the heavy folds that they had to hold back. Again and again they held the curtain back; and even when they had let it fall and the singers had disappeared and the orchestra were leaving their seats, the audience still stood clapping and waving their programmes.

Kitty turned to the young man in her box. He was leaning over the ledge. He was still clapping. He was shouting, 'Bravo! Bravo!' He had forgotten her. He had forgotten himself.

'Wasn't that marvellous?' he said at last, turning round.

There was an odd look on his face as if he were in two worlds at once and had to draw them together.

'Marvellous!' she agreed. She looked at him with a pang of envy.

'And now,' she said, gathering her things together, 'let us have dinner.'

At Hyams Place they had finished dinner. The table was cleared; only a few crumbs remained, and the pot of flowers stood in the middle of the table like a sentry. The only sound in the room was the stitching of a needle, pricking through silk, for Maggie was sewing. Sara sat hunched on the music stool, but she was not playing.

'Sing something,' said Maggie suddenly. Sara turned and struck the notes.

'Brandishing, flourishing my sword in my hand. . . ' she sang. The words were the words of some pompous eighteenth-century march, but her voice was reedy and thin. Her voice broke. She stopped singing.

She sat silent with her hands on the notes. 'What's the good of singing if one hasn't any voice?' she murmured. Maggie went on sewing.

'What did you do today?' she said at length, looking up abruptly.

'Went out with Rose,' said Sara.

'And what did you do with Rose?' said Maggie. She spoke absent-mindedly.

Sara turned and glanced at her. Then she began to play again. 'Stood on the bridge and looked into the water,' she murmured.

'Stood on the bridge and looked into the water,' she hummed, in time to the music. 'Running water; flowing water. May my bones turn to coral; and fish light their lanthorns; fish light their green lanthorns in my eyes.' She half turned and looked round at Maggie. But she was not attending. Sara was silent. She looked at the notes again. But she did not see the notes, she saw a garden; flowers; and her sister; and a young man with a big nose who stooped to pick a flower that was gleaming in the dark. And he held the flower out in his hand in the moonlight . . . Maggie interrupted her.

'You went out with Rose,' she said. 'Where to?'

Sara left the piano and stood in front of the fireplace.

'We got into a bus and went to Holborn,' she said. 'And we walked along a street,' she went on; 'and suddenly,' she jerked her hand out, 'I felt a clap on my shoulder. "Damned liar!" said Rose, 'and took me and flung me against a public-house wall!'

Maggie stitched on in silence.

'You got into a bus and went to Holborn,' she repeated mechanically after a time. 'And then?'

'Then we went into a room,' Sara continued, 'and there were people – multitudes of people. And I said to myself . . . ' she paused.

'A meeting?' Maggie murmured. 'Where?'

'In a room,' Sara answered. 'A pale greenish light. A woman hanging clothes on a line in the back garden; and someone went by rattling a stick on the railings.'

'I see,' said Maggie. She stitched on quickly.

'I said to myself,' Sara resumed, 'whose heads are those . . . ' she paused.

'A meeting,' Maggie interrupted her. 'What for? What about?'

'There were pigeons cooing,' Sara went on. 'Take two coos, Taffy. Take two coos . . . Tak . . . And then a wing darkened the air, and in came Kitty clothed in starlight; and sat on a chair.'

She paused. Maggie was silent. She went on stitching for a moment.

'Who came in?' she asked at length.

'Somebody very beautiful; clothed in starlight; with green in her hair,' said Sara. 'Whereupon' – here she changed her voice and imitated the tones in which a middle-class man might be supposed to welcome a lady of fashion, 'up jumps Mr Pickford, and says, "Oh, Lady Lasswade, won't you take this chair?" '

She pushed a chair in front of her.

'And then,' she went on, flourishing her hands, 'Lady Lasswade sits down; puts her gloves on the table' – she patted a cushion – 'like that.'

Maggie looked up over her sewing. She had a general impression of a room full of people; sticks rattling on the railings; clothes hanging out to dry; and someone coming in with beetles' wings in her hair.

'What happened then?' she asked.

'Then withered Rose, spiky Rose, tawny Rose, thorny Rose,' Sara burst out laughing, 'shed a tear.'

'No, no,' said Maggie. There was something wrong with the story; something impossible. She looked up. The light of a passing car slid across the ceiling. It was growing too dark to see. The lamp from the public house opposite made a yellow glare in the room; the ceiling trembled with a watery pattern of fluctuating light. There was a sound of brawling in the street outside; a scuffling and trampling as if the police were hauling someone along the street against his will. Voices jeered and shouted after him.

'Another row?' Maggie murmured, sticking her needle in the stuff.

Sara got up and went to the window. A crowd had gathered outside the public house. A man was being thrown out. There he came, staggering. He fell against a lamp-post to which he clung. The scene was lit up by the glare of the lamp over the public-house door. Sara stood for a moment at the window watching them. Then she turned; her face in the mixed light looked cadaverous and worn, as if she were no longer a girl, but an old woman worn out by a life of childbirth, debauchery and crime. She stood there hunched up, with her hands clenched together.

'In time to come,' she said, looking at her sister, 'people, looking into this room – this cave, this little antre, scooped out of mud and dung, will hold their fingers to their noses' – she held her fingers to her nose – 'and say, "Pah! They stink!" ' She fell down into a chair.

Maggie looked at her. Curled round, with her hair falling over her face and her hands screwed together she looked like some great ape, crouching there in a little cave of mud and dung. 'Pah!' Maggie repeated to herself, 'They stink' . . . She drove her needle through the stuff in a spasm of disgust. It was true, she thought; they were nasty little creatures, driven by uncontrollable lusts. The night was full of roaring and cursing; of violence and unrest, also of beauty and joy. She got up, holding the dress in her hands. The folds of silk fell down to the floor and she ran her hand over them.

'That's done. That's finished,' she said, laying the dress on the table. There was nothing more she could do with her hands. She folded the dress up and put it away. Then the cat, which had been asleep, rose very slowly, arched its back and stretched itself to its full length.

'You want your supper, do you?' said Maggie. She went into the kitchen and came back with a saucer of milk. 'There, poor puss,' she said, putting the saucer down on the floor. She stood watching the cat lap up its milk, mouthful by mouthful; then it stretched itself out again with extraordinary grace.

Sara, standing at a little distance, watched her. Then she imitated her.

'There, poor puss, there, poor puss,' she repeated. 'As you rock the cradle, Maggie,' she added.

Maggie raised her arms as if to ward off some implacable destiny; then let them fall. Sara smiled as she watched her; then tears brimmed, fell and ran slowly down her cheeks. But as she put up her hand to wipe them there was a sound of knocking; somebody was hammering on the door of the next house. The hammering stopped. Then it began again – hammer, hammer, hammer.

They listened.

'Upcher's come home drunk and wants to be let in,' said Maggie. The knocking ceased. Then it began again.

Sara dried her eyes, roughly, energetically.

'Bring up your children on a desert island where the ships only come when the moon's full!' she exclaimed.

'Or have none?' said Maggie. A window was thrown open. A woman's voice was heard shrieking abuse at the man. He bawled back in a thick drunken voice from the doorstep. Then the door slammed.

They listened.

'Now he'll stagger against the wall and be sick,' said Maggie. They could hear heavy footsteps lurching up the stairs in the next house. Then there was silence.

Maggie crossed the room to shut the window. The great windows of the factory opposite were all lit up; it looked like a palace of glass with thin black bars across it. A glaze of yellow light lit up the lower halves of the houses opposite; the slate roofs shone blue, for the sky hung down in a heavy canopy of yellow light. Footsteps tapped on the pavement, for people were still walking in the street. Far off a voice was crying hoarsely. Maggie leant out. The night was windy and warm.

'What's he crying?' she said.

The voice came nearer and nearer.

'Death . . . ?' she said.

'Death . . . ?' said Sara. They leant out. But they could not hear the rest of the sentence. Then a man who was wheeling a barrow along the street shouted up to them: 'The King's dead!'

1911

THE SUN WAS RISING. Very slowly it came up over the horizon shaking out light. But the sky was so vast, so cloudless, that to fill it with light took time. Very gradually the clouds turned blue; leaves on forest trees sparkled; down below a flower shone; eyes of beasts – tigers, monkeys, birds – sparkled. Slowly the world emerged from darkness. The sea became like the skin of innumerable scaled fish, glittering gold. Here in the South of France the furrowed vineyards caught the light; the little vines turned purple and yellow; and the sun coming through the slats of the blinds striped the white walls. Maggie, standing at the window, looked down on the courtyard, and saw her husband's book cracked across with shadow from the vine above; and the glass that stood beside him glowed yellow. Cries of peasants working came through the open window.

The sun, crossing the Channel, beat vainly on the blanket of thick sea mist. Light slowly permeated the haze over London; struck on the statues in Parliament Square, and on the Palace[37] where the flag flew though the King, borne under a white and blue Union Jack, lay in the caverns at Frogmore. It was hotter than ever. Horses' noses hissed as they drank from the troughs; their hoofs made ridges hard and brittle as plaster on the country roads. Fires tearing over the moors left charcoal twigs behind them. It was August, the holiday season. The glass roofs of the great railway stations were globes incandescent with light. Travellers watched the hands of the round yellow clocks as they followed porters, wheeling portmanteaus, with dogs on leashes. In all the stations trains were ready to bore their way through England: to the North, to the South, to the West. Now the guard standing with his hand raised dropped his flag and the tea-urn slid past. Off the trains swung through the public gardens with asphalt paths; past the factories; into open country. Men standing on bridges fishing looked up; horses cantered; women came to doors and shaded their eyes; the shadow of the smoke floated over the corn, looped down and caught a tree. And on they passed.

In the station yard at Wittering, Mrs Chinnery's old victoria stood waiting. The train was late; it was very hot. William the gardener sat on the box in his buff-coloured coat with the plated buttons flicking the flies off. The flies were troublesome. They had gathered in little brown clusters on the horses' ears. He flicked his whip; the old mare stamped her hoofs; and shook her ears, for the flies had settled again. It was very hot. The sun beat down on the station yard, on the carts and flies and traps waiting for the train. At last the signal dropped; a puff of smoke blew over the hedge; and in a minute people came streaming out into the yard, and here was Miss Pargiter carrying her bag in her hand and a white umbrella. William touched his hat.

'Sorry to be so late,' said Eleanor, smiling up at him, for she knew him; she came every year.

She put her bag on the seat and sat back under the shade of her white umbrella. The leather of the carriage was hot behind her back; it was very hot – hotter even than Toledo.[38] They turned into the High Street; the heat seemed to make everything drowsy and silent. The broad street was full of traps and carts with the reins hanging loose and the horses' heads drooping. But after the din of the foreign market-places how quiet it seemed! Men in gaiters were leaning against the walls; the shops had their awnings out; the pavement was barred with shadow. They had parcels to fetch. At the fishmonger's they stopped and a damp white parcel was handed out to them. At the ironmonger's they stopped and William came back with a scythe. Then they stopped at the chemist's; but there they had to wait, because the lotion was not yet ready.

Eleanor sat back under the shade of her white umbrella. The air seemed to hum with the heat. The air seemed to smell of soap and chemicals. How thoroughly people wash in England, she thought, looking at the yellow soap, the green soap and the pink soap in the chemist's window. In Spain she had hardly washed at all; she had dried herself with a pocket handkerchief standing among the white dry stones of the Guadalquivir. In Spain it was all parched and shrivelled. But here – she looked down the High Street – every shop was full of vegetables; of shining silver fish; of yellow-clawed, soft-breasted chickens; of buckets, rakes and wheelbarrows. And how friendly people were!

She noticed how often hats were touched; hands were grasped; people stopped, talking, in the middle of the road. But now the chemist came out with a large bottle wrapped in tissue paper. It was stowed away under the scythe.

'Midges very bad this year, William?' she asked, recognising the lotion.

'Tarrible bad, miss, tarrible,' he said, touching his hat. There hadn't been such a drought since the Jubilee she understood him to say; but his accent, his singsong and Dorsetshire rhythm, made it difficult to catch what he said. Then he flicked his whip and they drove on: past the market cross; past the red-brick town hall, with the arches under it; along a street of bow-windowed eighteenth-century houses, the residences of doctors and solicitors; past the pond with chains linking white posts together and a horse drinking; and so out into the country. The road was laid with soft white dust; the hedges, hung with wreaths of travellers' joy, seemed also thick with dust. The old horse settled down into his mechanical jog-trot, and Eleanor lay back under her white umbrella.

Every summer she came to visit Morris at his mother-in-law's house. Seven times, eight times she had come she counted; but this year it was different. This year everything was different. Her father was dead; her house was shut up; she had no attachment at the moment anywhere. As she jolted through the hot lanes she thought drowsily, What shall I do now? Live there? she asked herself, as she passed a very respectable Georgian villa in the middle of a street. No, not in a village, she said to herself; and they jogged through the village. What about that house then, she said to herself, looking at a house with a verandah among some trees. But then she thought, I should turn into a grey-haired lady cutting flowers with a pair of scissors and tapping at cottage doors. She did not want to tap at cottage doors. And the clergyman – a clergyman was wheeling his bicycle up the hill – would come to tea with her. But she did not want the clergyman to come to tea with her. How spick and span it all is she thought; for they were passing through the village. The little gardens were bright with red and yellow flowers. Then they began to meet village people: a procession. Some of the women carried parcels; there was a gleaming silver object on the quilt of a perambulator; and one old man clasped a hairy-headed coconut to his breast. There had been a fête she supposed; here it was, returning. They drew to the side of the road as the carriage trotted past, and cast steady curious looks at the lady sitting under her green-and-white umbrella. Now they came to a white gate; trotted briskly down a short avenue; and drew up with a flourish of the whip in front of two slender columns; door-scrapers like bristling hedgehogs; and a wide open hall door.

She waited for a moment in the hall. Her eyes were dimmed after the glare of the road. Everything seemed pale and frail and friendly. The rugs were faded; the pictures were faded. Even the admiral in his cocked hat over the fireplace wore a curious look of faded urbanity. In Greece one was always going back two thousand years. Here it was always the eighteenth century. Like everything English, she thought, laying down her umbrella on the refectory table beside the china bowl, with dried rose leaves in it, the past seemed near, domestic, friendly.

The door opened. 'Oh, Eleanor!' her sister-in-law exclaimed, running into the hall in her fly-away summer clothes. 'How nice to see you! How brown you look! Come into the cool!'

She led her into the drawing-room. The drawing-room piano was strewn with white baby-linen; pink and green fruit glimmered in glass bottles.

'We're in such a mess,' said Celia, sinking on to the sofa. 'Lady St Austell has only just this minute gone, and the Bishop.'

She fanned herself with a sheet of paper.

'But it's been a great success. We had the bazaar in the garden. They acted.' It was a programme with which she was fanning herself.

'A play?' said Eleanor.

'Yes, a scene from Shakespeare,' said Celia. '*Midsummer Night*? *As You Like It*? I forget which. Miss Green got it up. Happily it was so fine. Last year it poured. But how my feet are aching!' The long window opened on to the lawn. Eleanor could see people dragging tables.

'What an undertaking!' she said.

'It was!' Celia panted. 'We had Lady St Austell and the Bishop, coconut shies and a pig; but I think it all went off very well. They enjoyed it.'

'For the church?' Eleanor asked.

'Yes. The new steeple,' said Celia.

'What a business!' said Eleanor again. She looked out on to the lawn. The grass was already scorched and yellow; the laurel bushes looked shrivelled. Tables were standing against the laurel bushes. Morris passed, dragging a table.

'Was it nice in Spain?' Celia was asking. 'Did you see wonderful things?'

'Oh yes!' Eleanor exclaimed. 'I saw . . . ' She stopped. She had seen wonderful things – buildings, mountains, a red city in a plain. But how could she describe it?

'You must tell me all about it afterwards,' said Celia getting up. 'It's time we got ready. But I'm afraid,' she said, toiling rather painfully up the broad staircase, 'I must ask you to be careful, because we're very short of water. The well . . . ' she stopped. The well, Eleanor remembered, always gave out in a hot summer. They walked together down the broad passage, past the old yellow globe which stood under the pleasant eighteenth-century picture of all the little Chinnerys in long drawers and nankeen trousers standing round their father and mother in the garden. Celia paused with her hand on the bedroom door. The sound of doves cooing came in through the open window.

'We're putting you in the Blue Room this time,' she said. Generally Eleanor had the Pink Room. She glanced in. 'I hope you've got everything – ' she began.

'Yes, I'm sure I've got everything,' said Eleanor, and Celia left her.

The maid had already unpacked her things. There they were – laid on the bed. Eleanor took off her dress, and stood in her white petticoat washing herself, methodically but carefully, since they were short of water. The English sun still made her face prickle all over where the Spanish sun had burnt it. Her neck had been cut off from her chest as if it had been painted brown, she thought, as she slipped on her evening dress in front of the looking-glass. She twisted her thick hair, with the grey strand in it, rapidly into a coil; hung the jewel, a red blob like congealed raspberry jam with a gold seed in the centre, round her neck; and gave one glance at the woman who had been for fifty-five years so familiar that she no longer saw her – Eleanor Pargiter. That she was getting old was obvious; there were wrinkles across her forehead; hollows and creases where the flesh used to be firm.

And what was my good point? she asked herself, running the comb once more through her hair. My eyes? Her eyes laughed back at her as she looked at them. My eyes, yes, she thought. Somebody had once praised her eyes. She made herself open them instead of screwing them together. Round each eye were several little white strokes, where she had crinkled them up to avoid the glare on the Acropolis, at Naples, at Granada and Toledo. But that's over, she thought, people praising my eyes, and finished her dressing.

She stood for a moment looking at the burnt, dry lawn. The grass was almost yellow; the elm trees were beginning to turn brown; red-and-white cows were munching on the far side of the sunk hedge. But England was disappointing, she thought; it was small; it was pretty; she felt no affection for her native land – none whatever. Then she went down, for she wanted if possible to see Morris alone.

But he was not alone. He got up as she came in and introduced her to a stoutish, white-haired old man in a dinner-jacket.

'You know each other, don't you?' said Morris. 'Eleanor – Sir William Whatney.' He put a little stress humorously upon the 'Sir' which for a moment confused Eleanor.

'We used to know each other,' said Sir William, coming forward and smiling as he took her hand.

She looked at him. Could it be William Whatney – old Dubbin – who used to come to Abercorn Terrace years ago? It was. She had not seen him since he went to India.

But are we all like that? she asked herself, looking from the grisled, crumpled red-and-yellow face of the boy she had known – he was almost hairless – at her own brother Morris. He looked bald and thin; but surely he was in the prime of life, as she was herself? Or had they all suddenly become old fogies like Sir William? Then her nephew North and her niece Peggy came in with their mother and they went in to dinner. Old Mrs Chinnery dined upstairs.

How has Dubbin become Sir William Whatney? she wondered, glancing at him as they ate the fish that had been brought up in the damp parcel. She had last seen him – in a boat on the river. They had gone for a picnic; they had supped on an island in the middle of the river. Maidenhead, was it?

They were talking about the fête. Craster had won the pig; Mrs Grice had won the silver-plated salver.

'That's what I saw on the perambulator,' said Eleanor. 'I met the fête coming back,' she explained. She described the procession. And they talked about the fête.

'Don't you envy my sister-in-law?' said Celia, turning to Sir William. 'She's just back from a tour in Greece.'

'Indeed!' said Sir William. 'Which part of Greece?'

'We went to Athens, then to Olympia, then to Delphi,' Eleanor began, reciting the usual formula. They were on purely formal terms evidently – she and Dubbin.

'My brother-in-law, Edward,' Celia explained, 'takes these delightful tours.'

'You remember Edward?' said Morris. 'Weren't you up with him?'

'No, he was junior to me,' said Sir William. 'But I've heard of him, of course. He's – let me think – what is he – a great swell, isn't he?'

'Oh, he's at the top of his tree,' said Morris.

He was not jealous of Edward, Eleanor thought; but there was a certain note in his voice which told her that he was comparing his career with Edward's.

'They loved him,' she said. She smiled; she saw Edward lecturing troops of devout schoolmistresses on the Acropolis. Out came their notebooks and down they scribbled every word he said. But he had been very generous; very kind; he had looked after her all the time.

'Did you meet anyone at the embassy?' Sir William asked her. Then he corrected himself. 'Not an embassy though, is it?'

'No. Athens is not an embassy,' said Morris. Here there was a diversion; what was the difference between an embassy and a legation? Then they began to discuss the situation in the Balkans.

'There's going to be trouble there in the near future,' Sir William was saying. He turned to Morris; they discussed the situation in the Balkans.

Eleanor's attention wandered. What's he done? she wondered. Certain words and gestures brought him back to her as he had been thirty years ago. There were relics of the old Dubbin if one half-shut one's eyes. She half-shut her eyes. Suddenly she remembered – it was *he* who had praised her eyes. 'Your sister has the brightest eyes I ever saw,' he had said. Morris had told her. And she had hidden her face behind a newspaper in the train going home to conceal her pleasure. She looked at him again. He was talking. She listened. He seemed too big for the quiet, English dining-room; his voice boomed out. He wanted an audience.

He was telling a story. He spoke in clipped, nervous sentences as if there were a ring round them – a style she admired, but she had missed the beginning. His glass was empty.

'Give Sir William some more wine,' Celia whispered to the nervous parlour-maid. There was some juggling with decanters on the sideboard. Celia frowned nervously. A girl from the village who doesn't know her job, Eleanor reflected. The story was reaching its climax; but she had missed several links.

' . . . and I found myself in an old pair of riding-breeches standing under a peacock umbrella; and all the good people were crouching with their heads to the ground. "Good Lord," I said to myself, "if they only knew what a bally ass I feel!" ' He held out his glass to be filled. 'That's how we were taught our job in those days,' he added.

He was boasting, of course; that was natural. He came back to England after ruling a district 'about the size of Ireland', as they always said; and nobody had ever heard of him. She had a feeling that she would hear a great many more stories that sailed serenely to his own advantage, during the weekend. But he talked very well. He had done a great many interesting things. She wished that Morris would tell stories too. She wished that he would assert himself instead of leaning back and passing his hand – the hand with the cut on it – over his forehead.

Ought I to have urged him to go to the Bar? she thought. Her father had been against it. But once it's done there it is; he married; the children came; he had to go on, whether he wanted to or not. How irrevocable things are, she thought. We make our experiments, then they make theirs. She looked at her nephew North and at her niece Peggy. They sat opposite her with the sun on their faces. Their perfectly healthy eggshell faces looked extraordinarily young. Peggy's blue dress stuck out like a child's muslin frock; North was still a brown-eyed cricketing boy. He was listening intently; Peggy was looking down at her plate. She had the non-committal look which well-brought-up children have when they listen to the talk of their elders. She might be amused; or bored? Eleanor could not be sure which it was.

'There he goes,' Peggy said, suddenly looking up. 'The owl . . . ' she said, catching Eleanor's eye. Eleanor turned to look out of the window behind her. She missed the owl; she saw the heavy trees, gold in the setting sun; and the cows slowly moving as they munched their way across the meadow.

'You can time him,' said Peggy, 'he's so regular.' Then Celia made a move.

'Shall we leave the gentlemen to their politics,' she said, 'and have our coffee on the terrace?' and they shut the door upon the gentlemen and their politics.

'I'll fetch my glasses,' said Eleanor, and she went upstairs.

She wanted to see the owl before it got too dark. She was becoming more and more interested in birds. It was a sign of old age, she supposed, as she went into her bedroom. An old maid who washes and watches birds, she said to herself as she looked in the glass. There were her eyes – they still seemed to her rather bright, in spite of the lines round them – the eyes she had shaded in the railway carriage because Dubbin praised them. But now I'm labelled, she thought – an old maid who washes and watches birds. That's what they think I am. But I'm not – I'm not in the least like that, she said. She shook her head, and turned away from the glass. It was a nice room: shady, civilised, cool after the bedrooms in foreign inns, with marks on the wall where someone had squashed bugs and men brawling under the window. But where were her glasses? Put away in some drawer? She turned to look for them.

'Did father say Sir William was in love with her?' Peggy asked as they waited on the terrace.

'Oh I don't know about that,' said Celia. 'But I wish they could have married. I wish she had children of her own. And then they could have settled here,' she added. 'He's such a delightful man.'

Peggy was silent. There was a pause.

Celia resumed: 'I hope you were polite to the Robinsons this afternoon, dreadful as they are . . . '

'They give ripping parties anyhow,' said Peggy.

' "Ripping, ripping",' her mother complained, half laughing. 'I wish you wouldn't pick up all North's slang, my dear . . . Oh, here's Eleanor,' she broke off.

Eleanor came out on to the terrace with her glasses, and sat down beside Celia. It was still very warm; it was still light enough to see the hills in the distance.

'He'll be back in a minute,' said Peggy, drawing up a chair. 'He'll come along that hedge.'

She pointed to the dark line of hedge that went across the meadow. Eleanor focused her glasses and waited.

'Now,' said Celia, pouring out the coffee, 'there are so many things I want to ask you.' She paused. She always had a hoard of questions to ask; she had not seen Eleanor since April. In four months questions accumulated. Out they came drop by drop.

'In the first place,' she began. 'No . . . ' She rejected that question in favour of another. 'What's all this about Rose?' she asked.

'What?' said Eleanor absent-mindedly, altering the focus of her glasses. 'It's getting too dark,' she said; the field was blurred.

'Morris says she's been had up in a police-court,' said Celia. She dropped her voice slightly though they were alone.

'She threw a brick[39] – ' said Eleanor. She focused her glasses on the hedge again. She held them poised in case the owl should come that way again.

'Will she be put in prison?' Peggy asked quickly.

'Not this time,' said Eleanor. 'Next time – Ah, here he comes!' she broke off. The blunt-headed bird came swinging along the hedge. He looked almost white in the dusk. Eleanor got him within the circle of her lens. He held a little black spot in front of him.

'He's got a mouse in his claws!' she exclaimed.

'He's got a nest in the steeple,' said Peggy. The owl swooped out of the field of vision.

'Now I can't see him any more,' said Eleanor. She lowered her glasses. They were silent for a moment, sipping their coffee. Celia was thinking of her next question; Eleanor anticipated her.

'Tell me about William Whatney,' she said. 'When I last saw him he was a slim young man in a boat.'

Peggy burst out laughing. 'That must have been ages ago!' she said.

'Not so very long,' said Eleanor. She felt rather nettled. 'Well – ' she reflected, 'twenty years – twenty-five years perhaps.'

It seemed a very short time to her; but then, she thought, it was before Peggy was born. She could only be sixteen or seventeen.

'Isn't he a delightful man?' Celia exclaimed. 'He was in India, you know. Now he's retired, and we do hope he'll take a house here; but Morris thinks he'd find it too dull.'

They sat silent for a moment, looking out over the meadow. The cows coughed now and then as they munched and moved a step farther through the grass. A sweet scent of cows and grass was wafted up to them.

'It's going to be another hot day tomorrow,' said Peggy. The sky was perfectly smooth; it seemed made of innumerable grey-blue atoms the colour of an Italian officer's cloak; until it reached the horizon where there was a long bar of pure green. Everything looked very settled; very still; very pure. There was not a single cloud, and the stars were not yet showing.

It was small; it was smug; it was petty after Spain; but still, now that the sun had sunk and the trees were massed together without separate leaves, it had its beauty, Eleanor thought. The downs were becoming larger and simpler; they were becoming part of the sky.

'How lovely it is!' she exclaimed, as if she were making amends to England after Spain.

'If only Mr Robinson doesn't build!' sighed Celia; and Eleanor remembered – they were the local scourge: rich people who threatened to build. 'I did my best to be polite to them at the bazaar today,' Celia continued. 'Some people won't ask them; but I say one must be polite to neighbours in the country . . . '

Then she paused. 'There are so many things I want to ask you,' she said. The bottle was tilted on its end again. Eleanor waited obediently.

'Have you had an offer for Abercorn Terrace yet?' Celia demanded. Drop, drop, drop, out her questions came.

'Not yet,' said Eleanor. 'The agent wants me to cut it up into flats.' Celia pondered. Then she hopped on again.

'And now about Maggie – when's her baby going to be born?'

'In November, I think,' said Eleanor. 'In Paris,' she added.

'I hope it'll be all right,' said Celia. 'But I do wish it could have been born in England.' She reflected again. 'Her children will be French, I suppose?' she said.

'Yes; French, I suppose,' said Eleanor. She was looking at the green bar; it was fading; it was turning blue. It was becoming night.

'Everybody says he's a very nice fellow,' said Celia. 'But René – René,' her accent was bad, ' – it doesn't sound like a man's name.'

'You can call him Renny,' said Peggy, pronouncing it in the English way.

'But that reminds me of Ronny; and I don't like Ronny. We had a stable-boy called Ronny.'

'Who stole the hay,' said Peggy. They were silent again.

'It's such a pity – ' Celia began. Then she stopped. The maid had come to clear away the coffee.

'It's a wonderful night, isn't it?' said Celia, adapting her voice to the presence of servants. 'It looks as if it would never rain again. In which case I don't know . . . ' And she went on prattling about the drought; about the lack of water. The well always ran dry. Eleanor, looking at the hills, hardly listened. 'Oh, but there's quite enough for everybody at present,' she heard Celia saying. And for some reason she held the sentence suspended without a meaning in her mind's ear: ' – quite enough for everybody at present,' she repeated. After all the foreign languages she had been hearing, it sounded to her pure English. What a lovely language, she thought, saying over to herself again the commonplace words, spoken by Celia quite simply, but with some indescribable burr in the r's, for the Chinnerys had lived in Dorsetshire since the beginning of time.

The maid had gone.

'What was I saying?' Celia resumed. 'I was saying, it's such a pity. Yes . . . ' But there was a sound of voices; a scent of cigar smoke; the gentlemen were upon them. 'Oh, here they are!' she broke off. And the chairs were pulled up and rearranged.

They sat in a semicircle looking across the meadows at the fading hills. The broad bar of green that lay across the horizon had vanished. Only a tinge was left in the sky. It had become peaceful and cool; in them too something seemed to be smoothed out. There was no need to talk. The owl flew down the meadow again; they could just see the white of his wing against the dark of the hedge.

'There he goes,' said North, puffing at a cigar which was his first, Eleanor guessed, Sir William's gift. The elm trees had become dead black against the sky. Their leaves hung in a fretted pattern like black lace with holes in it. Through a hole Eleanor saw the point of a star. She looked up. There was another.

'It's going to be a fine day tomorrow,' said Morris, knocking out his pipe against his shoe. Far away on a distant road there was a rattle of cartwheels; then a chorus of voices singing – country people going home. This is England, Eleanor thought to herself; she felt as if she were slowly sinking into some fine mesh made of branches shaking, hills growing dark and leaves hanging like black lace with stars among them. But a bat swooped low over their heads.

'I hate bats!' Celia exclaimed, raising her hand to her head nervously.

'Do you?' said Sir William. 'I rather like them.' His voice was quiet and almost melancholy. Now Celia will say, They get into one's hair, Eleanor thought.

'They get into one's hair,' Celia said.

'But I haven't any hair,' said Sir William. His bald head, his large face gleamed out in the darkness.

The bat swooped again, skimming the ground at their feet. A little cool air stirred at their ankles. The trees had become part of the sky. There was no moon, but the stars were coming out. There's another, Eleanor thought, gazing at a twinkling light ahead of her. But it was too low; too yellow; it was another house she realised, not a star. And then Celia began talking to Sir William, whom she wanted to settle near them; and Lady St Austell had told her that The Grange was to let. Was that The Grange? Eleanor wondered, looking at a light, or a star? And they went on talking.

Tired of her own company, old Mrs Chinnery had come down early. There she sat in the drawing-room waiting. She had made a formal entry, but there was nobody there. Arrayed in her old lady's dress of black satin, with a lace cap on her head, she sat waiting. Her hawk-like nose was curved in her shrivelled cheeks; a little red rim showed on one of her drooping eyelids.

'Why don't they come in?' she said peevishly to Ellen, the discreet black maid who stood behind her. Ellen went to the window and tapped on the pane.

Celia stopped talking and turned round. 'That's mama,' she said. 'We must go in.' She got up and pushed back her chair.

After the dark, the drawing-room with its lamps lit had the effect of a stage. Old Mrs Chinnery sitting in her wheeled chair with her ear trumpet seemed to sit there awaiting homage. She looked exactly the same; not a day older; as vigorous as ever. As Eleanor bent to give her the customary kiss, life once more took on its familiar proportions. So she had bent, night after night, over her father. She was glad to stoop down; it made her feel younger herself. She knew the whole procedure by heart. They, the middle-aged, deferred to the very old; the very old were courteous to them; and then came the usual pause. They had nothing to say to her; she had nothing to say to them. What happened next? Eleanor saw the old lady's eyes suddenly brighten. What made the eyes of an old woman of ninety turn blue? Cards? Yes. Celia had fetched the green baize table; Mrs Chinnery had a passion for whist. But she too had her ceremony; she too had her manners.

'Not tonight,' she said, making a little gesture as if to push away the table. 'I am sure it will bore Sir William?' She gave a nod in the direction of the large man who stood there seeming a little outside the family party.

'Not at all. Not at all,' he said with alacrity. 'Nothing would please me more,' he assured her.

You're a good fellow, Dubbin, Eleanor thought. And they drew up the chairs; and dealt the cards; and Morris chaffed his mother-in-law down her ear-trumpet and they played rubber after rubber. North read a book; Peggy strummed on the piano; and Celia, dozing over her embroidery, now and then gave a sudden start and put her hand over her mouth. At last the door opened stealthily. Ellen, the discreet black maid, stood behind Mrs Chinnery's chair, waiting. Mrs Chinnery pretended to ignore her, but the others were glad to stop. Ellen stepped forward and Mrs Chinnery, submitting, was wheeled off to the mysterious upper chamber of extreme old age. Her pleasure was over.

Celia yawned openly.

'The bazaar,' she said, rolling up her embroidery. 'I shall go to bed. Come, Peggy. Come, Eleanor.'

North jumped up with alacrity to open the door. Celia lit the brass candlesticks and began, rather heavily, to climb the stairs. Eleanor followed after. But Peggy lagged behind. Eleanor heard her whispering with her brother in the hall.

'Come along, Peggy,' Celia called back over the banister as she toiled upstairs. When she got to the landing at the top she stopped under the picture of the little Chinnerys and called back again rather sharply: 'Come, Peggy.' There was a pause. Then Peggy came, reluctantly. She kissed her mother obediently; but she did not look in the least sleepy. She looked extremely pretty and rather flushed. She did not mean to go to bed, Eleanor felt sure.

She went into her room and undressed. All the windows were open and she heard the trees rustling in the garden. It was so hot still that she lay in her nightgown on top of the bed with only the sheet over her. The candle burnt its little pear-shaped flame on the table by her side. She lay listening vaguely to the trees in the garden; and watched the shadow of a moth that dashed round and round the room. Either I must get up and shut the window or blow out the candle, she thought drowsily. She did not want to do either. She wanted to lie still. It was a relief to lie in the semi-darkness after the talk, after the cards. She could still see the cards falling: black, red and yellow; kings, queens and knaves; on a green-baize table. She looked drowsily round her. A nice vase of flowers stood on the dressing-table; there was the polished wardrobe and a china box by her bedside. She lifted the lid. Yes; four biscuits and a pale piece of chocolate – in case she should be hungry in the night. Celia had provided books too, *The Diary of a Nobody*, *Ruff's Tour in Northumberland* and an odd volume of Dante, in case she should wish to read in the night. She took one of the books and laid it on the counterpane beside her. Perhaps because she had been travelling, it seemed as if the ship were still padding softly through the sea; as if the train were still swinging from side to side as it rattled across France. She felt as if things were moving past her as she lay stretched on the bed under the single sheet. But it's not the landscape any longer, she thought; it's people's lives, their changing lives.

The door of the pink bedroom shut. William Whatney coughed next door. She heard him cross the room. Now he was standing by the window, smoking a last cigar. What's he thinking, she wondered – about India? – how he stood under a peacock umbrella? Then he began moving about the room, undressing. She could hear him take up a brush and put it down again on his dressing-table. And it's to him, she thought, remembering the wide sweep of his chin and the floating stains of pink and yellow that lay underneath it, that I owe that moment, which had been more than pleasure, when she hid her face behind the newspaper in the corner of the third-class railway carriage.

Now there were three moths dashing round the ceiling. They made a little tapping noise as they dashed round and round from corner to corner. If she left the window open much longer the room would be full of moths. A board creaked in the passage outside. She listened. Peggy, was it, escaping, to join her brother? She felt sure there was some scheme afoot. But she could only hear the heavy-laden branches moving up and down in the garden; a cow lowing; a bird chirping; and then, to her delight, the liquid call of an owl going from tree to tree looping them with silver.

She lay looking at the ceiling. A faint watermark appeared there. It was like a hill. It reminded her of one of the great desolate mountains in Greece or in Spain, which looked as if nobody had ever set foot there since the beginning of time.

She opened the book that lay on the counterpane. She hoped it was *Ruff's Tour* or *The Diary of a Nobody*; but it was Dante, and she was too lazy to change it. She read a few lines, here and there. But her Italian was rusty; the meaning escaped her. There was a meaning, however; a hook seemed to scratch the surface of her mind.

> chè per quanti si dice più lì nostro
> tanto possiede più di ben ciascuno.

What did that mean? She read the English translation.

> For by so many more there are who say 'ours'
> So much the more of good doth each possess.

Brushed lightly by her mind that was watching the moths on the ceiling, and listening to the call of the owl as it looped from tree to tree with its liquid cry, the words did not give out their full meaning, but seemed to hold something furled up in the hard shell of the archaic Italian. I'll read it one of these days, she thought, shutting the book. When I've pensioned Crosby off, when . . . Should she take another house? Should she travel? Should she go to India, at last? Sir William was getting into bed next door, his life was over; hers was beginning. No, I don't mean to take another house, not another house, she thought, looking at the stain on the ceiling. Again the sense came to her of a ship padding softly through the waves; of a train swinging from side to side down a railway-line. Things can't go on for ever, she thought. Things pass, things change, she thought, looking up at the ceiling. And where are we going? Where? Where? . . . The moths were dashing round the ceiling; the book slipped on to the floor. Craster won the pig, but who was it won the silver salver? she mused; made an effort; turned round, and blew out the candle. Darkness reigned.

1913

IT WAS JANUARY. Snow was falling; snow had fallen all day. The sky spread like a grey goose's wing from which feathers were falling all over England. The sky was nothing but a flurry of falling flakes. Lanes were levelled; hollows filled; the snow clogged the streams, obscured windows and lay wedged against doors. There was a faint murmur in the air, a slight crepitation, as if the air itself were turning to snow; otherwise all was silent, save when a sheep coughed, snow flopped from a branch, or slipped in an avalanche down some roof in London. Now and again a shaft of light spread slowly across the sky as a car drove through the muffled roads. But as the night wore on, snow covered the wheel ruts, softened to nothingness the marks of the traffic and coated monuments, palaces and statues with a thick vestment of snow.

It was still snowing when the young man came from the house agent's to see over Abercorn Terrace. The snow cast a hard white glare upon the walls of the bathroom, showed up the cracks on the enamel bath, and the stains on the wall. Eleanor stood looking out of the window. The trees in the back garden were heavily lined with snow; all the roofs were softly moulded with snow; it was still falling. She turned. The young man turned too. The light was unbecoming to them both, yet the snow – she saw it through the window at the end of the passage – was beautiful, falling.

Mr Grice turned to her as they went downstairs,

'The fact is, our clients expect more lavatory accommodation nowadays,' he said, stopping outside a bedroom door.

Why can't he say 'baths' and have done with it, she thought. Slowly she went downstairs. Now she could see the snow falling through the panels of the hall door. As he went downstairs, she noticed the red ears which stood out over his high collar; and the neck which he had washed imperfectly in some sink at Wandsworth. She was annoyed; as he went round the house, sniffing and peering, he had indicted their cleanliness, their humanity; and he used absurd long words. He was hauling himself up into the class above him, she supposed, by means of long words. Now he stepped cautiously over the body of the sleeping dog, took his hat from the hall table and went down the front doorsteps in his businessman's buttoned boots, leaving yellow footprints in the thick white cushion of snow. A four-wheeler was waiting.

Eleanor turned. There was Crosby, dodging about in her best bonnet and mantle. She had been following Eleanor about the house like a dog all the morning; the odious moment could no longer be put off. Her four-wheeler was at the door; they had to say goodbye.

'Well, Crosby, it all looks very empty, doesn't it?' said Eleanor, looking in at the empty drawing-room. The white light of the snow glared in on the walls. It showed up the marks on the walls where the furniture had stood, where the pictures had hung.

'It does, Miss Eleanor,' said Crosby. She stood looking too. Eleanor knew that she was going to cry. She did not want her to cry. She did not want to cry herself.

'I can still see you all sitting round that table, Miss Eleanor,' said Crosby. But the table had gone. Morris had taken this; Delia had taken that; everything had been shared out and separated.

'And the kettle that wouldn't boil,' said Eleanor. 'D'you remember that?' She tried to laugh.

'Oh, Miss Eleanor,' said Crosby, shaking her head, 'I remember everything!' The tears were forming; Eleanor looked away into the farther room.

There too were marks on the wall, where the bookcase had stood, where the writing-table had stood. She thought of herself sitting there, drawing a pattern on the blotting-paper; digging a hole, adding up tradesmen's books . . . Then she turned. There was Crosby. Crosby was crying. The mixture of emotions was positively painful; she was so glad to be quit of it all, but for Crosby it was the end of everything.

She had known every cupboard, flagstone, chair and table in that large rambling house, not from five or six feet of distance as they had known it; but from her knees, as she scrubbed and polished; she had known every groove, stain, fork, knife, napkin and cupboard. They and their doings had made her entire world. And now she was going off, alone, to a single room at Richmond.

'I should think you'd be glad to be out of that basement anyhow, Crosby,' said Eleanor, turning into the hall again. She had never realised how dark, how low it was, until, looking at it with 'our Mr Grice', she had felt ashamed.

'It was my home for forty years, miss,' said Crosby. The tears were running. For forty years! Eleanor thought with a start. She had been a little girl of thirteen or fourteen when Crosby came to them, looking so stiff and smart. Now her blue gnat's eyes protruded and her cheeks were sunk.

Crosby was stooping to put Rover on the chain.

'You're sure you want him?' said Eleanor, looking at the rather smelly, wheezy and unattractive old dog. 'We could easily find a nice home for him in the country.'

'Oh, miss, don't ask me to give him up!' said Crosby. Tears checked her speech. Tears were running freely down her cheeks. For all Eleanor could do to prevent it, tears formed in her eyes too.

'Dear Crosby, goodbye,' she said. She bent and kissed her. She had a curious dry quality of skin she noticed. But her own tears were falling. Then Crosby, holding Rover on the chain, began to edge sideways down the slippery steps. Eleanor, holding the door open, looked after her. It was a dreadful moment; unhappy; muddled; altogether wrong. Crosby was so miserable; she was so glad. Yet as she held the door open her tears formed and fell. They had all lived here; she had stood here to wave Morris to school; there was the little garden in which they used to plant crocuses. And now Crosby, with flakes of snow falling on her black bonnet, climbed into the four-wheeler, holding Rover in her arms. Eleanor shut the door and went in.

Snow was falling as the cab trotted along the streets. There were long yellow ruts on the pavement where people, shopping, had pressed it into slush. It was beginning to thaw slightly; loads of snow slipped off the roofs and fell on to the pavement. Little boys, too, were snowballing; one of them threw a ball which struck the cab as it passed. But when it turned into Richmond Green the whole of the vast space was completely white. Nobody seemed to have crossed the snow there; everything was white. The grass was white; the trees were white; the railings were white; the only marks in the whole vista were the rooks, sitting huddled black on the tree-tops. The cab trotted on.

The carts had churned the snow to a yellowish clotted mixture by the time the cab stopped in front of the little house off the Green. Crosby, carrying Rover in her arms lest his feet should mark the stairs, went up the steps. There was Louisa Burt standing to welcome her; and Mr Bishop, the lodger from the top floor who had been a butler. He lent a hand with the luggage, and Crosby followed after, to her little room.

Her room was at the top, and at the back, overlooking the garden. It was small, but when she had unpacked her things it was comfortable enough. It had a look of Abercorn Terrace. Indeed for many years she had been hoarding odds and ends with a view to her retirement. Indian elephants, silver vases, the walrus that she had found in the waste-paper basket one morning, when the guns were firing for the old Queen's funeral – there they all were. She ranged them askew on the mantelpiece, and when she had hung the portraits of the family – some in wedding dress, some in wigs and gowns, and Mr Martin in his uniform in the middle because he was her favourite – it was quite like home.

But whether it was the change to Richmond, or whether he had caught cold in the snow, Rover sickened immediately. He refused his food. His nose was hot. His eczema broke out again. When she tried to take him shopping with her next morning he rolled over with his feet in the air as if he begged to be left alone. Mr Bishop had to tell Mrs Crosby – for she wore the courtesy title in Richmond – that in his opinion the poor old chap (here he patted his head) was better out of the way.

'Come along with me, my dear,' said Mrs Burt, putting her arm on Crosby's shoulder, 'and let Bishop do it.'

'He won't suffer, I can assure you,' said Mr Bishop, rising from his knees. He had put her ladyship's dogs to sleep scores of time before this. 'He'll just take one sniff' – Mr Bishop had his pocket-handkerchief in his hand – 'and he'll be off in a jiffy.'

'It'll be for his good, Annie,' Mrs Burt added, trying to draw her away.

Indeed, the poor old dog looked very miserable. But Crosby shook her head. He had wagged his tail; his eyes were open. He was alive. There was a gleam of what she had long considered a smile on his face. He depended on her, she felt. She was not going to hand him over to strangers. She sat by his side for three days and nights; she fed him with a teaspoon on Brand's Essence; but at last he refused to open his lips; his body grew stiffer and stiffer; a fly walked across his nose without its twitching. This was in the early morning with the sparrows twittering on the trees outside.

'It's a mercy she's got something to distract her,' said Mrs Burt as Crosby passed the kitchen window the day after the funeral in her best mantle and bonnet; for it was Thursday, when she fetched Mr Pargiter's socks from Ebury Street. 'But he ought to have been put down long ago,' she added, turning back to the sink. His breath had smelt.

Crosby took the District Railway to Sloane Square and then she walked. She walked slowly, with her elbows jutting out from her sides as if to protect herself from the haphazardry of the streets. She still looked sad; but the change from Richmond to Ebury Street did her good. She felt more herself in Ebury Street than in Richmond. A common sort of people lived in Richmond she always felt. Here the ladies and gentlemen had the same kind of way with them. She glanced approvingly into the shops as she passed. And General Arbuthnot, who used to visit the master, lived in Ebury Street she reflected as she turned into that gloomy thoroughfare. He was dead now; Louisa had shown her the notice in the papers. But when he was alive, he had lived here. She had reached Mr Martin's lodgings. She paused on the steps and adjusted her bonnet. She always had a word with Martin when she came to fetch his socks; it was one of her pleasures; and she enjoyed a gossip with Mrs Briggs, his landlady. Today she would have the pleasure of telling her of the death of Rover. Sidling cautiously down the area steps which were slippery with sleet she stood at the back door and rang the bell.

Martin sat in his room reading his newspaper. The war in the Balkans was over;[40] but there was more trouble brewing – of that he was sure. Quite sure. He turned the page. The room was very dark with the sleet falling. And he could never read while he was waiting. Crosby was coming; he could hear voices in the hall. How they gossiped! How they chattered! he thought impatiently. He threw the paper down and waited. Now she was coming; her hand was on the door. But what was he to say to her? he wondered, as he saw the handle turning. He made use of the usual formula: 'Well, Crosby, how's the world treating you?' as she came in.

She remembered Rover; and the tears started to her eyes.

Martin listened to the story; he wrinkled his brow sympathetically. Then he got up, went into his bedroom, and came back holding a pyjama jacket in his hand.

'What d'you call *that* , Crosby?' he said. He pointed to a hole under the collar, fringed with brown. Crosby adjusted her gold-rimmed spectacles.

'A burn, sir,' she said with conviction.

'Brand new pyjamas; only worn them twice,' said Martin, holding them extended. Crosby touched them. They were made of the finest silk, she could tell.

'Tut-tut-tut!' she said, shaking her head.

'Will you please take this pyjama to Mrs What's-her-name,' he went on, holding it out in front of him. He wanted to use a metaphor; but one had to be very literal and use only the simplest language, he remembered, when one talked to Crosby. 'Tell her to get another laundress,' he concluded, 'and send the old one to the devil.'

Crosby gathered the injured pyjama tenderly to her breast; Mr Martin never could abide wool next the skin, she remembered. Martin paused. One must pass the time of the day with Crosby, but the death of Rover had seriously limited their topics of conversation.

'How's the rheumatics?' he asked, as she stood very upright at the door of the room with the pyjamas on her arm. She had grown distinctly smaller, he thought. She shook her head. Richmond was very low compared with Abercorn Terrace, she said. Her face dropped. She was thinking of Rover, he supposed. He must get her mind off that; he could not bear tears.

'Seen Miss Eleanor's new flat?' he asked. Crosby had. But she did not like flats. In her opinion Miss Eleanor wore herself out.

'And the people's not worth it, sir,' she said, referring to the Zwinglers, Paravicinis and Cobbs who used to come to the back door for cast-off clothing in the old days.

Martin shook his head. He could not think what to say next. He hated talking to servants; it always made him feel insincere. Either one simpers, or one's hearty, he was thinking. In either case it's a lie.

'And are you keeping pretty well yourself, Master Martin?' Crosby asked him, using the diminutive, which was a perquisite of her long service.

'Not married yet, Crosby,' said Martin.

Crosby cast her eye round the room. It was a bachelor's apartment, with its leather chairs; its chessmen on top of a pile of books and its soda-water syphon on a tray. She ventured to say that she was sure that there were plenty of nice young ladies who would be very glad to take care of him.

'Ah, but I like lying in bed of a morning,' said Martin.

'You always did, sir,' she said, smiling. And then it was possible for Martin to take out his watch, step briskly to the window, exclaim as if he had suddenly remembered an appointment, 'By Jove, Crosby, I must be off!' and shut the door upon Crosby.

It was a lie. He had no engagement. One always lies to servants, he thought, looking out of the window. The mean outlines of the Ebury Street houses showed through the falling sleet. Everybody lies, he thought. His father had lied – after his death they had found letters from a woman called Mira tied up in his table-drawer. And he had seen Mira – a stout respectable lady who wanted help with her roof. Why had his father lied? What was the harm of keeping a mistress? And he had lied himself: about the room off the Fulham Road where he and Dodge and Erridge used to smoke cheap cigars and tell smutty stories. It was an abominable system, he thought: family life; Abercorn Terrace. No wonder the house would not let. It had one bathroom, and a basement; and there all those different people had lived, boxed up together, telling lies.

Then as he stood at the window looking at the little figures slinking along the wet pavement he saw Crosby come up the area steps with a parcel under her arm. She stood for a moment, like a frightened little animal, peering round her before she ventured to brave the dangers of the street. At last, off she trotted. He saw the snow falling on her black bonnet as she disappeared. He turned away.

1914

ITWAS A BRILLIANT SPRING; the day was radiant. Even the air seemed to have a burr in it as it touched the tree-tops; it vibrated, it rippled. The leaves were sharp and green. In the country old church clocks rasped out the hour; the rusty sound went over fields that were red with clover, and up went the rooks as if flung by the bells. Round they wheeled; then settled on the tree-tops.

In London all was gallant and strident; the season was beginning; horns hooted; the traffic roared; flags flew taut as trout in a stream. And from all the spires of all the London churches – the fashionable saints of Mayfair, the dowdy saints of Kensington, the hoary saints of the city – the hour was proclaimed. The air over London seemed a rough sea of sound through which circles travelled. But the clocks were irregular, as if the saints themselves were divided. There were pauses, silences . . . Then the clocks struck again.

Here in Ebury Street some distant frail-voiced clock was striking. It was eleven. Martin, standing at his window, looked down on the narrow street. The sun was bright; he was in the best of spirits; he was going to visit his stockbroker in the city. His affairs were turning out well. At one time, he was thinking, his father had made a lot of money; then he lost it; then he made it; but in the end he had done very well.

He stood at the window for a moment admiring a lady of fashion in a charming hat who was looking at a pot in the curiosity shop opposite. It was a blue pot on a Chinese stand with green brocade behind it. The sloping symmetrical body, the depth of blue, the little cracks in the glaze pleased him. And the lady looking at the pot was also charming.

He took his hat and stick and went out into the street. He would walk part of the way to the City. 'The King of Spain's daughter,' he hummed as he turned up Sloane Street, 'came to visit me. All for the sake of . . . ' He looked into the shop windows as he passed. They were full of summer dresses: charming confections of green and gauze, and there were flights of hats stuck on little rods. ' . . . all for the sake of,' he hummed as he walked on, 'my silver nutmeg tree.' But what was a silver nutmeg tree? he wondered. An organ was fluting its merry little jig farther down the street. The organ moved round and round, shifted this way and that, as if the old man who played it were half dancing to the tune. A pretty servant girl ran up the area steps and gave him a penny. His supple Italian face wrinkled all over as he whipped off his cap and bowed to her. The girl smiled and slipped back into the kitchen.

' . . . all for the sake of my silver nutmeg tree,' Martin hummed, peering down through the area railings into the kitchen where they were sitting. They looked very snug, with teapots and bread and butter on the kitchen table. His stick swung from side to side like the tail of a cheerful dog. Everybody seemed light-hearted and irresponsible, sallying out of their houses, flaunting along the streets with pennies for the organ-grinders and pennies for the beggars. Everybody seemed to have money to spend. Women clustered round the plate-glass windows. He too stopped, looked at the model of a toy boat; at dressing-cases, shining yellow with rows of silver bottles. But who wrote that song, he wondered, as he strolled on, about the King of Spain's daughter, the song that Pippy used to sing him, as she wiped his ears with a piece of slimy flannel? She used to take him on her knee and croak out in her wheezy rattle of a voice, 'The King of Spain's daughter came to visit me, all for the sake of . . . ' And then suddenly her knee gave, and down he was tumbled on to the floor.

Here he was at Hyde Park Corner. The scene was extremely animated. Vans, motor cars, motor omnibuses were streaming down the hill. The trees in the park had little green leaves on them. Cars with gay ladies in pale dresses were already passing in at the gates. Everybody was going about their business. And somebody, he observed, had written the words 'God is Love' in pink chalk on the gates of Apsley House. That must need some pluck, he thought, to write 'God is Love' on the gates of Apsley House when at any moment a policeman might nab you. But here came his bus; and he climbed on top.

'To St Paul's,' he said, handing the conductor his coppers.

The omnibuses swirled and circled in a perpetual current round the steps of St Paul's. The statue of Queen Anne seemed to preside over the chaos and to supply it with a centre, like the hub of a wheel. It seemed as if the white lady ruled the traffic with her sceptre; directed the activities of the little men in bowler hats and round coats; of the women carrying attaché cases; of the vans, the lorries and the motor omnibuses. Now and then single figures broke off from the rest and went up the steps into the church. The doors of the cathedral kept opening and shutting. Now and again a blast of faint organ music was blown out into the air. The pigeons waddled; the sparrows fluttered. Soon after midday a little old man carrying a paper bag took up his station halfway up the steps and proceeded to feed the birds. He held out a slice of bread. His lips moved. He seemed to be wheedling and coaxing them. Soon he was haloed by a circle of fluttering wings. Sparrows perched on his head and his hands. Pigeons waddled close to his feet. A little crowd gathered to watch him feeding the sparrows. He tossed his bread round him in a circle. Then there was a ripple in the air. The great clock, all the clocks of the city, seemed to be gathering their forces together; they seemed to be whirring a preliminary warning. Then the stroke struck. 'One' blared out. All the sparrows fluttered up into the air; even the pigeons were frightened; some of them made a little flight round the head of Queen Anne.

As the last ripple of the stroke died away, Martin came out in the open space in front of the cathedral.

He crossed over and stood with his back against a shop window looking up at the great dome. All the weights in his body seemed to shift. He had a curious sense of something moving in his body in harmony with the building; it righted itself: it came to a full stop. It was exciting – this change of proportion. He wished he had been an architect. He stood with his back pressed against the shop trying to get the whole of the cathedral clear. But it was difficult with so many people passing. They knocked against him and brushed in front of him. It was the rush hour, of course, when City men were making for their luncheons. They were taking short cuts across the steps. The pigeons were swirling up and then settling down again. The doors were opening and shutting as he mounted the steps. The pigeons were a nuisance, he thought, making a mess on the steps. He climbed up slowly.

'And who's that?' he thought, looking at someone who was standing against one of the pillars. 'Don't I know her?'

Her lips were moving. She was talking to herself.

'It's Sally!' he thought. He hesitated; should he speak to her, or should he not? But she was company; and he was tired of his own.

'A penny for your thoughts, Sal!' he said, tapping her on the shoulder.

She turned; her expression changed instantly. 'Just as I was thinking of you, Martin!' she exclaimed.

'What a lie!' he said, shaking hands.

'When I think of people, I always see them,' she said. She gave her queer little shuffle as if she were a bird, a somewhat dishevelled fowl, for her cloak was not in the fashion. They stood for a moment on the steps, looking down at the crowded street beneath. A gust of organ music came out from the cathedral behind them as the doors opened and shut. The faint ecclesiastical murmur was vaguely impressive, and the dark space of the cathedral seen through the door.

'What were you thinking . . . ?' he began. But he broke off. 'Come and lunch,' he said. 'I'll take you to a City chop-house,' and he shepherded her down the steps and along a narrow alley blocked by carts into which packages were being shot from the warehouses. They pushed through the swing doors into the chop-house.

'Very full today, Alfred,' said Martin affably, as the waiter took his coat and hat and hung them on the rack. He knew the waiter; he often lunched there; the waiter knew him too.

'Very full, captain,' he said.

'Now,' he said, sitting down, 'what shall we have?'

A vast brownish-yellow joint was being trundled from table to table on a lorry.

'That,' said Sara, waving her hand at it.

'And drink?' said Martin. He took the wine-list and consulted it.

'Drink – ' said Sara, 'drink, I leave to you.' She took off her gloves and laid them on a small reddish-brown book that was obviously a prayer-book.

'Drink you leave to me,' said Martin. Why, he wondered, do prayer-books always have their leaves gilt with red and gold? He chose the wine.

'And what were you doing,' he said, dismissing the waiter, 'at St Paul's?'

'Listening to the service,' she said. She looked round her. The room was very hot and crowded. The walls were covered with gold leaves encrusted on a brown surface. People were passing them and coming in and out all the time. The waiter brought the wine. Martin poured her out a glass.

'I didn't know you went to services,' he said, looking at her prayer-book.

She did not answer. She kept looking round her, watching the people come in and go out. She sipped her wine. The colour was coming into her cheeks. She took up her knife and fork and began to eat the admirable mutton. They ate in silence for a moment.

He wanted to make her talk.

'And what, Sal,' he said, touching the little book, 'd'you make of it?'

She opened the prayer-book at random and began to read: 'The father incomprehensible; the son incomprehensible – ' she spoke in her ordinary voice.

'Hush!' he stopped her. 'Somebody's listening.'

In deference to him she assumed the manner of a lady lunching with a gentleman in a City restaurant.

'And what were you doing,' she asked, 'at St Paul's?'

'Wishing I'd been an architect,' he said. 'But they sent me into the army instead, which I loathed.' He spoke emphatically.

'Hush,' she whispered. 'Somebody's listening.'

He looked round quickly; then he laughed. The waiter was setting their tart in front of them. They ate in silence. He filled her glass again. Her cheeks were flushed; her eyes were bright. He envied her the generalised sensation of universal wellbeing that he used to get from a glass of wine. Wine was good – it broke down barriers. He wanted to make her talk.

'I didn't know you went to services,' he said, looking at her prayer-book. 'And what do you think of it?'

She looked at it too. Then she tapped it with her fork. 'What do *they* think of it, Martin?' she asked. 'The woman praying and the man with a long white beard?'

'Much what Crosby thinks when she comes to see me,' he said. He thought of the old woman standing at the door of his room with the pyjama jacket over her arm, and the devout look on her face.

'I'm Crosby's God,' he said, helping her to brussels sprouts.

'Crosby's God! Almighty, all-powerful Mr Martin!' She laughed.

She raised her glass to him. Was she laughing at him? he wondered. He hoped she did not think him very old. 'You remember Crosby, don't you?' he said. 'She's retired, and her dog's dead.'

'Retired and her dog's dead?' she repeated. She looked again over her shoulder. Conversation in a restaurant was impossible; it was broken into little fragments. City men in their neat striped suits and bowler hats were brushing past them all the time.

'It's a fine church,' she said, turning round. She had hopped back to St Paul's, he supposed.

'Magnificent,' he replied. 'Were you looking at the monuments?'

Somebody had come in whom he recognised: Erridge, the stock-broker. He raised a finger and beckoned. Martin rose and went to speak to him. When he came back she had filled her glass again. She was sitting there, looking at the people, as if she were a child that he had taken to a pantomime.

'And what are you doing this afternoon?' he asked.

'The Round Pond at four,' she said. She drummed on the table, 'The Round Pond at four.' Now she had passed, he guessed, into the drowsy benevolence which waits on a good dinner and a glass of wine.

'Meeting somebody?' he asked.

'Yes. Maggie,' she said.

They ate in silence. Fragments of other people's talk reached them in broken sentences. Then the man to whom Martin had spoken touched him on the shoulder as he went out.

'Wednesday at eight,' he said.

'Right you are,' said Martin. He made a note in his pocket-book.

'And what are you doing this afternoon?' she asked.

'Ought to see my sister in prison,' he said, lighting a cigarette.

'In prison?' she asked.

'Rose. For throwing a brick,' he said.

'Red Rose, tawny Rose,' she began, reaching out her hand for the wine again, 'wild Rose, thorny Rose – '

'No,' he said, putting his hand over the mouth of the bottle, 'you've had enough.' A little excited her. He must damp her excitement. There were people listening. 'A damned unpleasant thing,' he said, 'being in prison.'

She drew back her glass and sat gazing at it, as if the engine of the brain were suddenly cut off. She was very like her mother – except when she laughed.

He would have liked to talk to her about her mother. But it was impossible to talk. Too many people were listening, and they were smoking. Smoke mixed with the smell of meat made the air heavy. He was thinking of the past when she exclaimed: 'Sitting on a three-legged stool having meat crammed down her throat!'[41]

He roused himself. She was thinking of Rose, was she?

'Crash came a brick!' she laughed, flourishing her fork.

' "Roll up the map of Europe," said the man to the flunkey. "I don't believe in force"!' She brought down her fork. A plum-stone jumped. Martin looked round. People were listening. He got up.

'Shall we go?' he said, ' – if you've had enough?'

She got up and looked for her cloak.

'Well, I've enjoyed it,' she said, taking her cloak. 'Thanks, Martin, for my good lunch.'

He beckoned to the waiter who came with alacrity and totted up the bill. Martin laid a sovereign on the plate. Sara began to thrust her arms into the sleeves of her cloak.

'Shall I come with you,' he said, helping her, 'to the Round Pond at four?'

'Yes!' she said, spinning round on her heel. 'To the Round Pond at four!'

She walked off, a little unsteadily he observed, past the City men who were still eating.

Here the waiter came up with the change and Martin began to slip it in his pocket. He kept back one coin for the tip. But as he was about to give it, he was struck by something shifty in Alfred's expression. He flicked up the flap of the bill; a two-shilling piece lay beneath. It was the usual trick. He lost his temper.

'What's this?' he said angrily.

'Didn't know it was there, sir,' the waiter stammered.

Martin felt his blood rise to his ears. He felt exactly like his father in a rage; as if he had white spots above his temples. He pocketed the coin that he had been going to give the waiter; and marched past him, brushing aside his hand. The man slunk back with a murmur.

'Let's be off,' he said, hustling Sara along the crowded room. 'Let's get out of this.'

He hurried her into the street. The fug, the warm meaty smell of the City chop-house, had suddenly become intolerable.

'How I hate being cheated!' he said as he put on his hat. 'Sorry, Sara,' he apologised. 'I oughtn't to have taken you there. It's a beastly hole.'

He drew in a breath of fresh air. The street noises, the unconcerned, businesslike look of things, were refreshing after the hot steamy room. There were the carts waiting, drawn up along the street; and the packages sliding down into them from the warehouses. Again they came out in front of St Paul's. He looked up. There was the same old man still feeding the sparrows. And there was the cathedral. He wished he could feel again the sense of weights changing in his body and coming to a stop; but the queer thrill of some correspondence between his own body and the stone no longer came to him. He felt nothing except anger. Also, Sara distracted him. She was about to cross the crowded road. He put out his hand to stop her. 'Take care,' he said. Then they crossed.

'Shall we walk?' he asked. She nodded. They began to walk along Fleet Street. Conversation was impossible. The pavement was so narrow that he had to step on and off in order to keep beside her. He still felt the discomfort of anger, but the anger itself was cooling. What ought I to have done? he thought, seeing himself brush past the waiter without giving him a tip. Not that; he thought, no, not that. People pressing against him made him step off the pavement. After all, the poor devil had to make a living. He liked being generous: he liked to leave people smiling; and two shillings meant nothing to him. But what's the use, he thought, now it's done? He began to hum his little song – and then stopped, remembering that he was with someone.

'Look at that, Sal,' he said, clutching at her arm. 'Look at that!'

He pointed at the splayed-out figure at Temple Bar; it looked as ridiculous as usual – something between a serpent and a fowl.

'Look at that!' he repeated laughing. They paused for a moment to look at the little flattened figures lodged so uncomfortably against the pediment of Temple Bar: Queen Victoria; King Edward. Then they walked on. It was impossible to talk because of the crowd. Men in wigs and gowns hurried across the street; some carried red bags, others blue bags.

'The Law Courts,' he said, pointing at the cold mass of decorated stone. It looked very gloomy and funereal, ' . . . where Morris spends his time,' he said aloud.

He still felt uncomfortable at having lost his temper. But the feeling was passing. Only a little ridge of roughness remained in his mind.

'D'you think I ought to have been . . . ' he began, a barrister he meant; but also: ought I to have done that – lost his temper with the waiter.

'Ought to have been – ought to have done?' she asked, bending towards him. She had not caught his meaning in the roar of the traffic. It was impossible to talk; but at any rate the feeling that he had lost his temper was diminishing. That little sting was being successfully smoothed over. Then back it came because he saw a beggar selling violets. And that poor devil, he thought, had to go without his tip because he cheated me . . . He fixed his eyes on a pillar-box. Then he looked at a car. It was odd how soon one got used to cars without horses, he thought. They used to look ridiculous. They passed the woman selling violets. She wore a hat over her face. He dropped a sixpence in her tray to make amends to the waiter. He shook his head. No violets, he meant; and indeed they were faded. But he caught sight of her face. She had no nose; her face was seamed with white patches; there were red rims for nostrils. She had no nose – she had pulled her hat down to hide that fact.

'Let's cross,' he said, abruptly. He took Sara's arm and made her cross between the omnibuses. She must have seen such sights often; he had, often; but not together – that made a difference. He hurried her on to the farther pavement.

'We'll get a bus,' he said. 'Come along.'

He took her by the elbow to make her step out briskly. But it was impossible: a cart blocked the way; there were people passing. They were approaching Charing Cross. It was like the piers of a bridge: men and women were sucked in instead of water. They had to stop. Newspaper boys held placards against their legs. Men were buying papers: some loitered; others snatched them. Martin bought one and held it in his hand.

'We'll wait here,' he said. 'The bus'll come.' An old straw hat with a purple ribbon round it, he thought opening his paper. The sight persisted. He looked up. The station clock's always fast, he assured a man who was hurrying to catch a train. Always fast, he said to himself as he opened the paper. But there was no clock. He turned to read the news from Ireland.[42] Omnibus after omnibus stopped, then swooped off again. It was difficult to concentrate on the news from Ireland; he looked up.

'This is ours,' he said, as the right bus came. They climbed on top and sat side by side overlooking the driver.

'Two to Hyde Park Corner,' he said, producing a handful of silver, and looked through the pages of the evening paper; but it was only an early edition.

'Nothing in it,' he said, stuffing the paper under the seat. 'And now – ' he began, filling his pipe. They were running smoothly down the incline of Piccadilly. ' – where my old father used to sit,' he broke off, waving his pipe at club windows. ' . . . and now – ' he lit a match, ' – and now, Sally, you can say whatever you like. Nobody's listening. Say something,' he added, throwing his match overboard, 'very profound.'

He turned to her. He wanted her to speak. Down they dipped; up they swooped again. He wanted her to speak; or he must speak himself. And what could he say? He had buried his feeling. But some emotion remained. He wanted her to speak it: but she was silent. No, he thought, biting the stem of his pipe. I won't say it. If I did she'd think me . . .

He looked at her. The sun was blazing on the windows of St George's Hospital. She was looking at it with rapture. But why with rapture? he wondered, as the bus stopped and they got down.

The scene since the morning had changed slightly. Clocks in the distance were just striking three. There were more cars; more women in pale summer dresses; more men in tail-coats and grey top-hats. The procession through the gates into the park was beginning. Everyone looked festive. Even the little dressmakers' apprentices with band-boxes looked as if they were taking part in some ceremonial. Green chairs were drawn up at the edge of the Row.[43] They were full of people looking about them as if they had taken seats at a play. Riders cantered to the end of the Row; pulled up their horses; turned and cantered the other way. The wind, coming from the west, moved white clouds grained with gold across the sky. The windows of Park Lane shone with blue and gold reflections.

Martin stepped out briskly.

'Come along,' he said; 'come – come!' He walked on. I'm young, he thought; I'm in the prime of life. There was a tang of earth in the air; even in the park there was some faint smell of spring, of the country.

'How I like – ' he said aloud. He looked round. He had spoken to the empty air. Sara had lagged behind; there she was, tying her shoelace. But he felt as if he had missed a step going downstairs.

'What a fool one feels when one talks aloud to oneself,' he said as she came up.

She pointed. 'But look,' she said, 'they all do it.'

A middle-aged woman was coming towards them. She was talking to herself. Her lips moved; she was gesticulating with her hand.

'It's the spring,' he said, as she passed them.

'No. Once in winter I came here,' she said, 'and there was a negro, laughing aloud in the snow.'

'In the snow,' said Martin. 'A negro.' The sun was bright on the grass; they were passing a bed in which the many-coloured hyacinths were curled and glossy.

'Don't let's think of the snow,' he said. 'Let's think – ' A young woman was wheeling a perambulator; a sudden thought came into his head. 'Maggie,' he said. 'Tell me. I haven't seen her since her baby was born. And I've never met the Frenchman – what d'you call him? – René?'

'Renny,' she said. She was still under the influence of the wine; of the wandering airs; of the people passing. He too felt the same distraction; but he wanted to end it.

'Yes. What's he like, this man René; Renny?'

He pronounced the word first in the French way; then, as she did, in the English. He wanted to wake her. He took her arm.

'Renny!' Sara repeated. She threw her head back and laughed. 'Let me see,' she said. 'He wears a red tie with white spots. And has dark eyes. And he takes an orange – suppose we're at dinner, and says, looking straight at you, "This orange, Sara – " ' She rolled her r's. She paused.

'There's another person talking to himself,' she broke off. A young man came past them in a closely buttoned-up coat as if he had no shirt. He was muttering as he walked. He scowled at them as he passed them.

'But Renny?' said Martin. 'We were talking about Renny,' he reminded her. 'He takes an orange – '

' . . . and pours himself out a glass of wine,' she resumed. ' "Science is the religion of the future!" '[44] she exclaimed, waving her hand as if she held a glass of wine.

'Of wine?' said Martin. Half listening, he had visualised an earnest French professor – a little picture to which now he must add inappropriately a glass of wine.

'Yes, wine,' she repeated. 'His father was a merchant,' she continued. 'A man with a black beard; a merchant at Bordeaux. And one day,' she continued, 'when he was a little boy, playing in the garden, there was a tap on the window. "Don't make so much noise. Play farther away," said a woman in a white cap. His mother was dead . . . And he was afraid to tell his father that the horse was too big to ride . . . and they sent him to England . . . '

She was skipping over railings.

'And then what happened?' said Martin, joining her. 'They became engaged?'

She was silent. He waited for her to explain – why they had married – Maggie and Renny. He waited, but she said no more. Well, she married him and they're happy he thought. He was jealous for a moment. The park was full of couples walking together. Everything seemed fresh and full of sweetness. The air puffed soft in their faces. It was laden with murmurs; with the stir of branches; the rush of wheels; dogs barking, and now and again the intermittent song of a thrush.

Here a lady passed them, talking to herself. As they looked at her she turned and whistled, as if to her dog. But the dog she had whistled was another person's dog. It bounded off in the opposite direction. The lady hurried on pursing her lips together.

'People don't like being looked at,' said Sara, 'when they're talking to themselves.'

Martin roused himself. 'Look here,' he said. 'We've gone the wrong way.'

Voices floated out to them.

They had been walking in the wrong direction. They were near the bald rubbed space where the speakers congregate. Meetings were in full swing. Groups had gathered round the different orators. Mounted on their platforms, or sometimes only on boxes, the speakers were holding forth. The voices became louder, louder and louder as they approached.

'Let's listen,' said Martin. A thin man was leaning forward holding a slate in his hand. They could hear him say, 'Ladies and gentlemen . . . ' They stopped in front of him. 'Fix your eyes on me,' he said. They fixed their eyes on him. 'Don't be afraid,' he said, crooking his finger. He had an ingratiating manner. He turned his slate over. 'Do I look like a Jew?' he asked. Then he turned his slate and looked on the other side. And they heard him say that his mother was born in Bermondsey, as they strolled on, and his father in the Isle of – The voice died away.

'What about this chap?' said Martin. Here was a large man, banging on the rail of his platform.

'Fellow citizens!' he was shouting. They stopped. The crowd of loafers, errand-boys and nursemaids gaped up at him with their mouths falling open and their eyes gazing blankly. His hand raked in the line of cars that was passing with a superb gesture of scorn. His shirt appeared under his waistcoat.

'Joostice and liberty,' said Martin, repeating his words, as the fist thumped on the railing. They waited. Then it all came over again.

'But he's a jolly good speaker,' said Martin, turning. The voice died away. 'And now, what's the old lady saying?' They strolled on.

The old lady's audience was extremely small. Her voice was hardly audible. She held a little book in her hand and she was saying something about sparrows. But her voice tapered off into a thin frail pipe. A chorus of little boys imitated her.

They listened for a moment. Then Martin turned again. 'Come along, Sall,' he said, putting his hand on her shoulder.

The voices grew fainter, fainter and fainter. Soon they ceased altogether. They strolled on across the smooth slope that rose and fell like a breadth of green cloth striped with straight brown paths in front of them. Great white dogs were gambolling; through the trees shone the waters of the Serpentine, set here and there with little boats. The urbanity of the park, the gleam of the water, the sweep and curve and composition of the scene, as if somebody had designed it, affected Martin agreeably.

'Joostice and liberty,' he said half to himself, as they came to the water's edge and stood a moment, watching the gulls cut the air into sharp white patterns with their wings.

'Did you agree with him?' he asked, taking Sara's arm to rouse her; for her lips were moving; she was talking to herself. 'That fat man,' he explained, 'who flung his arm out.'

She started. 'Oi, oi, oi!' she exclaimed, imitating his cockney accent.

Yes, thought Martin, as they walked on. Oi, oi, oi, oi, oi, oi. It's always that. There wouldn't be much justice or liberty for the likes of him if the fat man had his way – or beauty either.

'And the poor old lady whom nobody listened to?' he said, 'talking about the sparrows . . . '

He could still see in his mind's eye the thin man persuasively crooking his finger; the fat man who flung his arms out so that his braces showed;

and the little old lady who tried to make her voice heard above the cat-calls and whistles. There was a mixture of comedy and tragedy in the scene.

But they had reached the gate into Kensington Gardens. A long row of cars and carriages was drawn up by the kerb. Striped umbrellas were open over the little round tables where people were already sitting, waiting for their tea. Waitresses were hurrying in and out with trays; the season had begun. The scene was very gay.

A lady, fashionably dressed with a purple feather dipping down on one side of her hat, sat there sipping an ice. The sun dappled the table and gave her a curious look of transparency, as if she were caught in a net of light; as if she were composed of lozenges of floating colours. Martin half thought that he knew her; he half raised his hat. But she sat there looking in front of her; sipping her ice. No, he thought; he did not know her, and he stopped for a moment to light his pipe. What would the world be, he said to himself – he was still thinking of the fat man brandishing his arm – without 'I' in it? He lit the match. He looked at the flame that had become almost invisible in the sun. He stood for a second drawing at his pipe. Sara had walked on. She too was netted with floating lights from between the leaves. A primal innocence seemed to brood over the scene. The birds made a fitful sweet chirping in the branches; the roar of London encircled the open space in a ring of distant but complete sound. The pink and white chestnut blossoms rode up and down as the branches moved in the breeze. The sun dappling the leaves gave everything a curious look of insubstantiality as if it were broken into separate points of light. He too, himself, seemed dispersed. His mind for a moment was a blank. Then he roused himself, threw away his match, and caught up Sally.

'Come along!' he said. 'Come along . . . The Round Pond at four!'

They walked on arm in arm in silence, down the long avenue with the palace and the phantom church at the end of its vista. The size of the human figure seemed to have shrunk. Instead of full-grown people, children were now in the majority. Dogs of all sorts abounded. The air was full of barking and sudden shrill cries. Coveys of nursemaids pushed perambulators along the paths. Babies lay fast asleep in them like images of faintly tinted wax; their perfectly smooth eyelids fitted over their eyes as if they sealed them completely. He looked down; he liked children. Sally had looked like that the first time he saw her, asleep in her perambulator in the hall in Browne Street.

He stopped short. They had reached the pond.

'Where's Maggie?' he said. 'There – is that her?' He pointed to a young woman who was lifting a baby out of its perambulator under a tree.

'Where?' said Sara. She looked in the wrong direction.

He pointed. 'There, under that tree.'

'Yes,' she said, 'that's Maggie.'

They walked in that direction.

'But is it?' said Martin. He was suddenly doubtful; for she had the unconsciousness of a person who is unaware that she is being looked at. It made her unfamiliar. With one hand she held the child; with the other she arranged the pillows of the perambulator. She too was dappled with lozenges of floating light.

'Yes,' he said, noticing something about her gesture, 'that's Maggie.' She turned and saw them.

She held up her hand as if to warn them to approach quietly. She put a finger to her lips. They approached silently. As they reached her, the distant sound of a clock striking was wafted on the breeze. One, two, three, four it struck . . . Then it ceased.

'We met at St Paul's,' said Martin in a whisper. He dragged up two chairs and sat down. They were silent for a moment. The child was not asleep. Then Maggie bent over and looked at the child.

'You needn't talk in a whisper,' she said aloud. 'He's asleep.'

'We met at St Paul's,' Martin repeated in his ordinary voice. 'I'd been seeing my stockbroker.' He took off his hat and laid it on the grass. 'And when I came out,' he resumed, 'there was Sally . . . ' He looked at her. She had never told him, he remembered, what it was that she was thinking, as she stood there, with her lips moving, on the steps of St Paul's.

Now she was yawning. Instead of taking the little hard green chair which he had pulled up for her, she had thrown herself down on the grass. She had folded herself like a grasshopper with her back against the tree. The prayer-book, with its red and gold leaves, was lying on the ground tented over with trembling blades of grass. She yawned; she stretched. She was already half asleep.

He drew his chair beside Maggie's; and looked at the scene in front of them.

It was admirably composed. There was the white figure of Queen Victoria[45] against a green bank; beyond, was the red brick of the old palace; the phantom church raised its spire; and the Round Pond made a pool of blue. A race of yachts was going forward. The boats leant on their sides so that the sails touched the water. There was a nice little breeze.

'And what did you talk about?' said Maggie.

Martin could not remember. 'She was tipsy,' he said, pointing to Sara. 'And now she's going to sleep.' He felt sleepy himself. The sun for the first time was almost hot on his head.

Then he answered her question.

'The whole world,' he said. 'Politics; religion; morality.' He yawned. Gulls were screaming as they rose and sank over a lady who was feeding them. Maggie was watching them. He looked at her.

'I haven't seen you,' he said, 'since your baby was born.' It's changed her, having a child, he thought. It's improved her, he thought. But she was watching the gulls; the lady had thrown a handful of fish. The gulls swooped round and round her head.

'D'you like having a child?' he said.

'Yes,' she said, rousing herself to answer him. 'It's a tie though.'

'But it's nice having ties, isn't it?' he enquired. He was fond of children. He looked at the sleeping baby with its eyes sealed and its thumb in its mouth.

'D'you want them?' she asked.

'Just what I was asking myself,' he said, 'before – '

Here Sara made a click at the back of her throat; he dropped his voice to a whisper. 'Before I met her at St Paul's,' he said. They were silent. The baby was asleep; Sara was asleep; the presence of the two sleepers seemed to enclose them in a circle of privacy. Two of the racing yachts were coming together as if they must collide; but one passed just ahead of the other. Martin watched them. Life had resumed its ordinary proportions. Everything once more was back in its place. The boats were sailing; the men walking; the little boys dabbled in the pond for minnows; the waters of the pond rippled bright blue. Everything was full of the stir, the potency, the fecundity of spring.

Suddenly he said aloud: 'Possessiveness is the devil.'

Maggie looked at him. Did he mean herself – herself and the baby? No. There was a tone in his voice that told her he was thinking not of her.

'What are you thinking?' she asked.

'About the woman I'm in love with,' he said. 'Love ought to stop on both sides, don't you think, simultaneously?' He spoke without any stress on the words, so as not to wake the sleepers. 'But it won't – that's the devil,' he added in the same undertone.

'Bored, are you?' she murmured.

'Stiff,' he said. 'Bored stiff.' He stooped and disinterred a pebble in the grass.

'And jealous?' she murmured. Her voice was very low and soft.

'Horribly,' he whispered. It was true, now that she referred to it.

Here the baby half woke and stretched out its hand. Maggie rocked the perambulator. Sara stirred. Their privacy was imperilled. It would be destroyed at any moment, he felt; and he wanted to talk.

He glanced at the sleepers. The baby's eyes were shut, and Sara's too. Still they seemed encircled in a ring of solitude. Speaking in a low voice without accent, he told her his story; the story of the lady; how she wanted to keep him, and he wanted to be free. It was an ordinary story, but painful – mixed. As he told it, however, the sting was drawn. They sat silent, looking in front of them.

Another race was starting: men crouched at the edge of the pond, each with his stick resting on a toy boat. It was a charming scene, gay, innocent and a trifle ridiculous. The signal was given; off the boats went. And will he, Martin thought, looking at the sleeping baby, go through the same thing too? He was thinking of himself – of his jealousy.

'My father,' he said suddenly, but softly, 'had a lady . . . She called him "Bogy".' And he told her the story of the lady who kept a boarding-house at Putney – the very respectable lady, grown stout, who wanted help with her roof. Maggie laughed, but very gently, so as not to wake the sleepers. Both were still sleeping soundly.

'Was he in love,' Martin asked her, 'with your mother?'

She was looking at the gulls, cutting patterns on the blue distance with their wings. His question seemed to sink through what she was seeing; then suddenly it reached her.

'Are we brother and sister?' she asked; and laughed out loud. The child opened its eyes, and uncurled its fingers.

'We've woken him,' said Martin. He began to cry. Maggie had to soothe him. Their privacy was over. The child cried; and the clocks began striking. The sound came wafted gently towards them on the breeze. One, two, three, four, five . . .

'It's time to go,' said Maggie, as the last stroke died away. She laid the baby back on its pillow, and turned. Sara was still asleep. She lay crumpled up with her back to the tree. Martin stooped and threw a twig at her. She opened her eyes but shut them again.

'No, no,' she protested, stretching her arms over her head.

'It's time,' said Maggie.

She pulled herself up. 'Time is it?' she sighed. 'How strange . . . !' she murmured. She sat up and rubbed her eyes.

'Martin!' she exclaimed. She looked at him as he stood over her in his blue suit holding his stick in his hand. She looked at him as if she were bringing him back to the field of vision. 'Martin!' she said again.

'Yes, Martin!' he replied. 'Did you hear what we've been saying?' he asked her.

'Voices,' she yawned, shaking her head. 'Only voices.'

He paused for a moment, looking down at her. 'Well, I'm off,' he said, taking up his hat, 'to dine with a cousin in Grosvenor Square,' he added. He turned and left them.

He looked back at them after he had gone a little distance. They were still sitting by the perambulator under the trees. He walked on. Then he looked back again. The ground sloped, and the trees were hidden. A very stout lady was being tugged along the path by a small dog on a chain. He could see them no longer.

The sun was setting as he drove across the park an hour or two later. He was thinking that he had forgotten something; but what, he did not know. Scene passed over scene; one obliterated another. Now he was crossing the bridge over the Serpentine. The water glowed with sunset light; twisted poles of lamplight lay on the water, and there, at the end, the white bridge composed the scene. The cab entered the shadow of the trees, and joined the long line of cabs that was streaming towards the Marble Arch. People in evening dress were going to plays and parties. The light became yellower and yellower. The road was beaten to a metallic silver. Everything looked festive.

But I'm going to be late, he thought, for the cab was held up in a block by the Marble Arch. He looked at his watch – it was just on eight-thirty. But eight-thirty means eight-forty-five he thought, as the cab moved on. Indeed as it turned into the square there was a car at the door, and a man getting out. So I'm just on time, he thought, and paid the driver.

The door opened almost before he touched the bell, as if he had trod on a spring. The door opened and two footmen started forward to take his things directly he entered the black-and-white-paved hall. He followed another man up the imposing staircase of white marble, sweeping in a curve. A succession of large, dark pictures hung on the wall, and at the top outside the door was a yellow-and-blue picture of Venetian palaces and pale green canals.

'Canaletto[46] or the school of?' he thought, pausing to let the other man precede him. Then he gave his name to the footman.

'Captain Pargiter,' the man boomed out; and there was Kitty standing at the door. She was formal; fashionable; with a dash of red on her lips. She gave him her hand; but he moved on for other guests were arriving.

'A saloon?' he said to himself, for the room with its chandeliers, yellow panels, and sofas and chairs dotted about had the air of a grandiose waiting-room. Seven or eight people were already there. It's not going to work this time, he said to himself as he chatted with his host, who had been racing. His face shone as if it had only that moment been taken out of the sun. One almost expected, Martin thought, as he stood talking, to see a pair of glasses slung round his shoulders, just as there was a red mark across his forehead where his hat had been. No, it's not going to work, Martin thought as they talked about horses. He heard a paper-boy calling in the street below, and the hooting of horns. He preserved clearly his sense of the identity of different objects, and their differences. When a party worked all things, all sounds merged into one. He looked at an old lady with a wedge-shaped stone-coloured face sitting ensconced on a sofa. He glanced at Kitty's portrait by a fashionable portrait painter as he chatted, standing first on this foot, then on that, to the grizzled man with the bloodhound eyes and the urbane manner whom Kitty had married instead of Edward. Then she came up and introduced him to a girl all in white who was standing alone with her hand on the back of a chair.

'Miss Ann Hillier,' she said. 'My cousin, Captain Pargiter.'

She stood for a moment beside them as if to facilitate their introduction. But she was a little stiff always; she did nothing but flick her fan up and down.

'Been to the races, Kitty?' Martin said, because he knew that she hated racing, and he always felt a wish to tease her.

'I? No; I don't go to races,' she replied rather shortly. She turned away because somebody else had come in – a man in gold lace, with a star.

I should have been better off, Martin thought, reading my book.

'Have you been to the races?' he said aloud to the girl whom he was to take down to dinner. She shook her head. She had white arms; a white dress; and a pearl necklace. Purely virginal, he said to himself; and only an hour ago I was lying stark naked in my bath in Ebury Street, he thought.

'I've been watching polo,' she said. He looked down at his shoes, and noticed that they had creases across them; they were old; he had meant to buy a new pair, but had forgotten. That was what he had forgotten, he thought, seeing himself again in the cab, crossing the bridge over the Serpentine.

But they were going down to dinner. He gave her his arm. As they went down the stairs, and he watched the ladies' dresses in front of them trail from step to step, he thought, What on earth am I going to say to her? Then they crossed the black and white squares and went into the dining-room. It was harmoniously shrouded; pictures with hooded bars of light under them shone out; and the dinner table glowed; but no light shone directly on their faces. If this doesn't work, he thought, looking at the portrait of a nobleman with a crimson cloak and a star that hung luminous in front of him, I'll never do it again. Then he braced himself to talk to the virginal girl who sat beside him. But he had to reject almost everything that occurred to him – she was so young.

'I've thought of three subjects to talk about,' he began straight off, without thinking how the sentence was to end. 'Racing; the Russian ballet; and' – he hesitated for a moment – 'Ireland. Which interests you?' He unfolded his napkin.

'Please,' she said, bending slightly towards him, 'say that again.'

He laughed. She had a charming way of putting her head on one side and bending towards him.

'Don't let's talk of any of them,' he said. 'Let's talk of something interesting. Do you enjoy parties?' he asked her.

She was dipping her spoon in her soup. She looked up at him as she lifted it with eyes that seemed like bright stones under a film of water. They're like drops of glass under water, he thought. She was extra-ordinarily pretty.

'But I've only been to three parties in my life!' she said. She gave a charming little laugh.

'You don't say so!' he exclaimed. 'This is the third, then; or is it the fourth?'

He listened to the sounds in the street. He could just hear the cars hooting; but they had gone far away; they made a continuous rushing noise. It was beginning to work. He held out his glass. He would like her to say, he thought, as his glass was filled, 'What a charming man I sat next!' when she went to bed that night.

'This is my third *real* party,' she said, stressing the word 'real' in a way that seemed to him slightly pathetic. She must have been in the nursery three months ago, he thought, eating bread and butter.

'And I was thinking as I shaved,' he said, 'that I would never go to a party again.' It was true; he had seen a hole in the bookcase. Who's taken my life of Wren? he had thought, holding his razor out; and had wanted to stay and read, alone. But now – what little piece of his vast experience could he break off and give to her, he wondered?

'Do you live in London?' she asked.

'Ebury Street,' he told her. And she knew Ebury Street, because it was on the way to Victoria; she often went to Victoria, because they had a house in Sussex.

'And now tell me,' he said, feeling that they had broken the ice – when she turned her head to answer some remark of the man on the other side. He was annoyed. The whole fabric that he had been building, like a game of spillikins in which one frail little bone is hooked on top of another, was dashed to the ground. Ann was talking as if she had known the other man all her life; he had hair that looked as if a rake had been drawn through it; he was very young. Martin sat silent. He looked at the great portrait opposite. A footman was standing beneath it; a row of decanters obscured the folds of the cloak on the floor. That's the third earl, or the fourth? he asked himself. He knew his eighteenth century; it was the fourth earl who had made the great marriage. But after all, he thought, looking at Kitty at the head of the table, the Rigbys are a better family than they are. He smiled; he checked himself. I only think of 'better families' when I dine in this sort of place, he thought. He looked at another picture: a lady in sea green; the famous Gainsborough. But here Lady Margaret, the woman on his left, turned to him.

'I'm sure you'll agree with me,' she said, 'Captain Pargiter' – he noticed that she swept her eyes over the name on his card before she spoke it, although they had met often before – 'that it's a devilish thing to have done?'

She spoke so pouncingly that the fork she held upright seemed like a weapon with which she was about to pinion him. He threw himself into their conversation. It was about politics of course, about Ireland. 'Tell me – what's your opinion?' she asked, with her fork poised. For a moment he had the illusion that he too was behind the scenes. The screen was down; the lights were up; and he too was behind the scenes. It was an illusion of course; they were only throwing him scraps from their larder; but it was an agreeable sensation while it lasted. He listened. Now she was holding forth to a distinguished old man at the end of the table. He watched him. He had let down a mask of infinitely wise tolerance over his face as she harangued them. He was arranging three crusts of bread by the side of his plate as if he were playing a mysterious little game of profound significance. 'So,' he seemed to be saying. 'So,' as if they were fragments of human destiny, not crusts, that he held in his fingers. The mask might conceal anything – or nothing? Anyhow it was a mask of great distinction. But here Lady Margaret pinioned him too with her fork; and he raised his eyebrows and moved one of the crusts a little to one side before he spoke. Martin leant forward to listen.

'When I was in Ireland,' he began, 'in 1880 . . . ' He spoke very simply; he was offering them a memory; he told his story perfectly; it held its meaning without spilling a single drop. And he had played a great part. Martin listened attentively. Yes, it was absorbing. Here we are, he thought, going on and on and on . . . He leant forward trying to catch every word. But he was conscious of some interruption; Ann had turned to him.

'Do tell me' – she was asking him – 'who *he* is?' She bent her head to the right. She was under the impression that he knew everybody, apparently. He was flattered. He looked along the table. Who was it? Somebody he had met; somebody, he guessed, who was not quite at his ease.

'I know him,' he said. 'I know him – ' He had a rather white, fat face; he was talking away at a great rate. And the young married woman to whom he was talking was saying, 'I see; I see,' with little nods of her head. But there was a slight look of strain on her face. You needn't put yourself to all that trouble, my good fellow, Martin felt inclined to say to him. She doesn't understand a word you're saying.

'I can't put a name to him,' he said aloud. 'But I've met him – let me see – where? In Oxford or Cambridge?'

A faint look of amusement came into Ann's eyes. She had spotted the difference. She coupled them together. They were not her world – no.

'Have you seen the Russian dancers?' she was saying. She had been there with her young man, it seemed. And what's your world, Martin thought, as she rapped out her slender stock of adjectives – 'heavenly', 'amazing', 'marvellous', and so on. Is it 'the' world? he mused. He looked down the table. Anyhow no other world had a chance against it, he thought. And it's a good world too, he added: large; generous; hospitable. And very nice-looking. He glanced from face to face. Dinner was drawing to an end. They all looked as if they had been rubbed with wash leather, like precious stones; yet the bloom seemed ingrained; it went through the stone. And the stone was clear-cut; there was no blur, no indecision. Here a footman's white-gloved hand removing dishes knocked over a glass of wine. A red splash trickled on to the lady's dress. But she did not move a muscle; she went on talking. Then she straightened the clean napkin that had been brought her, nonchalantly, over the stain.

That's what I like, Martin thought. He admired that. She would have blown her nose on her fingers like an applewoman if she wanted to, he thought. But Ann was talking.

'And when he gives that leap!' she exclaimed – she raised her hand with a lovely gesture in the air – 'and then comes down!' She let her hand fall in her lap.

'Marvellous!' Martin agreed. He had got the very accent, he thought; he had got it from the young man whose hair looked as if a rake had gone through it.

'Yes: Nijinsky's[47] marvellous,' he agreed. 'Marvellous,' he repeated.

'And my aunt has asked me to meet him at a party,' said Ann.

'Your aunt?' he said aloud.

She mentioned a well-known name.

'Oh, she's your aunt, is she?' he said. He placed her. So *that* was her world. He wanted to ask her – for he found her charming in her youth, her simplicity – but it was too late. Ann was rising.

'I hope – ' he began. She bent her head towards him as if she longed to stay, catch his last word, his least word; but could not, since Lady Lasswade had risen; and it was time for her to go.

Lady Lasswade had risen; everybody rose. All the pink, grey, sea-coloured dresses lengthened themselves, and for a moment the tall women standing by the table looked like the famous Gainsborough hanging on the wall. The table, strewn with napkins and wine-glasses, had a derelict air as they left it. For a moment the ladies clustered at the door; then the little old woman in black hobbled past them with remarkable dignity; and Kitty, coming last, put her arm round Ann's shoulder and led her out. The door shut on the ladies.

Kitty paused for a moment.

'I hope you liked my old cousin?' she said to Ann as they walked upstairs together. She put her hand to her dress and straightened something as they passed a looking-glass.

'I thought him charming!' Ann exclaimed. 'And what a lovely tree!' She spoke of Martin and the tree in exactly the same tone. They paused for a moment to look at a tree that was covered with pink blossoms in a china tub standing at the door. Some of the flowers were fully out; others were still unopened. As they looked a petal dropped.

'It's cruel to keep it here,' said Kitty, 'in this hot air.'

They went in. While they dined the servants had opened the folding doors and lit lights in a further room so that it seemed as if they came into another room freshly made ready for them. There was a great fire blazing between two stately fire-dogs; but it seemed cordial and decorative rather than hot. Two or three of the ladies stood before it, opening and shutting their fingers as they spread them to the blaze; but they turned to make room for their hostess.

'How I love that picture of you, Kitty!' said Mrs Aislabie, looking up at the portrait of Lady Lasswade as a young woman. Her hair had been very red in those days; she was toying with a basket of roses. Fiery but tender, she looked, emerging from a cloud of white muslin.

Kitty glanced at it and then turned away.

'One never likes one's own picture,' she said.

'But it's the image of you!' said another lady.

'Not now,' said Kitty, laughing off the compliment rather awkwardly. Always after dinner women paid each other compliments about their clothes or their looks, she thought. She did not like being alone with women after dinner; it made her shy. She stood there, upright among them, while footmen went round with trays of coffee.

'By the way, I hope the wine – ' she paused and helped herself to coffee, 'the wine didn't stain your frock, Cynthia?' she said to the young married woman who had taken the disaster so coolly.

'And such a lovely frock,' said Lady Margaret, fondling the folds of golden satin between her finger and thumb.

'D'you like it?' said the young woman.

'It's perfectly lovely! I've been looking at it the whole evening!' said Mrs Treyer, an Oriental-looking woman, with a feather floating back from her head in harmony with her nose, which was Jewish.

Kitty looked at them admiring the lovely frock. Eleanor would have found herself out of it, she thought. She had refused her invitation to dinner. That annoyed her.

'Do tell me,' Lady Cynthia interrupted, 'who was the man I sat next? One always meets such interesting people at your house,' she added.

'The man you sat next?' said Kitty. She considered a moment. 'Tony Ashton,' she said.

'Is that the man who's been lecturing on French poetry at Mortimer House?' chimed in Mrs Aislabie. 'I longed to go to those lectures. I heard they were wonderfully interesting.'

'Mildred went,' said Mrs Treyer.

'Why should we all stand?' said Kitty. She made a movement with her hands towards the seats. She did things like that so abruptly that they called her, behind her back, 'The Grenadier'. They all moved this way and that, and she herself, after seeing how the couples sorted themselves, sat down by old Aunt Warburton, who was enthroned in the great chair.

'Tell me about my delightful godson,' the old lady began. She meant Kitty's second son, who was with the fleet at Malta.

'He's at Malta – ' she began. She sat down on a low chair and began answering her questions. But the fire was too hot for Aunt Warburton. She raised her knobbed old hand.

'Priestley wants to roast us all alive,' said Kitty. She got up and went to the window. The ladies smiled as she strode across the room and jerked down the top of the long window. Just for a moment, as the curtains hung apart, she looked at the square outside. There was a spatter of leaf-shadow and lamplight on the pavement; the usual police-man was balancing himself as he patrolled; the usual little men and women, foreshortened from this height, hurried along by the railings. So she saw them hurrying, the other way, when she brushed her teeth in the morning. Then she came back and sat down on a low stool beside old Aunt Warburton. The worldly old woman was honest, in her way.

'And the little red-haired ruffian whom I love?' she asked. He was her favourite; the little boy at Eton.

'He's been in trouble,' said Kitty. 'He's been swished.' She smiled. He was her favourite too.

The old lady grinned. She liked boys who got into trouble. She had a wedge-shaped yellow face with an occasional bristle on her chin; she was over eighty; but she sat as if she were riding a hunter, Kitty thought, glancing at her hands. They were coarse hands, with big finger-joints; red and white sparks flashed from her rings as she moved them.

'And you, my dear,' said the old lady, looking at her shrewdly under her bushy eyebrows, 'busy as usual?'

'Yes. Much as usual,' said Kitty, evading the shrewd old eyes; for she did things on the sly that they – the ladies over there – did not approve.

They were chattering together. Yet animated as it sounded, to Kitty's ear the talk lacked substance. It was battledore and shuttlecock talk, to be kept going until the door opened and the gentlemen came in. Then it would stop. They were talking about a by-election. She could hear Lady Margaret telling some story that was rather coarse presumably, in the eighteenth-century way, since she dropped her voice.

' – turned her upside down and slapped her,' she could hear her say. There was a twitter of laughter.

'I'm so delighted he got in in spite of them,' said Mrs Treyer. They dropped their voices.

'I'm a tiresome old woman,' said Aunt Warburton, raising one of her knobbed hands to her shoulder. 'But now I'm going to ask you to shut that window.' The draught was getting at her rheumatic joint.

Kitty strode to the window. 'Damn these women!' she said to herself. She laid hold of the long stick with a beak at the end that stood in the window and poked; but the window stuck. She would have liked to fleece them of their clothes, of their jewels, of their intrigues, of their gossip. The window went up with a jerk. There was Ann standing about with nobody to talk to.

'Come and talk to us, Ann,' she said, beckoning to her. Ann drew up a footstool and sat down at Aunt Warburton's feet. There was a pause. Old Aunt Warburton disliked young girls; but they had relations in common.

'Where's Timmy, Ann?' she asked.

'Harrow,' said Ann.

'Ah, you've always been to Harrow,' said Aunt Warburton. And then the old lady, with the beautiful breeding that simulated at least human charity, flattered the girl, likening her to her grandmother, a famous beauty.

'How I should love to have known her!' Ann exclaimed. 'Do tell me – what was she like?'

The old lady began making a selection from her memoirs; it was only a selection, an edition with asterisks; for it was a story that could hardly be told to a girl in white satin. Kitty's mind wandered. If Charles stayed much longer downstairs, she thought, glancing at the clock, she would miss her train. Could Priestley be trusted to whisper a message in his ear? She would give them another ten minutes; she turned to Aunt Warburton again.

'She must have been wonderful!' Ann was saying. She sat with her hands clasped round her knees looking up into the face of the hoary old dowager. Kitty felt a moment's pity. Her face will be like their faces, she thought, looking at the little group at the other side of the room. Their faces looked harassed, worried; their hands moved restlessly. Yet they're brave, she thought; and generous. They gave as much as they took. Had Eleanor after all any right to despise them? Had she done more with her life than Margaret Marrable? And I? she thought. And I? . . . Who's right? she thought. Who's wrong? . . . Here mercifully the door opened.

The gentlemen came in. They came in reluctantly, rather slowly, as if they had just stopped talking, and had to get their bearings in the drawing-room. They were a little flushed and still laughing, as if they had stopped in the middle of what they were saying. They filed in; and the distinguished old man moved across the room with the air of a ship making port, and all the ladies stirred without rising. The game was over; the battledores and shuttlecocks put away. They were like gulls settling on fish, Kitty thought. There was a rising and a fluttering. The great man let himself slowly down into a chair beside his old friend Lady Warburton. He put the tips of his fingers together and began, 'Well . . . ?' as if he were continuing a conversation left unfinished the night before. Yes, she thought, there was something – was it human? civilised? she could not find the word she wanted – about the old couple talking as they had talked for the past fifty years . . . They were all talking. They had all settled in to add another sentence to the story that was just ending, or in the middle, or about to begin.

But there was Tony Ashton standing by himself without a sentence to add to the story. She went up to him therefore.

'Have you seen Edward lately?' he asked her as usual.

'Yes, today,' she said. 'I lunched with him. We walked in the park . . . ' She stopped. They had walked in the park. A thrush had been singing; they had stopped to listen. 'That's the wise thrush that sings each song twice over . . . ' he had said. 'Does he?' she had asked innocently. And it had been a quotation. She had felt foolish; Oxford always made her feel foolish. She disliked Oxford; yet she respected Edward, and Tony too, she thought, looking at him. A snob on the surface; underneath a scholar . . . They had a standard . . . But she roused herself.

He would like to talk to some smart woman – Mrs Aislabie or Margaret Marrable. But they were both engaged – both were adding sentences with considerable vivacity. There was a pause. She was not a good hostess, she reflected; this sort of hitch always happened at her parties. There was Ann; Ann about to be captured by a youth she knew. But Kitty beckoned. Ann came instantly and submissively.

'Come and be introduced,' she said, 'to Mr Ashton. He's been lecturing at Mortimer House,' she explained, 'about – ' She hesitated.

'Mallarmé,' he said with his odd little squeak, as if his voice had been pinched off.

Kitty turned away. Martin came up to her.

'A very brilliant party, Lady Lasswade,' he said with his usual tiresome irony.

'This? Oh, not at all,' she said brusquely. This wasn't a party. Her parties were never brilliant. Martin was trying to tease her as usual. She looked down and saw his shabby shoes.

'Come and talk to me,' she said, feeling the old family affection return. She noticed with amusement that he was a little flushed, a little, as the nurses used to say, 'above himself'. How many 'parties' would it need, she wondered, to turn her satirical, uncompromising cousin into an obedient member of society?

'Let's sit down and talk sense,' she said, sinking on to a little sofa.

He sat down beside her.

'Tell me, what's Nell doing?' she asked.

'She sent her love,' said Martin. 'She told me to say how much she wanted to see you.'

'Then why wouldn't she come tonight?' said Kitty. She felt hurt. She could not help it.

'She hasn't the right kind of hairpin,' he said with a laugh, looking down at his shoes. Kitty looked down at them too.

'My shoes, you see, don't matter,' he said. 'But then I'm a man.'

'It's such nonsense . . . ' Kitty began. 'What does it matter . . . '

But he was looking round him at the groups of beautifully dressed women; then at the picture.

'That's a horrid daub of you over the mantelpiece,' he said, looking at the red-haired girl. 'Who did it?'

'I forget . . . Don't let's look at it,' she said. 'Let's talk . . . ' Then she stopped.

He was looking round the room. It was crowded: there were little tables with photographs; ornate cabinets with vases of flowers; and panels of yellow brocade let into the walls. She felt that he was criticising the room and herself too.

'I always want to take a knife and scrape it all off,' she said. But what's the use, she thought? If she moved a picture, 'Where's Uncle Bill on the old cob?' her husband would say, and back it had to go again.

'Like a hotel, isn't it?' she continued.

'A saloon,' he remarked. He did not know why he always wanted to hurt her; but he did; it was a fact.

'I was asking myself,' he dropped his voice, 'why have a picture like that – ' he nodded his head at the portrait – 'when they've a Gainsborough . . . '

'And why,' she dropped her voice, imitating his tone that was half sneering, half humorous, 'come and eat their food when you despise them?'

'I don't! Not a bit!' he exclaimed. 'I'm enjoying myself immensely. I like seeing you, Kitty,' he added. It was true – he always liked her. 'You haven't dropped your poor relations. That's very nice of you.'

'It's they who've dropped me,' she said.

'Oh, Eleanor,' he said. 'She's a queer old bird.'

'It's all so . . . ' Kitty began. But there was something wrong about the disposition of her party; she stopped in the middle of her sentence. 'You've got to come and talk to Mrs Treyer,' she said getting up.

Why does one do it? he wondered as he followed her. He had wanted to talk to Kitty; he had nothing to say to that Oriental-looking harpy with a pheasant's feather floating at the back of her head. Still, if you drink the good wine of the noble countess, he said bowing, you have to entertain her less desirable friends. He led her off.

Kitty went back to the fireplace. She dealt the coal a blow, and the sparks went volleying up the chimney. She was irritable; she was restless. Time was passing; if they stayed much longer she would miss her train. Surreptitiously she noted that the hands of the clock were close on eleven. The party was bound to break up soon; it was only the prelude to another party. Yet they were all talking, and talking, as if they would never go.

She glanced at the groups that seemed immovable. Then the clock chimed a succession of petulant little strokes, on the last of which the door opened and Priestley advanced. With his inscrutable butler's eyes and crooked forefinger he summoned Ann Hillier.

'That's mama fetching me,' said Ann, advancing down the room with a little flutter.

'She's taking you on?' said Kitty. She held her hand for a moment. Why? she asked herself, looking at the lovely face, empty of meaning, or character, like a page on which nothing has been written but youth. She held her hand for a moment. 'Must you go?' she said.

'I'm afraid I must,' said Ann, withdrawing her hand.

There was a general rising and movement, like the flutter of white-winged gulls.

'Coming with us?' Martin heard Ann say to the youth through whose hair the rake seemed to have been passed. They turned to leave together. As she passed Martin, who stood with his hand out, Ann gave him the least bend of her head, as if his image had been already swept from her mind. He was dashed; his feeling was out of all proportion to its object. He felt a strong desire to go with them, wherever it was. But he had not been asked; Ashton had; he was following in their wake.

'What a toady!' he thought to himself with a bitterness that surprised him. It was odd how jealous he felt for a moment. They were all 'going on', it seemed. He hung about a little awkwardly. Only the old fogies were left – no, even the great man was going on, it seemed. Only the old lady was left. She was hobbling across the room on Lasswade's arm. She wanted to confirm something that she had been saying about a miniature. Lasswade had taken it off the wall; he held it under a lamp so that she could pronounce her verdict. Was it grandpapa on the cob, or was it Uncle William?

'Sit down, Martin, and let us talk,' said Kitty. He sat down: but he had a feeling that she wanted him to go. He had seen her glance at the clock. They chatted for a moment. Now the old lady came back; she was proving, beyond a doubt, from her unexampled store of anecdotes, that it must be Uncle William on the cob; not grandpapa. She was going. But she took her time. Martin waited till she was fairly in the doorway, leaning on her nephew's arm. He hesitated; they were alone now; should he stay, or should he go? But Kitty was standing up. She was holding out her hand.

'Come again soon and see me alone,' she said. She had dismissed him, he felt.

That's what people always say, he said to himself as he made his way slowly downstairs behind Lady Warburton. Come again; but I don't know that I shall . . . Lady Warburton went downstairs like a crab, holding on to the banisters with one hand, to Lasswade's arm with the other. He lingered behind her. He looked at the Canaletto once more. A nice picture: but a copy, he said to himself. He peered over the banisters and saw the black and white slabs of the hall beneath.

It did work, he said to himself, descending step by step into the hall. Off and on; by fits and starts. But was it worth it? he asked himself, letting the footman help him into his coat. The double doors stood wide open into the street. One or two people were passing; they peered in curiously, looking at the footmen, at the bright big hall; and at the old lady who paused for a moment on the black and white squares. She was robing herself. Now she was accepting her cloak with a violet slash in it; now her furs. A bag dangled from her wrist. She was hung about with chains; her fingers were knobbed with rings. Her sharp stone-coloured face, riddled with lines and wrinkled into creases, looked out from its soft nest of fur and laces. The eyes were still bright.

The nineteenth century going to bed, Martin said to himself as he watched her hobble down the steps on the arm of her footman. She was helped into her carriage. Then he shook hands with that good fellow his host, who had had quite as much wine as was good for him, and walked off through Grosvenor Square.

Upstairs in the bedroom at the top of the house Kitty's maid Baxter was looking out of the window, watching the guests drive off. There – that was the old lady going. She wished they would hurry; if the party went on much longer her own little jaunt would be done for. She was going up the river tomorrow with her young man. She turned and looked round her. She had everything ready – her ladyship's coat, skirt, and the bag with the ticket in it. It was long past eleven. She stood at the dressing-table waiting. The three-folded mirror reflected silver pots, powder puffs, combs and brushes. Baxter stooped down and smirked at herself in the glass – that was how she would look when she went up the river – then she drew herself up; she heard footsteps in the passage. Her ladyship was coming. Here she was.

Lady Lasswade came in, slipping the rings from her fingers. 'Sorry to be so late, Baxter,' she said. 'Now I must hurry.'

Baxter, without speaking, unhooked her dress; slipped it dexterously to her feet, and bore it away. Kitty sat down at her dressing-table and kicked off her shoes. Satin shoes were always too tight. She glanced at the clock on her dressing-table. She just had time.

Baxter was handing her coat. Now she was handing her bag. 'The ticket's in there, m'lady,' she said, touching the bag.

'Now my hat,' said Kitty. She stooped to settle it in front of the mirror. The little tweed travelling-hat poised on the top of her hair made her look quite a different person; the person she liked being. She stood in her travelling-dress, wondering if she had forgotten anything. Her mind was a perfect blank for a moment. Where am I? she wondered. What am I doing? Where am I going? Her eyes fixed themselves on the dressing-table; vaguely she remembered some other room, and some other time when she was a girl. At Oxford was it?

'The ticket, Baxter?' she said perfunctorily.

'In your bag, m'lady,' Baxter reminded her. She was holding it in her hand.

'So that's everything,' said Kitty, glancing round her.

She felt a moment's compunction.

'Thanks, Baxter,' she said. 'I hope you'll enjoy your. . . ' – she hesitated; she did not know what Baxter did on her day off – ' . . . your play,' she said at a venture. Baxter gave a queer little bitten-off smile. Maids bothered Kitty with their demure politeness; with their inscrutable, pursed-up faces. But they were very useful.

'Good-night!' she said to Baxter at the door of the bedroom; for there Baxter turned back as if her responsibility for her mistress ended. Somebody else had charge of the stairs.

Kitty looked in at the drawing-room, in case her husband should be there. But the room was empty. The fire was still blazing; the chairs, drawn out in a circle, still seemed to hold the skeleton of the party in their empty arms. But the car was waiting for her at the door.

'Plenty of time?' she said to the chauffeur as he laid the rug across her knees. Off they started.

It was a clear still night and every tree in the square was visible: some were black, others were sprinkled with strange patches of green artificial light. Above the arc lamps rose shafts of darkness. Although it was close on midnight, it scarcely seemed to be night; but rather some ethereal disembodied day, for there were so many lamps in the streets; cars passing; men in white mufflers with their light overcoats open walking along the clean dry pavements, and many houses were still lit up, for everyone was giving parties. The town changed as they drew smoothly through Mayfair. The public houses were closing; here was a group clustered round a lamp-post at the corner. A drunken man was bawling out some loud song; a tipsy girl with a feather bobbing in her eyes was swaying as she clung to the lamp-post . . . but Kitty's eyes alone registered what she saw. After the talk, the effort and the hurry, she could add nothing to what she saw. And they swept on quickly. Now they had turned, and the car was gliding at full speed up a long bright avenue of great shuttered shops. The streets were almost empty. The yellow station clock showed that they had five minutes to spare.

Just in time, she said to herself. The usual exhilaration mounted in her as she walked along the platform. Diffused light poured down from a great height. Men's cries and the clangour of shunting carriages echoed in the immense vacancy. The train was waiting; travellers were making ready to start. Some were standing with one foot on the step of the carriage drinking out of thick cups as if they were afraid to go far from their seats. She looked down the length of the train and saw the engine sucking water from a hose. It seemed all body, all muscle; even the neck had been consumed into the smooth barrel of the body. This was 'the' train; the others were toys in comparison. She snuffed up the sulphurous air, which left a slight tinge of acid at the back of the throat, as if it already had a tang of the north.

The guard had seen her and was coming towards her with his whistle in his hand.

'Good-evening, m'lady,' he said.

'Good-evening, Purvis. Run it rather fine,' she said as he unlocked the door of her carriage.

'Yes, m'lady. Only just in time,' he replied.

He locked the door. Kitty turned and looked round the small lighted room in which she was to spend the night. Everything was ready; the bed was made; the sheets were turned down; her bag was on the seat. The guard passed the window, holding his flag in his hand.

A man who had only just caught the train ran across the platform with his arms spread out. A door slammed.

'Just in time,' Kitty said to herself as she stood there. Then the train gave a gentle tug. She could hardly believe that so great a monster could start so gently on so long a journey. Then she saw the tea-urn sliding past.

'We're off,' she said to herself, sinking back on to the seat. 'We're off!'

All the tension went out of her body. She was alone; and the train was moving. The last lamp on the platform slid away. The last figure on the platform vanished.

'What fun!' she said to herself, as if she were a little girl who had run away from her nurse and escaped. 'We're off!'

She sat still for a moment in her brightly lit compartment; then she tugged the blind and it sprang up with a jerk. Elongated lights slid past; lights in factories and warehouses; lights in obscure back streets. Then there were asphalt paths; more lights in public gardens; and then bushes and a hedge in a field. They were leaving London behind them; leaving that blaze of light which seemed, as the train rushed into the darkness, to contract itself into one fiery circle. The train rushed with a roar through a tunnel. It seemed to perform an act of amputation; now she was cut off from that circle of light.

She looked round the narrow little compartment in which she was isolated. Everything shook slightly. There was a perpetual faint vibration. She seemed to be passing from one world to another; this was the moment of transition. She sat still for a moment; then undressed and paused with her hand on the blind. The train had got into its stride now; it was rushing at full speed through the country. A few distant lights twinkled here and there. Black clumps of trees stood in the grey summer fields; the fields were full of summer grasses. The light from the engine lit up a quiet group of cows; and a hedge of hawthorn. They were in open country now.

She pulled down the blind and climbed into her bed. She laid herself out on the rather hard shelf with her back to the carriage wall, so that she felt a faint vibration against her head. She lay listening to the humming noise which the train made, now that it had got into its stride. Smoothly and powerfully she was being drawn through England to the north. I need do nothing, she thought, nothing, nothing, but let myself be drawn on. She turned and pulled the blue shade over the lamp. The sound of the train became louder in the darkness; its roar, its vibration, seemed to fall into a regular rhythm of sound, raking through her mind, rolling out her thoughts.

Ah, but not all of them, she thought, turning restlessly on her shelf. Some still jutted up. One's not a child, she thought, staring at the light under the blue shade, any longer. The years changed things; destroyed things; heaped things up – worries and bothers; here they were again.

Fragments of talk kept coming back to her; sights came before her. She saw herself raise the window with a jerk; and the bristles on Aunt Warburton's chin. She saw the women rising, and the men filing in. She sighed as she turned on her ledge. All their clothes are the same, she thought; all their lives are the same. And which is right? she thought, turning restlessly on her shelf. Which is wrong? She turned again.

The train rushed her on. The sound had deepened; it had become a continuous roar. How could she sleep? How could she prevent herself from thinking? She turned away from the light. *Now* where are we? she said to herself. Where is the train at this moment? *Now*, she murmured, shutting her eyes, we are passing the white house on the hill; *now* we are going through the tunnel; *now* we are crossing the bridge over the river . . . A blank intervened; her thoughts became spaced; they became muddled. Past and present became jumbled together. She saw Margaret Marrable pinching the dress in her fingers, but she was leading a bull with a ring through its nose . . . This is sleep, she said to herself, half opening her eyes; thank goodness, she said to herself, shutting them again, this is sleep. And she resigned herself to the charge of the train, whose roar now became dulled and distant.

There was a tap at her door. She lay for a moment, wondering why the room shook so; then the scene settled itself; she was in the train; she was in the country; they were nearing the station. She got up.

She dressed rapidly and stood in the corridor. It was still early. She watched the fields galloping past. They were the bare fields, the angular fields of the north. The spring was late here; the trees were not fully out yet. The smoke looped down and caught a tree in its white cloud. When it lifted, she thought how fine the light was: clear and sharp, white and grey. The land had none of the softness, none of the greenness of the land in the south. But here was the junction; here was the gasometer; they were running into the station. The train slowed down, and all the lamp-posts on the platform gradually came to a standstill.

She got out and drew in a deep breath of the cold raw air. The car was waiting for her; and directly she saw it she remembered – it was the new car; a birthday present from her husband. She had never driven in it yet. Cole touched his hat.

'Let's have it open, Cole,' she said, and he opened the stiff new hood, and she got in beside him. Very slowly, for the engine seemed to beat intermittently, starting and stopping and then starting again, they moved off. They drove through the town; all the shops were still shut; women were on their knees scrubbing doorsteps; blinds were still drawn in bedrooms and sitting-rooms; there was very little traffic about. Only milk-carts rattled past. Dogs roamed down the middle of the street on private errands of their own. Cole had to hoot again and again.

'They'll learn in time, m'lady,' he said as a great brindled cur slunk out of their way. In the town he drove carefully; but once they were outside he speeded up. Kitty watched the needle jump forward on the speedometer.

'She does it easily?' she asked, listening to the soft purr of the engine.

Cole lifted his foot to show how lightly it touched the accelerator. Then he touched it again and the car sped on. They were driving too fast, Kitty thought; but the road – she kept her eye on it – was still empty. Only two or three lumbering farm wagons passed them; the men went to the horses' heads and held them as they went by. The road stretched pearl-white in front of them; the hedges were decked with the little pointed leaves of early spring.

'Spring's very late up here,' said Kitty; 'cold winds I suppose?'

Cole nodded. He had none of the servile ways of the London flunkey; she was at her ease with him; she could be silent. The air seemed to have different grades of warmth and chill in it; now sweet; now – they were passing a farmyard – strong-smelling, acrid from the sour smell of manure. She leant back, holding her hat to her head as they rushed a hill. 'You won't get her up this in top, Cole,' she said. The pace slackened a little; they were climbing the familiar Crabbs Hill, with the yellow streaks where carters had put on their brakes. In the old days, when she drove horses, they used to get out here and walk. Cole said nothing. He was going to show off his engine, she suspected. The car swept up finely. But the hill was long; there was a level stretch; then the road mounted again. The car faltered. Cole coaxed her on. Kitty saw him jerk his body slightly backwards and forwards as if he were encouraging horses. She felt the tension of his muscles. They slowed – they almost stopped. No, now they were on the crest of the hill. She had done it in top!

'Well done!' she exclaimed. He said nothing; but he was very proud, she knew.

'We couldn't have done that in the old car,' she said.

'Ah, but it wasn't her fault,' said Cole.

He was a very humane man; the kind of man she liked, she reflected – silent, reserved. On they swept again. Now they were passing the grey stone house where the mad lady lived alone with her peacocks and her bloodhounds. They had passed it. Now the woods were on their right hand and the air came singing through them. It was like the sea, Kitty thought, looking, as they passed, down a dark green drive patched with yellow sunlight. On they went again. Now heaps of ruddy brown leaves lay by the roadside staining the puddles red.

'It's been raining?' she said. He nodded. They came out on the high ridge with woods beneath and there, in a clearing among the trees, was the grey tower of the castle. She always looked for it and greeted it as if she were raising a hand to a friend. They were on their own land now. Gateposts were branded with their initials; their arms swung above the doorways of inns; their crest was mounted over cottage doors. Cole looked at the clock. The needle leapt again.

Too fast, too fast! Kitty said to herself. But she liked the rush of the wind in her face. Now they reached the lodge gate; Mrs Preedy was holding it open with a white-haired child on her arm. They rushed through the park. The deer looked up and hopped away lightly through the fern.

'Two minutes under the quarter, m'lady,' said Cole as they swept in a circle and drew up at the door. Kitty stood for a moment looking at the car. She laid her hand on the bonnet. It was hot. She gave it a little pat. 'She did it beautifully, Cole,' she said. 'I'll tell his lordship.' Cole smiled; he was happy.

She went in. Nobody was about; they had arrived earlier than was expected. She crossed the great stone-flagged hall, with the armour and the busts, and went into the morning-room where breakfast was laid.

The green light dazzled her as she went in. It was as if she stood in the hollow of an emerald. All was green outside. The statues of grey French ladies stood on the terrace, holding their baskets; but the baskets were empty. In summer flowers would burn there. Green turf fell down in broad swaths between clipped yews; dipped to the river; and then rose again to the hill that was crested with woods. There was a curl of mist on the woods now – the light mist of early morning. As she gazed, a bee buzzed in her ear; she thought she heard the murmur of the river over the stones; pigeons crooned in the tree-tops. It was the voice of early morning, the voice of summer. But the door opened. Here was breakfast.

She breakfasted; she felt warm, restored and comfortable as she lay back in her chair. And she had nothing to do – nothing whatever. The whole day was hers. It was fine too. The sunlight suddenly quickened in the room, and laid a broad bar of light across the floor. The sun was on the flowers outside. A tortoiseshell butterfly flaunted across the window; she saw it settle on a leaf, and there it sat, opening its wings and shutting them, opening and shutting them, as if it feasted on the sunlight. She watched it. The down was soft rust-red on its wings. Off it flaunted again. Then, admitted by an invisible hand, the chow stalked in; came straight up to her; sniffed at her skirt, and flung himself down in a bright patch of sunlight.

Heartless brute! she thought, but his indifference pleased her. He asked nothing of her either. She stretched her hand for a cigarette. And what would Martin say, she wondered, as she took the enamel box that turned from green to blue, as she opened it. Hideous? Vulgar? Possibly – but what did it matter what people said? Criticism seemed light as smoke this morning. What did it matter what he said, what they said, what anybody said, since she had a whole day to herself? – since she was alone? And there they are, still asleep, in their houses, she thought, standing at the window, looking at the green-grey grass, after their dances, after their parties . . . The thought pleased her. She threw away her cigarette and went upstairs to change her clothes.

The sun was much stronger when she came down again. The garden had already lost its look of purity; the mist was off the woods. She could hear the squeak of the lawnmower as she stepped out of the window. The rubber-shoed pony was pacing up and down the lawns leaving a pale wake in the grass behind him. The birds were singing in their scattered way. The starlings in their bright mail were feeding on the grass. Dew shone, red, violet, gold on the trembling tips of the grass blades. It was a perfect May morning.

She sauntered slowly along the terrace. As she passed she glanced in at the long windows of the library. Everything was shrouded and shut up. But the long room looked more than usually stately, its proportions seemly; and the brown books in their long rows seemed to exist silently, with dignity, by themselves, for themselves. She left the terrace and strolled down the long grass path. The garden was still empty; only a man in his shirt sleeves was doing something to a tree; but she need speak to nobody. The chow stalked after her; he too was silent. She walked on past the flower-beds to the river. There she always stopped, on the bridge, with the cannon-balls at intervals. The water always fascinated her. The quick northern river came down from the moors; it was never smooth and green, never deep and placid like southern rivers. It raced; it hurried. It splayed itself, red, yellow and clear brown, over the pebbles on the bed. Resting her elbows on the balustrade, she watched it eddy round the arches; she watched it make diamonds and sharp arrow streaks over the stones. She listened. She knew the different sounds it made in summer and winter; now it hurried, it raced.

But the chow was bored; he marched on. She followed him. She went up the green ride towards the snuffer-shaped monument on the crest of the hill. Every path through the woods had its name. There was Keepers' Path, Lovers' Walk, Ladies' Mile, and here was the Earl's Ride. But before she went into the woods, she stopped and looked back at the house. Times out of number she had stopped here; the castle looked grey and stately; asleep this morning, with the blinds drawn, and no flag on the flagstaff. Very noble it looked, and ancient, and enduring. Then she went on into the woods.

The wind seemed to rise as she walked under the trees. It sang in their tops, but it was silent beneath. The dead leaves crackled under foot; among them sprang up the pale spring flowers, the loveliest of the year – blue flowers and white flowers, trembling on cushions of green moss. Spring was sad always, she thought; it brought back memories. All passes, all changes, she thought, as she climbed up the little path between the trees. Nothing of this belonged to her; her son would inherit; his wife would walk here after her. She broke off a twig; she picked a flower and put it to her lips. But she was in the prime of life; she was vigorous. She strode on. The ground rose sharply; her muscles felt strong and flexible as she pressed her thick-soled shoes to the ground. She threw away her flower. The trees thinned as she strode higher and higher. Suddenly she saw the sky between two striped tree trunks extraordinarily blue. She came out on the top. The wind ceased; the country spread wide all round her. Her body seemed to shrink; her eyes to widen. She threw herself on the ground, and looked over the billowing land that went rising and falling, away and away, until some-where far off it reached the sea. Uncultivated, uninhabited, existing by itself, for itself, without towns or houses it looked from this height. Dark wedges of shadow, bright breadths of light lay side by side. Then, as she watched, light moved and dark moved: light and shadow went travelling over the hills and over the valleys. A deep murmur sang in her ears – the land itself, singing to itself, a chorus, alone. She lay there listening. She was happy, completely. Time had ceased.

1917

A VERY COLD WINTER'S NIGHT, so silent that the air seemed frozen and, since there was no moon, congealed to the stillness of glass, spread over England. Ponds and ditches were frozen; the puddles made glazed eyes in the roads, and on the pavement the frost had raised slippery knobs. Darkness pressed on the windows; towns had merged themselves in open country. No light shone, save when a searchlight rayed round the sky, and stopped, here and there, as if to ponder some fleecy patch.

'If that is the river,' said Eleanor, pausing in the dark street outside the station, 'Westminster must be there.' The omnibus in which she had come, with its silent passengers looking cadaverous in the blue light, had already vanished. She turned.

She was dining with Renny and Maggie, who lived in one of the obscure little streets under the shadow of the Abbey. She walked on. The farther side of the street was almost invisible. The lamps were shrouded in blue. She flashed her torch on to a name on a street corner. Again she flashed her torch. Here it lit up a brick wall; there a dark green tuft of ivy. At last the number thirty, the number she was looking for, shone out. She knocked and rang at the same moment, for the darkness seemed to muffle sound as well as sight. Silence weighed on her as she stood there waiting. Then the door opened and a man's voice said, 'Come in!'

He shut the door behind him, quickly, as if to shut in the light. It looked strange after the streets – the perambulator in the hall; the umbrellas in the stand; the carpet, the pictures: they all seemed intensified.

'Come in!' said Renny again, and led her into the sitting-room ablaze with light. Another man was standing in the room, and she was surprised because she had expected to find them alone. But the man was somebody whom she did not know.

For a moment they stared at each other; then Renny said, 'You know Nicholas . . . ' but he did not speak the surname distinctly, and it was so long that she could not catch it. A foreign name, she thought. A foreigner. He was clearly not English. He shook hands with a bow like a foreigner, and he went on talking, as if he were in the middle of a sentence that he wished to finish . . . 'we are talking about Napoleon – ' he said, turning to her.

'I see,' she said. But she had no notion what he was saying. They were in the middle of an argument, she supposed. But it came to an end without her understanding a word of it, except that it had to do with Napoleon. She took off her coat and laid it down. They stopped talking.

'I will go and tell Maggie,' said Renny. He left them abruptly.

'You were talking about Napoleon?' Eleanor said. She looked at the man whose surname she had not heard. He was very dark; he had a rounded head and dark eyes. Did she like him or not? She did not know.

I've interrupted them, she felt, and I've nothing whatever to say. She felt dazed and cold. She spread her hands over the fire. It was a real fire; wood blocks were blazing; the flame ran along the streaks of shiny tar. A little trickle of feeble gas was all that was left her at home.

'Napoleon,' she said, warming her hands. She spoke without any meaning.

'We were considering the psychology of great men,' he said, 'by the light of modern science,' he added with a little laugh. She wished the argument had been more within her reach.

'That's very interesting,' she said shyly.

'Yes – if we knew anything about it,' he said.

'If we knew anything about it . . . ' she repeated. There was a pause. She felt numb all over – not only her hands, but her brain.

'The psychology of great men – ' she said, for she did not wish him to think her a fool, ' . . . was that what you were discussing?'

'We were saying – ' He paused. She guessed that he found it difficult to sum up their argument – they had evidently been talking for some time, judging by the newspapers lying about and the cigarette-ends on the table.

'I was saying,' he went on, 'I was saying we do not know ourselves, ordinary people; and if we do not know ourselves, how then can we make religions, laws, that – ' he used his hands as people do who find language obdurate, 'that – '

'That fit – that fit,' she said, supplying him with a word that was shorter, she felt sure, than the dictionary word that foreigners always used.

' – that fit, that fit,' he said, taking the word and repeating it as if he were grateful for her help.

' . . . that fit,' she repeated. She had no idea what they were talking about. Then suddenly, as she bent to warm her hands over the fire, words floated together in her mind and made one intelligible sentence. It seemed to her that what he had said was, 'We cannot make laws and religions that fit because we do not know ourselves.'

'How odd that you should say that!' she said, smiling at him, 'because I've so often thought it myself!'

'Why is that odd?' he said. 'We all think the same things; only we do not say them.'

'Coming along in the omnibus tonight,' she began, 'I was thinking about this war – I don't feel this, but other people do . . . ' She stopped. He looked puzzled; probably she had misunderstood what he had said; she had not made her own meaning plain.

'I mean,' she began again, 'I was thinking as I came along in the bus – '

But here Renny came in.

He was carrying a tray with bottles and glasses.

'It is a great thing,' said Nicholas, 'being the son of a wine merchant.'

It sounded like a quotation from the French grammar.

The son of the wine merchant, Eleanor repeated to herself, looking at his red cheeks, dark eyes and large nose. The other man must be Russian, she thought. Russian, Polish, Jewish? – she had no idea what he was, who he was.

She drank; the wine seemed to caress a knob in her spine. Here Maggie came in.

'Good-evening,' she said, disregarding the foreigner's bow as if she knew him too well to greet him.

'Papers,' she protested, looking at the litter on the floor, 'papers, papers.' The floor was strewn with papers.

'We dine in the basement,' she continued, turning to Eleanor, 'because we've no servants.' She led the way down the steep little stairs.

'But Magdalena,' said Nicholas, as they stood in the little low-ceilinged room in which dinner was laid, 'Sara said, "We shall meet tomorrow night at Maggie's . . . " She is not here.'

He stood; the others had sat down.

'She will come in time,' said Maggie.

'I shall ring her up,' said Nicholas. He left the room.

'Isn't it much nicer,' said Eleanor, taking her plate, 'not having servants . . . '

'We have a woman to do the washing-up,' said Maggie.

'And we are extremely dirty,' said Renny.

He took up a fork and examined it between the prongs.

'No, this fork, as it happens, is clean,' he said, and put it down again.

Nicholas came back into the room. He looked perturbed. 'She is not there,' he said to Maggie. 'I rang her up, but I could get no answer.'

'Probably she's coming,' said Maggie. 'Or she may have forgotten . . . '

She handed him his soup. But he sat looking at his plate without moving. Wrinkles had come on his forehead; he made no attempt to hide his anxiety. He was without self-consciousness. 'There!' he suddenly exclaimed, interrupting them as they talked. 'She is coming!' he added. He put down his spoon and waited. Someone was coming slowly down the steep stairs.

The door opened and Sara came in. She looked pinched with the cold. Her cheeks were white here and red there, and she blinked as if she were still dazed from her walk through the blue-shrouded streets. She gave her hand to Nicholas and he kissed it. But she wore no engagement ring, Eleanor observed.

'Yes, we are dirty,' said Maggie, looking at her; she was in her day clothes. 'In rags,' she added, for a loop of gold thread hung down from her own sleeve as she helped the soup.

'I was thinking how beautiful . . . ' said Eleanor, for her eyes had been resting on the silver dress with gold threads in it. 'Where did you get it?'

'In Constantinople, from a Turk,' said Maggie.

'A turbaned and fantastic Turk,' Sara murmured, stroking the sleeve as she took her plate. She still seemed dazed.

'And the plates,' said Eleanor, looking at the purple birds on her plate, 'Don't I remember them?' she asked.

'In the cabinet in the drawing-room at home,' said Maggie. 'But it seemed silly – keeping them in a cabinet.'

'We break one every week,' said Renny.

'They'll last the war,' said Maggie.

Eleanor observed a curious mask-like expression come down over Renny's face as she said 'the war'. Like all the French, she thought, he cares passionately for his country. But contradictorily, she felt, looking at him. He was silent. His silence oppressed her. There was something formidable about his silence.

'And why were you so late?' said Nicholas, turning to Sara. He spoke gently, reproachfully, rather as if she were a child. He poured her out a glass of wine.

Take care, Eleanor felt inclined to say to her; the wine goes to one's head. She had not drunk wine for months. She was feeling already a little blurred; a little light-headed. It was the light after the dark; talk after silence; the war, perhaps, removing barriers.

But Sara drank. Then she burst out: 'Because of that damned fool.'

'Damned fool?' said Maggie. 'Which?'

'Eleanor's nephew,' said Sara. 'North. Eleanor's nephew, North.' She held her glass towards Eleanor, as if she were addressing her. 'North . . . ' Then she smiled. 'There I was, sitting alone. The bell rang. "That's the wash," I said. Footsteps came up the stairs. There was North – North,' she raised her hand to her head as if in salute, 'cutting a figure like this – "What the devil's that for?" I asked. "I leave for the Front tonight," he said, clicking his heels together. "I'm a lieutenant in – " whatever it was – Royal Regiment of Rat-Catchers or something . . . And he hung his cap on the bust of our grandfather. And I poured out tea. "How many lumps of sugar does a lieutenant in the Royal Rat-Catchers require?" I asked. "One. Two. Three. Four . . . ?" '

She dropped pellets of bread on to the table. As each fell, it seemed to emphasise her bitterness. She looked older, more worn; though she laughed, she was bitter.

'Who is North?' Nicholas asked. He pronounced the word 'North' as if it were a point on the compass.

'My nephew. My brother Morris's son,' Eleanor explained.

'There he sat,' Sara resumed, 'in his mud-coloured uniform, with his switch between his legs, and his ears sticking out on either side of his pink, foolish face, and whatever I said, "Good," he said, "Good," "Good," until I took up the poker and tongs' – she took up her knife and fork – 'and played "God save the King, Happy and glorious, Long to reign over us – " ' She held her knife and fork as if they were weapons.

I'm sorry he's gone, Eleanor thought. A picture came before her eyes – the picture of a nice cricketing boy smoking a cigar on a terrace. I'm sorry . . . Then another picture formed. She was sitting on the same terrace; but now the sun was setting; a maid came out and said, 'The soldiers are guarding the line with fixed bayonets!' That was how she had heard of the war – three years ago. And she had thought, putting down her coffee-cup on a little table, Not if I can help it! overcome by an absurd but vehement desire to protect those hills; she had looked at the hills across the meadow . . . Now she looked at the foreigner opposite.

'How unfair you are,' Nicholas was saying to Sara. 'Prejudiced; narrow; unfair,' he repeated, tapping her hand with his finger.

He was saying what Eleanor felt herself.

'Yes. Isn't it natural . . . ' she began. 'Could you allow the Germans to invade England and do nothing?' she said, turning to Renny. She was sorry she had spoken; and the words were not the ones she had meant to use. There was an expression of suffering, or was it anger? on his face.

'I?' he said. 'I help them to make shells.'

Maggie stood behind him. She had brought in the meat. 'Carve,' she said. He was staring at the meat which she had put down in front of him. He took up the knife and began to carve mechanically.

'Now nurse,' she reminded him. He cut another helping.

'Yes,' said Eleanor awkwardly as Maggie took away the plate. She did not know what to say. She spoke without thinking. 'Let's end it as quickly as possible and then . . . ' She looked at him. He was silent. He turned away. He had turned to listen to what the others were saying, as if to take refuge from speaking himself.

'Poppycock, poppycock . . . don't talk such damned poppycock – that's what you really said,' Nicholas was saying. His hands were large and clean and the fingernails were trimmed very close, Eleanor noticed. He might be a doctor, she thought.

'What's "poppycock"?' she asked, turning to Renny. For she did not know the word.

'American,' said Renny. 'He's an American,' he said, nodding at Nicholas.

'No,' said Nicholas, turning round, 'I am a Pole.'

'His mother was a princess,' said Maggie as if she were teasing him. That explains the seal on his chain, Eleanor thought. He wore a large old seal on his chain.

'She was,' he said quite seriously. 'One of the noblest families in Poland. But my father was an ordinary man – a man of the people . . . You should have had more self-control,' he added, turning again to Sara.

'So I should,' she sighed. 'But then he gave his bridle reins a shake and said, "Adieu for evermore, adieu for evermore!" ' She stretched out her hand and poured herself another glass of wine.

'You shall have no more to drink,' said Nicholas, moving away the bottle. 'She saw herself,' he explained, turning to Eleanor, 'on top of a tower, waving a white handkerchief to a knight in armour.'

'And the moon was rising over a dark moor,' Sara murmured, touching a pepper-pot.

The pepper-pot's a dark moor, Eleanor thought, looking at it. A little blur had come round the edges of things. It was the wine; it was the war. Things seemed to have lost their skins; to be freed from some surface hardness; even the chair with gilt claws, at which she was looking, seemed porous; it seemed to radiate out some warmth, some glamour, as she looked at it.

'I remember that chair,' she said to Maggie. 'And your mother . . . ' she added. But she always saw Eugénie not sitting but in movement. ' . . . dancing,' she added.

'Dancing . . . ' Sara repeated. She began drumming on the table with her fork. 'When I was young, I used to dance,' she hummed. 'All men loved me when I was young . . . Roses and syringas hung, when I was young, when I was young. D'you remember, Maggie?' She looked at her sister as if they both remembered the same thing.

Maggie nodded. 'In the bedroom. A waltz,' she said.

'A waltz . . . ' said Eleanor. Sara was drumming a waltz rhythm on the table. Eleanor began to hum in time to it: 'Hoity te, toity te, hoity te . . . '

A long-drawn hollow sound wailed out.

'No, no!' she protested, as if somebody had given her the wrong note. But the sound wailed again.

'A fog-horn?' she said. 'On the river?'

But as she said it she knew what it was.

The siren wailed again.

'The Germans!' said Renny. 'Those damned Germans!' He put down his knife and fork with an exaggerated gesture of boredom.

'Another raid,' said Maggie, getting up. She left the room; Renny followed her.

'The Germans . . . ' said Eleanor as the door shut. She felt as if some dull bore had interrupted an interesting conversation. The colours began to fade. She had been looking at the red chair. It lost its radiance as she looked at it, as if a light had been extinguished underneath.

They heard the rush of wheels in the street. Everything seemed to be going past very quickly. There was the sound of feet tapping on the pavement. Eleanor got up and drew the curtains slightly apart. The basement was sunk beneath the pavement, so that she only saw people's legs and skirts as they went past the area railings. Two men came by walking very quickly; then an old woman, with her skirt swinging from side to side, walked past.

'Oughtn't we to ask people in?' she said, turning round. But when she looked back the old woman had disappeared. So had the men. The street was now quite empty. The houses opposite were completely curtained. She drew their own curtain carefully. The table, with the gay china and the lamp, seemed ringed in a circle of bright light as she turned back.

She sat down again. 'D'you mind air raids?' Nicholas asked, looking at her with his inquisitive expression. 'People differ so much.'

'Not at all,' she said. She would have crumbled a piece of bread to show him that she was at her ease; but as she was not afraid, the action seemed to her unnecessary. 'The chances of being hit oneself are so small,' she said. 'What were we saying?' she added.

It seemed to her that they had been saying something extremely interesting; but she could not remember what. They sat silent for a moment. Then they heard a shuffling on the stairs.

'The children . . . ' said Sara. They heard the dull boom of a gun in the distance.

Here Renny came in.

'Bring your plates,' he said. 'In here.' He led them into the cellar. It was a large cellar. With its crypt-like ceiling and stone walls it had a damp ecclesiastical look. It was used partly for coal, partly for wine. The light in the centre shone on glittering heaps of coal; bottles of wine wrapped in straw lay on their sides on stone shelves. There was a mouldy smell of wine, straw and damp. It was chilly after the dining-room. Sara came in carrying quilts and dressing-gowns which she had fetched from upstairs. Eleanor was glad to wrap herself in a blue dressing-gown; she wrapped it round her and sat holding her plate on her knees. It was cold.

'And now?' said Sara, holding her spoon erect.

They all looked as if they were waiting for something to happen. Maggie came in carrying a plum pudding.

'We may as well finish our dinner,' she said. But she spoke too sensibly; she was anxious about the children, Eleanor guessed. They were in the kitchen. She had seen them as she passed.

'Are they asleep?' she asked.

'Yes. But if the guns . . . ' she began, helping the pudding. Another gun boomed out. This time it was distinctly louder.

'They've got through the defences,' said Nicholas.

They began to eat their pudding.

A gun boomed again. This time there was a bark in its boom.

'Hampstead,' said Nicholas. He took out his watch. The silence was profound. Nothing happened. Eleanor looked at the blocks of stone arched over their heads. She noticed a spider's web in one corner. Another gun boomed. A sigh of air rushed up with it. It was right on top of them this time.

'The Embankment,' said Nicholas. Maggie put down her plate and went into the kitchen.

There was profound silence. Nothing happened. Nicholas looked at his watch as if he were timing the guns. There was something queer about him, Eleanor thought: medical? priestly? He wore a seal that hung down from his watch-chain. The number on the box opposite was

1397. She noticed everything. The Germans must be overhead now. She felt a curious heaviness on top of her head. One, two, three, four, she counted, looking up at the greenish-grey stone. Then there was a violent crack of sound, like the split of lightning in the sky. The spider's web oscillated.

'On top of us,' said Nicholas, looking up. They all looked up. At any moment a bomb might fall. There was dead silence. In the silence they heard Maggie's voice in the kitchen.

'That was nothing. Turn round and go to sleep.' She spoke very calmly and soothingly.

One, two, three, four, Eleanor counted. The spider's web was swaying. That stone may fall, she thought, fixing a certain stone with her eyes. Then a gun boomed again. It was fainter – farther away.

'That's over,' said Nicholas. He shut his watch with a click. And they all turned and shifted on their hard chairs as if they had been cramped.

Maggie came in.

'Well, that's over,' she said. ('He woke for a moment, but he went off to sleep again,' she said in an undertone to Renny, 'but the baby slept right through.') She sat down and took the plate that Renny was holding for her. 'Now let's finish our pudding,' she said, speaking in her natural voice.

'Now we will have some wine,' said Renny. He examined one bottle; then another; finally he took a third and wiped it carefully with the tail of his dressing-gown. He placed the bottle on a wooden case and they sat round in a circle.

'It didn't come to much, did it?' said Sara. She was tilting back her chair as she held out her glass.

'Ah, but we were frightened,' said Nicholas. 'Look – how pale we all are.'

They looked at each other. Draped in their quilts and dressing-gowns, against the grey-green walls, they all looked whitish, greenish.

'It's partly the light,' said Maggie. 'Eleanor,' she said, looking at her, 'looks like an abbess.'

The deep-blue dressing-gown which hid the foolish little ornaments, the tabs of velvet and lace on her dress, had improved her appearance. Her middle-aged face was crinkled like an old glove that has been creased into a multitude of fine lines by the gestures of a hand.

'Untidy, am I?' she said, putting her hand to her hair.

'No. Don't touch it,' said Maggie.

'And what were we talking about before the raid?' Eleanor asked. Again she felt that they had been in the middle of saying something very interesting when they were interrupted. But there had been a complete break; none of them could remember what they had been saying.

'Well, it's over now,' said Sara. 'So let's drink a health – Here's to the New World!' she exclaimed. She raised her glass with a flourish. They all felt a sudden desire to talk and laugh.

'Here's to the New World!' they all cried, raising their glasses, and clinking them together.

The five glasses filled with yellow liquid came together in a bunch.

'To the New World!' they cried and drank. The yellow liquid swayed up and down in their glasses.

'Now, Nicholas,' said Sara, setting her glass down with a tap on the box, 'a speech! A speech!'

'Ladies and gentlemen!' he began, flinging his hand out like an orator. 'Ladies and gentlemen . . . '

'We don't want speeches,' Renny interrupted him.

Eleanor was disappointed. She would have liked a speech. But he seemed to take the interruption good-humouredly; he sat there nodding and smiling.

'Let's go upstairs,' said Renny, pushing away the box.

'And leave this cellar,' said Sara, stretching her arms out, 'this cave of mud and dung . . . '

'Listen!' Maggie interrupted. She held up her hand. 'I thought I heard the guns again . . . '

They listened. The guns were still firing, but far away in the distance. There was a sound like the breaking of waves on a shore far away.

'They're only killing other people,' said Renny savagely. He kicked the wooden box.

'But you must let us think of something else,' Eleanor protested. The mask had come down over his face.

'And what nonsense, what nonsense Renny talks,' said Nicholas, turning to her privately. 'Only children letting off fireworks in the back garden,' he muttered as he helped her out of her dressing-gown. They went upstairs.

Eleanor came into the drawing-room. It looked larger than she remembered it, and very spacious and comfortable. Papers were strewn on the floor; the fire was burning brightly; it was warm; it was cheerful. She felt very tired. She sank down into an armchair. Sara and Nicholas had lagged behind. The others were helping the nurse to carry the children up to bed, she supposed. She lay back in the chair. Everything seemed to become quiet and natural again. A feeling of great calm possessed her. It was as if another space of time had been issued to her, but, robbed by the presence of death of something personal, she felt – she hesitated for a word – 'immune'? Was that what she meant? Immune, she said, looking at a picture without seeing it. Immune, she repeated. It was a picture of a hill and a village perhaps in the South of France; perhaps in Italy. There were olive trees; and white roofs grouped against a hillside. Immune, she repeated, looking at the picture.

She could hear a gentle thudding on the floor above: Maggie and Renny were settling the children into their beds again, she supposed. There was a little squeak, like a sleepy bird chirping in its nest. It was very private and peaceful after the guns. But here the others came in.

'Did they mind it?' she said, sitting up, ' – the children?'

'No,' said Maggie. 'They slept through it.'

'But they may have dreamt,' said Sara, pulling up a chair. Nobody spoke. It was very quiet. The clocks that used to boom out the hour in Westminster were silent.

Maggie took the poker and struck the wood blocks. The sparks went volleying up the chimney in a shower of gold eyes.

'How that makes me . . . ' Eleanor began.

She stopped.

'Yes?' said Nicholas.

' . . . think of my childhood,' she added.

She was thinking of Morris and herself, and old Pippy; but had she told them nobody would know what she meant. They were silent. Suddenly a clear flute-like note rang out in the street below.

'What's that?' said Maggie. She started; she looked at the window; she half rose.

'The bugles,' said Renny, putting out his hand to stop her.

The bugles blew again beneath the window. Then they heard them farther down the street; then farther away still down the next street. Almost directly the hooting of cars began again, and the rushing of wheels, as if the traffic had been released and the usual night life of London had begun again.

'It's over,' said Maggie. She lay back in her chair; she looked very tired for a moment. Then she pulled a basket towards her and began to darn a sock.

'I'm glad I'm alive,' said Eleanor. 'Is that wrong, Renny?' she asked. She wanted him to speak. It seemed to her that he hoarded immense supplies of emotion that he could not express. He did not answer. He was leaning on his elbow, smoking a cigar and looking into the fire.

'I have spent the evening sitting in a coal cellar while other people try to kill each other above my head,' he said suddenly. Then he stretched out and took up a paper.

'Renny, Renny, Renny,' said Nicholas, as if he were expostulating with a naughty child. He went on reading. The rush of wheels and the hooting of motor cars had run themselves into one continuous sound.

As Renny was reading and Maggie was darning there was silence in the room. Eleanor watched the fire run along veins of tar and blaze and sink.

'What are you thinking, Eleanor?' Nicholas interrupted her. He calls me Eleanor, she thought; that's right.

'About the new world . . . ' she said aloud. 'D'you think we're going to improve?' she asked.

'Yes, yes,' he said, nodding his head.

He spoke quietly as if he did not wish to rouse Renny who was reading, or Maggie who was darning, or Sara who was lying back in her chair half asleep. They seemed to be talking, privately, together.

'But how . . . ' she began, ' – how can we improve ourselves . . . live more. . . ' – she dropped her voice as if she were afraid of waking sleepers – ' . . . live more naturally . . . better . . . How can we?'

'It is only a question,' he said – he stopped. He drew himself close to her – 'of learning. The soul . . . ' Again he stopped.

'Yes – the soul?' she prompted him.

'The soul – the whole being,' he explained. He hollowed his hands as if to enclose a circle. 'It wishes to expand; to adventure; to form – new combinations.'

'Yes, yes,' she said, as if to assure him that his words were right.

'Whereas now' – he drew himself together; put his feet together; he looked like an old lady who is afraid of mice – 'this is how we live, screwed up into one hard little, tight little – knot.'

'Knot, knot – yes, that's right,' she nodded.

'Each is his own little cubicle; each with his own cross or holy book; each with his fire, his wife . . . '

'Darning socks,' Maggie interrupted.

Eleanor started. She had seemed to be looking into the future. But they had been overheard. Their privacy was ended.

Renny threw down his paper. 'It's all damned rot!' he said. Whether he referred to the paper, or to what they were saying, Eleanor did not know. But talk in private was impossible.

'Why d'you buy them then?' she said, pointing to the papers.

'To light fires with,' said Renny.

Maggie laughed and threw down the sock she was mending. 'There!' she exclaimed. 'Mended . . . '

Again they sat silent, looking at the fire. Eleanor wished that he would go on talking – the man she called Nicholas. When, she wanted to ask him, when will this new world come? When shall we be free? When shall we live adventurously, wholly, not like cripples in a cave? He seemed to have released something in her; she felt not only a new space of time, but new powers, something unknown within her. She watched his cigarette moving up and down. Then Maggie took the poker and struck the wood and again a shower of red-eyed sparks went volleying up the chimney. We shall be free, we shall be free, Eleanor thought.

'And what have you been thinking all this time?' said Nicholas, laying his hand on Sara's knee. She started. 'Or have you been asleep?' he added.

'I heard what you were saying,' she said.

'What were we saying?' he asked.

'The soul flying upwards like sparks up the chimney,' she said. The sparks were flying up the chimney.

'Not such a bad shot,' said Nicholas.

'Because people always say the same thing,' she laughed. She roused herself and sat up. 'There's Maggie – she says nothing. There's Renny – he says, "What damned rot!" Eleanor says, "That's just what I was thinking." And Nicholas, Nicholas' – she patted him on the knee – 'who ought to be in prison, says, "Oh, my dear friends, let us improve the soul!"'

'Ought to be in prison?' said Eleanor, looking at him.

'Because he loves – ' Sara explained. She paused. ' – the other sex,[48] the other sex, you see,' she said lightly, waving her hand in the way that was so like her mother's.

For a second a sharp shiver of repugnance passed over Eleanor's skin as if a knife had sliced it. Then she realised that it had touched nothing of importance. The sharp shiver passed. Underneath was – what? She looked at Nicholas. He was watching her.

'Does that,' he said, hesitating a little, 'make you dislike me, Eleanor?'

'Not in the least! Not in the least!' she exclaimed spontaneously. All the evening, off and on, she had been feeling about him this, that and the other; but now all the feelings came together and made one feeling, one whole – liking. 'Not in the least,' she said again. He gave her a little bow. She returned it with a little bow. But the clock on the mantelpiece was striking. Renny was yawning. It was late. She got up. She went to the window and parted the curtains and looked out. All the houses were still curtained. The cold winter's night was almost black. It was like looking into the hollow of a dark-blue stone. Here and there a star pierced the blue. She had a sense of immensity and peace – as if something had been consumed . . .

'Shall I get you a cab?' Renny interrupted.

'No, I'll walk,' she said, turning. 'I like walking in London.'

'We will come with you,' said Nicholas. 'Come, Sara,' he said. She was lying back in her chair swinging her foot up and down.

'But I don't want to come,' she said, waving him away. 'I want to stay; I want to talk; I want to sing – a hymn of praise – a song of thanksgiving . . . '

'Here is your hat; here is your bag,' said Nicholas, giving them to her.

'Come,' he said, taking her by the shoulder and pushing her out of the room. 'Come.'

Eleanor went up to say good-night to Maggie.

'I should like to stay too,' she said. 'There are so many things I should like to talk about – '

'But I want to go to bed – I want to go to bed,' Renny protested. He stood there with his hands stretched above his head, yawning.

Maggie rose. 'So you shall,' she laughed at him.

'Don't bother to come downstairs,' Eleanor protested as he opened the door for her. But he insisted. He is very rude and at the same time very polite, she thought, as she followed him down the stairs. A man who feels many different things, and all passionately, all at the same time, she thought . . . But they had reached the hall. Nicholas and Sara were standing there.

'Cease to laugh at me for once, Sara,' Nicholas was saying as he put on his coat.

'And cease to lecture me,' she said, opening the front door.

Renny smiled at Eleanor as they stood for a moment by the per-ambulator.

'Educating themselves!' he said.

'Good-night,' she said, smiling as she shook hands. That is the man, she said to herself, with a sudden rush of conviction, as she came out into the frosty air, that I should like to have married. She recognised a feeling which she had never felt. But he's twenty years younger than I am, she thought, and married to my cousin. For a moment she resented the passage of time and the accidents of life which had swept her away – from all that, she said to herself. And a scene came before her: Maggie and Renny sitting over the fire. A happy marriage, she thought, that's what I was feeling all the time. A happy marriage. She looked up as she walked down the dark little street behind the others. A broad fan of light, like the sail of a windmill, was sweeping slowly across the sky. It seemed to take what she was feeling and to express it broadly and simply, as if another voice were speaking in another language. Then the light stopped and examined a fleecy patch of sky, a suspected spot.

The raid! she said to herself. I'd forgotten the raid!

The others had come to the crossing; there they stood.

'I'd forgotten the raid!' she said aloud as she came up with them. She was surprised; but it was true.

They were in Victoria Street. The street curved away, looking wider and darker than usual. Little figures were hurrying along the pavement; they emerged for a moment under a lamp, then vanished into darkness again. The street was very empty.

'Will the omnibuses be running as usual?' Eleanor asked as they stood there.

They looked round them. Nothing was coming along the street at the moment.

'I shall wait here,' said Eleanor.

'Then I shall go,' said Sara abruptly. 'Goodnight!'

She waved her hand and walked away. Eleanor took it for granted that Nicholas would go with her.

'I shall wait here,' she repeated.

But he did not move. Sara had already vanished. Eleanor looked at him. Was he angry? Was he unhappy? She did not know. But here a great form loomed up through the darkness; its lights were shrouded with blue paint. Inside silent people sat huddled up; they looked cadaverous and unreal in the blue light. 'Good-night,' she said, shaking hands with Nicholas. She looked back and saw him still standing on the pavement. He still held his hat in his hand. He looked tall, impressive and solitary standing there alone, while the searchlights wheeled across the sky.

The omnibus moved on. She found herself staring at an old man in the corner who was eating something out of a paper bag. He looked up and caught her staring at him.

'Like to see what I've got for supper, lady?' he said, cocking one eyebrow over his rheumy, twinkling old eyes. And he held out for her inspection a hunk of bread on which was laid a slice of cold meat or sausage.

1918

AVEIL OF MIST covered the November sky: a many-folded veil, so fine-meshed that it made one density. It was not raining, but here and there the mist condensed on the surface into dampness and made pavements greasy. Here and there on a grass blade or on a hedge leaf a drop hung motionless. It was windless and calm. Sounds coming through the veil – the bleat of sheep, the croak of rooks – were deadened. The uproar of the traffic merged into one growl. Now and then as if a door opened and shut, or the veil parted and closed, the roar boomed and faded.

'Dirty brute,' Crosby muttered as she hobbled along the asphalt path across Richmond Green. Her legs were paining her. It was not actually raining, but the great open space was full of mist; and there was nobody near, so that she could talk aloud.

'Dirty brute,' she muttered again. She had got into the habit of talking aloud. There was nobody in sight; the end of the path was lost in mist. It was very silent. Only the rooks gathered on the tree-tops now and then let fall a queer little croak, and a leaf, spotted with black, fell to the ground. Her face twitched as she walked, as if her muscles had got into the habit of protesting, involuntarily, against the spites and obstacles that tormented her. She had aged greatly during the past four years. She looked so small and hunched that it seemed doubtful if she could make her way across the wide open space, shrouded in white mist. But she had to go to the High Street to do her shopping.

'The dirty brute,' she muttered again. She had had some words that morning with Mrs Burt about the count's bath. He spat in it, and Mrs Burt had told her to clean it.

'Count indeed – he's no more count than you are,' she continued. She was talking to Mrs Burt now. 'I'm quite willing to oblige you,' she went on. Even out here, in the mist, where she was free to say what she liked, she adopted a conciliatory tone, because she knew that they wanted to be rid of her. She gesticulated with the hand that was not carrying the bag as she told Louisa that she was quite ready to oblige her. She hobbled on. 'And I shouldn't mind going either,' she added bitterly, but this was spoken to herself only. It was no pleasure to her to live in the house any more; but there was nowhere else for her to go; that the Burts knew very well.

'And I'm quite ready to oblige you,' she added aloud, as indeed she had said to Louisa herself. But the truth was that she was no longer able to work as she had done. Her legs pained her. It took all the strength out of her to do her own shopping, let alone to clean the bath. But it was all take-it-or-leave-it now. In the old days she would have sent the whole lot packing.

'Drabs . . . hussies,' she muttered. She was now addressing the red-haired servant girl who had flung out of the house yesterday without warning. *She* could easily get another job. It didn't matter to her. So it was left to Crosby to clean the count's bath.

'Dirty brute, dirty brute,' she repeated; her pale-blue eyes glared impotently. She saw once more the blob of spittle that the count had left on the side of his bath – the Belgian who called himself a count. 'I've been used to work for gentlefolk, not for dirty foreigners like you,' she told him as she hobbled.

The roar of traffic sounded louder as she approached the ghostly line of trees. She could see houses now beyond the trees. Her pale-blue eyes peered forward through the mist as she made her way towards the railings. Her eyes alone seemed to express an unconquerable determination; she was not going to give in; she was bent on surviving. The soft mist was slowly lifting. Leaves lay damp and purple on the asphalt path. The rooks croaked and shuffled on the tree-tops. Now a dark line of railings emerged from the mist. The roar of traffic in the High Street sounded louder and louder. Crosby stopped and rested her bag on the railing before she went on to do battle with the crowd of shoppers in the High Street. She would have to shove and push, and be jostled this way and that; and her feet pained her. They didn't mind if you bought or not, she thought; and often she was pushed out of her place by some bold-faced drab. She thought of the red-haired girl again, as she stood there, panting slightly, with her bag on the railing. Her legs pained her. Suddenly the long-drawn note of a siren floated out its melancholy wail of sound; then there was a dull explosion.

'Them guns again,' Crosby muttered, looking up at the pale-grey sky with peevish irritation. The rooks, scared by the gunfire, rose and wheeled round the tree-tops. Then there was another dull boom. A man on a ladder who was painting the windows of one of the houses paused with his brush in his hand and looked round. A woman who was walking along carrying a loaf of bread that stuck half out of its paper wrapping stopped too. They both waited as if for something to happen.

A topple of smoke drifted over and flopped down from the chimneys. The guns boomed again. The man on the ladder said something to the woman on the pavement. She nodded her head. Then he dipped his brush in the pot and went on painting. The woman walked on. Crosby pulled herself together and tottered across the road into the High Street. The guns went on booming and the sirens wailed. The war was over[49] – so somebody told her as she took her place in the queue at the grocer's shop. The guns went on booming and the sirens wailed.

PRESENT DAY

IT WAS A SUMMER EVENING; the sun was setting; the sky was blue still, but tinged with gold, as if a thin veil of gauze hung over it, and here and there in the gold-blue amplitude an island of cloud lay suspended. In the fields the trees stood majestically caparisoned, with their innumerable leaves gilt. Sheep and cows, pearl white and parti-coloured, lay recumbent or munched their way through the half-transparent grass. An edge of light surrounded everything. A red-gold fume rose from the dust on the roads. Even the little red-brick villas on the high roads had become porous, incandescent with light, and the flowers in cottage gardens, lilac and pink like cotton dresses, shone veined as if lit from within. Faces of people standing at cottage doors or padding along pavements showed the same red glow as they fronted the slowly sinking sun.

Eleanor came out of her flat and shut the door. Her face was lit up by the glow of the sun as it sank over London, and for a moment she was dazzled and looked out over the roofs and spires that lay beneath. There were people talking inside her room, and she wanted to have a word with her nephew alone. North, her brother Morris's son, had just come back from Africa, and she had scarcely seen him alone. So many people had dropped in that evening – Miriam Parrish; Ralph Pickersgill; Antony Wedd; her niece Peggy; and on top of them all, that very talkative man, her friend Nicholas Pomjalovsky, whom they called Brown for short. She had scarcely had a word with North alone. For a moment they stood in the bright square of sunshine that fell on the stone floor of the passage. Voices were still talking within. She put her hand on his shoulder.

'It's so nice to see you,' she said. 'And you haven't changed . . . ' She looked at him. She still saw traces of the brown-eyed cricketing boy in the massive man, who was so burnt, and a little grey too over the ears. 'We shan't let you go back,' she continued, beginning to walk downstairs with him, 'to that horrid farm.'

He smiled. 'And you haven't changed either,' he said.

She looked very vigorous. She had been in India. Her face was tanned with the sun. With her white hair and her brown cheeks she scarcely looked her age, but she must be well over seventy, he was thinking. They walked downstairs arm in arm. There were six flights of stone steps to descend, but she insisted upon coming all the way down with him, to see him off.

'And North,' she said, when they reached the hall, 'you will be careful . . .' She stopped on the doorstep. 'Driving in London,' she said, 'isn't the same as driving in Africa.'

There was his little sports car outside; a man was going past the door in the evening sunlight crying, 'Old chairs and baskets to mend.'

He shook his head; his voice was drowned by the voice of the man crying. He glanced at a board that hung in the hall with names on it. Who was in and who was out was signified with a care that amused him slightly, after Africa. The voice of the man crying, 'Old chairs and baskets to mend,' slowly died away.

'Well, goodbye, Eleanor,' he said turning. 'We shall meet later.' He got into his car.

'Oh, but North – ' she cried, suddenly remembering something she wanted to say to him. But he had turned on the engine; he did not hear her voice. He waved his hand to her – there she stood at the top of the steps with her hair blowing in the wind. The car started off with a jerk. She gave another wave of her hand to him as he turned the corner.

Eleanor is just the same, he thought: more erratic perhaps. With a room full of people – her little room had been crowded – she had insisted upon showing him her new shower-bath. 'You press that knob,' she had said, 'and look – ' Innumerable needles of water shot down. He laughed aloud. They had sat on the edge of the bath together.

But the cars behind him hooted persistently; they hooted and hooted. What at? he asked. Suddenly he realised that they were hooting at him. The light had changed; it was green now, he had been blocking the way. He started off with a violent jerk. He had not mastered the art of driving in London.

The noise of London still seemed to him deafening, and the speed at which people drove was terrifying. But it was exciting after Africa. The shops even, he thought, as he shot past rows of plate-glass windows, were marvellous. Along the kerb, too, there were barrows of fruit and flowers. Everywhere there was profusion; plenty . . . Again the red light shone out; he pulled up.

He looked about him. He was somewhere in Oxford Street; the pavement was crowded with people; jostling each other; swarming round the plate-glass windows which were still lit up. The gaiety, the colour, the variety, were amazing after Africa. All these years, he thought to himself, looking at a floating banner of transparent silk, he had been used to raw goods: hides and fleeces; here was the finished article. A dressing-case, of yellow leather fitted with silver bottles, caught his eye. But the light was green again. On he jerked.

He had only been back ten days, and his mind was a jumble of odds and ends. It seemed to him that he had never stopped talking; shaking hands; saying, How-d'you-do? People sprang up everywhere: his father; his sister; old men got up from armchairs and said, You don't remember me? Children he had left in the nursery were grown-up men at college; girls with pigtails were now married women. He was still confused by it all; they talked so fast; they must think him very slow, he thought. He had to withdraw into the window and say, 'What, what, what do they mean by it?'

For instance, this evening at Eleanor's there was a man there with a foreign accent who squeezed lemon into his tea. Who might he be, he wondered? 'One of Nell's dentists,' said his sister Peggy, wrinkling her lip. For they all had lines cut; phrases ready-made. But that was the silent man on the sofa. It was the other one he meant – squeezing lemon into his tea. 'We call him Brown,' she murmured. Why Brown if he's a foreigner, he wondered. Anyhow they all romanticised solitude and savagery – 'I wish I'd done what you did,' said a little man called Pickersgill – except this man Brown, who had said something that interested him. 'If we do not know ourselves, how can we know other people?' he had said. They had been discussing dictators: Napoleon; the psychology of great men. But there was the green light – '*Go* '. He shot on again. And then the lady with the ear-rings gushed about the beauties of nature. He glanced at the name of the street on the left. He was going to dine with Sara but he had not much notion how to get there. He had only heard her voice on the telephone saying, 'Come and dine with me – Milton Street, fifty-two, my name's on the door.' It was near the Prison Tower. But this man Brown – it was difficult to place him at once. He talked, spreading his fingers out, with the volubility of a man who will in the end become a bore. And Eleanor wandered about, holding a cup, telling people about her shower-bath. He wished they would stick to the point. Talk interested him. Serious talk on abstract subjects. 'Was solitude good; was society bad?' That was interesting; but they hopped from thing to thing. When the large man said, 'Solitary confinement is the greatest torture we inflict,' the meagre old woman with the wispy hair at once piped up, laying her hand on her heart, 'It ought to be abolished!' She visited prisons, it seemed.

'Where the dickens am I now?' he asked, peering at the name on the street corner. Somebody had chalked a circle on the wall with a jagged line in it.[50] He looked down the long vista. Door after door, window after window, repeated the same pattern. There was a red-yellow glow over it all, for the sun was sinking through the London dust. Everything was tinged with a warm yellow haze. Barrows full of fruit and flowers were drawn up at the kerb. The sun gilded the fruit; the flowers had a blurred brilliance; there were roses, carnations and lilies too. He had half a mind to stop and buy a bunch to take to Sally. But the cars were hooting behind him. He went on. A bunch of flowers, he thought, held in the hand, would soften the awkwardness of meeting and the usual things that had to be said. 'How nice to see you – you've filled out,' and so on. He had only heard her voice on the telephone, and people changed after all these years. Whether this was the right street or not, he could not be sure; he filtered slowly round the corner. Then stopped; then went on again. This was Milton Street, a dusky street, with old houses, now let out as lodgings; but they had seen better days.

'The odds on that side; the evens on this,' he said. The street was blocked with vans. He hooted. He stopped. He hooted again. A man went to the horse's head, for it was a coal-cart, and the horse slowly plodded on. Fifty-two was just along the row. He dribbled up to the door. He stopped.

A voice pealed out across the street, the voice of a woman singing scales.

'What a dirty,' he said, as he sat still in the car for a moment – here a woman crossed the street with a jug under her arm – 'sordid,' he added, 'low-down street to live in.' He cut off his engine, got out and examined the names on the door. Names mounted one above another; here on a visiting-card, here engraved on brass – Foster; Abrahamson; Roberts; S. Pargiter was near the top, punched on a strip of aluminium. He rang one of the many bells. No one came. The woman went on singing scales, mounting slowly. The mood comes, the mood goes, he thought. He used to write poetry; now the mood had come again as he stood there waiting. He pressed the bell two or three times sharply. But no one answered. Then he gave the door a push; it was open. There was a curious smell in the hall of vegetables cooking; and the oily brown paper made it dark. He went up the stairs of what had once been a gentleman's residence. The banisters were carved; but they had been daubed over with some cheap yellow varnish. He mounted slowly and stood on the landing, uncertain which door to knock at. He was always finding himself now outside the doors of strange houses. He had a feeling that he was no one and nowhere in particular. From across the road came the voice of the singer deliberately ascending the scale, as if the notes were stairs; and here she stopped indolently, languidly, flinging out the voice that was nothing but pure sound. Then he heard somebody inside, laughing.

That's her voice, he said. But there is somebody with her. He was annoyed. He had hoped to find her alone. The voice was speaking and did not answer when he knocked. Very cautiously he opened the door and went in.

'Yes, yes, yes,' Sara was saying. She was kneeling at the telephone talking; but there was nobody there. She raised her hand when she saw him and smiled at him; but she kept her hand raised as if the noise he had made caused her to lose what she was trying to hear.

'What?' she said, speaking into the telephone. 'What?' He stood silent, looking at the silhouettes of his grandparents on the mantelpiece. There were no flowers, he observed. He wished he had brought her some. He listened to what she was saying; he tried to piece it together.

'Yes, now I can hear . . . Yes, you're right. Someone has come in . . . Who? North. My cousin from Africa . . . '

That's me, North thought. 'My cousin from Africa.' That's my label.

'You've met him?' she was saying. There was a pause. 'D'you think so?' she said. She turned and looked at him. They must be discussing him, he thought. He felt uncomfortable.

'Goodbye,' she said, and put down the telephone.

'He says he met you tonight,' she said, going up to him and taking his hand. 'And liked you,' she added, smiling.

'Who was that?' he asked, feeling awkward; but he had no flowers to give her.

'A man you met at Eleanor's,' she said.

'A foreigner?' he asked.

'Yes. Called Brown,' she said, pushing up a chair for him.

He sat down on the chair she had pushed out for him, and she curled up opposite with her foot under her. He remembered the attitude; she came back in sections; first the voice; then the attitude; but something remained unknown.

'You've not changed,' he said – the face he meant. A plain face scarcely changed; whereas beautiful faces wither. She looked neither young nor old; but shabby; and the room, with the pampas grass in a pot in the corner, was untidy. A lodging-house room tidied in a hurry, he guessed.

'And you – ' she said, looking at him. It was as if she were trying to put two different versions of him together; the one on the telephone perhaps and the one on the chair. Or was there some other? This half knowing people, this half being known, this feeling of the eye on the flesh, like a fly crawling – how uncomfortable it was, he thought; but inevitable, after all these years. The tables were littered; he hesitated, holding his hat in his hand. She smiled at him, as he sat there, holding his hat uncertainly.

'Who's the young Frenchman,' she said, 'with the top hat in the picture?'

'What picture?' he asked.

'The one who sits looking puzzled with his hat in his hand,' she said. He put his hat on the table, but awkwardly. A book fell to the floor.

'Sorry,' he said. She meant, presumably, when she compared him to the puzzled man in the picture, that he was clumsy; he always had been.

'This isn't the room where I came last time?' he asked.

He recognised a chair – a chair with gilt claws; there was the usual piano.

'No – that was on the other side of the river,' she said, 'when you came to say goodbye.'

He remembered. He had come to her the evening before he left for the war; and he had hung his cap on the bust of his great-grandfather – that had vanished. And she had mocked him.

'How many lumps of sugar does a lieutenant in His Majesty's Royal Regiment of Rat-Catchers require?' she had sneered. He could see her now dropping lumps of sugar into his tea. And they had quarrelled. And he had left her. It was the night of the raid, he remembered. He remembered the dark night; the searchlights that slowly swept over the sky; here and there they stopped to ponder a fleecy patch; little pellets of shot fell; and people scudded along the empty blue shrouded streets. He had been going to Kensington to dine with his family; he had said goodbye to his mother; he had never seen her again.

The voice of the singer interrupted. 'Ah – h–h, oh–h–h, ah – h–h, oh – h–h,' she sang, languidly climbing up and down the scale on the other side of the street.

'Does she go on like that every night?' he asked. Sara nodded. The notes coming through the humming evening air sounded slow and sensuous. The singer seemed to have endless leisure; she could rest on every stair.

And there was no sign of dinner, he observed; only a dish of fruit on the cheap lodging-house tablecloth, already yellowed with some gravy stain.

'Why d'you always choose slums – ' he was beginning, for children were screaming in the street below, when the door opened and a girl came in carrying a bunch of knives and forks. The regular lodging-house skivvy, North thought; with red hands, and one of those jaunty white caps that girls in lodging-houses clap on top of their hair when the lodger has a party. In her presence they had to make conversation. 'I've been seeing Eleanor,' he said. 'That was where I met your friend Brown . . .'

The girl made a clatter laying the table with the knives and forks she held in a bunch.

'Oh, Eleanor,' said Sara. 'Eleanor – ' But she watched the girl going clumsily round the table; she breathed rather hard as she laid it.

'She's just back from India,' he said. He too watched the girl laying the table. Now she stood a bottle of wine among the cheap lodging-house crockery.

'Gallivanting round the world,' Sara murmured.

'And entertaining the oddest set of old fogies,' he added. He thought of the little man with the fierce blue eyes who wished he had been in Africa; and the wispy woman with beads who visited prisons it seemed.

' . . . and that man, your friend – ' he began. Here the girl went out of the room, but she left the door open, a sign that she was about to come back.

'Nicholas,' said Sara, finishing his sentence. 'The man you call Brown.'

There was a pause.

'And what did you talk about?' she asked.

He tried to remember. 'Napoleon; the psychology of great men; if we don't know ourselves how can we know other people . . .' He stopped. It was difficult to remember accurately what had been said even one hour ago.

'And then,' she said, holding out one hand and touching a finger exactly as Brown had done, ' – how can we make laws, religions, that fit, that fit, when we don't know ourselves?'

'Yes! Yes!' he exclaimed. She had caught his manner exactly; the slight foreign accent; the repetition of the little word 'fit', as if he were not quite sure of the shorter words in English.

'And Eleanor,' Sara continued, 'says . . . "Can we improve – can we improve ourselves?" sitting on the edge of the sofa?'

'Of the bath,' he laughed, correcting her. 'You've had that talk before,' he said.

That was precisely what he was feeling. They had talked before.

'And then,' he continued, 'we discussed . . .'

But here the girl burst in again. She had plates in her hand this time: blue-ringed plates, cheap lodging-house plates.

' – society or solitude; which is best,' he finished his sentence.

Sara kept looking at the table. 'And which,' she asked, in the distracted way of someone who with their surface senses watches what is being done, but at the same time thinks of something else, 'which did you say? You who've been alone all these years – ' she said. The girl left the room again. ' – among your sheep, North.' She broke off; for now a trombone player had struck up in the street below, and as the voice of the woman practising her scales continued, they sounded like two people trying to express completely different views of the world in general at one and the same time. The voice ascended; the trombone wailed. They laughed.

' . . . Sitting on the verandah,' she resumed, 'looking at the stars.'

He looked up: was she quoting something? He remembered he had written to her when he first went out. 'Yes, looking at the stars,' he said.

'Sitting on the verandah in the silence,' she added. A van went past the window. All sounds were for the moment obliterated.

'And then . . . ' she said as the van rattled away – she paused as if she were referring to something else that he had written. ' – then you saddled a horse,' she said, 'and rode away!'

She jumped up, and for the first time he saw her face in the full light. There was a smudge on the side of her nose.

'D'you know,' he said, looking at her, 'that you've a smudge on your face?'

She touched the wrong cheek.

'Not that side – the other,' he said.

She left the room without looking in the glass. From which we deduce the fact, he said to himself, as if he were writing a novel, that Miss Sara Pargiter has never attracted the love of men. Or had she? He did not know. These little snapshot pictures of people left much to be desired, these little surface pictures that one made, like a fly crawling over a face and feeling here's the nose, here's the brow.

He strolled to the window. The sun must be setting, for the brick of the house at the corner blushed a yellowish pink. One or two high windows were burnished gold. The girl was in the room, and she distracted him; also the noise of London still bothered him. Against the dull background of traffic noises, of wheels turning and brakes squeaking, there rose near at hand the cry of a woman suddenly alarmed for her child; the monotonous cry of a man selling vegetables; and far away a barrel-organ was playing. It stopped; it began again. I used to write to her, he thought, late at night, when I felt lonely, when I was young. He looked at himself in the glass. He saw his sunburnt face with the broad cheek-bones and the little brown eyes.

The girl had been sucked down into the lower portion of the house. The door stood open. Nothing seemed to be happening. He waited. He felt an outsider. After all these years, he thought, everyone was paired off; settled down; busy with their own affairs. You found them telephoning, remembering other conversations; they went out of the room; they left one alone. He took up a book and read a sentence.

'A shadow like an angel with bright hair . . . '

Next moment she came in. But there seemed to be some hitch in the proceedings. The door was open; the table laid; but nothing happened. They stood together, waiting, with their backs to the fireplace.

'How strange it must be,' she resumed, 'coming back after all these years – as if you'd dropped from the clouds in an aeroplane,' she pointed to the table as if that were the field in which he had landed.

'On to an unknown land,' said North. He leant forward and touched a knife on the table.

' – and finding people talking,' she added.

' – talking, talking,' he said, 'about money and politics,' he added, giving the fender behind him a vicious little kick with his heel.

Here the girl came in. She wore an air of importance derived apparently from the dish she carried, for it was covered with a great metal cover. She raised the cover with a certain flourish. There was a leg of mutton underneath. 'Let's dine,' said Sara.

'I'm hungry,' he added.

They sat down and she took the carving-knife and made a long incision. A thin trickle of red juice ran out; it was underdone. She looked at it.

'Mutton oughtn't to be like that,' she said. 'Beef – but not mutton.'

They watched the red juice running down into the well of the dish.

'Shall we send it back,' she said, 'or eat it as it is?'

'Eat it,' he said. 'I've eaten far worse joints than this,' he added.

'In Africa . . . ' she said, lifting the lids of the vegetable dishes. There was a slabbed-down mass of cabbage in one oozing green water; in the other, yellow potatoes that looked hard. ' . . . in Africa, in the wilds of Africa,' she resumed, helping him to cabbage, 'in that farm you were on, where no one came for months at a time, and you sat on the verandah listening – '

'To sheep,' he said. He was cutting his mutton into strips. It was tough.

'And there was nothing to break the silence,' she went on, helping herself to potatoes, 'but a tree falling, or a rock breaking from the side of a distant mountain – ' She looked at him as if to verify the sentences that she was quoting from his letters.

'Yes,' he said. 'It was very silent.'

'And hot,' she added. 'Blazing hot at midday: an old tramp tapped on your door . . . ?'

He nodded. He saw himself again, a young man, and very lonely.

'And then – ' she began again. But a great lorry came crashing down the street. Something rattled on the table. The walls and the floor seemed to tremble. She parted two glasses that were jingling together. The lorry passed; they heard it rumbling away in the distance.

'And the birds,' she went on. 'The nightingales, singing in the moon-light?'

He felt uncomfortable at the vision she called up. 'I must have written you a lot of nonsense!' he exclaimed. 'I wish you'd torn them up – those letters!'

'No! They were beautiful letters! Wonderful letters!' she exclaimed, raising her glass. A thimbleful of wine always made her tipsy, he remembered. Her eyes shone; her cheeks glowed.

'And then you had a day off,' she went on, 'and jolted along a rough white road in a springless cart to the next town – '

'Sixty miles away,' he said.

'And went to a bar; and met a man from the next – ranch?' She hesitated as if the word might be the wrong one.

'Ranch, yes, ranch,' he confirmed her. 'I went to the town and had a drink at the bar – '

'And then?' she said.

He laughed. There were some things he had not told her. He was silent.

'Then you stopped writing,' she said. She put her glass down.

'When I forgot what you were like,' he said, looking at her. 'You gave up writing too,' he said.

'Yes, I too,' she said.

The trombone had moved his station and was wailing lugubriously under the window. The doleful sound, as if a dog had thrown back its head and were baying at the moon, floated up to them. She waved her fork in time to it.

'Our hearts full of tears, our lips full of laughter, we passed on the stairs' – she dragged her words out to fit the wail of the trombone – 'we passed on the stair–r–r–s' – but here the trombone changed its measure to a jig. 'He to sorrow, I to bliss,' she jigged with it, 'he to bliss and I to sorrow, we passed on the stair–r–r–s.'

She set her glass down.

'Another cut off the joint?' she asked.

'No, thank you,' he said, looking at the rather stringy disagreeable object which was still bleeding into the well. The willow-pattern plate was daubed with gory streaks. She stretched her hand out and rang the bell. She rang; she rang a second time. No one came.

'Your bells don't ring,' he said.

'No,' she smiled. 'The bells don't ring, and the taps don't run.' She thumped on the floor. They waited. No one came. The trombone wailed outside.

'But there was one letter you wrote me,' he continued as they waited. 'An angry letter; a cruel letter.'

He looked at her. She had lifted her lip like a horse that is going to bite. That, too, he remembered.

'Yes?' she said.

'The night you came in from the Strand,' he reminded her.

Here the girl came in with the pudding. It was an ornate pudding, semi-transparent, pink, ornamented with blobs of cream.

'I remember,' said Sara, sticking her spoon into the quivering jelly; 'a still autumn night; the lights lit; and people padding along the pavement with wreaths in their hands?'

'Yes,' he nodded. 'That was it.'

'And I said to myself,' she paused, 'this is hell. We are the damned?' He nodded.

She helped him to pudding.

'And I,' he said, as he took his plate, 'was among the damned.' He stuck his spoon into the quivering mass that she had given him. 'Coward; hypocrite; with your switch in your hand and your cap on your head – ' He seemed to quote from a letter that she had written him. He paused.

She smiled at him. 'But what was the word – the word I used?' she asked, as if she were trying to remember.

'Poppycock!' he reminded her. She nodded.

'And then I went over the bridge,' she resumed, raising her spoon half-way to her mouth, 'and stopped in one of those little alcoves, bays, what d'you call 'em? – scooped out over the water, and looked down – ' She looked down at her plate.

'When you lived on the other side of the river,' he prompted her.

'Stood and looked down,' she said, looking at her glass which she held in front of her, 'and thought: Running water, flowing water, water that crinkles up the lights; moonlight; starlight – ' She drank and was silent.

'Then the car came,' he prompted her.

'Yes; the Rolls-Royce. It stopped in the lamplight and there they sat – '

'Two people,' he reminded her.

'Two people. Yes,' she said. 'He was smoking a cigar. An upper-class Englishman with a big nose, in a dress suit. And she, sitting beside him, in a fur-trimmed cloak, took advantage of the pause under the lamplight to raise her hand' – she raised her hand – 'and polish that spade, her mouth.'

She swallowed her mouthful.

'And the peroration?' he prompted her.

She shook her head.

They were silent. North had finished his pudding. He took out his cigarette-case. Save for a dish of rather fly-blown apples and bananas, there was no more to eat apparently.

'We were very foolish when we were young, Sal,' he said, as he lit his cigarette, 'writing purple passages . . .'

'At dawn with the sparrows chirping,' she said, pulling the plate of fruit towards her. She began peeling a banana, as if she were unsheathing some soft glove. He took an apple and peeled it. The curl of apple-skin lay on his plate, coiled up like a snake's skin, he thought; and the banana-skin was like the finger of a glove that had been ripped open.

The street was now quiet. The woman had stopped singing. The trombone-player had moved off. The rush hour was over and nothing went down the street. He looked at her, biting little bits off her banana.

When she came to the Fourth of June, he remembered, she wore her skirt the wrong way round. She was crooked in those days too; and they had laughed at her – he and Peggy. She had never married; he wondered why not. He swept up the broken coils of apple-peel on his plate.

'What does he do,' he said suddenly, ' – that man who throws his hands out?'

'Like this?' she said. She threw her hands out.

'Yes,' he nodded. That was the man – one of those voluble foreigners with a theory about everything. Yet he had liked him – he gave off an aroma; a whirr; his flexible supple face worked amusingly; he had a round forehead; good eyes; and was bald.

'What does he do?' he repeated.

'Talks,' she replied, 'about the soul.' She smiled. Again he felt an outsider; so many talks there must have been between them; such intimacy.

'About the soul,' she continued, taking a cigarette. 'Lectures,' she added, lighting it. 'Ten and six for a seat in the front row,' she puffed her smoke out. 'There's standing room at half a crown;[51] but then,' she puffed, 'you don't hear so well. You only catch half the lesson of the teacher, the master,' she laughed.

She was sneering at him now; she conveyed the impression that he was a charlatan. Yet Peggy had said that they were very intimate – she and this foreigner. The vision of the man at Eleanor's changed slightly like an air ball blown aside.

'I thought he was a friend of yours,' he said aloud.

'Nicholas?' she exclaimed. 'I love him!'

Her eyes certainly glowed. They fixed themselves upon a salt cellar with a look of rapture that made North feel once more puzzled.

'You love him. . . ' he began. But here the telephone rang.

'There he is!' she exclaimed. 'That's him! That's Nicholas!'

She spoke with extreme irritation.

The telephone rang again. 'I'm not here!' she said. The telephone rang again. 'Not here! Not here! Not here!' she repeated in time to the bell. She made no attempt to answer it. He could stand the stab of her voice and the bell no longer. He went over to the telephone. There was a pause as he stood with the receiver in his hand.

'Tell him I'm not here!' she said.

'Hello,' he said, answering the telephone. But there was a pause. He looked at her sitting on the edge of her chair, swinging her foot up and down.

Then a voice spoke.

'I'm North,' he answered the telephone. 'I'm dining with Sara . . . Yes, I'll tell her . . . ' He looked at her again. 'She is sitting on the edge of her chair,' he said, 'with a smudge on her face, swinging her foot up and down.'

Eleanor stood holding the telephone. She smiled, and for a moment after she had put the receiver back stood there, still smiling, before she turned to her niece Peggy who had been dining with her.

'North is dining with Sara,' she said, smiling at the little telephone picture of two people at the other end of London, one of whom was sitting on the edge of her chair with a smudge on her face.

'He's dining with Sara,' she said again. But her niece did not smile, for she had not seen the picture, and she was slightly irritated because, in the middle of what they were saying, Eleanor had suddenly got up and said, 'I'll just remind Sara.'

'Oh, is he?' she said casually.

Eleanor came and sat down. 'We were saying – ' she began.

'You've had it cleaned,' said Peggy simultaneously. While Eleanor telephoned, she had been looking at the picture of her grandmother over the writing-table.

'Yes,' Eleanor glanced back over her shoulder. 'Yes. And do you see there's a flower fallen on the grass?' she said. She turned and looked at the picture. The face, the dress, the basket of flowers all shone softly, melting into each other, as if the paint were one smooth coat of enamel. There was a flower – a little sprig of blue – lying in the grass.

'It was hidden by the dirt,' said Eleanor. 'But I can just remember it, when I was a child. That reminds me, if you want a good man to clean pictures – '

'But was it like her?' Peggy interrupted.

Somebody had told her that she was like her grandmother; and she did not want to be like her. She wanted to be dark and aquiline: but in fact she was blue-eyed and round-faced – like her grandmother.

'I've got the address somewhere,' Eleanor went on.

'Don't bother – don't bother,' said Peggy, irritated by her aunt's habit of adding unnecessary details. It was age coming on, she supposed: age that loosened screws and made the whole apparatus of the mind rattle and jingle.

'Was it like her?' she asked again.

'Not as I remember her,' said Eleanor, glancing once more at the picture. 'When I was a child perhaps – no, I don't think even as a child. What's so interesting,' she continued, 'is that what they thought ugly – red hair for instance – we think pretty; so that I often ask myself,' she paused, puffing at her cheroot, ' "What is pretty?" '

'Yes,' said Peggy. 'That's what we were saying.'

For when Eleanor suddenly took it into her head that she must remind Sara of the party, they had been talking about Eleanor's childhood – how things had changed; one thing seemed good to one generation, another to another. She liked getting Eleanor to talk about her past; it seemed to her so peaceful and so safe.

'Is there any standard, d'you think?' she said, wishing to bring her back to what they were saying.

'I wonder,' said Eleanor absent-mindedly.

She was thinking of something else.

'How annoying!' she exclaimed suddenly. 'I had it on the tip of my tongue – something I want to ask you. Then I thought of Delia's party; then North made me laugh – Sally sitting on the edge of her chair with a smudge on her nose; and that's put it out of my head.' She shook her head. 'D'you know the feeling when one's been on the point of saying something, and been interrupted, how it seems to stick *here*,' she tapped her forehead, 'so that it stops everything else? Not that it was anything of importance,' she added. She wandered about the room for a moment. 'No, I give it up; I give it up,' she said, shaking her head. 'I shall go and get ready now, if you'll call a cab.'

She went into the bedroom. Soon there was the sound of running water.

Peggy lit another cigarette. If Eleanor were going to wash, as seemed likely from the sounds in the bedroom, there was no need to hurry about the cab. She glanced at the letters on the mantelpiece. An address stuck out on the top of one of them – 'Mon Repos, Wimbledon'. One of Eleanor's dentists, Peggy thought to herself. The man she went botanising with on Wimbledon Common perhaps. A charming man. Eleanor had described him. 'He says every tooth is quite unlike every other tooth. And he knows all about plants . . . ' It was difficult to get her to stick to her childhood.

She crossed to the telephone; she gave the number. There was a pause. As she waited she looked at her hands holding the telephone. Efficient, shell-like, polished but not painted, they're a compromise, she thought, looking at her fingernails, between science and . . . But here a voice said, 'Number, please,' and she gave it.

Again she waited. As she sat where Eleanor had sat she saw the telephone picture that Eleanor had seen – Sally sitting on the edge of her chair with a smudge on her face. What a fool, she thought bitterly, and a thrill ran down her thigh. Why was she bitter? For she prided herself upon being honest – she was a doctor – and that thrill she knew meant bitterness. Did she envy her because she was happy, or was it the croak of some ancestral prudery – did she disapprove of these friendships with men who did not love women? She looked at the picture of her grandmother as if to ask her opinion. But she had assumed the immunity of a work of art; she seemed as she sat there, smiling at her roses, to be indifferent to our right and wrong.

'Hello,' said a gruff voice, which suggested sawdust and a shelter, and she gave the address and put down the telephone just as Eleanor came in – she was wearing a red-gold Arab cloak with a silver veil over her hair.

'One of these days d'you think you'll be able to see things at the end of the telephone?' Peggy said, getting up. Eleanor's hair was her beauty, she thought; and her silver-washed dark eyes – a fine old prophetess, a queer old bird, venerable and funny at one and the same time. She was burnt from her travels so that her hair looked whiter than ever.

'What's that?' said Eleanor, for she had not caught her remark about the telephone. Peggy did not repeat it. They stood at the window waiting for the cab. They stood there side by side, silent, looking out, because there was a pause to fill up, and the view from the window, which was so high over the roofs, over the squares and angles of back gardens to the blue line of hills in the distance served, like another voice speaking, to fill up the pause. The sun was setting; one cloud lay curled like a red feather in the blue. She looked down. It was queer to see cabs turning corners, going round this street and down the other, and not to hear the sound they made. It was like a map of London: a section laid beneath them. The summer day was fading; lights were being lit, primrose lights, still separate, for the glow of the sunset was still in the air.

Eleanor pointed at the sky. 'That's where I saw my first aeroplane – there between those chimneys,' she said. There were high chimneys, factory chimneys, in the distance; and a great building – Westminster Cathedral was it? – over there riding above the roofs.

'I was standing here, looking out,' Eleanor went on. 'It must have been just after I'd got into the flat, a summer's day, and I saw a black spot in the sky, and I said to whoever it was – Miriam Parrish, I think, yes, for she came to help me to get into the flat – I hope Delia, by the way, remembered to ask her – ' . . . that's old age, Peggy noted, bringing in one thing after another.

'You said to Miriam – ' she prompted her.

'I said to Miriam, "Is it a bird? No, I don't think it can be a bird. It's too big. Yet it moves." And suddenly it came over me, that's an aeroplane! And it was! You know they'd flown the Channel not so very long before. I was staying with you in Dorset at the time; and I remember reading it out in the paper, and someone – your father, I think – said: 'The world will never be the same again!'

'Oh, well – ' Peggy laughed. She was about to say that aeroplanes hadn't made all that difference, for it was her line to disabuse her elders of their belief in science, partly because their credulity amused her, partly because she was daily impressed by the ignorance of doctors – when Eleanor sighed.

'Oh dear,' she murmured.

She turned away from the window.

Old age again, Peggy thought. Some gust blew open a door: one of the many millions in Eleanor's seventy-odd years; out came a painful thought; which she at once concealed – she had gone to her writing-table and was fidgeting with papers – with the humble generosity, the painful humility of the old.

'What, Nell – ?' Peggy began.

'Nothing, nothing,' said Eleanor. She had seen the sky; and that sky was laid with pictures – she had seen it so often – any one of which might come uppermost when she looked at it. Now, because she had been talking to North, it brought back the war; how she had stood there one night, watching the searchlights. She had come home, after a raid; she had been dining in Westminster with Renny and Maggie. They had sat in a cellar; and Nicholas – it was the first time she had met him – had said that the war was of no importance. 'We are children playing with fireworks in the back garden' . . . she remembered his phrase; and how, sitting round a wooden packing-case, they had drunk to a new world. 'A new world – a new world!' Sally had cried, drumming with her spoon on top of the packing-case. She turned to her writing-table, tore up a letter and threw it away.

'Yes,' she said, fumbling among her papers, looking for something. 'Yes – I don't know about aeroplanes, I've never been up in one; but motor cars – I could do without motor cars. I was almost knocked down by one, did I tell you? In the Brompton Road. All my own fault – I wasn't looking . . . And wireless – that's a nuisance – the people downstairs turn it on after breakfast; but on the other hand – hot water; electric light; and those new – ' She paused. 'Ah, there it is!' she exclaimed. She pounced upon some paper that she had been hunting for. 'If Edward's there tonight, do remind me – I'll tie a knot in my handkerchief . . . ' She opened her bag, took out a silk handkerchief, and proceeded solemnly to tie it into a knot . . . 'to ask him about Runcorn's boy.'

The bell rang.

'The taxi,' she said.

She glanced about to make sure that she had forgotten nothing. She stopped suddenly. Her eye had been caught by the evening paper, which lay on the floor with its broad bar of print and its blurred photograph. She picked it up.

'What a face!' she exclaimed, flattening it out on the table.

As far as Peggy could see, but she was short-sighted, it was the usual evening paper's blurred picture of a fat man gesticulating.[52]

'Damned – ' Eleanor shot out suddenly, 'bully!' She tore the paper across with one sweep of her hand and flung it on the floor. Peggy was shocked. A little shiver ran over her skin as the paper tore. The word 'damned' on her aunt's lips had shocked her.

Next moment she was amused; but still she had been shocked. For when Eleanor, who used English so reticently, said 'damned' and then 'bully', it meant much more than the words she and her friends used. And her gesture, tearing the paper . . . What a queer set they are, she thought, as she followed Eleanor down the stairs. Her red-gold cloak trailed from step to step. So she had seen her father crumple *The Times* and sit trembling with rage because somebody had said something in a newspaper. How odd!

And the way she tore it! she thought, half laughing, and she flung out her hand as Eleanor had flung hers. Eleanor's figure still seemed erect with indignation. It would be simple, she thought, it would be satisfactory, she thought, following her down flight after flight of stone steps, to be like that. The little knob on her cloak tapped on the stairs. They descended rather slowly.

'Take my aunt,' she said to herself, beginning to arrange the scene into an argument she had been having with a man at the hospital, 'take my aunt, living alone in a sort of workman's flat at the top of six flights of stairs . . . ' Eleanor stopped.

'Don't tell me,' she said, 'that I left the letter upstairs – Runcorn's letter that I want to show Edward, about the boy?' She opened her bag. 'No: here it is.' There it was in her bag. They went on downstairs.

Eleanor gave the address to the cabman and sat down with a jerk in her corner. Peggy glanced at her out of the corner of her eye.

It was the force that she had put into the words that impressed her, not the words. It was as if she still believed with passion – she, old Eleanor – in the things that man had destroyed. A wonderful generation, she thought, as they drove off. Believers . . .

'You see,' Eleanor interrupted, as if she wanted to explain her words, 'it means the end of everything we cared for.'

'Freedom?' said Peggy perfunctorily.

'Yes,' said Eleanor. 'Freedom and justice.'

The cab drove off down the mild respectable little streets where every house had its bow window, its strip of garden, its private name. As they drove on, into the big main street, the scene in the flat composed itself in Peggy's mind as she would tell it to the man in the hospital. 'Suddenly she lost her temper,' she said, 'took the paper and tore it across – my aunt, who's over seventy.' She glanced at Eleanor to verify the details. Her aunt interrupted her.

'That's where we used to live,' she said. She waved her hand towards a long lamp-starred street on the left. Peggy, looking out, could just see the imposing unbroken avenue with its succession of pale pillars and steps. The repeated columns, the orderly architecture, had even a pale pompous beauty as one stucco column repeated another stucco column all down the street.

'Abercorn Terrace,' said Eleanor; ' . . . the pillar-box,' she murmured as they drove past. Why the pillar-box? Peggy asked herself. Another door had been opened. Old age must have endless avenues, stretching away and away down its darkness, she supposed, and now one door opened and then another.

'Aren't people – ' Eleanor began. Then she stopped. As usual, she had begun in the wrong place.

'Yes?' said Peggy. She was irritated by this inconsequence.

'I was going to say – the pillar-box made me think,' Eleanor began; then she laughed. She gave up the attempt to account for the order in which her thoughts came to her. There was an order, doubtless; but it took so long to find it, and this rambling, she knew, annoyed Peggy, for young people's minds worked so quickly.

'That's where we used to dine,' she broke off, nodding at a big house at the corner of a square. 'Your father and I. The man he used to read with. What was his name? He became a judge . . . We used to dine there, the three of us. Morris, my father and I . . . They had very large parties in those days. Always legal people. And he collected old oak. Mostly shams,' she added with a little chuckle.

'You used to dine . . . ' Peggy began. She wished to get her back to her past. It was so interesting; so safe; so unreal – that past of the 'eighties; and to her, so beautiful in its unreality.

'Tell me about your youth . . . ' she began.

'But your lives are much more interesting than ours were,' said Eleanor. Peggy was silent.

They were driving along a bright crowded street; here stained ruby with the light from picture palaces;[53] here yellow from shop windows gay with summer dresses; for the shops, though shut, were still lit up, and people were still looking at dresses, at flights of hats on little rods, at jewels.

When my Aunt Delia comes to town, Peggy continued the story of Eleanor that she was telling her friend at the hospital, she says, We must have a party. Then they all flock together. They love it. As for herself, she hated it. She would far rather have stayed at home or gone to the pictures. It's the sense of the family, she added, glancing at Eleanor as if to collect another little fact about her to add to her portrait of a Victorian spinster. Eleanor was looking out of the window. Then she turned.

'And the experiment with the guinea-pig – how did that go off?' she asked. Peggy was puzzled.

Then she remembered and told her.

'I see. So it proved nothing. So you've got to begin all over again. That's very interesting. Now I wish you'd explain to me . . . ' There was another problem that puzzled her.

The things she wants explained, Peggy said to her friend at the hospital, are either as simple as two and two make four, or so difficult that nobody in the world knows the answer. And if you say to her, 'What's eight times eight?' – she smiled at the profile of her aunt against the window – she taps her forehead and says . . . but again Eleanor interrupted her.

'It's so good of you to come,' she said, giving her a little pat on the knee. (But did I show her, Peggy thought, that I hate coming?)

'It's a way of seeing people,' Eleanor continued. 'And now that we're all getting on – not you, us – one doesn't like to miss chances.'

They drove on. And how does one get *that* right? Peggy thought, trying to add another touch to the portrait. 'Sentimental' was it? Or, on the contrary, was it good to feel like that . . . natural . . . right? She shook her head. I'm no use at describing people, she said to her friend at the hospital. They're too difficult . . . She's not like that – not like that at all, she said, making a little dash with her hand as if to rub out an outline that she had drawn wrongly. As she did so, her friend at the hospital vanished.

She was alone with Eleanor in the cab. And they were passing houses. Where does she begin, and where do I end? she thought . . . On they drove. They were two living people, driving across London; two sparks of life enclosed in two separate bodies; and those sparks of life enclosed in two separate bodies are at this moment, she thought, driving past a picture palace. But what is this moment; and what are we? The puzzle was too difficult for her to solve it. She sighed.

'You're too young to feel that,' said Eleanor.

'What?' Peggy asked with a little start.

'About meeting people. About not missing chances of seeing them.'

'Young?' said Peggy. 'I shall never be as young as you are!' She patted her aunt's knee in her turn. 'Gallivanting off to India . . . ' she laughed.

'Oh, India. India's nothing nowadays,' said Eleanor. 'Travel's so easy. You just take a ticket; just get on board ship . . . But what I want to see before I die,' she continued, 'is something different . . . ' She waved her hand out of the window. They were passing public buildings; offices of some sort. ' . . . another kind of civilisation. Tibet, for instance. I was reading a book by a man called – now what was he called?'

She paused, distracted by the sights in the street. 'Don't people wear pretty clothes nowadays?' she said, pointing to a girl with fair hair and a young man in evening dress.

'Yes,' said Peggy perfunctorily, looking at the painted face and the bright shawl; at the white waistcoat and the smoothed back hair. Anything distracts Eleanor, everything interests her, she thought.

'Was it that you were suppressed when you were young?' she said aloud, recalling vaguely some childish memory; her grandfather with the shiny stumps instead of fingers; and a long dark drawing-room. Eleanor turned. She was surprised.

'Suppressed?' she repeated. She so seldom thought about herself now that she was surprised.

'Oh, I see what you mean,' she added after a moment. A picture – another picture – had swum to the surface. There was Delia standing in the middle of the room; Oh my God! Oh my God! she was saying; a hansom cab had stopped at the house next door; and she herself was watching Morris – was it Morris? – going down the street to post a letter . . . She was silent. I do not want to go back into my past, she was thinking. I want the present.

'Where's he taking us?' she said, looking out. They had reached the public part of London; the illuminated. The light fell on broad pavements; on white brilliantly lit-up public offices; on a pallid, hoary-looking church. Advertisements popped in and out. Here was a bottle of beer: it poured: then stopped: then poured again. They had reached the theatre quarter. There was the usual garish confusion. Men and women in evening dress were walking in the middle of the road. Cabs were wheeling and stopping. Their own taxi was held up. It stopped dead under a statue: the lights shone on its cadaverous pallor.

'Always reminds me of an advertisement for sanitary towels,' said Peggy, glancing at the figure of a woman in nurse's uniform[54] holding out her hand.

Eleanor was shocked for a moment. A knife seemed to slice her skin, leaving a ripple of unpleasant sensation; but what was solid in her body it did not touch, she realised after a moment. That she said because of Charles, she thought, feeling the bitterness in her tone – her brother, a nice dull boy who had been killed.

'The only fine thing that was said in the war,' she said aloud, reading the words cut on the pedestal.

'It didn't come to much,' said Peggy sharply.

The cab remained fixed in the block.

The pause seemed to hold them in the light of some thought that they both wished to put away.

'Don't people wear pretty clothes nowadays?' said Eleanor, pointing to another girl with fair hair in a long bright cloak and another young man in evening dress.

'Yes,' said Peggy briefly.

But why don't you enjoy yourself more? Eleanor said to herself. Her brother's death had been very sad, but she had always found North much the more interesting of the two. The cab threaded its way through the traffic and passed into a back street. He was stopped now by a red light. 'It's nice, having North back again,' Eleanor said.

'Yes,' said Peggy. 'He says we talk of nothing but money and politics,' she added. She finds fault with him because he was not the one to be killed; but that's wrong, Eleanor thought.

'Does he?' she said. 'But then . . . ' A newspaper placard, with large black letters, seemed to finish her sentence for her. They were approaching the square in which Delia lived. She began to fumble with her purse. She looked at the metre which had mounted rather high. The man was going the long way round.

'He'll find his way in time,' she said. They were gliding slowly round the square. She waited patiently, holding her purse in her hand. She saw a breadth of dark sky over the roofs. The sun had sunk. For a moment the sky had the quiet look of the sky that lies above fields and woods in the country.

'He'll have to turn, that's all,' she said. 'I'm not despondent,' she added, as the taxi turned. 'Travelling, you see: when one has to mix up with all sorts of other people on board ship, or in one of those little places where one has to stay – off the beaten track – ' The taxi was sliding tentatively past house after house – 'You ought to go there, Peggy,' she broke off; 'you ought to travel; the natives are so beautiful you know: half naked, going down to the river in the moonlight; – that's the house over there – ' She tapped on the window – the taxi slowed down. 'What was I saying? I'm not despondent, no, because people are so kind, so good at heart . . . So that if only ordinary people, ordinary people like ourselves . . . '

The cab drew up at a house whose windows were lit up. Peggy leant forward and opened the door. She jumped out and paid the driver. Eleanor bundled out after her. 'No, no, no, Peggy,' she began.

'It's my cab. It's my cab,' Peggy protested.

'But I insist on paying my share,' said Eleanor, opening her purse.

'That's Eleanor,' said North. He left the telephone and turned to Sara. She was still swinging her foot up and down.

'She told me to tell you to come to Delia's party,' he said.

'To Delia's party? Why to Delia's party?' she asked.

'Because they're old and want you to come,' he said, standing over her.

'Old Eleanor; wandering Eleanor; Eleanor with the wild eyes . . . ' she mused. 'Shall I, shan't I, shall I, shan't I?' she hummed, looking up at him. 'No,' she said, putting her feet to the ground, 'I shan't.'

'You must,' he said. For her manner irritated him – Eleanor's voice was still in his ears.

'I must, must I?' she said, making the coffee.

'Then,' she said, giving him his cup and picking up the book at the same time, 'read until we must go.'

She curled herself up again, holding her cup in her hand.

It was still early, it was true. But why, he thought as he opened the book again and turned over the pages, won't she come? Is she afraid? he wondered. He looked at her crumpled in her chair. Her dress was shabby. He looked at the book again, but he could hardly see to read. She had not lit the lamp.

'I can't see to read without a light,' he said. It grew dark soon in this street; the houses were so close. Now a car passed and a light slid across the ceiling.

'Shall I turn on the light?' she asked.

'No,' he said. 'I'll try to remember something.' He began to say aloud the only poem he knew by heart. As he spoke the words out into the semi-darkness they sounded extremely beautiful, he thought, because they could not see each other, perhaps.

He paused at the end of the verse.

'Go on,' she said.

He began again. The words going out into the room seemed like actual presences, hard and independent; yet as she was listening they were changed by their contact with her. But as he reached the end of the second verse –

> 'Society is all but rude –
> To this delicious solitude . . . '[55]

he heard a sound. Was it in the poem or outside of it, he wondered? Inside, he thought, and was about to go on when she raised her hand. He stopped. He heard heavy footsteps outside the door. Was someone coming in? Her eyes were on the door.

'The Jew,' she murmured.

'The Jew?' he said. They listened. He could hear quite distinctly now. Somebody was turning on taps; somebody was having a bath in the room opposite.

'The Jew having a bath,' she said.

'The Jew having a bath?' he repeated.

'And tomorrow there'll be a line of grease round the bath,' she said.

'Damn the Jew!' he exclaimed. The thought of a line of grease from a strange man's body on the bath next door disgusted him.

'Go on – ' said Sara: ' "Society is all but rude",' she repeated the last lines, ' "to this delicious solitude." '

'No,' he said.

They listened to the water running. The man was coughing and clearing his throat as he sponged.

'Who is this Jew?' he asked.

'Abrahamson, in the tallow trade,' she said.

They listened.

'Engaged to a pretty girl in a tailor's shop,' she added.

They could hear the sounds through the thin walls very distinctly.

He was snorting as he sponged himself.

'But he leaves hairs in the bath,' she concluded.

North felt a shiver run through him. Hairs in food, hairs on basins, other people's hairs made him feel physically sick.

'D'you share a bath with him?' he asked.

She nodded.

He made a noise like 'Pah!'

' "Pah." That's what I said,' she laughed. ' "Pah!" – when I went into the bathroom on a cold winter's morning – "Pah!" – she threw her hand out – ' "Pah!" ' She paused.

'And then – ?' he asked.

'And then,' she said, sipping her coffee, 'I came back into the sitting-room. And breakfast was waiting. Fried eggs and a bit of toast. Lydia with her blouse torn and her hair down. The unemployed singing hymns under the window. And I said to myself – ' she flung her hand out, ' "Polluted city, unbelieving city, city of dead fish and worn-out frying-pans" – thinking of a river's bank, when the tide's out,' she explained.

'Go on,' he nodded.

'So I put on my hat and coat and rushed out in a rage,' she continued, 'and stood on the bridge, and said, "Am I a weed, carried this way, that way, on a tide that comes twice a day without a meaning?" '

'Yes?' he prompted her.

'And there were people passing: the strutting; the tiptoeing; the
pasty; the ferret-eyed; the bowler-hatted, servile, innumerable army of
workers. And I said, "Must I join your conspiracy? Stain the hand, the
unstained hand," ' – he could see her hand gleam as she waved it in the
half-light of the sitting-room, ' " – and sign on, and serve a master; all
because of a Jew in my bath, all because of a Jew?" '

She sat up and laughed, excited by the sound of her own voice which
had run into a jog-trot rhythm.

'Go on, go on,' he said.

'But I had a talisman, a glowing gem, a lucent emerald' – she picked
up an envelope that lay on the floor – 'a letter of introduction. And I
said to the flunkey in peach-blossom trousers, "Admit me, sirrah," and
he led me along corridors piled with purple till I came to a door, a
mahogany door, and knocked; and a voice said, "Enter." And what did I
find?' She paused. 'A stout man with red cheeks. On his table three
orchids in a vase. Pressed into your hand, I thought, as the car crunches
the gravel by your wife at parting. And over the fireplace the usual
picture – '

'Stop!' North interrupted her. 'You have come to an office,' he tapped
the table. 'You are presenting a letter of introduction – but to whom?'

'Oh, to whom?' she laughed. 'To a man in sponge-bag trousers. "I
knew your father at Oxford," he said, toying with the blotting-paper,
ornamented in one corner with a cartwheel. But what do *you* find
insoluble, I asked him, looking at the mahogany man, the clean-shaven,
rosy-gilled, mutton-fed man – '

'The man in a newspaper office,' North checked her, 'who knew your
father. And then?'

'There was a humming and a grinding. The great machines went
round; and little boys popped in with elongated sheets; black sheets;
smudged; damp with printer's ink. "Pardon me a moment," he said, and
made a note in the margin. But the Jew's in my bath, I said – the Jew . . .
the Jew – ' She stopped suddenly and emptied her glass.

Yes, he thought, there's the voice; there's the attitude; and the
reflection in other people's faces; but then there's something true – in
the silence perhaps. But it was not silent. They could hear the Jew
thudding in the bathroom; he seemed to stagger from foot to foot as he
dried himself. Now he unlocked the door, and they heard him go
upstairs. The pipes began to give forth hollow gurgling sounds.

'How much of that was true?' he asked her. But she had lapsed into
silence. The actual words he supposed – the actual words floated
together and formed a sentence in his mind – meant that she was poor;

that she must earn her living, but the excitement with which she had spoken, due to wine perhaps, had created yet another person; another semblance, which one must solidify into one whole.

The house was quiet now, save for the sound of the bathwater running away. A watery pattern fluctuated on the ceiling. The street lamps jiggering up and down outside made the houses opposite a curious pale red. The uproar of the day had died away; no carts were rattling down the street. The vegetable-sellers, the organ-grinders, the woman practising her scales, the man playing the trombone, had all trundled away their barrows, pulled down their shutters and closed the lids of their pianos. It was so still that for a moment North thought he was in Africa, sitting on the verandah in the moonlight; but he roused himself. 'What about this party?' he said. He got up and threw away his cigarette. He stretched himself and looked at his watch. 'It's time to go,' he said. 'Go and get ready,' he urged her. For if one went to a party, he thought, it was absurd to go just as people were leaving. And the party must have begun.

'What were you saying – what were you saying, Nell?' said Peggy, in order to distract Eleanor from paying her share of the cab, as they stood on the doorstep. 'Ordinary people – ordinary people ought to do what?' she asked.

Eleanor was still fumbling with her purse and did not answer.

'No, I can't allow that,' she said. 'Here, take this – '

But Peggy brushed aside the hand, and the coins rolled on the doorstep. They both stooped simultaneously and their heads collided.

'Don't bother,' said Eleanor as a coin rolled away. 'It was all my fault.' The maid was holding the door open.

'And where do we take our cloaks off?' she said. 'In here?'

They went into a room on the ground floor which, though an office, had been arranged so that it could be used as a cloakroom. There was a looking-glass on the table and in front of it trays of pins and combs and brushes. She went up to the glass and gave herself one brief glance.

'What a gypsy I look!' she said, and ran a comb through her hair. 'Burnt as brown as a nigger!' Then she gave way to Peggy and waited.

'I wonder if this was the room . . . ' she said.

'What room?' said Peggy abstractedly: she was attending to her face.

' . . . where we used to meet,' said Eleanor. She looked about her. It was still used as an office apparently; but now there were a house-agent's placards on the wall.

'I wonder if Kitty'll come tonight,' she mused.

Peggy was gazing into the glass and did not answer.

'She doesn't often come to town now. Only for weddings and christenings and so on,' Eleanor continued.

Peggy was drawing a line with a tube of some sort round her lips.

'Suddenly you meet a young man six-foot-two and you realise this is the baby,' Eleanor went on.

Peggy was still absorbed in her face.

'D'you have to do that fresh every time?' said Eleanor.

'I should look a fright if I didn't,' said Peggy. The tightness round her lips and eyes seemed to her visible. She had never felt less in the mood for a party.

'Oh, how kind of you . . . ' Eleanor broke off. The maid had brought in a sixpence.

'Now, Peggy,' said she, proffering the coin, 'let me pay my share.'

'Don't be an ass,' said Peggy, brushing away her hand.

'But it was my cab,' Eleanor insisted. Peggy walked on. 'Because I hate going to parties,' Eleanor continued, following her, still holding out the coin, 'on the cheap. You don't remember your grandfather? He always said, "Don't spoil a good ship for a ha'porth of tar." If you went shopping with him,' she went on as they began mounting the stairs, ' "Show me the very best thing you've got," he'd say.'

'I remember him,' said Peggy.

'Do you?' said Eleanor. She was pleased that anyone should remember her father. 'They've lent these rooms, I suppose,' she added as they walked upstairs. Doors were open. 'That's a solicitor's,' she said, looking at some deed-boxes with white names painted on them.

'Yes, I see what you mean about painting – making-up,' she continued, glancing at her niece. 'You do look nice. You look lit-up. I like it on young people. Not for myself. I should feel bedizened – bedizzened? – how d'you pronounce it? And what am I to do with this sixpence and these coppers if you won't take them? I ought to have left them in my bag downstairs.' They mounted higher and higher. 'I suppose they've opened all these rooms,' she continued – they had now reached a strip of red carpet – 'so that if Delia's little room gets too full – but of course the party's hardly begun yet. We're early. Everybody's upstairs. I hear them talking. Come along. Shall I go first?'

A babble of voices sounded behind a door. A maid intercepted them.

'Miss Pargiter,' said Eleanor.

'Miss Pargiter!' the maid called out, opening the door.

*

'Go and get ready,' said North. He crossed the room and fumbled with
the switch.

He touched the switch, and the electric light in the middle of the
room came on. The shade had been taken off, and a cone of greenish
paper had been twisted round it.

'Go and get ready,' he repeated. Sara did not answer. She had pulled
a book towards her and pretended to read it.

'He's killed the king,' she said. 'So what'll he do next?' She held her
finger between the pages of the book and looked up at him; a device, he
knew, to put off the moment of action. He did not want to go either.
Still, if Eleanor wanted them to go – he hesitated, looking at his watch.

'What'll he do next?' she repeated.

'Comedy,' he said briefly. 'Contrast,' he said, remembering something he had read. 'The only form of continuity,' he added at a venture.

'Well, go on reading,' she said, handing him the book.

He opened it at random.

'The scene is a rocky island in the middle of the sea,' he said. He
paused.

Always before reading he had to arrange the scene; to let this sink;
that come forward. A rocky island in the middle of the sea, he said to
himself – there were green pools, tufts of silver grass, sand, and far away
the soft sigh of waves breaking. He opened his mouth to read. Then
there was a sound behind him; a presence – in the play or in the room?
He looked up.

'Maggie!' Sara exclaimed. There she was standing at the open door in
evening dress.

'Were you asleep?' she said, coming into the room. 'We've been ringing
and ringing.'

She stood smiling at them, amused, as if she had wakened sleepers.

'Why d'you trouble to have a bell when it's always broken?' said a
man who stood behind her.

North rose. At first he scarcely remembered them. The surface sight
was strange on top of his memory of them, as he had seen them years
ago.

'The bells don't ring, and the taps don't run,' he said, awkwardly. 'Or
they don't stop running,' he added, for the bathwater was still gurgling
in the pipes.

'Luckily the door was open,' said Maggie. She stood at the table
looking at the broken apple peel and the dish of fly-blown fruit. Some
beauty, North thought, withers; some, he looked at her, grows more

beautiful with age. Her hair was grey; her children must be grown up now, he supposed. But why do women purse their lips up when they look in the glass? he wondered. She was looking in the glass. She was pursing her lips. Then she crossed the room, and sat down in the chair by the fireplace.

'And why has Renny been crying?' said Sara. North looked at him. There were wet marks on either side of his large nose.

'Because we've been to a very bad play,' he said, 'and should like something to drink,' he added.

Sara went to the cupboard and began clinking glasses. 'Were you reading?' said Renny, looking at the book which had fallen on the floor.

'We were on a rocky island in the middle of the sea,' said Sara, putting the glasses on the table. Renny began to pour out whisky.

Now I remember him, North thought. Last time they had met was before he went to the war. It was in a little house in Westminster. They had sat in front of the fire. And a child had played with a spotted horse. And he had envied them their happiness. And they had talked about science. And Renny had said, 'I help them to make shells,' and a mask had come down over his face. A man who made shells; a man who loved peace; a man of science; a man who cried . . .

'Stop!' cried Renny. 'Stop!' Sara had spurted the soda water over the table.

'When did you get back?' Renny asked him, taking his glass and looking at him with eyes still wet with tears.

'About a week ago,' he said.

'You've sold your farm?' said Renny. He sat down with his glass in his hand.

'Yes, sold it,' said North. 'Whether I shall stay, or go back,' he said, taking his glass and raising it to his lips, 'I don't know.'

'Where was your farm?' said Renny, bending towards him. And they talked about Africa.

Maggie looked at them drinking and talking. The twisted cone of paper over the electric light was oddly stained. The mottled light made their faces look greenish. The two grooves on each side of Renny's nose were still wet. His face was all peaks and hollows; North's face was round and snub-nosed and rather blueish about the lips. She gave her chair a little push so that she got the two heads in relation side by side. They were very different. And as they talked about Africa their faces changed, as if some twitch had been given to the fine network under the skin and the weights fell into different sockets. A thrill ran through her as if the weights in her own body had changed too. But there was something about the light that puzzled her. She looked round. A lamp must be flaring in the street outside. Its light, flickering up and down, mixed with the electric light under the greenish cone of mottled paper. It was that which . . . She started; a voice had reached her.

'To Africa?' she said, looking at North.

'To Delia's party,' he said. 'I asked if you were coming . . . ' She had not been listening.

'One moment . . . ' Renny interrupted. He held up his hand like a policeman stopping traffic. And again they went on, talking about Africa.

Maggie lay back in her chair. Behind their heads rose the curve of the mahogany chairback. And behind the curve of the chairback was a crinkled glass with a red lip; then there was the straight line of the mantelpiece with little black and white squares on it; and then three rods ending in soft yellow plumes. She ran her eye from thing to thing. In and out it went, collecting, gathering, summing up into one whole, when, just as she was about to complete the pattern, Renny exclaimed: 'We must – we must!'

He had got up. He had pushed away his glass of whisky. He stood there like somebody commanding a troop, North thought; so emphatic was his voice, so commanding his gesture. Yet it was only a question of going round to an old woman's party. Or was there always, he thought, as he too rose and looked for his hat, something that came to the surface, inappropriately, unexpectedly, from the depths of people, and made ordinary actions, ordinary words, expressive of the whole being, so that he felt, as he turned to follow Renny to Delia's party, as if he were riding to the relief of a besieged garrison across a desert?

He stopped with his hand on the door. Sara had come in from the bedroom. She had changed; she was in evening dress; there was something odd about her – perhaps it was the effect of the evening dress estranging her?

'I am ready,' she said, looking at them.

She stooped and picked up the book that North had let fall.

'We must go – ' she said, turning to her sister.

She put the book on the table; she gave it a sad little pat as she shut it.

'We must go,' she repeated, and followed them down the stairs.

Maggie rose. She gave one more look at the cheap lodging-house room. There was the pampas grass in its terracotta pot; the green vase with the red crinkled lip; and the mahogany chair. On the dinner table lay the dish of fruit; the heavy sensual apples lay side by side with the spotted yellow bananas. It was an odd combination – the round and the tapering, the rosy and the yellow. She switched off the light. The room now was almost dark, save for a watery pattern fluctuating on the ceiling. In this phantom evanescent light only the outlines showed: ghostly apples, ghostly bananas, and the spectre of a chair. Colour was slowly returning, as her eyes grew used to the darkness, and substance . . . She stood there for a moment looking. Then a voice shouted: 'Maggie! Maggie!'

'I'm coming!' she cried, and followed them down the stairs.

'And your name, miss?' said the maid to Peggy as she hung back behind Eleanor.

'Miss Margaret Pargiter,' said Peggy.

'Miss Margaret Pargiter!' the maid called out into the room.

There was a babble of voices; lights opened brightly in front of her, and Delia came forward. 'Oh, Peggy!' she exclaimed. 'How nice of you to come!'

She went in; but she felt plated, coated over with some cold skin. They had come too early – the room was almost empty. Only a few people stood about, talking too loudly, as if to fill the room. Making believe, Peggy thought to herself as she shook hands with Delia and passed on, that something pleasant is about to happen. She saw with extreme clearness the Persian rug and the carved fireplace, but there was an empty space in the middle of the room.

What is the tip for this particular situation? she asked herself, as if she were prescribing for a patient. Take notes, she added. Do them up in a bottle with a glossy green cover, she thought. Take notes and the pain goes. Take notes and the pain goes, she repeated to herself as she stood there alone. Delia hurried past her. She was talking, but talking at random.

'It's all very well for you people who live in London – ' she was saying. But the nuisance of taking notes of what people say, Peggy went on as Delia passed her, is that they talk such nonsense . . . such complete nonsense, she thought, drawing herself back against the wall. Here her father came in. He paused at the door, put his head up as if he were looking for someone and advanced with his hand out.

And what's this? she asked, for the sight of her father in his rather worn shoes had given her a direct spontaneous feeling. This sudden warm spurt? she asked, examining it. She watched him cross the room. His shoes always affected her strangely. Part sex, part pity, she thought. Can one call it 'love'? But she forced herself to move. Now that I have drugged myself into a state of comparative insensibility, she said to herself, I will walk across the room boldly; I will go to Uncle Patrick, who is standing by the sofa picking his teeth, and I will say to him – what shall I say?

A sentence suggested itself for no rhyme or reason as she crossed the room: 'How's the man who cut his toes off with the hatchet?'

'How's the man who cut his toes off with the hatchet?' she said, speaking the words exactly as she thought them. The handsome old Irishman bent down, for he was very tall, and hollowed his hand, for he was hard of hearing.

'Hacket? Hacket?' he repeated. She smiled. The steps from brain to brain must be cut very shallow, if thought is to mount them, she noted.

'Cut his toes off with the hatchet when I was staying with you,' she said. She remembered how when she last stayed with them in Ireland the gardener had cut his foot with a hatchet.

'Hacket? Hacket?' he repeated. He looked puzzled. Then under-standing dawned.

'Oh, the Hackets!' he said. 'Dear old Peter Hacket – yes.' It seemed that there were Hackets in Galway, and the mistake, which she did not trouble to explain, was all to the good, for it set him off, and he told her stories about the Hackets as they sat side by side on the sofa.

A grown woman, she thought, crosses London to talk to a deaf old man about the Hackets, whom she's never heard of, when she meant to ask after the gardener who cut his toes off with a hatchet. But does it matter? Hackets or hatchets? She laughed, happily in time with a joke, so that it seemed appropriate. But one wants somebody to laugh with, she thought. Pleasure is increased by sharing it. Does the same hold good of pain? she mused. Is that the reason why we all talk so much of ill-health – because sharing things lessens things? Give pain, give pleasure an outer body, and by increasing the surface diminish them . . . But the thought slipped. He was off telling his old stories. Gently, methodically, like a man setting in motion some still serviceable but rather weary nag, he was off remembering old days, old dogs, old memories that slowly shaped themselves, as he warmed, into little figures of country-house life. She fancied as she half listened that she was looking at a faded snapshot of cricketers; of shooting parties on the many steps of some country mansion.

How many people, she wondered, listen? This 'sharing', then, is a bit of a farce. She made herself attend.

'Ah yes, those were fine old days!' he was saying. The light came into his faded eyes.

She looked once more at the snapshot of the men in gaiters, and the women in flowing skirts on the broad white steps with the dogs curled up at their feet. But he was off again.

'Did you ever hear from your father of a man called Roddy Jenkins who lived in the little white house on the right-hand side as you go along the road?' he asked. 'But you must know that story?' he added.

'No,' she said, screwing up her eyes as if she referred to the files of memory. 'Tell me.'

And he told her the story.

I'm good, she thought, at fact-collecting. But what makes up a person (she hollowed her hand), the circumference – no, I'm not good at that. There was her Aunt Delia. She watched her moving quickly about the room. What do I know about her? That she's wearing a dress with gold spots; has wavy hair, that was red, is white; is handsome; ravaged; with a past. But what past? She married Patrick . . . The long story that Patrick was telling her kept breaking up the surface of her mind like oars dipping into water. Nothing could settle. There was a lake in the story too, for it was a story about duck-shooting.

She married Patrick, she thought, looking at his battered weather-worn face with the single hairs on it. Why did Delia marry Patrick? she wondered. How do they manage it – love, childbirth? The people who touch each other and go up in a cloud of smoke: red smoke? His face reminded her of the red skin of a gooseberry with the little stray hairs. But none of the lines on his face was sharp enough, she thought, to explain how they came together and had three children. They were lines that came from shooting; lines that came from worry; for the old days were over, he was saying. They had to cut things down.

'Yes, we're all finding that,' she said perfunctorily. She turned her wrist cautiously so that she could read her watch. Fifteen minutes only had passed. But the room was filling with people she did not know. There was an Indian in a pink turban.

'Ah, but I'm boring you with these old stories,' said her uncle, wagging his head. He was hurt, she felt.

'No, no, no!' she said, feeling uncomfortable. He was off again, but out of good manners this time, she felt. Pain must outbalance pleasure by two parts to one, she thought; in all social relations. Or am I the exception, the peculiar person? she continued, for the others seemed happy enough. Yes, she thought, looking straight ahead of her, and feeling again the stretched skin round her lips and eyes tight from the tiredness of sitting up late with a woman in childbirth, I'm the exception; hard; cold; in a groove already; merely a doctor.

Getting out of grooves is damned unpleasant, she thought, before the

chill of death has set in, like bending frozen boots . . . She bent her head
to listen. To smile, to bend, to make believe you're amused when you're
bored, how painful it is, she thought. All ways, every way's painful, she
thought; staring at the Indian in the pink turban.

'Who's that fellow?' Patrick asked, nodding his head in his direction.

'One of Eleanor's Indians I expect,' she said aloud, and thought, If
only the merciful powers of darkness would obliterate the external
exposure of the sensitive nerve and I could get up and . . . There was a
pause.

'But I mustn't keep you here, listening to my old stories,' said Uncle
Patrick. His weather-beaten nag with the broken knees had stopped.

'But tell me, does old Biddy still keep the little shop,' she asked,
'where we used to buy sweets?'

'Poor old body – ' he began. He was off again. All her patients said
that, she thought. Rest – rest – let me rest. How to deaden; how to cease
to feel; that was the cry of the woman bearing children; to rest, to cease
to be. In the Middle Ages, she thought, it was the cell; the monastery;
now it's the laboratory; the professions; not to live; not to feel; to make
money, always money, and in the end, when I'm old and worn like a
horse, no, it's a cow. . . for part of old Patrick's story had imposed itself
upon her mind: ' . . . for there's no sale for the beasts at all,' he was
saying, 'no sale at all. Ah, there's Julia Cromarty – ' he exclaimed, and
waved his hand, his large loose-jointed hand, at a charming compatriot.

She was left sitting alone on the sofa. For her uncle rose and went off
with both hands outstretched to greet the bird-like old woman who had
come in chattering.

She was left alone. She was glad to be alone. She had no wish to talk.
But next moment somebody stood beside her. It was Martin. He sat
down beside her. She changed her attitude completely.

'Hello, Martin!' she greeted him cordially.

'Done your duty by the old mare, Peggy?' he said. He referred to the
stories that old Patrick always told them.

'Did I look very glum?' she asked.

'Well,' he said, glancing at her, 'not exactly enraptured.'

'One knows the end of his stories by now,' she excused herself, looking
at Martin. He had taken to brushing his hair up like a waiter's. He never
looked her fully in the face. He never felt entirely at his ease with her.
She was his doctor; she knew that he dreaded cancer. She must try to
distract him from thinking, Does she see any symptoms?

'I was wondering how they came to marry,' she said. 'Were they in
love?' She spoke at random to distract him.

'Of course he was in love,' he said. He looked at Delia. She was standing by the fireplace talking to the Indian. She was still a very handsome woman, with her presence, with her gestures.

'We were all in love,' he said, glancing sideways at Peggy. The younger generation were so serious.

'Oh, of course,' she said, smiling. She liked his eternal pursuit of one love after another love – his gallant clutch upon the flying tail, the slippery tail of youth – even he, even now.

'But you,' he said, stretching his feet out, hitching up his trousers, 'your generation I mean – you miss a great deal . . . you miss a great deal,' he repeated. She waited. 'Loving only your own sex,' he added.

He liked to assert his own youth in that way, she thought; to say things that he thought up to date.

'I'm not that generation,' she said.

'Well, well, well,' he chuckled, shrugging his shoulder and glancing at her sideways. He knew very little about her private life. But she looked serious; she looked tired. She works too hard, he thought.

'I'm getting on,' said Peggy. 'Getting into a groove. So Eleanor told me tonight.'

Or was it she, on the other hand, who had told Eleanor she was 'suppressed'? One or the other.

'Eleanor's a gay old dog,' he said. 'Look!' He pointed.

There she was, talking to the Indian in her red cloak.

'Just back from India,' he added. 'A present from Bengal, eh?' he said, referring to the cloak.

'And next year she's off to China,' said Peggy. 'But Delia – ' she asked; Delia was passing them. 'Was she in love?' (What you in your generation called 'in love', she added to herself.)

He wagged his head from side to side and pursed his lips. He always liked his little joke, she remembered.

'I don't know – I don't know about Delia,' he said. 'There was the cause, you know – what she called in those days The Cause.' He screwed his face up. 'Ireland, you know. Parnell. Ever heard of a man called Parnell?' he asked.

'Yes,' said Peggy. 'And Edward?' she added. He had come in; he looked very distinguished, too, in his elaborate, if conscious simplicity.

'Edward – yes,' said Martin. 'Edward was in love. Surely you know that old story – Edward and Kitty?'

'The one who married – what was his name? – Lasswade?' Peggy murmured as Edward passed them.

'Yes, she married the other man – Lasswade. But he was in love – he was very much in love,' Martin murmured. 'But you,' he gave her a quick little glance. There was something in her that chilled him. 'Of course, you have your profession,' he added. He looked at the ground. He was thinking of his dread of cancer, she supposed. He was afraid that she had noted some symptom.

'Oh, doctors are great humbugs,' she threw out at random.

'Why? People live longer than they used, don't they?' he said. 'They don't die so painfully anyhow,' he added.

'We've learnt a few little tricks,' she conceded. He stared ahead of him with a look that moved her pity.

'You'll live to be eighty – if you want to live to be eighty,' she said. He looked at her.

'Of course I'm all in favour of living to be eighty!' he exclaimed. 'I want to go to America. I want to see their buildings. I'm on that side, you see. I enjoy life.' He did, enormously.

He must be over sixty himself, she supposed. But he was wonderfully got up; as sprig and spruce as a man of forty, with his canary-coloured lady in Kensington.

'I don't know,' she said aloud.

'Come, Peggy, come,' he said. 'Don't tell me you don't enjoy – here's Rose.'

Rose came up. She had grown very stout.

'Don't you want to be eighty?' he said to her. He had to say it twice over. She was deaf.

'I do. Of course I do!' she said when she understood him. She faced them. She made an odd angle with her head thrown back, Peggy thought, as if she were a military man.

'Of course I do,' she said, sitting down abruptly on the sofa beside them.

'Ah, but then – ' Peggy began. She paused. Rose was deaf, she remembered. She had to shout. 'People hadn't made such fools of themselves in your day,' she shouted. But she doubted if Rose heard.

'I want to see what's going to happen,' said Rose. 'We live in a very interesting world,' she added.

'Nonsense,' Martin teased her. 'You want to live,' he bawled in her ear, 'because you enjoy living.'

'And I'm not ashamed of it,' she said. 'I like my kind – on the whole.'

'What you like is fighting them,' he bawled.

'D'you think you can get a rise out of me at this time o' day?' she said, tapping him on the arm.

Now they'll talk about being children; climbing trees in the back garden, thought Peggy, and how they shot somebody's cats. Each person had a certain line laid down in their minds, she thought, and along it came the same old sayings. One's mind must be crisscrossed like the palm of one's hand, she thought, looking at the palm of her hand.

'She always was a spitfire,' said Martin, turning to Peggy.

'And they always put the blame on me,' Rose said. '*He* had the school-room. Where was I to sit? "Oh, run away and play in the nursery!" ' she waved her hand.

'And so she went into the bathroom and cut her wrist with a knife,' Martin jeered.

'No, that was Erridge: that was about the microscope,' she corrected him.

It's like a kitten catching its tail, Peggy thought; round and round they go in a circle. But it's what they enjoy, she thought; it's what they come to parties for. Martin went on teasing Rose.

'And where's your red ribbon?' he was asking.

Some decoration had been given her, Peggy remembered, for her work in the war.

'Aren't we worthy to see you in your war paint?' he teased her.

'This fellow's jealous,' she said, turning to Peggy again. 'He's never done a stroke of work in his life.'

'I work – I work,' Martin insisted. 'I sit in an office all day long – '

'Doing what?' said Rose.

Then they became suddenly silent. That turn was over – the old-brother-and-sister turn. Now they could only go back and repeat the same thing over again.

'Look here,' said Martin, 'we must go and do our duty.' He rose. They parted.

'Doing what?' Peggy repeated, as she crossed the room. 'Doing what?' she repeated. She was feeling reckless; nothing that she did mattered. She walked to the window and twitched the curtain apart. There were the stars pricked in little holes in the blue-black sky. There was a row of chimney-pots against the sky. Then the stars. Inscrutable, eternal, indifferent – those were the words; the right words. But I don't feel it, she said, looking at the stars. So why pretend to? What they're really like, she thought, screwing up her eyes to look at them, is little bits of frosty steel. And the moon – there it was – is a polished dish-cover. But she felt nothing, even when she had reduced moon and stars to that. Then she turned and found herself face to face with a young man she thought she knew but could not put a name to. He had a fine brow but a receding chin, and he was pale, pasty.

'How-d'you-do?' she said. Was his name Leacock or Laycock?

'Last time we met,' she said, 'was at the races.' She connected him, incongruously, with a Cornish field, stone walls, farmers and rough ponies jumping.

'No, that's Paul,' he said. 'My brother Paul.' He was tart about it. What did he do, then, that made him superior in his own esteem to Paul?

'You live in London?' she said.

He nodded.

'You write?' she hazarded. But why, because he was a writer – she remembered now seeing his name in the papers – throw your head back when you say, 'Yes'? She preferred Paul; he looked healthy; this one had a queer face: knit up; nerve-drawn; fixed.

'Poetry?' she said.

'Yes.' But why bite off that word as if it were a cherry on the end of a stalk? she thought. There was nobody coming; they were bound to sit down side by side, on chairs by the wall.

'How do you manage, if you're in an office?' she said. Apparently in his spare time.

'My uncle,' he began. ' . . . You've met him?'

Yes, a nice commonplace man; he had been very kind to her about a passport once. This boy, of course, though she only half listened, sneered at him. Then why go into his office? she asked herself. My people, he was saying . . . hunted. Her attention wandered. She had heard it all before. I, I, I – he went on. It was like a vulture's beak pecking, or a vacuum-cleaner sucking, or a telephone bell ringing. I, I, I. But he couldn't help it, not with that nerve-drawn egotist's face, she thought, glancing at him. He could not free himself, could not detach himself. He was bound on the wheel with tight iron hoops. He had to expose, had to exhibit. But why let him? she thought, as he went on talking. For what do I care about his 'I, I, I'? Or his poetry? Let me shake him off then, she said to herself, feeling like a person whose blood has been sucked, leaving all the nerve-centres pale. She paused. He noted her lack of sympathy. He thought her stupid, she supposed.

'I'm tired,' she apologised. 'I've been up all night,' she explained. 'I'm a doctor – '

The fire went out of his face when she said 'I'. That's done it – now he'll go, she thought. He can't be 'you' – he must be 'I'. She smiled. For up he got and off he went.

*

She turned round and stood at the window. Poor little wretch, she thought: atrophied, withered; cold as steel; hard as steel; bald as steel. And I too, she thought, looking at the sky. The stars seemed pricked haphazard in the sky, except that there, to the right over the chimney-pots, hung that phantom wheelbarrow[56] – what did they call it? The name escaped her. I will count them, she thought, returning to her notebook, and had begun one, two, three, four . . . when a voice exclaimed behind her: 'Peggy! Aren't your ears tingling?' She turned. It was Delia of course, with her genial ways, her imitation Irish flattery. ' – because they ought to be,' said Delia, laying a hand on her shoulder, 'considering what *he's* been saying' – she pointed to a grey-haired man – 'what praises he's been singing of you.'

Peggy looked where she pointed. There was her teacher over there, her master. Yes, she knew he thought her clever. She was, she supposed. They all said so. Very clever.

'He's been telling me – ' Delia began. But she broke off. 'Just help me open this window,' she said. 'It's getting hot.'

'Let me,' said Peggy. She gave the window a jerk, but it stuck, for it was old and the frames did not fit.

'Here, Peggy,' said somebody, coming behind her. It was her father. His hand was on the window, his hand with the scar. He pushed; the window went up.

'Thanks, Morris, that's better,' said Delia. 'I was telling Peggy her ears ought to be tingling,' she began again: ' "My most brilliant pupil!" That's what *he* said,' Delia went on. 'I assure you I felt quite proud. "But she's my niece," I said. He hadn't known it – '

There, said Peggy, that's pleasure. The nerve down her spine seemed to tingle as the praise reached her father. Each emotion touched a different nerve. A sneer rasped the thigh; pleasure thrilled the spine; and also affected the sight. The stars had softened; they quivered. Her father brushed her shoulder as he dropped his hand; but neither of them spoke.

'D'you want it open at the top too?' he said.

'No, that'll do,' said Delia. 'The room's getting hot,' she said. 'People are beginning to come. They must use the rooms downstairs,' she said. 'But who's that out there?' she pointed. Opposite the house against the railings of the square was a group in evening dress.

'I think I recognise one of them,' said Morris, looking out. 'That's North, isn't it?'

'Yes, that's North,' said Peggy, looking out.

'Then why don't they come in?' said Delia, tapping on the window.

*

'But you must come and see it for yourselves,' North was saying. They had asked him to describe Africa. He had said that there were mountains and plains; it was silent, he had said, and birds sang. He stopped; it was difficult to describe a place to people who had not seen it. Then curtains in the house opposite parted, and three heads appeared at the window. They looked at the heads outlined on the window opposite them. They were standing with their backs to the railings of the square. The trees hung dark showers of leaves over them. The trees had become part of the sky. Now and then they seemed to shift and shuffle slightly as a breeze went through them. A star shone among the leaves. It was silent too; the murmur of the traffic was run together into one far hum. A cat slunk past; for a second they saw the luminous green of the eyes; then it was extinguished. The cat crossed the lighted space and vanished. Someone tapped again on the window and cried, 'Come in!'

'Come!' said Renny, and threw his cigar into the bushes behind him. 'Come, we must.'

They went upstairs, past the doors of offices, past long windows that opened on to back gardens that lay behind houses. Trees in full leaf stretched their branches across at different levels; the leaves, here bright green in the artificial light, here dark in shadow, moved up and down in the little breeze. Then they came to the private part of the house, where the red carpet was laid; and a roar of voices sounded from behind a door as if a flock of sheep were penned there. Then music, a dance, swung out.

'Now,' said Maggie, pausing for a moment, outside the door. She gave their names to the servant.

'And you, sir?' said the maid to North, who hung behind.

'Captain Pargiter,' said North, touching his tie.

'And Captain Pargiter!' the maid called out.

Delia was upon them instantly. 'And Captain Pargiter!' she exclaimed, as she came hurrying across the room. 'How very nice of you to come!' she exclaimed. She took their hands at random, here a left hand, there a right hand, in her left hand, in her right hand.

'I thought it was you,' she exclaimed, 'standing in the square. I thought I could recognise Renny – but I wasn't sure about North. Captain Pargiter!' she wrung his hand, 'you're quite a stranger – but a very welcome one! Now who d'you know? Who don't you know?'

She glanced round, twitching her shawl rather nervously.

'Let me see, there's all your uncles and aunts; and your cousins; and your sons and daughters – yes, Maggie, I saw your lovely couple not long ago. They're somewhere . . . Only all the generations in our family are so mixed; cousins and aunts, uncles and brothers – but perhaps it's a good thing.'

She stopped rather suddenly as if she had used up that vein. She twitched her shawl.

'They're going to dance,' she said, pointing at the young man who was putting another record on the gramophone. 'It's all right for dancing,' she added, referring to the gramophone. 'Not for music.' She became simple for a moment. 'I can't bear music on the gramophone. But dance music – that's another thing. And young people – don't you find that? – must dance. It's right they should. Dance or not – just as you like.' She waved her hand.

'Yes, just as you like,' her husband echoed her. He stood beside her, dangling his hands in front of him like a bear on which coats are hung in a hotel. 'Just as you like,' he repeated, shaking his paws.

'Help me to move the tables, North,' said Delia. 'If they're going to dance, they'll want everything out of the way – and the rugs rolled up.' She pushed a table out of the way. Then she ran across the room to whisk a chair against the wall.

Now one of the vases was upset, and a stream of water flowed across the carpet.

'Don't mind it, don't mind it – it doesn't matter at all!' Delia exclaimed, assuming the manner of a harum-scarum Irish hostess. But North stooped and swabbed up the water.

'And what are you going to do with that pocket handkerchief?' Eleanor asked him; she had joined them in her flowing red cloak.

'Hang it on a chair to dry,' said North, walking off.

'And you, Sally?' said Eleanor, drawing back against the wall since they were going to dance. 'Going to dance?' she asked, sitting down.

'I?' said Sara, yawning. 'I want to sleep.' She sank down on a cushion beside Eleanor.

'But you don't come to parties,' Eleanor laughed, looking down at her, 'to sleep, do you?' Again she saw the little picture she had seen at the end of the telephone. But she could not see her face; only the top of her head.

'Dining with you, wasn't he?' she said, as North passed them with his handkerchief.

'And what did you talk about?' she asked. She saw her, sitting on the edge of a chair, swinging her foot up and down, with a smudge on her nose.

'Talk about?' said Sara. 'You, Eleanor.' People were passing them all the time; they were brushing against their knees; they were beginning to dance. It made one feel a little dizzy, Eleanor thought, sinking back in her chair.

'Me?' she said. 'What about me?'

'Your life,' said Sara.

'My life?' Eleanor repeated. Couples began to twist and turn slowly past them. It was a fox-trot that they were dancing, she supposed.

My life, she said to herself. That was odd, it was the second time that evening that somebody had talked about her life. And I haven't got one, she thought. Oughtn't a life to be something you could handle and produce? – a life of seventy odd years. But I've only the present moment, she thought. Here she was alive, now, listening to the fox-trot. Then she looked round. There was Morris; Rose; Edward with his head thrown back talking to a man she did not know. I'm the only person here, she thought, who remembers how he sat on the edge of my bed that night, crying – the night Kitty's engagement was announced. Yes, things came back to her. A long strip of life lay behind her. Edward crying; Mrs Levy talking; snow falling; a sunflower with a crack in it; the yellow omnibus trotting along the Bayswater Road. And I thought to myself, I'm the youngest person in this omnibus; now I'm the oldest ... Millions of things came back to her. Atoms danced apart and massed themselves. But how did they compose what people called a life? She clenched her hands and felt the hard little coins she was holding. Perhaps there's 'I' at the middle of it, she thought; a knot; a centre; and again she saw herself sitting at her table drawing on the blotting-paper, digging little holes from which spokes radiated. Out and out they went; thing followed thing, scene obliterated scene. And then they say, she thought, 'We've been talking about you!'

'My life ... ' she said aloud, but half to herself.

'Yes?' said Sara, looking up.

Eleanor stopped. She had forgotten her. But there was somebody listening. Then she must put her thoughts into order; then she must find words. But no, she thought, I can't find words; I can't tell anybody.

'Isn't that Nicholas?' she said, looking at a rather large man who stood in the doorway.

'Where?' said Sara. But she looked in the wrong direction. He had disappeared. Perhaps she had been mistaken. My life's been other people's lives, Eleanor thought – my father's; Morris's; my friends' lives; Nicholas's ... Fragments of a conversation with him came back to her. Either I'd been lunching with him or dining with him, she thought.

It was in a restaurant. There was a parrot with a pink feather in a cage on the counter. And they had sat there talking – it was after the war – about the future; about education. And he wouldn't let me pay for the wine, she suddenly remembered, though it was I who ordered it . . .

Here somebody stopped in front of her. She looked up. 'Just as I was thinking of you!' she exclaimed.

It was Nicholas.

'Good-evening, madame!' he said, bending over her in his foreign way.

'Just as I was thinking of you!' she repeated. Indeed it was like a part of her, a sunk part of her, coming to the surface. 'Come and sit beside me,' she said, and pulled up a chair.

'D'you know who that chap is, sitting by my aunt?' said North to the girl he was dancing with. She looked round; but vaguely.

'I don't know your aunt,' she said. 'I don't know anybody here.'

The dance was over and they began walking towards the door.

'I don't even know my hostess,' she said. 'I wish you'd point her out to me.'

'There – over there,' he said. He pointed to Delia in her black dress with the gold spangles.

'Oh, that,' she said, looking at her. 'That's my hostess, is it?' He had not caught the girl's name, and she knew none of them either. He was glad of it. It made him seem different to himself – it stimulated him. He shepherded her towards the door. He wanted to avoid his relations. In particular he wanted to avoid his sister Peggy; but there she was, standing alone by the door. He looked the other way; he conveyed his partner out of the door. There must be a garden or a roof somewhere, he thought, where they could sit, alone. She was extraordinarily pretty and young.

'Come along,' he said, 'downstairs.'

'And what were you thinking about me?' said Nicholas, sitting down beside Eleanor.

She smiled. There he was in his rather ill-assorted dress-clothes, with the seal engraved with the arms of his mother the princess, and his swarthy wrinkled face that always made her think of some loose-skinned, furry animal, savage to others but kind to herself. But what was she thinking about him? She was thinking of him in the lump; she could not break off little fragments. The restaurant had been smoky she remembered.

'How we dined together once in Soho,' she said. ' . . . d'you remember?'

'All the evenings with you I remember, Eleanor,' he said. But his glance was a little vague. His attention was distracted. He was looking at a lady who had just come in; a well-dressed lady, who stood with her back to the bookcase equipped for every emergency. If I can't describe my own life, Eleanor thought, how can I describe him? For what he was she did not know; only that it gave her pleasure when he came in; relieved her of the need of thinking; and gave her mind a little jog. He was looking at the lady. She seemed upheld by their gaze; vibrating under it. And suddenly it seemed to Eleanor that it had all happened before. So a girl had come in that night in the restaurant: had stood, vibrating, in the door. She knew exactly what he was going to say. He had said it before, in the restaurant. He is going to say, She is like a ball on the top of a fishmonger's fountain. As she thought it, he said it. Does everything then come over again a little differently? she thought. If so, is there a pattern; a theme, recurring, like music; half remembered, half foreseen? . . . a gigantic pattern, momentarily perceptible? The thought gave her extreme pleasure: that there was a pattern. But who makes it? Who thinks it? Her mind slipped. She could not finish her thought.

'Nicholas . . . ' she said. She wanted him to finish it; to take her thought and carry it out into the open unbroken; to make it whole, beautiful, entire.

'Tell me, Nicholas . . .' she began; but she had no notion how she was going to finish her sentence, or what it was that she wanted to ask him. He was talking to Sara. She listened. He was laughing at her. He was pointing at her feet.

' . . . coming to a party,' he was saying, 'with one stocking that is white, and one stocking that is blue.'

'The Queen of England asked me to tea;' Sara hummed in time to the music; 'and which shall it be; the gold or the rose; for all are in holes, my stockings, said she.' This is their love-making, Eleanor thought, half listening to their laughter, to their bickering. Another inch of the pattern, she thought, still using her half-formulated idea to stamp the immediate scene. And if this love-making differs from the old, still it has its charm; it was 'love', different from the old love, perhaps, but worse, was it? Anyhow, she thought, they are aware of each other; they live in each other; what else is love, she asked, listening to their laughter.

' . . . Can you never act for yourself?' he was saying. 'Can you never even choose stockings for yourself?'

'Never! Never!' Sara was laughing.

' . . . Because you have no life of your own,' he said. 'She lives in dreams,' he added, turning to Eleanor, 'alone.'

'The professor preaching his little sermon,' Sara sneered, laying her hand on his knee.

'Sara singing her little song,' Nicholas laughed, pressing her hand.

But they are very happy, Eleanor thought: they laugh at each other. 'Tell me, Nicholas . . . ' she began again. But another dance was beginning. Couples came flocking back into the room. Slowly, intently, with serious faces, as if they were taking part in some mystic rite which gave them immunity from other feelings, the dancers began circling past them, brushing against their knees, almost treading on their toes. And then someone stopped in front of them.

'Oh, here's North,' said Eleanor, looking up.

'North!' Nicholas exclaimed. 'North! We met this evening,' he stretched out his hand to North, ' – at Eleanor's.'

'We did,' said North warmly. Nicholas crushed his fingers; he felt them separate again when the hand was removed. It was effusive; but he liked it. He was feeling effusive himself. His eyes shone. He had lost his puzzled look completely. His adventure had turned out well. The girl had written her name in his pocket-book. 'Come and see me tomorrow at six,' she had said.

'Good-evening again, Eleanor,' he said, bowing over her hand. 'You're looking very young. You're looking extraordinarily handsome. I like you in those clothes,' he said, looking at her Indian cloak.

'The same to you, North,' she said. She looked up at him. She thought she had never seen him look so handsome, so vigorous.

'Aren't you going to dance?' she asked. The music was in full swing.

'Not unless Sally will honour me,' he said, bowing to her with exaggerated courtesy. What has happened to him? Eleanor thought. He looks so handsome, so happy. Sally rose. She gave her hand to Nicholas.

'I will dance with you,' she said. They stood for a moment waiting; and then they circled away.

'What an odd-looking couple!' North exclaimed. He screwed his face up into a grin as he watched them. 'They don't know how to dance!' he added. He sat down by Eleanor in the chair that Nicholas had left empty.

'Why don't they marry?' he asked.

'Why should they?' she said.

'Oh, everybody ought to marry,' he said. 'And I like him, though he's a bit of a – shall we say "bounder"?'[57] he suggested, as he watched them circling rather awkwardly in and out.

' "Bounder"?' Eleanor echoed him.

'Oh it's his fob, you mean,' she added, looking at the gold seal which swung up and down as Nicholas danced.

'No, not a bounder,' she said aloud. 'He's – '

But North was not attending. He was looking at a couple at the farther end of the room. They were standing by the fireplace. Both were young; both were silent; they seemed held still in that position by some powerful emotion. As he looked at them, some emotion about himself, about his own life, came over him, and he arranged another background for them or for himself – not the mantelpiece and the bookcase, but cataracts roaring, clouds racing, and they stood on a cliff above a torrent . . .

'Marriage isn't for everyone,' Eleanor interrupted.

He started. 'No. Of course not,' he agreed. He looked at her. She had never married. Why not? he wondered. Sacrificed to the family, he supposed – old grandpapa without any fingers. Then some memory came back to him of a terrace, a cigar and William Whatney. Was not that her tragedy, that she had loved him? He looked at her with affection. He felt fond of everyone at the moment.

'What luck to find you alone, Nell!' he said, laying his hand on her knee.

She was touched; the feel of his hand on her knee pleased her.

'Dear North!' she exclaimed. She felt his excitement through her dress; he was like a dog on a leash; straining forward with all his nerves erect, she felt, as he laid his hand on her knee.

'But don't marry the wrong woman!' she said.

'I?' he asked. 'What makes you say that?' Had she seen him, he wondered, shepherding the girl downstairs?

'Tell me – ' she began. She wanted to ask him, coolly and sensibly, what his plans were, now that they were alone; but as she spoke she saw his face change; an exaggerated expression of horror came over it.

'Milly!' he muttered. 'Damn her!'

Eleanor glanced quickly over her shoulder. Her sister Milly, voluminous in draperies proper to her sex and class, was coming towards them. She had grown very stout. In order to disguise her figure, veils with beads on them hung down over her arms. They were so fat that they reminded North of asparagus: pale asparagus tapering to a point.

'Oh, Eleanor!' she exclaimed. For she still kept relics of a younger sister's doglike devotion.

'Oh, Milly!' said Eleanor, but not so cordially.

'How nice to see you, Eleanor!' said Milly, with her little old woman's chuckle; yet there was something deferential in her manner. 'And you too, North!'

She gave him her fat little hand. He noticed how the rings were sunk in her fingers, as if the flesh had grown over them. Flesh grown over diamonds disgusted him.

'How very nice that you're back again!' she said, settling slowly down into her chair. Everything, he felt, became dulled. She cast a net over them; she made them all feel one family; he had to think of their relations in common; but it was an unreal feeling.

'Yes, we're staying with Connie,' she said; they had come up for a cricket match.

He sunk his head. He looked at his shoes.

'And I've not heard a word about your travels, Nell,' she went on. They fall and fall, and cover all, he went on, as he listened to the damp falling patter of his aunt's little questions. But he was in such a super-fluity of high spirits that he could still make her words jingle. Did the tarantulas bite, she was asking him, and were the stars bright? And where shall I spend tomorrow night? he added, for the card in his waistcoat pocket rayed out of its own accord without regard for the context scenes which obliterated the present moment. They were staying with Connie, she went on, who was expecting Jimmy, who was home from Uganda . . . his mind slipped a few words, for he was seeing a garden, a room, and the next word he heard was 'adenoids' – which is a good word, he said to himself, separating it from its context: wasp-waisted; pinched in the middle; with a hard, shining, metallic abdomen, useful to describe the appearance of an insect – but here a vast bulk approached: chiefly white waistcoat, lined with black; and Hugh Gibbs stood over them. North sprang up to offer him his chair.

'My dear boy, you don't expect me to sit on *that*?' said Hugh, deriding the rather spindly seat that North offered him.

'You must find me something – ' he looked about him, holding his hands to the sides of his white waistcoat, 'more substantial.'

North pulled a stuffed seat towards him. He lowered himself cautiously.

'Chew, chew, chew,' he said as he sat down.

And Milly said, 'Tut-tut-tut,' North observed.

That was what it came to – thirty years of being husband and wife – tut-tut-tut, and chew, chew, chew. It sounded like the half-inarticulate munchings of animals in a stall. Tut-tut-tut and chew, chew, chew – as they trod out the soft steamy straw in the stable; as they wallowed in the primeval swamp, prolific, profuse, half-conscious, he thought; listening vaguely to the good-humoured patter, which suddenly fastened itself upon him.

'What d'you weigh, North?' his uncle was asking, sizing him up. He looked him up and down as if he were a horse.

'We must get you to fix a date,' Milly added, 'when the boys are home.'

They were inviting him to stay with them at the Towers in September for cub-hunting. The men shot, and the women – he looked at his aunt as if she might be breaking into young even there, on that chair – the women broke off into innumerable babies. And those babies had other babies; and the other babies had – adenoids. The word recurred; but it now suggested nothing. He was sinking; he was falling under their weight; the name in his pocket even was fading. Could nothing be done about it? he asked himself. Nothing short of revolution, he thought. The idea of dynamite, exploding dumps of heavy earth, shooting earth up in a tree-shaped cloud, came to his mind, from the war. But that's all poppycock, he thought; war's poppycock, poppycock. Sara's word 'poppycock' returned. So what remains? Peggy caught his eye, where she stood talking to an unknown man. You doctors, he thought, you scientists, why don't you drop a little crystal into a tumbler, something starred and sharp, and make them swallow it? Common sense; reason; starred and sharp. But would they swallow it? He looked at Hugh. He had a way of blowing his cheeks in and out, as he said tut-tut-tut and chew, chew, chew. Would you swallow it? he said silently to Hugh.

Hugh turned to him again.

'And I hope you're going to stay in England now, North,' he said, 'though I dare say it's a fine life out there?'

And so they turned to Africa and the paucity of jobs. His exhilaration was oozing. The card no longer rayed out pictures. The damp leaves were falling. They fall and fall and cover all, he murmured to himself and looked at his aunt, colourless save for a brown stain on her forehead; and her hair colourless save for a stain like the yolk of egg on it. All over he suspected she must be soft and discoloured like a pear that has gone sleepy. And Hugh himself – his great hand was on his knee – was bound round with raw beef-steak. He caught Eleanor's eye. There was a strained look in it.

'Yes, how they've spoilt it,' she was saying.

But the resonance had gone out of her voice.

'Brand-new villas everywhere,' she was saying. She had been down in Dorsetshire apparently.

'Little red villas all along the road,' she went on.

'Yes, that's what strikes me,' he said, rousing himself to help her, 'how you've spoilt England while I've been away.'

'But you won't find many changes in our part of the world, North,' said Hugh. He spoke with pride.

'No. But then we're lucky,' said Milly. 'We have several large estates. We're very lucky,' she repeated. 'Except for Mr Phipps,' she added. She gave a tart little laugh.

North woke up. She meant that, he thought. She spoke with an acerbity that made her real. Not only did she become real, but the village, the great house, the little house, the church and the circle of old trees also appeared before him in complete reality. He would stay with them.

'That's our parson,' Hugh explained. 'Quite a good chap in his way; but high – very high. Candles – that sort of thing.'

'And his wife . . . ' Milly began.

Here Eleanor sighed. North looked at her. She was dropping off to sleep. A glazed look, a fixed expression, had come over her face. She looked terribly like Milly for a moment; sleep brought out the family likeness. Then she opened her eyes wide; by an effort of will she kept them open. But obviously she saw nothing.

'You must come down and see what you make of us,' Hugh said. 'What about the first week in September, eh?' He swayed from side to side as if his benevolence rolled about in him. He was like an old elephant who may be going to kneel. And if he does kneel, how will he ever get up again, North asked himself. And if Eleanor falls sound asleep and snores, what am I going to do, left sitting here between the knees of the elephant?

He looked round for an excuse to go.

There was Maggie coming along, not looking where she was going. They saw her. He felt a strong desire to cry out, 'Take care! Take care!' for she was in the danger zone. The long white tentacles that amorphous bodies leave floating so that they can catch their food, would suck her in. Yes, they saw her: she was lost.

'Here's Maggie!' Milly exclaimed, looking up.

'Haven't seen you for an age!' said Hugh, trying to heave himself up.

She had to stop; to put her hand into that shapeless paw. Using the last ounce of energy that remained to him, from the address in his waistcoat pocket, North rose. He would carry her off. He would save her from the contamination of family life.

But she ignored him. She stood there, answering their greetings with perfect composure as if using an outfit provided for emergencies. Oh Lord, North said to himself, she's as bad as they are. She was glazed; insincere. They were talking about *her* children now.

'Yes. That's the baby,' she was saying, pointing to a boy who was dancing with a girl.

'And your daughter, Maggie?' Milly asked, looking round.

North fidgeted. This is the conspiracy, he said to himself; this is the steamroller that smooths, obliterates; rounds into identity; rolls into balls. He listened. Jimmy was in Uganda; Lily was in Leicestershire; *my* boy – *my* girl . . . they were saying. But they're not interested in other people's children, he observed. Only in their own; their own property; their own flesh and blood, which they would protect with the unsheathed claws of the primeval swamp, he thought, looking at Milly's fat little paws; even Maggie, even she. For she too was talking about my boy, my girl. How then can we be civilised? he asked himself.

Eleanor snored. She was nodding off, shamelessly, helplessly. There was an obscenity in unconsciousness, he thought. Her mouth was open; her head was on one side.

But now it was his turn. Silence gaped. One has to egg it on, he thought; somebody has to say something, or human society would cease. Hugh would cease; Milly would cease; and he was about to apply himself to find something to say, something with which to feed the immense vacancy of that primeval maw, when Delia, either from the erratic desire of a hostess always to interrupt or divinely inspired by human charity – which he could not say – came beckoning.

'The Ludbys!' she exclaimed. 'The Ludbys!'

'Oh where? The dear Ludbys!' said Milly, and up they heaved and off they went, for the Ludbys, it appeared, seldom left Northumberland.

'Well, Maggie?' said North, turning to her – but here Eleanor made a little click at the back of her throat. Her head pitched forward. Sleep, now that she slept soundly, had given her dignity. She looked peaceful, far from them, rapt in the calm which sometimes gives the sleeper the look of the dead. They sat silent, for a moment, alone together, in private.

'Why – why – why – ' he said at last, making a gesture as if he were plucking tufts of grass from the carpet.

'Why?' Maggie asked. 'Why what?'

'The Gibbses,' he murmured. He jerked his head at them, where they stood talking by the fireplace. Gross, obese, shapeless, they looked to him like a parody, a travesty, an excrescence that had overgrown the form within, the fire within. 'What's wrong?' he asked.

She looked too. But she said nothing. Couples came dancing slowly past them. A girl stopped, and her gesture as she raised her hand, unconsciously, had the seriousness of the very young anticipating life in its goodness which touched him.

'Why – ?' he jerked his thumb in the direction of the young, 'when they're so lovely – '

She too looked at the girl, who was fastening a flower that had come undone in the front of her frock. She smiled. She said nothing. Then half consciously she echoed his question without a meaning in her echo, 'Why?'

He was dashed for a moment. It seemed to him that she refused to help him. And he wanted her to help him. Why should she not take the weight off his shoulders and give him what he longed for – assurance, certainty? Because she too was deformed like the rest of them? He looked down at her hands. They were strong hands; fine hands; but if it were a question, he thought, watching the fingers curl slightly, of 'my' children, of 'my' possessions, it would be one rip down the belly; or teeth in the soft fur of the throat. We cannot help each other, he thought, we are all deformed. Yet, disagreeable as it was to him to remove her from the eminence upon which he placed her, perhaps she was right, he thought, and we who make idols of other people, who endow this man, that woman, with power to lead us, only add to the deformity, and stoop ourselves.

'I'm going to stay with them,' he said aloud.

'At the Towers?' she asked.

'Yes,' he said. 'For cubbing in September.'

She was not listening. Her eyes were on him. She was getting him into relation with something else he felt. It made him uneasy. She was looking at him as if he were not himself but somebody else. He felt again the discomfort that he had felt when Sally described him on the telephone.

'I know,' he said, stiffening the muscles of his face, 'I'm like the picture of a Frenchman holding his hat.'

'Holding his hat?' she asked.

'And getting fat,' he added.

' . . . Holding a hat . . . who's holding a hat?' said Eleanor, opening her eyes.

She glanced about her in bewilderment. Since her last recollection, and it seemed only a second ago, was of Milly talking of candles in a church, something must have happened. Milly and Hugh had been there; but they were gone. There had been a gap – a gap filled with the golden light of lolling candles, and some sensation which she could not name.

She woke up completely.

'What nonsense are you talking?' she said. 'North's not holding a hat! And he's not fat,' she added. 'Not at all, not at all,' she repeated, patting him affectionately on the knee.

She felt extraordinarily happy. Most sleep left some dream in one's mind – some scene or figure remained when one woke up. But this sleep, this momentary trance, in which the candles had lolled and lengthened themselves, had left her with nothing but a feeling; a feeling, not a dream.

'He's not holding a hat,' she repeated.

They both laughed at her.

'You've been dreaming, Eleanor,' said Maggie.

'Have I?' she said. A deep gulf had been cut in the talk, it was true. She could not remember what they had been saying. There was Maggie; but Milly and Hugh had gone.

'Only a second's nap,' she said. 'But what are you going to do, North? What are your plans?' she said, speaking rather quickly. 'We musn't let him go back, Maggie,' she said. 'Not to that horrid farm.'

She wished to appear extremely practical, partly to prove that she had not slept, partly to protect the extraordinary feeling of happiness that still remained with her. Covered up from observation it might survive, she felt.

'You've saved enough, haven't you?' she said aloud.

'Saved enough?' he said. Why, he wondered, did people who had been asleep always want to make out that they were extremely wide-awake? 'Four or five thousand,' he added at random.

'Well, that's enough,' she insisted. 'Five per cent; six per cent – ' She tried to do the sum in her head. She appealed to Maggie for help. 'Four or five thousand – how much would that be, Maggie? Enough to live on, wouldn't it?'

'Four or five thousand,' repeated Maggie.

'At five or six per cent . . . ' Eleanor put in. She could never do sums in her head at the best of times; but for some reason it seemed to her very important to bring things back to facts. She opened her bag, found a letter, and produced a stubby little pencil.

'There – work it out on that,' she said. Maggie took the paper and drew a few lines with the pencil as if to test it. North glanced over her shoulder. Was she solving the problem before her – was she considering his life, his needs? No. She was drawing, apparently a caricature – he looked – of a big man opposite in a white waistcoat. It was a farce. It made him feel slightly ridiculous.

'Don't be so silly,' he said.

'That's my brother,' she said, nodding at the man in the white waist-coat. 'He used to take us for rides on an elephant . . . ' She added a flourish to the waistcoat.

'And we're being very sensible,' Eleanor protested. 'If you want to live in England, North – if you want – '

He cut her short. 'I don't know what I want,' he said.

'Oh, I see!' she said. She laughed. Her feeling of happiness returned to her, her unreasonable exaltation. It seemed to her that they were all young, with the future before them. Nothing was fixed; nothing was known; life was open and free before them.

'Isn't that odd?' she exclaimed. 'Isn't that queer? Isn't that why life's a perpetual – what shall I call it? – miracle? . . . I mean,' she tried to explain, for he looked puzzled, 'old age they say is like this; but it isn't. It's different; quite different. So when I was a child; so when I was a girl; it's been a perpetual discovery, my life. A miracle.' She stopped. She was rambling on again. She felt rather light-headed, after her dream.

'There's Peggy!' she exclaimed, glad to attach herself to something solid. 'Look at her! Reading a book!'

Peggy, marooned when the dance started, over by the bookcase, stood as close to it as she could. In order to cover her loneliness she took down a book. It was bound in green leather; and had, she noted as she turned it in her hands, little gilt stars tooled upon it. Which is all to the good, she thought, turning it over, because then it'll seem as if I were admiring the binding . . . But I can't stand here admiring the binding, she thought. She opened it. He'll say what I'm thinking, she thought as she did so. Books opened at random always did.

'La médiocrité de l'univers m'étonne et me révolte,' she read. That was it. Precisely. She read on. ' . . . la petitesse de toutes choses m'emplit de dégoût . . . ' She lifted her eyes. They were treading on her toes. ' . . . la pauvreté des êtres humains m'anéantit.'[58] She shut the book and put it back on the shelf.

Precisely, she said.

She turned her watch on her wrist and looked at it surreptitiously. Time was getting on. An hour is sixty minutes, she said to herself; two hours are one hundred and twenty minutes. How many have I still to stay here? Could she go yet? She saw Eleanor beckoning. She put the book back on the shelf. She went towards them.

'Come, Peggy, come and talk to us,' Eleanor called out, beckoning.

'D'you know what time it is, Eleanor?' said Peggy, coming up to them. She pointed to her watch. 'Don't you think it's time to be going?' she said.

'I'd forgotten the time,' said Eleanor.

'But you'll be so tired tomorrow,' Peggy protested, standing beside her.

'How like a doctor!' North twitted her. 'Health, health, health!' he exclaimed. 'But health's not an end in itself,' he said, looking up at her.

She ignored him.

'D'you mean to stay to the end?' she said to Eleanor. 'This'll go on all night.' She looked at the twisting couples gyrating in time to the tune on the gramophone, as if some animal were dying in slow but exquisite anguish.

'But we're enjoying ourselves,' said Eleanor. 'Come and enjoy yourself too.'

She pointed to the floor at her side. Peggy let herself down on to the floor at her side. Give up brooding, thinking, analysing, Eleanor meant she knew. Enjoy the moment – but could one? she asked, pulling her skirts round her feet as she sat down.

Eleanor bent over and tapped her on the shoulder. 'I want you to tell me,' she said, drawing her into the conversation, since she looked so glum, 'you're a doctor – you know these things – what do dreams mean?'

Peggy laughed. Another of Eleanor's questions. Does two and two make four – and what is the nature of the universe?

'I don't mean dreams exactly,' Eleanor went on. 'Feelings – feelings that come when one's asleep?'

'My dear Nell,' said Peggy, glancing up at her, 'how often have I told you? Doctors know very little about the body; absolutely nothing about the mind.' She looked down again.

'I always said they were humbugs!' North exclaimed.

'What a pity!' said Eleanor. 'I was hoping you'd be able to explain to me – ' She was bending down. There was a flush on her cheek, Peggy noted; she was excited; but what was there to be excited about?

'Explain – what?' she asked.

'Oh, nothing,' said Eleanor. Now I've snubbed her, Peggy thought. She looked at her again. Her eyes were bright; her cheeks were flushed, or was it only the tan from her voyage to India? And a little vein stood out on her forehead. But what was there to be excited about? She leant back against the wall. From her seat on the floor she had a queer view of people's feet: feet pointing this way, feet pointing that way; patent leather pumps; satin slippers; silk stockings and socks. They were dancing rhythmically, insistently, to the tune of the fox-trot. And what about the cocktail and the tea, said he to me, said he to me – the tune seemed to repeat over and over again. And voices went on over her head. Odd little gusts of inconsecutive conversations reached her . . . down in Norfolk where my brother-in-law has a boat . . . Oh, a complete washout, yes I agree . . . People talked nonsense at parties. And beside her Maggie was talking; North was talking; Eleanor was talking. Suddenly Eleanor swept her hand out.

'There's Renny!' she was saying. 'Renny, whom I never see. Renny whom I love . . . Come and talk to us, Renny.' And a pair of pumps crossed Peggy's field of vision and stopped in front of her. He sat down beside Eleanor. She could just see the line of his profile: the big nose; the thin cheek. And what about the cocktails and the tea, said he to me, said he to me, the music ground out; the couples danced past. But the little group on the chairs above her were talking; they were laughing.

'I know you'll agree with me . . . ' Eleanor was saying. Through her half-shut eyes Peggy could see Renny turn towards her. She saw his thin cheek; his big nose; his nails, she noticed, were very close cut.

'Depends what you were saying . . . ' he said.

'What were we saying?' Eleanor pondered. She's forgotten already, Peggy suspected.

' . . . That things have changed for the better,' she heard Eleanor's voice.

'Since you were a girl?' That she thought was Maggie's voice.

Then a voice from a skirt with a pink bow on the hem interrupted. ' . . . I don't know how it is but the heat doesn't affect me as much as it used to do . . . ' She looked up. There were fifteen pink bows on the dress, accurately stitched, and wasn't that Miriam Parrish's little saint-like, sheep-like head on top?

'What I mean is, we've changed in ourselves,' Eleanor was saying. 'We're happier – we're freer – '

What does she mean by 'happiness', by 'freedom'? Peggy asked herself, lapsing against the wall again.

'Take Renny and Maggie,' she heard Eleanor saying. And then she stopped. And then she went on again: 'D'you remember, Renny, the night of the raid? When I met Nicholas for the first time . . . when we sat in the cellar? . . . Going downstairs I said to myself, That's a happy marriage – ' There was another pause. 'I said to myself,' she continued, and Peggy saw her hand laid on Renny's knee, 'if I'd known Renny when I was young . . . ' She stopped. Does she mean she would have fallen in love with him? Peggy wondered. Again the music interrupted . . . said he to me, said he to me . . .

'No, never . . . ' she heard Eleanor say. 'No, never . . . ' Was she saying she had never been in love, never wanted to marry? Peggy wondered. They were laughing.

'Why, you look like a girl of eighteen!' she heard North say.

'And I feel like one!' Eleanor exclaimed. But you'll be a wreck tomorrow morning Peggy thought, looking at her. She was flushed, the veins stood out on her forehead.

'I feel . . . ' she stopped. She put her hand to her head: 'as if I'd been in another world! So happy!' she exclaimed.

'Tosh, Eleanor, tosh,' said Renny.

I thought he'd say that, Peggy said to herself with some queer satisfaction. She could see his profile as he sat on the other side of her aunt's knee. The French are logical; they are sensible, she thought. Still, she added, why not let Eleanor have her little flutter if she enjoys it?

'Tosh? What d'you mean by "tosh"?' Eleanor was asking. She was leaning forward; she held her hand up as if she wanted him to speak.

'Always talking of the other world,' he said. 'Why not this one?'

'But I meant this world!' she said. 'I meant, happy in this world – happy with living people.' She waved her hand as if to embrace the miscellaneous company, the young, the old, the dancers, the talkers; Miriam with her pink bows, and the Indian in his turban. Peggy sank back against the wall. Happy in this world, she thought, happy with living people!

The music stopped. The young man who had been putting records on the gramophone had walked off. The couples broke apart and began to push their way through the door. They were going to eat perhaps; they were going to stream out into the back garden and sit on hard sooty chairs. The music which had been cutting grooves in her mind had ceased. There was a lull – a silence. Far away she heard the sounds of the London night: a horn hooted; a siren wailed on the river. The far-away sounds, the suggestion they brought in of other worlds, indifferent to this world, of people toiling, grinding, in the heart of darkness,[59] in the depths of night, made her say over Eleanor's words, Happy in this world, happy with living people. But how can one be 'happy'? she asked herself, in a world bursting with misery. On every placard at every street corner was death; or worse – tyranny; brutality; torture; the fall of civilisation; the end of freedom. We here, she thought, are only sheltering under a leaf, which will be destroyed. And then Eleanor says the world is better, because two people out of all those millions are 'happy'. Her eyes had fixed themselves on the floor; it was empty now save for a wisp of muslin torn from some skirt. But why do I notice everything? she thought. She shifted her position. Why must I think? She did not want to think. She wished that there were blinds like those in railway carriages that came down over the light and hooded the mind. The blue blind that one pulls down on a night journey, she thought. Thinking was torment; why not give up thinking, and drift and dream? But the misery of the world, she thought, forces me to think. Or was that a pose? Was she not seeing herself in the becoming attitude of one who points to his bleeding heart? to whom the miseries of the world are misery, when in fact, she thought, I do not love my kind. Again she saw the ruby-splashed pavement, and faces mobbed at the door of a picture palace; apathetic, passive faces; the faces of people drugged with cheap pleasures; who had not even the courage to be themselves, but must dress up, imitate, pretend. And here, in this room, she thought, fixing her eyes on a couple . . . But I will not think, she repeated; she would force her mind to become a blank and lie back, and accept quietly, tolerantly, whatever came.

She listened. Scraps reached her from above. ' . . . flats in Highgate have bathrooms,' they were saying. ' . . . Your mother . . . Digby . . . Yes, Crosby's still alive – ' It was family gossip, and they were enjoying it. But how can I enjoy it? she said to herself. She was too tired; the skin round her eyes felt taut; a hoop was bound tight over her head; she tried to think herself away into the darkness of the country. But it was impossible; they were laughing. She opened her eyes, exacerbated by their laughter.

That was Renny laughing. He held a sheet of paper in his hand; his head was flung back; his mouth was wide open. From it came a sound like Ha! Ha! Ha! That is laughter, she said to herself. That is the sound people make when they are amused.

She watched him. Her muscles began to twitch involuntarily. She could not help laughing too. She stretched out her hand and Renny gave her the paper. It was folded; they had been playing a game. Each of them had drawn a different part of a picture. On top there was a woman's head like Queen Alexandra, with a fuzz of little curls; then a bird's neck; the body of a tiger; and stout elephant's legs dressed in child's drawers completed the picture.

'I drew that – I drew that!' said Renny pointing to the legs from which a long trail of ribbon depended. She laughed, laughed, laughed; she could not help laughing.

'The face that launched a thousand ships!'[60] said North, pointing to another part of the monster's person. They all laughed again. She stopped laughing; her lips smoothed themselves out. But her laughter had had some strange effect on her. It had relaxed her, enlarged her. She felt, or rather she saw, not a place, but a state of being, in which there was real laughter, real happiness, and this fractured world was whole; whole, and free. But how could she say it?

'Look here . . . ' she began. She wanted to express something that she felt to be very important; about a world in which people were whole, in which people were free . . . But they were laughing; she was serious. 'Look here . . . ' she began again.

Eleanor stopped laughing.

'Peggy wants to say something,' she said. The others stopped talking, but they had stopped at the wrong moment. She had nothing to say when it came to the point, and yet she had to speak.

'Here,' she began again, 'here you all are – talking about North –' He looked up at her in surprise. It was not what she had meant to say, but she must go on now that she had begun. Their faces gaped at her like birds with their mouths open. ' . . . How he's to live, where he's to live,' she went on. ' . . . But what's the use, what's the point of saying that?'

She looked at her brother. A feeling of animosity possessed her. He was still smiling, but his smile smoothed itself out as she looked at him.

'What's the use?' she said, facing him. 'You'll marry. You'll have children. What'll you do then? Make money. Write little books to make money . . . '

She had got it wrong. She had meant to say something impersonal, but she was being personal. It was done now however; she must flounder on now.

'You'll write one little book, and then another little book,' she said viciously, 'instead of living . . . living differently, differently.'

She stopped. There was the vision still, but she had not grasped it. She had broken off only a little fragment of what she meant to say, and she had made her brother angry. Yet there it hung before her, the thing she had seen, the thing she had not said. But as she fell back with a jerk against the wall, she felt relieved of some oppression; her heart thumped; the veins on her forehead stood out. She had not said it, but she had tried to say it. Now she could rest; now she could think herself away under the shadow of their ridicule, which had no power to hurt her, into the country. Her eyes half shut; it seemed to her that she was on a terrace, in the evening; an owl went up and down, up and down; its white wing showed on the dark of the hedge; and she heard country people singing and the rattle of wheels on a road.

Then gradually the blur became distinct; she saw the line of the bookcase opposite; the wisp of muslin on the floor; and two large feet, in tight shoes, so that the bunions showed, stopped in front of her.

For a moment nobody moved; nobody spoke. Peggy sat still. She did not want to move, or to speak. She wanted to rest, to lean, to dream. She felt very tired. Then more feet stopped, and the hem of a black skirt.

'Aren't you people coming down to supper?' said a chuckling little voice. She looked up. It was her Aunt Milly, with her husband by her side.

'Supper's downstairs,' said Hugh. 'Supper's downstairs.' And they passed on.

'How prosperous they've grown!' said North's voice, laughing at them.

'Ah, but they're so good to people . . . ' Eleanor protested. The sense of the family again, Peggy noted.

Then the knee against which she was sheltering herself moved.

'We must go,' said Eleanor. Wait, wait, Peggy wanted to implore her. There was something she wanted to ask her; something she wanted to add to her outburst, since nobody had attacked her, and nobody had laughed at her. But it was useless; the knees straightened themselves; the red cloak elongated itself; Eleanor had risen. She was hunting for her bag or her handkerchief; she was ferreting in the cushions of her chair. As usual, she had lost something.

'I'm sorry to be such an old muddler,' she apologised. She shook a cushion; coins rolled out on to the floor. A sixpenny bit spun on its edge across the carpet, reached a pair of silver shoes on the floor and fell flat.

'There!' Eleanor exclaimed. 'There! . . . But that's Kitty! isn't it?' she exclaimed.

Peggy looked up. A handsome elderly woman, with curled white hair and something shining in her hair was standing in the doorway looking round her, as if she had just come in and were looking for her hostess, who was not there. It was at her feet that the sixpence had fallen.

'Kitty!' Eleanor repeated. She went towards her with her hands stretched out. They all got up. Peggy got up. Yes, it was over; it was destroyed she felt. Directly something got together, it broke. She had a feeling of desolation. And then you have to pick up the pieces, and make something new, something different, she thought, and crossed

the room, and joined the foreigner, the man she called Brown, whose
real name was Nicholas Pomjalovsky.

'Who is that lady,' Nicholas asked her, 'who appears to come into a
room as if the whole world belonged to her?'

'That's Kitty Lasswade,' said Peggy. As she stood in the door, they
could not pass.

'I'm afraid I'm dreadfully late,' they heard her saying in her clear,
authoritative tones. 'But I've been to the ballet.'

That's Kitty, is it? North said to himself, looking at her. She was one
of those well-set-up rather masculine old ladies who repelled him
slightly. He thought he remembered that she was the wife of one of
our governors; or was it the Viceroy of India? He could see her, as she
stood there, doing the honours of Government House. 'Sit here. Sit
there. And you, young man, I hope you take plenty of exercise?' He
knew the type. She had a short straight nose and blue eyes very wide
apart. She might have looked very dashing in the eighties, he thought;
in a tight riding-habit; worn a small hat, with a cock's feather in it;
perhaps had an affair with an aide-de-camp; and then settled down,
become dictatorial, and told stories about her past. He listened.

'Ah, but he's not a patch on Nijinsky!' she was saying.

The sort of thing she would say, he thought. He examined the books
in the bookcase. He took one out and held it upside down. One little
book, and then another little book – Peggy's taunt returned to him.
The words had stung him out of all proportion to their surface meaning.
She had turned on him with such violence, as if she despised him; she
had looked as if she were going to burst into tears. He opened the little
book. Latin, was it? He broke off a sentence and let it swim in his mind.
There the words lay, beautiful, yet meaningless, yet composed in a
pattern – *nox est perpetua una dormienda*.[61] He remembered his master
saying, Mark the long word at the end of the sentence. There the words
floated; but just as they were about to give out their meaning, there was
a movement at the door. Old Patrick had come ambling up, had given
his arm gallantly to the widow of the governor-general, and they were
proceeding with a curious air of antiquated ceremony down the stairs.
The others began to follow them. The younger generation following in
the wake of the old, North said to himself as he put the book back on
the shelf and followed. Only, he observed, they were not so very young;
Peggy – there were white hairs on Peggy's head – she must be thirty-
seven, thirty-eight?

*

'Enjoying yourself, Peg?' he said as they hung back behind the others. He had a vague feeling of hostility towards her. She seemed to him bitter, disillusioned, and very critical of everyone, especially of himself.

'You go first, Patrick,' they heard Lady Lasswade boom out in her genial loud voice. 'These staircases are not adapted . . . ' she paused, as she advanced what was probably a rheumatic leg, 'for old people who've . . . ' there was another pause as she descended another step, 'been kneeling on damp grass killing slugs.'

North looked at Peggy and laughed. He had not expected the sentence to end like that, but the widows of viceroys, he thought, always have gardens, always kill slugs. Peggy smiled too. But he felt uncomfortable with her. She had attacked him. There they stood, however, side by side.

'Did you see old William Whatney?' she said, turning to him.

'No!' he exclaimed, '*he* still alive? That old white walrus with the whiskers?'

'Yes – that's him,' she said. There was an old man in a white waistcoat standing in the door.

'The old Mock Turtle,' he said. They had to fall back on childish slang, on childish memories, to cover their distance, their hostility.

'D'you remember . . . ' he began.

'The night of the row?' she said. 'The night I let myself out of the window by a rope.'

'And we picnicked in the Roman camp,' he said.

'We should never have been found out if that horrid little scamp hadn't told on us,' she said, descending a step.

'A little beast with pink eyes,' said North.

They could think of nothing else to say, as they stood blocked, waiting for the others to move on, side by side. And he used to read her his poetry in the apple-loft, he remembered, and as they walked up and down by the rose bushes. And now they had nothing to say to each other.

'Perry,' he said, descending another step, suddenly remembering the name of the pink-eyed boy who had seen them coming home that morning and had told on them.

'Alfred,' she added.

She still knew certain things about him, he thought; they still had something very profound in common. That was why, he thought, she had hurt him by what she had said, before the others, about his 'writing little books'. It was their past condemning his present. He glanced at her.

Damn women, he thought, they're so hard; so unimaginative. Curse their little inquisitive minds. What did their 'education' amount to? It only made her critical, censorious. Old Eleanor, with all her rambling and stumbling, was worth a dozen of Peggy any day. She was neither one thing nor the other, he thought, glancing at her; neither in the fashion nor out of it.

She felt him look at her and look away. He was finding fault with something about her, she knew. Her hands? Her dress? No, it was because she criticised him, she thought. Yes, she thought as she descended another step, now I'm going to be trounced; now I'm going to be paid back for telling him he'd write 'little books'. It takes from ten to fifteen minutes, she thought, to get an answer; and then it'll be something off the point but disagreeable – very, she thought. The vanity of men was immeasurable. She waited. He looked at her again. And now he's comparing me with the girl I saw him talking to, she thought, and saw again the lovely, hard face. He'll tie himself up with a red-lipped girl and become a drudge. He must, and I can't, she thought. No, I've a sense of guilt always. I shall pay for it, I shall pay for it, I kept saying to myself even in the Roman camp, she thought. She would have no children, and he would produce little Gibbses, more little Gibbses, she thought, looking in at the door of a solicitor's office, unless she leaves him at the end of the year for some other man . . . The solicitor's name was Alridge, she noted. But I will take no more notes; I will enjoy myself, she thought suddenly. She put her hand on his arm.

'Met anybody amusing tonight?' she said.

He guessed that she had seen him with the girl.

'One girl,' he said briefly.

'So I saw,' she said. She looked away. 'I thought her lovely,' she said, carefully observing a tinted picture of a bird with a long beak that hung on the stairs.

'Shall I bring her to see you?' he asked.

So he cared for her opinion, did he? Her hand was still on his arm; she felt something hard and taut beneath the sleeve, and the touch of his flesh, bringing back to her the nearness of human beings and their distance, so that if one meant to help one hurt, yet they depended on each other, produced in her such a tumult of sensation that she could scarcely keep herself from crying out, North! North! North! But I mustn't make a fool of myself again, she said to herself.

'Any evening after six,' she said aloud, carefully descending another step, and they reached the bottom of the stairs.

A roar of voices sounded from behind the door of the supper room. She withdrew her hand from his arm. The door burst open.

'Spoons! spoons! spoons!' cried Delia, brandishing her arms in a rhetorical manner as if she were still declaiming to someone inside. She caught sight of her nephew and niece. 'Be an angel, North, and fetch spoons!' she cried, throwing her hands out towards him.

'Spoons for the widow of the governor-general!' North cried, catching her manner, imitating her dramatic gesture.

'In the kitchen, in the basement!' Delia cried, waving her arm at the kitchen stairs. 'Come, Peggy, come,' she said, catching Peggy's hand in hers, 'we're all sitting down to supper.' She burst into the room where they were having supper. It was crowded. People were sitting on the floor, on chairs, on office stools. Long office tables, little typewriting tables, had been pressed into use. They were strewn with flowers, frilled with flowers. Carnations, roses, daisies, were flung down higgledy-piggledy. 'Sit on the floor, sit anywhere,' Delia commanded, waving her hand promiscuously.

'Spoons are coming,' she said to Lady Lasswade, who was drinking her soup out of a mug.

'But I don't want a spoon,' said Kitty. She tilted the mug and drank.

'No, you wouldn't,' said Delia, 'but other people do.'

North brought in a bunch of spoons and she took them from him.

'Now who wants a spoon and who doesn't?' she said, brandishing the bunch of spoons in front of her. Some people do and some don't, she thought. Her sort of people, she thought, did not want spoons; the others – the English – did. She had been making that distinction between people all her life.

'A spoon? A spoon?' she said, looking round her at the crowded room with some complacency. All sorts of people were there, she noted. That had always been her aim: to mix people; to do away with the absurd conventions of English life. And she had done it tonight, she thought. There were nobles and commoners; people dressed and people not dressed; people drinking out of mugs, and people waiting with their soup getting cold for a spoon to be brought to them.

'A spoon for me,' said her husband, looking up at her.

She wrinkled her nose. For the thousandth time he had dashed her dream. Thinking to marry a wild rebel, she had married the most king-respecting, empire-admiring of country gentlemen, and for that very reason partly – because he was, even now, such a magnificent figure of a man. 'A spoon for your uncle,' she said dryly, and sent North off with the bunch. Then she sat down beside Kitty, who was gulping her soup like a child at a school treat. She set down her mug empty, among the flowers.

'Poor flowers,' she said, taking up a carnation that lay on the table-cloth and putting it to her lips. 'They'll die, Delia – they want water.'

'Roses are cheap today,' said Delia. 'Twopence a bunch off a barrow in Oxford Street,' she said. She took up a red rose and held it under the light, so that it shone, veined, semi-transparent.

'What a rich country England is!' she said, laying it down again. She took up her mug.

'What I'm always telling you,' said Patrick, wiping his mouth. 'The only civilised country in the whole world,' he added.

'I thought we were on the verge of a smash,' said Kitty. 'Not that it looked much like it at Covent Garden tonight,' she added.

'Ah, but it's true,' he sighed, going on with his own thoughts. 'I'm sorry to say it – but we're savages compared with you.'

'He won't be happy till he's got Dublin Castle.[62] back again,' Delia twitted him.

'You don't enjoy your freedom?' said Kitty, looking at the queer old man whose face always made her think of a hairy gooseberry. But his body was magnificent.

'It seems to me that our new freedom is a good deal worse than our old slavery,'.[63] said Patrick, fumbling with his toothpick.

Politics as usual, money and politics, North thought, overhearing them as he went round with the last of his spoons.

'You're not going to tell me that all that struggle has been in vain, Patrick?' said Kitty.

'Come to Ireland and see for yourself, m'lady,' he said grimly.

'It's too early – too early to tell,' said Delia.

Her husband looked past her with the sad innocent eyes of an old sporting dog whose hunting days are over. But they could not keep their fixity for long. 'Who's this chap with the spoons?' he said, resting his eyes on North, who stood just behind them, waiting.

'North,' said Delia. 'Come and sit by us, North.'

'Good-evening to you, sir,' said Patrick. They had met already, but he had already forgotten.

'What, Morris's son?' said Kitty, turning round abruptly. She shook hands cordially. He sat down and took a gulp of soup.

'He's just back from Africa. He's been on a farm there,' said Delia.

'And how does the old country strike you?' said Patrick, leaning towards him genially.

'Very crowded,' he said, looking round the room. 'And you all talk,' he added, 'about money and politics.' That was his stock phrase. He had said it twenty times already.

'You were in Africa?' said Lady Lasswade. 'And what made you give up your farm?' she demanded. She looked him in the eyes and spoke just as he expected she would speak: too imperiously for his liking. What business is that of yours, old lady? he asked himself.

'I'd had about enough of it,' he said aloud.

'And I'd have given anything to be a farmer!' she exclaimed. That was a little out of the picture, North thought. So were her eyes; she ought to have worn a pince-nez; but she did not.

'But in my youth,' she said, rather fiercely – her hands were rather stubby, and the skin was rough, but she gardened, he remembered – 'that wasn't allowed.'

'No,' said Patrick. 'And it's my belief,' he continued, drumming on the table with a fork, 'that we should all be very glad, very glad, to go back to things as they were. What's the war done for us, eh? Ruined me for one.' He wagged his head with melancholy tolerance from side to side.

'I'm sorry to hear that,' said Kitty. 'But speaking for myself, the old days were bad days, wicked days, cruel days . . . ' Her eyes turned blue with passion.

What about the aide-de-camp, and the hat with a cock's feather in it? North asked himself.

'Don't you agree with me, Delia?' said Kitty, turning to her.

But Delia was talking across her, using her rather exaggerated Irish sing-song to someone at the next table. Don't I remember this room, Kitty thought; a meeting; an argument. But what was it about? Force . . .

'My dear Kitty,' Patrick interrupted, patting her hand with his great paw. 'That's another instance of what I'm telling you. Now these ladies have got the vote,' he said, turning to North, 'are they any better off?'

Kitty looked fierce for a moment; then she smiled. 'We won't argue, my old friend,' she said, giving him a little pat on the hand.

'And it's just the same with the Irish,' he went on. North saw that he was bent on treading out the round of his familiar thoughts like an old broken-winded horse. 'They'd be glad enough to join the empire again, I assure you. I come of a family,' he said to North, 'that has served its king and country for three hundred – '

'English settlers,'.[64] said Delia, rather shortly, returning to her soup.

That's what they quarrel about when they're alone, North thought.

'We've been three hundred years in the country,' old Patrick continued, padding out his round – he laid a hand on North's arm, 'and what strikes an old fellow like me, an old fogy like me – '

'Nonsense, Patrick,' Delia struck in, 'I've never seen you look younger. Might be fifty, mightn't he, North?'

But Patrick shook his head.

'I shan't see seventy again,' he said simply. ' . . . But what strikes an old fellow like me,' he continued, patting North's arm, 'is with such a lot of good feeling about,' he nodded rather vaguely at a placard that was pinned to the wall – 'and nice things too,' – he referred perhaps to the flowers, but his head jerked involuntarily as he talked – 'what do these fellows want to be shooting each other for? I don't join any societies; I don't sign any of these' – he pointed to the placard – 'what d'you call 'em? manifestos – I just go to my friend Mike, or it may be Pat – they're all good friends of mine, and we – '

He stooped and pinched his foot. 'Lord, these shoes!' he complained.

'Tight, are they?' said Kitty. 'Kick 'em off.'

Why had the poor old boy been brought over here, North wondered, and stuck into those tight shoes? He was clearly talking to his dogs. There was a look in his eyes now when he raised them again and tried to recover the drift of what he had been saying that was like the look of a sportsman who saw the birds rising in a semicircle over the wide green bog. But they were out of shot. He could not remember where he had got to. ' . . . We talk things over,' he said, 'round a table.' His eyes became mild and vacant as if the engine were cut off, and his mind glided on silently.

'The English talk too,' said North perfunctorily. Patrick nodded, and looked vaguely at a group of young people. But he was not interested in what other people were saying. His mind could no longer stretch beyond its beat. His body was still beautifully proportioned; it was his mind that was old. He would say the same thing all over again, and when he had said it he would pick his teeth and sit gazing in front of him. There he sat now, holding a flower between his finger and thumb, loosely, without looking at it, as if his mind were gliding on . . . But Delia interrupted.

'North must go and talk to his friends,' she said. Like so many wives, she saw when her husband was becoming a bore, North thought, as he got up.

'Don't wait to be introduced,' said Delia, waving her hand. 'Do just what you like – just what you like,' her husband echoed her, beating on the table with his flower.

*

North was glad to go; but where was he to go now? He was an outsider, he felt again, as he glanced round the room. All these people knew each other. They called each other – he stood on the outskirts of a little group of young men and women – by their Christian names, by their nicknames. Each was already part of a little group, he felt as he listened, keeping on the outskirts. He wanted to hear what they were saying; but not to be drawn in himself. He listened. They were arguing. Politics and money, he said to himself; money and politics. That phrase came in handy. But he could not understand the argument, which was already heated. Never have I felt so lonely, he thought. The old platitude about solitude in a crowd was true: for hills and trees accept one; human beings reject one. He turned his back and pretended to read the par-ticulars of a desirable property at Bexhill which Patrick had called for some reason 'a manifesto'. 'Running water in all the bedrooms,' he read. He overheard scraps of talk. That's Oxford, that's Harrow, he continued, recognising the tricks of speech that were caught at school and college. It seemed to him that they were still cutting little private jokes about Jones minor winning the long jump; and old Foxy, or whatever the headmaster's name was. It was like hearing small boys at a private school, hearing these young men talk politics. 'I'm right . . . you're wrong.' At their age, he thought, he had been in the trenches; he had seen men killed. But was that a good education? He shifted from one foot to another. At their age, he thought, he had been alone on a farm sixty miles from a white man, in control of a herd of sheep. But was that a good education? Anyhow it seemed to him, half hearing their argument, looking at their gestures, catching their slang, that they were all the same sort. Public school and university, he sized them up as he looked over his shoulder. But where are the Sweeps and the Sewermen, the Seamstresses and the Stevedores? he thought, making a list of trades that began with the letter S. For all Delia's pride in her promiscuity, he thought, glancing at the people, there were only Dons and Duchesses, and what other words begin with D? he asked himself, as he scrutinised the placard again – Drabs and Drones?

He turned. A nice fresh-faced boy with a freckled nose in ordinary day clothes was looking at him. If he didn't take care he would be drawn in too. Nothing would be easier than to join a society, to sign what Patrick called 'a manifesto'. But he did not believe in joining societies, in signing manifestos. He turned back to the desirable residence with its three-quarters of an acre of garden and running water in all the bed-rooms. People met, he thought, pretending to read, in hired halls. And one of them stood on a platform. There was the pump-handle gesture;

the wringing-wet-clothes gesture; and then the voice, oddly detached from the little figure and tremendously magnified by the loudspeaker, went booming and bawling round the hall: Justice! Liberty! For a moment, of course, sitting among knees, wedged in tight, a ripple, a nice emotional quiver, went over the skin; but next morning, he said to himself as he glanced again at the house-agent's placard, there's not an idea, not a phrase that would feed a sparrow. What do they mean by Justice and Liberty? he asked, all these nice young men with two or three hundred a year. Something's wrong, he thought; there's a gap, a dislocation, between the word and the reality. If they want to reform the world, he thought, why not begin there, at the centre, with themselves? He turned on his heel and ran straight into an old man in a white waistcoat.

'Hello!' he said, holding out his hand.

It was his Uncle Edward. He had the look of an insect whose body has been eaten out, leaving only the wings, the shell.

'Very glad to see you back, North,' said Edward, and shook him warmly by the hand.

'Very glad,' he repeated. He was shy. He was spare and thin. He looked as if his face had been carved and graved by a multitude of fine instruments; as if it had been left out on a frosty night and frozen over. He threw his head back like a horse champing a bit; but he was an old horse, a blue-eyed horse whose bit no longer irked him. His movements were from habit, not from feeling. What had he been doing all these years? North wondered, as they stood there surveying each other. Editing Sophocles? What would happen if Sophocles one of these days were edited? What would they do then, these eaten out hollow-shelled old men?

'You've filled out,' said Edward, looking him up and down. 'You've filled out,' he repeated.

There was a subtle deference in his manner. Edward, the scholar, paid tribute to North, the soldier. Yes, but they found it difficult to talk. He had the air of being stamped, North thought; he had kept something, after all, out of the hubbub.

'Shan't we sit down?' said Edward, as if he wished to talk to him seriously about interesting things. They looked about for a quiet place. He had not frittered his time away talking to old red setters and raising his gun, North thought, glancing about him to see if by chance there was a quiet place in the room where they could sit down and talk. But there were only two office stools empty beside Eleanor over there in the corner.

She saw them and called out, 'Oh, there's Edward! I know there was something I wanted to ask. . . ' she began.

It was a relief that the interview with the headmaster should be broken up by this impulsive, foolish old woman. She was holding out her pocket-handkerchief.

'I made a knot,' she was saying. Yes, there it was, a knot in her pocket-handkerchief. 'Now what did I make a knot for?' she said, looking up.

'It is an admirable habit to make a knot,' said Edward in his courteous, clipped way, lowering himself a little stiffly on to the chair beside her. 'But at the same time it is advisable . . . ' He stopped. That's what I like about him, North thought, taking the other chair: he left half his sentence unfinished.

'It was to remind me – ' said Eleanor putting her hand to her thick crop of white hair. Then she stopped. What is it that makes him look so calm, so carved, North thought, stealing a look at Edward, who waited with admirable serenity for his sister to remember why she had made a knot in her handkerchief. There was something final about him; he left half his sentences unfinished. He hadn't worried himself about politics and money, he thought. There was something sealed up, stated, about him. Poetry and the past, was it? But as he fixed his eyes upon him, Edward smiled at his sister.

'Well, Nell?' he said.

It was a quiet smile, a tolerant smile.

North broke in, for Eleanor was still ruminating over her knot. 'I met a man at the Cape who was a tremendous admirer of yours, Uncle Edward,' he said. The name came back to him – 'Arbuthnot,' he said.

'R. K.?' said Edward. And he raised his hand to his head and smiled. It pleased him, that compliment. He was vain; he was touchy; he was – North stole a glance to add another impression – established. Glazed over with the smooth glossy varnish that those in authority wear. For he was now – what? North could not remember. A professor? A master? Somebody who had an attitude fixed on him, from which he could not relax any longer. Still, Arbuthnot, R. K., had said, with emotion, that he owed more to Edward than to any man.

'He said he owed more to you than to any man,' he said aloud.

Edward brushed aside the compliment; but it pleased him. He had a way of putting his hand to his head that North remembered. And Eleanor called him 'Nigs'. She laughed at him; she preferred failures, like Morris. There she sat holding her pocket-handkerchief in her hand, smiling ironically, covertly, at some memory.

'And what are your plans?' said Edward. 'You deserve a holiday.'

There was something flattering in his manner, North thought, like a schoolmaster welcoming back to school an old boy who had won distinction. But he meant it; he doesn't say what he doesn't mean, North thought, and that was alarming too. They were silent.

'Delia's got a wonderful lot of people here tonight, hasn't she?' said Edward, turning to Eleanor. They sat looking at the different groups. His clear blue eyes surveyed the scene amiably but sardonically. But what's he thinking, North asked himself. He's got something behind that mask, he thought. Something that's kept him clear of this muddle. The past? Poetry? he thought, looking at Edward's distinct profile. It was finer than he remembered.

'I'd like to brush up my classics,' he said suddenly. 'Not that I ever had much to brush,' he added, foolishly, afraid of the schoolmaster.

Edward did not seem to be listening. He was raising his eyeglass and letting it fall as he looked at the queer jumble. There his head rested, with the chin thrown up, on the back of his chair. The crowd, the noise, the clatter of knives and forks, made it unnecessary to talk. North stole another glance at him. The past and poetry, he said to himself, that's what I want to talk about, he thought. He wanted to say it aloud. But Edward was too formed and idiosyncratic; too black and white and linear, with his head tilted up on the back of his chair, to ask him questions easily.

Now he was talking about Africa, and North wanted to talk about the past and poetry. There it was, he thought, locked up in that fine head, the head that was like a Greek boy's head grown white; the past and poetry. Then why not prise it open? Why not share it? What's wrong with him, he thought, as he answered the usual intelligent Englishman's questions about Africa and the state of the country. Why can't he flow? Why can't he pull the string of the shower bath? Why's it all locked up, refrigerated? Because he's a priest, a mystery monger, he thought; feeling his coldness; this guardian of beautiful words.

But Edward was speaking to him.

'We must arrange a date,' he was saying, 'next autumn.' He meant it too.

'Yes,' North said aloud, 'I'd love to . . . In the autumn . . . ' And he saw before him a house with creeper-shaded rooms, butlers creeping, decanters, and someone handing a box of good cigars.

Unknown young men coming round with trays pressed different eatables upon them.

'How very kind of you!' said Eleanor, taking a glass. He himself took a glass of some yellow liquid. It was some kind of claret cup, he supposed. The little bubbles kept rising to the top and exploding. He watched them rise and explode.

'Who's that pretty girl,' said Edward, inclining his head, 'over there, standing in the corner, talking to the youth?'

He was benignant and urbane.

'Aren't they lovely?' said Eleanor. 'Just what I was thinking . . . Everyone looks so young. That's Maggie's daughter . . . But who's that talking to Kitty?'

'That's Middleton,' said Edward. 'What, don't you remember him? You must have met him in the old days.'

They chatted, basking there at their ease. Spinners and sitters in the sun,[65] North thought, taking their ease when the day's work is over; Eleanor and Edward each in their own niche, with their hands on the fruit, tolerant, assured.

He watched the bubbles rising in the yellow liquid. For them it's all right, he thought; they've had their day; but not for him, not for his generation. For him a life modelled on the jet (he was watching the bubbles rise), on the spring, of the hard-leaping fountain; another life; a different life. Not halls and reverberating megaphones; not marching in step after leaders, in herds, groups, societies, caparisoned. No; to begin inwardly, and let the devil take the outer form, he thought, looking up at a young man with a fine forehead and a weak chin. Not black shirts, green shirts, red shirts – always posing in the public eye; that's all poppycock. Why not down barriers and simplify? But a world, he thought, that was all one jelly, one mass, would be a rice-pudding world, a white-counterpane world. To keep the emblems and tokens of North Pargiter – the man Maggie laughs at; the Frenchman holding his hat; but at the same time spread out, make a new ripple in human consciousness, be the bubble and the stream, the stream and the bubble – myself and the world together – he raised his glass. Anonymously, he said, looking at the clear yellow liquid. But what do I mean, he wondered – I, to whom ceremonies are suspect, and religion's dead; who don't fit, as the man said, don't fit in anywhere? He paused. There was the glass in his hand; in his mind a sentence. And he wanted to make other sentences. But how can I, he thought – he looked at Eleanor, who sat with a silk handkerchief in her hands – unless I know what's solid, what's true; in my life, in other people's lives?

'Runcorn's boy,' Eleanor suddenly ejaculated. 'The son of the porter at my flat,' she explained. She had untied the knot in her handkerchief.

'The son of the porter at your flat,' Edward repeated. His eyes were like a field on which the sun rests in winter, North thought, looking up – the winter's sun, that has no heat left in it but some pale beauty.

'Commissionaire they call him, I think,' she said.

'How I hate that word!' said Edward with a little shudder. 'Porter's good English, isn't it?'

'That's what I say,' said Eleanor. 'The son of the *porter* at my flat . . . Well, he wants, they want him to go to college. So I said if I saw you, I'd ask you – '

'Of course, of course,' said Edward kindly.

And that's all right, North said to himself. That's the human voice at its natural speaking level. Of course, of course, he repeated.

'He wants to go to college, does he?' Edward went on. 'What examinations has he passed, eh?'

What examinations has he passed, eh? North repeated. He repeated that too, but critically, as if he were actor and critic; he listened but he commented. He surveyed the thin yellow liquid in which the bubbles rose more slowly, one by one. Eleanor did not know what examinations he had passed. And what was I thinking? North asked himself. He felt that he had been in the middle of a jungle; in the heart of darkness; cutting his way towards the light; but provided only with broken sentences, single words, with which to break through the briar bush of human bodies, human wills and voices, that bent over him, binding him, blinding him . . . He listened.

'Well then, tell him to come and see me,' said Edward, briskly.

'But that's asking too much of you, Edward?' Eleanor protested.

'That's what I'm for,' said Edward.

That's the right tone of voice too, North thought. Not carapaced – the words 'caparison' and 'carapace' collided in his mind, and made a new word that was no word. What I mean is, he added, taking a drink of his claret cup, underneath there's the fountain; the sweet nut. The fruit, the fountain that's in all of us; in Edward; in Eleanor; so why caparison ourselves on top? He looked up.

A big man had stopped in front of them. He bent over and very politely gave Eleanor his hand. He had to bend, for his white waistcoat enclosed so magnificent a sphere. 'Alas,' he was saying in a voice that was oddly mellifluous for one of his bulk, 'I'd love nothing more; but I have a meeting at ten tomorrow morning.' They were inviting him to sit down and talk. He was tittupping up and down on his little feet in front of them.

'Throw it over!' said Eleanor, smiling up at him, just as she used to

smile when she was a girl with her brother's friends, thought North.
Then why hadn't she married one of them, he wondered. Why do we
hide all the things that matter? he asked himself.

'And leave my directors cooling their heels? As much as my place is
worth!' the old friend was saying, and swung round on his heel with the
agility of a trained elephant.

'Seems a long time since he acted in the Greek play, doesn't it?' said
Edward. ' . . . in a toga,' he added with a grin, following the well-
rounded person of the great railway magnate as he went with a certain
celerity, for he was a perfect man of the world, through the crowd to
the door.

'That's Chipperfield, the great railway man,' he explained to North. 'A
very remarkable fellow,' he went on. 'Son of a railway porter.' He made
little pauses between each sentence. 'Done it all off his own bat . . . A
delightful house . . . Perfectly restored . . . Two or three hundred acres, I
suppose . . . Has his shooting . . . Asks me to direct his reading . . . And
buys old masters.'

'And buys old masters,' North repeated. The deft little sentences
seemed to build up a pagoda; sparely but accurately; and through it all
ran some queer breath of mockery tinged with affection.

'Shams, I should think,' Eleanor laughed.

'Well, we needn't go into that,' Edward chuckled. Then they were
silent. The pagoda floated off. Chipperfield had vanished through the
door.

'How nice this drink is,' Eleanor said above his head. North could see
her glass held at the level of his head on her knee. A thin green leaf
floated on top of it. 'I hope it's not intoxicating?' she said, raising it.

North took up his glass again. What was I thinking last time I looked
at it? he asked himself. A block had formed in his forehead as if two
thoughts had collided and had stopped the passage of the rest. His mind
was a blank. He swayed the liquid from side to side. He was in the
middle of a dark forest.

'So, North . . . ' His own name roused him with a start. It was Edward
speaking. He jerked forward. ' . . . you want to brush up your classics, do
you?' Edward went on. 'I'm glad to hear you say that. There's a lot in
those old fellows. But the younger generation,' he paused, ' . . . don't
seem to want 'em.'

'How foolish!' said Eleanor. 'I was reading one of them the other
day . . . the one you translated. Now which was it?' She paused. She
never could remember names. 'The one about the girl who . . . '

'The *Antigone*?' Edward suggested.

'Yes! The *Antigone*!' she exclaimed. 'And I thought to myself, just what you say, Edward – how true – how beautiful . . . '

She broke off, as if afraid to continue.

Edward nodded. He paused. Then suddenly he jerked his head back and said some words in Greek: 'οὗτοι συνέχθειν, ἀλλὰ συμφιλεῖν ἔφυν.'.[66]

North looked up.

'Translate it,' he said.

Edward shook his head. 'It's the language,' he said.

Then he shut up. It's no go, North thought. He can't say what he wants to say; he's afraid. They're all afraid; afraid of being laughed at; afraid of giving themselves away. He's afraid too, he thought, looking at the young man with a fine forehead and a weak chin who was gesticulating too emphatically. We're all afraid of each other, he thought; afraid of what? Of criticism; of laughter; of people who think differently . . . He's afraid of me because I'm a farmer (and he saw again his round face: high cheekbones and small brown eyes). And I'm afraid of him because he's clever. He looked at the big forehead, from which the hair was already receding. That's what separates us; fear, he thought.

He shifted his position. He wanted to get up and talk to him. Delia had said, 'Don't wait to be introduced.' But it was difficult to speak to a man whom he did not know, and say: 'What's this knot in the middle of my forehead? Untie it.' For he had had enough of thinking alone. Thinking alone tied knots in the middle of the forehead; thinking alone bred pictures, foolish pictures. The man was moving off. He must make the effort. Yet he hesitated. He felt repelled and attracted, attracted and repelled. He began to rise; but before he had got on his feet somebody thumped on a table with a fork.

A large man sitting at a table in the corner was thumping on the table with his fork. He was leaning forward as if he wanted to attract attention, as if he were about to make a speech. It was the man Peggy called Brown; the others called Nicholas; whose real name he did not know. Perhaps he was a little drunk.

'Ladies and gentlemen!' he said. 'Ladies and gentlemen!' he repeated rather more loudly.

'What, a speech?' said Edward quizzically. He half turned his chair; he raised his eyeglass, which hung on a black silk ribbon as if it were a foreign order.

People were buzzing about with plates and glasses. They were stumbling over cushions on the floor. A girl pitched head foremost.

'Hurt yourself?' said a young man, stretching out his hand.

No, she had not hurt herself. But the interruption had distracted attention from the speech. A buzz of talk had risen like the buzz of flies over sugar. Nicholas sat down again. He was lost apparently in contemplation of the red stone in his ring; or of the strewn flowers: the white, waxy flowers, the pale, semi-transparent flowers, the crimson flowers that were so full-blown that the gold heart showed and the petals had fallen and lay among the hired knives and forks, the cheap tumblers on the table. Then he roused himself.

'Ladies and gentlemen!' he began. Again he thumped the table with his fork. There was a momentary lull. Rose marched across the room.

'Going to make a speech, are you?' she demanded. 'Go on, I like hearing speeches.' She stood beside him, with her hand hollowed round her ear like a military man. Again the buzz of talk had broken out.

'Silence!' she exclaimed. She took a knife and rapped on the table. 'Silence! Silence!' She rapped again.

Martin crossed the room.

'What's Rose making such a noise about?' he asked.

'I'm asking for silence!' she said, flourishing her knife in his face. 'This gentleman wants to make a speech!'

But he had sat down and was regarding his ring with equanimity.

'Isn't she the very spit and image,' said Martin, laying his hand on Rose's shoulder and turning to Eleanor as if to confirm his words, 'of old Uncle Pargiter of Pargiter's Horse?'

'Well, I'm proud of it!' said Rose, brandishing her knife in his face. 'I'm proud of my family; proud of my country; proud of . . . '

'Your sex?' he interrupted her.

'I am,' she asseverated. 'And what about you?' she went on, tapping him on the shoulder. 'Proud of yourself, are you?'

'Don't quarrel, children, don't quarrel!' cried Eleanor, giving her chair a little edge nearer. 'They always would quarrel,' she said, 'always . . . always . . . '

'She was a horrid little spitfire,' said Martin, squatting down on the floor, and looking up at Rose, 'with her hair scraped off her forehead . . . '

' . . . wearing a pink frock,' Rose added. She sat down abruptly, holding her knife erect in her hand. 'A pink frock; a pink frock . . . ' she repeated, as if the words recalled something.

'But go on with your speech, Nicholas,' said Eleanor, turning to him. He shook his head.

'Let us talk about pink frocks,' he smiled.

' . . . in the drawing-room at Abercorn Terrace, when we were children,' said Rose. 'D'you remember?' She looked at Martin. He nodded his head.

'In the drawing-room at Abercorn Terrace . . . ' said Delia. She was going from table to table with a great jug of claret cup. She stopped in front of them. 'Abercorn Terrace!' she exclaimed, filling a glass. She flung her head back and looked for a moment astonishingly young, handsome, and defiant.

'It was hell!' she exclaimed. 'It was hell!' she repeated.

'Oh come, Delia . . . ' Martin protested, holding out his glass to be filled.

'It was hell,' she said, dropping her Irish manner, and speaking quite simply, as she poured out the drink.

'D'you know,' she said, looking at Eleanor, 'when I go to Paddington, I always say to the man, "Drive the other way round!" '

'That's enough . . . ' Martin stopped her; his glass was full. 'I hated it too . . . ' he began.

But here Kitty Lasswade advanced upon them. She held her glass in front of her as though it were a bauble.

'What's Martin hating now?' she said, facing him.

A polite gentleman pushed forward a little gilt chair upon which she sat down.

'He always was a hater,' she said, holding her glass out to be filled. 'What was it you hated that night, Martin, when you dined with us?' she asked him. 'I remember how angry you made me . . . '

She smiled at him. He had grown cherubic: pink and plump; with his hair brushed back like a waiter's.

'Hated? I never hated anybody,' he protested. 'My heart's full of love; my heart's full of kindness,' he laughed, waving his glass at her.

'Nonsense,' said Kitty. 'When you were young you hated . . . everything!' she flung her hand out. 'My house . . . my friends . . . ' She broke off with a quick little sigh. She saw them again – the men filing in; the women pinching some dress between their thumbs and fingers. She lived alone now, in the north. ' . . . and I dare say I'm better off as I am,' she added, half to herself, 'with just a boy to chop up wood.'

There was a pause.

'Now let him get on with his speech,' said Eleanor.

'Yes. Get on with your speech!' said Rose. Again she rapped her knife on the table; again he half rose.

'Going to make a speech, is he?' said Kitty, turning to Edward who had drawn his chair up beside her.

'The only place where oratory is now practised as an art . . . ' Edward began. Then he paused, drew his chair a little closer, and adjusted his glasses, ' . . . is the church,' he added.

That's why I didn't marry you, Kitty said to herself. How the voice, the supercilious voice, brought it back! The tree half fallen; rain falling; undergraduates calling; bells tolling; she and her mother . . .

But Nicholas had risen. He took a deep breath which expanded his shirt front. With one hand he fumbled with his fob; the other he flung out with an oratorical gesture.

'Ladies and gentlemen!' he began again. 'In the name of all who have enjoyed themselves tonight . . . '

'Speak up! Speak up!' the young men cried who were standing in the window.

('Is he a foreigner?' Kitty whispered to Eleanor.)

' . . . in the name of all who have enjoyed themselves tonight,' he repeated more loudly, 'I wish to thank our host and hostess . . . '

'Oh, don't thank me!' said Delia brushing past them with her empty jug.

Again the speech was brought to the ground. He must be a foreigner, Kitty thought to herself, because he has no self-consciousness. There he stood holding his wine-glass and smiling.

'Go on, go on,' she urged him. 'Don't mind them.' She was in the mood for a speech. A speech was a good thing at parties. It gave them a fillip. It gave them a finish. She rapped her glass on the table.

'It's very nice of you,' said Delia, trying to push past him, but he had laid his hand on her arm, 'but don't thank me.'

'But Delia,' he expostulated, still holding her, 'it's not what *you* want; it's what *we* want. And it is fitting,' he continued, waving his hand out, 'when our hearts are full of gratitude. . . '

Now he's getting into his stride, Kitty thought. I dare say he's a bit of an orator. Most foreigners are.

' . . . when our hearts are full of gratitude,' he repeated, touching one finger.

'What for?' said a voice abruptly.

Nicholas stopped again.

('Who is that dark man?' Kitty whispered to Eleanor. 'I've been wondering all the evening.'

'Renny,' Eleanor whispered. 'Renny,' she repeated.)

'What for?' said Nicholas. 'That is what I am about to tell you . . . ' He paused, and drew a deep breath which again expanded his waistcoat. His eyes beamed; he seemed full of spontaneous subterraneous benevolence.

But here a head popped up over the edge of the table; a hand swept up a fistful of flower petals; and a voice cried: 'Red Rose, thorny Rose, brave Rose, tawny Rose!' The petals were thrown, fan-shape, over the stout old woman who was sitting on the edge of her chair. She looked up in surprise. Petals had fallen on her. She brushed them where they had lodged upon the prominences of her person. 'Thank you! Thank you!' she exclaimed. Then she took up a flower and beat it energetically upon the edge of the table. 'But I want my speech!' she said, looking at Nicholas.

'No, no,' he said. 'This is not a time for making speeches,' and sat down again.

'Let's drink then,' said Martin. He raised his glass. 'Pargiter of Pargiter's Horse!' he said. 'I drink to her!' He put his glass down with a thump on the table.

'Oh, if you're all drinking healths,' said Kitty, 'I'll drink too. Rose, your health. Rose is a fine fellow,' she said, raising her glass. 'But Rose was wrong,' she added. 'Force is always wrong – don't you agree with me, Edward?' She tapped him on the knee. I'd forgotten the war, she muttered half to herself. 'Still,' she said aloud, 'Rose had the courage of her convictions. Rose went to prison. And I drink to her!' She drank.

'The same to you, Kitty,' said Rose, bowing to her.

'She smashed his window,' Martin jeered at her, 'and then she helped him to smash other people's windows. Where's your decoration, Rose?'

'In a cardboard box on the mantelpiece,' said Rose. 'You can't get a rise out of me at this time of day, my good fellow.'

'But I wish you had let Nicholas finish his speech,' said Eleanor.

Down through the ceiling, muted and far away, came the preliminary notes of another dance. The young people, hastily swallowing what remained in their glasses, rose and began to move off upstairs. Soon there was the sound of feet thudding, rhythmically, heavily on the floor above.

'Another dance?' said Eleanor. It was a waltz. 'When we were young,' she said, looking at Kitty, 'we used to dance . . . ' The tune seemed to take her words and to repeat them – when I was young I used to dance – I used to dance . . .

'And how I hated it!' said Kitty, looking at her fingers, which were short and pricked. 'How nice it is,' she said, 'not to be young! How nice not to mind what people think! Now one can live as one likes,' she added, ' . . . now that one's seventy.'

She paused. She raised her eyebrows as if she remembered something. 'Pity one can't live again,' she said. But she broke off.

'Aren't we going to have our speech after all, Mr – ?' she said, looking at Nicholas, whose name she did not know. He sat gazing benevolently in front of him, paddling his hands among the flower petals.

'What's the good?' he said. 'Nobody wants to listen.' They listened to the feet thudding upstairs, and to the music repeating, it seemed to Eleanor, when I was young I used to dance, all men loved me when I was young . . .

'But I want a speech!' said Kitty in her authoritative manner. It was true; she wanted something – something that gave a fillip, a finish – what she scarcely knew. But not the past – not memories. The present, the future: that was what she wanted.

'There's Peggy!' said Eleanor, looking round. She was sitting on the edge of a table, eating a ham sandwich.

'Come, Peggy!' she called out. 'Come and talk to us!'

'Speak for the younger generation, Peggy!' said Lady Lasswade, shaking hands.

'But I'm not the younger generation,' said Peggy. 'And I've made my speech already,' she said. 'I made a fool of myself upstairs,' she said, sinking down on the floor at Eleanor's feet.

'Then, North . . . ' said Eleanor, looking down on the parting of North's hair as he sat on the floor beside her.

'Yes, North,' said Peggy, looking at him across her aunt's knee. 'North says we talk of nothing but money and politics,' she added. 'Tell us what we ought to do.' He started. He had been dozing off, dazed by the music and voices. What we ought to do? he said to himself, waking up. What ought we to do?

He jerked up into a sitting posture. He saw Peggy's face looking at him. Now she was smiling; her face was gay; it reminded him of his grandmother's face in the picture. But he saw it as he had seen it upstairs – scarlet, puckered – as if she were about to burst into tears. It was her face that was true; not her words. But only her words returned to him – to live differently – differently. He paused. This is what needs courage, he said to himself: to speak the truth. She was listening. The old people were already gossiping about their own affairs.

' . . . It's a nice little house,' Kitty was saying. 'An old mad woman used to live there . . . You'll have to come and stay with me, Nell. In the spring . . . '

Peggy was watching him over the rim of her ham sandwich.

'What you said was true,' he blurted out, ' . . . quite true.' It was what she meant that was true, he corrected himself; her feeling, not her words. He felt her feeling now; it was not about him; it was about other people; about another world, a new world . . .

The old aunts and uncles were gossiping above him.

'What was the name of the man I used to like so much at Oxford?' Lady Lasswade was saying. He could see her silver body bending towards Edward.

'The man you liked at Oxford?' Edward was repeating. 'I thought you never liked anyone at Oxford . . . ' And they laughed.

But Peggy was waiting, she was watching him. He saw again the glass with the bubbles rising; he felt again the constriction of a knot in his forehead. He wished there were someone, infinitely wise and good, to think for him, to answer for him. But the young man with the receding forehead had vanished.

' . . . To live differently . . . differently,' he repeated. Those were her words; they did not altogether fit his meaning; but he had to use them. Now I've made a fool of myself too, he thought, as a ripple of some disagreeable sensation went across his back as if a knife had sliced it, and he leant against the wall.

'Yes, it was Robson!' Lady Lasswade exclaimed. Her trumpet voice rang out over his head.

'How one forgets things!' she went on. 'Of course – Robson. That was his name. And the girl I used to like – Nelly? The girl who was going to be a doctor?'

'Died, I think,' said Edward.

'Died, did she – died – ' said Lady Lasswade. She paused for a moment. 'Well, I wish you'd make your speech,' she said, turning and looking down at North.

He drew himself back. No more speech-making for me, he thought. He had his glass in his hand still. It was still half full of pale yellow liquid. The bubbles had ceased to rise. The wine was clear and still. Stillness and solitude, he thought to himself; silence and solitude . . . that's the only element in which the mind is free now.

Silence and solitude, he repeated; silence and solitude. His eyes half closed themselves. He was tired; he was dazed; people talked; people talked. He would detach himself, generalise himself, imagine that he was lying in a great space on a blue plain with hills on the rim of the horizon. He stretched out his feet. There were the sheep cropping; slowly tearing the grass; advancing first one stiff leg and then another. And babbling – babbling. He made no sense of what they were saying. Through his half-open eyes he saw hands holding flowers – thin hands, fine hands; but hands that belonged to no one. And were they flowers the hands held? Or mountains? Blue mountains with violet shadows? Then petals fell. Pink, yellow, white with violet shadows, the petals fell. They fall and fall and cover all, he murmured. And there was the stem of a wine-glass; the rim of a plate; and a bowl of water. The hands went on picking up flower after flower; that was a white rose; that was a yellow rose; that was a rose with violet valleys in its petals. There they hung, many folded, many coloured, drooping over the rim of the bowl. And petals fell. There they lay, violet and yellow, little shallops, boats on a river. And he was floating, and drifting, in a shallop, in a petal, down a river into silence, into solitude . . . which is the worst torture, the words came back to him as if a voice had spoken them, that human beings can inflict . . .

'Wake up, North . . . we want your speech!' a voice interrupted him. Kitty's red handsome face was hanging over him.

'Maggie!' he exclaimed, pulling himself up. It was she who was sitting there, putting flowers into water.

'Yes, it's Maggie's turn to speak,' said Nicholas, putting his hand on her knee.

'Speak, speak!' Renny urged her.

But she shook her head. Laughter took her and shook her. She laughed, throwing her head back as if she were possessed by some genial spirit outside herself that made her bend and rise, as a tree, North thought, is tossed and bent by the wind. No idols, no idols, no idols, her laughter seemed to chime as if the tree were hung with innumerable bells, and he laughed too.

Their laughter ceased. Feet thudded, dancing on the floor above. A siren hooted on the river. A van crashed down the street in the distance. There was a rush and quiver of sound; something seemed to be released; it was as if the life of the day were about to begin, and this were the chorus, the cry, the chirp, the stir, which salutes the London dawn.

Kitty turned to Nicholas.

'And what was your speech going to have been about, Mr . . . I'm afraid I don't know your name?' she said. ' . . . the one that was interrupted?'

'My speech?' he laughed. 'It was to have been a miracle!' he said. 'A masterpiece! But how can one speak when one is always interrupted? I begin: I say, Let us give thanks. Then Delia says, Don't thank me. I begin again: I say, Let us give thanks to someone, to somebody . . . And Renny says, What for? I begin again, and look – Eleanor is sound asleep.' (He pointed at her.) 'So what's the good?'

'Oh, but there is some good – ' Kitty began.

She still wanted something – some finish, some fillip – what she did not know. And it was getting late. She must go.

'Tell me, privately, what you were going to have said, Mr – ?' she asked him.

'What I was going to have said? I was going to have said – ' he paused and stretched his hand out; he touched each finger separately.

'First I was going to have thanked our host and hostess. Then I was going to have thanked this house – ' he waved his hand round the room hung with the placards of the house agent, 'which has sheltered the lovers, the creators, the men and women of goodwill. And finally – ' he took his glass in his hand, 'I was going to drink to the human race. The human race,' he continued, raising his glass to his lips, 'which is now in its infancy, may it grow to maturity! Ladies and gentlemen!' he exclaimed, half rising and expanding his waistcoat, 'I drink to that!'

He brought his glass down with a thump on the table. It broke.

'That's the thirteenth glass broken tonight!' said Delia, coming up and stopping in front of them. 'But don't mind – don't mind. They're very cheap – glasses.'

'What's very cheap?' Eleanor murmured. She half opened her eyes. But where was she? In what room? In which of the innumerable rooms? Always there were rooms; always there were people. Always from the beginning of time . . . She shut her hands on the coins she was holding, and again she was suffused with a feeling of happiness. Was it because this had survived – this keen sensation (she was waking up) – and the other thing, the solid object – she saw an ink-corroded walrus – had vanished? She opened her eyes wide. Here she was; alive; in this room, with living people. She saw all the heads in a circle. At first they were without identity. Then she recognised them. That was Rose; that was Martin; that was Morris. He had hardly any hair on the top of his head. There was a curious pallor on his face.

There was a curious pallor on all their faces as she looked round. The brightness had gone out of the electric lights; the tablecloths looked whiter. North's head – he was sitting on the floor at her feet – was rimmed with whiteness. His shirt-front was a little crumpled.

He was sitting on the floor at Edward's feet with his hands bound round his knees, and he gave little jerks and looked up at him as if he appealed to him about something.

'Uncle Edward,' she heard him say, 'tell me this . . . '

He was like a child asking to be told a story.

'Tell me this,' he repeated, giving another little jerk. 'You're a scholar. About the classics now. Aeschylus. Sophocles. Pindar.'[67]

Edward bent towards him.

'And the chorus,' North jerked on again. She leant towards them. 'The chorus – ' North repeated.

'My dear boy,' she heard Edward say as he smiled benignly down at him, 'don't ask me. I was never a great hand at that. No, if I'd had my way' – he paused and passed his hand over his forehead – 'I should have been . . . ' A burst of laughter drowned his words. She could not catch the end of the sentence. What had he said – what had he wished to be? She had lost his words.

There must be another life, she thought, sinking back into her chair, exasperated. Not in dreams; but here and now, in this room, with living people. She felt as if she were standing on the edge of a precipice with her hair blown back; she was about to grasp something that just evaded her. There must be another life, here and now, she repeated. This is too short, too broken. We know nothing, even about ourselves. We're only just beginning, she thought, to understand, here and there. She hollowed her hands in her lap, just as Rose had hollowed hers round her ears. She held her hands hollowed; she felt that she wanted to enclose the present moment; to make it stay; to fill it fuller and fuller, with the past, the present and the future, until it shone, whole, bright, deep with understanding.

'Edward,' she began, trying to attract his attention. But he was not listening to her; he was telling North some old college story. It's useless, she thought, opening her hands. It must drop. It must fall. And then? she thought. For her too there would be the endless night; the endless dark. She looked ahead of her as though she saw opening in front of her a very long dark tunnel. But, thinking of the dark, something baffled her; in fact it was growing light. The blinds were white.

There was a stir in the room.

Edward turned to her.

'Who are *they*?' he asked her, pointing to the door.

She looked. Two children stood in the door. Delia had her hands on their shoulders as if to encourage them. She was leading them over to the table in order to give them something to eat. They looked awkward and clumsy.

Eleanor glanced at their hands, at their clothes, at the shape of their ears. 'The children of the caretaker, I should think,' she said. Yes, Delia was cutting slices of cake for them, and they were larger slices of cake

than she would have cut had they been the children of her own friends.
The children took the slices and stared at them with a curious fixed
stare as if they were fierce. But perhaps they were frightened, because
she had brought them up from the basement into the drawing-room.

'Eat it!' said Delia, giving them a little pat.

They began to munch slowly, gazing solemnly round them.

'Hello, children!' cried Martin, beckoning to them. They stared at
him solemnly.

'Haven't you got a name?' he said. They went on eating in silence.
He began to fumble in his pocket.

'Speak!' he said. 'Speak!'

'The younger generation,' said Peggy, 'don't mean to speak.'

They turned their eyes on her now; but they went on munching.

'No school tomorrow?' she said. They shook their heads from side to
side.

'Hurrah!' said Martin. He held the coins in his hand; pressed between
his thumb and finger. 'Now – sing a song for sixpence!'.[68] he said.

'Yes. Weren't you taught something at school?' Peggy asked.

They stared at her but remained silent. They had stopped eating.
They were a centre of a little group. They swept their eyes over the
grown-up people for a moment, then, each giving the other a little
nudge, they burst into song:

> Etho passo tanno hai,
> Fai donk to tu do,
> Mai to, kai to, lai to see
> Toh dom to tuh do –

That was what it sounded like. Not a word was recognisable. The
distorted sounds rose and sank as if they followed a tune. They stopped.

They stood with their hands behind their backs. Then with one
impulse they attacked the next verse:

> Fanno to par, etto to mar,
> Timin tudo, tido,
> Foll to gar in, mitno to par,
> Eido, teido, meido –

They sang the second verse more fiercely than the first. The rhythm
seemed to rock and the unintelligible words ran themselves together
almost into a shriek. The grown-up people did not know whether to
laugh or to cry. Their voices were so harsh; the accent was so hideous.

They burst out again:

Chree to gay ei,
Geeray didax . . . .[69]

Then they stopped. It seemed to be in the middle of a verse. They stood there grinning, silent, looking at the floor. Nobody knew what to say. There was something horrible in the noise they made. It was so shrill, so discordant and so meaningless. Then old Patrick ambled up.

'Ah, that's very nice, that's very nice. Thank you, my dears,' he said in his genial way, fiddling with his toothpick. The children grinned at him. Then they began to make off. As they sidled past Martin, he slipped coins into their hands. Then they made a dash for the door.

'But what the devil were they singing?' said Hugh Gibbs. 'I couldn't understand a word of it, I must confess.' He held his hands to the sides of his large white waistcoat.

'Cockney accent, I suppose,' said Patrick. 'What they teach 'em at school, you know.'

'But it was . . . ' Eleanor began. She stopped. What was it? As they stood there they had looked so dignified; yet they had made this hideous noise. The contrast between their faces and their voices was astonishing; it was impossible to find one word for the whole. 'Beautiful?' she said, with a note of interrogation, turning to Maggie.

'Extraordinarily,' said Maggie.

But Eleanor was not sure that they were thinking of the same thing.

She gathered together her gloves, her bag and two or three coppers, and got up. The room was full of a queer pale light. Objects seemed to be rising out of their sleep, out of their disguise, and to be assuming the sobriety of daily life. The room was making ready for its use as an estate agent's office. The tables were becoming office tables; their legs were the legs of office tables, and yet they were still strewn with plates and glasses, with roses, lilies and carnations.

'It's time to go,' she said, crossing the room. Delia had gone to the window. Now she jerked the curtains open.

'The dawn!' she exclaimed rather melodramatically.

The shapes of houses appeared across the square. Their blinds were all drawn; they seemed fast asleep still in the morning pallor.

'The dawn!' said Nicholas, getting up and stretching himself. He too walked across to the window.

Renny followed him. 'Now for the peroration,' he said, standing with him in the window. 'The dawn – the new day – '

He pointed at the trees, at the roofs, at the sky.

'No,' said Nicholas, holding back the curtain. 'There you are mistaken. There is going to be no peroration – no peroration!' he exclaimed, throwing his arm out, 'because there was no speech.'

'But the dawn has risen,' said Renny, pointing at the sky.

It was a fact. The sun had risen. The sky between the chimneys looked extraordinarily blue.

'And I am going to bed,' said Nicholas after a pause. He turned away.

'Where is Sara?' he said, looking round him. There she was curled up in a corner with her head against a table asleep apparently.

'Wake your sister, Magdalena,' he said, turning to Maggie. Maggie looked at her. Then she took a flower from the table and tossed it at her. She half-opened her eyes. 'It's time,' said Maggie, touching her on the shoulder.

'Time, is it?' she sighed. She yawned and stretched herself. She fixed her eyes on Nicholas as if she were bringing him back to the field of vision. Then she laughed.

'Nicholas!' she exclaimed.

'Sara!' he replied. They smiled at each other. Then he helped her up and she balanced herself uncertainly against her sister, and rubbed her eyes.

'How strange,' she murmured, looking round her, ' . . . how strange . . . '

There were the smeared plates, and the empty wine-glasses; the petals and the breadcrumbs. In the mixture of lights they looked prosaic but unreal; cadaverous but brilliant. And there against the window, gathered in a group, were the old brothers and sisters.

'Look, Maggie,' she whispered, turning to her sister, 'Look!' She pointed at the Pargiters, standing in the window.

The group in the window, the men in their black-and-white evening dress, the women in their crimsons, golds and silvers, wore a statuesque air for a moment, as if they were carved in stone. Their dresses fell in stiff sculptured folds. Then they moved; they changed their attitudes; they began to talk.

'Can't I give you a lift back, Nell?' Kitty Lasswade was saying. 'I've a car waiting.'

Eleanor did not answer. She was looking at the curtained houses across the square. The windows were spotted with gold. Everything looked clean swept, fresh and virginal. The pigeons were shuffling on the tree-tops.

'I've a car . . . ' Kitty repeated.

'Listen . . . ' said Eleanor, raising her hand. Upstairs they were playing 'God Save the King' on the gramophone; but it was the pigeons she meant; they were crooning.

'That's wood pigeons, isn't it?' said Kitty. She put her head on one side to listen. Take two coos, Taffy, take two coos . . . tak . . . they were crooning.

'Wood pigeons?' said Edward, putting his hand to his ear.

'There on the tree-tops,' said Kitty. The green-blue birds were shuffling about on the branches, pecking and crooning to themselves.

Morris brushed the crumbs off his waistcoat.

'What an hour for us old fogies to be out of bed!' he said. 'I haven't seen the sun rise since . . . since . . . '

'Ah, but when we were young,' said old Patrick, slapping him on the shoulder, 'we thought nothing of making a night of it! I remember going to Covent Garden and buying roses for a certain lady. . . '

Delia smiled as if some romance, her own or another's, had been recalled to her.

'And I . . . ' Eleanor began. She stopped. She saw an empty milk jug and leaves falling. Then it had been autumn. Now it was summer. The sky was a faint blue; the roofs were tinged purple against the blue; the chimneys were a pure brick red. An air of ethereal calm and simplicity lay over everything.

'And all the tubes have stopped, and all the omnibuses,' she said turning round. 'How are we going to get home?'

'We can walk,' said Rose. 'Walking won't do us any harm.'

'Not on a fine summer morning,' said Martin.

A breeze went through the square. In the stillness they could hear the branches rustle as they rose slightly, and fell, and shook a wave of green light through the air.

Then the door burst open. Couple after couple came flocking in, dishevelled, gay, to look for their cloaks and their hats, to say good-night.

'It's been so good of you to come!' Delia exclaimed, turning towards them with her hands outstretched.

'Thank you – thank you for coming!' she cried.

'And look at Maggie's bunch!' she said, taking a bunch of many coloured flowers that Maggie held out to her.

'How beautifully you've arranged them!' she said. 'Look, Eleanor!' She turned to her sister.

But Eleanor was standing with her back to them. She was watching a taxi that was gliding slowly round the square. It stopped in front of a house two doors down.

'Aren't they lovely?' said Delia, holding out the flowers.

Eleanor started.

'The roses? Yes . . . ' she said. But she was watching the cab. A young man had got out; he paid the driver. Then a girl in a tweed travelling suit followed him. He fitted his latchkey to the door. 'There,' Eleanor murmured, as he opened the door and they stood for a moment on the threshold. 'There!' she repeated, as the door shut with a little thud behind them.

Then she turned round into the room. 'And now?' she said, looking at Morris, who was drinking the last drops of a glass of wine. 'And now?' she asked, holding out her hands to him.

The sun had risen, and the sky above the houses wore an air of extraordinary beauty, simplicity and peace.

1 (p. 7) *Whiteley's and the Army and Navy Stores*   Whiteley's, a large store in Bayswater; the Army and Navy Stores, founded in 1871 as a co-operative to provide goods at discount prices to military families

2 (p. 7) *landaus, victorias and hansom cabs*   types of Victorian horse-drawn carriages

3 (p. 7) *Hyde Park*   the largest royal park in London and a location for suffragette protests, and earlier, in the nineteenth century, of demonstrations in support of the Chartists and the Reform League

4 (p. 7) *the Princess*   Princess Alexandra of Denmark, who became the Princess of Wales in 1863 on her marriage to Queen Victoria's eldest son, Albert Edward, and was crowned queen as the consort of Albert (Edward VII) on Victoria's death

5 (p. 8) *broughams*   closed horse-drawn carriages

6 (p. 11) *sovereign . . . one pound eight and sixpence*   The gold sovereign, minted irregularly from the reign of Henry VIII until 1917, was originally so called because it showed the monarch in full splendour; from 1817, it was the standard one-pound coin worth twenty shillings, a shilling being worth twelve pence; the sixpence was a small silver coin worth half a shilling.

7 (p. 14) *florins*   The name for gold coins struck in Florence in 1253 came to be applied to English two-shilling coins, struck between 1849 and 1970.

8 (p. 14) *the Mutiny*   the Indian Mutiny of 1857, which began as a mutiny of sepoys, Muslim and Hindu soldiers, against the East India Company in response to changes in their conditions of service, pressure to convert to Christianity and rumour that their gun cartridges were greased with pork fat which was regarded as unclean by Muslims

9 (p. 20) *Charles Stewart Parnell*   (1846–91), founder of the Irish Parliamentary Party and a strong advocate of Home Rule for Ireland

10 (p. 25) *the Levys, the Grubbs . . . and the Cobbs*   family names suggesting the multi-ethnic community of London

11 (p. 25) *Shoreditch*   a district of London associated with clothing manufacture and dependent upon immigrant labour

12 (p. 27) *the Bar*   To be 'called to the Bar', a phrase originating in the Middle Ages, means to qualify for and to take up the profession of barrister in courts of law.

13 (p. 39) *Antigone*   a tragedy by the Greek dramatist Sophocles, written about 442 BC, in which Antigone defies the order of Creon, the ruler of Thebes, that her brother be left unburied on the battle-field, and subsequently commits suicide to avoid Creon's having her buried alive.

14 (p. 44) *Katharine's*   a fictitious Oxford College at this time

15 (p. 44) *Bodleian*   the famous Oxford University library founded in 1602

16 (p. 46) *Balliol*   an Oxford College, founded in 1282

17 (p. 52) *stunner*   a slang term, originating in the nineteenth century, for an attractive woman

18 (p. 52) *Gainsborough*   Sir Thomas Gainsborough (1727–88), an English portrait and landscape painter

19 (p. 54) *Taffy*   a derogatory English nickname for a Welshman and one of several allusions in the novel to the oppression by the English of people they perceived as 'other'. (See Note 30, below.)

20 (p. 55) *Chingachgook*   a Native American chief in *The Last of the Mohicans* by the American novelist James Fenimore Cooper (1789–1851)

21 (p. 57) *Pope, Tennyson*   Alexander Pope (1688–1744), on whom Virginia Woolf's father wrote a book, and Lord Alfred Tennyson (1809–92), significant English poets

22 (p. 57) *Mr Gladstone*   William Ewart Gladstone (1809–98), Prime Minister 1868–74, 1880–86 and 1892–4. He was critical of the imperial foreign policy of Benjamin Disraeli (1874–80) and an advocate of Irish Home Rule.

23 (pp. 61–3) *I am the resurrection and the life . . . Man that is born of a woman . . . this sinful world*   extracts from 'The Order for the Burial of the Dead' in the *Book of Common Prayer*

24 (p. 64) *St Martin's*   St Martin-in-the-Fields Church, Trafalgar Square, London

25 (p. 65) *Sur le pont d'Avignon*   a French song from the fifteenth century about the bridge straddling the Avignon, a popular spot for fairs and revelry

26 (p. 76) *Chancery Lane*   a famous street in London consisting mainly of legal offices

27 (p. 77) *the lion and the unicorn*   on the Royal Arms, representing England and Scotland

28 (p. 82) *Whitehall*   the Government, referring to the street on which many Government offices are located.

29 (p. 82) *nonsense talked about the divorce case*   the 1890 divorce case involving Charles Stewart Parnell (see Note 9, above) who was forced to resign from public office over his affair with Katherine ('Kitty') O'Shea

30 (p. 83) *dagos*   offensive English slang for Spanish, Portuguese or Italian people

31 (p. 86) *Lido*   outdoor bathing area or resort; originally a Venetian bathing resort

32 (p. 91) *Covent Garden*   a market in central London selling fruit, vegetables and flowers; originally located near the river in a district which became infamous for crime, drunkenness and prostitution

33 (p. 92) *the Government in a fix . . . that young man*   The events referred to here occurred in 1909, not 1907; the House of Lords rejected the radical budget of the Chancellor of the Exchequer, David Lloyd George (1863–1945). Lloyd George went on to become the first Welsh and Welsh-speaking and last liberal Prime Minister and led Britain during the latter half of the First World War (1916–18). He ushered in many of the reforms that laid the foundations of the modern Welfare State.

34 (p. 96) *She was buried alive*   a reference to *Antigone*. (See Note 13, above.)

35 (p. 103) *Isle of Dogs*   a peninsula opposite Greenwich created by the River Thames, once marshland and known as Stepney Marsh

36 (p. 128) *The doctors have given him up*   Edward VII died after a series of heart attacks at Sandringham.

37 (p. 134) *the Palace*   Buckingham Palace

38 (p. 135) *Toledo*   capital of Castile in Spain, besieged by republicans in the Spanish Civil War

39 (p. 142) *She threw a brick*   Suffragettes broke windows to publicise their cause; Rose becomes one of many suffragettes to be sent to prison, like Woolf's friend Ethel Smyth.

40 (p. 153) *The war in the Balkans was over*   the second of two wars in south-eastern Europe, 1912–13, involving Bulgaria, Greece, Montenegro and Serbia

41 (p. 161) *meat crammed down her throat*   force-feeding of suffragettes who went on hunger strike when they were imprisoned

42 (p. 164) *the news from Ireland*   concerning the Curragh Mutiny in Curragh, Kildare, in March 1914, involving the newly formed Irish Volunteers who were bitterly opposed to the Home Rule Bill which had its third reading that year

43 (p. 164) *The Row*   a wide avenue in Hyde Park where fashionable Londoners went to ride, to meet and to be seen; perhaps named the Rotten Row after a former row of tumbledown cottages

44 (p. 165) *Science is the religion of the future*   an allusion to the ideas of the French philosopher Ernest Renan (1823–92)

45 (p. 169) *the white figure of Queen Victoria*   the statue of the Queen and her daughter near Kensington Palace

46 (p. 172) *Canaletto*   Giovani Antonio Canal (1697–1768), a Venetian painter famous for his landscapes of Venice

47 (p. 177) *Nijinsky*   Vaslav Vatslav Fomich Nizhinsky (1889–1950), an internationally celebrated Russian ballet dancer and choreographer

48 (p. 205) *ought to be in prison . . . the other sex*   Sexual intercourse between males was made illegal in 1533 and carried the death penalty until 1861; consensual sexual relationships between men were legalised in England and Wales in 1967.

49 (p. 210) *The war was over*   The Armistice was declared on 11 November 1918 at 11 a.m.

50 (p. 214) *a circle on the wall with a jagged line in it*   the symbol of the British Union of Fascists

51 (p. 223) *half a crown*   worth two shillings and sixpence. (See Note 6, above.)

52 (p. 227) *a fat man gesticulating*   Benito Mussolini (1883–1945), Fascist leader and 40th prime minister of Italy, 1942–3

53 (p. 229) *picture palaces*   large, elaborately decorated cinemas built between 1910 and the 1940s

54 (p. 231) *the figure of a woman in nurse's uniform*   monument in London to Edith Cavell (1865–1915), a British nurse, now known to have been a British spy, executed for assisting Allied soldiers to escape German-occupied Belgium during the First World War

55 (p. 233) *society . . . solitude*   from the poem 'The Garden' by Andrew Marvell (1621–78), an English metaphysical poet and friend of John Milton

56 (p. 249) *that phantom wheelbarrow* the constellation Ursa Major, known as the Plough

57 (p. 255) *bounder* old-fashioned British slang for a morally reprehensible person

58 (p. 263) *La médiocrité . . . m'anéantit* 'The mediocrity of the universe surprises and revolts me . . . the pettiness of everything fills me with disgust . . . the poverty of human beings destroys me.'

59 (p. 266) *in the heart of darkness* *Heart of Darkness*, a novella (1902) by Joseph Conrad (1857–1924), in which the narrator recalls his disturbing experiences as a steamboat captain on the (Congo) river. His story exposes the huge gap between the rhetoric of the (Western) Christian 'civilising' mission and the coloniser's brutal, contemptuous exploitation. As the repeated use of the title suggests, Woolf is thinking of the darkness of the human heart that renders both self-knowledge and the knowledge of others difficult.

60 (p. 268) *The face that launched a thousand ships* Helen of Troy was a princess of legendary beauty in Greek mythology, whose abduction brought about the Trojan War; the line is from *Dr Faustus* (1604) by Christopher Marlowe (1564–93).

61 (p. 270) *nox est perpetua una dormienda* 'night is a never ending sleep', from Catullus (*c*.84–54 BC), Poem 5, v.6, referring to what follows death

62 (p. 274) *Dublin Castle* the seat of government in Ireland

63 (p. 274) *our new freedom is a good deal worse than our old slavery* The Irish Free State, created on 6 December 1922, under the Anglo-Irish treaty replaced the self-proclaimed Irish Republic of 21 January 1919. (Northern Ireland opted out of the Irish Free State within two days of its inclusion.) The Free State disappointed many republicans who wanted a fully independent Ireland. Civil war (1922–3) broke out between the Free State government and the republicans which was concluded with a victory for the government. The Irish Free State was replaced by the Irish Republic in 1937.

64 (p. 275) *English settlers* Catholic Ireland posed a threat to Protestant England from the sixteenth century, as Catholic Europe could invade Britain via Ireland, mustering support there on the way. Following the slaughter of Irish Catholic priests by Oliver Cromwell in the mid-seventeenth century, the English and Scottish were encouraged to settle on Irish land in an attempt to anglicise the country and create what, in the eighteenth century, became known as a 'Protestant Ascendancy' in Ireland.

65 (p. 281) *Spinners and sitters in the sun* an adaptation of the line 'The spinsters and the knitters in the sun', in Shakespeare's *Twelfth Night* (Act 2, Scene 4, line 44)

66 (p. 284) *said some words in Greek* from *Antigone* (see Note 13, above), where Antigone tells Creon that it is not in her to hate but to love. Edward's inability to provide a translation reinforces how characters in the novel cannot communicate with or understand each other.

67 (p. 293) *Aeschylus . . . Pindar* Aeschylus (525–456 BC), a Greek dramatist; Pindar (518–438 BC), a Greek poet

68 (p. 294) *Sing a song for sixpence* an adaptation of the nursery rhyme, 'Sing a song of sixpence', referring to bakers putting strange items in pies, which usually ended with tweaking a child's nose

69 (pp. 294–5) *Etho passo . . . to tuh do – . . . Fanno to par . . . meido – . . . Chree . . . didax* a mixture of Latin, Greek and cockney English which deliberately makes little sense

Between the Acts

◆

VIRGINIA WOOLF

A novel by
VIRGINIA WOOLF
first published in 1941

Note

The manuscript of this book had been completed, but had not been finally revised for the printer, at the time of Virginia Woolf's death. She would not, I believe, have made any large or material alterations in it, though she would probably have made a good many small corrections or revisions before passing the final proofs.

LEONARD WOOLF

I T WAS A SUMMER'S NIGHT and they were talking, in the big room with the windows open to the garden, about the cesspool. The county council had promised to bring water to the village, but they hadn't.

Mrs Haines, the wife of the gentleman farmer, a goose-faced woman with eyes protruding as if they saw something to gobble in the gutter, said affectedly: 'What a subject to talk about on a night like this!'

Then there was silence; and a cow coughed; and that led her to say how odd it was, as a child, she had never feared cows, only horses. But, then, as a small child in a perambulator, a great cart-horse had brushed within an inch of her face. Her family, she told the old man in the armchair, had lived near Liskeard[1] for many centuries. There were the graves in the churchyard to prove it.

A bird chuckled outside. 'A nightingale?' asked Mrs Haines. No, nightingales didn't come so far north. It was a daylight bird, chuckling over the substance and succulence of the day, over worms, snails, grit, even in sleep.

The old man in the armchair – Mr Oliver, of the Indian Civil Service, retired – said that the site they had chosen for the cesspool was, if he had heard aright, on the Roman road. From an aeroplane, he said, you could still see, plainly marked, the scars made by the Britons; by the Romans; by the Elizabethan manor house; and by the plough, when they ploughed the hill to grow wheat in the Napoleonic wars.

'But you don't remember . . . ' Mrs Haines began. No, not that. Still he did remember – and he was about to tell them what, when there was a sound outside, and Isa, his son's wife, came in with her hair in pigtails; she was wearing a dressing-gown with faded peacocks on it. She came in like a swan swimming its way; then was checked and stopped; was surprised to find people there; and lights burning. She had been sitting with her little boy who wasn't well, she apologised. What had they been saying?

'Discussing the cesspool,' said Mr Oliver.

'What a subject to talk about on a night like this!' Mrs Haines exclaimed again.

What had *he* said about the cesspool; or indeed about anything? Isa wondered, inclining her head towards the gentleman farmer, Rupert Haines. She had met him at a bazaar; and at a tennis party. He had handed her a cup and a racquet – that was all. But in his ravaged face she always felt mystery; and in his silence, passion. At the tennis party she had felt this, and at the bazaar. Now a third time, if anything more strongly, she felt it again.

'I remember,' the old man interrupted, 'my mother . . . ' Of his mother he remembered that she was very stout; kept her tea-caddy[2] locked; yet had given him in that very room a copy of Byron. It was over sixty years ago, he told them, that his mother had given him the works of Byron in that very room. He paused.

' "She walks in beauty like the night",' he quoted. Then again: ' "So we'll go no more a-roving by the light of the moon".'

Isa raised her head. The words made two rings, perfect rings, that floated them, herself and Haines, like two swans downstream. But his snow-white breast was circled with a tangle of dirty duckweed; and she, too, in her webbed feet was entangled, by her husband, the stockbroker. Sitting on her three-cornered chair she swayed, with her dark pigtails hanging, and her body like a bolster in its faded dressing-gown.

Mrs Haines was aware of the emotion circling them, excluding her. She waited, as one waits for the strain of an organ to die out before leaving church. In the car going home to the red villa in the cornfields, she would destroy it, as a thrush pecks the wings off a butterfly. Allowing ten seconds to intervene, she rose; paused; and then, as if she had heard the last strain die out, offered Mrs Giles Oliver her hand.

But Isa, though she should have risen at the same moment that Mrs Haines rose, sat on. Mrs Haines glared at her out of goose-like eyes, gobbling, 'Please, Mrs Giles Oliver, do me the kindness to recognise my existence . . . ' which she was forced to do, rising at last from her chair, in her faded dressing-gown, with the pigtails falling over each shoulder.

Pointz Hall was seen in the light of an early summer morning to be a middle-sized house. It did not rank among the houses that are mentioned in guide books. It was too homely. But this whitish house with the grey roof, and the wing thrown out at right angles, lying unfortunately low on the meadow with a fringe of trees on the bank above it so that smoke curled up to the nests of the rooks, was a desirable house to live in. Driving past, people said to each other: 'I wonder if that'll ever come into the market?' And to the chauffeur: 'Who lives there?'

The chauffeur didn't know. The Olivers, who had bought the place something over a century ago, had no connection with the Warings, the Elveys, the Mannerings or the Burnets; the old families who had all intermarried, and lay in their deaths intertwisted, like the ivy roots, beneath the churchyard wall.

Only something over a hundred and twenty years the Olivers had been there. Still, on going up the principal staircase – there was another, a mere ladder at the back for the servants – there was a portrait. A length of yellow brocade was visible halfway up; and, as one reached the top, a small powdered face, a great head-dress slung with pearls, came into view: an ancestress of sorts. Six or seven bedrooms opened out of the corridor. The butler had been a soldier; had married a lady's maid; and, under a glass case there was a watch that had stopped a bullet on the field of Waterloo.

It was early morning. The dew was on the grass. The church clock struck eight times. Mrs Swithin drew the curtain in her bedroom – the faded white chintz that so agreeably from the outside tinged the window with its green lining. There with her old hands on the hasp, jerking it open, she stood: old Oliver's married sister; a widow. She always meant to set up a house of her own; perhaps in Kensington, perhaps at Kew, so that she could have the benefit of the gardens.[3] But she stayed on all through the summer; and when winter wept its damp upon the panes, and choked the gutters with dead leaves, she said: 'Why, Bart, did they build the house in the hollow, facing north?' Her brother said, 'Obviously to escape from nature. Weren't four horses needed to drag the family coach through the mud?' Then he told her the famous story of the great eighteenth-century winter; when for a whole month the house had been blocked by snow. And the trees had fallen. So every year, when winter came, Mrs Swithin retired to Hastings.

But it was summer now. She had been waked by the birds. How they sang! attacking the dawn like so many choirboys attacking an iced cake. Forced to listen, she had stretched for her favourite reading – an *Outline of History*[4] – and had spent the hours between three and five thinking of rhododendron forests in Piccadilly; when the entire continent, not then, she understood, divided by a channel, was all one; populated, she understood, by elephant-bodied, seal-necked, heaving, surging, slowly writhing and, she supposed, barking monsters: the iguanodon, the mammoth and the mastodon; from whom presumably, she thought, jerking the window open, we descend.

It took her five seconds in actual time, in mind time ever so much longer, to separate Grace herself, with blue china on a tray, from the leather-covered grunting monster who was about, as the door opened, to demolish a whole tree in the green steaming undergrowth of the primeval forest. Naturally, she jumped as Grace put the tray down and said: 'Good-morning, ma'am.' 'Batty,' Grace called her, as she felt on her face the divided glance that was half meant for a beast in a swamp, half for a maid in a print frock and white apron.

'How those birds sing!' said Mrs Swithin, at a venture. The window was open now; the birds certainly were singing. An obliging thrush hopped across the lawn; a coil of pinkish rubber twisted in its beak. Tempted by the sight to continue her imaginative reconstruction of the past, Mrs Swithin paused; she was given to increasing the bounds of the moment by flights into past or future; or sidelong down corridors and alleys; but she remembered her mother – her mother in that very room rebuking her. 'Don't stand gaping, Lucy, or the wind'll change . . . ' How often her mother had rebuked her in that very room – 'but in a very different world', as her brother would remind her. So she sat down to morning tea, like any other old lady with a high nose, thin cheeks, a ring on her finger and the usual trappings of rather shabby but gallant old age, which included in her case a cross gleaming gold on her breast.

The nurses after breakfast were trundling the perambulator up and down the terrace; and as they trundled they were talking – not shaping pellets of information or handing ideas from one to another, but rolling words like sweets on their tongues; which, as they thinned to transparency, gave off pink, green, and sweetness. This morning that sweetness was: 'How cook had told 'im off about the asparagus; how when she rang I said: how it was a sweet costume with blouse to match;' and that was leading to something about a feller as they walked up and down the terrace rolling sweets, trundling the perambulator.

It was a pity that the man who had built Pointz Hall had pitched the house in a hollow, when beyond the flower garden and the vegetables there was this stretch of high ground. Nature had provided a site for a house; man had built his house in a hollow. Nature had provided a stretch of turf half a mile in length and level, till it suddenly dipped to the lily pool. The terrace was broad enough to take the entire shadow of one of the great trees laid flat. There you could walk up and down, up and down, under the shade of the trees. Two or three grew close together; then there were gaps. Their roots broke the turf, and among those bones were green waterfalls and cushions of grass in which violets grew in spring or in summer the wild purple orchis.

Amy was saying something about a feller when Mabel, with her hand on the pram, turned sharply, her sweet swallowed. 'Leave off grubbing,' she said sharply. 'Come along, George.'

The little boy had lagged and was grouting in the grass. Then the baby, Caro, thrust her fist out over the coverlet and the furry bear was jerked overboard. Amy had to stoop. George grubbed. The flower blazed between the angles of the roots. Membrane after membrane was torn. It blazed a soft yellow, a lambent light under a film of velvet; it filled the caverns behind the eyes with light. All that inner darkness became a hall, leaf smelling, earth smelling of yellow light. And the tree was beyond the flower; the grass, the flower and the tree were entire. Down on his knees grubbing he held the flower complete. Then there was a roar and a hot breath and a stream of coarse grey hair rushed between him and the flower. Up he leapt, toppling in his fright, and saw coming towards him a terrible peaked eyeless monster moving on legs, brandishing arms.

'Good-morning, sir,' a hollow voice boomed at him from a beak of paper.

The old man had sprung upon him from his hiding-place behind a tree.

'Say good-morning, George; say, "Good-morning, Grandpa",' Mabel urged him, giving him a push towards the man. But George stood gaping. George stood gazing. Then Mr Oliver crumpled the paper which he had cocked into a snout and appeared in person. A very tall old man, with gleaming eyes, wrinkled cheeks, and a head with no hair on it. He turned.

'Heel!' he bawled, 'heel, you brute!' And George turned; and the nurses turned holding the furry bear; they all turned to look at Sohrab[5] the Afghan hound bounding and bouncing among the flowers.

'Heel!' the old man bawled, as if he were commanding a regiment. It was impressive, to the nurses, the way an old boy of his age could still bawl and make a brute like that obey him. Back came the Afghan hound, sidling, apologetic. And as he cringed at the old man's feet, a string was slipped over his collar; the noose that old Oliver always carried with him.

'You wild beast . . . you bad beast,' he grumbled, stooping. George looked at the dog only. The hairy flanks were sucked in and out; there was a blob of foam on its nostrils. He burst out crying.

Old Oliver raised himself, his veins swollen, his cheeks flushed; he was angry. His little game with the paper hadn't worked. The boy was a cry-baby. He nodded and sauntered on, smoothing out the crumpled paper and muttering, as he tried to find his line in the column, 'A cry-baby – a cry-baby.' But the breeze blew the great sheet out; and over the edge he surveyed the landscape – flowing fields, heath and woods.

Framed, they became a picture. Had he been a painter, he would have fixed his easel here, where the country, barred by trees, looked like a picture. Then the breeze fell.

'M. Daladier,'[6] he read finding his place in the column, 'has been successful in pegging down the franc . . .'

Mrs Giles Oliver drew the comb through the thick tangle of hair which, after giving the matter her best attention, she had never had shingled or bobbed;[7] and lifted the heavily embossed silver brush that had been a wedding present and had its uses in impressing chambermaids in hotels. She lifted it and stood in front of the three-folded mirror, so that she could see three separate versions of her rather heavy, yet handsome, face; and also, outside the glass, a slip of terrace, lawn and tree tops.

Inside the glass, in her eyes, she saw what she had felt overnight for the ravaged, the silent, the romantic gentleman farmer. 'In love' was in her eyes. But outside, on the washstand, on the dressing-table, among the silver boxes and toothbrushes, was the other love: love for her husband, the stockbroker – 'The father of my children,' she added, slipping into the cliché conveniently provided by fiction. Inner love was in the eyes; outer love on the dressing-table. But what feeling was it that stirred in her now when above the looking-glass, out of doors, she saw coming across the lawn the perambulator; two nurses; and her little boy George, lagging behind?

She tapped on the window with her embossed hairbrush. They were too far off to hear. The drone of the trees was in their ears; the chirp of birds; other incidents of garden life, inaudible, invisible to her in the bedroom, absorbed them. Isolated on a green island, hedged about with snowdrops, laid with a counterpane of puckered silk, the innocent island floated under her window. Only George lagged behind.

She returned to her eyes in the looking-glass. 'In love' she must be; since the presence of his body in the room last night could so affect her; since the words he said, handing her a teacup, handing her a tennis racquet, could so attach themselves to a certain spot in her; and thus lie between them like a wire, tingling, tangling, vibrating – she groped, in the depths of the looking-glass, for a word to fit the infinitely quick vibrations of the aeroplane propeller that she had seen once at dawn at Croydon. Faster, faster, faster, it whizzed, whirred, buzzed, till all the flails became one flail and up soared the plane away and away . . .

'Where we know not, where we go not, neither know nor care,' she hummed. 'Flying, rushing through the ambient, incandescent, summer silent . . .'

The rhyme was 'air'. She put down her brush. She took up the telephone.

'Three, four, eight, Pyecombe,' she said. 'Mrs Oliver speaking . . . What fish have you this morning? Cod? Halibut? Sole? Plaice?'

'There to lose what binds us here,' she murmured. 'Soles. Filleted. In time for lunch please,' she said aloud. 'With a feather, a blue feather . . . flying mounting through the air . . . there to lose what binds us here . . . ' The words weren't worth writing in the book bound like an account book in case Giles suspected. 'Abortive', was the word that expressed her. She never came out of a shop, for example, with the clothes she admired; nor did her figure, seen against the dark roll of trousering in a shop window, please her. Thick of waist, large of limb, and, save for her hair, fashionable in the tight modern way, she never looked like Sappho,[8] or one of the beautiful young men whose photographs adorned the weekly papers. She looked what she was: Sir Richard's daughter; and niece of the two old ladies at Wimbledon who were so proud, being O'Neils, of their descent from the kings of Ireland.

A foolish, flattering lady, pausing on the threshold of what she once called 'the heart of the house', the threshold of the library, had once said: 'Next to the kitchen, the library's always the nicest room in the house.' Then she added, stepping across the threshold: 'Books are the mirrors of the soul.'

In this case a tarnished, a spotted soul. For as the train took over three hours to reach this remote village in the very heart of England, no one ventured so long a journey without staving off possible mind-hunger, without buying a book on a bookstall. Thus the mirror that reflected the soul sublime, reflected also the soul bored. Nobody could pretend, as they looked at the shuffle of shilling shockers that week-enders had dropped, that the looking-glass always reflected the anguish of a queen or the heroism of King Harry.

At this early hour of a June morning the library was empty. Mrs Giles had to visit the kitchen. Mr Oliver still tramped the terrace. And Mrs Swithin was of course at church. The light but variable breeze, foretold by the weather expert, flapped the yellow curtain, tossing light, then shadow. The fire greyed, then glowed, and the tortoiseshell butterfly beat on the lower pane of the window; beat, beat, beat; repeating that if no human being ever came, never, never, never, the books would be mouldy, the fire out and the tortoiseshell butterfly dead on the pane.

Heralded by the impetuosity of the Afghan hound, the old man entered. He had read his paper; he was drowsy; and so sank down into the chintz-covered chair with the dog at his feet – the Afghan hound. His nose on his paws, his haunches drawn up, he looked a stone dog, a crusader's dog,[9] guarding even in the realms of death the sleep of his master. But the master was not dead; only dreaming; drowsily, seeing as in a glass, its lustre spotted, himself, a young man helmeted; and a cascade falling. But no water; and the hills, like grey stuff pleated; and in the sand a hoop of ribs; a bullock maggot-eaten in the sun; and in the shadow of the rock, savages; and in his hand a gun.[10] The dream hand clenched; the real hand lay on the chair arm, the veins swollen but only with a brownish fluid now.

The door opened.

'Am I,' Isa apologised, 'interrupting?'

Of course she was – destroying youth and India. It was his fault, since she had persisted in stretching his thread of life so fine, so far. Indeed he was grateful to her, watching her as she strolled about the room, for continuing.

Many old men had only their India – old men in clubs, old men in rooms off Jermyn Street. She in her striped dress continued him, murmuring, in front of the bookcases: 'The moor is dark beneath the moon, rapid clouds have drunk the last pale beams of even . . . I have ordered the fish,' she said aloud, turning, 'though whether it'll be fresh or not I can't promise. But veal is dear, and everybody in the house is sick of beef and mutton . . . Sohrab,' she said, coming to a standstill in front of them, 'what's *he* been doing?'

His tail never wagged. He never admitted the ties of domesticity. Either he cringed or he bit. Now his wild yellow eyes gazed at her, gazed at him. He could outstare them both.

Then Oliver remembered: 'Your little boy's a cry-baby,' he said scornfully.

'Oh,' she sighed, pegged down on a chair arm, like a captive balloon, by a myriad of hair-thin ties into domesticity. 'What's been happening?'

'I took the newspaper,' he explained, 'so . . . '

He took it and crumpled it into a beak over his nose. 'So,' he had sprung out from behind a tree on to the children.

'And he howled. He's a coward, your boy is.'

She frowned. He was not a coward, her boy wasn't. And she loathed the domestic, the possessive; the maternal. And he knew it and did it on purpose to tease her, the old brute, her father-in-law.

She looked away.

'The library's always the nicest room in the house,' she quoted, and ran her eyes along the books. 'The mirror of the soul' books were. *The*

Faerie Queene[11] and Kinglake's *Crimea*;[12] Keats[13] and *The Kreutzer Sonata*.[14] There they were, reflecting. What? What remedy was there for her at her age – the age of the century, thirty-nine – in books? Book-shy she was, like the rest of her generation; and gun-shy too. Yet as a person with a raging tooth runs her eye in a chemist's shop over green bottles with gilt scrolls on them lest one of them may contain a cure, she considered: Keats and Shelley; Yeats and Donne. Or perhaps not a poem; a life. The life of Garibaldi.[15] The life of Lord Palmerston.[16] Or perhaps not a person's life; a county's. *The Antiquities of Durham*; *The Proceedings of the Archaeological Society of Nottingham*. Or not a life at all, but science – Eddington, Darwin or Jeans.[17]

None of them stopped her toothache. For her generation the news-paper was a book; and, as her father-in-law had dropped *The Times*, she took it and read: 'A horse with a green tail[18] . . . ' which was fantastic. Next, 'The guard at Whitehall . . . ' which was romantic, and then, building word upon word, she read: 'The troopers told her the horse had a green tail; but she found it was just an ordinary horse. And they dragged her up to the barrack room where she was thrown upon a bed. Then one of the troopers removed part of her clothing, and she screamed and hit him about the face . . . '

That was real; so real that on the mahogany door panels she saw the Arch in Whitehall; through the Arch the barrack room; in the barrack room the bed; and on the bed the girl was screaming and hitting him about the face, when the door (for in fact it was a door) opened and in came Mrs Swithin carrying a hammer.

She advanced, sidling, as if the floor were fluid under her shabby garden shoes, and, advancing, pursed her lips and smiled, sidelong, at her brother. Not a word passed between them as she went to the cupboard in the corner and replaced the hammer, which she had taken without asking leave, together – she unclosed her fist – with a handful of nails.

'Cindy – Cindy,' he growled, as she shut the cupboard door.

Lucy, his sister, was three years younger than he was. The name Cindy, or Sindy, for it could be spelt either way, was short for Lucy. It was by this name that he had called her when they were children; when she had trotted after him as he fished, and had made the meadow flowers into tight little bunches, winding one long grass stalk round and round and round. Once, she remembered, he had made her take the fish off the hook herself. The blood had shocked her – 'Oh!' she had cried – for the gills were full of blood. And he had growled: 'Cindy!' The ghost of that morning in the meadow was in her mind as she replaced the hammer where it belonged on one shelf; and the nails where they belonged on another; and shut the cupboard about which, for he still kept his fishing tackle there, he was still so very particular.

'I've been nailing the placard on the barn,' she said, giving him a little pat on the shoulder.

The words were like the first peal of a chime of bells. As the first peals, you hear the second; as the second peals, you hear the third. So when Isa heard Mrs Swithin say: 'I've been nailing the placard to the barn,' she knew she would say next:

'For the pageant.'

And he would say:

'Today? By Jupiter! I'd forgotten!'

'If it's fine,' Mrs Swithin continued, 'they'll act on the terrace . . . '

'And if it's wet,' Bartholomew continued, 'in the barn.'

'And which will it be?' Mrs Swithin continued. 'Wet or fine?'

Then, for the seventh time in succession, they both looked out of the window.

Every summer, for seven summers now, Isa had heard the same words: about the hammer and the nails; the pageant and the weather. Every year they said, would it be wet or fine; and every year it was – one or the other. The same chime followed the same chime, only this year beneath the chime she heard: 'The girl screamed and hit him about the face with a hammer.'

'The forecast,' said Mr Oliver, turning the pages till he found it, 'says: variable winds; fair average temperature; rain at times.'

He put down the paper, and they all looked at the sky to see whether the sky obeyed the meteorologist. Certainly the weather was variable. It was green in the garden one moment; grey the next. Here came the sun – an illimitable rapture of joy, embracing every flower, every leaf. Then in compassion it withdrew, covering its face, as if it forebore to look on human suffering. There was a fecklessness, a lack of symmetry and order in the clouds as they thinned and thickened. Was it their own law, or no law, they obeyed? Some were wisps of white hair merely. One, high up, very distant, had hardened to golden alabaster; was made of immortal marble. Beyond that was blue, pure blue, black blue; blue that had never filtered down; that had escaped registration. It never fell as sun, shadow, or rain upon the world, but disregarded the little coloured ball of earth entirely. No flower felt it; no field; no garden.

Mrs Swithin's eyes glazed as she looked at it. Isa thought her gaze was fixed because she saw God there, God on his throne. But as a shadow fell next moment on the garden Mrs Swithin loosed and lowered her fixed look and said: 'It's very unsettled. It'll rain, I'm afraid. We can only pray,' she added, and fingered her crucifix.

'And provide umbrellas,' said her brother.

Lucy flushed. He had struck her faith. When she said 'pray', he added 'umbrellas'. She half covered the cross with her fingers. She shrank; she cowered; but next moment she exclaimed: 'Oh there they are – the darlings!'

The perambulator was passing across the lawn.

Isa looked too. What an angel she was – the old woman! Thus to salute the children; to beat up against those immensities and the old man's irreverences her skinny hands, her laughing eyes! How courageous to defy Bart and the weather!

'He looks blooming,' said Mrs Swithin.

'It's astonishing how they pick up,' said Isa.

'He ate his breakfast?' Mrs Swithin asked.

'Every scrap,' said Isa.

'And baby? No sign of measles?'

Isa shook her head. 'Touch wood,' she added, tapping the table.

'Tell me, Bart,' said Mrs Swithin turning to her brother, 'what's the origin of that? Touch wood . . . Antaeus, didn't he touch earth?'

She would have been, he thought, a very clever woman, had she fixed her gaze. But this led to that; that to the other. What went in at this ear, went out at that. And all were circled, as happens after seventy, by one recurring question. Hers was, should she live at Kensington or at Kew? But every year, when winter came, she did neither. She took lodgings at Hastings.

'Touch wood; touch earth; Antaeus,'[19] he muttered, bringing the scattered bits together. Lemprière would settle it; or the *Encyclopaedia*. But it was not in books the answer to his question – why, in Lucy's skull, shaped so much like his own, there existed a prayable being? She didn't, he supposed, invest it with hair, teeth or toe-nails. It was, he supposed more of a force or a radiance, controlling the thrush and the worm; the tulip and the hound; and himself, too, an old man with swollen veins. It got her out of bed on a cold morning and sent her down the muddy path to worship it, whose mouthpiece was Streatfield. A good fellow, who smoked cigars in the vestry. He needed some solace, doling out preachments to asthmatic elders, perpetually repairing the perpetually falling steeple by means of placards nailed to barns. The love, he was thinking, that they should give to flesh and blood they give to the church . . . when Lucy rapping her fingers on the table said: 'What's the origin – the origin – of that?'

'Superstition,' he said.

She flushed, and the little breath too was audible that she drew in as once more he struck a blow at her faith. But, brother and sister, flesh and blood was not a barrier, but a mist. Nothing changed their affection; no argument; no fact; no truth. What she saw he didn't; what he saw she didn't – and so on, *ad infinitum*.

'Cindy,' he growled. And the quarrel was over.

The barn to which Lucy had nailed her placard was a great building in the farmyard. It was as old as the church, and built of the same stone, but it had no steeple. It was raised on cones of grey stone at the corners to protect it from rats and damp. Those who had been to Greece always said it reminded them of a temple. Those who had never been to Greece – the majority – admired it all the same. The roof was weathered red-orange; and inside it was a hollow hall, sun-shafted, brown, smelling of corn, dark when the doors were shut, but splendidly illuminated when the doors at the end stood open, as they did to let the wagons in – the long low wagons, like ships of the sea, breasting the corn, not the sea, returning in the evening shagged with hay. The lanes caught tufts where the wagons had passed.

Now benches were drawn across the floor of the barn. If it rained, the actors were to act in the barn; planks had been laid together at one end to form a stage. Wet or fine, the audience would take tea there. Young men and women – Jim, Iris, David, Jessica – were even now busy with garlands of red and white paper roses left over from the Coronation.[20] The seeds and the dust from the sacks made them sneeze. Iris had a handkerchief bound round her forehead; Jessica wore breeches. The young men worked in shirt sleeves. Pale husks had stuck in their hair, and it was easy to run a splinter of wood into the fingers.

'Old Flimsy' (Mrs Swithin's nickname) had been nailing another placard on the barn. The first had been blown down, or the village idiot, who always tore down what had been nailed up, had done it, and was chuckling over the placard under the shade of some hedge. The workers were laughing too, as if old Swithin had left a wake of laughter behind her. The old girl with a wisp of white hair flying, knobbed shoes as if she had claws corned like a canary's, and black stockings wrinkled over the ankles, naturally made David cock his eye and Jessica wink back as she handed him a length of paper roses. Snobs they were; long enough stationed that is in that one corner of the world to have taken indelibly the print of some three hundred years of customary behaviour. So they laughed; but respected. If she wore pearls, pearls they were.

'Old Flimsy on the hop,' said David. She would be in and out twenty times, and finally bring them lemonade in a great jug and a plate of sandwiches. Jessie held the garland; he hammered. A hen strayed in; a file of cows passed the door; then a sheepdog; then the cowman, Bond, who stopped.

He contemplated the young people hanging roses from one rafter to another. He thought very little of anybody, simples or gentry. Leaning, silent, sardonic, against the door he was like a withered willow, bent over a stream, all its leaves shed, and in his eyes the whimsical flow of the waters.

'Hi – huh!' he cried suddenly. It was cow language presumably, for the parti-coloured cow, who had thrust her head in at the door, lowered her horns, lashed her tail and ambled off. Bond followed after.

'That's the problem,' said Mrs Swithin. While Mr Oliver consulted the *Encyclopaedia* searching under Superstition for the origin of the expression 'Touch wood', she and Isa discussed fish: whether, coming from a distance, it would be fresh.

They were so far from the sea. A hundred miles away, Mrs Swithin said; no, perhaps a hundred and fifty. 'But they do say,' she continued, 'one can hear the waves on a still night. After a storm, they say, you can hear a wave break . . . I like that story,' she reflected. ' "Hearing the waves in the middle of the night he saddled a horse and rode to the sea." Who was it, Bart, who rode to the sea?'

He was reading.

'You can't expect it brought to your door in a pail of water,' said Mrs Swithin, 'as I remember when we were children, living in a house by the sea. Lobsters, fresh from the lobster pots. How they pinched the stick cook gave them! And salmon. You know if they're fresh because they have lice in their scales.'

Bartholomew nodded. A fact that was. He remembered, the house by the sea. And the lobster.

They were bringing up nets full of fish from the sea; but Isa was seeing – the garden, variable as the forecast said, in the light breeze. Again, the children passed, and she tapped on the window and blew them a kiss. In the drone of the garden it went unheeded.

'Are we really,' she said, turning round, 'a hundred miles from the sea?'

'Thirty-five only,' her father-in-law said, as if he had whipped a tape-measure from his pocket and measured it exactly.

'It seems more,' said Isa. 'It seems from the terrace as if the land went on for ever and ever.'

'Once there was no sea,' said Mrs Swithin. 'No sea at all between us and the continent. I was reading that in a book this morning. There were rhododendrons in the Strand; and mammoths in Piccadilly.'

'When we were savages,' said Isa.

Then she remembered; her dentist had told her that savages could perform very skilful operations on the brain. Savages had false teeth, he said. False teeth were invented, she thought he said, in the time of the Pharaohs.

'At least so my dentist told me,' she concluded.

'Which man d'you go to now?' Mrs Swithin asked her.

'The same old couple: Batty and Bates in Sloane Street.'

'And Mr Batty told you they had false teeth in the time of the Pharaohs?' Mrs Swithin pondered.

'Batty? Oh not Batty. Bates,' Isa corrected her.

Batty, she recalled, only talked about royalty. Batty, she told Mrs Swithin, had a patient a princess. 'So he kept me waiting well over an hour. And you know, when one's a child, how long that seems.'

'Marriages with cousins,' said Mrs Swithin, 'can't be good for the teeth.'

Bart put his finger inside his mouth and projected the upper row outside his lips. They were false. Yet, he said, the Olivers hadn't married cousins. The Olivers couldn't trace their descent for more than two or three hundred years. But the Swithins could. The Swithins were there before the Conquest.[19]

'The Swithins,' Mrs Swithin began. Then she stopped. Bart would crack another joke about saints if she gave him the chance. And she had had two jokes cracked at her already; one about an umbrella; another about superstition.

So she stopped and said, 'How did we begin this talk?' She counted on her fingers. 'The Pharaohs. Dentists. Fish . . . Oh yes, you were saying, Isa, you'd ordered fish; and you were afraid it wouldn't be fresh. And I said, "That's the problem . . . "'

The fish had been delivered. Mitchell's boy, holding them in the crook of his arm, jumped off his motor bike. There was no feeding the pony with lumps of sugar at the kitchen door, nor time for gossip, since his round had been increased. He had to deliver right over the hill at Bickley; also go round by Waythorn, Roddam and Pyeminster, whose names, like his own, were in Domesday Book.[20] But the cook – Mrs Sands she was called, but by old friends Trixie – had never in all her fifty years been over the hill, nor wanted to.

He dabbed them down on the kitchen table, the filleted soles, the semi-transparent boneless fish. And before Mrs Sands had time to peel the paper off, he was gone, giving a slap to the very fine yellow cat who rose majestically from the basket chair and advanced superbly to the table, winding the fish.

Were they a bit whiffy? Mrs Sands held them to her nose. The cat rubbed itself this way, that way against the table legs, against her legs. She would save a slice for Sunny – his drawing-room name Sung-Yen had undergone a kitchen change into Sunny. She took them, the cat attendant, to the larder, and laid them on a plate in that semi-ecclesiastical apartment. For the house before the Reformation, like so many houses in that neighbourhood, had a chapel; and the chapel had become a larder, changing, like the cat's name, as religion changed. The Master (his drawing-room name; in the kitchen they called him Bartie) would bring gentlemen sometimes to see the larder – often when cook wasn't dressed. Not to see the hams that hung from hooks, or the butter on a blue slate, or the joint for tomorrow's dinner, but to see the cellar that opened out of the larder and its carved arch. If you tapped – one gentleman had a hammer – there was a hollow sound; a reverberation; undoubtedly, he said, a concealed passage where once somebody had hid. So it might be. But Mrs Sands wished they wouldn't come into her kitchen telling stories with the girls about. It put ideas into their silly heads. They heard dead men rolling barrels. They saw a white lady walking under the trees. No one would cross the terrace after dark. If a cat sneezed, 'There's the ghost!'

Sunny had his little bit off the fillet. Then Mrs Sands took an egg from the brown basket full of eggs; some with yellow fluff sticking to the shells; then a pinch of flour to coat those semi-transparent slips; and a crust from the great earthenware crock full of crusts. Then, returning to the kitchen, she made those quick movements at the oven, cinder raking, stoking, damping, which sent strange echoes through the house, so that in the library, the sitting-room, the dining-room and the nursery, whatever they were doing, thinking, saying, they knew, they all knew, it was getting on for breakfast, lunch or dinner.

'The sandwiches . . . ' said Mrs Swithin, coming into the kitchen. She refrained from adding 'Sands' to 'sandwiches', for Sands and sandwiches clashed. 'Never play,' her mother used to say, 'on people's names.' And Trixie was not a name that suited, as Sands did, the thin, acid woman, red-haired, sharp and clean, who never dashed off masterpieces, it was true; but then never dropped hairpins in the soup. 'What in the name of thunder?' Bart had said, raising a hairpin in his spoon, in the old days, fifteen years ago, before Sands came, in the time of Jessie Pook.

Mrs Sands fetched bread; Mrs Swithin fetched ham. One cut the bread; the other the ham. It was soothing, it was consolidating, this handwork together. The cook's hands cut, cut, cut. Whereas Lucy, holding the loaf, held the knife up. Why's stale bread, she mused, easier to cut than fresh? And so skipped, sidelong, from yeast to alcohol; so to fermentation; so to inebriation; so to Bacchus;[23] and lay under purple lamps in a vineyard in Italy, as she had done, often; while Sands heard the clock tick; saw the cat; noted a fly buzz; and registered, as her lips showed, a grudge she mustn't speak against people making work in the kitchen while they had a high old time hanging paper roses in the barn.

'Will it be fine?' asked Mrs Swithin, her knife suspended. In the kitchen they humoured old Mother Swithin's fancies.

'Seems like it,' said Mrs Sands, giving her sharp look-out of the kitchen window.

'It wasn't last year,' said Mrs Swithin. 'D'you remember what a rush we had – when the rain came – getting in the chairs?' She cut again. Then she asked about Billy, Mrs Sands's nephew, apprenticed to the butcher.

'He's been doing,' Mrs Sands said, 'what boys shouldn't; cheeking the master.'

'That'll be all right,' said Mrs Swithin, half meaning the boy, half meaning the sandwich, as it happened a very neat one, trimmed, triangular. 'Mr Giles may be late,' she added, laying it, complacently, on top of the pile.

For Isa's husband, the stockbroker, was coming from London. And the local train, which met the express train, arrived by no means punctually, even if he caught the early train which was by no means certain. In which case it meant – but what it meant to Mrs Sands, when people missed their trains, and she, whatever she might want to do, must wait, by the oven, keeping meat hot, no one knew.

'There!' said Mrs Swithin, surveying the sandwiches, some neat, some not, 'I'll take 'em to the barn.' As for the lemonade, she assumed, without a flicker of doubt, that Jane the kitchenmaid would follow after.

Candish paused in the dining-room to move a yellow rose. Yellow, white, carnation red – he placed them. He loved flowers, and arranging them, and placing the green sword- or heart-shaped leaf that came, fitly, between them. Queerly, he loved them, considering his gambling and drinking. The yellow rose went there. Now all was ready – silver and white, forks and napkins, and in the middle the splashed bowl of variegated roses. So, with one last look, he left the dining-room.

Two pictures hung opposite the window. In real life they had never met, the long lady and the man holding his horse by the rein. The lady was a picture,[24] bought by Oliver because he liked the picture; the man was an ancestor. He had a name. He held the rein in his hand. He had said to the painter: 'If you want my likeness, dang it, sir, take it when the leaves are on the trees.' There were leaves on the trees. He had said: 'Ain't there room for Colin as well as Buster?' Colin was his famous hound. But there was only room for Buster. It was, he seemed to say, addressing the company not the painter, a damned shame to leave out Colin whom he wished buried at his feet, in the same grave, about 1750; but that skunk the Reverend Whatshisname wouldn't allow it.

He was a talk producer, that ancestor. But the lady was a picture. In her yellow robe, leaning, with a pillar to support her, a silver arrow in her hand, and a feather in her hair, she led the eye up, down, from the curve to the straight, through glades of greenery and shades of silver, dun and rose into silence. The room was empty.

Empty, empty, empty; silent, silent, silent. The room was a shell, singing of what was before time was; a vase stood in the heart of the house, alabaster, smooth, cold, holding the still, distilled essence of emptiness, silence.

Across the hall a door opened. One voice, another voice, a third voice came wimpling and warbling: gruff – Bart's voice; quavering – Lucy's voice; middle-toned – Isa's voice. Their voices impetuously, impatiently, protestingly came across the hall saying: 'The train's late'; saying: 'Keep it hot'; saying: 'We won't, no Candish, we won't wait.'

Coming out from the library the voices stopped in the hall. They encountered an obstacle evidently: a rock. Utterly impossible was it, even in the heart of the country, to be alone? That was the shock. After that, the rock was raced round, embraced. If it was painful, it was essential. There must be society. Coming out of the library it was painful, but pleasant, to run slap into Mrs Manresa and an unknown young man with tow-coloured hair and a twisted face. No escape was possible; meeting was inevitable. Uninvited, unexpected, droppers-in, lured off the high road by the very same instinct that caused the sheep and the cows to desire propinquity, they had come. But they had brought a lunch basket. Here it was.

'We couldn't resist when we saw the name on the signpost,' Mrs Manresa began in her rich fluty voice. 'And this is a friend – William Dodge. We were going to sit all alone in a field. And I said: "Why not ask our dear friends," seeing the signpost, "to shelter us?" A seat at the table – that's all we want. We have our grub. We have our glasses. We ask nothing but – ' society apparently, to be with her kind.

And she waved her hand upon which there was a glove, and under the glove it seemed rings, at old Mr Oliver.

He bowed deep over her hand; a century ago, he would have kissed it. In all this sound of welcome, protestation, apology and again welcome, there was an element of silence, supplied by Isabella, observing the unknown young man. He was of course a gentleman: witness socks and trousers; brainy – tie spotted, waistcoat undone; urban, professional, that is putty coloured, unwholesome; very nervous, exhibiting a twitch at this sudden introduction, and fundamentally infernally conceited, for he deprecated Mrs Manresa's effusion, yet was her guest.

Isa felt antagonised, yet curious. But when Mrs Manresa added, to make all shipshape: 'He's an artist,' and when William Dodge corrected her: 'I'm a clerk in an office' – she thought he said Education or Somerset House[25] – she had her finger on the knot which had tied itself so tightly, almost to the extent of squinting, certainly of twitching, in his face.

Then they went in to lunch, and Mrs Manresa bubbled up, enjoying her own capacity to surmount, without turning a hair, this minor social crisis – this laying of two more places. For had she not complete faith in flesh and blood? and aren't we all flesh and blood? and how silly to make bones of trifles when we're all flesh and blood under the skin – men and women too! But she preferred men – obviously.

'Or what are your rings for, and your nails, and that really adorable little straw hat?' said Isabella addressing Mrs Manresa silently and thereby making silence add its unmistakable contribution to talk. Her hat, her rings, her fingernails red as roses, smooth as shells, were there for all to see. But not her life history. That was only scraps and fragments to all of them, excluding perhaps William Dodge, whom she called 'Bill' publicly – a sign perhaps that he knew more than they did. Some of the things that he knew – that she strolled the garden at midnight in silk pyjamas, had the loudspeaker playing jazz, and a cocktail bar – of course they knew also. But nothing private; no strict biographical facts.

She had been born, but it was only gossip said so, in Tasmania: her grandfather had been exported for some hanky-panky mid-Victorian scandal; malversation of trusts was it? But the story got no further the only time Isabella heard it than 'exported', for the husband of the communicative lady – Mrs Blencowe of the Grange – took exception, pedantically, to 'exported', said 'expatriated' was more like it, but not the right word, which he had on the tip of his tongue, but couldn't get at. And so the story dwindled away. Sometimes she referred to an uncle, a bishop. But he was thought to have been a colonial bishop only. They forgot and forgave very easily in the colonies. Also it was said her diamonds and rubies had been dug out of the earth with his own hands by a 'husband' who was not Ralph Manresa. Ralph, a Jew, got up to look the very spit and image of the landed gentry, supplied from directing City companies – that was certain – tons of money; and they had no child. But surely with George VI on the throne it was old fashioned, dowdy, savoured of moth-eaten furs, bugles, cameos and black-edged notepaper, to go ferreting into people's pasts?

'All I need,' said Mrs Manresa ogling Candish, as if he were a real man, not a stuffed man, 'is a corkscrew.' She had a bottle of champagne, but no corkscrew.

'Look, Bill,' she continued, cocking her thumb – she was opening the bottle – 'at the pictures. Didn't I tell you you'd have a treat?'

Vulgar she was in her gestures, in her whole person, over-sexed, over-dressed for a picnic. But what a desirable, at least valuable, quality it was – for everybody felt, directly she spoke, 'She's said it, she's done it, not I,' and could take advantage of the breach of decorum, of the fresh air that blew in, to follow like leaping dolphins in the wake of an ice-breaking vessel. Did she not restore to old Bartholomew his spice islands, his youth?

'I told him,' she went on, ogling Bart now, 'that he wouldn't look at our things' (of which they had heaps and mountains) 'after yours. And I promised him you'd show him the – the – ' here the champagne fizzed up and she insisted upon filling Bart's glass first. 'What is it all you learned gentlemen rave about? An arch? Norman? Saxon? Who's the last from school? Mrs Giles?'

She ogled Isabella now, conferring youth upon her; but always when she spoke to women, she veiled her eyes, for they, being conspirators, saw through it.

So with blow after blow, with champagne and ogling, she staked out her claim to be a wild child of nature, blowing into this – she did give one secret smile – sheltered harbour; which did make her smile, after London; yet it did, too, challenge London. For on she went to offer them a sample of her life; a few gobbets of gossip; mere trash; but she gave it for what it was worth; how last Tuesday she had been sitting next so and so; and she added, very casually a Christian name; then a nickname; and he'd said – for, as a mere nobody, they didn't mind what they said to her – and 'in strict confidence, I needn't tell you,' she told them. And they all pricked their ears. And then, with a gesture of her hands as if tossing overboard that odious crackling-under-the-pot London life – so – she exclaimed, 'There! . . . And what's the first thing I do when I come down here?' They had only come last night, driving through June lanes, alone with Bill it was understood, leaving London, suddenly become dissolute and dirty, to sit down to dinner. 'What do I do? Can I say it aloud? Is it permitted, Mrs Swithin? Yes, everything can be said in this house. I take off my stays' (here she pressed her hands to her sides – she was stout) 'and roll in the grass. Roll – you'll believe that . . . ' She laughed wholeheartedly. She had given up dealing with her figure and thus gained freedom.

'That's genuine,' Isa thought. Quite genuine. And her love of the country too. Often when Ralph Manresa had to stay in town she came down alone; wore an old garden hat; taught the village women *not* how to pickle and preserve; but how to weave frivolous baskets out of coloured straw. Pleasure's what they want she said. You often heard her, if you called, yodelling among the hollyhocks, 'Hoity te doity te ray do . . . '

A thorough good sort she was. She made old Bart feel young. Out of the corner of his eye, as he raised his glass, he saw a flash of white in the garden. Someone passing.

The scullery maid, before the plates came out, was cooling her cheeks by the lily pond.

There had always been lilies there, self-sown from wind-dropped seed, floating red and white on the green plates of their leaves. Water, for hundreds of years, had silted down into the hollow, and lay there four or five feet deep over a black cushion of mud. Under the thick plate of green water, glazed in their self-centred world, fish swam – gold, splashed with white, streaked with black or silver. Silently they manoeuvred in their water world, poised in the blue patch made by the sky, or shot silently to the edge where the grass, trembling, made a fringe of nodding shadow. On the water-pavement spiders printed their delicate feet. A grain fell and spiralled down; a petal fell, filled and sank. At that the fleet of boat-shaped bodies paused: poised; equipped; mailed; then with a waver of undulation off they flashed.

It was in that deep centre, in that black heart, that the lady had drowned herself. Ten years since the pool had been dredged and a thigh bone recovered. Alas, it was a sheep's, not a lady's. And sheep have no ghosts, for sheep have no souls. But, the servants insisted, they must have a ghost; the ghost must be a lady's; who had drowned herself for love. So none of them would walk by the lily pool at night, only now when the sun shone and the gentry still sat at table.

The flower petal sank; the maid returned to the kitchen; Bartholomew sipped his wine. Happy he felt as a boy; yet reckless as an old man; an unusual, an agreeable sensation. Fumbling in his mind for something to say to the adorable lady, he chose the first thing that came handy; the story of the sheep's thigh. 'Servants,' he said, 'must have their ghost.' Kitchen-maids must have their drowned lady.

'But so must I!' cried the wild child of nature, Mrs Manresa. She became, of a sudden, solemn as an owl. She *knew*, she said, pinching a bit of bread to make this emphatic, that Ralph, when he was at the war, couldn't have been killed without her seeing him – 'wherever I was, whatever I was doing,' she added, waving her hands so that the diamonds flashed in the sun.

'I don't feel that,' said Mrs Swithin, shaking her head.

'No,' Mrs Manresa laughed. 'You wouldn't. None of you would. You see I'm on a level with . . . ' she waited till Candish had retired, 'the servants. I'm nothing like so grown up as you are.'

She preened, approving her adolescence. Rightly or wrongly? A spring of feeling bubbled up through her mud. They had laid theirs with blocks of marble. Sheep's bones were sheep's bones to them, not the relics of the drowned Lady Ermyntrude.

'And which camp,' said Bartholomew turning to the unknown guest, 'd'you belong to? The grown, or the ungrown?'

Isabella opened her mouth, hoping that Dodge would open his, and so enable her to place him. But he sat staring. 'I beg your pardon, sir?' he said. They all looked at him. 'I was looking at the pictures.'

The picture looked at nobody. The picture drew them down the paths of silence.

Lucy broke it.

'Mrs Manresa, I'm going to ask you a favour – If it comes to a pinch this afternoon, will you sing?'

This afternoon? Mrs Manresa was aghast. Was it the pageant? She had never dreamt it was this afternoon. They would never have thrust themselves in – had they known it was this afternoon. And, of course, once more the chime pealed. Isa heard the first chime; and the second; and the third – If it was wet, it would be in the barn; if it was fine on the terrace. And which would it be, wet or fine? And they all looked out of the window. Then the door opened. Candish said Mr Giles had come. Mr Giles would be down in a moment.

*

Giles had come. He had seen the great silver-plated car at the door with the initials R. M. twisted so as to look at a distance like a coronet. Visitors, he had concluded, as he drew up behind; and had gone to his room to change. The ghost of convention rose to the surface, as a blush or a tear rises to the surface at the pressure of emotion; so the car touched his training. He must change. And he came into the dining-room looking like a cricketer, in flannels, wearing a blue coat with brass buttons; though he was enraged. Had he not read, in the morning paper, in the train, that sixteen men had been shot, others prisoned, just over there, across the gulf, in the flat land which divided them from the continent? Yet he changed. It was Aunt Lucy, waving her hand at him as he came in, who made him change. He hung his grievances on her, as one hangs a coat on a hook, instinctively. Aunt Lucy, foolish, free; always, since he had chosen, after leaving college, to take a job in the City, expressing her amazement, her amusement, at men who spent their lives, buying and selling – ploughs? glass beads was it? or stocks and shares? – to savages who wished most oddly – for were they not beautiful naked? – to dress and live like the English? A frivolous, a malignant statement hers was of a problem which, for he had no special gift, no capital, and had been furiously in love with his wife – he nodded to her across the table – had afflicted him for ten years. Given his choice, he would have chosen to farm. But he was not given his choice. So one thing led to another; and the conglomeration of things pressed you flat; held you fast, like a fish in water. So he came for the weekend, and changed.

'How d'you do?' he said all round; nodded to the unknown guest; took against him; and ate his fillet of sole.

He was the very type of all that Mrs Manresa adored. His hair curled; far from running away, as many chins did, his was firm; the nose straight, if short; the eyes, of course, with that hair, blue; and finally to make the type complete, there was something fierce, untamed, in the expression which incited her, even at forty-five, to furbish up her ancient batteries.

'He is my husband,' Isabella thought, as they nodded across the bunch of many-coloured flowers. 'The father of my children.' It worked, that old cliché; she felt pride; and affection; then pride again in herself, whom he had chosen. It was a shock to find, after the morning's look in the glass, and the arrow of desire shot through her last night by the gentleman farmer, how much she felt when he came in, not a dapper City gent, but a cricketer, of love; and of hate.

They had met first in Scotland, fishing – she from one rock, he from another. Her line had got tangled; she had given over, and had watched him with the stream rushing between his legs, casting, casting – until, like a thick ingot of silver bent in the middle, the salmon had leapt, had been caught, and she had loved him.

Bartholomew too loved him; and noted his anger – about what? But he remembered his guest. The family was not a family in the presence of strangers. He must, rather laboriously, tell them the story of the pictures at which the unknown guest had been looking when Giles came in.

'That,' he indicated the man with a horse, 'was my ancestor. He had a dog. The dog was famous. The dog has his place in history. He left it on record that he wished his dog to be buried with him.'

They looked at the picture.

'I always feel,' Lucy broke the silence, 'he's saying: "Paint my dog." '

'But what about the horse?' said Mrs Manresa.

'The horse,' said Bartholomew, putting on his glasses. He looked at the horse. The hindquarters were not satisfactory.

But William Dodge was still looking at the lady.

'Ah,' said Bartholomew who had bought that picture because he liked that picture, 'you're an artist.'

Dodge denied it, for the second time in half an hour, or so Isa noted.

What for did a good sort like the woman Manresa bring these half-breeds in her trail? Giles asked himself. And his silence made its contribution to talk – Dodge that is, shook his head. 'I like that picture.' That was all he could bring himself to say.

'And you're right,' said Bartholomew. 'A man – I forget his name – a man connected with some Institute,[26] a man who goes about giving advice, gratis, to descendants like ourselves, degenerate descendants, said . . . said . . . ' He paused. They all looked at the lady. But she looked over their heads, looking at nothing. She led them down green glades into the heart of silence.

'Said it was by Sir Joshua?' Mrs Manresa broke the silence abruptly.

'No, no,' William Dodge said hastily, but under his breath.

'Why's he afraid?' Isabella asked herself. A poor specimen he was; afraid to stick up for his own beliefs – just as she was afraid, of her husband. Didn't she write her poetry in a book bound like an account book lest Giles might suspect? She looked at Giles.

He had finished his fish; he had eaten quickly, not to keep them waiting. Now there was cherry tart. Mrs Manresa was counting the stones.

'Tinker, tailor, soldier, sailor, apothecary, ploughboy . . . that's me!' she cried, delighted to have it confirmed by the cherry stones that she was a wild child of nature.

'You believe,' said the old gentleman, courteously chaffing her, 'in that too?'

'Of course, of course I do!' she cried. Now she was on the rails again. Now she was a thorough good sort again. And they too were delighted; now they could follow in her wake and leave the silver and dun shades that led to the heart of silence.

'I had a father,' said Dodge beneath his breath to Isa who sat next him, 'who loved pictures.'

'Oh, I too!' she exclaimed. Flurriedly, disconnectedly, she explained. She used to stay when she was a child, when she had the whooping cough, with an uncle, a clergyman; who wore a skull cap; and never did anything; didn't even preach; but made up poems, walking in his garden, saying them aloud.

'People thought him mad,' she said. 'I didn't . . . '

She stopped.

'Tinker, tailor, soldier, sailor, apothecary, ploughboy . . . It appears,' said old Bartholomew, laying down his spoon, 'that I am a thief. Shall we take our coffee in the garden?' He rose.

Isa dragged her chair across the gravel, muttering: 'To what dark antre of the unvisited earth, or wind-brushed forest, shall we go now? Or spin from star to star and dance in the maze of the moon? Or . . . '

She held her deckchair at the wrong angle. The frame with the notches was upside down.

'Songs my uncle taught me?' said William Dodge, hearing her mutter. He unfolded the chair and fixed the bar into the right notch.

She flushed, as if she had spoken in an empty room and someone had stepped out from behind a curtain.

'Don't you, if you're doing something with your hands, talk nonsense?' she stumbled. But what did he do with his hands, the white, the fine, the shapely?

Giles went back to the house and brought more chairs and placed them in a semi-circle, so that the view might be shared, and the shelter of the old wall. For by some lucky chance a wall had been built continuing the house, it might be with the intention of adding another wing, on the raised ground in the sun. But funds were lacking; the plan was abandoned, and the wall remained, nothing but a wall. Later, another generation had planted fruit trees, which in time had spread their arms widely across the red-orange weathered brick. Mrs Sands called it a good year if she could make six pots of apricot jam from them – the fruit was never sweet enough for dessert. Perhaps three apricots were worth enclosing in muslin bags. But they were so beautiful, naked, with one flushed cheek, one green, that Mrs Swithin left them naked, and the wasps burrowed holes.

The ground sloped up so that, to quote Figgis's *Guide Book* (1833), 'it commanded a fine view of the surrounding country . . . The spire of Bolney Minster, Rough Norton woods, and on an eminence rather to the left, Hogben's Folly, so called because . . . '

The *Guide Book* still told the truth; 1833 was true in 1939. No house had been built; no town had sprung up. Hogben's Folly was still eminent; the very flat, field-parcelled land had changed only in this – the tractor had to some extent superseded the plough. The horse had gone; but the cow remained. If Figgis were here now, Figgis would have said the same. So they always said when in summer they sat there to drink coffee, if they had guests. When they were alone, they said nothing. They looked at the view; they looked at what they knew, to see if what they knew might perhaps be different today. Most days it was the same.

'That's what makes a view so sad,' said Mrs Swithin, lowering herself into the deckchair which Giles had brought her. 'And so beautiful. It'll be there,' she nodded at the strip of gauze laid upon the distant fields, 'when we're not.'

Giles nicked his chair into position with a jerk. Thus only could he show his irritation, his rage with old fogies who sat and looked at views over coffee and cream when the whole of Europe – over there – was bristling like . . . He had no command of metaphor. Only the ineffective word 'hedgehog' illustrated his vision of Europe, bristling with guns, poised with planes. At any moment guns would rake that land into furrows; planes splinter Bolney Minster into smithereens and blast the Folly. He, too, loved the view. And blamed Aunt Lucy, looking at views, instead of – doing what? What she had done was to marry a squire now dead; she had borne two children, one in Canada, the other, married, in Birmingham. His father, whom he loved, he exempted from censure; as for himself, one thing followed another; and so he sat, with old fogies, looking at views.

'Beautiful,' said Mrs Manresa, 'beautiful . . . ' she mumbled. She was lighting a cigarette. The breeze blew out her match. Giles hollowed his hand and lit another. She too was exempted – why, he could not say.

'Since you're interested in pictures,' said Bartholomew, turning to the silent guest, 'why, tell me, are we, as a race, so incurious, irresponsive and insensitive' – the champagne had given him a flow of unusual three-decker words – 'to that noble art, whereas, Mrs Manresa, if she'll allow me my old man's liberty, has her Shakespeare by heart?'

'Shakespeare by heart!' Mrs Manresa protested. She struck an attitude. ' "To be, or not to be, that is the question. Whether 'tis nobler . . . " Go on!' she nudged Giles, who sat next her.

' "Fade far away and quite forget what thou amongst the leaves hast never known . . . " ' Isa supplied the first words that came into her head by way of helping her husband out of his difficulty.

' "The weariness, the torture, and the fret . . . " ' William Dodge added, burying the end of his cigarette in a grave between two stones.

'There!' Bartholomew exclaimed, cocking his forefinger aloft. 'That proves it! What spring's touched, what secret drawer displays its treasures, if I say' – he raised more fingers – 'Reynolds! Constable! Crome!'[27]

'Why called "Old"?' Mrs Manresa thrust in.

'We haven't the words – we haven't the words,' Mrs Swithin protested. 'Behind the eyes; not on the lips; that's all.'

'Thoughts without words,' her brother mused. 'Can that be?'

'Quite beyond me!' cried Mrs Manresa, shaking her head. 'Much too clever! May I help myself? I know it's wrong. But I've reached the age – and the figure – when I do what I like.'

She took the little silver cream jug and let the smooth fluid curl luxuriously into her coffee, to which she added a shovel full of brown sugar candy. Sensuously, rhythmically, she stirred the mixture round and round.

'Take what you like! Help yourself!' Bartholomew exclaimed. He felt the champagne withdrawing and hastened, before the last trace of geniality was withdrawn, to make the most of it, as if he cast one last look into a lit-up chamber before going to bed.

The wild child, afloat once more on the tide of the old man's benignity, looked over her coffee cup at Giles, with whom she felt in conspiracy. A thread united them – visible, invisible, like those threads, now seen, now not, that unite trembling grass blades in autumn before the sun rises. She had met him once only, at a cricket match. And then had been spun between them an early-morning thread before the twigs and leaves of real friendship emerge. She looked before she drank. Looking was part of drinking. Why waste sensation, she seemed to ask, why waste a single drop that can be pressed out of this ripe, this melting, this adorable world? Then she drank. And the air round her became threaded with sensation. Bartholomew felt it; Giles felt it. Had he been a horse, the thin brown skin would have twitched, as if a fly had settled. Isabella twitched too. Jealousy, anger pierced her skin.

'And now,' said Mrs Manresa, putting down her cup, 'about this entertainment – this pageant, into which we've gone and butted' – she made it, too, seem ripe like the apricot into which the wasps were burrowing. 'Tell me, what's it to be?' She turned. 'Don't I hear?' She listened. She heard laughter, down among the bushes, where the terrace dipped to the bushes.

Beyond the lily pool the ground sank again, and in that dip of the ground, bushes and brambles had mobbed themselves together. It was always shady; sun-flecked in summer, dark and damp in winter. In the summer there were always butterflies; fritillaries darting through; red admirals feasting and floating; cabbage whites unambitiously fluttering round a bush, like muslin milkmaids, content to spend a life there. Butterfly catching, for generation after generation, began there; for Bartholomew and Lucy; for Giles; for George it had began only the day before yesterday, when, in his little green net, he had caught a cabbage white.

It was the very place for a dressing-room, just as, obviously, the terrace was the very place for a play.

'The very place!' Miss La Trobe had exclaimed the first time she came to call and was shown the grounds. It was a winter's day. The trees were leafless then.

'That's the place for a pageant, Mr Oliver!' she had exclaimed. 'Winding in and out between the trees . . . ' She waved her hand at the trees standing bare in the clear light of January.

'There the stage; here the audience; and down there among the bushes a perfect dressing-room for the actors.'

She was always all agog to get things up. But where did she spring from? With that name she wasn't presumably pure English. From the Channel Islands perhaps? Only her eyes and something about her always made Mrs Bingham suspect that she had Russian blood in her. 'Those deep-set eyes; that very square jaw' reminded her – not that she had been to Russia – of the Tartars. Rumour said that she had kept a tea shop at Winchester; that had failed. She had been an actress. That had failed. She had bought a four-roomed cottage and shared it with an actress. They had quarrelled. Very little was actually known about her. Outwardly she was swarthy, sturdy and thick set; strode about the fields in a smock frock; sometimes with a cigarette in her mouth; often with a whip in her hand; and used rather strong language – perhaps, then, she wasn't altogether a lady? At any rate, she had a passion for getting things up.

*

The laughter died away.

'Are they going to act?' Mrs Manresa asked.

'Act; dance; sing; a little bit of everything,' said Giles.

'Miss La Trobe is a lady of wonderful energy,' said Mrs Swithin.

'She makes everyone do something,' said Isabella.

'Our part,' said Bartholomew, 'is to be the audience. And a very important part too.'

'Also, we provide the tea,' said Mrs Swithin.

'Shan't we go and help?' said Mrs Manresa. 'Cut up bread and butter?'

'No, no,' said Mr Oliver. 'We are the audience.'

'One year we had *Gammer Gurton's Needle*,'[28] said Mrs Swithin. 'One year we wrote the play ourselves. The son of our blacksmith – Tony? Tommy? – had the loveliest voice. And Elsie at the Crossways – how she mimicked! Took us all off. Bart; Giles; Old Flimsy – that's me. People are gifted – very. The question is – how to bring it out? That's where she's so clever – Miss La Trobe. Of course, there's the whole of English literature to choose from. But how can one choose? Often on a wet day I begin counting up; what I've read; what I haven't read.'

'And leaving books on the floor,' said her brother. 'Like the pig in the story; or was it a donkey?'

She laughed, tapping him lightly on the knee.

'The donkey who couldn't choose between hay and turnips and so starved,' Isabella explained, interposing – anything – between her aunt and her husband, who hated this kind of talk this afternoon. Books open; no conclusion come to; and he sitting in the audience.

'We remain seated' – 'We are the audience.' Words this afternoon ceased to lie flat in the sentence. They rose, became menacing and shook their fists at you. This afternoon he wasn't Giles Oliver come to see the villagers act their annual pageant; manacled to a rock he was, and forced passively to behold indescribable horror. His face showed it; and Isa, not knowing what to say, abruptly, half purposely, knocked over a coffee cup.

William Dodge caught it as it fell. He held it for a moment. He turned it. From the faint blue mark, as of crossed daggers, in the glaze at the bottom he knew that it was English, made perhaps at Nottingham; date about 1760. His expression, considering the daggers, coming to this conclusion, gave Giles another peg on which to hang his rage as one hangs a coat on a peg, conveniently. A toady; a lickspittle; not a downright plain man of his senses but a teaser and twitcher; a fingerer of sensations; picking and choosing; dillying and dallying; not a man to have straightforward love for a woman – his head was close to Isa's head – but simply a — At this word, which he could not speak in public, he pursed his lips; and the signet-ring on his little finger looked redder, for the flesh next it whitened as he gripped the arm of his chair.

'Oh what fun!' cried Mrs Manresa in her fluty voice. 'A little bit of everything. A song; a dance; then a play acted by the villagers themselves. Only,' here she turned with her head on one side to Isabella, 'I'm sure *she's* written it. Haven't you, Mrs Giles?'

Isa flushed and denied it.

'For myself,' Mrs Manresa continued, 'speaking plainly, I can't put two words together. I don't know how it is – such a chatterbox as I am with my tongue, once I hold a pen – ' She made a face, screwed her fingers as if she held a pen in them. But the pen she held thus on the little table absolutely refused to move. 'And my handwriting – so huge – so clumsy – ' She made another face and dropped the invisible pen.

Very delicately William Dodge set the cup in its saucer. 'Now *he*,' said Mrs Manresa, as if referring to the delicacy with which he did this, and imputing to him the same skill in writing, 'writes beautifully. Every letter perfectly formed.'

Again they all looked at him. Instantly he put his hands in his pockets.

Isabella guessed the word that Giles had not spoken. Well, was it wrong if he was that word? Why judge each other? Do we know each other? Not here, not now. But somewhere, this cloud, this crust, this doubt, this dust – She waited for a rhyme, it failed her; but somewhere surely one sun would shine and all, without a doubt, would be clear.

She started. Again, sounds of laughter reached her.

'I think I hear them,' she said. 'They're getting ready. They're dressing up in the bushes.'

Miss La Trobe was pacing to and fro between the leaning birch trees. One hand was deep stuck in her jacket pocket; the other held a foolscap sheet. She was reading what was written there. She had the look of a commander pacing his deck. The leaning graceful trees with black bracelets circling the silver bark were distant about a ship's length.

Wet would it be, or fine? Out came the sun; and, shading her eyes in the attitude proper to an admiral on his quarter-deck, she decided to risk the engagement out of doors. Doubts were over. All stage properties, she commanded, must be moved from the barn to the bushes. It was done. And the actors, while she paced, taking all responsibility and plumping for fine not wet, dressed among the brambles. Hence the laughter.

The clothes were strewn on the grass. Cardboard crowns, swords made of silver paper, turbans that were sixpenny dishcloths, lay on the grass or were flung on the bushes. There were pools of red and purple in the shade; flashes of silver in the sun. The dresses attracted the butterflies. Red and silver, blue and yellow gave off warmth and sweetness. Red admirals gluttonously absorbed richness from dishcloths, cabbage whites drank icy coolness from silver paper. Flitting, tasting, returning, they sampled the colours.

Miss La Trobe stopped her pacing and surveyed the scene. 'It has the makings . . . ' she murmured. For another play always lay behind the play she had just written. Shading her eyes, she looked. The butterflies circling; the light changing; the children leaping; the mothers laughing – 'No, I don't get it,' she muttered and resumed her pacing.

'Bossy' they called her privately, just as they called Mrs Swithin 'Flimsy'. Her abrupt manner and stocky figure; her thick ankles and sturdy shoes; her rapid decisions barked out in guttural accents – all this 'got their goat'. No one liked to be ordered about singly. But in little troops they appealed to her. Someone must lead. Then too they could put the blame on her. Suppose it poured?

'Miss La Trobe!' they hailed her now. 'What's the idea about this?' She stopped. David and Iris each had a hand on the gramophone. It must be hidden; yet must be close enough to the audience to be heard. Well, hadn't she given orders? Where were the hurdles covered in leaves? Fetch them. Mr Streatfield had said he would see to it. Where was Mr Streatfield? No clergyman was visible. Perhaps he's in the barn? 'Tommy, cut along and fetch him.' 'Tommy's wanted in the first scene.' 'Beryl then . . . ' The mothers disputed. One child had been chosen; another not. Fair hair was unjustly preferred to dark. Mrs Ebury had forbidden Fanny to act because of the nettle-rash. There was another name in the village for nettle-rash.

Mrs Ball's cottage was not what you might call clean. In the last war Mrs Ball lived with another man while her husband was in the trenches. All this Miss La Trobe knew, but refused to be mixed up in it. She splashed into the fine mesh like a great stone into the lily pool. The criss-cross was shattered. Only the roots beneath the water were of use to her. Vanity, for example, made them all malleable. The boys wanted the big parts; the girls wanted the fine clothes. Expenses had to be kept down. Ten pounds was the limit. Thus conventions were outraged. Swathed in conventions, they couldn't see, as she could, that a dishcloth wound round a head in the open looked much richer than real silk. So they squabbled; but she kept out of it. Waiting for Mr Streatfield, she paced between the birch trees.

The other trees were magnificently straight. They were not too regular; but regular enough to suggest columns in a church; in a church without a roof; in an open-air cathedral, a place where swallows darting seemed, by the regularity of the trees, to make a pattern, dancing, like the Russians, only not to music but to the unheard rhythm of their own wild hearts.

The laughter died away.

'We must possess our souls in patience,' said Mrs Manresa again. 'Or could we help?' she suggested, glancing over her shoulder, 'with those chairs?'

Candish, a gardener and a maid were all bringing chairs – for the audience. There was nothing for the audience to do. Mrs Manresa suppressed a yawn. They were silent. They stared at the view, as if something might happen in one of those fields to relieve them of the intolerable burden of sitting silent, doing nothing, in company. Their minds and bodies were too close, yet not close enough. We aren't free, each one of them felt separately, to feel or think separately, nor yet to fall asleep. We're too close; but not close enough. So they fidgeted.

The heat had increased. The clouds had vanished. All was sun now. The view laid bare by the sun was flattened, silenced, stilled. The cows were motionless; the brick wall, no longer sheltering, beat back grains of heat. Old Mr Oliver sighed profoundly. His head jerked; his hand fell. It fell within an inch of the dog's head on the grass by his side. Then up he jerked it again on to his knee.

Giles glared. With his hands bound tight round his knees he stared at the flat fields. Staring, glaring, he sat silent.

Isabella felt prisoned. Through the bars of the prison, through the sleep haze that deflected them, blunt arrows bruised her; of love, then of hate. Through other people's bodies she felt neither love nor hate distinctly. Most consciously she felt – she had drunk sweet wine at luncheon – a desire for water. 'A beaker of cold water, a beaker of cold water,' she repeated, and saw water surrounded by walls of shining glass.

Mrs Manresa longed to relax and curl in a corner with a cushion, a picture paper and a bag of sweets.

Mrs Swithin and William surveyed the view aloofly, and with detachment.

How tempting, how very tempting, to let the view triumph; to reflect its ripple; to let their own minds ripple; to let outlines elongate and pitch over – so – with a sudden jerk.

Mrs Manresa yielded, pitched, plunged, then pulled herself up.

'What a view!' she exclaimed, pretending to dust the ashes of her cigarette, but in truth concealing her yawn. Then she sighed, pretending to express not her own drowsiness, but something connected with what she felt about views.

Nobody answered her. The flat fields glared green yellow, blue yellow, red yellow, then blue again. The repetition was senseless, hideous, stupefying.

'Then,' said Mrs Swithin, in a low voice, as if the exact moment for speech had come, as if she had promised, and it was time to fulfil her promise, 'come, come and I'll show you the house.'

She addressed no one in particular. But William Dodge knew she meant him. He rose with a jerk, like a toy suddenly pulled straight by a string.

'What energy!' Mrs Manresa half sighed, half yawned.

'Have I the courage to go too?' Isabella asked herself. They were going; above all things, she desired cold water, a beaker of cold water; but desire petered out, suppressed by the leaden duty she owed to others. She watched them go – Mrs Swithin tottering yet tripping; and Dodge unfurled and straightened, as he strode beside her along the blazing tiles under the hot wall, till they reached the shade of the house.

A matchbox fell – Bartholomew's. His fingers had loosed it; he had dropped it. He gave up the game; he couldn't be bothered. With his head on one side, his hand dangling above the dog's head he slept; he snored.

Mrs Swithin paused for a moment in the hall among the gilt-clawed tables.

'This,' she said, 'is the staircase. And now – up we go.'

She went up, two stairs ahead of her guest. Lengths of yellow satin unfurled themselves on a cracked canvas as they mounted.

'Not an ancestress,' said Mrs Swithin, as they came level with the head in the picture. 'But we claim her because we've known her – Oh, ever so many years. Who was she?' she gazed. 'Who painted her?' She shook her head. She looked lit up, as if for a banquet, with the sun pouring over her.

'But I like her best in the moonlight,' Mrs Swithin reflected, and mounted more stairs.

She panted slightly, going upstairs. Then she ran her hand over the sunk books in the wall on the landing, as if they were pan pipes.

'Here are the poets from whom we descend by way of the mind,

Mr . . . ' she murmured. She had forgotten his name. Yet she had singled him out.

'My brother says, they built the house north for shelter, not south for sun. So they're damp in the winter.' She paused. 'And now what comes next?'

She stopped. There was a door.

'The morning room.' She opened the door. 'Where my mother received her guests.'

Two chairs faced each other on either side of a fine fluted mantelpiece. He looked over her shoulder.

She shut the door.

'Now up, now up again.' Again they mounted. 'Up and up they went,' she panted, seeing, it seemed, an invisible procession, 'up and up to bed. A bishop; a traveller – I've forgotten even their names. I ignore. I forget.'

She stopped at a window in the passage and held back the curtain. Beneath was the garden, bathed in sun. The grass was sleek and shining. Three white pigeons were flirting and tiptoeing as ornate as ladies in ball dresses. Their elegant bodies swayed as they minced with tiny steps on their little pink feet upon the grass. Suddenly, up they rose in a flutter, circled, and flew away.

'Now,' she said, 'for the bedrooms.' She tapped twice very distinctly on a door. With her head on one side, she listened. 'One never knows,' she murmured, 'if there's somebody there.' Then she flung open the door.

He half expected to see somebody there, naked, or half dressed, or knelt in prayer. But the room was empty. The room was tidy as a pin, not slept in for months, a spare room. Candles stood on the dressing-table. The counterpane was straight. Mrs Swithin stopped by the bed.

'Here,' she said, 'yes, here,' she tapped the counterpane, 'I was born. In this bed.'

Her voice died away. She sank down on the edge of the bed. She was tired, no doubt, by the stairs, by the heat.

'But we have other lives, I think, I hope,' she murmured. 'We live in others, Mr . . . We live in things.'

She spoke simply. She spoke with an effort. She spoke as if she must overcome her tiredness out of charity towards a stranger, a guest. She had forgotten his name. Twice she had said 'Mr' and stopped.

The furniture was mid-Victorian, bought at Maples,[29] perhaps, in the forties. The carpet was covered with small purple dots. And a white circle marked the place where the slop pail had stood by the washstand.

Could he say 'I'm William'? He wished to. Old and frail she had climbed the stairs. She had spoken her thoughts, ignoring – not caring – if he thought her, as he had, inconsequent, sentimental, foolish. She had lent him a hand to help him up a steep place. She had guessed his trouble. Sitting on the bed he heard her sing, swinging her little legs, 'Come and see my sea weeds, come and see my sea shells, come and see my dicky bird hop upon its perch' – an old child's nursery rhyme to help a child. Standing by the cupboard in the corner he saw her reflected in the glass. Cut off from their bodies, their eyes smiled, their bodiless eyes, at their eyes in the glass.

Then she slipped off the bed.

'Now,' she said, 'what comes next?' and pattered down the corridor. A door stood open. Everyone was out in the garden. The room was like a ship deserted by its crew. The children had been playing – there was a spotted horse in the middle of the carpet. The nurse had been sewing – there was a piece of linen on the table. The baby had been in the cot. The cot was empty.

'The nursery,' said Mrs Swithin.

Words raised themselves and became symbolical. 'The cradle of our race,' she seemed to say.

Dodge crossed to the fireplace and looked at the Newfoundland dog in the *Christmas Annual* that was pinned to the wall. The room smelt warm and sweet: of clothes drying; of milk; of biscuits and warm water. 'Good Friends' the picture was called. A rushing sound came in through the open door. He turned. The old woman had wandered out into the passage and leant against the window.

He left the door open for the crew to come back to and joined her.

Down in the courtyard beneath the window cars were assembling. Their narrow black roofs were laid together like the blocks of a floor. Chauffeurs were jumping down; here old ladies gingerly advanced black legs with silver-buckled shoes; old men striped trousers. Young men in shorts leapt out on one side; girls with skin-coloured legs on the other. There was a purring and a churning of the yellow gravel. The audience was assembling. But they, looking down from the window, were truants, detached. Together they leant half out of the window.

And then a breeze blew and all the muslin blinds fluttered out, as if some majestic goddess, rising from her throne among her peers, had tossed her amber-coloured raiment, and the other gods, seeing her rise and go, laughed, and their laughter floated her on.

Mrs Swithin put her hands to her hair, for the breeze had ruffled it.

'Mr . . . ' she began.

'I'm William,' he interrupted.

At that she smiled a ravishing girl's smile, as if the wind had warmed the wintry blue in her eyes to amber.

'I took you,' she apologised, 'away from your friends, William, because I felt wound tight here . . . ' She touched her bony forehead upon which a blue vein wriggled like a blue worm. But her eyes in their caves of bone were still lambent. He saw her eyes only. And he wished to kneel before her, to kiss her hand, and to say: 'At school they held me under a bucket of dirty water, Mrs Swithin; when I looked up, the world was dirty, Mrs Swithin; so I married; but my child's not my child, Mrs Swithin. I'm a half-man, Mrs Swithin; a flickering, mind-divided little snake in the grass, Mrs Swithin; as Giles saw; but you've healed me . . . ' So he wished to say; but said nothing; and the breeze went lolloping along the corridors, blowing the blinds out.

Once more he looked and she looked down on to the yellow gravel that made a crescent round the door. Pendant from her chain her cross swung as she leant out and the sun struck it. How could she weight herself down by that sleek symbol? How stamp herself, so volatile, so vagrant, with that image? As he looked at it, they were truants no more. The purring of the wheels became vocal. 'Hurry, hurry, hurry,' it seemed to say, 'or you'll be late. Hurry, hurry, hurry, or the best seats'll be taken.'

'Oh,' cried Mrs Swithin, 'there's Mr Streatfield!' And they saw a clergyman, a strapping clergyman, carrying a hurdle, a leafy hurdle. He was striding through the cars with the air of a person of authority, who is awaited, expected, and now comes.

'Is it time,' said Mrs Swithin, 'to go and join – ' She left the sentence unfinished, as if she were of two minds, and they fluttered to right and to left, like pigeons rising from the grass.

The audience was assembling. They came streaming along the paths and spreading across the lawn. Some were old; some were in the prime of life. There were children among them. Among them, as Mr Figgis might have observed, were representatives of our most respected families – the Dyces of Denton; the Wickhams of Owlswick; and so on. Some had been there for centuries, never selling an acre. On the other hand there were newcomers, the Manresas, bringing the old houses up to date, adding bathrooms. And a scatter of odds and ends, like Cobbet of Cobbs Corner, retired, it was understood, on a pension from a tea plantation. Not an asset. He did his own housework and dug in his garden. The building of a car factory and of an aerodrome in the neighbourhood had attracted a number of unattached floating residents. Also there was Mr Page, the reporter, representing the local paper.

Roughly speaking, however, had Figgis been there in person and called a roll call, half the ladies and gentlemen present would have said: '*Adsum*; I'm here, in place of my grandfather or great-grandfather,' as the case might be. At this very moment, half-past three on a June day in 1939, they greeted each other, and as they took their seats, finding if possible a seat next one another, they said: 'That hideous new house at Pyes Corner! What an eyesore! And those bungalows! – have you seen 'em?'

Again, had Figgis called the names of the villagers, they too would have answered. Mrs Sands was born Iliffe; Candish's mother was one of the Perrys. The green mounds in the churchyard had been cast up by their molings, which for centuries had made the earth friable. True, there were absentees when Mr Streatfield called his roll call in the church. The motor bike, the motor bus and the movies – when Mr Streatfield called his roll call, he laid the blame on them.

Rows of chairs, deckchairs, gilt chairs, hired cane chairs and indigenous garden seats had been drawn up on the terrace. There were plenty of seats for everybody. But some preferred to sit on the ground. Certainly Miss La Trobe had spoken the truth when she said: 'The very place for a pageant!' The lawn was as flat as the floor of a theatre. The terrace, rising, made a natural stage. The trees barred the stage like pillars. And the human figure was seen to great advantage against a background of sky. As for the weather, it was turning out, against all expectation, a very fine day. A perfect summer afternoon.

'What luck!' Mrs Carter was saying. 'Last year . . . ' Then the play began. Was it, or was it not, the play? Chuff, chuff, chuff sounded from the bushes. It was the noise a machine makes when something has gone wrong. Some sat down hastily; others stopped talking guiltily. All looked at the bushes. For the stage was empty. Chuff, chuff, chuff, the machine buzzed in the bushes. While they looked apprehensively and some finished their sentences, a small girl, like a rosebud in pink, advanced, took her stand on a mat behind a conch hung with leaves, and piped:

Gentles and simples, I address you all . . .

So it was the play then. Or was it the prologue?

Come hither for our festival (she continued);

This is a pageant, all may see,

Drawn from our island history.

　England am I . . .

'She's England,' they whispered. 'It's begun. The prologue,' they added, looking down at the programme.

'*England am I,*' she piped again; and stopped.

She had forgotten her lines.

'Hear! Hear!' said an old man in a white waistcoat briskly. 'Bravo! Bravo!'

'Blast 'em!' cursed Miss La Trobe, hidden behind the tree. She looked along the front row. They glared as if they were exposed to a frost that nipped them and fixed them all at the same level. Only Bond the cowman looked fluid and natural.

'Music!' she signalled. 'Music!' But the machine continued: Chuff, chuff, chuff.

'*A child new born . . .*' she prompted.

'*A child new born,*' Phyllis Jones continued,

Sprung from the sea,
Whose billows blown by mighty storm
Cut off from France and Germany
This isle.

She glanced back over her shoulder. Chuff, chuff, chuff, the machine buzzed. A long line of villagers in shirts made of sacking began passing in and out in single file behind her between the trees. They were singing, but not a word reached the audience.

England am I, Phyllis Jones continued, facing the audience,

Now weak and small,
A child, as all may see . . .

Her words peppered the audience as with a shower of hard little stones. Mrs Manresa in the very centre smiled; but she felt as if her skin cracked when she smiled. There was a vast vacancy between her, the singing villagers and the piping child.

Chuff, chuff, chuff went the machine like a corn-cutter on a hot day. The villagers were singing, but half their words were blown away.

Cutting the roads . . . up to the hilltop . . . we climbed. Down in the valley . . . sow, wild boar, hog, rhinoceros, reindeer . . . Dug ourselves into the hilltop . . . Ground roots between stones . . . Ground corn . . . till we too . . . lay underg–r–o–u–n–d . . .

The words petered away. Chuff, chuff, chuff, the machine ticked. Then at last the machine ground out a tune!

Armed against fate,
The valiant Rhoderick,
Armed and valiant,
Bold and blatant,
Firm, elatant,
See the warriors – here they come . . .

The pompous popular tune brayed and blared. Miss La Trobe watched from behind the tree. Muscles loosened; ice cracked. The stout lady in the middle began to beat time with her hand on her chair. Mrs Manresa was humming:

My home is at Windsor, close to the Inn.

Royal George is the name of the pub.

And boys you'll believe me,

I don't want no asking . . .

She was afloat on the stream of the melody. Radiating royalty, complacency, good humour, the wild child was queen of the festival. The play had begun.

But there was an interruption. 'Oh,' Miss La Trobe growled behind her tree, 'the torture of these interruptions!'

'Sorry I'm so late,' said Mrs Swithin. She pushed her way through the chairs to a seat beside her brother. 'What's it all about? I've missed the prologue. England? That little girl? Now she's gone . . . '

Phyllis had slipped off her mat.

'And who's this?' asked Mrs Swithin.

It was Hilda, the carpenter's daughter. She now stood where England had stood.

'*Oh, England's grown* . . . ' Miss La Trobe prompted her.

'*Oh, England's grown a girl now,*' Hilda sang out

('What a lovely voice!' someone exclaimed),

With roses in her hair,

Wild roses, red roses,

She roams the lanes and chooses

A garland for her hair.

'A cushion? Thank you so much,' said Mrs Swithin, stuffing the cushion behind her back. Then she leant forward.

'That's England in the time of Chaucer, I take it. She's been maying, nutting. She has flowers in her hair . . . But those passing behind her – ' she pointed. 'The Canterbury pilgrims? Look!'

All the time the villagers were passing in and out between the trees. They were singing; but only a word or two was audible ' . . . *wore ruts in the grass* . . . *built the house in the lane* . . . ' The wind blew away the connecting words of their chant, and then, as they reached the tree at the end, they sang: '*To the shrine of the saint* . . . *to the tomb* . . . *lovers* . . . *believers* . . . *we come* . . . '

They grouped themselves together.

Then there was a rustle and an interruption. Chairs were drawn back. Isa looked behind her. Mr and Mrs Rupert Haines, detained by a breakdown on the road, had arrived. He was sitting to the right, several rows back, the man in grey.

Meanwhile the pilgrims, having done their homage to the tomb, were, it appeared, tossing hay on their rakes.

> *I kissed a girl and let her go,*
> *Another did I tumble*
> *In the straw and in the hay . . .*

– that was what they were singing, as they scooped and tossed the invisible hay, when she looked round again.

'Scenes from English history,' Mrs Manresa explained to Mrs Swithin. She spoke in a loud cheerful voice, as if the old lady were deaf. 'Merrie England.'

She clapped energetically.

The singers scampered away into the bushes. The tune stopped. Chuff, chuff, chuff, the machine ticked. Mrs Manresa looked at her programme. It would take till midnight unless they skipped. Early Briton; Plantagenets; Tudors; Stuarts – she ticked them off, but probably she had forgotten a reign or two.

'Ambitious, ain't it?' she said to Bartholomew, while they waited. Chuff, chuff, chuff went the machine. Could they talk? Could they move? No, for the play was going on. Yet the stage was empty; only the cows moved in the meadows; only the tick of the gramophone needle was heard. The tick, tick, tick seemed to hold them together, tranced. Nothing whatsoever appeared on the stage.

'I'd no notion we looked so nice,' Mrs Swithin whispered to William. Hadn't she? The children; the pilgrims; behind the pilgrims the trees, and behind them the fields – the beauty of the visible world took his breath away. Tick, tick, tick, the machine continued.

'Marking time,' said old Oliver beneath his breath.

'Which don't exist for us,' Lucy murmured. 'We've only the present.'

'Isn't that enough?' William asked himself. Beauty – isn't that enough? But here Isa fidgetted. Her bare brown arms went nervously to her head. She half turned in her seat. 'No, not for us, who've the future,' she seemed to say. The future disturbing our present. Who was she looking for? William, turning, following her eyes, saw only a man in grey.

The ticking stopped. A dance tune was put on the machine. In time to it, Isa hummed: 'What do I ask? To fly away, from night and day, and issue where – no partings are – but eye meets eye – and . . . Oh,' she cried aloud, 'look at her!'

Everyone was clapping and laughing. From behind the bushes issued Queen Elizabeth – Eliza Clark, licensed to sell tobacco. Could she be Mrs Clark of the village shop? She was splendidly made up. Her head, pearl-hung, rose from a vast ruff. Shiny satins draped her. Sixpenny brooches glared like cats' eyes and tigers' eyes; pearls looked down; her cape was made of cloth of silver – in fact swabs used to scour saucepans. She looked the age in person. And when she mounted the soap box in the centre, representing perhaps a rock in the ocean, her size made her appear gigantic. She could reach a flitch of bacon or haul a tub of oil with one sweep of her arm in the shop. For a moment she stood there, eminent, dominant, on the soap box with the blue and sailing clouds behind her. The breeze had risen.

The Queen of this great land . . .

– those were the first words that could be heard above the roar of laughter and applause.

Mistress of ships and bearded men (she bawled),
Hawkins, Frobisher, Drake,[30]
Tumbling their oranges, ingots of silver,
Cargoes of diamonds, ducats of gold,
Down on the jetty, there in the west land –
(she pointed her fist at the blazing blue sky)
Mistress of pinnacles, spires and palaces –
(her arm swept towards the house)
For me Shakespeare sang –
(a cow mooed; a bird twittered)
The throstle, the mavis (she continued)
In the green wood, the wild wood,
Carolled and sang, praising England, the Queen.
Then there was heard too
On granite and cobble
From Windsor to Oxford
Loud laughter, low laughter
Of warrior and lover,
The fighter, the singer.
The ashen-haired babe
(she stretched out her swarthy, muscular arm)
Stretched his arm in contentment
As home from the Isles came
The seafaring men . . .

Here the wind gave a tug at her head dress. Loops of pearls made it top-heavy. She had to steady the ruffle which threatened to blow away.

'Laughter, loud laughter,' Giles muttered. The tune on the gramophone reeled from side to side as if drunk with merriment. Mrs Manresa began beating her foot and humming in time to it.

'Bravo! Bravo!' she cried. 'There's life in the old dog yet!' And she trolloped out the words of the song with an abandonment which, if vulgar, was a great help to the Elizabethan age. For the ruff had become unpinned and great Eliza had forgotten her lines. But the audience laughed so loud that it did not matter.

'I fear I am not in my perfect mind,' Giles muttered to the same tune. Words came to the surface – he remembered ' "a stricken deer in whose lean flank the world's harsh scorn has struck its thorn . . . Exiled from its festival, the music turned ironical . . . A churchyard haunter at whom the owl hoots and the ivy mocks tap-tap-tapping on the pane . . . For they are dead, and I . . . I . . . I," ' he repeated, forgetting the words, and glaring at his Aunt Lucy who sat craned forward, her mouth gaping, and her bony little hands clapping.

What were they laughing at?

At Albert, the village idiot, apparently. There was no need to dress him up. There he came, acting his part to perfection. He came ambling across the grass, mopping and mowing.

I know where the tit nests, he began –
In the hedgerow. I know, I know –
What don't I know?
All your secrets, ladies,
And yours too, gentlemen . . .

He skipped along the front row of the audience, leering at each in turn. Now he was picking and plucking at Great Eliza's skirts. She cuffed him on the ear. He tweaked her back. He was enjoying himself immensely.

'Albert having the time of his life,' Bartholomew muttered.

'Hope he don't have a fit,' Lucy murmured.

'*I know . . . I know . . .* ' Albert tittered, skipping round the soap box.

'The village idiot,' whispered a stout black lady – Mrs Elmhurst – who came from a village ten miles distant where they, too, had an idiot. It wasn't nice. Suppose he suddenly did something dreadful? There he was pinching the queen's skirts. She half covered her eyes, in case he did do – something dreadful.

Hoppety, jiggety, Albert resumed,
In at the window, out at the door,
What does the little bird hear? (he whistled on his fingers).

And see! There's a mouse . . . (he made as if chasing it through the grass).

Now the clock strikes! (he stood erect, puffing out his cheeks as if he were blowing a dandelion clock)

One, two, three, four . . .

And off he skipped, as if his turn was over.

'Glad that's over,' said Mrs Elmhurst, uncovering her face. 'Now what comes next? A tableau. . . ?'

For helpers, issuing swiftly from the bushes, carrying hurdles, had enclosed the queen's throne with screens papered to represent walls. They had strewn the ground with rushes. And the pilgrims who had continued their march and their chant in the background, now gathered round the figure of Eliza on her soap box as if to form the audience at a play.

Were they about to act a play in the presence of Queen Elizabeth? Was this, perhaps, the Globe Theatre?[31]

'What does the programme say?' Mrs Herbert Winthrop asked, raising her lorgnettes. She mumbled through the blurred carbon sheet. Yes; it was a scene from a play.

'About a false duke; and a princess disguised as a boy; then the long lost heir turns out to be the beggar, because of a mole on his cheek; and Carinthia – that's the duke's daughter, only she's been lost in a cave – falls in love with Ferdinando who had been put into a basket as a baby by an aged crone. And they marry. That's I think what happens,' she said, looking up from the programme.

'*Play out the play*,' great Eliza commanded.

An aged crone tottered forward.

('Mrs Otter of the End House,' someone murmured.)

She sat herself on a packing case, and made motions, plucking her dishevelled locks and rocking herself from side to side as if she were an aged beldame in a chimney corner.

('The crone, who saved the rightful heir,' Mrs Winthrop explained.)

'Twas a winter's night (she croaked out),

I mind me that, I to whom all's one now, summer or winter.

You say the sun shines? I believe you, sir . . .

'*Oh, but it's winter, and the fog's abroad,*'

All's one to Elsbeth, summer or winter,

By the fireside, in the chimney corner, telling her beads.

I've cause to tell 'em.

Each bead (she held a bead between thumb and finger)

A crime!

'Twas a winter's night, before cockcrow,

Yet the cock did crow ere he left me –

The man with a hood on his face, and the bloody hands,

And the babe in the basket.

'*Tee hee,*' *he mewed, as who should say,* '*I want my toy.*'

Poor witling!
'Tee hee, tee hee!' I could not slay him!
For that, Mary in heaven forgive me
The sins I've sinned before cockcrow!
Down to the creek i' the dawn I slipped,
Where the gull haunts and the heron stands
Like a stake on the edge of the marshes . . .
Who's here?

(Three young men swaggered on to the stage and accosted her.)

'Are you come to torture me, sirs?
There is little blood in this arm

(she extended her skinny forearm from her ragged shift),

Saints in heaven preserve me!

She bawled. They bawled. All together they bawled, and so loud that it was difficult to make out what they were saying: apparently it was: *Did she remember concealing a child in a cradle among the rushes some twenty years previously? A babe in a basket, crone! A babe in a basket?* they bawled. *The wind howls and the bittern shrieks*, she replied.

'There is little blood in my arm,' Isabella repeated.

That was all she heard. There was such a medley of things going on, what with the beldame's deafness, the bawling of the youths and the confusion of the plot, that she could make nothing of it.

Did the plot matter? She shifted and looked over her right shoulder. The plot was only there to beget emotion. There were only two emotions: love and hate. There was no need to puzzle out the plot. Perhaps Miss La Trobe meant that when she cut this knot in the centre?

Don't bother about the plot: the plot's nothing.

But what was happening? The prince had come.

Plucking up his sleeve, the beldame recognised the mole; and, staggering back in her chair, shrieked:

My child! My child!

Recognition followed. The young prince (Albert Perry) was almost smothered in the withered arms of the beldame. Then suddenly he started apart.

'Look where she comes!' he cried.

They all looked where she came – Sylvia Edwards in white satin.

Who came? Isa looked. The nightingale's song? The pearl in night's black ear? Love embodied.

All arms were raised; all faces stared.

'Hail, sweet Carinthia!' said the prince, sweeping his hat off.

And she to him, raising her eyes:

'*My love! My lord!*'

'It was enough. Enough. Enough,' Isa repeated.

All else was verbiage, repetition.

The beldame meanwhile, because that was enough, had sunk back on her chair, the beads dangling from her fingers.

'*Look to the beldame there – old Elsbeth's sick!*'

(They crowded round her.)

Dead, sirs!

She fell back lifeless. The crowd drew away. *Peace, let her pass. She to whom all's one now, summer or winter.*

Peace was the third emotion. Love. Hate. Peace. Three emotions made the ply of human life. Now the priest, whose cotton-wool moustache confused his utterance, stepped forward and pronounced benediction.

From the distaff of life's tangled skein, unloose her hands.

(They unloosed her hands.)

Of her frailty, let nothing now remembered be.

Call for the robin redbreast and the wren.

And roses fall your crimson pall.

(Petals were strewn from wicker baskets.)

Cover the corpse. Sleep well.

(They covered the corpse.)

On you, fair sirs (he turned to the happy couple),

Let heaven rain benediction!

Haste ere the envying sun

Night's curtain hath undone. Let music sound

And the free air of heaven waft you to your slumber!

Lead on the dance!

The gramophone blared. Dukes, priests, shepherds, pilgrims and serving men took hands and danced. The idiot scampered in and out. Hands joined, heads knocking, they danced round the majestic figure of the Elizabethan age personified by Mrs Clark, licensed to sell tobacco, on her soap box.

It was a mellay; a medley; an entrancing spectacle (to William) of dappled light and shade on half-clothed, fantastically coloured, leaping, jerking, swinging legs and arms. He clapped till his palms stung.

Mrs Manresa applauded loudly. Somehow she was the queen; and he (Giles) was the surly hero.

'Bravo! Bravo!' she cried, and her enthusiasm made the surly hero squirm on his seat. Then the great lady in the bath chair, the lady whose marriage with the local peer had obliterated in his trashy title a name that had been a name when there were brambles and briars where the church now stood – so indigenous was she that even her body, crippled by arthritis, resembled an uncouth, nocturnal animal, now nearly extinct – clapped and laughed loud – the sudden laughter of a startled jay.

'Ha, ha, ha!' she laughed and clutched the arms of her chair with ungloved twisted hands.

'A-maying, a-maying,' they bawled. 'In and out and round about, a-maying, a-maying . . .'

It didn't matter what the words were; or who sang what. Round and round they whirled, intoxicated by the music. Then, at a sign from Miss La Trobe behind the tree, the dance stopped. A procession formed. Great Eliza descended from her soap box. Taking her skirts in her hand, striding with long strides, surrounded by dukes and princes, followed by the lovers arm in arm, with Albert the idiot playing in and out, and the corpse on its bier concluding the procession, the Elizabethan age passed from the scene.

'Curse! Blast! Damn 'em!' Miss La Trobe in her rage stubbed her toe against a root. Here was her downfall; here was the Interval. Writing this skimble-skamble stuff in her cottage, she had agreed to cut the play here; a slave to her audience – to Mrs Sands's grumble about tea; about dinner – she had gashed the scene here. Just as she had brewed emotion, she spilt it. So she signalled: Phyllis! And, summoned, Phyllis popped up on the mat again in the middle.

Gentles and simples, I address you all (she piped).
Our act is done, our scene is over.
Past is the day of crone and lover.
The bud has flowered; the flower has fallen.
But soon will rise another dawning,
For time whose children small we be
Hath in his keeping, you shall see,
You shall see . . .

Her voice petered out. No one was listening. Heads bent, they read 'Interval' on the programme. And, cutting short her words, the megaphone announced in plain English: 'An interval.' Half an hour's interval, for tea. Then the gramophone blared out:

> *Armed against fate,*
> > *The valiant Rhoderick,*
> *Bold and blatant,*
> > *Firm, elatant, etc., etc.*

At that, the audience stirred. Some rose briskly; others stooped, retrieving walking-sticks, hats, bags. And then, as they raised themselves and turned about, the music modulated. The music chanted: *Dispersed are we*. It moaned: *Dispersed are we*. It lamented: *Dispersed are we*, as they streamed, spotting the grass with colour, across the lawns, and down the paths: *Dispersed are we*.

Mrs Manresa took up the strain. *Dispersed are we*. 'Freely, boldly, fearing no one' (she pushed a deckchair out of her way), 'youths and maidens' (she glanced behind her; but Giles had his back turned), 'follow, follow, follow me . . . Oh, Mr Parker, what a pleasure to see *you* here! I'm for tea!'

'Dispersed are we,' Isabella followed her, humming. 'All is over. The wave has broken. Left us stranded, high and dry. Single, separate on the shingle. Broken is the three-fold ply . . . Now I follow' (she pushed her chair back . . . The man in grey was lost in the crowd by the ilex) 'that old strumpet' (she invoked Mrs Manresa's tight, flowered figure in front of her) 'to have tea.'

Dodge remained behind. 'Shall I,' he murmured, 'go or stay? Slip out some other way? Or follow, follow, follow the dispersing company?'

Dispersed are we, the music wailed; *dispersed are we*. Giles remained like a stake in the tide of the flowing company.

'Follow?' He kicked his chair back. 'Whom? Where?' He stubbed his light tennis shoes on the wood. 'Nowhere. Anywhere.' Stark still he stood.

Here Cobbet of Cobbs Corner, alone under the monkey-puzzle tree, rose and muttered: 'What was in her mind, eh? What idea lay behind, eh? What made her indue the antique with this glamour – this sham lure, and set 'em climbing, climbing, climbing up the monkey-puzzle tree?'

Dispersed are we, the music wailed. *Dispersed are we*. He turned and sauntered slowly after the retreating company.

Now Lucy, retrieving her bag from beneath the seat, chirruped to her brother: 'Bart, my dear, come with me . . . D'you remember, when we were children, the play we acted in the nursery?'

He remembered. Red Indians the game was; a reed with a note wrapped up in a pebble.

'But for us, my old Cindy' – he picked up his hat – 'the game's over.' The glare and the stare and the beat of the tom-tom, he meant. He gave her his arm. Off they strolled. And Mr Page, the reporter, noted, 'Mrs Swithin, Mr B. Oliver,' then turning, added further, 'Lady Haslip, of

Haslip Manor,' as he spied that old lady wheeled in her chair by her footman winding up the procession.

To the valediction of the gramophone hid in the bushes the audience departed. *Dispersed*, it wailed, *Dispersed are we*.

Now Miss La Trobe stepped from her hiding. Flowing, and streaming, on the grass, on the gravel, still for one moment she held them together – the dispersing company. Hadn't she, for twenty-five minutes, made them see? A vision imparted was relief from agony . . . for one moment . . . one moment. Then the music petered out on the last word *we*. She heard the breeze rustle in the branches. She saw Giles Oliver with his back to the audience. Also Cobbet of Cobbs Corner. She hadn't made them see. It was a failure, another damned failure! As usual. Her vision escaped her. And turning, she strode to the actors, undressing, down in the hollow, where butterflies feasted upon swords of silver paper; where the dishcloths in the shadow made pools of yellow.

Cobbet had out his watch. Three hours till seven, he noted; then water the plants. He turned.

Giles, nicking his chair into its notch, turned too, in the other direction. He took the short cut by the fields to the barn. This dry summer the path was hard as brick across the fields. This dry summer the path was strewn with stones. He kicked – a flinty yellow stone, a sharp stone, edged as if cut by a savage for an arrow. A barbaric stone; a prehistoric. Stone-kicking was a child's game. He remembered the rules. By the rules of the game, one stone, the same stone, must be kicked to the goal. Say a gate, or a tree. He played it alone. The gate was a goal; to be reached in ten. The first kick was Manresa (lust). The second, Dodge (perversion). The third himself (coward). And the fourth and the fifth and all the others were the same.

He reached it in ten. There, couched in the grass, curled in an olive-green ring, was a snake. Dead? No, choked with a toad in its mouth. The snake was unable to swallow, the toad was unable to die. A spasm made the ribs contract; blood oozed. It was birth the wrong way round – a monstrous inversion. So, raising his foot, he stamped on them. The mass crushed and slithered. The white canvas on his tennis shoes was bloodstained and sticky. But it was action. Action relieved him. He strode to the barn, with blood on his shoes.

The barn, the Noble Barn, the barn that had been built over seven hundred years ago and reminded some people of a Greek temple, others of the middle ages, most people of an age before their own, scarcely anybody of the present moment, was empty.

The great doors stood open. A shaft of light like a yellow banner sloped from roof to floor. Festoons of paper roses, left over from the Coronation, drooped from the rafters. A long table, on which stood an urn, plates and cups, cakes and bread and butter, stretched across one end. The barn was empty. Mice slid in and out of holes or stood upright, nibbling. Swallows were busy with straw in pockets of earth in the rafters. Countless beetles and insects of various sorts burrowed in the dry wood. A stray bitch had made the dark corner where the sacks stood a lying-in ground for her puppies. All these eyes, expanding and narrowing, some adapted to light, others to darkness, looked from different angles and edges. Minute nibblings and rustlings broke the silence. Whiffs of sweetness and richness veined the air. A bluebottle had settled on the cake and stabbed its yellow rock with its short drill. A butterfly sunned itself sensuously on a sunlit yellow plate.

But Mrs Sands was approaching. She was pushing her way through the crowd. She had turned the corner. She could see the great open doors. But butterflies she never saw, mice were only black pellets in kitchen drawers; moths she bundled in her hands and put out of the window. Bitches suggested only servant girls misbehaving. Had there been a cat she would have seen it – any cat, a starved cat with a patch of mange on its rump opened the flood gates of her childless heart. But there was no cat. The barn was empty. And so running, panting, set upon reaching the barn and taking up her station behind the tea urn before the company came, she reached the barn. And the butterfly rose and the bluebottle.

Following her in a scud came the servants and helpers – David, John, Irene, Lois. Water boiled. Steam issued. Cake was sliced. Swallows swooped from rafter to rafter. And the company entered.

'This fine old barn . . . ' said Mrs Manresa, stopping in the doorway. It was not for her to press ahead of the villagers. It was for her, moved by the beauty of the barn, to stand still; to draw aside; to gaze; to let other people come first.

'We have one, much like it, at Lathom,' said Mrs Parker, stopping, for the same reasons. 'Perhaps,' she added, 'not quite so large.'

The villagers hung back. Then, hesitating, dribbled past.

'And the decorations . . . ' said Mrs Manresa, looking round for someone to congratulate. She stood smiling, waiting. Then old Mrs Swithin came in. She was gazing up too, but not at the decorations. At the swallows apparently.

'They come every year,' she said, 'the same birds.' Mrs Manresa smiled benevolently, humouring the old lady's whimsy. It was unlikely, she thought, that the birds were the same.

'The decorations, I suppose, are left over from the Coronation,' said Mrs Parker. 'We kept ours too. We built a village hall.'

Mrs Manresa laughed. She remembered. An anecdote was on the tip of her tongue, about a public lavatory built to celebrate the same occasion, and how the mayor . . . Could she tell it? No. The old lady, gazing at the swallows, looked too refined. 'Refeened' – Mrs Manresa qualified the word to her own advantage, thus confirming her approval of the wild child she was, whose nature was somehow 'just human nature'. Somehow she could span the old lady's 'refeenment', also the boy's fun – Where was that nice fellow Giles? She couldn't see him; nor Bill either. The villagers still hung back. They must have someone to start the ball rolling.

'Well, I'm dying for my tea!' she said in her public voice; and strode forward. She laid hold of a thick china mug. Mrs Sands giving precedence, of course, to one of the gentry, filled it at once. David gave her cake. She was the first to drink, the first to bite. The villagers still hung back. 'It's all my eye about democracy,' she concluded. So did Mrs Parker, taking her mug too. The people looked to them. They led; the rest followed.

'What delicious tea!' each exclaimed, disgusting though it was, like rust boiled in water, and the cake fly-blown. But they had a duty to society.

'They come every year,' said Mrs Swithin, ignoring the fact that she spoke to the empty air. 'From Africa.' As they had come, she supposed, when the barn was a swamp.

The barn filled. Fumes rose. China clattered; voices chattered. Isa pressed her way to the table.

'Dispersed are we,' she murmured. And held her cup out to be filled. She took it. 'Let me turn away,' she murmured, turning, 'from the array' – she looked desolately round her – 'of china faces, glazed and hard. Down the ride, that leads under the nut tree and the may tree, away, till I come to the wishing well, where the washerwoman's little boy – ' she dropped sugar, two lumps, into her tea, 'dropped a pin. He got his horse, so they say. But what wish should I drop into the well?' She looked round. She could not see the man in grey, the gentleman farmer; nor anyone known to her. 'That the waters should cover me,' she added, 'of the wishing well.'

The noise of china and chatter drowned her murmur. 'Sugar for you?' they were saying. 'Just a spot of milk? And you?' 'Tea without milk or sugar. That's the way I like it.' 'A bit too strong? Let me add water.'

'That's what I wished,' Isa added, 'when I dropped my pin. Water. Water . . . '

'I must say,' the voice said behind her, 'it's brave of the King and Queen. They're said to be going to India. She looks such a dear. Someone I know said his hair . . . '

'There,' Isa mused, 'would the dead leaf fall, when the leaves fall, on the water. Should I mind not again to see may tree or nut tree? Not again to hear on the trembling spray the thrush sing, or to see, dipping and diving as if he skimmed waves in the air, the yellow woodpecker?' She was looking at the canary-yellow festoons left over from the Coronation.

'I thought they said Canada, not India,' the voice said behind her back.

To which the other voice answered: 'D'you believe what the papers say? For instance, about the Duke of Windsor. He landed on the south coast. Queen Mary met him. She'd been buying furniture – that's a fact. And the papers say she met him . . . '

'Alone, under a tree, the withered tree that keeps all day murmuring of the sea and hears the Rider gallop . . . '

Isa filled in the phrase. Then she started. William Dodge was by her side.

He smiled. She smiled. They were conspirators; each murmuring some song my uncle taught me.

'It's the play,' she said. 'The play keeps running in my head.'

' "Hail, sweet Carinthia. My love. My life," ' he quoted.

' "My lord, my liege," ' she bowed ironically.

She was handsome. He wanted to see her, not against the tea urn, but with her glass-green eyes and thick body, the neck was broad as a pillar, against an arum lily or a vine. He wished she would say: 'Come along. I'll show you the greenhouse, the pig sty, or the stable.' But she said nothing, and they stood there holding their cups, remembering the play. Then he saw her face change, as if she had got out of one dress and put on another. A small boy battled his way through the crowd, striking against skirts and trousers as if he were swimming blindly.

'Here!' she cried raising her arm.

He made a bee-line for her. He was her little boy, apparently, her son, her George. She gave him cake; then a mug of milk. Then Nurse came up. Then again she changed her dress. This time, from the expression in her eyes, it was apparently something in the nature of a strait waistcoat. Hirsute, handsome, virile, the young man in blue jacket and brass buttons, standing in a beam of dusty light, was her husband.

And she his wife. Their relations, as he had noted at lunch, were as people say in novels 'strained'. As he had noted at the play, her bare arm had raised itself nervously to her shoulder when she turned – looking for whom? But here he was; and the muscular, the hirsute, the virile plunged him into emotions in which the mind had no share. He forgot how she would have looked against vine leaf in a greenhouse. Only at Giles he looked; and looked and looked. Of whom was he thinking as he stood with his face turned? Not of Isa. Of Mrs Manresa?

Mrs Manresa halfway down the barn had gulped her cup of tea. How can I rid myself, she asked, of Mrs Parker? If they were of her own class, how they bored her – her own sex! Not the class below – cooks, shopkeepers, farmers' wives; nor the class above – peeresses, countesses; it was the women of her own class that bored her. So she left Mrs Parker, abruptly.

'Oh Mrs Moore,' she hailed the keeper's wife. 'What did you think of it? And what did baby think of it?' Here she pinched baby. 'I thought it every bit as good as anything I'd seen in London . . . But we mustn't be outdone. We'll have a play of our own. In *our* barn. We'll show 'em' (here she winked obliquely at the table; so many bought cakes, so few made at home) 'how *we* do it.'

Then cracking her jokes, she turned; saw Giles; caught his eye; and swept him in, beckoning. He came. And what – she looked down – had he done with his shoes? They were bloodstained. Vaguely some sense that he had proved his valour for her admiration flattered her. If vague it was sweet. Taking him in tow, she felt: I am the queen, he my hero, my sulky hero.

'That's Mrs Neale!' she exclaimed. 'A perfect marvel of a woman, aren't you, Mrs Neale! She runs our post office, Mrs Neale. She can do sums in her head, can't you, Mrs Neale? Twenty-five halfpenny stamps, two packets of stamped envelopes and a packet of postcards – how much does that come to, Mrs Neale?'

Mrs Neale laughed; Mrs Manresa laughed; Giles too smiled, and looked down at his shoes.

She drew him down the barn, in and out, from one to another. She knew 'em all. Everyone was a thorough good sort. No, she wouldn't allow it, not for a moment – Pinsent's bad leg. 'No, no. We're not going to take that for an excuse, Pinsent.' If he couldn't bowl, he could bat. Giles agreed. A fish on a line meant the same to him and Pinsent; also jays and magpies. Pinsent stayed on the land; Giles went to an office. That was all. And she was a thorough good sort, making him feel less of an audience, more of an actor, going round the barn in her wake.

Then, at the end by the door, they came upon the old couple, Lucy and Bartholomew, sitting on their Windsor chairs.

Chairs had been reserved for them. Mrs Sands had sent them tea. It would have caused more bother than it was worth – asserting the democratic principle; standing in the crowd at the table.

'Swallows,' said Lucy, holding her cup, looking at the birds. Excited by the company they were flitting from rafter to rafter. Across Africa, across France they had come to nest here. Year after year they came. Before there was a channel, when the earth, upon which the Windsor chair was planted, was a riot of rhododendrons, and humming birds quivered at the mouths of scarlet trumpets, as she had read that morning in her *Outline of History*, they had come . . . Here Bart rose from his chair.

But Mrs Manresa absolutely refused to take his seat. 'Go on sitting, go on sitting,' she pressed him down again. 'I'll squat on the floor.' She squatted. The surly knight remained in attendance.

'And what did you think of the play?' she asked.

Bartholomew looked at his son. His son remained silent.

'And you, Mrs Swithin?' Mrs Manresa pressed the old lady.

Lucy mumbled, looking at the swallows.

'I was hoping you'd tell me,' said Mrs Manresa. 'Was it an old play? Was it a new play?'

No one answered.

'Look!' Lucy exclaimed.

'The birds?' said Mrs Manresa, looking up.

There was a bird with a straw in its beak; and the straw dropped.

Lucy clapped her hands. Giles turned away. She was mocking him as usual, laughing.

'Going?' said Bartholomew. 'Time for the next act?'

And he heaved himself up from his chair. Regardless of Mrs Manresa and of Lucy, off he strolled too.

'Swallow, my sister, O sister swallow,' he muttered, feeling for his cigar case, following his son.

Mrs Manresa was nettled. What for had she squatted on the floor then? Were her charms fading? Both were gone. But, woman of action as she was, deserted by the male sex, she was not going to suffer tortures of boredom from the refeened old lady. Up she scrambled, putting her hands to her hair as if it were high time that she went too, though it was nothing of the kind and her hair was perfectly tidy. Cobbet in his corner saw through her little game. He had known human nature in the

East. It was the same in the West. Plants remained – the carnation, the zinnia and the geranium. Automatically he consulted his watch; noted time to water at seven; and observed the little game of the woman following the man to the table in the West as in the East.

William at the table, now attached to Mrs Parker and Isa, watched him approach. Armed and valiant, bold and blatant, firm, elatant – the popular march tune rang in his head. And the fingers of William's left hand closed firmly, surreptitiously, as the hero approached.

Mrs Parker was deploring to Isa in a low voice the village idiot.

'Oh that idiot!' she was saying. But Isa was immobile, watching her husband. She could feel the Manresa in his wake. She could hear in the dusk in their bedroom the usual explanation. It made no difference, his infidelity – but hers did.

'The idiot?' William answered Mrs Parker for her. 'He's in the tradition.'

'But surely,' said Mrs Parker, and told Giles how creepy the idiot – 'We have one in our village' – had made her feel. 'Surely, Mr Oliver, we're more civilised?'

'*We?*' said Giles. '*We?*' He looked, once, at William. He knew not his name; but what his left hand was doing. It was a bit of luck – that he could despise him, not himself. Also Mrs Parker. But not Isa – not his wife. She had not spoken to him, not one word. Nor looked at him either.

'Surely,' said Mrs Parker, looking from one to the other. 'Surely we are?'

Giles then did what to Isa was his little trick; shut his lips; frowned; and took up the pose of one who bears the burden of the world's woe, making money for her to spend.

'No,' said Isa, as plainly as words could say it, 'I don't admire you,' and looked, not at his face, but at his feet. 'Silly little boy, with blood on his boots.'

Giles shifted his feet. Whom then did she admire? Not Dodge. That he could take for certain. Who else? Some man he knew. Some man, he was sure, in the barn. Which man? He looked round him.

Then Mr Streatfield, the clergyman, interrupted. He was carrying cups.

'So I shake hands with my heart!' he exclaimed, nodding his handsome, grizzled head and depositing his burden safely.

Mrs Parker took the tribute to herself.

'Mr Streatfield!' she exclaimed. 'Doing all the work! While we stand gossiping!'

'Like to see the greenhouse?' said Isa suddenly, turning to William Dodge.

Oh not now, he could have cried. But had to follow, leaving Giles to welcome the approaching Manresa, who had him in thrall.

The path was narrow. Isa went ahead. And she was broad; she fairly filled the path, swaying slightly as she walked, and plucking a leaf here and there from the hedge.

'Fly then, follow,' she hummed, 'the dappled herds in the cedar grove, who, sporting, play, the red with the roe, the stag with the doe. Fly, away. I grieving stay. Alone I linger. I pluck the bitter herb by the ruined wall, the churchyard wall, and press its sour, its sweet, its sour, long grey leaf, so, twixt thumb and finger . . . '

She threw away the shred of old man's beard that she had picked in passing and kicked open the greenhouse door. Dodge had lagged behind. She waited. She picked up a knife from the plank. He saw her standing against the green glass, the fig tree and the blue hydrangea, knife in hand.

'She spake,' Isa murmured. 'And from her bosom's snowy antre drew the gleaming blade. "Plunge blade!" she said. And struck. "Faithless!" she cried. Knife, too! It broke. So too my heart,' she said.

She was smiling ironically as he came up.

'I wish the play didn't run in my head,' she said. Then she sat down on a plank under the vine. And he sat beside her. The little grapes above them were green buds; the leaves thin and yellow as the web between birds' claws.

'Still the play?' he asked. She nodded. 'That was your son,' he said, 'in the barn?'

She had a daughter too, she told him, in the cradle.

'And you – married?' she asked. From her tone he knew she guessed, as women always guessed, everything. They knew at once they had nothing to fear, nothing to hope. At first they resented – serving as statues in a greenhouse. Then they liked it. For then they could say – as she did – whatever came into their heads. And hand him, as she handed him, a flower.

'There's something for your buttonhole, Mr . . . ' she said, handing him a sprig of scented geranium.

'I'm William,' he said, taking the furry leaf and pressing it between thumb and finger.

'I'm Isa,' she answered. Then they talked as if they had known each other all their lives; which was odd, she said, as they always did, considering she'd known him perhaps one hour. Weren't they, though, conspirators, seekers after hidden faces? That confessed, she paused and wondered, as they always did, why they could speak so plainly to each other. And added: 'Perhaps because we've never met before, and never shall again.'

'The doom of sudden death hanging over us,' he said. 'There's no retreating and advancing' – he was thinking of the old lady showing him the house – 'for us as for them.'

The future shadowed their present, like the sun coming through the many-veined transparent vine leaf; a criss-cross of lines making no pattern.

They had left the greenhouse door open, and now music came through it. A B C, A B C, A B C – someone was practising scales. C A T, C A T, C A T . . . Then the separate letters made one word 'Cat'. Other words followed. It was a simple tune, like a nursery rhyme –

> The king is in his counting house,
> Counting out his money,
> The queen is in her parlour,
> Eating bread and honey.

They listened. Another voice, a third voice, was saying something simple. And they sat on in the greenhouse, on the plank with the vine over them, listening to Miss La Trobe, or whoever it was, practising her scales.

He could not find his son. He had lost him in the crowd. So old Bartholomew left the barn, and went to his own room, holding his cheroot and murmuring:

> 'O sister swallow, O sister swallow,
> How can thy heart be full of the spring?

'How can my heart be full of the spring?' he said aloud, standing in front of the bookcase. Books: the treasured life-blood of immortal spirits. Poets; the legislators of mankind. Doubtless, it was so. But Giles was unhappy. 'How can my heart, how can my heart,' he repeated, puffing at his cheroot. 'Condemned in life's infernal mine, condemned in solitude to pine . . . ' Arms akimbo, he stood in front of his country gentleman's library. Garibaldi; Wellington; Irrigation Officers' Reports; and Hibbert on *The Diseases of the Horse*. A great harvest the mind had reaped; but for all this, compared with his son, he did not care one damn.

'What's the use, what's the use,' he sank down into his chair muttering,

'O sister swallow, O sister swallow, of singing your song?' The dog, who had followed him, flopped down on to the floor at his feet. Flanks sucked in and out, the long nose resting on his paws, a fleck of foam on the nostril, there he was, his familiar spirit, his Afghan hound.

The door trembled and stood half open. That was Lucy's way of coming in – as if she did not know what she would find. Really! It was her brother! And his dog! She seemed to see them for the first time. Was it that she had no body? Up in the clouds, like an air ball, her mind touched ground now and then with a shock of surprise. There was nothing in her to weight a man like Giles to the earth.

She perched on the edge of a chair like a bird on a telegraph wire before starting for Africa.

'Swallow, my sister, O sister swallow . . . ' he murmured.

From the garden – the window was open – came the sound of someone practising scales. A B C, A B C, A B C. Then the separate letters formed one word 'Dog'. Then a phrase. It was a simple tune, another voice speaking.

'Hark, hark, the dogs do bark,

The beggars are coming to town . . . '

Then it languished and lengthened, and became a waltz. As they listened and looked – out into the garden – the trees tossing and the birds swirling seemed called out of their private lives, out of their separate avocations, and made to take part.

The lamp of love burns high, over the dark cedar groves,

The lamp of love shines clear, clear as a star in the sky . . .

Old Bartholomew tapped his fingers on his knee in time to the tune.

Leave your casement and come, lady, I love till I die,

He looked sardonically at Lucy, perched on her chair. How, he wondered, had she ever borne children?

For all are dancing, retreating and advancing,

The moth and the dragonfly . . .

She was thinking, he supposed, God is peace. God is love. For she belonged to the unifiers; he to the separatists.

Then the tune with its feet always on the same spot, became sugared, insipid; bored a hole with its perpetual invocation to perpetual adoration. Had it – he was ignorant of musical terms – gone into the minor key?

For this day and this dance and this merry, merry May

Will be over (he tapped his forefinger on his knee)

With the cutting of the clover this retreating and advancing –

the swifts seemed to have shot beyond their orbits –

Will be over, over, over,
And the ice will dart its splinter, and the winter,
Oh the winter, will fill the grate with ashes,
And there'll be no glow, no glow on the log.
He knocked the ash off his cheroot and rose.
'So we must,' said Lucy; as if he had said aloud, 'It's time to go.'

The audience was assembling. The music was summoning them. Down the paths, across the lawns they were streaming again. There was Mrs Manresa, with Giles at her side, heading the procession. In taut plump curves her scarf blew round her shoulders. The breeze was rising. She looked, as she crossed the lawn to the strains of the gramophone, goddess-like, buoyant, abundant, her cornucopia running over. Bartholomew, following, blessed the power of the human body to make the earth fruitful. Giles would keep his orbit so long as she weighted him to the earth. She stirred the stagnant pool of his old heart even – where bones lay buried, but the dragonflies shot and the grass trembled as Mrs Manresa advanced across the lawn to the strains of the gramophone.

Feet crunched the gravel. Voices chattered. The inner voice, the other voice was saying: How can we deny that this brave music, wafted from the bushes, is expressive of some inner harmony? 'When we wake' (some were thinking) 'the day breaks us with its hard mallet blows.' 'The office' (some were thinking) 'compels disparity. Scattered, shattered, hither thither summoned by the bell. "Ping-ping-ping" that's the phone. "Forward!" "Serving!" – that's the shop.' So we answer to the infernal, age-long and eternal order issued from on high. And obey. 'Working, serving, pushing, striving, earning wages – to be spent – here? Oh dear no. Now? No, by and by. When ears are deaf and the heart is dry.'

Here Cobbet of Cobbs Corner who had stooped – there was a flower – was pressed on by people pushing from behind.

For I hear music, they were saying. Music wakes us. Music makes us see the hidden, join the broken. Look and listen. See the flowers, how they ray their redness, whiteness, silverness and blue. And the trees with their many-tongued much syllabling, their green and yellow leaves hustle us and shuffle us, and bid us, like the starlings, and the rooks, come together, crowd together, to chatter and make merry while the red cow moves forward and the black cow stands still.

The audience had reached their seats. Some sat down; others stood a moment, turned, and looked at the view. The stage was empty; the actors were still dressing up among the bushes. The audience turned to one another and began to talk. Scraps and fragments reached Miss La Trobe where she stood, script in hand, behind the tree.

'They're not ready . . . I hear 'em laughing' (they were saying). '. . . Dressing up. That's the great thing, dressing up. And it's pleasant now, the sun's not so hot . . . That's one good the war brought us – longer days . . . Where did we leave off? D'you remember? The Elizabethans . . . Perhaps she'll reach the present, if she skips . . . D'you think people change? Their clothes, of course . . . But I meant ourselves . . . Clearing out a cupboard, I found my father's old top hat . . . But ourselves – do we change?'

'No, I don't go by politicians. I've a friend who's been to Russia. He says . . . And my daughter, just back from Rome, she says the common people, in the cafés, hate dictators . . . Well, different people say different things . . . '

'Did you see it in the papers – the case about the dog? D'you believe dogs can't have puppies? . . . And Queen Mary and the Duke of Windsor on the south coast? . . . D'you believe what's in the papers? I ask the butcher or the grocer . . . That's Mr Streatfield, carrying a hurdle . . . The good clergyman, I say, does more work for less pay than all the lot . . . It's the wives that make the trouble . . . '

'And what about the Jews? The refugees . . . the Jews . . . People like ourselves, beginning life again . . . But it's always been the same . . . My old mother, who's over eighty, can remember . . . Yes, she still reads without glasses . . . How amazing! Well, don't they say, after eighty . . . Now they're coming . . . No, that's nothing . . . I'd make it penal, leaving litter. But then, who's, my husband says, to collect the fines? . . . Ah there she is, Miss La Trobe, over there, behind that tree . . . '

Over there behind the tree Miss La Trobe gnashed her teeth. She crushed her manuscript. The actors delayed. Every moment the audience slipped the noose; split up into scraps and fragments.

'Music!' she signalled. 'Music!'

'What's the origin,' said a voice, 'of the expression "with a flea in his ear"?'

Down came her hand peremptorily. 'Music, music,' she signalled.

And the gramophone began A B C, A B C.

> The king is in his counting house,
> Counting out his money,
> The queen is in her parlour,
> Eating bread and honey . . .

*

Miss La Trobe watched them sink down peacefully into the nursery rhyme. She watched them fold their hands and compose their faces. Then she beckoned. And at last, with a final touch to her head-dress, which had been giving trouble, Mabel Hopkins strode from the bushes, and took her place on the raised ground facing the audience.

Eyes fed on her as fish rise to a crumb of bread on the water. Who was she? What did she represent? She was beautiful – very. Her cheeks had been powdered; her colour glowed smooth and clear underneath. Her grey satin robe (a bedspread), pinned in stone-like folds, gave her the majesty of a statue. She carried a sceptre and a little round orb. England was she? Queen Anne was she? Who was she? She spoke too low at first; all they heard was . . . *reason holds sway.*

Old Bartholomew applauded. 'Hear! Hear!' he cried. 'Bravo! Bravo!'

Thus encouraged Reason spoke out.

Time, leaning on his sickle, stands amazed. While commerce from her cornucopia pours the mingled tribute of her different ores. In distant mines the savage sweats; and from the reluctant earth the painted pot is shaped. At my behest, the armed warrior lays his shield aside; the heathen leaves the altar steaming with unholy sacrifice. The violet and the eglantine over the riven earth their flowers entwine. No longer fears the unwary wanderer the poisoned snake. And in the helmet, yellow bees their honey make.

She paused. A long line of villagers in sacking were passing in and out of the trees behind her.

Digging and delving, ploughing and sowing they were singing, but the wind blew their words away.

Beneath the shelter of my flowing robe (she resumed, extending her arms) *the arts arise. Music for me unfolds her heavenly harmony. At my behest the miser leaves his hoard untouched; at peace the mother sees her children play . . . Her children play . . .* she repeated, and at the waving of her sceptre, figures advanced from the bushes.

Let swains and nymphs lead on the play, while Zephyr sleeps, and the unruly tribes of heaven confess my sway.

A merry little old tune was played on the gramophone. Old Bartholomew joined his fingertips; Mrs Manresa smoothed her skirts about her knees.

> *Young Damon said to Cynthia,*
> *Come out now with the dawn*
> *And don your azure tippet*
> *And cast your cares adown,*
> *For peace has come to England,*
> *And reason now holds sway.*

> *What pleasure lies in dreaming*
> *When blue and green's the day?*
> *Now cast your cares behind you.*
> *Night passes: here is day.*

Digging and delving, the villagers sang, passing in single file in and out between the trees, *for the earth is always the same, summer and winter and spring; and spring and winter again; ploughing and sowing, eating and growing; time passes* . . .

The wind blew the words away.

The dance stopped. The nymphs and swains withdrew. Reason held the centre of the stage alone. Her arms extended, her robes flowing, holding orb and sceptre, Mabel Hopkins stood sublimely looking over the heads of the audience. The audience gazed at her. She ignored the audience. Then while she gazed, helpers from the bushes arranged round her what appeared to be the three sides of a room. In the middle they stood a table. On the table they placed a china tea service. Reason surveyed this domestic scene from her lofty eminence unmoved. There was a pause.

'Another scene from another play, I suppose,' said Mrs Elmhurst, referring to her programme. She read out for the benefit of her husband, who was deaf: '*Where there's a Will there's a Way*. That's the name of the play. And the characters . . . ' She read out: 'Lady Harpy Harraden, in love with Sir Spaniel Lilyliver. Deb, her maid. Flavinda, her niece, in love with Valentine. Sir Spaniel Lilyliver, in love with Flavinda. Sir Smirking Peace-be-with-you-all, a clergyman. Lord and Lady Fribble. Valentine, in love with Flavinda. What names for real people! But look – here they come!'

Out they came from the bushes – men in flowered waistcoats, white waistcoats and buckled shoes; women wearing brocades tucked up, hooped and draped; glass stars, blue ribands and imitation pearls made them look the very image of lords and ladies.

'The first scene,' Mrs Elmhurst whispered into her husband's ear, 'is Lady Harraden's dressing-room . . . That's her . . . ' She pointed. 'Mrs Otter, I think, from the End House; but she's wonderfully made up. And that's Deb her maid. Who she is, I don't know.'

'Hush, hush, hush,' someone protested.

Mrs Elmhurst dropped her programme. The play had begun.

Lady Harpy Harraden entered her dressing-room, followed by Deb her maid.

Lady H. H. *Give me the pounce-box. Then the patch. Hand me the mirror, girl. So. Now my wig . . . A pox on the girl – she's dreaming!*

DEB ... *I was thinking, my lady, what the gentleman said when he saw you in the Park.*

LADY H. H. (gazing in the glass) *So, so – what was it? Some silly trash! Cupid's dart – hah, hah! lighting his taper – tush – at my eyes . . . pooh! That was in milord's time, twenty years since . . . But now – what'll he say of me now?* (She looks in the mirror) *Sir Spaniel Lilyliver, I mean . . .* (a rap at the door) *Hark! That's his chaise at the door. Run child. Don't stand gaping.*

DEB (going to the door) *Say? He'll rattle his tongue as a gambler rattles dice in a box. He'll find no words to fit you. He'll stand like a pig in a poke . . . Your servant, Sir Spaniel.* (Enter Sir Spaniel.)

SIR S. L. *Hail, my fair saint! What, out o' bed so early? Methought as I came along the Mall the air was something brighter than usual. Here's the reason . . . Venus, Aphrodite, upon my word a very galaxy, a constellation! As I'm a sinner, a very Aurora Borealis!* (He sweeps his hat off.)

LADY H. H. *Oh flatterer, flatterer! I know your ways. But come. Sit down . . . A glass of Aqua Vitae. Take this seat, Sir Spaniel. I've something very private and particular to say to you . . . You had my letter, sir?*

SIR S. L. *Pinned to my heart!* (He strikes his breast.)

LADY H. H. *I have a favour to ask of you, sir.*

SIR S. L. (singing) *What favour could fair Chloe ask that Damon would not get her? . . . A-done with rhymes. Rhymes are still a-bed. Let's speak prose. What can Asphodilla ask of her plain servant Lilyliver? Speak out, madam. An ape with a ring in his nose, or a strong young jackanapes to tell tales of us when we're no longer here to tell truth about ourselves?*

LADY H. H. (flirting her fan) *Fie, fie, Sir Spaniel. You make me blush – you do indeed. But come closer.* (She shifts her seat nearer to him.) *We don't want the whole world to hear us.*

SIR S. L. (aside) *Come closer? A pox on my life! The old hag stinks like a red herring that's been stood over head in a tar barrel!* (Aloud) *Your meaning, madam? You were saying?*

LADY H. H. *I have a niece, Sir Spaniel, Flavinda by name.*

SIR S. L. (aside) *Why that's the girl I love, to be sure!* (Aloud) *You have a niece, madam? I seem to remember hearing so. An only child, left by your brother, so I've heard, in your ladyship's charge – him that perished at sea.*

LADY H. H. *The very same, sir. She's of age now and marriageable. I've kept her close as a weevil, Sir Spaniel, wrapped in the sere cloths of her virginity. Only maids about her, never a man to my knowledge, save Clout the serving man, who has a wart on his nose and a face like a nutgrater. Yet some fool has caught her fancy. Some gilded fly – some Harry, Dick; call him what you will.*

Sir S. L. (aside) *That's young Valentine, I warrant. I caught 'em at the play together.* (Aloud) *Say you so, madam?*

Lady H. H. *She's not so ill favoured, Sir Spaniel – there's beauty in our line – but that a gentleman of taste and breeding like yourself now might take pity on her.*

Sir S. L. *Saving your presence, madam. Eyes that have seen the sun are not so easily dazzled by the lesser lights – the Cassiopeias, Aldebarans, Great Bears and so on – A fig for them when the sun's up!*

Lady H. H. (ogling him) *You praise my hairdresser, sir, or my ear-rings* (she shakes her head).

Sir S. L. (aside) *She jingles like a she-ass at a fair! She's rigged like a barber's pole of a May Day.* (Aloud) *Your commands, madam?*

Lady H. H. *Well, sir, t'was this way, sir. Brother Bob, for my father was a plain country gentleman and would have none of the fancy names the foreigners brought with 'em – Asphodilla I call myself, but my Christian name's plain Sue – brother Bob, as I was telling you, ran away to sea; and, so they say, became Emperor of the Indies; where the very stones are emeralds and the sheep-crop rubies. Which, for a tenderer-hearted man never lived, he would have brought back with him, sir, to mend the family fortunes, sir. But the brig, frigate or what they call it, for I've no head for sea terms – never crossed a ditch without saying the Lord's Prayer backwards – struck a rock. The whale had him. But the cradle was by the bounty of heaven washed ashore. With the girl in it; Flavinda here. What's more to the point, with the will in it; safe and sound; wrapped in parchment. Brother Bob's will. Deb, there! Deb, I say! Deb!* (She hollas for Deb.)

Sir S. L. (aside) *Ah hah! I smell a rat! A will, quotha! Where there's a will there's a way.*

Lady H. H. (bawling) *The will, Deb! The will! In the ebony box by the right hand of the escritoire opposite the window . . . A pox on the girl! She's dreaming. It's these romances, Sir Spaniel – these romances. Can't see a candle gutter but its her heart that's melting, or snuff a wick without reciting all the names in Cupid's Calendar . . .* (Enter Deb carrying a parchment.)

Lady H. H. *So . . . Give it here. The will. Brother Bob's will* (she mumbles over the will).

Lady H. H. *To cut the matter short, sir, for these lawyers even at the Antipodes are a long-winded race –*

Sir S. L. *To match their ears, ma'am –*

Lady H. H. *Very true, very true. To cut the matter short, sir, my brother Bob left all he died possessed of to his only child Flavinda; with this proviso, mark ye. That she marry to her aunt's liking. Her aunt; that's me. Otherwise, mark ye, all – to wit ten bushels of diamonds; item of rubies; item two hundred square miles of fertile territory bounding the River Amazon to the nor-nor-east; item his snuff box; item his flageolet – he was always one to love a tune, sir, brother Bob; item six macaws and as many concubines as he had with him at the time of his decease – all this with other trifles needless to specify he left, mark ye, should she fail to marry to her aunt's liking – that's me – to found a chapel, Sir Spaniel, where six poor virgins should sing hymns in perpetuity for the repose of his soul – which, to speak the truth, Sir Spaniel, poor brother Bob stands in need of, perambulating the Gulf Stream as he is and consorting with Sirens. But take it; read the will yourself, sir.*

SIR S. L. (reading) *'Must marry to her aunt's liking'. That's plain enough.*

LADY H. H. *Her aunt, sir. That's me. That's plain enough.*

SIR S. L. (aside) *She speaks the truth there!* (Aloud) *You would have me understand, madam . . . ?*

LADY H. H. *Hist! Come closer. Let me whisper in your ear . . . You and I have long entertained a high opinion of one another, Sir Spaniel. Played at ball together. Bound our wrists with daisy chains together. If I mind aright, you called me little bride – 'tis fifty years since. We might have made a match of it, Sir Spaniel, had fortune favoured . . . You take my meaning, sir?*

SIR S. L. *Had it been written in letters of gold, fifty feet high, visible from Paul's Churchyard to the Goat and Compasses at Peckham, it could have been no plainer . . . Hist, I'll whisper it. I, Sir Spaniel Lilyliver, do hereby bind myself to take thee – what's the name of the green girl that was cast up in a lobster pot covered with seaweed? Flavinda, eh? Flavinda, so – to be my wedded wife . . . Oh for a lawyer to have it all in writing!*

LADY H. H. *On condition, Sir Spaniel –*

SIR S. L. *On condition, Asphodilla –* (both speak together) *that the money is shared between us.*

LADY H. H. *We want no lawyer to certify that! Your hand on it, Sir Spaniel!*

SIR S. L. *Your lips, madam!* (They embrace)

SIR S. L. *Pah! She stinks!*

'Ha! Ha! Ha!' laughed the indigenous old lady in her bath chair.

'Reason, begad! Reason!' exclaimed old Bartholomew, and looked at his son as if exhorting him to give over these womanish vapours and be a man, sir.

Giles sat straight as a dart, his feet tucked under him.

Mrs Manresa had out her mirror and lipstick and attended to her lips and nose.

The gramophone, while the scene was removed, gently stated certain facts which everybody knows to be perfectly true. The tune said, more or less, how Eve, gathering her robes about her, stands reluctant still to let her dewy mantle fall. The herded flocks, the tune continued, in peace repose. The poor man to his cot returns, and, to the eager ears of wife and child, the simple story of his toil relates: what yield the furrow bears; and how the team the plover on the nest has spared; while Wat her courses ran; and speckled eggs in the warm hollow lay. Meanwhile the good wife on the table spreads her simple fare; and to the shepherd's flute, from toil released, the nymphs and swains join hands and foot it on the green. Then Eve lets down her sombre tresses brown and spreads her lucent veil o'er hamlet, spire and mead, etc., etc. And the tune repeated itself once more.

The view repeated in its own way what the tune was saying. The sun was sinking; the colours were merging; and the view was saying how after toil men rest from their labours; how coolness comes; reason prevails; and having unharnessed the team from the plough, neighbours dig in cottage gardens and lean over cottage gates.

The cows, making a step forward, then standing still, were saying the same thing to perfection.

Folded in this triple melody, the audience sat gazing; and beheld gently and approvingly without interrogation, for it seemed inevitable, a box tree in a green tub take the place of the lady's dressing-room; while on what seemed to be a wall was hung a great clock face; the hands pointing to three minutes to the hour; which was seven.

Mrs Elmhurst roused herself from her reverie; and looked at her programme. 'Scene Two. The Mall,' she read out. 'Time; early morning. Enter Flavinda. Here she comes!'

Here came Millie Loder (shop assistant at Messrs Hunt and Dickson's, drapery emporium), in sprigged satin, representing Flavinda.

FLAV. *Seven he said, and there's the clock's word for it. But Valentine – where's Valentine? La! How my heart beats! Yet it's not the time o' day, for I'm often afoot before the sun's up in the meadows . . . See – the fine folk passing! All a-tiptoeing like peacocks with spread tails! And I in my petticoat that looked so fine by my aunt's cracked mirror. Why, here it's a dish clout . . . And they heap their hair up like a birthday cake stuck about with candles . . . That's a diamond – that's a ruby . . . Where's Valentine? The Orange Tree in the Mall, he said. The tree – there. Valentine – nowhere. That's a courtier, I'll warrant, that old fox with his tail between*

*his legs. That's a serving wench out without her master's knowledge.
That's a man with a broom to sweep paths for the fine ladies' flounces . . .
La! the red in their cheeks! They never got that in the fields, I warrant!
O faithless, cruel, hard-hearted Valentine. Valentine! Valentine.* (She
wrings her hands, turning from side to side.) *Didn't I leave my bed
a-tiptoe and steal like a mouse in the wainscot for fear of waking aunt?
And lard my hair from her powder box? And scrub my cheeks to make
'em shine? And lie awake watching the stars climb the chimney pots?
And give my gold guinea that Godfather hid behind the mistletoe last
Twelfth Night to Deb so she shouldn't tell on me? And grease the key in
the lock so that aunt shouldn't wake and shriek Flavvy! Flavvy! Val, I
say, Val – That's him coming . . . No, I could tell him a mile off the way
he strides the waves like what d'you call him in the picture book . . .
That's not Val . . . That's a cit; that's a fop; raising his glass, prithee, to
have his fill of me . . . I'll be home then . . . No, I won't . . . That's to play
the green girl again and sew samplers . . . I'm of age, ain't I, come
Michaelmas? Only three turns of the moon and I inherit . . . Didn't I
read it in the will the day the ball bounced on top of the old chest where
aunt keeps her furbelows, and the lid opened? . . . 'All I die possessed of to
my daughter . . . ' So far I'd read when the old lady came tapping down
the passage like a blind man in an alley . . . I'm no castaway, I'd have you
know, sir; no fishtailed mermaid with a robe of seaweed, at your mercy.
I'm a match for any of 'em – the chits you dally with, and bid me meet you
at the Orange Tree when you're drowsing the night off spent in their
arms . . . Fie upon you, sir, making sport with a poor girl so . . . I'll not
cry, I swear I won't. I'll not brew a drop of the salt liquid for a man who's
served me so . . . Yet to think on't – how we hid in the dairy the day the cat
jumped. And read romances under the holly tree. La! how I cried when the
duke left poor Polly . . . And my aunt found me with eyes like red jellies.
'What stung, niece?' says she. And cried, 'Quick, Deb, the blue bag.' I told
ye . . . La, to think I read it all in a book and cried for another! . . . Hist,
what's there among the trees? It's come – it's gone. The breeze is it? In the
shade now – in the sun now . . . Valentine on my life! It's he! Quick, I'll
hide. Let the tree conceal me!* (Flavinda hides behind the tree.)*

He's here . . . He turns . . . He casts about . . . He's lost the scent . . . He
gazes – this way, that way . . . Let him feast his eyes on the fine faces –
taste 'em, sample 'em, say: 'That's the fine lady I danced with . . . that I lay
with . . . that I kissed under the mistletoe . . . ' Ha! How he spews 'em out!
Brave Valentine! How he casts his eyes upon the ground! How his frowns
become him! 'Where's Flavinda?' he sighs. 'She I love like the heart in my
breast.' See him pull his watch out! 'O faithless wretch!' he sighs. See how*

he stamps the earth! Now turns on his heel . . . He sees me – no, the sun's in his eyes. Tears fill 'em . . . Lord, how he fingers his sword! He'll run it through his breast like the duke in the story book! . . . Stop, sir, stop! (She reveals herself.)

VALENTINE *Oh Flavinda, Oh!*

FLAVINDA *Oh Valentine, Oh!* (They embrace as the clock strikes nine.)

'All that fuss about nothing!' a voice exclaimed. People laughed. The voice stopped. But the voice had seen; the voice had heard. For a moment Miss La Trobe behind her tree glowed with glory. The next, turning to the villagers who were passing in and out between the trees, she barked: 'Louder! Louder!'

For the stage was empty; the emotion must be continued; the only thing to continue the emotion was the song; and the words were inaudible.

'Louder! Louder!' She threatened them with her clenched fists.

Digging and delving (they sang), *hedging and ditching, we pass . . . Summer and winter, autumn and spring return . . . All passes but we, all changes . . . but we remain for ever the same . . .* (the breeze blew gaps between their words).

'Louder, louder!' Miss La Trobe vociferated.

Palaces tumble down (they resumed), *Babylon, Nineveh, Troy . . . And Caesar's great house . . . all fallen they lie . . . Where the plover nests was the arch . . . through which the Romans trod . . . Digging and delving we break with the share of the plough the clod . . . Where Clytemnestra watched for her lord . . . saw the beacons blaze on the hills . . . we see only the clod . . . Digging and delving we pass . . . and the queen and the watchtower fall . . . for Agamemnon has ridden away . . . Clytemnestra is nothing but . . .*

The words died away. Only a few great names – Babylon, Nineveh, Clytemnestra, Agamemnon, Troy – floated across the open space. Then the wind rose, and in the rustle of the leaves even the great words became inaudible; and the audience sat staring at the villagers, whose mouths opened, but no sound came.

And the stage was empty. Miss La Trobe leant against the tree, paralysed. Her power had left her. Beads of perspiration broke on her forehead. Illusion had failed. 'This is death,' she murmured, 'death.'

Then suddenly, as the illusion petered out, the cows took up the burden. One had lost her calf. In the very nick of time she lifted her great moon-eyed head and bellowed. All the great moon-eyed heads laid themselves back. From cow after cow came the same yearning bellow. The whole world was filled with dumb yearning. It was the primeval voice sounding loud in the ear of the present moment. Then the whole herd caught the infection. Lashing their tails, blobbed like pokers, they tossed their heads high, plunged and bellowed, as if Eros had planted his dart in their flanks and goaded them to fury. The cows annihilated the gap; bridged the distance; filled the emptiness and continued the emotion.

Miss La Trobe waved her hand ecstatically at the cows.

'Thank heaven!' she exclaimed.

Suddenly the cows stopped; lowered their heads, and began browsing. Simultaneously the audience lowered their heads and read their programmes.

'The producer,' Mrs Elmhurst read out for her husband's benefit, 'craves the indulgence of the audience. Owing to lack of time a scene has been omitted; and she begs the audience to imagine that in the interval Sir Spaniel Lilyliver has contracted an engagement with Flavinda; she had been about to plight her troth when Valentine, hidden inside the grandfather clock, steps forward; claims Flavinda as his bride; reveals the plot to rob her of her inheritance; and, during the confusion that ensues, the lovers fly together, leaving Lady Harpy and Sir Spaniel alone together.'

'We're asked to imagine all that,' she said, putting down her glasses.

'That's very wise of her,' said Mrs Manresa, addressing Mrs Swithin. 'If she'd put it all in, we should have been here till midnight. So we've got to imagine, Mrs Swithin.' She patted the old lady on the knee.

'Imagine?' said Mrs Swithin. 'How right! Actors show us too much. The Chinese, you know, put a dagger on the table and that's a battle. And so Racine . . . '[32]

'Yes, they bore one stiff,' Mrs Manresa interrupted, scenting culture, resenting the snub to the jolly human heart. 'T'other day I took my nephew – such a jolly boy at Sandhurst[33] – to *Pop Goes the Weasel*. Seen it?' She turned to Giles.

'Up and down the City Road,' he hummed by way of an answer.

'Did your nanny sing that!' Mrs Manresa exclaimed. 'Mine did. And when she said "Pop" she made a noise like a cork being drawn from a ginger-beer bottle. Pop!'

She made the noise.

'Hush, hush,' someone whispered.

'Now I'm being naughty and shocking your aunt,' she said. 'We must be good and attend. This is Scene Three. Lady Harpy Harraden's closet. The sound of horses' hooves is heard in the distance.'

The sound of horses' hooves, energetically represented by Albert the idiot with a wooden spoon on a tray, died away.

*

Lady H. H. *Halfway to Gretna Green*[34] *already! Oh my deceitful niece! You that I rescued from the brine and stood on the hearthstone dripping! Oh that the whale had swallowed you whole! Perfidious porpoise, Oh! Didn't the hornbook teach you Honour thy Great Aunt? How have you misread it and misspelt it, learnt thieving and cheating and reading of wills in old boxes and hiding of rascals in honest time-pieces that have never missed a second since King Charles's day! Oh Flavinda! Oh porpoise, Oh!*

Sir S. L. (trying to pull on his jack boots) *Old – old – old. He called me 'old' – 'To your bed, old fool, and drink hot posset!'*

Lady H. H. *And she, stopping at the door and pointing the finger of scorn at me, said 'old', sir – 'woman', sir – I that am in the prime of life and a lady!*

Sir S. L. (tugging at his boots) *But I'll be even with him. I'll have the law on 'em! I'll run 'em to earth . . .* (He hobbles up and down, one boot on, one boot off.)

Lady H. H. (laying her hand on his arm) *Have mercy on your gout, Sir Spaniel. Bethink you, sir – let's not run mad, we that are on the sunny side of fifty. What's this youth they prate on? Nothing but a goose feather blown on a north wind. Sit you down, Sir Spaniel. Rest your leg – so –* (She pushes a cushion under his leg.)

Sir S. L. *'Old' he called me . . . jumping from the clock like a jack-in-the-box . . . And she, making mock of me, points to my leg and cries, 'Cupid's darts, sir Spaniel, Cupid's darts.' Oh that I could braise 'em in a mortar and serve 'em up smoking hot on the altar of – Oh my gout, Oh my gout!*

Lady H. H. *This talk, sir, ill befits a man of sense. Bethink you, sir, only t'other day you were invoking – ahem – the constellations. Cassiopeia; Aldebaran; the Aurora Borealis . . . It's not to be denied that one of 'em has left her sphere, has shot, has eloped, to put it plainly, with the entrails of a time-piece, the mere pendulum of a grandfather clock. But, Sir Spaniel, there are some stars that – ahem – stay fixed; that shine, to put it in a nutshell, never so bright as by a sea-coal fire on a brisk morning.*

Sir S. L. *Oh that I were five and twenty with a sharp sword at my side!*

Lady H. H. (bridling) *I take your meaning, sir. Te hee – To be sure, I regret it as you do. But youth's not all. To let you into a secret, I've passed the meridian myself. Am on t'other side of the equator too. Sleep sound o' nights without turning. The dog days are over . . . But bethink you, sir. Where there's a will there's a way.*

Sir S. L. *God's truth, ma'am . . . ah, my foot's like a burning, burning horseshoe on the devil's anvil, ah! – what's your meaning?*

Lady H. H. *My meaning, sir? Must I disrupt my modesty and unquilt that which has been laid in lavender since, my lord, peace be to his name – 'tis twenty years since – was lapped in lead? In plain words, sir, Flavinda's flown. The cage is empty. But we that have bound our wrists with cowslips might join 'em with a stouter chain. To have done with fallals and figures. Here am I, Asphodilla – but my plain name is Sue. No matter what my name is – Asphodilla or Sue – here am I, hale and hearty, at your service. Now that the plot's out, brother Bob's bounty must go to the virgins. That's plain. Here's Lawyer Quill's word for it. 'Virgins . . . in perpetuity . . . sing for his soul' And I warrant you, he has need of it . . . But no matter. Though we have thrown that to the fishes that might have wrapped us in lambswool, I'm no beggar. There's messuages; tenements; napery; cattle; my dowry; an inventory, I'll show you, engrossed on parchment; enough I'll warrant you to keep us handsomely, for what's to run of our time, as husband and wife.*

SIR S. L. *Husband and wife! So that's the plain truth of it! Why, madam, I'd rather lash myself to a tar barrel, be bound to a thorn tree in a winter's gale. Faugh!*

LADY H. H. *A tar barrel, quotha! A thorn tree – quotha! You that were harping on galaxies and milky ways! You that were swearing I outshone 'em all! A pox on you – you faithless! You shark, you! You serpent in jack boots, you! So you won't have me? Reject my hand, do you?* (She proffers her hand; he strikes it from him.)

SIR S. L. *Hide your chalk stones in a woollen mit! pah! I'll none of 'em! Were they diamond, pure diamond, and half the habitable globe and all its concubines strung upon a string round your throat, I'd none of it . . . none of it. Unhand me, scritch owl, witch, vampire! Let me go!*

LADY H. H. *So all your fine words were tinsel wrapped round a Christmas cracker!*

SIR S. L. *Bells hung on an ass's neck! Paper roses on a barber's pole . . . Oh my foot, my foot . . . Cupid's darts, she mocked me . . . Old, old, he called me old . . .* (He hobbles away.)

LADY H. H. (left alone) *All gone. Following the wind. He's gone; she's gone; and the old clock that the rascal made himself into a pendulum for is the only one of 'em all to stop. A pox on 'em – turning an honest woman's house into a brothel. I that was Aurora Borealis am shrunk to a tar barrel. I that was Cassiopeia am turned to a she-ass. My head turns. There's no trusting man nor woman; nor fine speeches; nor fine looks. Off comes the sheep's skin; out creeps the serpent. Get ye to Gretna Green; couch on the wet grass and breed vipers. My head spins . . . Tar barrels, quotha. Cassiopeia . . . Chalk stones . . . Andromeda . . . Thorn trees . . . Deb, I say, Deb!* (She holloas.) *Unlace me. I'm fit to burst . . . Bring me my green-baize table and set the cards . . . And my fur-lined slippers,*

Deb. And a dish of chocolate . . . I'll be even with 'em . . . I'll outlive 'em all. . . Deb, I say! Deb! A pox on the girl! Can't she hear me? Deb, I say, you gipsy's spawn that I snatched from the hedge and taught to sew samplers! Deb! Deb! (She throws open the door leading to the maid's closet.) *Empty! She's gone too! . . . Hist, what's that on the dresser?* (She picks up a scrap of paper and reads.) *'What care I for your goose-feather bed? I'm off with the raggle-taggle gipsies, O! Signed: Deborah, one time your maid.'* So! *She that I fed on apple parings and crusts from my own table, she that I taught to play cribbage and sew chemises . . . she's gone too. O ingratitude, thy name is Deborah! Who's to wash the dishes now; who's to bring me my posset now, suffer my temper and unlace my stays? . . . All gone. I'm alone then. Sans niece, sans lover – and sans maid.*

> *And so to end the play, the moral is*
> *The God of love is full of tricks;*
> *Into the foot his dart he sticks,*
> *But the way of the will is plain to see;*
> *Let holy virgins hymn perpetually:*
> *'Where there's a will there's a way.'*
> *Good people all, farewell.*

(Dropping a curtsey, Lady H. H. withdrew.)

The scene ended. Reason descended from her plinth. Gathering her robes about her, serenely acknowledging the applause of the audience, she passed across the stage; while lords and ladies in stars and garters followed after; Sir Spaniel limping escorted Lady Harraden smirking; and Valentine and Flavinda arm in arm bowed and curtsied.

'God's truth!' cried Bartholomew catching the infection of the language. 'There's a moral for you!'

He threw himself back in his chair and laughed, like a horse whinnying.

A moral. What? Giles supposed it was: Where there's a will there's a way. The words rose and pointed a finger of scorn at him. Off to Gretna Green with his girl; the deed done. Damn the consequences.

'Like to see the greenhouse?' he said abruptly, turning to Mrs Manresa.

'Love to!' she exclaimed, and rose.

Was there an interval? Yes, the programme said so. The machine in the bushes went chuff, chuff, chuff. And the next scene?

'The Victorian age,' Mrs Elmhurst read out. Presumably there was time then for a stroll round the gardens, even for a look over the house. Yet somehow they felt – how could one put it – a little not quite here or there. As if the play had jerked the ball out of the cup; as if what I call myself was still floating unattached, and didn't settle. Not quite themselves, they felt. Or was it simply that they felt clothes conscious? Skimpy out-of-date voile dresses; flannel trousers; panama hats; hats wreathed with raspberry-coloured net in the style of the royal duchess's hat at Ascot seemed flimsy somehow.

'How lovely the clothes were,' said someone, casting a last look at Flavinda disappearing. 'Most becoming. I wish . . . '

Chuff, chuff, chuff went the machine in the bushes, accurately, insistently.

Clouds were passing across the sky. The weather looked a little unsettled. Hogben's Folly was for a moment ashen white. Then the sun struck the gilt vane of Bolney Minster.

'Looks a little unsettled,' said someone.

'Up you get . . . Let's stretch our legs,' said another voice. Soon the lawns were floating with little moving islands of coloured dresses. Yet some of the audience remained seated.

'Major and Mrs Mayhew,' Page the reporter noted, licking his pencil. As for the play, he would collar Miss Whatshername and ask for a synopsis. But Miss La Trobe had vanished.

Down among the bushes she worked like a nigger. Flavinda was in her petticoats. Reason had thrown her mantle on a holly hedge. Sir Spaniel was tugging at his jack boots. Miss La Trobe was scattering and foraging.

'The Victorian mantle with the bead fringe . . . Where is the damned thing? Chuck it here . . . Now the whiskers . . . '

Ducking up and down she cast her quick bird's eye over the bushes at the audience. The audience was on the move. The audience was strolling up and down. They kept their distance from the dressing-room; they respected the conventions. But if they wandered too far, if they began exploring the grounds, going over the house, then . . . Chuff, chuff, chuff went the machine. Time was passing. How long would time hold them together? It was a gamble; a risk . . . And she laid about her energetically, flinging clothes on the grass.

Over the tops of the bushes came stray voices, voices without bodies, symbolical voices they seemed to her, half hearing, seeing nothing, but still, over the bushes, feeling invisible threads connecting the bodiless voices.

'It all looks very black.'

'No one wants it – save those damned Germans.'

There was a pause.

'I'd cut down those trees . . . '

'How they get their roses to grow!'

'They say there's been a garden here for five hundred years . . . '

'Why even old Gladstone,[35] to do him justice . . . '

Then there was silence. The voices passed the bushes. The trees rustled. Many eyes, Miss La Trobe knew, for every cell in her body was absorbent, looked at the view. Out of the corner of her eye she could see Hogben's Folly; then the vane flashed.

'The glass is falling,' said a voice.

She could feel them slipping through her fingers, looking at the view.

'Where's that damned woman, Mrs Rogers? Who's seen Mrs Rogers?' she cried, snatching up a Victorian mantle.

Then, ignoring the conventions, a head popped up between the trembling sprays: Mrs Swithin's.

'Oh, Miss La Trobe!' she exclaimed; and stopped. Then she began again; 'Oh, Miss La Trobe, I do congratulate you!'

She hesitated. 'You've given me . . . ' She skipped, then alighted – 'Ever since I was a child I've felt . . . ' A film fell over her eyes, shutting off the present. She tried to recall her childhood; then gave it up; and, with a little wave of her hand, as if asking Miss La Trobe to help her out, continued: 'This daily round; this going up and down stairs; this saying, "What am I going for? My specs? I have 'em on my nose" . . . '

She gazed at Miss La Trobe with a cloudless old-aged stare. Their eyes met in a common effort to bring a common meaning to birth. They failed; and Mrs Swithin, laying hold desperately of a fraction of her meaning, said: 'What a small part I've had to play! But you've made me feel I could have played . . . Cleopatra!'

She nodded between the trembling bushes and ambled off.

The villagers winked. 'Batty' was the word for old Flimsy, breaking through the bushes.

' "I might have been – Cleopatra," ' Miss La Trobe repeated. 'You've stirred in me my unacted part, she meant. Now for the skirt, Mrs Rogers,' she said.

Mrs Rogers stood grotesque in her black stockings. Miss La Trobe pulled the voluminous flounces of the Victorian age over her head. She tied the tapes. 'You've twitched the invisible strings,' was what the old lady meant; and revealed – of all people – Cleopatra! Glory possessed her. Ah, but she was not merely a twitcher of individual strings; she was one who seethes wandering bodies and floating voices in a cauldron, and makes rise up from its amorphous mass a recreated world. Her moment was on her – her glory.

'There!' she said, tying the black ribbons under Mrs Rogers' chin. 'That's done it! Now for the gentleman. Hammond!'

She beckoned Hammond. Sheepishly he came forward, and submitted to the application of black side whiskers. With his eyes half shut, his head leant back, he looked, Miss La Trobe thought, like King Arthur – noble, knightly, thin.

'Where's the Major's old frock coat?' she asked, trusting to the effect of that to transform him.

Tick, tick, tick, the machine continued. Time was passing. The audience was wandering, dispersing. Only the tick, tick of the gramophone held them together. There, sauntering solitary far away by the flower-beds, was Mrs Giles escaping.

'The tune!' Miss La Trobe commanded. 'Hurry up! The tune! The next tune! Number Ten!'

'Now may I pluck,' Isa murmured, picking a rose, 'my single flower. The white or the pink? And press it so, twixt thumb and finger . . . '

She looked among the passing faces for the face of the man in grey. There he was for one second; but surrounded, inaccessible. And now vanished.

She dropped her flower. What single, separate leaf could she press? None. Nor stray by the beds alone. She must go on; and she turned in the direction of the stable.

'Where do I wander?' she mused. 'Down what draughty tunnels? Where the eyeless wind blows? And there grows nothing for the eye. No rose. To issue where? In some harvestless dim field where no evening lets fall her mantle; nor sun rises. All's equal there. Unblowing, ungrowing are the roses there. Change is not; nor the mutable and lovable; nor greetings, nor partings; nor furtive findings and feelings, where hand seeks hand and eye seeks shelter from the eye.'

She had come into the stable yard where the dogs were chained; where the buckets stood; where the great pear tree spread its ladder of branches against the wall. The tree whose roots went beneath the flags was weighted with hard green pears. Fingering one of them she murmured: 'How am I burdened with what they drew from the earth; memories; possessions. This is the burden that the past laid on me, last little donkey in the long caravanserai crossing the desert. "Kneel down," said the past. "Fill your pannier from our tree. Rise up, donkey. Go your way till your heels blister and your hoofs crack."'

The pear was hard as stone. She looked down at the cracked flags beneath which the roots spread . 'That was the burden,' she mused, 'laid on me in the cradle; murmured by waves; breathed by restless elm trees; crooned by singing women; what we must remember; what we would forget.'

She looked up. The gilt hands of the stable clock pointed inflexibly at two minutes to the hour. The clock was about to strike.

'Now comes the lightning,' she muttered, 'from the stone blue sky. The thongs are burst that the dead tied. Loosed are our possessions.'

Voices interrupted. People passed the stable yard, talking.

'It's a good day, some say, the day we are stripped naked. Others, it's the end of the day. They see the Inn and the Inn's keeper. But none speaks with a single voice. None with a voice free from the old vibrations. Always I hear corrupt murmurs; the chink of gold and metal. Mad music . . . '

More voices sounded. The audience was streaming back to the terrace. She roused herself. She encouraged herself. 'On little donkey, patiently stumble. Hear not the frantic cries of the leaders who in that they seek to lead desert us. Nor the chatter of china faces glazed and hard. Hear rather the shepherd, coughing by the farmyard wall; the withered tree that sighs when the Rider gallops; the brawl in the barrack room when they stripped her naked; or the cry which in London when I thrust the window open someone cries . . . ' She had come out on to the path that led past the greenhouse. The door was kicked open. Out came Mrs Manresa and Giles. Unseen, Isa followed them across the lawns to the front row of seats.

The chuff, chuff, chuff of the machine in the bushes had stopped. In obedience to Miss La Trobe's command, another tune had been put on the gramophone. Number Ten. London street cries it was called. 'A Pot Pourri'.

'Lavender, sweet lavender, who'll buy my sweet lavender' the tune trilled and tinkled, ineffectively shepherding the audience. Some ignored it. Some still wandered. Others stopped, but stood upright. Some, like Colonel and Mrs Mayhew, who had never left their seats, brooded over the blurred carbon sheet which had been issued for their information.

'The Nineteenth Century.' Colonel Mayhew did not dispute the producer's right to skip two hundred years in less than fifteen minutes. But the choice of scenes baffled him.

'Why leave out the British Army? What's history without the army, eh?' he mused. Inclining her head, Mrs Mayhew protested after all one mustn't ask too much. Besides, very likely there would be a Grand Ensemble, round the Union Jack, to end with. Meanwhile, there was the view. They looked at the view.

'Sweet lavender . . . sweet lavender . . . ' Humming the tune old Mrs Lynn-Jones (of the Mount) pushed a chair forward. 'Here, Etty,' she said, and plumped down, with Etty Springett, with whom, since both were widows now, she shared a house.

'I remember . . . ' she nodded in time to the tune, 'you remember too – how they used to cry it down the streets.' They remembered – the curtains blowing, and the men crying: 'All a-blowing, all a-growing,' as they came with geraniums, sweet william, in pots, down the street.

'A harp, I remember, and a hansom and a growler.[36] So quiet the street was then. Two for a hansom, was it? One for a growler? And Ellen, in cap and apron, whistling in the street? D'you remember? And the runners, my dear, who followed, all the way from the station, if one had a box.'

The tune changed. 'Any old iron, any old iron to sell?' 'D'you remember? That was what the men shouted in the fog. Seven Dials[37] they came from. Men with red handkerchiefs. Garotters,[38] did they call them? You couldn't walk – Oh, dear me, no – home from the play. Regent Street. Piccadilly. Hyde Park Corner. The loose women . . . And everywhere loaves of bread in the gutter. The Irish you know round Covent Garden . . . Coming back from a ball, past the clock at Hyde Park Corner, d'you remember the feel of white gloves? . . . My father remembered the old Duke[39] in the Park. Two fingers like that – he'd touch his hat . . . I've got my mother's album. A lake and two lovers. She'd copied out Byron, I suppose, in what was called then the Italian hand . . . '

'What's that? "Knocked 'em in the Old Kent Road".[40] I remember the bootboy whistled it. Oh, my dear, the servants . . . Old Ellen . . . Sixteen pound a year wages . . . And the cans of hot water! And the crinolines! And the stays! D'you remember the Crystal Palace,[41] and the fireworks, and how Mira's slipper got lost in the mud?'

'That's young Mrs Giles . . . I remember her mother. She died in India . . . We wore, I suppose, a great many petticoats then. Unhygienic? I dare say . . . Well, look at my daughter. To the right, just behind you. Forty, but slim as a wand. Each flat has its refrigerator . . . It took my mother half the morning to order dinner . . . We were eleven. Counting servants, eighteen in family . . . Now they simply ring up the Stores . . . That's Giles coming, with Mrs Manresa. She's a type I don't myself fancy. I may be wrong . . . And Colonel Mayhew, as spruce as ever . . . And Mr Cobbet of Cobbs Corner, there, under the monkey-puzzle tree. One don't see him often . . . That's what's so nice – it brings people together. These days, when we're all so busy, that's what one wants . . . The programme? Have you got it? Let's see what comes next . . . The Nineteenth Century . . . Look, there's the chorus, the villagers, coming on now, between the trees. First, there's a prologue . . . '

A great box, draped in red baize festooned with heavy gold tassels had been moved into the middle of the stage. There was a swish of dresses, a stir of chairs. The audience seated themselves, hastily, guiltily. Miss La Trobe's eye was on them. She gave them ten seconds to settle their faces. Then she flicked her hand. A pompous march tune brayed. 'Firm, elatant, bold and blatant,' etc . . . And once more a huge symbolical figure emerged from the bushes. It was Budge the publican; but so disguised that even cronies who drank with him nightly failed to recognise him; and a little titter of enquiry as to his identity ran about among the villagers. He wore a long black many-caped cloak: water-proof; shiny; of the substance of a statue in Parliament Square; a helmet which suggested a policeman; a row of medals crossed his breast; and in his right hand he held extended a special-constable's baton (loaned by Mr Willert of the Hall). It was his voice, husky and rusty, issuing from a thick black cotton-wool beard that gave him away.

'Budge, Budge. That's Mr Budge,' the audience whispered.

Budge extended his truncheon and spoke: *It ain't an easy job, directing the traffic at 'Yde Park Corner. Buses and 'ansom cabs. All a-clatter on the cobbles. Keep to the right, can't you? Hi there, Stop!* (He waved his truncheon.)

There she goes, the old party with the umbrella right under the 'orse's nose. (The truncheon pointed markedly at Mrs Swithin.)

She raised her skinny hand as if in truth she had fluttered off the pavement on the impulse of the moment to the just rage of authority. Got her, Giles thought, taking sides with authority against his aunt.

Fog or fine weather, I does my duty (Budge continued). *At Piccadilly Circus; at 'Yde Park Corner, directing the traffic of 'Er Majesty's Empire. The Shah of Persia; Sultan of Morocco; or it may be 'Er Majesty in person; or Cook's tourists; black men; white men; sailors, soldiers; crossing the ocean; to proclaim her Empire; all of 'em Obey the Rule of my truncheon.* (He flourished it magnificently from right to left.)

But my job don't end there. I take under my protection and direction the purity and security of all Her Majesty's minions; in all parts of her dominions; insist that they obey the laws of God and Man.

The laws of God and Man (he repeated and made as if to consult a statute, engrossed on a sheet of parchment, which with great deliberation he now produced from his trouser pocket.)

Go to church on Sunday; on Monday, nine sharp, catch the City bus. On Tuesday it may be, attend a meeting at the Mansion House[42] *for the redemption of the sinner; at dinner on Wednesday attend another – turtle soup. Some bother it may be in Ireland. Famine. Fenians. What not. On Thursday it's the natives of Peru require protection and correction; we give 'em what's due. But mark you, our rule don't end there. It's a Christian country, our Empire; under the White Queen Victoria. Over thought and religion; drink; dress; manners; marriage too, I wield my truncheon. Prosperity and respectability always go, as we know, 'and in 'and. The ruler of an Empire must keep his eye on the cot; spy too in the kitchen; drawing-room; library; wherever one or two, me and you, come together. Purity our watchword; prosperity and respectability. If not, why, let 'em fester in . . .* (he paused – no, he had not forgotten his words) *Cripplegate; St Giles's; Whitechapel; the Minories.*[43] *Let 'em sweat at the mines; cough at the looms; rightly endure their lot. That's the price of Empire; that's the white man's burden. And, I can tell you, to direct the traffic orderly, at 'Yde Park Corner, Piccadilly Circus, is a whole-time, white man's job.*

He paused, eminent, dominant, glaring from his pedestal. A very fine figure of a man he was, everyone agreed, his truncheon extended; his waterproof pendant. It only wanted a shower of rain, a flight of pigeons round his head and the pealing bells of St Paul's and the Abbey to transform him into the very spit and image of a Victorian constable; and to transport them to a foggy London afternoon, with the muffin bells ringing and the church bells pealing, at the very height of Victorian prosperity.

There was a pause. The voices of the pilgrims singing, as they wound in and out between the trees, could be heard; but the words were inaudible. The audience sat waiting.

'Tut-tut-tut,' Mrs Lynn-Jones expostulated. 'There were grand men among them . . .' Why she did not know, yet somehow she felt that a sneer had been aimed at her father; therefore at herself.

Etty Springett tutted too. Yet, children did draw trucks in mines; there was the basement; yet papa read Walter Scott aloud after dinner; and divorced ladies were not received at court. How difficult to come to any conclusion! She wished they would hurry on with the next scene. She liked to leave a theatre knowing exactly what was meant. Of course this was only a village play . . . They were setting another scene, round the red-baize box. She read out from her programme: 'The Picnic Party. About 1860. Scene: A lake. Characters – '

She stopped. A sheet had been spread on the terrace. It was a lake apparently. Roughly painted ripples represented water. Those green stakes were bulrushes. Rather prettily, real swallows darted across the sheet.

'Look, Minnie!' she exclaimed. 'Those are real swallows!'

'Hush, hush,' she was admonished. For the scene had begun. A young man in peg-top trousers and side whiskers carrying a spiked stick appeared by the lake.

EDGAR T. *Let me help you, Miss Hardcastle! There!* (he helps Miss Eleanor Hardcastle, a young lady in crinoline and mushroom hat to the top. They stand for a moment panting slightly, looking at the view.)

ELEANOR *How small the church looks down among the trees!*

EDGAR *So this is Wanderer's Well, the trysting-place.*

ELEANOR *Please, Mr Thorold, finish what you were saying before the others come. You were saying, 'Our aim in life . . . '*

EDGAR *Should be to help our fellow men.*

ELEANOR (sighing deeply) *How true – how profoundly true!*

EDGAR *Why sigh, Miss Hardcastle? – You have nothing to reproach yourself with – you whose whole life is spent in the service of others. It was of myself that I was thinking. I am no longer young. At twenty-four the best days of life are over. My life has passed* (he throws a pebble on to the lake) *like a ripple in water.*

ELEANOR *Oh Mr Thorold, you do not know me. I am not what I seem. I too –*

EDGAR *Do not tell me, Miss Hardcastle – no, I cannot believe it – You have doubted?*

ELEANOR *Thank heaven not that, not that . . . But safe and sheltered as I am, always at home, protected as you see me, as you think me . . . Oh what am I saying? But yes, I will speak the truth, before mama comes. I too have longed to convert the heathen!*

EDGAR *Miss Hardcastle . . . Eleanor . . . You tempt me! Dare I ask you? No – so young, so fair, so innocent. Think, I implore you, before you answer.*

ELEANOR *I have thought – on my knees!*

EDGAR (taking a ring from his pocket) *Then . . . My mother with her last breath charged me to give this ring only to one to whom a lifetime in the African desert among the heathens would be –*

ELEANOR (taking the ring) *Perfect happiness! But hist!* (She slips the ring into her pocket.) *Here's mama!* (They start asunder.)

(Enter Mrs Hardcastle, a stout lady in black bombazine, upon a donkey, escorted by an elderly gentleman in a deer-stalker's cap.)

MRS H. *So you stole a march upon us, young people. There was a time, Sir John, when you and I were always first on top. Now . . .*

(He helps her to alight. Children, young men, young women, some carrying hampers, others butterfly nets, others spy-glasses, others tin botanical cases arrive. A rug is thrown by the lake and Mrs H. and Sir John seat themselves on camp stools.)

MRS H. *Now who'll fill the kettles? Who'll gather the sticks? Alfred* (to a small boy), *don't run about chasing butterflies or you'll make yourself sick . . . Sir John and I will unpack the hampers, here where the grass is burnt, where we had the picnic last year.* (The young people scatter off in different directions. Mrs H. and Sir John begin to unpack the hamper.)

MRS H. *Last year poor dear Mr Beach was with us. It was a blessed release.* (She takes out a black-bordered handkerchief and wipes her eyes.) *Every year one of us is missing. That's the ham . . . That's the grouse . . . There in that packet are the game pasties . . .* (She spreads the eatables on the grass.) *As I was saying, poor dear Mr Beach . . . I do hope the cream hasn't curdled. Mr Hardcastle is bringing the claret. I always leave that to him. Only when Mr Hardcastle gets talking with Mr Pigott about the Romans . . . last year they quite came to words . . . But it's nice for gentlemen to have a hobby, though they do gather the dust – those skulls and things . . . But I was saying – poor dear Mr Beach . . . I wanted to ask you* (she drops her voice), *as a friend of the family, about the new clergyman – they can't hear us, can they? No, they're picking up sticks . . . Last year, such a disappointment. Just got the things out . . . down came the rain. But I wanted to ask you about the new clergyman, the one who's come in place of dear Mr Beach. I'm told the name's Sibthorp. To be sure, I hope I'm right, for I had a cousin who married a girl of that name, and as a friend of the family, we don't stand on ceremony . . . And when one has daughters – I'm sure I quite envy you, with only one daughter, Sir John, and I have four! So I was asking you to tell me in confidence, about this young – if that's his name – Sibthorp, for I must tell you the day before yesterday our Mrs Potts happened to say, as she passed the Rectory, bringing our laundry, they were unpacking the furniture; and what did she see on top of the wardrobe? A tea cosy! But of course she might be mistaken . . . But it occurred to me to ask you, as a friend of the family, in confidence, has Mr Sibthorp a wife?*

Here a chorus composed of villagers in Victorian mantles, side whiskers and top hats sang in concert: *Oh has Mr Sibthorp a wife? Oh has Mr Sibthorp a wife? That is the hornet, the bee in the bonnet, the screw in the cork and the drill that whirling and twirling are for ever unfurling the folds of the motherly heart; for a mother must ask, if daughters she has, begot in the feathery billowy fourposter family bed, Oh did he unpack, with his prayer book and bands; his gown and his cane; his*

*rod and his line; and the family album and gun; did he also display the
connubial respectable tea-table token, a cosy with honeysuckle embossed.
Has Mr Sibthorp a wife? Oh has Mr Sibthorp a wife?*

While the chorus was sung, the picnickers assembled. Corks popped.
Grouse, ham, chickens were sliced. Lips munched. Glasses were drained.
Nothing was heard but the chump of jaws and the chink of glasses.

'They did eat,' Mrs Lynn-Jones whispered to Mrs Springett. 'That's
true. More than was good for them, I dare say.'

MR HARDCASTLE (brushing flakes of meat from his whiskers) *Now . . .*

'Now what?' whispered Mrs Springett, anticipating further travesty.

*Now that we have gratified the inner man, let us gratify the desire of the
spirit. I call upon one of the young ladies for a song.*

CHORUS OF YOUNG LADIES *Oh not me . . . not me . . . I really couldn't .
. . No, you cruel thing, you know I've lost my voice . . . I can't sing without
the instrument . . . etc., etc.*

CHORUS OF YOUNG MEN *Oh bosh! Let's have 'The Last Rose of Summer'.
Let's have 'I Never Loved a Dear Gazelle'.*

MRS H. (authoritatively) *Eleanor and Mildred will now sing 'I'd be a
Butterfly'.*

(Eleanor and Mildred rise obediently and sing a duet: 'I'd be a
Butterfly'.)

MRS H. *Thank you very much, my dears. And now gentlemen, Our Country!*

(Arthur and Edgar sing 'Rule Britannia'.)

MRS H. *Thank you very much. Mr Hardcastle –*

MR HARDCASTLE (rising to his feet, clasping his fossil) *Let us pray.*

(The whole company rise to their feet.)

'This is too much, too much,' Mrs Springett protested.

MR H. *Almighty God, giver of all good things, we thank thee for our food
and drink; for the beauties of nature; for the understanding with which
thou hast enlightened us* (he fumbled with his fossil); *and for thy great
gift of peace. Grant us to be thy servants on earth; grant us to spread the
light of thy . . .*

Here the hindquarters of the donkey, represented by Albert the idiot,
became active. Intentional was it, or accidental? 'Look at the donkey!
Look at the donkey!' A titter drowned Mr Hardcastle's prayer; and then
he was heard saying:

*. . . a happy homecoming with bodies refreshed by thy bounty, and minds
inspired by thy wisdom. Amen.*

Holding his fossil in front of him, Mr Hardcastle marched off.
The donkey was captured; hampers were loaded; and forming into a
procession, the picnickers began to disappear over the hill.

EDGAR (winding up the procession with Eleanor) *To convert the heathen!*

ELEANOR *To help our fellow men!* (The actors disappeared into the bushes.)

BUDGE *It's time, gentlemen, time, ladies, time to pack up and be gone. From where I stand, truncheon in hand, guarding respectability, and prosperity, and the purity of Victoria's land, I see before me* – (he pointed: there was Pointz Hall; the rooks cawing; the smoke rising) – 'Ome, Sweet 'Ome.

The gramophone took up the strain: *Through pleasures and palaces, etc. there's no place like home.*

BUDGE *Home, gentlemen; home, ladies, it's time to pack up and go home. Don't I see the fire* (he pointed: one window blazed red) *blazing ever higher? In kitchen and nursery; drawing-room and library? That's the fire of 'Ome. And see! Our Jane has brought the tea. Now, children, where's the toys? Mama, your knitting, quick. For here* (he swept his truncheon at Cobbet of Cobbs Corner) *comes the breadwinner, home from the City, home from the counter, home from the shop. 'Mama, a cup o' tea.' 'Children, gather round my knee. I will read aloud. Which shall it be? Sindbad the sailor? Or some simple tale from the Scriptures? And show you the pictures? What none of 'em? Then out with the bricks. Let's build: a conservatory? a laboratory? a mechanics' institute? Or shall it be a tower; with our flag on top; where our widowed Queen, after tea, calls the royal orphans round her knee? For it's 'Ome, ladies, 'Ome, gentlemen. Be it never so humble, there's no place like 'Ome.'*

The gramophone warbled 'Home, Sweet Home', and Budge, swaying slightly, descended from his box and followed the procession off the stage.

There was an interval.

'Oh, but it was beautiful,' Mrs Lynn-Jones protested. Home she meant; the lamplit room; the ruby curtains; and papa reading aloud.

They were rolling up the lake and uprooting the bulrushes. Real swallows were skimming over real grass. But she still saw the home.

'It was . . . ' she repeated, referring to the home.

'Cheap and nasty, I call it,' snapped Etty Springett, referring to the play, and shot a vicious glance at Dodge's green trousers, yellow spotted tie and unbuttoned waistcoat.

But Mrs Lynn-Jones still saw the home. Was there, she mused, as Budge's red-baize pediment was rolled off, something – not impure, that wasn't the word – but perhaps 'unhygienic' about the home? Like a bit of meat gone sour, with whiskers, as the servants called it? Or why had it perished? Time went on and on like the hands of the kitchen clock. (The machine chuffed in the bushes.) If they had met with no resistance, she mused, nothing wrong, they'd still be going round and round and round. The home would have remained; and papa's beard, she thought, would have grown and grown; and mama's knitting – what did she do with all her knitting? Change had to come, she said to herself, or there'd have been yards and yards of papa's beard, of mama's knitting. Nowadays her son-in-law was clean-shaven. Her daughter had a refrigerator . . . Dear, how my mind wanders, she checked herself. What she meant was, change had to come, unless things were perfect; in which case she supposed they resisted time. Heaven was changeless.

'Were they like that?' Isa asked abruptly. She looked at Mrs Swithin as if she had been a dinosaur or a very diminutive mammoth. Extinct she must be, since she had lived in the reign of Queen Victoria.

Tick, tick, tick went the machine in the bushes.

'The Victorians,' Mrs Swithin mused. 'I don't believe' she said with her odd little smile, 'that there ever were such people. Only you and me and William dressed differently.'

'You don't believe in history,' said William.

The stage remained empty. The cows moved in the field. The shadows were deeper under the trees.

Mrs Swithin caressed her cross. She gazed vaguely at the view. She was off, they guessed, on a circular tour of the imagination – one-making. Sheep, cows, grass, trees, ourselves – all are one. If discordant, producing harmony – if not to us, to a gigantic ear attached to a gigantic head. And thus – she was smiling benignly – the agony of the particular sheep, cow or human being is necessary; and so – she was beaming seraphically at the gilt vane in the distance – we reach the conclusion that *all* is harmony, could we hear it. And we shall. Her eyes now rested on the white summit of a cloud. Well, if the thought gave her comfort, William and Isa smiled across her, let her think it.

Tick, tick, tick, the machine reiterated.

'D'you get her meaning?' said Mrs Swithin alighting suddenly. 'Miss La Trobe's?'

Isa, whose eyes had been wandering, shook her head.

'But you might say the same of Shakespeare,' said Mrs Swithin.

'Shakespeare and the musical glasses!' Mrs Manresa intervened. 'Dear, what a barbarian you all make me feel!'

She turned to Giles. She invoked his help against this attack upon the jolly human heart.

'Tosh,' Giles muttered.

Nothing whatever appeared on the stage.

Darts of red and green light flashed from the rings on Mrs Manresa's fingers. He looked from them at Aunt Lucy. From her to William Dodge. From him to Isa. She refused to meet his eyes. And he looked down at his blood-stained tennis shoes.

He said (without words), 'I'm damnably unhappy.'

'So am I,' Dodge echoed.

'And I too,' Isa thought.

They were all caught and caged; prisoners; watching a spectacle. Nothing happened. The tick of the machine was maddening.

'On, little donkey,' Isa murmured, 'crossing the desert . . . bearing your burden . . .'

She felt Dodge's eye upon her as her lips moved. Always some cold eye crawled over the surface like a winter bluebottle! She flicked him off.

'What a time they take!' she exclaimed irritably.

'Another interval,' Dodge read out, looking at the programme.

'And after that, what?' asked Lucy.

'Present time. Ourselves,' he read.

'Let's hope to God that's the end,' said Giles gruffly.

'Now you're being naughty,' Mrs Manresa reproved her little boy, her surly hero.

No one moved. There they sat, facing the empty stage, the cows, the meadows and the view, while the machine ticked in the bushes.

'What's the object,' said Bartholomew, suddenly rousing himself, 'of this entertainment?'

'The profits,' Isa read out from her blurred carbon copy, 'are to go to a fund for installing electric light in the church.'

'All our village festivals,' Mr Oliver snorted turning to Mrs Manresa, 'end with a demand for money.'

'Of course, of course,' she murmured, deprecating his severity, and the coins in her bead bag jingled.

'Nothing's done for nothing in England,' the old man continued.

Mrs Manresa protested. It might be true, perhaps, of the Victorians; but surely not of ourselves?

Did she really believe that we were disinterested? Mr Oliver demanded.

'Oh you don't know my husband!' the wild child exclaimed, striking an attitude.

Admirable woman! You could trust her to crow when the hour struck like an alarm clock; to stop like an old bus horse when the bell rang. Oliver said nothing.

Mrs Manresa had out her mirror and attended to her face.

All their nerves were on edge. They sat exposed. The machine ticked.

There was no music. The horns of cars on the high road were heard. And the swish of trees. They were neither one thing nor the other; neither Victorians nor themselves. They were suspended, without being, in limbo. Tick, tick, tick went the machine.

Isa fidgeted; glancing to right and to left over her shoulder.

'Four and twenty blackbirds, strung upon a string,' she muttered.

'Down came an ostrich, an eagle, an executioner,

"Which of you is ripe," he said, "to bake in my pie?

Which of you is ripe, which of you is ready,

Come, my pretty gentleman,

Come, my pretty lady" . . . '

How long was she going to keep them waiting? 'The present time. Ourselves.' They read it on the programme. Then they read what came next: 'The profits are to go to a fund for installing electric light in the church.' Where was the church? Over there. You could see the spire among the trees.

'Ourselves . . . ' They returned to the programme. But what could she know about ourselves? The Elizabethans, yes; the Victorians, perhaps; but ourselves sitting here on a June day in 1939 – it was ridiculous. 'Myself' – it was impossible. Other people, perhaps . . . Cobbet of Cobbs Corner; the Major; old Bartholomew; Mrs Swithin – them, perhaps. But she won't get me – no, not me. The audience fidgeted. Sounds of laughter came from the bushes. But nothing whatsoever appeared on the stage.

'What's she keeping us waiting for?' Colonel Mayhew asked irritably. 'They don't need to dress up if it's present time.'

Mrs Mayhew agreed. Unless of course she was going to end with a Grand Ensemble. Army; Navy; Union Jack; and behind them perhaps – Mrs Mayhew sketched what she would have done had it been her pageant – the church. In cardboard. One window, looking east, brilliantly illuminated to symbolise – she could work that out when the time came.

'There she is, behind the tree,' she whispered, pointing at Miss La Trobe.

Miss La Trobe stood there with her eye on her script. 'After Vic.,' she had written, 'try ten mins of present time. Swallows, cows, etc.' She wanted to expose them, as it were, to douche them with present-time reality. But something was going wrong with the experiment. 'Reality too strong,' she muttered. 'Curse 'em!' She felt everything they felt. Audiences were the devil. Oh to write a play without an audience – *the* play. But here she was fronting her audience. Every second they were slipping the noose. Her little game had gone wrong. If only she'd a backcloth to hang between the trees – to shut out cows, swallows, present time! But she had nothing. She had forbidden music. Grating her fingers in the bark, she damned the audience. Panic seized her. Blood seemed to pour from her shoes. This is death, death, death she noted in the margin of her mind; when illusion fails. Unable to lift her hand, she stood facing the audience.

And then the shower fell, sudden, profuse.

No one had seen the cloud coming. There it was, black, swollen, on top of them. Down it poured like all the people in the world weeping. Tears, Tears. Tears.

'Oh that our human pain could here have ending!' Isa murmured. Looking up she received two great blots of rain full in her face. They trickled down her cheeks as if they were her own tears. But they were all people's tears, weeping for all people. Hands were raised. Here and there a parasol opened. The rain was sudden and universal. Then it stopped. From the grass rose a fresh earthy smell.

'That's done it,' sighed Miss La Trobe, wiping away the drops on her cheeks. Nature once more had taken her part. The risk she had run acting in the open air was justified. She brandished her script. Music began – A B C – A B C. The tune was as simple as could be. But now that the shower had fallen, it was the other voice speaking, the voice that was no one's voice. And the voice that wept for human pain unending said:

> The king is in his counting house,
> Counting out his money,
> The queen is in her parlour . . .

'Oh that my life could here have ending,' Isa murmured (taking care not to move her lips). Readily would she endow this voice with all her treasure if so be tears could be ended. The little twist of sound could have the whole of her. On the altar of the rain-soaked earth she laid down her sacrifice . . .

'Oh look!' she cried aloud.

That was a ladder. And that (a cloth roughly painted) was a wall. And that a man with a hod on his back. Mr Page the reporter, licking his pencil, noted: 'With the very limited means at her disposal, Miss La Trobe conveyed to the audience civilisation (the wall) in ruins; rebuilt (witness man with hod) by human effort; witness also woman handing bricks.' Any fool could grasp that. 'Now issued black man in fuzzy wig; coffee-coloured ditto in silver turban; they signify presumably the League of . . . '

A burst of applause greeted this flattering tribute to ourselves. Crude of course. But then she had to keep expenses down. A painted cloth must convey – what *The Times* and the *Telegraph* both said in their leaders that very morning.

The tune hummed:

> *The king is in his counting house,*
> *Counting out his money,*
> *The queen is in her parlour,*
> *Eating . . .*

Suddenly the tune stopped. The tune changed. A waltz, was it? Something half known, half not. The swallows danced it. Round and round, in and out they skimmed. Real swallows. Retreating and advancing. And the trees, oh the trees, how gravely and sedately like senators in council, or the spaced pillars of some cathedral church . . . Yes, they barred the music, and massed and hoarded; and prevented what was fluid from overflowing. The swallows – or martins were they? – The temple-haunting martins who come, have always come . . . Yes, perched on the wall, they seemed to foretell what after all *The Times* was saying yesterday. Homes will be built. Each flat with its refrigerator, in the crannied wall. Each of us a free man; plates washed by machinery; not an aeroplane to vex us; all liberated; made whole . . .

The tune changed; snapped; broke; jagged. Foxtrot was it? Jazz? Anyhow the rhythm kicked, reared, snapped short. What a jangle and a jingle! Well, with the means at her disposal, you can't ask too much. What a cackle, a cacophony! Nothing ended. So abrupt. And corrupt. Such an outrage; such an insult. And not plain. Very up to date, all the same. What is her game? To disrupt? Jog and trot? Jerk and smirk? Put the finger to the nose? Squint and pry? Peak and spy? Oh the irreverence of the generation which is only momentarily – thanks be – 'the young'. The young, who can't make, but only break; shiver into splinters the old vision; smash to atoms what was whole. What a cackle, what a rattle, what a yaffle – as they call the woodpecker, the laughing bird that flits from tree to tree.

Look! Out they come, from the bushes – the riff-raff. Children? Imps – elves – demons. Holding what? Tin cans? Bedroom candlesticks? Old jars? My dear, that's the cheval glass from the Rectory! And the mirror – that I lent her. My mother's. Cracked. What's the notion? Anything that's bright enough to reflect, presumably, ourselves?

Ourselves! Ourselves!

Out they leapt, jerked, skipped. Flashing, dazzling, dancing, jumping. Now old Bart . . . he was caught. Now Manresa. Here a nose . . . There a skirt . . . Then trousers only . . . Now perhaps a face . . . Ourselves? But that's cruel. To snap us as we are, before we've had time to assume . . . And only, too, in parts . . . That's what's so distorting and upsetting and utterly unfair.

Mopping, mowing, whisking, frisking, the looking glasses darted, flashed, exposed. People in the back rows stood up to see the fun. Down they sat, caught themselves . . . What an awful show-up! Even for the old who, one might suppose, hadn't any longer any care about their faces . . . And Lord! the jangle and the din! The very cows joined in. Walloping, tail lashing, the reticence of nature was undone, and the barriers which should divide Man the Master from the Brute were dissolved. Then the dogs joined in. Excited by the uproar, scurrying and worrying, here they came! Look at them! And the hound, the Afghan hound . . . look at him!

Then once more, in the uproar which by this time has passed quite beyond control, behold Miss Whatshername behind the tree summoned from the bushes – or was it *they* who broke away – Queen Bess; Queen Anne; and the girl in the Mall; and the Age of Reason; and Budge the policeman. Here they came. And the pilgrims. And the lovers. And the grandfather clock. And the old man with a beard. They all appeared. What's more, each declaimed some phrase or fragment from their parts . . . *I am not* (said one) *in my perfect mind* . . . Another, *Reason am I* . . . *And I? I'm the old top hat* . . . *Home is the hunter, home from the hill* . . . *Home? Where the miner sweats, and the maiden faith is rudely strumpeted* . . . *Sweet and low; sweet and low, wind of the western sea* . . . *Is that a dagger that I see before me?* . . . *The owl hoots and the ivy mocks tap-tap-tapping on the pane* . . . *Lady I love till I die, leave thy chamber and come* . . . *Where the worm weaves its winding sheet* . . . *I'd be a butterfly. I'd be a butterfly* . . . *In thy will is our peace* . . . *Here, papa, take your book and read aloud* . . . *Hark, hark, the dogs do bark and the beggars* . . .

It was the cheval glass that proved too heavy. Young Bonthorp for all his muscle couldn't lug the damned thing about any longer. He stopped. So did they all – hand glasses, tin cans, scraps of scullery glass, harness-room glass and heavily embossed silver mirrors – all stopped. And the audience saw themselves, not whole by any means, but at any rate sitting still.

The hands of the clock had stopped at the present moment. It was now. Ourselves.

So that was her little game! To show us up, as we are, here and how. All shifted, preened, minced; hands were raised, legs shifted. Even Bart, even Lucy, turned away. All evaded or shaded themselves – save Mrs Manresa who, facing herself in the glass, used it as a glass; had out her mirror; powdered her nose; and moved one curl, disturbed by the breeze, to its place.

'Magnificent!' cried old Bartholomew. Alone she preserved unashamed her identity, and faced without blinking herself. Calmly she reddened her lips.

The mirror bearers squatted: malicious; observant; expectant; expository.

'That's them,' the back rows were tittering. 'Must we submit passively to this malignant indignity?' the front row demanded. Each turned ostensibly to say – oh, whatever came handy – to his neighbour. Each tried to shift an inch or two beyond the inquisitive insulting eye. Some made as if to go.

'The play's over, I take it,' muttered Colonel Mayhew, retrieving his hat. 'It's time . . . '

But before they had come to any common conclusion, a voice asserted itself. Whose voice it was no one knew. It came from the bushes – a megaphonic, anonymous, loud-speaking affirmation. The voice said: *Before we part, ladies and gentlemen, before we go . . .* (Those who had risen sat down.) *. . . let's talk in words of one syllable, without larding, stuffing or cant. Let's break the rhythm and forget the rhyme. And calmly consider ourselves. Ourselves. Some bony. Some fat.* (The glasses confirmed this.) *Liars most of us. Thieves too.* (The glasses made no comment on that.) *The poor are as bad as the rich are. Perhaps worse. Don't hide among rags. Or let our cloth protect us. Or for the matter of that book learning; or skilful practice on pianos; or laying on of paint. Or presume there's innocency in childhood. Consider the sheep. Or faith in love. Consider the dogs. Or virtue in those that have grown white hairs. Consider the gun slayers, bomb droppers here or there. They do openly what we do slyly. Take for example* (here the megaphone adopted a colloquial, conversational tone) *Mr M.'s bungalow. A view spoilt for ever. That's murder . . . Or Mrs E.'s lipstick and blood-red nails . . . A tyrant, remember, is half a slave. Item the vanity of Mr H. the writer, scraping in the dunghill for sixpenny fame . . . Then there's the amiable condescension of the lady of the manor – the upper-class manner. And buying shares in the market to sell 'em . . . Oh we're all the same. Take myself now. Do I escape my own reprobation, simulating indignation, in the bush, among the leaves? There's a rhyme, to suggest, in spite of protestation and the desire for immolation, I too have had some, what's called, education . . . Look at ourselves, ladies and gentlemen! Then at the wall; and ask how's this wall, the great wall, which we call, perhaps miscall, civilisation, to be built by* (here the mirrors flicked and flashed) *orts, scraps and fragments like ourselves?*

All the same here I change (by way of the rhyme mark ye) *to a loftier strain – there's something to be said: for our kindness to the cat; note too in today's paper, 'Dearly loved by his wife'; and the impulse which leads us – mark you, when no one's looking – to the window at midnight to smell the bean. Or the resolute refusal of some pimpled dirty little scrub in sandals to sell his soul. There is such a thing – you can't deny it. What? You can't descry it? All you can see of yourselves is scraps, orts and fragments? Well then listen to the gramophone affirming . . .*

A hitch occurred here. The records had been mixed. Foxtrot; Sweet lavender; Home, Sweet Home; Rule Britannia – sweating profusely, Jimmy, who had charge of the music, threw them aside and fitted the right one – was it Bach, Handel, Beethoven, Mozart or nobody famous, but merely a traditional tune? Anyhow, thank heaven, it was somebody speaking after the anonymous bray of the infernal megaphone.

Like quicksilver sliding, filings magnetised, the distracted united. The tune began; the first note meant a second; the second a third. Then down beneath a force was born in opposition; then another. On different levels they diverged. On different levels ourselves went forward; flower gathering some on the surface; others descending to wrestle with the meaning; but all comprehending; all enlisted. The whole population of the mind's immeasurable profundity came flocking; from the unprotected, the unskinned; and dawn rose; and azure; from chaos and cacophony measure; but not the melody of surface sound alone controlled it; but also the warring battle-plumed warriors straining asunder: To part? No. Compelled from the ends of the horizon; recalled from the edge of appalling crevasses; they crashed; solved; united. And some relaxed their fingers; and others uncrossed their legs.

Was that voice ourselves? Scraps, orts and fragments, are we, also, that? The voice died away.

As waves withdrawing uncover; as mist uplifting reveals; so, raising their eyes (Mrs Manresa's were wet; for an instant tears ravaged her powder), they saw, as waters withdrawing leave visible a tramp's old boot, a man in a clergyman's collar surreptitiously mounting a soap-box.

'The Reverend G. W. Streatfield,' the reporter licked his pencil and noted, 'then spoke . . . '

All gazed. What an intolerable constriction, contraction and reduction to simplified absurdity he was to be sure! Of all incongruous sights a clergyman in the livery of his servitude to the summing up was the most grotesque and entire. He opened his mouth. O Lord, protect and preserve us from words the defilers, from words the impure! What need have we of words to remind us? Must I be Thomas, you Jane?

As if a rook had hopped unseen to a prominent bald branch, he touched his collar and hemmed his preliminary croak. One fact mitigated the horror: his forefinger, raised in the customary manner, was stained with tobacco juice. He wasn't such a bad fellow, the Reverend G. W. Streatfield; a piece of traditional church furniture; a corner cupboard; or the top beam of a gate, fashioned by generations of village carpenters after some lost-in-the-mists-of-antiquity model.

He looked at the audience; then up at the sky. The whole lot of them, gentles and simples, felt embarrassed, for him, for themselves. There he stood, their representative spokesman; their symbol; themselves; a butt, a clod, laughed at by looking-glasses; ignored by the cows; condemned by the clouds which continued their majestic rearrangement of the celestial landscape; an irrelevant forked stake in the flow and majesty of the summer silent world.

His first words (the breeze had risen; the leaves were rustling) were lost. Then he was heard saying: 'What.' To that word he added another: 'Message'; and at last a whole sentence emerged; not comprehensible; say rather audible. 'What message,' it seemed he was asking, 'was our pageant meant to convey?'

They folded their hands in the traditional manner as if they were seated in church.

'I have been asking myself' – the words were repeated – 'what meaning, or message, this pageant was meant to convey?'

If he didn't know, calling himself Reverend, also M.A., who after all could?

'As one of the audience,' he continued (words now put on meaning), 'I will offer, very humbly, for I am not a critic' – and he touched the white gate that enclosed his neck with a yellow forefinger – 'my interpretation. No, that is too bold a word. The gifted lady . . . ' He looked round. La Trobe was invisible. He continued: 'Speaking merely as one of the audience, I confess I was puzzled. For what reason, I asked, were we shown these scenes? Briefly, it is true. The means at our disposal this afternoon were limited. Still we were shown different groups. We were shown, unless I mistake, the effort renewed. A few were chosen; the many passed in the background. That surely we were shown. But again, were we not given to understand – am I too presumptuous? Am I treading, like angels, where as a fool I should absent myself? To me at least it was indicated that we are members one of another. Each is part of the whole. Yes, that occurred to me, sitting among you in the audience. Did I not perceive Mr Hardcastle here' (he pointed) 'at one time a Viking? And in Lady Harridan – excuse me, if I get the names wrong – a Canterbury pilgrim? We act different parts; but are the same.

That I leave to you. Then again, as the play or pageant proceeded, my attention was distracted. Perhaps that too was part of the producer's intention? I thought I perceived that nature takes her part. Dare we, I asked myself, limit life to ourselves? May we not hold that there is a spirit that inspires, pervades . . . ' (the swallows were sweeping round him. They seemed cognisant of his meaning. Then they swept out of sight.) 'I leave that to you. I am not here to explain. That role has not been assigned me. I speak only as one of the audience, one of ourselves. I caught myself too reflected, as it happened in my own mirror . . . ' (Laughter) 'Scraps, orts and fragments! Surely, we should unite?'

'But' ('but' marked a new paragraph) 'I speak also in another capacity. As Treasurer of the Fund. In which capacity' (he consulted a sheet of paper) 'I am glad to be able to tell you that a sum of thirty-six pounds ten shillings and eightpence has been raised by this afternoon's entertainment towards our object: the illumination of our dear old church.'

'Applause,' the reporter reported.

Mr Streatfield paused. He listened. Did he hear some distant music?

He continued: 'But there is still a deficit' (he consulted his paper) 'of one hundred and seventy-five pounds odd. So that each of us who has enjoyed this pageant has still an opp . . . '

The word was cut in two. A zoom severed it. Twelve aeroplanes in perfect formation like a flight of wild duck came overhead. *That* was the music. The audience gaped; the audience gazed. Then zoom became drone. The planes had passed.

' . . . portunity,' Mr Streatfield continued, 'to make a contribution.' He signalled. Instantly collecting boxes were in operation. Hidden behind glasses they emerged. Coppers rattled. Silver jingled. But oh what a pity – how creepy it made one feel! Here came Albert, the idiot, jingling his collecting box – an aluminium saucepan without a lid. You couldn't very well deny him, poor fellow. Shillings were dropped. He rattled and sniggered; chattered and jibbered. As Mrs Parker made her contribution – half a crown as it happened – she appealed to Mr Streatfield to exorcise this evil, to extend the protection of his cloth.

The good man contemplated the idiot benignly. His faith had room, he indicated, for him too. He too, Mr Streatfield appeared to be saying, is part of ourselves. But not a part we like to recognise, Mrs Springett added silently, dropping her sixpence.

Contemplating the idiot, Mr Streatfield had lost the thread of his discourse. His command over words seemed gone. He twiddled the cross on his watch-chain. Then his hand sought his trouser pocket. Surreptitiously he extracted a small silver box. It was plain to all that the natural desire of the natural man was overcoming him. He had no further use for words.

'And now,' he resumed, cuddling the pipe lighter in the palm of his hand, 'for the pleasantest part of my duty. To propose a vote of thanks to the gifted lady . . . ' He looked round for an object corresponding to this description. None such was visible. '. . . who wishes it seems to remain anonymous.' He paused. 'And so . . . ' He paused again.

It was an awkward moment. How to make an end? Whom to thank? Every sound in nature was painfully audible: the swish of the trees; the gulp of a cow; even the skim of the swallows over the grass could be heard. But no one spoke. Whom could they make responsible? Whom could they thank for their entertainment? Was there no one?

Then there was a scuffle behind the bush; a preliminary premonitory scratching. A needle scraped a disc; chuff, chuff, chuff; then having found the rut, there was a roll and a flutter which portended God . . . they all rose to their feet . . . Save the King.

Standing, the audience faced the actors; who also stood, with their collecting boxes quiescent, their looking-glasses hidden, and the robes of their various parts hanging stiff.

> *Happy and glorious,*
> *Long to reign over us,*
> *God save the King.*

The notes died away.

Was that the end? The actors were reluctant to go. They lingered; they mingled. There was Budge the policeman talking to old Queen Bess. And the Age of Reason hobnobbed with the foreparts of the donkey. And Mrs Hardcastle patted out the folds of her crinoline. And little England, still a child, sucked a peppermint-drop out of a bag. Each still acted the unacted part conferred on them by their clothes. Beauty was on them. Beauty revealed them. Was it the light that did it? – the tender, the fading, the uninquisitive but searching light of evening that reveals depths in water and makes even the red-brick bungalow radiant?

'Look,' the audience whispered. 'Oh look, look, look – ' And once more they applauded; and the actors joined hands and bowed.

Old Mrs Lynn-Jones, fumbling for her bag, sighed, 'What a pity – must they change?'

But it was time to pack up and be off.

'Home, gentlemen; home ladies; it's time to pack up and be off,' the reporter whistled, snapping the band round his notebook.

And Mrs Parker was stooping. 'I'm afraid I've dropped my glove. I'm so sorry to trouble you. Down there, between the seats . . . '

The gramophone was affirming in tones there was no denying, triumphant yet valedictory: *Dispersed are we; who have come together. But*, the gramophone asserted, *let us retain whatever made that harmony.*

Oh let us, the audience echoed (stooping, peering, fumbling), keep together. For there is joy, sweet joy, in company.

Dispersed are we, the gramophone repeated.

And the audience turning saw the flaming windows, each daubed with golden sun; and murmured: 'Home, gentlemen; sweet. . . ' yet delayed a moment, seeing through the golden glory perhaps a crack in the boiler; perhaps a hole in the carpet; and hearing, perhaps, the daily drop of the daily bill.

Dispersed are we, the gramophone informed them. And dismissed them. So, straightening themselves for the last time, each grasping, it might be a hat, or a stick, or a pair of suede gloves, for the last time they applauded Budge and Queen Bess; the trees; the white road; Bolney Minster; and the Folly. One hailed another, and they dispersed, across lawns, down paths, past the house to the gravel-strewn crescent, where cars, push bikes and cycles were crowded together.

Friends hailed each other in passing.

'I do think,' someone was saying, 'Miss Whatshername should have come forward and not left it to the rector . . . After all, she wrote it . . . I thought it brilliantly clever . . . Oh my dear, I thought it utter bosh. Did *you* understand the meaning? Well, he said she meant we all act all parts . . . He said, too, if I caught his meaning, nature takes part . . . Then there was the idiot . . . Also, why leave out the army, as my husband was saying, if it's history? And if one spirit animates the whole, what about the aeroplanes? . . . Ah, but you're being too exacting. After all, remember, it was only a village play . . . For my part, I think they should have passed a vote of thanks to the owners. When we had our pageant, the grass didn't recover till autumn . . . Then we had tents . . . That's the man, Cobbet of Cobbs Corner, who wins all the prizes at all the shows. I don't myself admire prize flowers, nor yet prize dogs . . . '

Dispersed are we, the gramophone triumphed, yet lamented, *Dispersed are we . . .*

'But you must remember,' the old cronies chatted, 'they had to do it on the cheap. You can't get people, at this time o' year, to rehearse. There's the hay, let alone the movies . . . What we need is a centre. Something to bring us all together . . . The Brookes have gone to Italy, in spite of everything. Rather rash? . . . If the worst should come – let's hope it won't – they'd hire an aeroplane, so they said . . . What amused me was old Streatfield, feeling for his pouch. I like a man to be natural,

not always on a perch . . . Then those voices from the bushes . . .
Oracles? You're referring to the Greeks? Were the oracles, if I'm not
being irreverent, a foretaste of our own religion? Which is what? . . .
Crêpe soles? That's so sensible . . . They last much longer and protect
the feet . . . But I was saying: can the Christian faith adapt itself? In
times like these . . . At Larting no one goes to church . . . There's the
dogs, there's the pictures . . . It's odd that science, so they tell me, is
making things (so to speak) more spiritual . . . The very latest notion, so
I'm told, is nothing's solid . . . There, you can get a glimpse of the
church through the trees . . .

'Mr Umphelby! How nice to see you! Do come and dine . . . No,
alas, we're going back to town. The House is sitting . . . I was telling
them, the Brookes have gone to Italy. They've seen the volcano. Most
impressive, so they say – they were lucky – in eruption. I agree – things
look worse than ever on the continent. And what's the Channel, come
to think of it, if they mean to invade us? The aeroplanes, I didn't like to
say it, made one think . . . No, I thought it much too scrappy. Take the
idiot. Did she mean, so to speak, something hidden, the unconscious as
they call it? But why always drag in sex . . . It's true, there's a sense in
which we all, I admit, are savages still. Those women with red nails.
And dressing up – what's that? The old savage, I suppose . . . That's the
bell. Ding dong. Ding . . . Rather a cracked old bell . . . And the
mirrors! Reflecting us . . . I called that cruel. One feels such a fool,
caught unprotected . . . There's Mr Streatfield, going, I suppose to take
the evening service. He'll have to hurry or he won't have time to
change . . . He said she meant we all act. Yes, but whose play? Ah, that's
the question! And if we're left asking questions, isn't it a failure, as a
play? I must say I like to feel sure if I go to the theatre that I've grasped
the meaning . . . Or was that, perhaps, what she meant? . . . Ding dong.
Ding . . . that if we don't jump to conclusions, if you think, and I think,
perhaps one day, thinking differently, we shall think the same?

'There's dear old Mr Carfax . . . Can't we give you a lift, if you don't
mind playing bodkin? We were asking questions, Mr Carfax, about the
play. The looking-glasses now – did they mean the reflection is the
dream; and the tune – was it Bach, Handel, or no one in particular – is
the truth? Or was it t'other way about?

'Bless my soul, what a dither! Nobody seems to know one car from
another. That's why I have a mascot, a monkey . . . But I can't see it . . .
While we're waiting, tell me, did you feel when the shower fell someone
wept for us all? There's a poem, *Tears tears tears*, it begins. And goes on
Oh then the unloosened ocean . . . but I can't remember the rest.

'Then when Mr Streatfield said: One spirit animates the whole – the aeroplanes interrupted. That's the worst of playing out of doors . . . Unless of course she meant that very thing . . . Dear me, the parking arrangements are not what you might call adequate . . . I shouldn't have expected either so many Hispano-Suizas . . . That's a Rolls . . . That's a Bentley . . . That's the new type of Ford . . . To return to the meaning – Are machines the devil, or do they introduce a discord . . . Ding dong, ding . . . by means of which we reach the final . . . Ding dong . . . Here's the car with the monkey . . . Hop in . . . And goodbye, Mrs Parker . . . Ring us up. Next time we're down, don't forget . . . Next time . . . Next time . . . '

The wheels scrurred on the gravel. The cars drove off.

The gramophone gurgled *Unity–Dispersity*. It gurgled *Un . . . dis . . .* and ceased.

The little company who had come together at luncheon were left standing on the terrace. The pilgrims had bruised a lane on the grass. Also, the lawn would need a deal of clearing up. Tomorrow the telephone would ring: 'Did I leave my handbag? . . . A pair of spectacles in a red leather case? . . . A little old brooch of no value to anyone but me?' Tomorrow the telephone would ring. Now Mr Oliver said: 'Dear lady,' and, taking Mrs Manresa's gloved hand in his, pressed it, as if to say: 'You have given me what you now take from me.' He would have liked to hold on for a moment longer to the emeralds and rubies dug up, so people said, by thin Ralph Manresa in his ragamuffin days. But alas, sunset light was unsympathetic to her make-up; plated it looked, not deeply interfused. And he dropped her hand; and she gave him an arch roguish twinkle, as if to say – but the end of that sentence was cut short. For she turned, and Giles stepped forward; and the light breeze which the meteorologist had foretold fluttered her skirts; and she went, like a goddess, buoyant, abundant, with flower-chained captives following in her wake.

All were retreating, withdrawing and dispersing; and he was left with the ash grown cold and no glow, no glow on the log. What word expressed the sag at his heart, the effusion in his veins, as the retreating Manresa, with Giles attendant, admirable woman, all sensation, ripped the rag doll and let the sawdust stream from his heart?

The old man made a guttural sound, and turned to the right. On with the hobble, on with the limp, since the dance was over. He strolled alone past the trees. It was here, early that very morning, that he had destroyed the little boy's world. He had popped out with his newspaper; the child had cried.

Down in the dell, past the lily pool, the actors were undressing. He could see them among the brambles. In vests and trousers; unhooking; buttoning up; on all fours stuffing clothes into cheap attaché cases; with silver swords, beards and emeralds on the grass. Miss La Trobe in coat and skirt – too short, for her legs were stout – battled with the billows of a crinoline. He must respect the conventions. So he stopped, by the pool. The water was opaque over the mud.

Then, coming up behind him, 'Oughtn't we to thank her?' Lucy asked him. She gave him a light pat on the arm.

How imperceptive her religion made her! The fumes of that incense obscured the human heart. Skimming the surface, she ignored the battle in the mud. After La Trobe had been excruciated by the rector's interpretation, by the maulings and the manglings of the actors . . . 'She don't want our thanks, Lucy,' he said gruffly. What she wanted, like that carp (something moved in the water), was darkness in the mud; a whisky and soda at the pub; and coarse words descending like maggots through the waters.

'Thank the actors, not the author,' he said. 'Or ourselves, the audience.'

He looked over his shoulder. The old lady, the indigenous, the prehistoric, was being wheeled away by a footman. He rolled her through the arch. Now the lawn was empty. The line of the roof, the upright chimneys, rose hard and red against the blue of the evening. The house emerged; the house that had been obliterated. He was damned glad it was over – the scurry and the scuffle, the rouge and the rings. He stooped and raised a peony that had shed its petals. Solitude had come again. And reason and the lamplit paper . . . But where was his dog? Chained in a kennel? The little veins swelled with rage on his temples. He whistled. And here, released by Candish, racing across the lawn with a fleck of foam on the nostril, came his dog.

Lucy still gazed at the lily pool. 'All gone,' she murmured, 'under the leaves.' Scared by shadows passing, the fish had withdrawn. She gazed at the water. Perfunctorily she caressed her cross. But her eyes went water searching, looking for fish. The lilies were shutting: the red lily, the white lily, each on its plate of leaf. Above, the air rushed; beneath was water. She stood between two fluidities, caressing her cross. Faith required hours of kneeling in the early morning. Often the delight of the roaming eye seduced her – a sunbeam, a shadow. Now the jagged leaf at the corner suggested, by its contours, Europe. There were other leaves. She fluttered her eye over the surface, naming leaves India, Africa, America. Islands of security, glossy and thick.

'Bart . . . ' She spoke to him. She had meant to ask him about the dragon-fly – couldn't the blue thread settle, if we destroyed it here, then there? But he had gone into the house.

Then something moved in the water; her favourite fantail. The golden orfe followed. Then she had a glimpse of silver – the great carp himself, who came to the surface so very seldom. They slid on, in and out between the stalks – silver; pink; gold; splashed; streaked; pied.

'Ourselves,' she murmured. And retrieving some glint of faith from the grey waters, hopefully, without much help from reason, she followed the fish: the speckled, streaked and blotched; seeing in that vision beauty, power and glory in ourselves.

Fish had faith, she reasoned. They trust us because we've never caught 'em. But her brother would reply: 'That's greed.' 'Their beauty!' she protested. 'Sex,' he would say. 'Who makes sex susceptible to beauty?' she would argue. He shrugged who? Why? Silenced, she returned to her private vision: of beauty which is goodness; the sea on which we float. Mostly impervious, but surely every boat sometimes leaks?

He would carry the torch of reason till it went out in the darkness of the cave. For herself, every morning, kneeling, she protected her vision. Every night she opened the window and looked at leaves against the sky. Then slept. Then the random ribbons of birds' voices woke her.

The fish had come to the surface. She had nothing to give them – not a crumb of bread. 'Wait, my darlings,' she addressed them. She would trot into the house and ask Mrs Sands for a biscuit. Then a shadow fell. Off they flashed. How vexatious! Who was it? Dear me, the young man whose name she had forgotten; not Jones; nor Hodge . . .

Dodge had left Mrs Manresa abruptly. All over the garden he had been searching for Mrs Swithin. Now he found her; and she had forgotten his name.

'I'm William,' he said. At that she revived, like a girl in a garden in white, among roses, who came running to meet him – an unacted part.

'I was going to get a biscuit – no, to thank the actors,' she stumbled, virginal, blushing. Then she remembered her brother. 'My brother,' she added, 'says one mustn't thank the author, Miss La Trobe.'

It was always 'my brother . . . my brother' who rose from the depths of her lily pool.

As for the actors, Hammond had detached his whiskers and was now buttoning up his coat. When the chain was inserted between the buttons he was off.

Only Miss La Trobe remained, bending over something in the grass. 'The play's over,' he said. 'The actors have departed.'

'And we mustn't, my brother says, thank the author,' Mrs Swithin repeated, looking in the direction of Miss La Trobe.

'So I thank you,' he said. He took her hand and pressed it. Putting one thing with another, it was unlikely that they would ever meet again.

The church bells always stopped, leaving you to ask: Won't there be another note? Isa, halfway across the lawn, listened . . . Ding, dong, ding . . . There was not going to be another note. The congregation was assembled, on their knees, in the church. The service was beginning. The play was over; swallows skimmed the grass that had been the stage.

There was Dodge, the lip reader, her semblable, her conspirator, a seeker like her after hidden faces. He was hurrying to rejoin Mrs Manresa who had gone in front with Giles – 'the father of my children,' she muttered. The flesh poured over her, the hot, nerve-wired, now lit up, now dark as the grave, physical body. By way of healing the rusty fester of the poisoned dart she sought the face that all day long she had been seeking. Preening and peering, between backs, over shoulders, she had sought the man in grey. He had given her a cup of tea at a tennis party; handed her, once, a racquet. That was all. But, she was crying, had we met before the salmon leapt like a bar of silver . . . had we met, she was crying. And when her little boy came battling through the bodies in the barn, 'Had he been his son,' she had muttered . . . In passing, she stripped the bitter leaf that grew, as it happened, outside the nursery window. Old man's beard. Shrivelling the shreds in lieu of words, for no words grew there, nor roses either, she swept past her conspirator, her semblable, the seeker after vanished faces – 'like Venus,' he thought, making a rough translation, 'to her prey . . . ' – and followed after.

Turning the corner, they saw Giles attached to Mrs Manresa. She was standing at the door of her car. Giles had his foot on the edge of the running-board. Did they perceive the arrows about to strike them?

'Jump in, Bill,' Mrs Manresa chaffed him.

And the wheels scurred on the gravel, and the car drove off.

At last, Miss La Trobe could raise herself from her stooping position. It had been prolonged to avoid attention. The bells had stopped; the audience had gone; also the actors. She could straighten her back. She could open her arms. She could say to the world, You have taken my gift! Glory possessed her – for one moment. But what had she given? A cloud that melted into the other clouds on the horizon. It was in the giving that the triumph was. And the triumph faded. Her gift meant nothing. If they had understood her meaning; if they had known their parts; if the pearls had been real and the funds illimitable – it would have been a better gift. Now it had gone to join the others.

'A failure,' she groaned, and stooped to put away the records.

Then suddenly the starlings attacked the tree behind which she had hidden. In one flock they pelted it like so many winged stones. The whole tree hummed with the whizz they made, as if each bird plucked a wire. A whizz, a buzz rose from the bird-buzzing, bird-vibrant, bird-blackened tree. The tree became a rhapsody, a quivering cacophony, a whizz and vibrant rapture, branches, leaves, birds syllabling discordantly life, life, life, without measure, without stop, devouring the tree. Then up! Then off!

What interrupted? It was old Mrs Chalmers, creeping through the grass with a bunch of flowers – pinks apparently – to fill the vase that stood on her husband's grave. In winter it was holly, or ivy. In summer, a flower. It was she who had scared the starlings. Now she passed.

Miss La Trobe nicked the lock and hoisted the heavy case of gramophone records to her shoulder. She crossed the terrace and stopped by the tree where the starlings had gathered. It was here that she had suffered triumph, humiliation, ecstasy, despair – for nothing. Her heels had ground a hole in the grass.

It was growing dark. Since there were no clouds to trouble the sky, the blue was bluer, the green greener. There was no longer a view – no Folly, no spire of Bolney Minster. It was land merely, no land in particular. She put down her case and stood looking at the land. Then something rose to the surface.

'I should group them,' she murmured, 'here.' It would be midnight; there would be two figures, half concealed by a rock. The curtain would rise. What would the first words be? The words escaped her.

Again she lifted the heavy suitcase to her shoulder. She strode off across the lawn. The house was dormant; one thread of smoke thickened against the trees. It was strange that the earth, with all those flowers incandescent – the lilies, the roses, and clumps of white flowers and bushes of burning green – should still be hard. From the earth green waters seemed to rise over her. She took her voyage away from the shore, and, raising her hand, fumbled for the latch of the iron entrance gate.

She would drop her suitcase in at the kitchen window, and then go on up to the inn. Since the row with the actress who had shared her bed and her purse the need of drink had grown on her. And the horror and the terror of being alone. One of these days she would break – which of the village laws? Sobriety? Chastity? Or take something that did not properly belong to her?

At the corner she ran into old Mrs Chalmers returning from the grave. The old woman looked down at the dead flowers she was carrying and cut her. The women in the cottages with the red geraniums always did that. She was an outcast. Nature had somehow set her apart from her kind. Yet she had scribbled in the margin of her manuscript: 'I am the slave of my audience.'

She thrust her suitcase in at the scullery window and walked on, till at the corner she saw the red curtain at the bar window. There would be shelter; voices; oblivion. She turned the handle of the public-house door. The acrid smell of stale beer saluted her; and voices talking. They stopped. They had been talking about Bossy as they called her – it didn't matter. She took her chair and looked through the smoke at a crude glass painting of a cow in a stable; also at a cock and a hen. She raised her glass to her lips. And drank. And listened. Words of one syllable sank down into the mud. She drowsed; she nodded. The mud became fertile. Words rose above the intolerably laden dumb oxen plodding through the mud. Words without meaning – wonderful words.

The cheap clock ticked; smoke obscured the pictures. Smoke became tart on the roof of her mouth. Smoke obscured the earth-coloured jackets. She no longer saw them, yet they upheld her, sitting arms akimbo with her glass before her. There was the high ground at midnight; there the rock; and two scarcely perceptible figures. Suddenly the tree was pelted with starlings. She set down her glass. She heard the first words.

Down in the hollow, at Pointz Hall, beneath the trees, the table was cleared in the dining-room. Candish, with his curved brush, had swept the crumbs; had spared the petals and finally left the family to dessert. The play was over, the strangers gone, and they were alone – the family.

Still the play hung in the sky of the mind – moving, diminishing, but still there. Dipping her raspberry in sugar, Mrs Swithin looked at the play. She said, popping the berry into her mouth, 'What did it mean?' and added: 'The peasants; the kings; the fool; and' (she swallowed) 'ourselves?'

They all looked at the play: Isa, Giles and Mr Oliver. Each of course saw something different. In another moment it would be beneath the horizon, gone to join the other plays. Mr Oliver, holding out his cheroot, said: 'Too ambitious.' And, lighting his cheroot, he added: 'Considering her means.'

It was drifting away to join the other clouds: becoming invisible. Through the smoke Isa saw not the play but the audience dispersing.

Some drove; others cycled. A gate swung open. A car swept up the drive to the red villa in the cornfields. Low hanging boughs of acacia brushed the roof. Acacia-petalled the car arrived.

'The looking-glasses and the voices in the bushes,' she murmured. 'What did she mean?'

'When Mr Streatfield asked her to explain, she wouldn't,' said Mrs Swithin.

Here, with its sheaf sliced in four, exposing a white cone, Giles offered his wife a banana. She refused it. He stubbed his match on the plate. Out it went with a little fizz in the raspberry juice.

'We should be thankful,' said Mrs Swithin, folding her napkin, 'for the weather, which was perfect, save for one shower.'

Here she rose, Isa followed her across the hall to the big room.

They never pulled the curtains till it was too dark to see, nor shut the windows till it was too cold. Why shut out the day before it was over? The flowers were still bright; the birds chirped. You could see more in the evening often when nothing interrupted, when there was no fish to order, no telephone to answer. Mrs Swithin stopped by the great picture of Venice – school of Canaletto. Possibly in the hood of the gondola there was a little figure – a woman, veiled; or a man?

Isa, sweeping her sewing from the table, sank, her knee doubled, into the chair by the window. Within the shell of the room she overlooked the summer night. Lucy returned from her voyage into the picture and stood silent. The sun made each pane of her glasses shine red. Silver sparkled on her black shawl. For a moment she looked like a tragic figure from another play.

Then she spoke in her usual voice. 'We made more this year than last, he said. But then last year it rained.'

'This year, last year, next year, never . . . ' Isa murmured. Her hand burnt in the sun on the window sill.

Mrs Swithin took her knitting from the table. 'Did you feel,' she asked, 'what he said: we act different parts but are the same?'

'Yes,' Isa answered. 'No,' she added. It was Yes, No. Yes, yes, yes, the tide rushed out embracing. No, no no, it contracted. The old boot appeared on the shingle.

'Orts, scraps and fragments,' she quoted what she remembered of the vanishing play.

Lucy had just opened her lips to reply, and had laid her hand on her cross caressingly, when the gentlemen came in. She made her little chirruping sound of welcome. She shuffled her feet to clear a space. But in fact there was more space than was needed, and great hooded chairs.

They sat down, ennobled both of them by the setting sun. Both had changed. Giles now wore the black coat and white tie of the professional classes, which needed – Isa looked down at his feet – patent-leather pumps. 'Our representative, our spokesman,' she sneered. Yet he was extraordinarily handsome. 'The father of my children, whom I love and hate.' Love and hate – how they tore her asunder! Surely it was time someone invented a new plot, or that the author came out from the bushes . . .

Here Candish came in. He brought the second post on a silver salver. There were letters; bills; and the morning paper – the paper that obliterated the day before. Like a fish rising to a crumb of biscuit, Bartholomew snapped at the paper. Giles slit the flap of an apparently business document. Lucy read a criss-cross from an old friend at Scarborough. Isa had only bills.

The usual sounds reverberated through the shell: Sands making up the fire; Candish stoking the boiler. Isa had done with her bills. Sitting in the shell of the room, she watched the pageant fade. The flowers flashed before they faded. She watched them flash.

The paper crackled. The second hand jerked on. M. Daladier had pegged down the franc. The girl had gone skylarking with the troopers. She had screamed. She had hit him . . . What then?

When Isa looked at the flowers again, the flowers had faded.

Bartholomew flicked on the reading lamp. The circle of the readers, attached to white papers, was lit up. There in that hollow of the sun-baked field were congregated the grasshopper, the ant and the beetle, rolling pebbles of sun-baked earth through the glistening stubble. In that rosy corner of the sun-baked field, Bartholomew, Giles and Lucy polished and nibbled and broke off crumbs. Isa watched them.

Then the newspaper dropped.

'Finished?' said Giles, taking it from his father.

The old man relinquished his paper. He basked. One hand caressing the dog, resting on the rippled folds of skin towards the collar.

The clock ticked. The house gave little cracks as if it were very brittle, very dry. Isa's hand on the window felt suddenly cold. Shadow had obliterated the garden. Roses had withdrawn for the night.

Mrs Swithin folding her letter murmured to Isa: 'I looked in and saw the babies, sound asleep, under the paper roses.'

'Left over from the Coronation,' Bartholomew muttered, half asleep.

'But we needn't have been to all that trouble with the decorations,' Lucy added, 'for it didn't rain this year.'

'This year, last year, next year, never,' Isa murmured.

'Tinker, tailor, soldier, sailor,' Bartholomew echoed. He was talking in his sleep.

Lucy slipped her letter into its envelope. It was time to read now, her *Outline of History*. But she had lost her place. She turned the pages looking at pictures – mammoths, mastodons, prehistoric birds. Then she found the page where she had stopped.

The darkness increased. The breeze swept round the room. With a little shiver Mrs Swithin drew her sequined shawl about her shoulders. She was too deep in the story to ask for the window to be shut. 'England,' she was reading, 'was then a swamp. Thick forests covered the land. On the top of their matted branches birds sang . . . '

The great square of the open window showed only sky now. It was drained of light, severe, stone cold. Shadows fell. Shadows crept over Bartholomew's high forehead; over his great nose. He looked leafless, spectral, and his chair monumental. As a dog shudders its skin, his skin shuddered. He rose, shook himself, glared at nothing and stalked from the room. They heard the dog's paws padding on the carpet behind him.

Lucy turned the page, quickly, guiltily, like a child who will be told to go to bed before the end of the chapter.

'Prehistoric man,' she read, 'half-human, half-ape, roused himself from his semi-crouching position and raised great stones.'

She slipped the letter from Scarborough between the pages to mark the end of the chapter, rose, smiled and tiptoed silently out of the room.

The old people had gone up to bed. Giles crumpled the newspaper and turned out the light. Left alone together for the first time that day, they were silent. Alone, enmity was bared; also love. Before they slept, they must fight; after they had fought, they would embrace. From that embrace another life might be born. But first they must fight, as the dog fox fights with the vixen, in the heart of darkness, in the fields of night.

Isa let her sewing drop. The great hooded chairs had become enormous. And Giles too. And Isa too against the window. The window was all sky without colour. The house had lost its shelter. It was night before roads were made, or houses. It was the night that dwellers in caves had watched from some high place among rocks.

Then the curtain rose. They spoke.

1 (p. 307) *Liskeard* a town in south-east Cornwall, once the location of a Norman castle

2 (p. 308) *tea-caddy locked* Lockable tea caddies were used in the eighteenth and early nineteenth centuries when tea was very expensive.

3 (p. 309) *the gardens* Kensington Gardens and Kew Botanical Gardens in London

4 (p. 309) *Outline of History* a fictitious text, conflating two works of the time: H. G. Wells, *The Outline of History: Being a Plain History of Life and Mankind* (1920) and G. M. Trevelyan, *History of England* (1926)

5 (p. 311) *Sohrab* an allusion to 'Sohrab and Rustum' by Matthew Arnold (1822–88), a poem about Persian warriors who indulge in single combat to spare the lives of the men under their command. (Rustum discovers, as Sohrab lies dying, that he has unwittingly killed his only son.)

6 (p. 312) *M. Daladier* Edouard Daladier (1884–1970), a leading member of the Radicals and Prime Minster of France, 1838–40

7 (p. 312) *shingled and bobbed* a fashionable short hairstyle for women introduced in 1924 and associated with flappers, young women who wore their hair and their skirts short, listened to jazz and flouted the sexual and social norms of the 1920s

8 (p. 313) *Sappho* a bisexual Greek poet who was born on the island of Lesbos between 630 and 613BC and died around 570BC

9 (p. 314) *a crusader's dog* Medieval church monuments to crusaders often depicted a dog at their feet.

10 (p. 314) *But the master was not dead . . . in his hand a gun* See 'The Burial of the Dead', in T. S Eliot's poem, *The Waste Land*, ll. 19–24.

11 (p. 315) *The Faerie Queene* an incomplete epic poem by Edmund Spenser (1596), written in praise of Queen Elizabeth I, examining moral, philosophical and religious values

12 (p. 315) *Kinglake's Crimea* Alexander William Kinglake (1809–91), travel writer and historian, published *Invasion of the Crimea* in eight volumes between 1863 and 1887.

13 (p. 315) *Keats* the poet John Keats (1795–1821)

14 (p. 315) *Kreutzer Sonata* a novella by Leo Tolstoy (1890) in which the principal character, Pozdnyshev, relates the events leading up to his murder of his wife. Immediately banned by the Russian authorities, it is full of sex and might be seen as an argument in favour of sexual abstinence.

15 (p. 315) *Garibaldi* Giuseppe Garibaldi (1807–82), Italian states- man and soldier who played a significant role in the unification of Italy – known as Il Rissorgimento (or The Resurgence)

16 (p. 315) *Palmerston* Henry John Temple Palmerston (1784–1865), Prime Minister 1855–65

17 (p. 315) *Eddington, Darwin or Jeans* Sir Arthur Eddington (1882– 1944), an astrophysicist who sought to explain Einstein's theory of relativity to the general public; Charles Darwin (1809–82), credited with the theory of evolution propounded in *The Origin of Species* (1859); and Sir James Jeans (1877–1946), a physicist and astronomer who worked on interstellar clouds in space

18 (p. 315) *A horse with a green tail* The incident occurred in the year before that in which Woolf's novel was set; it was covered in *The Times* in June and July 1938 (see Introduction).

19 (p. 317) *Touch wood; touch earth; Antaeus* The giant Antaeus, son of the Greek god of the sea, Poseidon, challenged travellers to wrestle him. He was of indefatigable strength while he was in contact with the ground; learning of his secret, Heracles crushed him by lifting him off the ground so that he lost his strength.

20 (p. 318) *the Coronation* of George VI in 1937

21 (p. 320) *before the Conquest* the Norman Conquest, 1066

22 (p. 320) *Domesday Book* William the Conqueror's record compiled in 1086 listing ownership of lands, buildings and cattle

23 (p. 322) *Bacchus* the ancient Greek god of wine and carnival celebration

24 (p. 323) *The lady was a picture* a reference to a painting by Sir Thomas Gainsborough (1727–88)

25 (p. 324) *Somerset House* a repository of wills and other documents in London

26 (p. 329) *some Institute* the Courtauld Institute, University of London, specialising in the study of the history of art

27 (p. 332) *Reynolds! Constable! Crome!* landscape painters, Sir Joshua Reynolds (1723–92); John Constable (1776–1837); and John Crome (1768–1821)

28 (p. 334) *Gammer Gurton's Needle* an English comedy, 1553, possibly by John Still

29 (p. 339) *Maples* a famous furniture store in Tottenham Court Road, London

30 (p. 346) *Hawkins, Frobisher and Drake* Elizabethan explorers, Sir Richard Hawkins (1562–1622), Sir Martin Frobisher (1535–1594) and Sir Francis Drake (1540–1596), who were significant in building English trade and influence overseas

31 (p. 348) *Globe Theatre* built in London in 1599 and associated with Shakespeare's company of players, the Lord Chamberlain's Men. (It was destroyed by fire in 1613 and a second theatre was built on the site which opened in 1614 and closed in 1642.)

32 (p. 373) *Racine* Jean Racine (1639–99), a French classical dramatist, who wrote mainly tragedies, impressive for their passion, psychological insight and the elegance of their verse

33 (p. 373) *Sandhurst* the Royal Military Academy, Sandhurst, for the initial training of British army officers

34 (p. 374) *Gretna Green* the nearest village in the south of Scotland to England where eloping couples could take advantage of Scotland's permissive marriage laws

35 (p. 378) *Gladstone* W. E. Gladstone, four times British prime minister. (See Note 22 to *The Years*, above.)

36 (p. 381) *hansom . . . growler* two-wheeled and four-wheeled horse-drawn carriages

37 (p. 381) *Seven Dials* in Covent Garden, London, a district notorious as a haunt of criminals

38 (p. 381) *Garotters* criminals who strangled their victims

39 (p. 381) *the old Duke* nickname for the Duke of Wellington (1769–1852), an Anglo-Irish Protestant, Prime Minister 1828–30 and 1834

40 (p. 381) *Old Kent Road* a street in south-east London

41 (p. 381) *Crystal Palace* a glass structure erected in Hyde Park to house the Great Exhibition (1851)

42 (p. 383) *the Mansion House* the official residence of the Lord Mayor of London

43 (p. 383) *Cripplegate; St Giles; Whitechapel; the Minories* poor, working-class districts in London